THE
ABSENT GODS
TRILOGY

THE SILVER SERPENT
KEEPER OF THE MISTS
THE GATESOF IRON

DAVID DEBORD

GRYPHONWOOD

The Absent Gods Trilogy
Published by Gryphonwood Press
www.gryphonwoodpress.com
Copyright 2005, 2015 by David Debord
Cover art by Drazenka Kimpel
Edite by Michael Dunne

ISBN: 978-1-940095-34-9

Books by David Debord
The Absent Gods
The Silver Serpent
Keeper of the Mists
The Gates of Iron

The Impostor Prince (with Ryan A. Span- forthcoming)

Writing as David Wood

The Dane Maddock Adventures
Dourado
Cibola
Quest
Icefall
Buccaneer
Atlantis
Ark (forthcoming)

Dane and Bones Origins
Freedom (with Sean Sweeney)
Hell Ship (with Sean Ellis)
Splashdown (with Rick Chesler)
Dead Ice (with Steven Savile)
Liberty (with Edward G. Talbot)
Electra (with Rick Chesler)\
Amber (with Rick Chesler- forthcoming)
Justice (with Edward G. Talbot- forthcoming)

Jade Ihara Adventures
Oracle (with Sean Ellis)
Changeling (with Sean Ellis-forthcoming)

Myrmidon Files
Destiy (with Sean Ellis)

Other Works
Dark Rite (with Alan Baxter)
Into the Woods (with David S. Wood)
Callsign Queen (with Jeremy Robinson)
The Zombie-Driven Life
You Suck
Arena of Souls

THE
SILVER
SERPENT

For my daughters, Kyla Renee and Erin Elizabeth, with pride and love.

Chapter 1

The branch spun as it rode the river. It shot through a stretch of white water, bouncing in the froth. How far would it go? To the sea? No. It lodged against a rock. Held fast by the current, the stick seemed to strain against the immovable object, trying to break free, but to no avail. Likely, it would remain there until it became waterlogged, then sink to the bottom, forever mired in plain view of the world around it, but stuck.

"Just like life. You dream about what lies ahead, and then something grabs you. For the rest of your life you're stuck." Shanis swatted at an insect hovering near her brow, and cursed when she succeeded only in slapping herself in the face.

"Are you all right?"

The voice took her by surprise. She whipped her head around, annoyed that she had not heard anyone approaching.

"I've been looking for you," the young man said. "Aren't you coming to the ceremony?"

"Wouldn't that be wonderful?" She hefted a stone and hurled it into the river. "Stand by smiling like a good girl while you boys are told you are now men. What possible reason could I have to watch that?"

"Because you're my best friend?" he asked, laying a hand on her shoulder and turning her to the path that led back to town. "Because you're happy for me? Because you cannot bear to be away from me for more than a few moment's time? Because you admire my unsurpassed swordsmanship?"

"Nice try, Hierm." She gave him a shove that sent him stumbling into the thick bole of a chanbor tree. "You can't handle me. You need someone shorter and weaker than you."

"You are not taller than me," he said. "And you're not stronger than me, either." He saw the expression on her face and raised his hands in a defensive pose. "We are of even height and strength. Fair enough?"

"If that is what you need to believe, so be it." She had inherited her father's height, and at least some of his breadth. She was taller than most of the men in Galsbur, and as strong as many of the young men, making her the subject of stares and whispers among the other girls in town. "Just don't try to claim you're better with the sword."

"So that's what's bothering you," he said, grinning. "You think you are bigger, stronger and better than everyone else, yet we are the ones who are going to be recognized as men, while you are still a girl. Is that what you want? A sixteenth nameday ceremony, so you don't have to wait for your wedding before you're considered a woman?"

"You are truly a stone head sometimes," she said. She could not believe that he didn't understand. "I'm not saying I'm better than everyone else. What bothers me is that some of you young men will be chosen as apprentices. One of you in particular." She folded her arms and turned to face him, tapping her foot on the hard-packed earth.

Shafts of slanting morning sunlight filtered through the trees and shone in his pale blond hair, making him appear to glow as realization dawned on his face.

"Master Yurg has never chosen an apprentice," he said. "No one knows why

Galsbur even has a swordmaster. Ham Lurel might choose Oskar, but only because Oskar is strong enough to heft a hammer. I shudder to think what kind of damage the oaf would do at a forge."

Shanis could not help but smile at the thought of the big, bookish Oskar trying to shape iron.

"Truly, I think you need not worry. Most likely, I will end up working for my father. Laman is already learning to run the business, so I suppose I will guard the wagons or something equally unimportant. At least it will be a good use of my sword." His sheepish smile and the twinkle in his blue-gray eyes belied his sincerity.

"You know Yurg is going to choose you," she said, resuming their trek through the cool, shady forest. "He works with you almost every day." She omitted the fact that the swordmaster also included her in these lessons. Her father had raised her like a boy, and arranged at an early age for Master Yurg to instruct her in weaponry. But now that she was approaching marriageable age, it felt like everyone expected her to suddenly become something she was not.

"Shanis, I know how you feel."

"No, you don't. You are a man, so you could not possibly know how I feel. What's more, you are going to be the swordmaster's apprentice. Your father could afford to send you to the academy if he wanted. In the meantime, I'm stuck here waiting for some farmer to make me his bride. And you want me to stand by and pretend to be happy while you take what should be mine?" There, she had said it, and it sounded every bit as selfish as she feared it would, but it was true nonetheless.

"Why shouldn't he choose me?" Hierm's voice was tinged with hurt and a touch of defensiveness. "It has nothing to do with my father being firstman. He disapproves of my learning the sword, and only tolerates it because I'm the younger son. As far as the other youth my age, I am the best swordsman in Galsbur, and if Master Yurg wants to choose me as his apprentice, then that is precisely what he should do.

"You are the best of the young men in Galsbur," she said, her implied meaning clear.

"Is that a challenge?" Hierm asked, neither looking at her nor breaking stride. "Because if it is, there is still time before the ceremony for me to correct your misconception."

"I'll make you a wager," Shanis replied, glancing down at the man's tunic and hose she wore in part for comfort and in part because it offended most of the townspeople. "The loser wears a dress to the ceremony."

"Are you mad?" Hierm's eyes were wide with surprise, and he missed a step. "My father would murder me."

"So you admit that I'll win?" She was taking a reckless chance here. Master Yurg seldom let them practice against one another, but they had squared off with makeshift wooden swords enough to know that they were almost evenly matched, though Shanis believed herself to be the more skilled, if only by an eyelash.

"Fine," Hierm said through gritted teeth. "My mother says you need to learn a touch of humility." His cheeks went red and he looked away.

"Your mother," Shanis said, envisioning Mistress Faun Van Derin's pinched features and severe expression, "would have me in skirts, learning to dance. Maybe she'll teach you once she sees how lovely you look in a dress."

Shanis swept the weighted wooden practice sword in a vicious arc, all the time scowling at Hierm, who pointedly ignored her while shrugging on his padded leather vest. It was a good thing that no one was home at Master Yurg's house. He would not approve, but Shanis had a need to release the frustration boiling within her. Hierm was, perhaps unfairly, the focal point, but he was taking what should rightly be hers. Being born female was not something that should be punished.

"You know how this is done," she said. "Three points or a killing blow. And you may not leave the circle. Are you ready?"

"Let's get on with it," Hierm said, glancing at the sun with narrowed eyes. "My father will have my hide if I am late."

They faced one another in the center of the circle she had scratched on the ground. Hierm held his practice sword motionless before him in a two-handed grip. Shanis' hold on her weapon was relaxed, her anger held barely in check beneath an icy calm.

"Begin!" she said.

Hierm leapt forward with an overhead blow. She parried his stroke, the loud clack of solid wood ringing in her ears. She felt the vibration all the way down to her elbow, and relished it. She never felt more complete than when she held a sword. It brought back distant memories of her father teaching her the basics of swordplay with branches almost too heavy for her little arms. She had always felt she was meant to wield a sword.

She countered Hierm's attack with a waist-high slash. There would be no surprises. Years of training together had revealed their strengths and weaknesses. Hierm continued his furious offensive, seeking to keep her off balance. Shanis took a different tack, utilizing forms which made use of her agility. She warded off Hierm's blows with relative ease, waiting for him to make a mistake.

The error came quickly. Hierm reeled off a series of blows that she immediately recognized would culminate with an upward slash to her midsection. She risked a quick thrust at his throat. A bob of the head was all that he needed to avoid the half-hearted attack, but his footwork was now off. Something, most likely stubbornness knowing Hierm, led him to complete the attack. Or, rather, to try and complete it, because when he spun to deliver the final blow, Shanis scored with a deft thrust to the midsection.

"Point," she shouted, stepping back and waiting for Hierm to acknowledge the blow.

A chorus of cheers drew their attention to a cluster of children who had stumbled across their makeshift dueling ground in the woods behind Yurg's house. The little girls were taking great pleasure in Shanis' success, while the boys urged Hierm on.

They returned to their places and resumed their match. This time Shanis took the offensive with quick, short strokes that Hierm was hard-pressed to ward off. She forced him to give ground, knowing that if she drove him from the circle, she would be the winner. She took a nasty swipe at his head. He ducked underneath the stroke and circled to his right, trying to gain maneuvering room.

Shanis' concentration slipped for a moment as she savored the way Hierm's face reddened at the taunts from the girls who watched them. Was he thinking about what his father would say, or was he just angry at the thought of being whipped by a girl?

Hierm gritted his teeth, growled and barreled forward. He reeled off three vicious swings, lowered his head and threw his shoulder into her chest, knocking her backward. She pretended to stumble. Thinking he had the advantage, Hierm pressed the attack. Shanis dove forward, rolling under his down stroke and inside his guard. She sprang to her feet with the point of her sword at his throat.

"Yield." All trace of anger was gone from her voice. Hierm had no choice. He let his wooden sword clatter to the ground and stared at her, his eyes dull and his face without expression. "Say it," she urged.

"The ice take you if I'll ever yield to you," he muttered. "I have to go." He stalked away, ignoring the children who whispered and laughed as he passed by. He stripped off his leather vest and tossed it on the ground.

She immediately felt remorse. What had changed, save the fact that her best friend was now angry with her? No one would care that she had beaten him with wooden swords. She was still a young woman, and in Galsbur that counted for very little. Small hands tugged at her tunic, and she looked down at the beaming faces looking up at her in adoration.

"Will you teach me to do that?" A little girl with brown eyes and a freckled face asked.

"Perhaps another time," Shanis said. "I really have to go. Detaching herself from the children as gently as she could, she gathered the swords and Hierm's vest and hastened away.

She returned the items to Master Yurg's barn and caught up with Hierm at the edge of the town green. A crowd had gathered around the ancient oak in the center of the grassy oval. Before she could apologize, Mistress Faun emerged from the throng, followed by Lord Hiram.

"What have you been at?" Faun scolded her son. "You are a mess. Your clothes are dirty and you are all sweaty." She smoothed his hair and tried to straighten his clothing, but soon surrendered with an exasperated sigh. She glared at Shanis with cold eyes, making it clear she knew to whom she should affix blame.

"Everyone has been waiting for you," Lord Hiram said. Hierm lacked his father's angular body, long chin and hooked nose, but Hiram's blue-gray eyes, so like a stormy sky, were the twin of his son's. "Let us go before you embarrass me further." Hierm shot her an unreadable glance as he followed his parents.

Shanis let them get well ahead of her before making her way over to the crowd ringing the tree. She spotted Mistress Anna, Master Yurg's wife, and shouldered through the throng to stand beside her. The white-haired woman greeted her with a kind smile. She wore a simple blue dress, and her snowy hair pulled up in a bun. Despite her age, the beauty she had once been was evident in her high forehead and delicate cheekbones. She was Shanis' image of nobility; not Mistress Faun with her expensive clothes and jewels.

"They are starting, child," Anna whispered, laying her hand on Shanis' shoulder. Shanis' mother had died when Shanis was only a baby, and Mistress Anna had been, if not a mother to her, a grandmother. She adored the kindly woman, though Master Yurg remained a stolid, distant figure.

A hush drew over the crowd like a thick blanket. Lord Hiram had donned his sign of office: seven cords of different colors braided into a rope worn draped around the back of his neck and down his chest like a stole. Each color symbolized one of the gods of Gameryah. Unlike most nations, Galdora did not adhere to a single god, but worshiped all seven. He stood in front of a fabric-draped table in the shade of the ancient tree. The items needed for the ceremony lined the edge.

Shanis' eyes flitted to the carvings in the oak. They had fascinated her for as long as she could remember. Some of the primitive images were obvious: The sun symbol for Rantor, the whirlwind for Vesala. All the gods were represented, but some of the icons defied interpretation. No one talked much about it, but Shanis wondered how this tree could be old enough to be adorned with symbols older than memory.

At Hiram's signal, the young men came forward to kneel before him. Four youths from the town and surrounding area had reached their sixteenth summer: Hierm, Oskar Clehn, Natin Marwel and one she did not recognize. The annual ceremony drew families from remote parts of the countryside; families whom the townspeople would not otherwise see, save at harvest time and the occasional Seventhday market.

"We gather to recognize and honor the passage from boy to man," Lord Hiram said. "May the gods look with favor upon us gathered here, and those who submit themselves this day." He turned his attention to those who knelt before him. "Recite with me the Vow of Manhood."

Despite her frustrations, Shanis could not help but feel a tremor of excitement as the young men recited the ritual vow in unison.

"Upon my honor and in the sight of the gods, I pledge to uphold the obligations of manhood. I will protect and provide for myself and mine through the strength of my hand and the fruits of my labor. My words and deeds will be worthy of honor and respect. This is my vow."

Lord Hiram took a stone disc and one-by-one touched it to each young man's forehead, and said the ritual words. "May Kordlak grant you strength, wisdom and courage." He repeated the ritual with two more objects; a golden disc inscribed with a stylized sun image for Rantor and an alabaster stone carved in the shape of the moon for Lunmar. He used an eagle feather to fan each young man's forehead in honor of Vesala the wind goddess, and anointed them with earth and water for Dagdar and Boana respectively. For the fire god Arscla he lit a bowl of lamp oil and carried it down the line, with each youth passing his hand through the flame. Each time, Hiram repeated the ritual words, changing only the name of the god or goddess.

When the ritual was finished, Hiram ordered the group to stand and face the crowd. One by one, he introduced them. He saved Hierm for last, placing a hand on his younger son's shoulder and saying, "I present to you Hierm Van Derin, this day a man." His smile looked odd on his usually stolid face.

The ceremony was not over, though. The town council, comprised primarily of tradesmen, formed a line behind the table. There was little suspense in this part of the ceremony. Most of the townspeople's needs were supplied through Lord Hiram. The town mercer, he bought and hauled produce to market, and brought in and sold most of the items people needed. Thus, there was little call for many of the craftsmen and tradesmen a larger town would have. Consequently, there was little need for apprentices, but it was a part of the annual rite nonetheless.

"Master Ralman," he addressed the town thatcher, "do you take an apprentice?"

"I do not," the small, wiry man replied. The question was posed to each man. Oskar, notoriously lazy, relaxed visibly when Ham Lurel declined to take an apprentice. Master Yurg was last.

"Master Yurg," Hiram's voice had an odd tone, "do you take an apprentice?"

Shanis bit her lip. A part of her, albeit a small part, wanted to be happy for Hierm, but she could not. Now she was determined not to let her disappointment show. That was the best she could offer him today. She looked at Hierm, who was making a point not to meet her eye, and then to Master Yurg, who was slow to answer.

"I do not," he finally said, twisting his lips into a tight frown beneath his thick, white moustache. He folded his arms across his chest and stared at Lord Hiram with a defiant expression on his face.

Shanis sucked in her breath. Mistress Anna made a puzzled sound and squeezed Shanis' shoulder as Yurg made his announcement.

Hiram, for his part, was unfazed. He returned his attention to the assembled. "Let us share words of congratulations with these, the newest men of our community." He stepped back as well-wishers converged on the young men.

Shanis lost sight of Hierm in the crowd. She was uncertain as to whether or not he would want to see her, so she held back. Mistress Anna excused herself and left Shanis standing alone among the milling throng. Her head was abuzz with possibilities. What did it mean that Master Yurg was not taking Hierm as an apprentice? Had Lord Hiram put a stop to it? She could easily imagine Hierm's father doing that very thing.

She felt a strong hand take her by the shoulder and turn her about. Master Yurg's cold stare withered her. Though he was a hair shorter than her, he always seemed to be looking down at her.

"Are you pleased with yourself?" His deep, raspy voice resonated with anger. His moustache and bushy eyebrows seemed even whiter against his reddened face.

"I don't know what you mean," she said, painfully aware of the timidity in her voice. It galled her the way Yurg could still make her feel like a small child. She had no reservations about shouting, stamping her feet and even breaking things to get what she wanted from her father. Yurg was, for some reason, a different story.

"You and my other pupil," his lips twisted as if the word was souring in his mouth, "held a duel." He pointed a scarred finger at her. "Without my consent and without my supervision. I would know why."

She hung her head and scuffed the toe of her boot against the soft turf, kicking up a clump of grass. The conversations around them quieted as people took notice of the exchange.

"Hierm and I were talking. Well, we were arguing," the right words would not come. "I couldn't abide the things he said to me. He thinks himself the better swordsman. I wanted to show him he was wrong. I was so angry."

Her words hung in silence between them. She looked up at Yurg, who was staring daggers at her. The creases at the corners of his eyes deepened. When he finally answered, his voice was as cold as a midwinter gale.

"He made you angry? If an opponent can make you angry, he can kill you just as easily. For all the gifts you have with the blade, you cannot grasp that most simple concept."

She caught sight of Mistress Faun approaching. "Must we talk about this right here? Right now?"

"We are not talking about anything. You are the student and I am the teacher. I am pointing out a mistake that you made." Yurg's glare challenged her to defy him. "I will not have a pupil who chooses not to meet my expectations."

"Is that why you did not take Hierm as an apprentice?" Shanis was horrorstruck by the sudden thought, but she had to ask. "Master Yurg, please don't hold him responsible for what I goaded him into doing."

"Hierm is a man now, and responsible for the choices he makes. As are you. In any case, it is not the place of the student to question the master. Is that clear?"

"What is unclear to me," Shanis said in a harsh whisper, "is why you ever took me as a student in the first place." The familiar anger enveloped her like a mother's arms, and her courage rose. "You will not take me as an apprentice because I am a girl. For as long as I can remember, I have wanted nothing more than to be a swordsman." She forced a cynical laugh. "Do you hear me? A swordsman! None of it has been to any purpose!"

"It has been of more purpose than you know," Yurg whispered, taking her by the shoulders and pulling her close. "You will keep a civil tongue, do you hear?"

"Is this how you train your pupils, Master Yurg?" Mistress Faun's words dripped with contempt as she glided up next to Yurg. "I always said that such a long-legged girl should be taught to dance. Truly a shame."

"Dance?" Her temper had finally gotten the better of her. She rounded on Mistress Faun, her fists clenched. "Lady, I'll teach you to dance!"

White light flashed across Shanis' vision. Her cheek stung where Yurg struck her. She shook her head to clear the ringing in her ears, and looked at Yurg through teary eyes.

"I told you to keep a civil tongue," he said, still in that infuriatingly calm, cold voice. "You go to my house right now. Anna and I will be along soon, and we will talk about respect for your elders."

"I'm not going anywhere with you," she said, tears streaming down her face. Yurg had slapped her once before, years ago, for taking a similar tone with him. But to do it here, today, in front of everyone. To treat her like a child while her friends were named as men? It was too much. "I'm leaving this town forever." She turned on her heel and dashed away, Yurg's calls ringing in her ears.

Chapter 2

"Boy! Where have you gone?" Mistress Faun's footfalls echoed in the narrow stairwell. "Answer me, Boy!"

"So much for the manhood ceremony," Oskar mumbled, stashing the book under a pile of rags and looking about for something to help him appear industrious. The morning ritual now felt like a distant memory, and he was back to ordinary life. "I'm up here, Missus!"

"What are you doing up here, young oaf? Oh, never mind. I have something for you." Faun proffered a small cloth bundle. "Scraps of meat," she said. "I was going to give them to the dogs, but I though your family might like to have them instead."

A tall, slender woman, one needn't look twice at Faun Van Derin to know where Hierm had gotten his golden locks, and most of his other features. Only her face kept Mistress Faun from being considered beautiful. Not that hers was an ugly face. Rather, it was severe. Her features appeared to have been carved in granite. Her eyes were not the deep blue of Hierm's, but the pale, icy blue of a harsh winter morning. At any rate, she was striking.

He forced a grin and accepted the greasy bundle. Faun knew very well that his family was not poor, yet she took great pleasure in lording over him, even going so far as to refer to him as "the poor boy," with emphasis on "poor." Once she had even walked him outside to show him to a visitor from Archstone, and boast of her generosity in providing a job for him.

He ignored her as always. It was not for the meager wages that he worked in the Van Derin's warehouse. It was the books. Lord Hiram owned three books, which was, as far as Oskar knew, three more than anyone else in Galsbur. They were ancient, musty-smelling tomes with delicate brown pages and cracked leather covers. He loved the feel of them in his hands, and the odor of the old pages. The fading text, painstakingly copied by some nameless scholar, held stories that set his imagination awhirl. Hiram's interest in books was limited strictly to possessing them. Oskar had never seen the man so much as look at one. Consequently, he had not yet noticed when Oskar slipped one of the battered tomes from the office and secreted himself in this upstairs room, poring over the stories and histories, copying maps and interesting passages on whatever scraps of paper he could scavenge.

"Thank you, Missus. Most kind of you." Clutching the bag to his chest like it was the greased pig at Arskhain, he aped a foolish grin, hoping she would go away. His hope was in vain.

"Why are you up here?" Faun scanned the room through narrow eyes, delicate hands on rounded hips. "You should be down in the warehouse unloading wagons."

"No wagons as yet," he replied. "I was just looking to see if there was something up here I could clean or organize. Don't want the Master to send me home, you know."

"Well aren't we the industrious one?" Her voice had a patronizing tone that would have been lost on Oskar had he been half as slow-minded as she thought him. Her gaze fell on the pile of rags. "Hand me those old bits of cloth. I'll have them washed and your mother can make herself a dress from them."

"No thank you, Missus," he said, desperately trying to think of a reason not to pick up the bundle. "Mother has dresses."

"For your sisters then," she said. Her eyes locked with his, and for a moment he thought she was angry. But then she laughed, or at least he thought it was a laugh. It sounded more like dead corn husks rattling in the breeze.

"You need not worry that it will be taken from your pay," she said. "No, you simple boy. This is a gift from someone fortunate," she touched her chest, "to someone unfortunate." She tapped his shoulder. "Do you understand?" She asked the question in a loud, flat voice, as if he were hard of hearing.

His face reddened. "Yes Missus," he said, his voice low. What was he going to do? "I'll bring them along in just a moment."

"Oh, just stop," she said, her voice exasperated. "I'll get them myself." Before he could protest, she glided past him and retrieved the bundle. Her eyes widened when she found the book.

"This is one of the Master's books. What are you doing with it?" Her icy tone froze his marrow. He could do nothing but stare at the floor. At the very least, this would be the end of his employment with Van Derin and Sons. He held his breath, waiting for the explosion. Strangely, Faun's face registered surprise, then comprehension.

"You wanted to learn to read, you poor fool." She threw her head back and laughed. "Even if you could learn to read, you could never read this." Again she laughed. "Do you know what this is? Of course you do not. This is *Patrin's Conquests*! It's all maps and military history."

One by one, Oskar tensed and relaxed each muscle of his body: first his shoulders, then his back, his hips. Anything to hold his emotions in check. The laughter continued unabated. He knew what was in the book: the tales of kingdoms conquered and riches plundered, and the quest for the lost city of Murantha. He had spent most of the morning copying the maps onto scraps of paper using a bit of charcoal. He was no idiot.

Mistress Van Derin had regained some degree of composure.

"You poor young fool," she crooned, reaching up to stroke his cheek as if he were a favorite pet. "You just didn't know any better, but not to worry. We shan't tell the Master. Just you keep yourself out of his office. Am I understood?"

Even if he had wanted to answer, he could not. Hot anger clamped the muscles of his jaws closed, and he merely nodded.

"Very well. Don't worry too much, Boy. Someone of your station has no need of reading." She whisked away, leaving him to watch her graceful retreat.

His anger dissolved when he realized how close he had come to being head down in the manure pile, as his gran was fond of saying. Twisting his mouth into a self-deprecating smile, he contented himself with admiring Faun's backside as she descended the stairs. She certainly was not shaped like a woman of nearly forty summers. Cursing himself, he followed her down the stairs.

Faun left him in the warehouse with an admonition to stay out of further mischief until a wagon arrived. When he was certain she was gone, he headed to the back corner where he had rearranged some old crates to make a hiding place. His breadth of shoulder and ample waist made it a tight squeeze, but it was a comfortable spot to while away his time, and he could be on his feet at the first sound of someone entering the building.

Cracks in the wall filtered in adequate light for reading. He reached into his cloak and fished out the crude map he had copied the day before. He held it in a dusty, golden beam and whispered the names that conjured up fantastic images in his mind.

"Halvala, Riza, Cardith, the Claws." He longed to see these places that existed for him only in faded ink and weathered paper. Sometimes he thought himself the only one in Galsbur who knew there was a world beyond their quiet village.

A slamming door snatched him from his daydream.

"How could you do it?" Oskar sat with his back resting against the wall of Lord Hiram's office, and Hierm's voice came through clearly. "You know that's not the life I want!"

"Settle yourself." Lord Hiram sounded agitated. "I have my reasons. You are a boy no longer."

"Then let me make my own choice, Father! Stop controlling me. Have you forgotten that this very morning you declared me a man?"

Oskar smiled. It seemed that neither Van Derin put much stock in the manhood ceremony. He felt only a slight tinge of guilt at eavesdropping. Life in Galsbur was too tedious to pass up something as interesting as a quarrel within its leading family.

"A ceremony does not make you a man any more than that fool sword makes you a blademaster. You will be a man when you begin acting like one. And while we are on the subject, I have written to Marak Lane in Archstone. He has a daughter your age whom I'd like you to meet."

"No, Father. I won't hear it. No betrothal. No job in the warehouse. I want to learn the sword. Just because I do not choose your life does not make me less of a man."

The bang he heard was most likely Hiram's fist on his desk.

"What makes you believe you can apprentice the swordmaster when you cannot even best a girl? Oh yes, I have heard about your little duel, as has most everyone else in town. A fine show indeed. When I went to see your precious Master Yurg yesterday, I believed I would have to persuade him with gold, but it turns out he had already decided not to take you on. What say you to that?"

Oskar winced. If Hiram was telling the truth, that bit of news would cut Hierm to the quick. He did not hear the young man's reply because a wagoner, a paunchy fellow with a sour face and gray-streaked brown hair, chose that very moment to pull his wagon into the warehouse. With a sigh, he hauled himself to his feet.

Some day he would escape from all of this.

Shanis sat alone. A single candle cast long shadows across her sparsely furnished room. She stared at nothing, her lips mouthing curses at unseen recipients. A deep growl in the pit of her stomach interrupted the silence. The aroma of roast venison still hung in the air, but she was not about to eat. Perhaps after Papa went to bed.

Rising from her chair, she moved the three steps across the room to her bed, where her belongings lay in a heap. Twice already, she had packed everything, once even going so far as to don her travel cloak, and twice she had changed her mind. Now the urge rose anew.

Her sword hung in its scabbard on a post at the foot of the bed. She drew the blade with loving care and held it aloft, watching the candlelight waver on its shiny surface.

"Do you ever put that thing down?"

She leapt to her feet and thrust the sword in front of her as if preparing to ward off an attack. So much of Master Yurg's training was ingrained her that she felt she scarcely needed to think with a sword in her hand.

Chin cupped in his hands, Hierm leaned on the windowsill, beaming like a fool. "Careful, or you're going to hurt me one of these days." He heaved his lanky form over the sill and fell hard on the dirt floor.

"What do you want, hairy mule?" She turned her back so he would not see her smile, and sheathed her sword. It slid home with a wicked whisper.

"Not much." He shifted into a sitting position, his back against the log wall beneath the window. "I just thought I'd give you the chance to apologize."

"Apologize to you?" She clenched her fist as the anger shot through her. Then she saw his impudent grin and relaxed. "You're right. I apologize."

Hierm looked as though he had been run over by one of his father's wagons. He clutched his chest, crumpled to the floor and began twitching. His foot struck the wall with a loud thump.

"Sorry," he whispered, sitting back up and brushing his cloak.

"Don't worry. I've been hitting and throwing things for most of the evening. Papa started ignoring me after a while." As if to emphasize her point, she aimed a fierce kick at the wall between her room and Papa's. The thud resounded through the modest cabin, but predictably, her father ignored her.

"Your father builds a sturdy house." Hierm whispered, still seated on the floor.

"I don't give him much choice," Shanis laughed. "I've kicked a few walls and doors in my lifetime."

"Remember when he made you sleep in the barn for a week?" Hierm rolled onto his back and laced his fingers behind his neck. "It was wintertime, as I recall."

"Don't remind me. I nearly froze." She shivered at the memory, still feeling the cold seeping into her bones. She had thought she would never be warm again.

"Considering the condition of your room, I dare say you were better off in the barn." Hierm's eyes danced with mischief.

"It wasn't my fault. Thatch just makes for a weak roof." Shanis shielded her face from her friend's incredulous stare.

"Shanis, you climbed onto the roof and hacked a hole in it with your sword."

"Not a large hole. I fell through before I could do much damage." She paused. "Of course that made me so mad I threw a chair and broke it. Papa was livid."

"He laughed about it when he told my father." Hierm smiled and stared at his boots. "Did you know that you're the reason you don't have glass in your windows?"

"Wait! Papa laughed?" Stunned, Shanis dropped to the floor alongside Hierm. "But he made me sleep in the barn, with bugs."

"He thought it was what you deserved. My father suggested that you be put out with the pigs." Hierm grimaced as he spoke of his father. "You do sometimes get a bit out of control."

"Tonight was another of those times," she said, forcing a smile as she sank to the floor next to him. "I asked him why he made me spend my life learning the sword when he knew I could be anything more than someone's wife. He said he could not talk about it, and that I should trust him. I started screaming, and he told me that my mother would not approve of my behavior. That's when I started throwing things." Hierm chuckled, but she could not share his mirth. "I don't even remember my mother, and he never talks about her. Why now? None of it makes any sense."

A warm tear slid down her cheek. She tasted salt in the corner of her mouth. Before she could wipe her face, she felt Hierm's arm around her shoulders, pulling her close to him. She lay her head on his shoulder and tried to imagine they were children again, exploring the forests, battling imaginary monsters with swords of reed plucked from the banks of the Vulltu. She could be anything she wanted back then, but now she was a young woman and everything had changed. Rather, nothing at all had changed. Galsburans would always be the same. One of them in particular.

"How is your loving father?" she asked, straightening and pulling away from

Hierm. "Still pretending I'm invisible?"

"He took notice of you today," Hierm said. "I got the rough edge of his tongue for losing to you." He was silent after that. For so long, in fact, that she wondered if he had fallen asleep. Finally, he took a deep breath. "My father asked Master Yurg not to make me his apprentice. He wants me to join the family business. He thinks the sword was just childish folly."

A sudden determination filled her, and she sprang to her feet. Taking him by the hand, she hauled him up to stand in front of her. "Hierm, I will never be anything if I don't get out of here. Perhaps you should do the same." She placed a finger across his lips before he could reply. "You need to be home. We'll talk soon." With that, she gave him a rough shove toward the window. He climbed out and headed down the path toward the road, with only a single glance back. She leaned out the window to watch him go. Diamond stars scattered across a velvet sky colored the world a faint gray. Elbows propped on the sill, she watched until his tall, lean form faded into the darkness.

Chapter 3

Oskar hurried through the crush of the Seventhday market. People filled the green at the town's center. Wagons laden with produce jutted out above the throng. The sounds of laughter, calls of greeting, and good-natured dickering sang a happy tune in his ear. Seventhday was his favorite day. People from the countryside gathered to exchange goods, news, and gossip, not necessarily in that order.

He dodged a woman carrying a basket of tomatoes, only to careen into a cart loaded with apples.

"Watch yourself, boy." Lars Harim shot a tobacco-stained grin in his direction before turning back to haggle with a potential customer.

"Sorry, Master Harim." How long would it be until people thought of him as a man? Obviously longer than one day.

Certain that Master Harim's attention was diverted, Oskar filched an early summer apple, small and dark red, and hurried away. Reaching a safe distance, he paused to take a bite. Sweet juice ran from the corners of his mouth and down his chin. He located a comfortable fencepost and contentedly munched his prize. The smell of freshly baked bread wafted through the air, and he looked around for the source of the delicious aroma.

He dropped the remains of his snack to the ground, scrubbed his face with the back of a sweaty hand, and set off along the hard beaten dirt path that encircled the green. His nose guided him to the front porch of the Dry Birch, Galsbur's only inn, in front of which a local youth stood holding a basket of bread.

"Natin," Oskar hailed the young man. "What do you have for me?"

The slender, brown-haired youth greeted Oskar with a gap-toothed smile. "First, I want to know what you have for me. You still owe me for a loaf."

"May we consider it a manhood gift?" At Natin's answering smirk, Oskar dug into the pocket inside his cloak. His fingertips found a bit of string, a smooth stone he had found on the riverbank, and finally a single copper. "What will this buy?" he asked, handing it to his friend.

Natin accepted the coin and motioned for Oskar to join him on the front porch. They sat down together on the top step. Natin took a loaf from his basket and broke it in half. Oskar gratefully accepted his half, savoring the yeasty aroma. He tore off a warm crust and stuffed it in his mouth. Natin's mother was quite the baker.

"Ordinarily I wouldn't accept the coin, but things are hard." Natin did not meet Oskar's eye.

The bread was doughy, and Oskar could only answer with a sympathetic "Mmhmm!" Natin's family farmed a plot owned by the Van Derins. Each year Lord Hiram took most of their crop for rent, leaving Natin's family to make do the best they could. Natin sold or traded his mother's bread each Seventhday. Otherwise, when he wasn't working on their small farm, he was fishing for the fat speckled trout that made the Vulltu their home. Oskar could think of nothing to say, so he took another large bite of bread, and looked out over the town.

Galsbur was centered on an oval-shaped green. The dirt road that encircled the green was ringed on its outer edge by various shops, homes, and buildings. The Dry Birch lay on the west side of the green, directly opposite the main road that led toward civilization. On either side of the main road stood the Van Derin and Sons warehouse and the Van Derin home. Its whitewashed exterior and wooden shingles made it stand out like a pearl in a pigsty among the log and thatch buildings. He regarded the town with a disheartened stare. It was so small, so insignificant.

"Oskar," Natin whispered. "Look over there. Have you ever seen that man before?"

He immediately located the person of whom Natin spoke. Even with farmers from outlying villages in attendance, a stranger was a rare site on Seventhday, or any other for that matter. The man was tall; fully a head taller than Hierm. His auburn hair was pulled to the left side of his head and was plaited in a thick braid that hung down past his shoulder. His travel-stained cloak was dark brown stitched with intertwining vines of green and gray. His face and clothes looked as worn as his cloak. A sword hilt, its grip worn smooth, with a plain, round pommel was just visible inside the cloak. The stranger strode directly toward them, his wide-set hazel eyes fell upon them with a disinterested gaze.

"Pardon," the man said in a voice that was like rough stones grinding together. "There a common room in there?"

"There is," Oskar said. His voice sounded boyish compared to the stranger's deep baritone.

Nodding, the man took the steps in two strides and seemed to melt through the door.

"Did you see that? He had a sword." Natin said. "Who wears a sword in Galsbur, save Master Yurg?"

Master Yurg! All thoughts of the stranger were forgotten as Oskar recalled the reason for slipping out of the Van Derin's warehouse in the first place. He mumbled an apology around another mouthful of bread and ran for the swordmaster's house.

He reached his destination out of breath. Sparing a few moments to lean against the split rail fence and let the stitch in his side release, he scanned the enclosed yard behind Master Yurg's home.

Hierm and Master Yurg were working forms. The youngest Van Derin would not be giving up the sword after all. Shanis, however, was nowhere to be seen. A cluster of girls hovered nearby, feigning disinterest while watching every move Hierm made. He was the most popular and eligible young man in the area, thus all the older girls strove to catch his eye.

For a moment Oskar tried to imagine Shanis wearing a dress and giggling at the first glance from a young man. The image made him laugh. Who would marry her? If you could see past her height and muscles, she was pretty enough, with her soft red hair and gray-green eyes, but could anyone handle her temper and stubbornness? Her father was the most physically imposing man Oskar had ever seen, yet he scarcely managed to keep her in check.

"Do you find something funny?" Khalyndryn Serrill eyed him over her tiny, upturned nose. Oskar shook his head. Her golden hair and emerald eyes always put him ill at ease. He fancied her, but so did every other young man in town, and he was no prize catch. No one in Galsbur seemed to share his desire to learn what lay beyond the horizon. He was an outcast in his own way, but it did not matter. He was not going to stay in this town forever. He would visit those places in Lord Hiram's books and have his own adventures. And then someday he would write them all down in a book of his own.

"Oskar, shouldn't you be off pilfering books?" Hierm and Master Yurg halted their lesson and came over to where Oskar leaned against the fence.

"Have you seen Shanis?" Oskar asked. "I need to talk to her. And you too."

"I haven't seen her since yesterday." Hierm blushed and turned his head. He pushed back his sweaty mop of blond hair. "I thought I would see her today. Why do you need to talk to us?"

Oskar had to force himself not to go ahead and tell Hierm what he had heard while listening at the wall of Lord Hiram's office. The news seemed to be trying to claw its way out of him. But he wanted to tell Hierm and Shanis together. They were his best friends and both would be thrilled by his news. That, and he was not going to admit in Master Yurg's presence that he had been eavesdropping on the firstman of Galsbur.

"I have the most amazing news," he said. You won't believe it. But I want to tell the two of you together." Nearby, Khalyndryn and her friends had ceased their conversation and were actively pretending not to listen.

"Are you certain that she's not around market somewhere?" Hierm asked.

"I haven't seen her anywhere. Strange, she never misses market. What is it?" Hierm's eyes were suddenly wide, as if something had frightened him.

"She wouldn't," Hierm mumbled. "Yes she would. Swordmaster," he said to Yurg, "may I be excused from my lesson?"

Yurg arched an eyebrow at his pupil, looking like a hawk that had spotted a wounded rabbit. "Would either of you young men care to tell me what this is about?"

"It's Shanis," Hierm said. "She isn't here."

Yurg pretended to scrutinize the empty sword yard. "Truly? I had not noticed." He smirked. "She is not very pleased with me right now, but she'll come around once she's had time to calm that fool head of hers. Why is it of concern to you?"

"She told me last night that she wanted to go away. I didn't believe her then, but now I don't know."

Yurg ran his fingers through his closely cropped silver beard before venturing to speak. "Van Derin, one day you'll learn that women say a lot of things they don't mean, simply to get a reaction." This comment elicited angry whispers from the group of girls nearby. Oskar smirked. He had never heard Yurg talk about anything but swords and tales of his battles. "I do feel a bit guilty about the way I treated her yesterday. You are dismissed."

Hierm wasted no time. Ignoring the nearby gate, he vaulted the fence.

"Van Derin," Yurg said. "Let me know what you find out." He sounded unconcerned, but there was an intensity in his eyes that belied his tone.

Hierm nodded and set of at a trot. Oskar groaned and stuffed the last bite of bread in his mouth. He was a firm believer that running should be reserved strictly for those moments when a vicious predator was snapping at your heels.

"Do you really think Shanis has left?" Oskar gasped, trying to keep pace.

Hierm grimaced. "I certainly hope not."

The Malan's home was just far enough from town to make the run exhausting. When the tidy cabin and small log barn were in sight, Hierm stopped running. Oskar trotted forward until he had caught up with his friend.

"Why are stopping now? he gasped, resting his hands on his knees. His face felt like it was on fire and salty sweat burned his lips. "We're almost there." A rasping cough cut him short.

"Look," Hierm pointed to a white horse that stood cropping a tuft of thick grass in the corral that adjoined the barn. "She wouldn't go anywhere without Shine."

Oskar dropped onto his backside, panting. A rock dug painfully into his bottom, but he ignored it. "Then we're in no hurry. Van Derin, one of these days you're going to kill me. I really mean it. You're going to kill me." He lay back on the hard-packed trail and looked up at the blue sky. He wondered if this was the color of the sea of which he had read in one of Lord Hiram's books. A cotton cloud drifted slowly past, and for a moment he imagined it was a sailing ship come to carry him away to adventure.

"Come on," Hierm said, his voice earnest. "I'm worried about her. She's never been like this. Something isn't right."

"I'll help if I can," Oskar said. His cheeks heated. How could he help? In his mind, his words flowed from his lips like prose from the pages of Lord Hiram's books, but in reality, everything he said sounded wrong. He stared at the ground, feeling foolish.

Hierm seemed to understand what he was saying. "I'm not sure we can help. Shanis wants to learn the sword, to be a soldier. People around here are not going to let that happen. Of course, I don't know where she could go."

"Hallind," Oskar stated. "It's an island, actually an island nation. They have male and female soldiers. Some of their elite troops are made up entirely of women. I was just reading about it. It's fascinating." He stopped when he saw the look on Hierm's face.

Hierm pressed his hands to his temples. "Women soldiers? Elite troops? Is this some fairy tale you read somewhere?"

"You've never heard of it? Haven't you read any of your father's books?"

Hierm shook his head.

"Seriously? Why not? Oh." Compassion welled up inside of him. He tried to make his voice sympathetic as he placed a hand on Hierm's arm. "I'm sorry. I just assumed that all you wealthy people learned to read."

Hierm slapped the hand away. "Of course I can read, you dolt. I just don't like to."

Oskar stared for a moment. He didn't understand. "Well, in that case, you're just dense." He pushed past Hierm and began walking toward the Malan house. Hierm followed. Oskar could feel his friend's scowl burning into his back. "Don't you think Shanis might feel a little better if she knew about Hallind?"

"Oskar, don't you say a word to her. The way Shanis has been acting, the last thing she needs to hear about is this Hallind. No telling what she might do."

Oskar felt a cold tightness in his chest. He could sense a big fight just around the corner. How to avoid it? He stopped and turned around.

"What do you say we just go back to town? I mean, now that we know Shanis is all right." He was talking very fast. "We don't want to upset her or anything."

Just then, Shanis emerged from the house. "Aren't the two of you missing Seventhday?" She walked past without meeting either boy's eye. "I've a stall to clean, so if you laggards insist on gawking at me, do it in the barn." Hierm fell in step beside her. Oskar lagged a few paces behind, debating whether or not he would be able to slip away quietly. His eyes drifted to the wagon track that led back to town. After a moment's debate, he uttered a resigned sigh and followed his friends into the barn.

The dusty air assailed him immediately. He brushed a sleeve across his nose and suppressed a sneeze.

"We were worried about you," Hierm was saying. "I was afraid you had gone, oh, I don't know." Hierm threw up his arms.

"Where would I go Hierm?" Shanis' tone was mocking. "Who has any use for a girl with a sword?" She took a pitchfork down from the wall and headed to one of the stalls. It was a small barn, with only two stalls, which Shanis kept clean. She loved horses.

Oskar leaned against a post and watched as Hierm took up a shovel and helped Shanis muck out the stall.

"I'm actually quite satisfied with my lot in life," Shanis continued. "I mean, who wouldn't enjoy this?" A flick of her wrist sent a clump of manure hurtling at Oskar's head. Almost too late, he ducked out of the way. The dung projectile struck the post against which he was leaning, spattering dirty clumps on his tunic. "Nice reflexes for such a stout lad. As I was saying, I can spend the rest of my years cleaning stalls, washing clothes and pulling weeds. Quite an exciting life, full of adventure. If I'm lucky, I might even have the opportunity to face down some evil foe. Perhaps a garden spider, or a rat.

"Ho there, little field mouse," she said in a deep voice, thrusting her pitchfork at an imaginary opponent. "Surrender, or I shall skewer thee in the foulest of ways!" Dancing around the stall, she jabbed at Hierm's face. He raised his shovel in a half-hearted defense. Oskar stepped back a few paces just to be safe. Laughing, Shanis feinted high twice before sweeping Hierm's feet out from under him with the end of the pitchfork handle. "For shame, young rodent. Next time I shall seek combat with a worthier adversary."

Hierm fanned at the cloud of dust that engulfed him. From his seat on the barn floor, he pointed an accusing finger at Shanis. "What is going on? The last time we talked, you were ready to challenge the world to a duel, to run away. Now you're acting like nothing happened."

Shanis smiled. "I'm sorry. It was good of the two of you to worry about me."

"We couldn't help but worry. Even Master Yurg is wondering where you are." Hierm picked himself up and brushed at the straw that clung to his backside. "Will you be coming back to sword?"

"Of course. I just felt like making Yurg sweat a bit. I might not be an apprentice, but I won't stop with the sword until I choose." Shanis returned to her work in the stall. "I'm still angry, mind you, but I was a bit in the wrong myself. I know Yurg. He will probably stop in tonight to apologize, and that will be that." She dismissed the thought with a shrug.

"You don't think you owe him an apology?" Hierm placed his hands on his hips, a posture which reminded Oskar just how much his friend resembled Mistress Faun. "Either way, that doesn't solve your real problem. You can't be his informal student forever. What do you plan to do?"

Oskar could have kicked Hierm for blurting the question out so hastily. He didn't want Shanis to lose her good humor.

Shanis stopped her work in the stall. "Didn't you tell him, Oskar?" Oskar waved his hands to silence her, but the gesture was futile. "Hallind. It's a country where women can be soldiers."

Hierm's face contorted in a scowl. "I know about Hallind, and it's crazy." He rounded on Oskar, grabbing his tunic. "What were you thinking? You had no business telling her about that blasted place."

Oskar ripped Hierm's hands away, and gave the boy a shove that sent him careening into a stall door. "Enough! My business is just that, Van Derin. Mine. Who are you to tell us what to do anyway? You're more like your father than you think." Shanis' sharp intake of breath indicated that Oskar had gone too far. Hierm hung his head, unable to speak. A pang of guilt swept through Oskar. From where had that anger arisen?

"Sorry. You just get too bossy sometimes."

"You're right." Hierm raised his head to meet Oskar's gaze. "I'm the one who's sorry. I don't want to be like my father." He turned to Shanis. "You are leaving?"

It seemed to Oskar that something passed between Hierm and Shanis. It was not a question but a benediction. An affirmation of something that those closest to Shanis had always known. Galsbur was not for her, nor she for it. She had never fit in.

"You know I have to go. There's no other way," Shanis replied firmly. "I'll keep working with Yurg while I make preparations. Don't think I haven't thought this through."

"How can you have thought this through?" Hierm waved his arms in frustration. "How long ago did Oskar tell you about this place? A few days ago?"

"The place is not important. I've been thinking about leaving for a long time." Her face grew serious. "This is my home. I don't take leaving lightly."

"May I interrupt here?" In the midst of all the concern over Shanis, Oskar had forgotten the reason he had been searching for her in the first place. Hierm and Shanis looked at him with mild surprise, as if they had forgotten his presence. "I was looking for the two of you this morning because I have something to tell you.

It might be the solution to your problem."

"My, aren't we full of useful information?" Shanis mocked.

"Useless is more like it," Hierm scoffed. "What is this solution you've come up with?"

Oskar ignored their sarcasm. "A man came into town today. He was wearing the livery of the prince's guard. He came to talk to Lord Hiram. I was listening at the door." He paused and cleared his throat. "Anyway, there's going to be a tournament."

"The Prince's Tournament? That's not held again for months, and even then a town sends only its most talented apprentice." Hierm argued. "Even if Shanis could somehow become an apprentice, my father would never stand for her to represent Galsbur. Not at the capital."

"Hierm is right," Shanis said. "That tournament is for the very best. In the best of circumstances I wouldn't be ready to try for a spot in the academy for another two years or more. I don't think I'll ever have the opportunity. Some day Hierm will, but not me."

Oskar stood silent until he again had their attention. "Are the two of you finished arguing with me yet? I know what the Prince's Tournament is. It's an annual event at which apprentice swordsmen who are ready to become journeymen compete for places in the prince's elite units. Those who don't make it join the army, or become free swords."

"All right, Oskar, you're very smart," Hierm jibed. "Now tell us what you learned while you were eavesdropping on my father."

Oskar ignored that. "There's going to be a tournament here." He hurried on despite the suddenly stunned looks on their faces. "It won't be just swords, either. Archery, wrestling, you name it. Prince Lerryn himself will be here."

"But why hold a tournament here?" Hierm asked. Shanis remained silent, her face an unreadable mask of thought. "Why Galsbur?"

"There's a rumor that we might go to war with Kyrin. There will be tournaments like these in many of the larger towns. The best will go to the academy. Others can sign on as foot soldiers. Lerryn hopes to double the size of the standing army in the next year. They need good soldiers. If they see Shanis fight, maybe they'll give her a chance. They'd have to, wouldn't they? She's the best." Feeling quite proud of himself, Oskar folded his arms across his chest and nodded, waiting for their reactions.

"This doesn't make sense," Hierm protested. "You said the larger towns would have tournaments. We're a nothing town three leagues from nowhere."

Shanis grabbed Hierm's shoulders and gave him a firm shake. "Who cares about that? Oskar may have something here. This could be my chance." If the prospect of her nation going to war fazed her at all, she didn't show it. "If I can put on a good enough showing, they won't care that I'm a girl. If we go to war with Kyrin, they'll need all the fighters they can get."

"I'm not so sure," Hierm replied. "Do you honestly think they'll let a girl compete? If Oskar has it right, this will be the most important thing that has ever happened in Galsbur. Mother will be in rare form, and Father will not be much better. They won't take a chance on embarrassing themselves."

"You're right about one thing," Oskar said. "They won't want to embarrass themselves. That's why they have to let her compete. Shanis is the best. And you, of course," he added, noticing Hierm's frown. "All of the small towns and most of the villages in this part of the kingdom will send people to compete. Master Yurg isn't going to let them beat us if he can help it. I wouldn't be surprised if your father felt the same way. Besides, won't it take the vinegar out of them to be beaten by a girl?"

Shanis squeezed Oskar in a bear hug and planted a noisy kiss on his cheek. Her lips were softer than he expected, and the sensation was uncomfortably pleasant.

"That settles it," she said. "I don't need to be an apprentice. All I need is the chance to compete. Once they see me fight, all they'll see is my skill." She dashed out of the stall. "Besides," she called over her shoulder, "Yurg owes me!"

Chapter 4

Excitement, tempered by a heavy dose of skepticism, greeted word of the tournament. Sensible Galsburans were not quick to believe the crown had suddenly taken notice of their remote corner of the kingdom. Mistress Faun, eager to be the first to spread the news, had hurried to the Dry Birch's common room only to be treated with flat disbelief. Her vehement insistence won her only a small battle, bringing a touch of condescending acceptance, the way one would indulge a child's fancy. She finally stormed out with her skirts clutched in white-knuckled fists, raucous laughter nipping at her heels. But when word came from both Lord Hiram and Master Yurg, that gave the townspeople something to think about. And when a squadron of soldiers arrived in town, tacked up a notice to the same effect, and proceeded to drink Master Serrill dry in an impressive display, the like of which none could remember seeing in these parts, the remaining holdouts were finally persuaded.

Once reality set in, Lord Hiram and the town leaders set to work. They chose a nearby pasture ringed on three sided by gently sloping hills, forming a natural amphitheater. On the open end they built a viewing platform for Prince Lerryn and any dignitaries who might accompany him. Word was, Mistress Faun had arranged the seating to place herself next to the prince.

"I scarcely recognize this place anymore," Shanis said as she and Hierm jostled through the crowd.

The flow of visitors had begun as a trickle as soon as word of the tournament spread. In these last days before the event, they poured in, turning the countryside into a bustling anthill of activity. Some planned to enter the tournament, while others had come to witness the spectacle. So much had changed in the span of ten days. The common room was packed; music and laughter rolled forth in steady waves at all hours. Seventhday market was now an everyday market, and had grown with the influx of "outlanders" as the locals called anyone who lived more than a day's ride from Galsbur. Familiar faces mixed with those of strangers in a whirl of festivity. Shanis drank in the sights, the sounds, everything.

The practice yard brimmed with swordsmen. Master Yurg was watching as young men practiced. Shanis felt a touch of resentment that their swordmaster was providing any assistance at all to outsiders, but that was Yurg. From what she could see it was evident that few of the young men had the skill to go far in the competition, but the opportunity to be a part of such an important event was too much for any youth with imagination to pass upon. The usual crowd of girls milled about, but they were not watching the drills. They focused instead on a young man standing in their midst. He was slightly taller and broader of chest than Hierm. His glossy black hair fell almost to his shoulders and his hawkish brown eyes seemed to glow against his pale skin. His clothing was fine by Galsbur standards. He was working forms, all the while carrying on in a voice loud enough to be heard beyond the throng of young ladies.

"Of course I shall make it good sport. I'll permit my opponents to stand with me a few moments. The spectacle would be ruined for the onlookers of course, should I make quick work of the entire field."

Shanis leaned close to Hierm's ear. "Fascinating," she whispered, "how he can work his forms and his tongue at the same time."

"Perhaps he means to talk his opponents into submission," Hierm mumbled.

She clamped a hand over her mouth, trying without success to stifle a giggle. She caught the attention of one of the girls, Madelaine Halton, a chubby, brown-haired farmer's daughter with one green eye slightly bigger than the other, who turned and glared at the pair.

The young man also noticed, and broke off his form. "What have we here?" The look in his eyes belied his forced smile. "Admiring my forms, are you?"

Shanis felt an immediate aversion to this pompous stranger. "Amusing ourselves with them might be more accurate."

The youth was unfazed. "And what makes a girl such an expert at swordsmanship?" He flourished his sword in emphasis. To Shanis' practiced eye, it was nothing more than a silly affectation, but given the burst of hushed whispers among the onlookers, it must have appeared quite impressive.

"Didn't you know?" A voice piped up from the crowd. "She's fighting in the tournament."

Shanis did not try to stifle her impudent grin, but she remained silent. It was not altogether certain that she would be fighting in the tournament. Master Yurg planned to enter her name. Whether or not the prince would allow it was still in question.

The lad sheathed his sword. His eyes appraised Shanis for a moment before he replied. "That's not what I hear. I'm told Prince Lerryn will not allow any *woman*," he spat the word with disgust, "to disgrace his tournament with her ineptitude. The very idea is an affront to the gods and to common sense."

"Shanis is good." Natin had wandered up to the gathered crowd. "She's the best among us."

The dark-haired young man took a long, level look at the bread basket hooked over Natin's arm, smirked, and made a mocking face that elicited giggles from the girls. "I do not doubt that one bit." He looked around at the crowd that encircled him, seeming to challenge each person individually. "Of course, that is only a reflection of the sad state of the local manhood." The rumblings that arose from the onlookers only encouraged him. "My dear ladies," he shouted, "I am very sorry! Sorry that your birth has condemned you to live in a hamlet where masculinity is so obviously in short supply. Sorry that you have to live in a town full of large boys." Nervous laughter tittered from the girls not bright enough to realize he was insulting their home, their fathers and their brothers. "I do so hope you ladies will not hold it against me when I thrash your local lads."

Shanis rolled her eyes. She had heard more than enough from this flatulent sheep's bladder. She grabbed Hierm by the arm and turned to leave, but he shook his head and pointed to Natin, who had dropped his basket of bread and was shouting at the stranger.

"Who are you to come here and mock us?" Natin's face was scarlet, and his hands trembled. He had been humiliated, but what could he do? He was no swordsman. "You are not so great!"

Smiling wickedly, the stranger turned on Natin. "Perhaps you are right. Mayhap I have not nearly the skill of your local, ah, swordsmen." The face he made for the benefit of the onlookers said that the very idea was absurd to him. Another smattering of laughter arose. "What I am certain of is that you are not man enough to prove it." His predatory gaze locked on Natin.

"I guess we will find out at the tournament, won't we?" Shanis said in a raised voice, pushing her way past the cluster of girls. She gave Madelaine an elbow to the ribs on the way past, eliciting a satisfying grunt.

"Why wait until then? Surely this gentleman would not object to making a few passes with me. He seems the brave sort."

Natin did not meet the stranger's eye. He was staring at the ground, probably trying to think of a way to extricate himself from the situation without losing more face.

"Go ahead Natin," Khalyndryn piped up from behind Shanis. "Show us what you can do. You aren't afraid, are you?"

It was time to put a stop to this foolishness. She was about to say just that when she felt a hand clamp down on her shoulder. "Don't interfere," Hierm hissed. "You can't."

Did Hierm not realize what was happening? "He's just trying to pick a fight. To show off," she whispered back, turning to face her friend. "Natin can't handle a sword. He'd stand a better chance fighting with one of his loaves of bread."

Hierm's gaze was stern. "Shanis, if you stop this, you will shame him. You must not do it." The look in his eyes one of sadness, but resolution.

Shanis sniffed. Men and their ridiculous sense of pride! Hierm was right, of course. But if it did become necessary, she would put a stop to it. And she and Khalyndryn were going to have a long talk.

Khalyndryn's coaxing was all that Natin required. By the time Shanis turned back around, he had borrowed a sword from one of the bystanders. The crowd drew back from the combatants. With a cruel smile, his opponent prepared himself. Natin, his face ashen, raised his blade, and nodded.

The dark-haired stranger leapt to the attack. His first strokes were clumsy. Natin easily warded off the blows, and took the offensive. A murmur arose from the observers as Natin's assault was barely deflected. Shanis was not fooled. The stranger was toying with Natin. She needed only to see his footwork to know that he was, at the very least, experienced.

The crowd around the two combatants grew. A few of those drilling in the practice yard had taken notice, and now perched precariously on the fence, trying to gain a better vantage point. Master Yurg was busy on the far end of the yard, unaware of what transpired.

Shanis was struck by a sudden thought.

"Get Master Yurg! If he puts a stop to it, Natin won't be shamed. Hurry!"

Hierm nodded and pushed his way back out of the crowd.

Natin's advantage was short-lived. His adversary returned to the offensive with strokes that were increasingly precise. The rain of blows became a torrent. Natin backpedaled, all attention to form forsaken in a desperate attempt to defend himself. Shanis watched as the attack pressed on, and the concern in Natin's eyes became outright fear as it became apparent to all that the outsider had no intention of stopping.

A distant voice rang out. Shanis breathed a sigh of relief as she saw Master Yurg running toward them. The dueling boys neither heard nor saw the swordmaster's approach. Natin was tiring visibly. Stumbling and falling to one knee, he raised his blade in a gesture that was part defensive and part supplication.

"Hold! Hold!" Shanis shouted. The dark-haired outlander ignored her cry. He struck down hard in a sweeping slash. Natin screamed as the blade sliced through his wrist, spraying a hot, bloody froth across his face. His sword fell useless to the ground.

Then all was bedlam. People pushed and shouted. Shanis tried to fight through the throng that milled about Natin. She stumbled over Khalyndryn, who was bent over at the waist, retching. The dark-haired boy's head bobbed above the crowd, and she took off after him in mindless fury. Before she could reach her quarry, two men in white cloaks grabbed her by the arms and lifted her off the ground. She was too surprised to cry out. She looked about her and saw that several similarly garbed men were dispersing the crowd.

The men wore polished chain mail under their cloaks. All were armed. These were the prince's guard! Things began to quiet as the soldiers chased people away with sharp commands and more than a few threats of flogging.

Natin still lay on the ground. Master Yurg knelt over him along with two of the soldiers. His sword lay a few feet away in the blood-soaked grass. Another of them held Hierm by the upper arm. Natin's assailant stood with his arm pinned behind his back by an angular man in a flamboyant red and yellow checked cloak. The strange man seemed to wear a permanent smile along with the harp that was strapped to his back.

A stout soldier, his yellow beard streaked with gray, stalked up to them and inspected the three with a look not much short of contempt. "Come with me." He led them down the crowded dirt path that ringed the green in Galsbur's center. The soldiers half-dragged them up the steps of the Dry Birch, through the common room, where everyone paused to stare and shout japes, and into the small, private room in the back of the inn.

Lord Hiram sat at a small table in the corner with two men in merchant dress and a young man who could only be Prince Lerryn

The Prince was a tall man; even seated, that much was evident. His curly brown hair was cut short, just above his high, red collar. His skin was deeply tanned, unusual for royalty, but Lerryn's reputation was that of a soldier, and a good one. He spent little time at the palace in Archstone, preferring instead to remain in the field with his guard. He took in the scene with an amused expression.

"New recruits, Captain Tabars?" His laugh, deep and rich, cascaded over the three youths. Shanis hated him instantly.

Captain Tabars' face reddened. "Dueling, Highness. This one here," Tabars gestured at the young stranger, "near killed a local boy. Cut his hand 'most clean off!'"

The Prince was no longer smiling. His brown eyes bored into the three young people. "And the other two?"

"Had to grab them too." Tabars shook his head and directed a scowl at Shanis and Hierm. "Were going to dispense a little local justice, they were."

The Prince cupped his hand in his chin and gazed at Shanis with an intensity that took her breath. "The girl too?"

Shanis' heart sank. She had been deluding herself. The Prince was as bad as the rest of the men. He'd never let her fight in the tournament.

"Yes, Highness," Tabars said. His bearded chin twitched. "Oh yes, indeed."

"Master Van Derin," Lerryn inquired, turning his attention to Lord Hiram, who was staring daggers at his son. "Do you know these young people?"

The question hung in the silence as they awaited his reply. Shanis wondered if he was going to deny them, but he finally spoke, his voice a tired drone. "Your Highness, the boy to your right is my wayward son Hierm. The girl is Shanis Malan, the daughter of a man in my employ."

Hierm bowed as his father introduced him. Shanis knew that she should probably curtsy, or something ridiculously ladylike. After an awkward moment, she nodded and bent her knee slightly. Smiling, the Prince inclined his head in return.

"The other I do not know," Hiram continued. "He is not from these parts."

The jet-haired young man piped up right away. "Pedric Karst, Highness." He bowed deeply. "My father is the Duke of Kurnsbur, to the east and south."

If this name meant anything to Lerryn, it did not register on his face. He turned to the man who had brought Karst in. "And who might you be?"

"Sandrin Skedane at your service, Highness." The man made a graceful bow. "I am a loremaster," Skedane continued, "and a man of songs. I have come to see your tournament, and perhaps memorialize it in story and verse."

Shanis took a long look at him. His flamboyant red and yellow cloak was not all that was odd about him. His puffy, black hair was sprinkled with silver, and his chin whiskers, the only hair on his face, was twisted into a hands-length braid, with red and yellow ribbon woven in. His weathered face suggested that he had seen as many summers as Lord Hiram, but he seemed as spry and agile as a youth. He had easily taken Karst in hand.

"I see." Lerryn's tone said that he did not care one whit why Skedane was here. "Would you care to tell me what you witnessed?"

"I am sorry, Highness," Skedane said, holding out his hands in supplication. "I happened upon the scene just as the boy was injured. I took this one in hand," he said, nodding toward Karst, "before things grew even more heated."

"I thank you for your assistance. I assume you can find your way out?"

Skedane's face fell for a moment, but he caught himself and smiled at the prince. "Of course, Highness. Happy to be of service." He backed out of the room, his smile fading to a grin.

Lerryn waited until the man was well away and Tabars had closed the door before he spoke.

"Master Karst," he said, leaning forward and placing his hands on the table, fingers interlaced, "can you tell me how you came to cross blades with this other young man?"

"We were only making a few passes, Highness," Karst replied smoothly. "Practicing for the tournament. At least I was practicing."

Shanis clenched her fists and glared at the boy. Captain Tabars saw the expression on her face, and shook his head. The message was clear; do not interrupt.

"I have to admit I had teased him a bit," the boy continued, "all in good fun, mind. I guess he was angry. Things got out of hand, and I just...." Karst hung his head.

"You just cut off his hand." Lerryn's voice held no emotion.

"No Highness," Karst shook his head. "I mean, yes, but I didn't intend to. He fell and I was going to knock the blade from his hands to finish it, impressively, I suppose. But at the last moment, he flung his hands in the air. I didn't expect that. There was no time to stop."

Lerryn now turned his attention to Hierm and Shanis. "I suppose the two of you do not believe that this was an accident?"

"This was no accident. Natin was giving up. This ox brain didn't have to do what he did." Lord Hiram sat up straight and cleared his throat, but she ignored him. "Natin was no match for him to begin with. This boy knew what he was doing the entire time." Silence and expectant stares answered her. She looked quizzically at Lerryn before realizing what everyone was waiting for. "Um, Your Highness," she added. Tabars snorted, but the slight crinkle around Lerryn's eyes told Shanis that he, at least, found her lack of formality amusing.

Lerryn turned to Hierm. "And you, young Van Derin? Do you concur with the opinion of this girl?"

"Yes Highness," Hierm replied instantly. "He could have stopped himself." He did not meet the eye of his scowling father. "There is no doubt in my mind."

Lerryn propped his feet on the table, rocked back on his chair, hands folded behind his head, and stared at the ceiling. "Did this Natin raise his hands just before Master Karst delivered his blow?"

"He did, Highness, but with all due respect, I maintain that the blow could have been stopped."

"He raised his hands," Lerryn said, frowning at the ceiling. "Perhaps the girl is correct, and this Natin was trying to yield. Be that as it may, it would be totally unexpected to one practiced at swordplay." He removed his feet from the table, and turned back to Lord Hiram. "Is your son an adept bladesman?"

Hiram nodded. "Fair, Your Highness. Better than some, not as good as others."

Shanis did not miss the man's meaningful glance in her direction.

"Very well." Lerryn clapped his hands together. "Young Van Derin, in your opinion, had this Natin attempted to block Master Karst's blow, would his sword have been knocked from his grasp?"

Hierm paused for a moment before answering quietly. "I cannot say for certain, Highness. I think it likely, though." He let his head hang.

Shanis was incensed. Had it not occurred to the Prince that she might have an opinion herself? She was about to voice that opinion when someone entered the room.

"And what say you, Swordmaster?" Lerryn looked to the door, where Yurg had just walked in. The prince seemed unfazed by the blood covering Yurg's tunic.

Yurg made a hasty bow. "The boy will live, Highness." He paused a moment, glowering at Karst. "We had to take his hand."

Lerryn shook his head. "Did you happen to witness this incident?"

"I saw that a duel was taking place. I hurried to put a stop to it. But I regret to say I did not see the blow that cost the boy his hand."

"Did the injured boy have anything to say about what happened?" Lerryn gestured to a servant standing against the wall, who hastily refilled the prince's wine glass.

"He is scarcely coherent. He said that he did not know the intent of his opponent." Yurg's voice was flat, but Shanis could tell that he was having a difficult time keeping his temper in check. "Natin was not a student of the sword, but he is a good young man."

Lerryn sipped his wine and seemed to contemplate those words. When he finally spoke, his voice carried a tone that said he would brook no nonsense. "I cannot judge whether or not Master Karst intended the injury that he inflicted on Master Natin. It is, however, my judgment that Master Karst, as a young man of allegedly noble birth, has no business starting duels with farm boys."

"Tabars! What sort of coin is Master Karst carrying?"

After a brief search, the soldier relieved Karst of a small purse. He sorted through the contents. "Two golds, a few silvers, and some coppers." The soldier shrugged.

Lerryn nodded. "The gold shall be given to the boy's parents. A poor repayment for his hand."

"Give them the entire purse. I have another." Karst smirked.

Shanis clenched a fist and took a step in Karst's direction. Lerryn waved her back to her place without taking his eyes from Karst.

"Master Karst, do you wish to participate in my tournament?"

"I do, Highness." The boy's face paled as he realized he had said too much.

"You will control your words and your actions. My tournament is two days hence. I want neither to see your face nor hear your name until that time. Am I understood?"

"Yes. I swear it."

Lerryn nodded, and gestured toward the door. Karst bowed, and scurried out of the room. The Prince now turned his attention to Hierm and Shanis, who stood shoulder to shoulder in front of him.

"I expect that all thoughts of retribution will be forgotten immediately."

"Yes, Highness." Hierm's voice was a rough whisper.

Shanis stood, arms folded across her chest, staring back at Lerryn, who seemed content to wait her out. A few coins? That was all? Karst should be whipped. She controlled her tongue; no use in arguing with the second-most powerful man in Galdora. At long last she nodded in agreement.

Lerryn smiled and turned to Yurg. "Swordmaster, I understand this young woman is one of your students. Is that usual for Galsbur?"

"It is most unusual, Highness, but she is an exceptional talent. She and Master Van Derin are the best students I have ever trained."

The prince seemed to look at her with new eyes, taking stock of her: her face, chest, arms and legs. He looked at her not as a man might leer at a young girl, but as a man might inspect a horse.

"The two of you may go," he said at long last, nodding toward the door.

Relieved, Shanis turned to leave when Lerryn called to her.

"Miss Malan."

"Your Highness?" She turned to face the Prince.

"I look forward to witnessing your skills firsthand in my tournament!"

His words were like a shock of cold water. She gasped, but realization dawned within her, warming her very soul.

"Thank you, Highness," she whispered, as if a loud voice might wake her from what must be a dream. "Thank you." She made another failed attempt at a curtsy, then made a quick bow instead before darting from the room, fearful he might change his mind or say he had only been kidding.

She had to contain herself to keep from skipping through the common room. When they emerged into the street, she caught Hierm in a bear hug. "I'm going to do it, Hierm. I'm really going to do it." She couldn't take revenge on Karst, but perhaps she could beat him in the tournament. She could do no more for Natin than that.

Hierm merely smiled and squeezed her tightly.

She thought that nothing could spoil her mood, but then she noticed the figure standing a few paces from them. Karst waited on the edge of the green, across the dirt track from the inn. Pushing away from Hierm, she stared into Karst's eyes. He had regained his cruel glare, and any semblance of humility had vanished once he left Lerryn's presence.

"I am Pedric Karst," he hissed. "Remember my name." Without further word, he turned and stalked away.

Chapter 5

Lerryn's procession snaked through the crush of onlookers. Most were rural folk who might never again have the chance to witness royalty firsthand. The royal family of Galdora had not condescended to visit Galsbur or the surrounding area in remembered history. The guards, seven squadrons of seven soldiers, were the elite of Lerryn's corps. Called the White Fang, the unit garbed each warrior in a cloak of pure white over black tunic and hose, and a mail shirt of highly polished silver. The only visible marking was on the back, where a serpent's fang was outlined in black. A crimson drop of venom kissed the needle tip. Many in the crowd found their enthusiasm replaced with awe as these legendary fighters passed by. Nearby, Lars Harim stood dumbstruck, mouth agape, arms hanging loosely at his sides. Oskar chuckled at the farmer's reaction.

Oskar regarded the leader of one of the squadrons. His uniform devoid of any signs of rank, his standing was denoted by the silver armlet worn just above his wrist. Oskar had overheard someone explain the meaning of the armlets. One band signified a squad leader. More bands denoted higher rank. The soldier kept his gaze fixed immediately in front of him, but his countenance was enough to shake even the stoutest Galsburan. This was a man to be feared. Only a brief look at the other soldiers was needed to include them all in that category.

"Glad they're on our side," Oskar muttered, his stomach fluttering at the site. A man standing nearby bobbed a bald head in agreement. Oskar's cheeks reddened.

He had not intended to speak aloud.

Prince Lerryn rode in the middle of the procession. Unlike his soldiers, Lerryn wore no armor. His tunic and hose were crimson, with matching fringe trimming his snow-white cape. A black viper adorned his cape. Lerryn smiled, a stark contrast to his guard. The easy air about the prince seemed to soften the mood of the crowd. Cheers erupted. Fathers hoisted children onto their shoulders. A few young women wept openly. The Prince acknowledged the assemblage with an occasional wave, or nod of his head. A girl somewhere in the back of the throng squealed, "He looked at me! He looked at me!" The ensuing thud told Oskar that she had likely fainted.

When the last rider had passed, the cheers abated, but only for a moment. Shouts, whistles, and peals of laughter rang in Oskar's ears. Oskar looked around for the source of the crowd's reaction. He did not have to look far. Another procession made its way toward the tournament grounds, led by a group of what appeared, at first glance, to be soldiers escorting a shiny black carriage. The top was down, revealing several people seated within. One passenger was standing and waving to the crowd. As the carriage drew near, Oskar recognized Mistress Faun. She wore a black dress, which exposed a generous amount of cleavage. Her golden tresses were piled high atop her head, encircled by a sparkling tiara.

Oskar noticed that the carriage was escorted not by soldiers, but by various local farmers and craftsmen who had apparently allowed Faun to talk them into serving as an ill-assorted honor guard. Faun had garbed them all in black cloaks to match her dress. Nothing else about them was uniform. Their clothing was a motley assortment of brown, dark green, and dark blue tunics and hose. Black dye was rare and expensive, thus few common folk actually owned black clothing. A few of the men had belted on ancient swords, likely family heirlooms. The remainder carried a variety of weapons or farm implements. Unlike the men of the White Fang, it was easy to read the expressions on the faces of these men. Most were deeply embarrassed, probably regretting what had seemed like a good idea a few days earlier. Oskar hoped that Faun had at least paid them.

Mistaking the laughter for cries of approval, Faun continued to wave daintily. Hiram sat next to her, his face a mask of serenity. He stared at the sky, not acknowledging Faun or the host of mocking faces. Oskar almost felt sorry for him. Hierm's older brother Laman sat alongside his father. Where Hierm favored their mother, Laman was the spitting image of Hiram. Tall, angular, almost handsome, but not quite. The only feature that he and Hierm shared was their mother's golden hair. Ever the dutiful son, Laman kept a smile on his face, and stared straight ahead, never letting his embarrassment show. Joining the Van Derins in the coach was Master and Mistress Serrill, along with Khalyndryn. The three of them were decked out in their finest clothing. Though her parents appeared mortified by the jeers of the throng, Khalyndryn seemed not to notice. Her gaze was locked on the knot of white riders in the distance. After the Van Derin's coach passed, the crowd closed in behind and followed it down the road.

The hills surrounding the tournament ground were nearly filled. Some people had staked out spots two days before, and camped until the day of the event. He found an open space near the top of the hill, directly opposite the viewing platform.

Lerryn mounted the dais, recognized the crowd with an imperious wave, and spoke. Despite the distance and the roar of the massed throng, Oskar could clearly make out every word. Sorcery? A chill crawled up his spine, and he shivered. Galsburans were a practical sort. They knew that such things were supposed to exist but did not really believe. Given the response that Lerryn was receiving, most of those in attendance either did not realize that sorcery was being employed, or did not care.

"People of Galsbur. My friends!" A roar of adoration answered Lerryn's greeting. He paused momentarily to acknowledge the praise with a smile and nod. "It is truly an honor to be with you this day." Another cheer, another pause. "Our nation has need of good men! Of strong men!" Oskar wondered how Shanis was reacting to that particular choice of words. "I am pleased to see many such young men standing here before me." His gesture swept across the entirety of the tournament entrants, who stood arrayed before the dais.

"Today we shall honor the most promising of your swordsmen, your archers." He paused and extended his arms outward, fingers spread, as if to embrace the entire throng of people at once. "Today, the eyes of the realm are on Galsbur." A wave of joy and pride crashed into the dais, rolling across the platform with visible effect. In her seat, Mistress Faun flinched. Several members of the prince's entourage sat up straighter. Lerryn merely smiled, soaking it up. Ordinarily a cynic, Oskar was startled to hear his own voice joining the din.

When the cheers died down, a member of Lerryn's entourage, whose rich, green robes and blue stole marked him an ecclesiast, offered a prayer to the seven gods. The invocation went largely ignored by the Galsburans and other locals, who were impatient for the tournament to commence. Oskar noted that Faun raised her hands in prayer in imitation of the dignitaries seated around her. He was pleased to see that Lord Hiram, at least, kept his hands in his lap and retained his usual, implacable stare. If the ecclesiast thought any of them impious, he did not show it. When he finished his prayer, he merely bowed to Lerryn, and returned to his seat.

Anticipation rose anew, the tension taut like a bowstring stretched to its limit. To Oskar's mind, everyone seemed to be leaning forward slightly, tensed as if they were about to sprint onto the field. He could almost feel the collective energy of the crowd dancing in the air.

On the platform, Lerryn nodded to a guardsman, who raised his war horn. The rumble of the crowd ascended to a roar. While seven lengthy blasts issued from the horn, the flag of Galdora was raised atop a pole just behind the Prince's stand. The tournament had begun!

The day began with footraces. After several heats, Hanos Herran, a local boy, bested the field. Two members of the White Fang led him to the dais, and Lerryn himself placed a crown of what looked like ivy upon his head. Hanos, quivering nervously, bowed so deeply that the crown fell off his head. Many in the crowd laughed, but Lerryn merely returned the bow. A soldier then led Hanos into to a tent next to the viewing platform. Oskar's gaze returned to the field, where the wrestling competition had begun.

Oskar did not thoroughly understand the rules of formal wrestling. Neither did many of the entrants. After a great deal of eye gouging and hair pulling in the first few matches, one of the soldiers called a halt, and launched into an animated explanation, accompanied by demonstrations on an unwilling-looking young man who had been the worst of the hair-pullers. While the demonstration continued,

Oskar scanned the perimeter of the field looking for Shanis and Hierm. He located Shanis quickly enough. Her red hair stood out in any crowd.

She sat at the far end of the field, far to Oskar's right. Nearby, a large wall made of bales of straw would serve as the backdrop for the archery competition. Several of the more antsy swordsmen were stabbing the straw. Shanis was not looking at them. Rather, she was staring off to her left, where a tall boy with jet-black hair stood with his arms folded across his chest. The boy's smug countenance said that he thought himself superior to these country folk. Oskar knew from Shanis and Hierm's descriptions that this was Pedric Karst, the young man who had taken Natin's hand. Oskar's fists clenched. A primordial part of him that rarely surfaced wanted to force his way down through the crowd and strangle the youth with his bare hands. He took a deep breath and closed his eyes until the urge subsided.

"I hope Shanis gets a chance at him," he whispered. "I hope, I hope, I hope."

"You all right, boy?" Lars Harim, apparently recovered from his shock at seeing the White Fang at close range, cocked his head and stared at Oskar.

"Yes sir," Oskar replied, a bit abashed. He pointedly fixed his gaze on the wrestlers, so as to cut off any further embarrassing conversation.

The wrestling competition resumed with several spirited matches taking place simultaneously. As the less-experienced wrestlers were eliminated, the matches began to look less like melees and more like sport. Each contest took place inside a small square, with boundaries marked off by ropes only a hand's length above the ground. Oskar deduced most of the rules by watching. The rest he learned by listening to conversations going on around him. A wrestler earned a point for throwing his opponent to the ground, or by forcing him out of the designated area. A soldier oversaw each match, and awarded points. Kicking and punching were not allowed. Tripping was legal, but one did not receive a point for taking down an opponent in this manner. In the absence of a "throw down" or an "out", the overseer could award a point for "controlling the action."

It quickly became evident that the class of the tournament was a veritable giant of a boy from one of the outlying communities. Towering head and shoulder above the rest of the combatants, the young man combined incredible strength with surprising speed for one of his size. He quickly became the crowd favorite as he plowed through the tournament field. Not knowing his name, someone on the hill to Oskar's left began shouting "Bull! Bull!" The rest of the spectators picked up the chant. Oskar thought that the boy's matted black curls and lack of a neck made him look more like a troll than a bull.

In the finals, the Bull faced off against a lean fellow of above-average height. The boy had some muscle on him, but next to the Bull, he appeared woefully thin. He also seemed overly preoccupied with his hair, which he combed thoroughly between matches before knotting it atop his head in some strange sort of bun. In his mind, Oskar had already nicknamed this boy "Hair". The hairstyle, coupled with his perpetual grin made him appear almost effeminate.

"This fellow's going to be killed." Oskar voiced the thought that must have been in everyone's mind.

To everyone's surprise and pleasure, the match was competitive. Bull, though quick for his size, was not as fast as Hair, who managed to trip Bull a few times, all the while avoiding his clutches. When Hair managed to send Bull stumbling out of the ring, earning his first point, the chants of "Bull! Bull!" subsided for a moment.

Oskar filled the gap by shouting, "Hair! Hair! Hair!" Most of the people looked at him as if he were deranged, but a few laughed, and joined in. Within moments, chants of "Bull!" met shouts of "Hair!" as the two boys went at one another. Oskar did not think it possible, but the smile on the blond boy's face actually seemed to grow broader.

The match ended when Bull finally got a solid grip on his opponent, and crushed him in a bear hug. When he finally dropped Hair onto the ground, the boy lay motionless on the thick grass. The soldier overseeing the match knelt over the boy, examining him at length before pronouncing him "out".

Concern for the fallen wrestler tempered the crowd's enthusiasm. Oskar was impressed to see Bull drop to his knees and speak to the young man who lay on the ground. Apparently satisfied with whatever response he received, Bull stood and allowed himself to be led to Lerryn's dais. By the time the prince had crowned the wrestling champion, the runner-up was on his feet to the sound of applause and a few shouts of "Hair". He was still smiling. Oskar noted that this time, both young men were taken into the tent.

The archery competition opened with a nervous contestant sending his first shot over the protective backdrop and into the crowd. The arrow struck a man in the leg, but the victim was so drunk that he ripped the arrow from his thigh and held it aloft. Laughing, he staggered several steps through the crowd before his legs melted and he fell in an incoherent heap. A few of the spectators, overcoming their surprise, hurried over to tend to the man. The shaken young archer recovered his composure enough that he was able to hit the target with his remaining shots, but did not come near the bullseye.

As the contest progressed, Oskar determined that archery was not a great spectator sport. The better archers came close to the center of the target with nearly every shot. Only the observers who sat near the front could tell who had made the best shots. Thankfully, the competition moved along at a brisk pace until Edrin Kalloh, a local boy, emerged the winner. As he received his crown, the crowd roared with excitement. Not so much, Oskar thought, in support of the archer, but instead because it was time for the swords.

A chill ran up Shanis' spine as she listened to the roar of the crowd, rising to a tumult as the swordsmen were called onto the field. She had never been nervous about using the sword, it having always come easily to her. Besting the boys had been fun, the pressure always being on them not to lose to a girl. But today it was Shanis who felt the pressure. For the first time, something important was dependent on her performance. This was the chance to live her dream. The chance to attend the Prince's Academy. But she had to win.

The winner of the tournament would gain a place in the Prince's Academy, but others might also be invited if they were deemed worthy. Gossip among the contestants held that two wrestlers and three archers had been invited. The young men needed only to acquit themselves well in order to be considered. Shanis knew that that would not be enough in her case.

She did not know why Prince Lerryn had been so agreeable to her competing. Likely, he was amused by the novelty of it all. A girl with a sword! Doubtless, he did not expect her to win. He probably expected her to make a fool of herself. She would show him. If she won the tournament, he would be bound to admit her into the academy. She would have earned that right in front of thousands of witnesses. Anything less than a victory might give Lerryn an excuse to exclude her.

She scanned the crowd in search of her father. She did not expect to see him. He had left early that morning, hauling goods for Lord Hiram. He had not wished her luck. In fact, they had not spoken of the tournament since the day she had learned that she could compete. Arriving home, she had leapt into her father's arms like a young girl. For a moment he was his old self, laughing a deep, hearty laugh as he clutched her tight to his barrel chest.

Upon hearing the news, though, her father hung his head, shrugged his bear-like shoulders and whispered, "If it must be." He then retired to his room, and did not come out until morning.

Shanis' mother had died during childbirth, but this tragedy had not stopped Colin from filling his daughter's life with happiness and love. Her earliest memories were of walks in the woods with him. He taught her scout craft, how to track, hunt and survive in the wilderness. He taught her hand-to-hand fighting and trained her in the use of the knife and the bow.

He presented her with her first sword in her seventh summer: a blunt-edged tournament sword that was just right for her size and strength. Colin taught her the basics and then turned her over to Master Yurg for training.

Colin Malan had also taught her to read and to do sums. He was truly a remarkable man. How many simple teamsters had the breadth of knowledge and experience that Shanis' father had? Moreover, how many men would commit the time to raising a daughter alone?

The thing she most remembered was that he had taught her that being a girl should never hold her back. "You can do anything, Shanis. Anything. Always believe." How many times had he said those words to her? Shanis felt that she no longer knew this sad, strange man. His ill temper had grown worse over the past few months. The closer she came to her sixteenth birthday, the less supportive Colin became. All of the things he had taught her no longer seemed to matter. Suddenly he wanted her to be another one of the girls, which made the note he had left for her all the more puzzling.

She had risen early to find that her father had already left. A piece of parchment lay beneath her sword.

Shanis,
The sword is your destiny. I thought I could keep you from it, but I was wrong. I cannot be with you today because I would try to stop you. A man does not always know when he is beaten. Trust Yurg. Know that I will always be your father.
Papa

The note was strange in many ways. Apparently, her father was resigned to her pursuit of the sword. What did he mean, "Trust Yurg"? She had always trusted Yurg. He was like a second father to her. And why tell her that he would always be her father? It was strange.

The bark of a soldier giving instructions jolted her back to awareness. She recognized Captain Tabars from the encounter between Natin and Pedric Karst. She ground her teeth at the thought of Karst. She hoped that she would have the chance to make him pay for what he had done to Natin. She had only a moment to think before Tabars began moving people around. The contestants were divided into rows, each person several paces away from the others. Tabars explained that they would begin by working through some basic forms.

Shanis drew her sword, and ran through the mental exercises that Yurg had taught her. One with the blade. In her mind's eye, the blade became an extension of her body. She shed her emotions, her random thoughts, whittled away by the sword's razor edge. Her blood flowed through the sword. The sword breathed with her. She was the sword. The sword was her.

She flowed through the forms with a practiced ease, calming her nerves and focusing only on the sword. Her mind regarded the activity about her with a detached curiosity. Next to her, an awkward young man with a bulbous nose barely averted hacking off his own foot as he feebly attempted to follow along with the group. One of the Prince's guards intervened, and removed the boy from the group. Some part of Shanis heard the boy's sobs as he was led away. Another part of her wondered who had signed for the boy to enter. Probably he was the son of some nobleman who thought himself worthy because of his station.

The forms came to an end. Shanis noted that several hopefuls had been weeded from the field during the working of the forms. All the better. Even using a tournament sword, a novice could be seriously injured.

Three dueling circles were marked off in a triangle in front of the dais. Almost immediately, a soldier called Shanis to the one nearest Lerryn and the other guests.

A tall, grim-looking soldier with a pockmarked face approached her. "Get a jerkin and a sword. Give your own sword to me." He waited while Shanis unbelted her sword and handed it over. He carelessly tossed it to the side, and then addressed her opponent in the same way. If he had treated her sword casually, nothing else about him was casual. His every move spoke of barely contained danger, like a snake poised to strike.

Shanis chose a jerkin from a nearby pile. The tournament armor was a thick leather vest padded with wool. Shanis chose the lightest one she could find. She took more time choosing from the stack of blunted tournament swords. The weight was not of great concern to her, but proper balance was paramount. After testing several blades, she finally found one to her liking, and moved into the circle. Her opponent was waiting for her, as was the swarthy soldier. She wondered if he would be annoyed at the delay, but instead he gave her an appraising look, and a nod. Obviously, he understood what she had been doing.

Her adversary was a tall, broad-shouldered boy who looked to be of an age with her. The fine cut of his clothing marked him as someone of affluence, if not nobility. He had unruly auburn hair and a freckled face. He made no effort to hide his contempt for her, chuckling as she took her place in the circle. He must have misinterpreted the delay as hesitation on her part.

Out of the corner of her eye, Shanis spied Lerryn smirking. Mistress Faun, face twisted in revulsion, was whispering in Hiram's ear. Hot rage surged inside of her, and she had to fight to control her temper. Focus.

"I am Squadron Leader Khattre," the soldier said. "You will obey my instructions at all times. I will call all points. No points for strikes to the head and neck. Three points wins." With that, he handed each of them a light helm. "Ready positions!"

Hastily, Shanis donned her helm and moved to the center of the circle. She stood sideways to her opponent, looking at him across her right shoulder. She held her sword point-down in front of her. Her grip was tighter than it should have been. She was too tense. Her mind raced.

Calm yourself! Be one with the blade!

A few cheers arose from the crowd, but only a few. Taunts and jeers drowned them out. One man made an extremely profane proposition to her, which was received with much laughter. This was not at all how it was supposed to be! Her calm evaporated. Faun and her superior airs. Lerryn making sport of her. The smirking boy facing her in the circle. She wanted to destroy them all. When Khattre called "Begin!" she leapt into her opponent, hacking through him with unbound fury.

Taken by surprise, the boy backpedaled momentarily, then moved to the side, sliding past her. "Point!"

That was too fast. What happened?

More catcalls from the crowd. Shanis looked down. The point was not hers. Her opponent had stabbed her in the very center of the abdomen. With a real sword it would have been a killing blow. A painful one. She felt her face flush. She had lost control. The rage she had felt only moments ago drained away, replaced by humiliation. Khattre looked disappointed. She glanced up at the dais, where Faun veritably glowed with satisfaction. Lerryn maintained his amused grin. Hiram stared through her, as if he wished she were invisible. Everything was amplified. The laughter rang in her ears. She stepped back and shook her head vigorously, as if she could make it all go away.

Glancing up she noticed Yurg seated to Lerryn's left. Why hadn't she noticed him before? Her gaze locked with his. A brief narrowing of the eyes was the only response he gave, but it was enough. She remembered an argument not so long ago. 'If an opponent can make you angry, he can kill you just as easily. For all the gifts you have with the blade, you can't grasp that simple concept!' His voice echoed in her mind. Now she understood his anger, his frustration. Calm. Like the forms. Calm.

"One with the blade." she whispered. "One with the blade". She moved back to the center of the circle, as if in a trance. She sliced away her feelings, and discarded them one by one. Frustration, confusion, embarrassment, anger, all gone. She was one with the blade. She was the blade.

No longer did animosity of any sort show on her opponent's face. In fact, he no longer seemed to regard her in any way at all. She was no longer worthy of his concern. It showed in his posture, in the lazy way he held the sword. His eyes darted toward Khattre, impatiently waiting to dispatch this foolish girl. This time, Shanis did not care what he thought of her. She did not care what anyone thought. She was the blade.

"Begin!" Shanis easily deflected a broad, sweeping stroke that had been aimed at her head. She flowed smoothly into an attack. She pressed forward, this time under control. Her adversary cocked an eyebrow. Once again she had surprised him. This time it cost him.

"Point!" Khattre shouted.

The boy stared at her for a moment. He suppressed a chuckle, then returned to the center of the circle. When the duel resumed, he leapt to the attack.

Shanis glided into a defensive posture. The blows rained down. She deflected them with ease. She danced around the circle with a grace borne of years of training. Her attacker redoubled his efforts to no avail. His blade never came close. Shanis remained on the defensive. She now knew the extent of the young man's abilities.

Around the circle they spun, the boy hacking away in frustration. His chest heaved, sweat poured down his face, his footwork was sloppy, his strokes long and looping. He was clearly exhausted.

Shanis decided to give him a rest. She neatly deflected his blade and stabbed for the heart.

"Point!" If Khattre was surprised at this turn of events, his serious demeanor gave no hint.

This time, a few people in the crowd cheered. Most still taunted her. Those who did not understand swordplay believed that they had seen a superior swordsman drive his opponent around the circle, only to fall victim to a lucky stab. Khattre met her eye with a lengthy stare, as if taking stock of her. Her opponent received only a sympathetic shake of the head before they were recalled to action. This time Shanis would leave no doubt in anyone's mind.

A tight, measured attack drew the boy's blade in close to his body. He mounted a feeble defense, Shanis' blade coming ever closer. Four strokes to the abdomen in quick succession. A forehand slash across the bridge of the nose came just short of blinding the young man. Shanis had intended to miss. In a panic, the boy threw his blade up to protect his face. With a loud smack, Shanis' backhand stroke cracked across his stomach, driving the wind from him and buckling his knees.

"Match!" Khattre thrust his left fist into the air and pointed his right hand at Shanis.

This time the cheers almost equaled the whistles and insults that were hurled her way. Shanis turned toward the dais, removed her helm, and knelt in an exaggerated bow. More applause, and many more jeers. Lerryn stood, and returned her bow along with a flourish of his cape.

Mistress Faun looked scandalized. Shanis treated her to a mock-curtsy, difficult to do while wearing leather armor and holding a sword. Lerryn clapped his hands, and nudged Faun with an elbow to the ribs. It took Faun only a moment to decide this was all Lord Hiram's fault. She ignored both Shanis and the Prince, and laid into her husband with a vengeance. As usual, Hiram took it all with a stony detachment. Lerryn shook his head at Faun and continued to applaud.

"Girl! On guard!"

At the sound of Khattre's voice, Shanis spun around. Her vanquished opponent, now on his feet, charged at her. Reflexively, Shanis ducked under a stroke that would have caved in her skull. She somersaulted on her left shoulder, and came up underneath her assailant. With a deft thrust, she drove the pommel of her sword up into his groin. He made surprisingly little sound as he toppled and fell. The crowd roared its approval. Somewhere beneath the calm of the sword, Shanis smiled. This might be fun, after all.

Chapter 6

Hierm swept the sodden mass of hair from his forehead. He mopped his brow, then retied the cloth around his temple. Taking a moment to rest, he leaned against a nearby wagon, and tried to catch a glimpse of Shanis. He had seen little of her, but he was able to follow her progress by the roaring of the crowd. He had watched the beginning of Shanis' first match. It was not a pretty sight. He had agonized as he watched her struggle. He knew that she was better than what she displayed. But somehow, almost magically, the old Shanis had emerged. Even knowing her capabilities as he did, Hierm was amazed at the progressive ease with which she dispatched her opponents. As her performance improved, so did the crowd's reaction to her. She quickly became the favorite. From then on, every eruption told Hierm that Shanis had again emerged the victor.

Things had not been as easy for Hierm. His first opponent had been a young man obviously of moderate experience, and Hierm had made quick work of him. Since then, each match had grown increasingly difficult, each opponent more skilled. In fact, he had scarcely managed to win his last match. Only a foolish slip by his opponent had allowed him to claim the victory.

He stole a glance at the dais. No one was looking at Hierm. They were all waiting for Shanis' next match. His mother noticed him, and waved. Alongside her, Hiram looked at him and nodded. Strange, that simple gesture from his father meant more to Hierm than all of his mother's smiles and waves. His reverie was broken by the sound of his name being called.

"Van Derin! To the circle."

He made his way back toward the circle. As he walked, a soldier clapped a meaty hand on his shoulder. Hierm looked down at him.

The man looked like a walking tree stump. His arms were as thick as Hierm's thighs, and his legs were so muscular that the man seemed to step to-and-fro in order to keep his thighs from touching. A broad scar, puckered and faded with age, ran across the back of his thick neck. Despite his intimidating physical appearance, the soldier wore a relaxed smile, and his clear, brown eyes matched his pleasant demeanor.

"This is it, boy. Win this and you fight for the championship!" Hierm could not stifle a grin. Surely that would make his father proud. The soldier noticed his smile, but misunderstood the thought behind it. "Want a crack at that redhead, do you? She's a good one."

Hierm missed a step. In all of the excitement leading up to this day, it had not occurred to him that he might face Shanis. He should have considered the possibility, he supposed, but he had not truly expected to make it this far. Shanis was the crowd favorite. If he fought her and won, he would be reviled. And if he lost, he shuddered to think what is father would say. What was he thinking? If he won? The way Shanis was fighting today the whole of the White Fang could not beat her.

"I don't want to fight Shanis," he muttered. "This is not good. Not good at all."

"Not good, you say?" the soldier laughed. "Win this one before you worry about the next." They arrived at the circle. The soldier removed his hand from

Hierm's shoulder, and gestured across the ring. "Watch this one. He's as bad as she is good." With that, he turned and walked away.

Hierm watched his bulky form recede into the crowd. Odd that the fellow had taken an interest in him. Hierm didn't recall having ever seen him before. Too bad he had not gotten the man's name. Regardless, it was now time for the business at hand. He stepped into the ring, and looked across at his opponent. He stifled a curse when he saw whom he was to face. Beady black eyes stared at him from a frame of ink black hair. Karst! Hierm had completely forgotten the ill-disposed young noble. His surprise must have showed. Karst's lips curved back in a wicked smile. The whiteness of his teeth and the pallor of his skin made his lips appear to be the color of blood.

The two contestants were called to the center of the circle. Hierm stared dispassionately into Karst's eyes as they were given the same instructions they had received before each match. The surprise at seeing Karst had faded quickly. Hierm forced himself to regain his focus. This was simply another opponent. Hierm sized him up. Slightly taller than himself. Perhaps a slightly longer reach. Lanky, probably strong and quick. He tried to remember what he had seen when Karst had fought Natin. It had all happened so fast. The only things he could glean from the memory were that Karst was skilled and wicked.

Everything seemed to accelerate as Hierm analyzed his opponent. His heart pounded, and his senses seemed heightened. He felt the warmth of the sun on his scalp, the track of a single bead of sweat as it traced a path through the dust on his cheek. The roar of the crowd thundered in his ears, yet it seemed that he could pick out each individual voice. A fly buzzed past his face. Somewhere nearby, someone was roasting meat. The green expanse of the field, the deep blue sky, and the white cloaks of the Prince's guard took on a striking clarity. Objects seemed to rush toward him, then instantly recede. All of these things flashed through his consciousness in an instant. He took a deep breath, and fought to regain control of himself.

The instructions were nearly finished. Think! Think! Hierm told himself. Everyone has a weakness! Shanis' weakness was anger. Hierm had his weaknesses. What was Karst's weakness?

The instructions were completed. Hierm and Karst were ordered to step back and make ready. As they moved apart, Karst spoke to him softly enough that no one else heard. "I can't wait to see what passes for nobility in this cow pasture of a town." Hierm looked at Karst's sneering face and laughed. How had he not seen it before?

Shanis wondered what Hierm's laugh could mean. Her last match had been as easy as the rest. Not that her opponents weren't good. Today, she was better than she'd ever been in her life. Now, only one match remained. Her opponent would either be Karst or Hierm. She felt torn. She didn't want Hierm to lose to Karst. On the other hand, she would relish beating Karst. And she would beat him. He was good, but she believed that today, no one could beat her. Everything was flowing perfectly. This was the day that she would finally show everyone that they had been wrong to have discouraged her from pursuing the sword. She would hate to have to beat Hierm, but if that was what it took to win, she would do it. She was a swordsman. Swordsperson, Khalyndryn used to say, half-teasingly. Swordsman sounded just fine to Shanis. Anything else cheapened it, made it sound second-best. She was the best swordsman on the field today, and soon she would prove it.

She watched as Hierm and Karst made ready. At the signal, the two leapt together, swords meeting in midair with a resounding ring. They parted as quickly as they had come together. They circled one another nimbly, thrusting and parrying. Karst twisted his upper lip in a dismissive sneer as he crossed blades with his opponent. His footwork was smooth and his reflexes quick. He did not miss a step when Hierm stepped up the attack. He was better than Shanis had thought.

Hierm, for his part, wore a look of intense concentration. Shanis thought that was strange. Hierm normally kept his face blank, regardless of what he might be feeling on the inside. He was fighting well, but seemed to need every mental faculty to match Karst. Shanis watched as Hierm slowed his attack, and slid to his right, drawing Karst to him. Karst continued to smile as he pursued Hierm around the circle. Gradually, the dark-haired young man began to increase the pace of his attack. Stroke by stroke, Hierm's defenses began to fail.

Hierm parried awkwardly. Each stroke from Karst came increasingly closer to striking home. Shanis clenched her fists. His form was all wrong. Everything was slightly off. The angle of his elbow, his grip, and his footwork were those of a beginner; an experienced one, perhaps, but still a beginner. He was better than this. Karst noticed too, and pressed his attack with a reckless ferocity. Hierm wavered under the attack. He stumbled, ducked under a vicious two-handed strike that would have parted his head from his body, tournament sword or no, then thrust desperately.

"Point!"

A cheer went up from the crowd. It seemed that Karst had not endeared himself to the onlookers. Shanis smiled. It had appeared to be a lucky blow, but she now realized exactly what her friend was up to. Hierm looked winded, confused. A glance at Karst revealed that a mixture of rage and contempt had replaced his knowing grin. Right then, rage appeared to be winning. His black eyes glistened with intensity. His entire body quivered.

As they were again called to start, Karst leapt to the attack. Hierm fell back quickly. Desperately he fended off blows. Shanis bit her lip as she watched Hierm stumble as he retreated. Seeing his opponent off-balance, Karst prepared to deliver a crushing blow. Shanis wanted to cry out in glee when a sudden transformation took place in her friend. Hierm, who had been stumbling awkwardly, regained his feet. Nimbly he ducked under Karst's strike. He spun to the side, bringing his sword around as he pivoted. The blade landed solidly across the dark haired boy's stomach with a sickening thud. Karst's sharp exhale of breath could be heard over the hushed onlookers, who appeared to be shocked at this turn of events. Karst crumpled to his knees, the wind knocked from him. Lucky for him this was a tournament, Shanis mused. With a real sword, and without the protective padding, he'd have been dead. As it stood, the boy would have a nasty bruise by this evening.

The surprise began to wear off, and a smattering of applause arose, accompanied by a few hurrahs from the local boys. Karst stared up at Hierm, his face a mask of shock and disbelief. Spittle ran down his chin. His breath was returning to him in deep rasps. He no longer wore his haughty expression. Instead his eyes bore mute testimony to more unadulterated hate than Shanis had ever seen. Hierm's face was serene. His poise had returned. He glanced in her direction, and their eyes met briefly.

"Finish it," she whispered.

Hierm had fed Karst's illusion by pretending to be exactly what Karst expected him to be; an awkward country boy who couldn't handle a blade. Karst had foolishly left himself open for the first point. Even after surrendering a point, it had not registered with Karst that he faced a capable opponent. He had waded in recklessly and had been made to pay. Hierm knew that he could no longer fool his adversary. Now would come the test. Who was the better swordsman?

When the match resumed, Karst was no longer the overconfident opponent Hierm had faced. He circled Hierm, trading blows not cautiously, but carefully. Around they went. Hierm called upon all of his skill, whirling, feinting, slashing. Karst faltered, but before Hierm could take advantage, he leapt at Hierm, driving his shoulder into the shorter boys face. Hierm fell flat on his back.

"Halt!" the soldier called. "That's a warning Karst!" Karst did not respond. The soldier offered his hand, but Hierm leapt quickly to his feet. His cheekbone stung from the blow, and his left eye felt puffy. He might have a blackened eye when this was over.

Karst seemed to have regained his self-assuredness, and came at Hierm with a determined assault. Hierm parried, but could not return the attack. He could only defend himself. His head rung a bit from the collision, and his eye seemed to be swelling already. Karst whirled, struck low, then high.

"Point!"

Hierm cursed under his breath. He hadn't been focused, and Karst had taken advantage. Sweat dripped into his eye, making it sting. He swiped at it with his sleeve, and sucked in his breath sharply. Fire seemed to scorch the left side of his face. He reeled from the pain. What was wrong? He felt a firm hand clamp his shoulder.

"Come on boy!" the soldier barked at him. "He barely touched you. Make ready!"

Hierm gritted his teeth and tried to regain his calm. Things happened too fast. He had scarcely taken up his position when the match resumed. Karst attacked quickly, thrusting and dodging to his right. He kept Hierm pivoting toward what was fast becoming his blind side. The eye was swelling closed. This can't be happening! Hierm thought to himself. He didn't hit me that hard! It quickly became a losing battle. Karst kept up the pressure, dancing to Hierm's left before Hierm could strike. If this keeps up much longer he'll have me. Hierm had to try something.

Deflecting a slash, Hierm spun hard to his right, bringing his blade around in a vicious backhand swipe. From the corner of his good eye, he saw Pedric circling directly into the blade's path. A whirl. A heavy thud.

"Point!"

Hierm looked down to see the tip of Karst's sword pressed into the center of his stomach. Karst was balanced on the balls of his feet and the fingertips of his left hand. He had rolled under Hierm's swipe, and struck before Hierm could recover. Two points apiece. The next point would decide the match.

A stinging heat rose up along the side of Hierm's face. His eye was nearly swollen shut now, and the burning sensation had not subsided. He raised his hand to rub at it again, but thought the better of it. The memory of the last time he had tried that was still fresh in his mind. He shook his head vigorously, as if that would somehow solve the problem. He made ready.

At the signal, Karst again attacked quickly. He struck fast and bounced away, always staying to Hierm's left. Karst did not try any looping strokes that might open his defenses. He stabbed quickly, then pulled away. Hierm feinted a thrust of his own. The attempt was so feeble that Karst did not even react, but drove another lightning quick attack into Hierm's defenses. Hierm barely deflected it. Another. Then another. Karst was a shadow just out of the sight of Hierm's good eye.

Hierm was now so blind that he was fighting mostly on instinct, anticipating where each next stroke would fall. A sense of desperation welled up inside of him. He felt an icy cold in the pit of his stomach. I can't last much longer, he thought. A moment's panic seized him as, in his mind's eye, he saw Karst's sword slicing off Natin's hand. These were only tournament swords, but they could still do some damage. He threw his blade up, and felt the force of Karst's stroke all the way up to his elbow. He struck back awkwardly, and danced away, his sword raised to fend off the next attack. So far he had guessed correctly. But how much longer?

Chapter 7

Shanis watched the match with an increasing sense of despair. She couldn't believe Hierm's misfortune. The collision with Karst must have been worse than it looked. Hierm's face was swelling up like an angry bullfrog. Worse, Hierm was losing. Badly. He had managed to fight off his opponent's attack, but just barely. Hierm appeared desperate, almost frantic. Karst's smirk had returned. Shanis knew that it was only a matter of moments before he pointed Hierm. Hierm had obviously reached the same conclusion. He ducked his head, and plowed into Karst. It was the same trick he had used against Shanis with occasional success. This time it did not work.

Unlike Shanis, Karst outweighed Hierm by at least a stone. Rather than knocking his opponent off balance, Hierm merely bounced off the bigger boy and stumbled to his left. As Hierm tried to regain his balance, Karst's blade drove home.

"Match!" A collective groan arose from the audience, none of whom seemed to like Karst. The dark- haired youth did not seem to notice. Still smirking, he turned and genuflected deeply toward Prince Lerryn. Shanis kicked the ground. Even Karst's bows were arrogant. She had to beat him. She wanted it with every fiber of her being.

She watched as Hierm clambered to his feet, tossed the tournament sword to the ground, and pushed his way through the throng of onlookers. Finding his own sword, he slammed it into its scabbard, and stormed off. Shanis watched him go. He would probably want some time to himself. She noticed Khalyndryn following Hierm. Not good. Khalyndryn would be the last person Hierm would want to talk to right now, except his father, of course. Shanis quickly followed behind the retreating heads of Hierm and Khalyndryn.

Squad Leader Khattre seized her arm in a strong hand. "It will be a while yet, girl. The Prince likes to make a speech before the final match. Listen for us to call you!"

Shanis nodded, then made her way in the direction Hierm had gone. She quickly lost sight of him in the crowd, but she easily followed Khalyndryn's golden hair and red bow bobbing through the throng. Several times, she was forced to hastily shake off well-wishers. Not too rudely, she hoped. Gradually, Khalyndryn moved farther ahead of her. Shanis lost sight of the girl once. Climbing atop a nearby cart, she finally spotted Khalyndryn disappearing into the woods that bordered Galsbur to the west. Hierm must be going to the river. She'd grab Khalyndryn, and get back to the field in plenty of time for the match. She hopped down from the cart, and made her way hastily into the forest.

She dodged between trees and skipped across roots. Khalyndryn had disappeared quickly. Behind her, she heard a distant roar. Stopping, she inclined her ear and listened. Even at this distance, she could easily recognize Lerryn's voice. Strange. Oskar would have called it sorcery, but likely it was some sort of trick. At any rate, if Lerryn was just starting his speech, she had time to spare. Where had Khalyndryn gone?

"Khalyndryn!" Shanis called out. "I need to talk to you!" A muffled sound came from somewhere ahead of her. It sounded almost like a cry. She trotted off in the general direction from which the sound had come. "Khalyndryn?" Again the sound, it was definitely a cry, but muffled. She hurried ahead. "Hierm? Khalyndryn?" Now she heard it clearly. A whimpering sound coming from a thicket of fir trees to her right. She leapt through.

Khalyndryn was flat on her back. Her skirt was pushed up to her chin. A bulky soldier in a wine-stained uniform of the White Fang knelt atop her. One meaty hand was clamped down over her mouth. The other worked at his belt. The look in Khalyndryn's eyes was a mixture of terror and disbelief. Shanis did not hesitate.

"Get off of her!" Shanis sprinted across the gap separating them. She delivered a solid kick to the man's chin just as he turned to look in her direction. The blow knocked his head back a bit, but he did not release his grip on Khalyndryn. Shanis aimed another kick at his head. This time, he reached out and caught her by the ankle. A swift yank, and Shanis was on her back alongside her friend. The man was quicker than he looked. Before she could get up, his hand was at her throat. His breath reeked of sour wine. His oily black hair brushed her cheeks as he leaned down toward her.

"Well now. I've found me a little spitfire here." She struggled. She tried to pull his hand away from her throat, but his muscles were like iron. "This one's a fighter. I like that much better." She fought harder, driving a punch into his kidneys. He grunted, but his face registered no response.

Out of the corner of her eye Shanis watched her assailant release his grip on Khalyndryn, but only long enough to hit the blonde girl hard in the temple. Khalyndryn crumpled to the ground. The man then turned his full attention to Shanis. Keeping his grip on her throat, he began to remove his hose. Stark realization froze Shanis' heart. She struggled desperately, first punching at him, then trying to heave him off of her. As the soldier tried to force his hose below his knees, he shifted awkwardly. Shanis felt something cold and hard against her palm. Something in the back of her mind knew that it was his belt knife. A vicious yank and it was free in her hand. She thrust upward with all of her might.

A jolt ran up her arm as the blade met with resistance. Another stab. Nothing. His mail shirt! The inebriated soldier fumbled with his smallclothes, still oblivious to the fact that she was now armed. Somewhere in the far reaches of Shanis' mind, a voice told her that it was time to scream.

Hierm winced at the sounds of crashing brush and snapping twigs that grew ever closer. He had no desire to talk with anyone, especially Khalyndryn. He had been so close. So close! What had gone wrong? A stray lock of hair dangled over his swollen eye. He brushed it away reflexively and was jolted by the sharp pain. He cursed.

"Watch your language, Van Derin. Your mother might hear you." Oskar emerged from a thicket in front of Hierm. He walked directly over to his friend and inspected Hierm's eye. "This is bad," he declared flatly.

"It's not that bad," Hierm replied. "He only hit me with his shoulder. It hurts, but the swelling has already gone down." He tried to turn away, but Oskar seized his shoulders, and spun him back around so that the two faced one another.

"That's not what I mean. Karst put something in your eye." Hierm could tell by the look on Oskar's face that his skepticism must have been evident. "That's why I followed you. He cheated. We have to tell someone."

"He didn't put anything in my eye. You saw the match. He hit me in the eye, that's all. I lost." He brushed Oskar's hands away. "Who would cheat right in front of the prince? It's unthinkable."

Oskar shook his head. "That's no blackened eye I'm looking at. Your eye is bright red. He put something in it, something that made your eye swell shut."

Hierm was surprised at Oskar's intensity. He thought for a moment. The burning, the searing pain, the way his eye had swelled so quickly. It made sense. "He must have put something on his clothing." Realization tumbled fully upon him.

Oskar picked up where he left off. "I saw him rubbing his shoulder in between points. I thought he was hurt. Once I saw the way your eye was swelling, I knew what must have happened."

"Why didn't someone realize what he was doing? Why didn't I see it?"

Oskar stared off into the distance for a few moments, his palms upraised. "I guess it's like you said. No one would ever dream of cheating going on right in front of Lerryn. You see what you expect to see, I suppose, and nothing more." Oskar's dark eyes stared at the ground. Regret was painted across his face. "I tried to get to you, to get to the ring, but the crowd was too much. It was over before I got there. I'm sorry."

Hierm was touched by his friend's earnest apology. "It's all right, Oskar. You tried. I couldn't ask for a better friend." He placed a hand on his friend's beefy arm and gave him a quick squeeze. "Let's go watch Shanis whip Karst."

"What do you mean?" Oskar shook his fists in frustration. "We have got to tell someone. I'll support you."

"Who would we tell?"

"I don't know. The prince? Your mother could tell him." Even as he said the words, Oskar scratched his head and looked quizzically at the sky. "That won't work, will it?"

Hierm chuckled despite himself. "No, it won't work. Even if we're right, we can't prove anything. Doubtless he's washed off whatever it was. I'd just look like a poor loser. My father's going to be disappointed enough without me acting the fool in front of royalty." Hierm winced. He had been so disappointed at losing that he hadn't even thought about his father.

Oskar seemed to read his thoughts. "Well, Van Derin, there's one good thing that's come of all this." He didn't wait for Hierm to ask. "Your father would be much more upset if you'd lost to Shanis than to Karst."

Hierm had to admit that his friend was right, though it did little to improve his mood. A loud cry startled him from his reverie. "Did you hear that?" Oskar shook his head. Hierm began walking in the direction from which the sound had come. Silence. "I heard something!" He quickened his pace. He didn't know who had shouted, but his instincts told him that all was not right.

"I didn't hear anything," Oskar said, following along behind him. "What did you hear? Slow down!"

Hierm kept moving. Toward what, he did not know.

She ought to be frightened, should have kept crying out for help. But instinct took over. One with the blade! A voice seemed to whisper inside of her. One with the blade. There was no more thought. The blade slashed her captor across the wrist. That got his attention! But before he could make a sound, Shanis struck again. Hot blood splashed over her face as she opened his throat. She clamped her lips together against the sickly salty taste. The man's hands went to his throat, as if he could keep the life in. When he raised his arms, Shanis plunged the knife deep into his armpit, where his mail did not cover. The man convulsed, then fell slowly to the side. Shanis shoved him away and sprang to her feet.

Molten rage burned inside of her as she watched the man's final moments. Frothy blood bubbled from his lips as he futilely fought for breath. With a cry of bestial rage, she lashed out. She kicked the dying man. She fell to her knees and pummeled him. She fought to drive the rage out of her body. She screamed at him, willing her anger out of her, but nothing helped. The anger, the hurt, the fear roiled inside, raging in a furious storm. She had to get it out, or it would rip her apart. She clutched her head in her hands and screamed in anguish.

Her scream seemed to last forever. She felt someone's arms around her, lifting her to her feet. She opened her eyes to the sight of Hierm looking down at her. His blue eyes shone with feelings too deep and too many for her to read. His hair had fallen in front of his eyes again, partially covering his swollen face. His chest was covered with blood. If he was that bloody simply from helping her up, what must she look like? She tried to speak, but the words wouldn't come. Hierm also seemed to be having trouble finding words. A voice spoke from behind her.

"Shanis? What happened?" Oskar asked.

Shanis shrugged out of Hierm's embrace and turned to see the husky boy cradling Khalyndryn against his chest. Her fair skin had gone stark white. The slender girl seemed little more than a child, trembling against Oskar's broad chest. Shanis shook her head. She was still angry, but it was no longer the fiery rage that had shaken her so badly. Even spoiled, manipulative Khalyndryn, didn't deserve this.

Shanis found her strength had returned, and with it her resolve. "You know what happened! I killed him." She was surprised at how easy it was to say. "I killed him." The second time was easier than the first. She felt the anger slowly draining away. Hierm still had not found his voice. "I've got to get away from here. I've got to get away fast!"

"Are you sure?" Oskar asked in little more than a whisper. "If you tell the truth, maybe you can see your way clear of this." His words held more obligation than conviction.

"I'm certain, Oskar. I killed one of the Prince's guard. The blood is literally on my hands." She held out her hands to show them. "You two don't have to let anyone know that you saw me. Take Khalyndryn home."

"I'm not going back!" Khalyndryn cried. She wriggled from Oskar's grasp. "You're taking me with you. I can't go back." She looked at Shanis with pleading eyes.

"No one is going anywhere." Hierm finally spoke up. "We all know what happened. You were defending Khalyndryn. She can be your witness."

"Nothing happened to me!" Khalyndryn shrieked. "I'm not telling anything to anyone because nothing happened to me!" She turned back to Oskar and buried her face in his chest. Her body heaved with her sobbing. Hierm opened his mouth to speak, but Shanis gently placed a hand on his lips.

"The truth doesn't matter, Hierm." She was surprised at how calm she felt. "Khalyndryn can't tell what happened. Everyone will consider her soiled no matter what the truth is. They'll assume the worst. People always do. She'll be ruined."

Khalyndryn's weeping grew louder and more aggrieved. Hierm shook his head, but Shanis continued. "Even if both of us told the truth, it wouldn't make a difference. This is one of the Prince's guard. One of his own. This wouldn't be a trial before your father and the city leaders. The Prince can do anything he wants. What do you think he would do to me?" She let the question hang there in the silence. After a moment, she took Khalyndryn by the hand. She couldn't believe what she was about to do.

"You can come with me if you want." The look of gratitude in Khalyndryn's face was almost enough to make her forget her dislike of the wispy blonde. Almost. "We should go now." Where would they go? They'd have to get to her house quickly, and get her horse, and what money she had. That wouldn't do. They'd be searching the roads for her. Through the forest? They'd make little headway. And how would Khalyndryn manage days in the wilderness, being the soft, spoiled girl that she was? Her head began to ache. What was she going to do?

"I want to go with you," Oskar blurted. "I have a plan. I have money, too. A lot of money."

Shanis knew that she should refuse. Two lives had already been ruined today. Oskar should stay with his family. He didn't have to be a part of this. But the truth was, she wanted Oskar to come. She had never felt so alone or so uncertain. She smiled. Oskar seemed to take heart. "I've been planning for years. I can help." Shanis clutched him in a tight embrace.

"Thank you," she whispered. "I know it's selfish, but I want you to come." She gave him another hug. "I'm sorry to do this to you."

Oskar smiled. "Don't be!" Before he could say more, Hierm stepped between them.

"You're not, I mean, I won't let you. He struggled for the words. "If you're going, I'm going!"

"Hierm!" Shanis was shocked. "You can't." As much as she wanted Oskar to go, she wanted Hierm with her even more. He was her best friend. She couldn't imagine leaving him. And yet, he had the most to lose.

"I'm going with you." Hierm cupped her face in his hands. His gaze locked with hers. "I have no choice."

Shanis was startled at the look of longing in his eyes. He had never looked at her like that. No one had. What could she say? She wanted to protest, but her words were cut off by the sound of someone rustling through the underbrush.

"Borram!" A deep voice boomed. "Borram, we're due to be on watch." Through the trees, Shanis caught a glimpse of white cloth and silver mail. A soldier was coming right at them.

"Run," she whispered. No one moved. She raised her voice. "Run!" She gave Oskar a shove, and followed on his heels, Khalyndryn in tow. Hierm brought up the rear.

Behind them, the voice called out again. "Who's there? Come back here."

They ran harder. Branches slapped Shanis in the face, and gnarled roots seemed to reach up to ensnare her. Their pursuer must have found the body by now. His footsteps no longer rustled behind them. She heard a shout of surprise, then a mournful cry.

"Borram!" A string of curses ensued.

They continued to run. It soon became apparent that the man was not going to follow them. Still their pace did not slow. He would notify the guard, and time would be short. She hoped that Oskar's "plan" was a good one.

It took only a short while to reach the Clehn farm. The small house was kept in good repair. A barn and a few outbuildings separated the main house from the broad expanse of farmland that stretched northward for leagues, hugging the west bank of the Vulltu. The local farmers thought Master Clehn a bit foolish to plant so close to the river. In Shanis' memory, she could not recall the Clehns ever losing a crop to the rains. Master Clehn claimed to be "lucky that way."

Oskar took command immediately. "Hierm, you and Khalyndryn get a sack from the barn. The kitchen garden is around the back of the house. Get as much food as you can carry." Hierm responded to this new, confident Oskar without question. Khalyndryn, who still seemed to be stunned by her experience, stumbled along behind Hierm. Oskar turned to Shanis.

"Find some clothes for you girls. You know where my sister's room is." Shanis smirked. Oskar blushed. "Sorry. You can wear something of my brother's." Oskar did not wait for a response. He ran into the house ahead of Shanis, and disappeared into the room shared by him and his younger brother.

Shanis felt badly about taking anything that was not hers, so she took only one set of clothing for Khalyndryn. In Oskar's room, she selected something for herself from among his brother's things. Oskar stuffed the clothes into an oilcloth bag he had been filling. Her friend assuaged some of her guilt by leaving coins on both his brother's bed and that of his sister. They rushed out the back door to find Hierm and Khalyndryn waiting for them. Oskar continued to bark orders.

"Shanis, look in the rafters of the old smokehouse." His arms were full, so he gestured with his chin in the general vicinity of the barn. "There's a bundle up there that we'll need. Meet us at the river." Again he was off without waiting for a response.

Shanis hurried to the old smokehouse. Inside, she fought her way through a mass of dust-encased farm implements and other items she did not recognize. In the far corner, tucked high in the rafters, was a large bundle of what appeared to be canvas. The smokehouse ceiling was low and it took her only a few jumps to grab hold of the bundle, which promptly came crashing down on top of her. With a curse, she fell heavily onto a pile of old crates. Thankfully, they were empty, and cushioned her fall somewhat. She heaved the bundle onto her shoulder, wondering what it might be.

Outside, in the light, she stopped to examine her burden. She was surprised at what she found. "A tent! Why does Oskar have this?" She knew that she had little time to waste. Hefting the bundle, she trotted to the river, where a bigger surprise greeted her.

Hierm and Khalyndryn stood at the river's edge alongside a strange-looking boat. It was long and narrow, and appeared to have been hollowed out of a log. Each end came to a point. Shanis could not tell the front from the back. "What is that thing?" Hierm looked down at it and shrugged.

"Oskar called it a canoe. He read about it in one of his books." Hierm shook his head. "He says the Baghma, or something like that, use it. It's supposed to be good for river travel." Shanis could not believe it. Oskar expected her to get into that thing?

"This is his plan? This? Float away on a log?" She kicked the odd craft, and found it to be solid. "We can't take a boat downriver. Boats never travel the Vulltu. Papa says it's too narrow, rocky, and shallow!" She held one palm slightly above the other to illustrate her point.

"That's why we need the canoe." She had not heard Oskar walk up behind her during her ranting. "It sits high in the water, so it will clear most of the shallows. It's narrow, so we can guide it between rocks, and it's light enough that we can carry it if we have to." The burly youth fondly caressed the edge of the craft. "I read about it in one of Lord Hiram's books. It took me more than a year to carve it." Shanis was impressed.

"You did this yourself?" She wasn't impressed with the craftsmanship, so much as she was surprised that Oskar had kept his head out of the clouds long enough to see a task through to completion. Then another thought struck her. "Oskar, are you certain that it floats?" Oskar started to reply, then seemed to realize that he was being mocked.

"We'd better hurry. No one should have any idea that we've come here, but we should waste no time." He heaved the tent into the center of the canoe. He had drilled a small hole in each side of the canoe's center, near the top edges. Through these holes, he strung a rope, with which he secured the tent, the bag of food, and the oilcloth sack which held their spare clothing and whatever other items he had squirreled away. He pushed the canoe out into the water until only one end of the canoe was on land.

"Shanis, you'll be in front. Get in and try and stay in the very center. Lean too far and you'll tip it over!" Shanis paused, looking first at the canoe, then at Oskar, then back at the canoe. "What are you waiting for?"

Shanis hoped that she was not blushing. "Which end is the front? They both look alike."

Hierm chuckled, but nodded his agreement. Oskar's shoulders slumped in seeming disbelief.

"That end." He nodded to the end that extended into the water. "And take a paddle with you." Shanis assumed that a paddle was one of the giant wooden spoons that lay on the bank nearby. Not willing to add to her embarrassment by asking another question, she took a chance and grabbed one. Oskar did not contradict her, so she assumed that her guess was correct. Following Oskar's gestures, she climbed into the canoe, and clambered out to the far end. She sat down, facing back toward shore. Oskar shook his head. With a curse, she realized that she was facing the wrong way. "Don't say a word," she cautioned the young man. She whirled around, nearly upsetting the craft, and dropped cautiously to her knees, making certain not to overbalance.

"Good," Oskar called out. "Hierm, you and Khalyndryn get in. Take a paddle." Hierm half-dragged Khalyndryn into the canoe. He helped her climb across the pile of supplies secured in the center of the tent. She sat down limply, leaning back against the bulk of the bundled tent. She stared blankly at Shanis' back. She did not speak. Hierm positioned himself just behind the supplies, kneeling as Shanis had.

Shanis felt a sudden jolt as the canoe shot forward into the water. The front end heaved up, and then wobbled. Stealing a glance behind her, she saw that Oskar had pushed the craft into deeper water, and was awkwardly trying to climb in. She laughed. She had been feeling a little inept, but seeing Oskar struggle so valiantly somehow put everything back where it should be.

Instinctively she leaned away from the side to which Oskar clung. Hierm followed her lead, and soon Oskar was able to haul himself in.

"All right then," Shanis called back to him, "what do we do now?"

Oskar demonstrated how the paddle was used, and explained how best to propel the wobbly boat. Being strong, and having a good sense of balance, Shanis quickly had the hang of it. Hierm was also a quick study. The three of them soon had the canoe skimming down the river, leaving home behind.

Chapter 8

It was all wrong. The thought tickled at the back of Lerryn's consciousness like an itch he could not reach. Plans that had been years in the making had unraveled. Or had they? He shook his head, seeking to brush away the web of questions that clung to his thoughts. He just didn't know.

He sat in one of the inn's two rooms. The floors were of rough-hewn boards, worn smooth by the passage of time. The wood plank walls were unpainted and without ornamentation. His furnishings included a bed with a goose-down mattress, doubtless borrowed from Mistress Van Derin, a small wooden table, and two chairs. His own tent would have afforded more luxurious accommodations, but he had no desire to offend these kind, if provincial, people.

He swirled his cup of wine, trying to decide if his need for a drink outweighed his distaste for this provincial vintage. He held it up to the light, and noted with disappointment the murky lack of clarity. The bouquet was not much better, cloyingly sweet, almost oppressively heavy. He sighed. He had exhausted his personal store, and bad wine was better than none at all. Two gulps and the cup was almost drained. He shuddered at the taste, but the warmth that spread through his middle was comforting. If nothing else, the wine was strong.

"Highness?" Xaver, his vizier, poked his head through the door. "All is ready."

"Is it?" Lerryn posed the question to no one in particular. "It doesn't feel ready, Xaver. It feels *off*." The word hung there as he searched for something more to say. Finding nothing, he remained silent.

With a deep sigh, Xaver bustled past him. Reaching the table in the room's center, the gaunt, graying man replaced the stopper in Lerryn's wine decanter. He picked up the nearly empty cup, and strode to the open window. He threw a challenging stare at the prince and pitched the dregs out the window. If the vizier heard the angry cry from below, his face did not show it.

"Truly Highness," he intoned, absently dragging his palms across the folds of his purple cloak, "this conversation has become most tedious. And this," he pointed to the decanter, "helps you not at all. I have told you that all is in readiness, and I meant all!"

"I don't think so."

"Don't think so?" Xaver's condescending tone would have sent any other man to the headsman. "I shall explain it once more. Do you agree that we have chosen the correct place and time?" Lerryn nodded grudgingly as Xaver continued. "Do you agree that we are six?"

"I number them five."

"Five?" Xaver began to count on long, claw-like fingers. "You and I, the victor...."

"We do not have a victor!" Lerryn shouted, no longer able to hold his tongue. "There was no final match. There can be no victor." He pulled a chair away from the table, spun it around, and straddled the seat. He folded his arms across the chair's back, and rested his chin on the back of a hand. Freeze it all!

The Malan girl had vanished prior to the final match, along with the Van Derin boy and two other locals. The body of one of his Guard, a drunkard named Borram, had been found in the forest. It had taken very little investigation to get to the bottom of the matter.

According to Squad Leader Khattre, Borram had had wandered away from his post during the latter rounds of the previous day's tournament, declaring his intent to 'have a bit of fun with one of the farm girls'. One of Borram's friends, a guard named Arric, had found him dead in the forest, reeking of ale, hose around his knees, his own knife buried in his side. Arric had spotted a red-haired girl running away, along with several others. Probably scared out of their wits, Lerryn mused.

Scouts were turned out in search of the four, with no success. Their tracks led to a farm some distance from the village, and disappeared. Both sides of the river were scoured, but to no avail. The owners of the farm, parents of one of the missing boys, had been at the tournament all day, and were of no help. Mistress Van Derin had followed them, and had seemed oddly put out over the condition of the farm. Strange, he thought, it seemed to be quite a nice place as farms go.

"Highness?" Xaver's voice snatched him from his reverie.

"Do you truly believe that Karst is the one?" Lerryn had lain awake half the night trying to accept that Pedric Karst could be the one. It did not fit.

Xaver's face did not change. "It matters not what I believe. He is the one."

"He is arrogant, deceitful. I don't care for the boy one bit." Karst was not what he had envisioned when he began this search. How could this boy be the one?

"I did not realize that was a requirement." Xaver sat down opposite Lerryn. "We have a task before us. A task too sacred to be held back by your reservations."

"If conditions are not met, your sacred task cannot succeed." Why did Xaver not see what was wrong?

"Your Highness, I have dedicated my life to this quest. You know the sacrifices I have made. And you may believe me when I say that conditions have been met."

Lerryn gazed into Xaver's eyes. They were a dark violet, almost black. "You are not the only one who has sacrificed, Xaver. You're just the only one to whom it came easily."

"Need I remind you that it was you who came to me, Your Highness?" When Lerryn did not answer, Xaver chuckled, a dry, raspy sound that reminded Lerryn of the closing of a crypt door. "It is of no importance. We have a victor. Perhaps not one of your liking, but a victor none the less. Pedric Karst is your tournament champion. No one defeated him."

"No one defeated the Malan girl either," Lerryn stubbornly insisted. "Did we ever find her father?"

"He is gone." Xaver shook his head. "Hauling something or other for his Lord Hiram."

"Don't be so hard on Van Derin. You've met his wife." Lerryn forced a smile. "Wonder how long it took our friend Hiram to realize the mistake he'd made in marrying her?"

Xaver actually smiled in return. "I believe he got exactly what he deserved." The wizened man stood and returned to the window. He looked out and shook his head.

Lerryn could see past Xaver's rail-thin body and out the window. Across the green, Faun Van Derin stood on the porch of her home, gesticulating wildly to a group of workers who were attempting to erect a statue of some sort. While the Prince and his advisor watched, the statue teetered, and fell to the ground with a resounding crash. Despite the distance, he heard Faun's shrill cries quite clearly.

"She plays a dangerous game, that one." Xaver stroked his chin whiskers and smiled, a predatory baring of teeth.

"Pretending to be nobility, you mean?"

Xaver did not answer. He strode to the door. "Your party is waiting, Highness. Your destiny is waiting."

"Destiny has waited a long time. It can wait while I have another drink."

"We all have our priorities, Highness," Xaver sighed. "If you will be so kind as to join us once you have finished your bottle of courage." The gaunt man slipped from the room with wraithlike silence.

With a shrug, Lerryn put the bottle of wine to his lips, and downed it in a series of loud gulps. Finished, he slammed the bottle to the table, belched loudly, and threw a look of comic defiance at the empty doorway. Standing, he belted on his sword and proceeded down the stairs and out onto the front steps of the inn.

The innkeeper and his wife waited on the porch. Lerryn couldn't remember their names. "You have honored our home with your presence, Highness," the stocky man said with a bow. Lerryn inclined his head in return.

"You will find our daughter, won't you, your Highness?" The innkeeper's wife, an attractive woman, wrung her hands. Lerryn paused to think.

"We are certain that your daughter will return home soon," Xaver interrupted. "But we, as well as Captain Tabars and his men, will continue the search."

Of course! Their daughter was one of the three who had run away with the Malan girl. Perhaps Xaver was right about his drinking.

"Thank you, your Highness. Thank you." Though it had been Xaver who answered, the woman knelt before Lerryn. "We are so worried."

Lerryn placed a hand on her shoulder. "Worry no more. She will be returned to you. I am certain of it." Lerryn groaned inside at the look of complete trust in the woman's eyes. He was only a man, yet a word from him, and she believed that all would be made right. He just didn't understand.

He turned away from his hosts, and strode down the front steps. The bright morning sun stung his eyes. Squinting against the glare, he made his way down to the street.

Captain Tabars stood at the foot of the steps. "I don't like leaving you, Highness." The burly soldier stood with his arms folded across his chest, his face twisted in disapproval.

"You have your instructions, Tabars. Take the new recruits to Archstone, and then place yourself at my father's disposal."

"Khattre can take the recruits back. You need me and the men with you."

"Tabars," Lerryn's voice held a note of warning. "You have been given your orders."

"Highness, you didn't give me these," Tabars raised a muscular arm to Lerryn's face. His three silver bands of command reflected the sunlight in Lerryn's eyes, making him flinch, "because I meekly follow orders. You have always relied on me. Now you are leaving, the gods only know to where, with only these boys as your escort. Of course I question your orders."

"You are a good man and a good officer." Lerryn clapped a hand on Tabars' mailed shoulder. "I know that what I do is a poor repayment for the loyalty you have shown me. But I can tell you only that we must be six, or we will fail. When our task is complete, I will send for you and the men. Until that time, I must insist on your obedience." He met his underling with a level gaze.

Tabars stared intently at Lerryn for a long moment before nodding his acquiescence. "We'll be waiting for you, Highness. May the gods smile on you." The two men clasped hands.

"And on you as well, my friend," Lerryn replied.

Tabars rejoined the rest of the White Fang, now numbering forty-eight. The veteran soldier mounted his horse with ease, and shouted a terse command to the Guard. With a clatter of hoofs, the white-cloaked soldiers set off, Lerryn's new recruits following behind. "Keep up, or be left behind," Tabars called to the bewildered-looking farm boys. Lerryn watched until his men had circled the green and disappeared down the east road.

Sighing, he turned to the five men who waited for him. He used the term "men" rather loosely. Xaver sat upon his gray gelding, holding the reins of Kreege, Lerryn's warhorse. Behind him, the archery champion, Edrin something-or-other, sat astride the plainest-looking brown horse Lerryn had ever seen. Next to him, riding equally nondescript mounts of varying shades of brown, were the wrestlers. Lerryn had not bothered to learn their names. 'Bull' and 'Hair' suited him fine.

Hair! Lerryn chuckled. What a wonder it had been finding him!

"Why aren't we going with the others?" Several paces away, Pedric Karst sat upon a skittish black stallion. He looked down at Lerryn with ill-concealed impatience.

Lerryn took a deep breath and held it. Must everyone be so impertinent today? "You'll have your answer very soon, Master Karst." Accepting Kreege's reins from Xaver, he nimbly mounted the white horse. "And if you ever address me in that tone again, you will find yourself looking up at me from the flat of your back." He touched his heels to the horses' flanks, and the powerful creature set off at a trot. The others followed behind.

"Gentlemen," Lerryn began, "I have a long story to tell you."

Chapter 9

Shanis stared into the flames of the campfire, watching as the wood was consumed, reduced to ashes. She was stiff and suffering. Days of paddling had taken their toll. Her back ached, her hands were blistered, and her legs were stiff from lack of use. Gingerly she touched the bruises on her face, sustained when the canoe had capsized the previous day. The river had finally proven too much for the sturdy little craft. A jagged rock had smashed a hole in its bottom, sending its four occupants into the angry current. She thought her body had found every rock in the river on her way downstream.

They had finally come to a stretch of shallows where they were able to recover most of their belongings and make their way to shore. Thankfully, no one had been seriously injured, and they had spent the night and the next day sleeping in a thicket of pine near the river.

She had killed a man. How should she feel? Strangely, she didn't feel anything. Shouldn't she be upset? Feel guilty? Then again, didn't he deserve to die for what he tried to do to her? For what he tried to do to Khalyndryn? She looked across the campfire to where the girl lay.

Khalyndryn was wrapped in a blanket, staring blankly at the fire while Oskar hovered over her like a grandmother. He was making a fool of himself, Shanis mused. Khalyndryn's condition had not improved. Still in a stupor, she had been no help during the trip down the river. In fact, she had not even tried to save herself when they capsized. Shanis had been forced to drag the girl from the river to save her from drowning.

Hierm sat down beside her. He stared at the fire for a time without speaking. Finally he looked at Shanis. "How are you doing?" he asked tentatively.

Shanis shrugged. "All right, I guess." She didn't know what to say, but she appreciated Hierm's concern. "How should I be doing?"

"Shanis, you shouldn't feel bad," Hierm consoled. "I mean, well, I don't know how you should feel. But you did the right thing." He fell silent again.

"I think what bothers me is that I don't feel anything. Shouldn't I feel something? Am I some kind of monster?" She felt Hierm's hand gently touch her shoulder.

"I'm no expert, but it seems to me that a monster wouldn't care enough to ask the question." He didn't say anything else.

"Thanks," Shanis said dryly, "you've been a big help." He had made his point, though. From the corner of her eye, she saw him grin ruefully. "No, really," she reached up and grasped his hand in both of hers. Her voice softened. "You're a good friend. Better than I deserve." They sat that way for a long time, listening to the crackle of the flames.

Oskar appeared from the direction of the river. As the bulky youth dropped down next to them, Hierm yanked his hand out of Shanis' grasp and hopped to his feet. Shanis looked up at him, failing to stifle a giggle. Men! Or boys, rather. Hierm looked embarrassed. He strode away quickly, and found a seat on the opposite side of the fire. He evidently found something interesting to study in the dirt, because he didn't look up. Oskar's gaze flitted from one to the other.

"Did I miss something?" The moon-faced boy frowned at Shanis and shook his head. "Never mind." He looked up at the branches over their head, his eyes taking on a faraway cast, and he smiled.

"Can you believe it? We're on an adventure. We rode a river and crashed and nearly died. Now we're in a mysterious forest far from home. It's all so, I don't know." His gaze snapped back to Shanis, his eyes clear. "Did you see the Saikur?"

"Did I see what?" Shanis sat upright, suddenly nervous. What is a...whatever that word was?

"A saikur. Some people call them seekers. I saw one of them watching us from the forest just before we hit the rapids."

"So he could be nearby?" Alarm rang in Hierm's voice.

"I suppose," Oskar said. "He was on the other side of the river though, and quite a ways back. Why? Do you think we should try and find him?"

"No," Hierm said with a tone of finality. He did not elaborate.

"What's wrong?" Shanis asked. "Are these seekers dangerous? If so, we should move on quickly."

"Probably not," Hierm said, shaking his head. "My mother always told me not to trust them, but she never gave a reason." He shrugged. "Not that we would ever see one in Galsbur."

"I was wondering something," Oskar said, redirecting the conversation. "Where do you want to go?"

The question gave Shanis pause. She had not thought about anything other than getting away quickly as possible.

"I don't really know," she mused. "I definitely want to get as far away from Galsbur as possible. How about that country with women soldiers? Hallind, isn't it?" She had no idea how far away Hallind might be. "What about the two of you?"

Oskar shrugged. "I don't care where we go," he said with a bounce in his voice. "I want to see everything. I suppose Hallind is as good a place as any to get started. I'll get my maps." He sprang to his feet with surprising agility and strode purposefully to where their belongings lay. He returned with a bulky package wrapped in oilcloth. Unwrapping the bundle, he produced a sheaf of papers bound with string.

"These are all the things I've copied down from Lord Hiram's books. Maps, stories, sketches." He studiously bent to the pile and began furiously shuffling papers. "Where is it? Ha!" He flourished a folded sheet. Smoothing a place on the ground, he spread the paper in front of them. "This is a map of most of the known world," he announced with pride.

Shanis frowned at the mass of lines, dots, and squiggles. She shook her head, and squinted, leaning closer to the paper, as if proximity were the key to understanding. "You'll have to tell me what this all means. I can't make sense of it." She turned to Hierm. "Want to have a look?" The blond youth thrust his palms toward the map, as if to keep it at bay. Oskar laughed. Shanis knew that Oskar could not comprehend Hierm's lack of interest in all things scholarly.

Oskar pressed the tip of a thick finger into the center of the map. "This is home," he stated firmly.

Shanis felt an aching in her chest at the thought of home. Was her father home yet? If so, had he heard about what happened? What did he think of her now? She forced down the memories, and returned her attention to Oskar.

"Here," his finger traced a wavy line down the page, "is the Vulltu. I'd guess we've come about this far." He pointed to a spot not far below Galsbur on the map. Shanis winced. "Don't worry," he assured her, "It's farther than it looks." He waited for her to nod, then proceeded. "Hallind is over here." He pointed to an oblong shape on the far edge of the map. "We should move south to get out of Galdora as quickly as possible. Then, we'll cut east across land. Hallind is an island nation, so we'll have to book passage on a ship once we get to the coast!"

Hierm perked up. "A ship? You mean a big, wooden boat out in deep water? Not a chance. The canoe was one thing, but not a ship. I don't like the idea of water so deep that I can't see the bottom."

"Come on Van Derin," Oskar chided, "where's your spirit of adventure? We're going to see the world!" He swept his arms apart. "Think of all the things we're going to see." His round face shone in the semi-darkness.

"He's right," Shanis said, finding herself caught up in Oskar's infectious enthusiasm. "Imagine the places we'll see. We can go anywhere." Something tickled the back of her neck. Absentmindedly she scratched at it and came away with the biggest bug she'd ever seen. With a shout, she furiously shook her hand. The insect fell into the fire, where it burned with a satisfying crackle. "Anywhere without bugs," she added with a shiver. Someone giggled. She spun about, ready to confront the culprit, but was stopped short.

Khalyndryn was sitting up. Her eyes were bright, and her laughter was carefree. "I thought you weren't afraid of anything. I was sure of it." The blonde girl stood and walked to the fireside where she sat down alongside Oskar. The husky lad scooted aside to make room in front of his map. With a hint of self-satisfaction in his voice, he began going over the particulars with Khalyndryn.

Shanis cleared her throat. "I'm not afraid of bugs," she said to no one in particular. "I just don't like them." She turned to Hierm, daring him to say anything. Her friend smirked, but held his silence. Wanting to change the subject, she sat down alongside Khalyndryn. "What are all these other places on the map?"

Oskar's face split into a broad grin. He launched into a lengthy description of their part of the world. He shared his knowledge with such enthusiasm that even Hierm seemed to take interest.

The continent on which they lived was bisected by The Walls of Stone, a mountain range that ran from north to south in almost a straight line. Little was known of the lands to the west of the mountains. That side of the continent was sketched out in a rough semi-circle, with the words "The Lands West" written in the center. To the east of the mountains lay the lands that were more familiar.

To the extreme north was the kingdom of Halvala. Immediately to the south of Halvala lay Kyrin, and south of Kyrin lay Galdora. Both nations were landlocked, bordered by the mountains to the west, and the coastal nations of Cardith and Diyonus to the east. Galdora was bounded on the south by Lothan. Lothan, according to Oskar, was a "geographic nightmare of a nation," comprised of hilly country in the west and swamps in the east.

The river Jorran ran south from central Kyrin through Galdora, and into Lothan, where it forked. The western branch cut through the hills of Lothan before emptying into the Great South Sea. The Minor Jorran, the eastern branch, fed the swampy lands that divided Lothan and Diyonus. Lying at the center of the fork lay Karkwall, the capital city of Lothan.

"Galdora is shaped funny" Khalyndryn exclaimed. Shanis frowned. "Look," the fair haired girl pointed to Galdora. "It's a rectangle. Why?" She turned an inquisitive eye toward Oskar, who beamed like a proud father.

"You're right. Galdora isn't like other countries. Other borders were determined over time, either by war or by the lay of the land. Galdora was formed by a committee." Oskar bathed them in an expectant smile, and waited.

"All right, I'll bite. What do you mean, formed by a committee?" Shanis rolled her eyes.

Oskar ignored her sarcasm. "For years, Kyrin and Lothan were at war with one another. Most of the time, they fought over the fertile land where the border between their countries lay. Although they would fight for any reason, sometimes no reason at all."

"Sounds like someone I know," Hierm kidded, elbowing Shanis. Shanis punched him hard on the shoulder.

"Finally, the Kings of Cardith and Halvala, and the Council of Diyonus, had enough. They decided to create a country that would serve as a buffer between Kyrin and Lothan. They left each country a bit of the farmland. The rest of it became Galdora." Oskar traced the outline of their homeland.

"What about the people who lived there?" Khalyndryn asked. "Did anybody ask them if they wanted to be part of this new country?"

"They were just happy to finally have peace. A nation's flag doesn't mean much when your stomach is empty and you've seen nothing but death all your life."

"I hate soldiers. All they do is hurt people." Khalyndryn pulled her knees up to her chin, wrapped her arms tightly around her legs, and rocked in silent contemplation.

"Is that why Kyrinians hate Galdorans so much?' Hierm queried.

Oskar nodded. "For years, the combined armies had to protect Galdora from invasion. Meanwhile, they put a Cardithian on the throne, and married him off to a Halvalan girl. They put a Diyonan in charge of raising an army. In time, Galdora became strong enough to stand on its own."

Something didn't make sense to Shanis. "But why don't we ever hear about war with Lothan? Shouldn't they hate us just as much?"

"They're too busy hating each other. Lothan has two distinct groups of people: the Malgog and the Monaghan. The Malgog live in the highlands. The Monaghan live in the swamps and wetlands. They've always feuded. Fighting with Kyrin kept them distracted, but once that wasn't an option, they went back to fighting each other. There's been civil war there ever since.

"Kyrin is a different story. It's a landlocked country, like Galdora, and that's always made relations with other nations touchy. Kyrinians hate Lothans because of their historical enmity, hate Galdorans because we took their land, and they hate the other nations for giving us their land."

"What can they really do about it?" Hierm asked. They're only one country against five.

"Four," Oskar corrected. "Lothan isn't going to fight anyone in its present state. But don't underestimate Kyrin. Every boy grows up training to be a soldier. They are always ready for war." He lowered his voice to a whisper. "Some even say that they've had dealings beyond the mountains."

Shanis' skin prickled and a shiver ran down her spine. "Did you feel that?" she whispered.

"What?" Hierm regarded her with a frown.

"I heard, no, I felt something." She could not explain what it was, but it was very real. She was certain of it.

"What do you mean, felt something?" Hierm rose to his feet and looked around.

"Something is out there." Shanis scanned the clearing, eyes straining to see beyond the perimeter of the firelight. The feeling was stronger now. Gooseflesh covered her arms. She cautiously climbed to her feet and drew her sword, which slid free of its scabbard with a metallic hiss.

"What is it?" Khalyndryn's voice quavered. She clambered to her feet, and edged closer to the fire. "Where do you see it? I don't see anything."

Oskar and Hierm moved to either side of Khalyndryn. Firelight danced along the edge of Hierm's blade. Oskar wielded a chunk of firewood, holding it aloft like a club.

Shanis senses screamed. Her body quaked and her breath was coming in gasps. What was wrong with her?

"Don't be afraid." The pleading tone of Khalyndryn's voice belied her words of reassurance. "I'm sure it's all right."

"I'm not afraid. I'm cold." Shanis had to clench her jaws to keep her teeth from chattering. She felt like she was back in the icy river. Had she taken ill?

"How can you be cold? The fire's plenty warm enough." Oskar kept his eyes on the dark forest around them.

"I don't know. I feel strange."

The attack came from two sides at once. Large gray shapes hurtled out of the darkness with dizzying speed. Their bodies were vaguely human in form. Long, gangly arms hung from thick, powerful shoulders. Their barrel-like torsos ended in short, heavily muscled legs. They had feet and hands, but their fingers and toes ended in wicked looking claws. Their heads were roughly cat-like, shaped like that of a mountain lion. Their eyes, however, were startlingly human. Sleek, gray fur covered their entire bodies. Shanis took all of this in during the moment that it took for one of the creatures to cross the space between them and hurl itself at her.

Shanis ducked beneath the leaping creature, thrusting upward with her sword. A high pitched snarl pierced her ears, and something cold and wet splashed over her face. The sudden weight on her sword dragged her over backward as the monster flew past her. The snarl ascended to an ethereal scream as the creature fell into the fire. Shanis face and hair were singed by the cloud of sparks swirling about her. She yanked her sword free, scarcely avoiding the claws that flailed madly in the beast's death throes.

Before she could turn around, something slammed into her side. Her sword flew from her grip, and she tumbled to the ground, falling heavily onto her face. She felt an oppressive weight on her back. Black claws shredded the loam on either side of her head. The creature hissed, its breath icy on the back of her neck. As suddenly as the creature had pounced on her, it was gone.

Spitting out a mouthful of dirt, Shanis forced herself up to her knees and looked around for her assailant. What she saw made her gasp.

Oskar had forsaken his club and sat astride the beast's chest, gripping its wrists, and struggling vainly to pin it to the ground. The monster's rear legs kicked wildly, rending the back of Oskar's cloak. It fought to break free, contorting like a snake pinned under a stick. Veins bulged in Oskar's neck with the effort of holding it back.

Shanis quickly found her sword, and turned back to the fight. The beast had pushed Oskar back off of its chest, closer to the deadly talons that tipped its feet. Its powerful legs were flexed, poised to rip into the boy's back. Shanis shouted in fear and anger and sprinted to her friend's aid, all the while fearing she would be too late.

With unexpected suddenness, Hierm leapt from the shadows behind Oskar. His fair skin and hair gave him a wraithlike appearance in the dim light. With all the precision of a lumberjack, he struck with his sword across the back of the monster's upraised legs, hamstringing the beast. It threw its head back and screamed.

Shanis quickly closed the gap, reversed her sword, and struck downward with all her might, plunging her blade through the beast's throat and burying the point of the weapon in the soft soil below. The creature's thrashing slowed until it finally went limp as its life drained away.

Oskar rolled off the beast, and crawled a few paces before crumbling to the ground in a heap. Shanis hurried to his side. The boy's breath came in sobbing gasps. Gingerly, she drew back the tattered remains of his cloak. To her relief, he had somehow avoided injury. The beast's claws had cut his clothing, but had not penetrated his skin.

Hierm appeared at her side. "Is he all right?" Hierm asked.

"I think so." Shanis laid a gentle hand on Oskar's shoulder. "Oskar?"

With a groan, Oskar rolled over onto his back. "Am I dead?" He spread his arms out, and lay gazing up at the canopy of branches that enveloped them. "I definitely feel dead."

Shanis felt a surge of affection for this big, clumsy boy who had risked his life to save her. Grasping his shoulders, she hauled him up into a sitting position, and clenched him in a crushing embrace. "You're not dead, you big oaf. You should be, but you're not." She felt Oskar's arms tentatively encircle her. "You have got to be the biggest fool in the world."

"Van Derin," Oskar groaned, "next time I decide to save her life, remind me of the thanks I got for it." Shanis drew away from her friend and punched him in the shoulder, eliciting a satisfying grunt.

Khalyndryn appeared at Hierm's side. "Are you hurt?" she whispered.

"I don't think he's injured, just bruised." Shanis suddenly realized that

Khalyndryn was not asking about Oskar. The blonde girl was running her fingers through Hierm's hair, cooing softly to him like a mother bird.

"I'm fine," Hierm pushed her away, not gently. "You should be worried about Oskar."

Khalyndryn's face puckered. Her lower lip thrust forth. "I was concerned about you, that's all. Shanis was already seeing to Oskar."

"Khalyndryn, you'd better pull that lip in before a bird lands on it," Shanis jibed. With a loud sob, Khalyndryn whirled and ran away.

"Now you've done it," Hierm reproved. His grin contradicted the words. "I'll go and see to her." He turned and paced off into the darkness.

Shanis turned her attention to the creature she had slain. A chill ran down her spine as she knelt down alongside it. She reached out tentatively to touch its silvery gray fur. With a hiss she drew her hand back. The creature was ice cold!

"What is it?" Oskar's head appeared over her shoulder. "Is it still alive?"

"It's cold," Shanis replied, rubbing her hand. "I've never felt anything like it. Just being close to it gives me the chills. And the smell. It's like winter air. So icy it almost hurts.

Oskar squatted down next to her. He reached out a tentative hand to touch the beast. He tapped it, instantly drawing back as if it were a hot stove. A frown creased his brow. He again touched the creature, prodding it. He turned back to Shanis.

"Why do you say it's cold? The body is still warm."

"Not funny, Oskar. The thing nearly gave me frostbite." She hopped to her feet and moved closer to the fire, leaning precariously close to the flames as if its meager warmth could seep into her frozen bones. "What is that thing, anyway?"

"I don't know," Oskar replied. "But I'm not fooling. It's warm. You can feel it yourself if you don't believe me."

Shanis turned back toward Oskar. His deep brown eyes stared directly into her own. His broad face was a firm mask of sincerity. "You're serious, aren't you?" He nodded. Baffled, Shanis returned to her friend's side. She gingerly extended her hand toward the lifeless corpse. Again an icy cold gripped her and she yanked her hand back.

"You didn't even touch it."

"Look," she thrust her hand in front of Oskar's face. She drew back the sleeve of her tunic to reveal a forearm covered in chill bumps. "It's freezing. It's so cold I can't even put my hand to it." Her voice trailed off as she looked down to see Oskar stroking the fur of the cat-like monster.

"I believe you," he said. "But I'm telling you, it isn't cold." He did not say it, but the thought was evident in his eyes. Creatures of ice. The possibility, however remote, was unthinkable. Did he truly think the creatures were warm-blooded, or did he only want them to be?

The sound of approaching footsteps drew her away from frightening thoughts. Hierm appeared with Khalyndryn in tow. He nodded to the blonde girl, who looked down at the ground for a moment before speaking.

"I'm sorry," she began. "Oskar, is there anything I can do for you?" The stout boy shook his head. "I'm glad none of you are hurt. I've had a difficult few days." Her delicate fists scrubbed at the tears that spilled down her cheeks.

Something inside Shanis ached for this pitiful girl. She stood and wrapped her in a tight embrace.

Khalyndryn laid her head on Shanis' shoulder. "I wish I were strong like you," she sobbed.

"It's going to be all right," Shanis whispered. "You are much stronger than you know." Shanis was surprised to realize that she really meant it. Her heart held a tender spot for this spoiled, silly girl, who had endured so much in such a short time. They clung to one another for a moment longer. Shanis gave the blonde girl a firm pat on the back, and drew back a step, clasping her shoulders. "Can you see to the tent and our supplies? Make certain everything is all right?"

Khalyndryn nodded, and slipped away quietly.

Hierm and Oskar were inspecting the corpses of the slain beasts. Shanis joined them.

"Do you think we should stay here tonight?" Hierm's eyes searched the waves of inky blackness that strained against the flickering light of the campfire. "There could be more of them."

"I think we should stay," Shanis replied after a moment's thought. "If there are more of them, I'd sooner be here by the fire than out there." She pointed into the darkness of the forest. The boys nodded their agreement. "We'll build up the fire and take turns keeping watch."

"What about these?" Oskar nodded at the dead animals. Alive in his eyes was a duel between his evident fear and unquenchable curiosity.

"Let's drag them away from the camp. Perhaps their friends will think twice about coming after us." Shanis hoped she sounded more positive than she felt. Whatever their attackers were, they didn't look like beings who thought about much beyond killing.

Shanis took the first watch. She added fuel to the fire, and sat down cross-legged with her back to the cheery blaze. The light ruined her night vision, she knew, but she needed its warmth. The chilled feeling had not left her body. She shuddered at the memory of cold breath on her neck. A shuffling sound caught her attention, and she leapt to her feet, hand on the hilt of her sword.

"May I sit with you for a while?" Khalyndryn asked. Without waiting for an answer, the girl sat down near the fire. Shanis stared blankly for a moment, then joined her by the fire. Khalyndryn smiled at her, a thin, tight grin. "I'm not brave yet," she whispered, "but I want to be." She reached out her hand to Shanis, who clasped it tightly in hers. Silently, the girls turned to face the darkness of the night together.

Chapter 10

Shanis grimaced as she waved in futility at the swarm of bugs hovering just in front of her face. Bugs. Why not snakes? Or some more of those gray monsters? Anything but bugs. She muttered a curse under her breath.

"I know," Oskar commiserated. His eyes firmly fixed on the trail ahead, he obviously misunderstood the reason for her oath. "I'm tired of walking too." Shanis didn't bother to correct him.

It had been three days since the strange creatures attacked their camp. They waited through the night for another assault, but none came. The next morning they had determined to head east until they found a road, since they did not know exactly where they were. Oskar expressed his hope that the time spent on the river had brought them far enough south that they were beyond the bounds of Galdora and into Lothan. When they found a road they would make their way south to Karkwall, Lothan's capitol. From there, well, Oskar said they would figure that out later.

Shanis ran her fingers through her raven tresses, newly colored by a concoction of berries Khalyndryn had cooked up the previous night. The girl reasoned that, on the chance that they were not yet clear of the prince's writ, Shanis should be as inconspicuous as possible.

She protested at first, unaccustomed to admitting that Khalyndryn could be right about anything, but soon relented. She was not certain how black hair looked on her. She had tried to catch a glimpse of her reflection in a stream when no one was looking, but couldn't see much. Khalyndryn had assured her that it looked "positively lovely", but hers was not an opinion Shanis valued.

"Oskar, will you carry me on your shoulders?" Khalyndryn's voice had taken on a whiny tone that was even more annoying than usual.

Shanis whirled about to see Khalyndryn leaning against Oskar's shoulder, making calf eyes at the stout boy.

"Oskar, if you carry her one step, so help me, I'll break your arm." The threat was enough to squelch any words of protest from Khalyndryn, though the flaxen-haired girl glared at her with eyes afire. The two girls stared at one another for a long moment before Khalyndryn broke off her gaze with a "humph", and fell back alongside Hierm, nose upturned. Nonplussed, Shanis turned back to Oskar. The lad shrugged, flashing a guilty smile.

"Where is this road of yours?" Shanis knew that she need not be so short with her friend, but the days of walking, the bugs, and Khalyndryn's incessant complaining had her nerves on edge. At least there had been no more sign of the strange beasts.

"I truly think we'll find one soon," Oskar replied. "The forest has thinned out, so we're obviously on our way out."

The boy was right. The first day had been slow going as they fought their way through dense underbrush and hungry, barbed creepers that seemed to reach up to ensnare them at every step. In truth, only three of them fought their way through while Khalyndryn waited for them to clear a path. Gradually, the way had grown easier. At first there was only the occasional shaft of sunlight peeking through the dense canopy of greenery to offer them hope. Eventually the dense cluster of trees and tangled roots gave way to larger, more widely-spaced hardwoods. A thick mulch of leaves replaced the snarls of briars and vines that had hindered their steps.

Though their way had grown easier, Shanis' tension remained firmly entrenched. The memory of the creatures still made her shiver. What were they? Such beasts existed only in campfire tales, stories told to frighten young children. Yet they were real, flesh and blood.

She shook her head. Not so long ago, she had been a village girl who wanted to apprentice the sword. Now what could she call herself? An almost-tournament champion? A heroine who had saved her friend from the clutches of a foul suitor? A killer fleeing the wrath of her prince? A slayer of mysterious monsters of the night? She chuckled in spite of herself. She still felt like the same person. All around her, however, the world had suddenly become a complicated place.

Loud cries and the ring of steel upon steel up ahead of them interrupted her thoughts. She exchanged a quick glance with Hierm. Drawing their swords, they moved forward as one, trotting toward the commotion. As they drew closer, Shanis could see movement, flashes of color, and the sunlight glinting on metal. They broke through the thin barrier of shrubbery and tree limbs, and the whirling colors coalesced into several men locked in combat.

Two of the combatants could not properly be called men. They were young, not much older than Hierm or Oskar. They were dressed in plain woolen clothes, but of a fine cut, and they sat astride mounts that might have appeared nondescript to the untrained eye. Shanis noted immediately the deep, wide chests, well-sprung ribs, and strong, powerful hindquarters, well-muscled and nicely rounded. These were solid horses, well-equipped for traversing rough terrain. Each of the youths led a packhorse that was equally fine. These were not common travelers; nobility, or perhaps the sons of a merchant.

The two were desperately fighting off a half-dozen rough-looking characters in filthy garments. Despite their inferior numbers, the young men were acquitting themselves well. Two of the ruffians were already down. The others struggled in vain to penetrate the young men's defenses. One of their number cried out in pain and defiance as one of his potential victims, a lean youth with dark brown hair, penetrated his defenses with a deft thrust. The man staggered back momentarily, but returned to the attack. While he and another bandit pressed the attack, another of their partners slipped behind the defender, trying to liberate the packhorse. Their three comrades were attempting a similar ploy on the other lad.

Shanis wasted no time. She dashed forward, with Hierm on her heels. The body of a fallen brigand lay in her path. Leaping over him, she noted absently the feathered shaft that emerged from his throat. Something in the recesses of her mind told her that she ought to cringe at the sight of the dead man and the coppery smell of blood that wafted through the air. Strangely, she felt nothing except the surge of adrenaline and the strong conviction that she must help these two boys. Teeth gritted, she hurled herself into the fray.

The combatants did not hear the sound of their footfalls over the cacophony of hoofbeats and ringing of swords. Rushing in from behind, Shanis took the first bandit unaware, clouting him across the base of the skull with the pommel of her sword. He crumpled noiselessly to the ground. The youth astride the horse spared only a surprised glance at his unexpected reinforcements before furiously redoubling his efforts in a ferocious blur of steel.

Shanis lashed out at the man closest to her, an ugly fellow in a greasy tunic and patched hose. She drove him across the clearing with short, crisp strokes. Her adversary gave way quickly, backpedaling awkwardly as he struggled to fend off her assault. Bleary eyes peeked out from an unkempt shock of black hair and overgrown beard. His surprise at facing a woman was quickly replaced by alarm as he found himself badly outmatched. With a shout and an awkward swing, he leapt back, hurling his blade at her. She fell hard to the ground, dodging the missile. She saw her opponent turn and run. Regaining her feet quickly, she spun about, looking for a new opponent.

The attackers were in full retreat. The man she had struck down had come to, and was reeling down the roadway. The blond youth on the horse calmly nocked an arrow and drew a bead on the fleeing figure.

"Allyn," called the dark-haired rider. "Let him go. They won't try us again." The blond lad nodded his acquiescence, and returned the arrow to its quiver with a half-smile. The speaker turned to them and nodded.

"It seems that our thanks are due you." He glanced past Shanis for a moment as Oskar and Khalyndryn emerged from the forest. "My name is Larris. My companion is Allyn." He paused, waiting for them to return the introductions.

Shanis stared at Larris. He was tall, with wavy brown hair and eyes nearly as dark. They had never met before, of that she was certain, yet he seemed familiar somehow.

Khalyndryn spoke up first. "I am Khalyndryn. My friends are Hierm, Oskar, and Shanis."

Shanis swallowed an oath. They had agreed to give false names should they meet anyone along the way. She glanced at Khalyndryn. The deep blush on her cheeks indicated that she had realized her error too late.

"We are traveling south," Hierm interrupted, launching into the story they had concocted. "Is this the road to Apelmond?"

"It is," Larris replied, "but you are still well north of there." Shanis groaned. "A long way to go with no horses."

"Stolen," Hierm lied smoothly, "from our campsite. I fear that I fell asleep on sentry duty."

"A shame," Larris intoned. A slight furrowing of his brow indicated that he perhaps did not entirely believe their story. "As you can see, we have extra mounts, and we happen to be traveling in the same direction. Perhaps you would care to join us? The ladies, at least, can ride."

He seemed a friendly sort, but Shanis feared her party attaching themselves to any stranger. She was about to object, but in the moment she took trying to decide whether to do so on the grounds that she did not need to ride, or that she was no lady, Khalyndryn interjected.

"That is very kind of you. We accept your generous offer." Despite her soiled face and travel-stained dress, she managed to look every bit the lady as she curtsied deeply.

Shanis wanted to kick her.

"You are most welcome," Allyn replied smoothly, if not with the warmth that his friend Larris exuded. "Give me a moment to move some of our gear to my horse, and my spare mount is yours." He dismounted, and began rearranging their supplies. Larris did the same, and soon the group was on their way.

As they rode, Larris explained that he was the son of a merchant from Archstone. He was headed to Karkwall, in Lothan, to make inquiries of the local merchants regarding trade. Allyn had come along for companionship and security.

"We will pass through Apelmond along the way," he said. "I confess I am comforted by your presence. There is strength in numbers, and the prince's writ holds little weight this far from Galdora."

Prince's writ! She tensed at the words. How dearly she hoped that the young man was correct.

They walked their horses, maintaining a pace that Hierm and Oskar could keep afoot. Oskar looked up at her wistfully. Shanis flashed him her most innocent smile. She would let him suffer a while longer. She had forgotten how good it felt to ride. She thought of her own horse, and had to force down wistful memories of long rides in the countryside outside Galsbur. She hoped her father was treating her horse well. The two had never gotten along. Shine was as spirited as she.

Larris proved to be the more talkative of their new companions. "You handle the blade very well," he praised her. "Most impressive for a woman. No offense intended," he added quickly.

"None taken," she lied again. Mendacity was coming quite easily to her. "You are not the first to notice I'm not a man." That part was true.

"How did you develop such skill?" Larris was looking straight ahead, but the sharp tone of the question indicated his attention was firmly fixed on her.

Shanis did not wish to answer questions about herself. She tried to turn the conversation back toward Larris.

"You are obviously no stranger to the sword yourself," she complimented the young noble. "I'm not certain that the two of you needed our help."

"Oh, that we did indeed," Larris chuckled, "That we did indeed. But I thank you for the compliment. Allyn is a fair bladesman himself, and an even better archer. Had I given him leave to loose his arrow on that last brigand, you would have seen for yourself."

"I have no doubt of that," Shanis replied. This time she spoke the truth. Larris was nice enough, she supposed, but there was something about Allyn. The way he sat his horse, the unhurried way in which he went about everything he did, spoke volumes about his self-assuredness. The detached half-grin he had worn as he calmly lined up his sights on the fleeing man made him seem removed from his surroundings. He was above fear, above distraction He was a young man who knew what he was about. Shanis could believe him capable of almost anything.

"How is it that you are friends, yet you give the orders?"

"His father is my father's man," Larris replied, as if that explained everything. Her own father was Lord Hiram's man, but you would never catch her taking orders from Hierm. She was about to tell Larris that very thing when he cut her short with another question.

"You never told me why the four of you were headed to Apelmond."

"Oh, that," Shanis replied. "Hierm's father is a merchant as well." Oskar had told them that the best lie contains as much truth as possible, so they had concocted what they hoped was a plausible story. "Oskar works for him, as does my father." Here came the lie. "Hierm and Khalyndryn are betrothed. Her uncle in Apelmond is old and infirm. Hierm is going to take over his business."

"So you and Hierm are not..." Larris let the question hang unspoken between them.

"No!" she replied, perhaps a bit too vehemently. "No, we are friends. Oskar and I came along mostly for the adventure. Neither of us has ever traveled anywhere before."

"You are his betrothed?" Allyn asked Khalyndryn. Both she and Hierm nodded. "Perhaps I can change your mind before we get to Apelmond," he laughed, winking at Khalyndryn.

Shanis scowled at the back of Khalyndryn's head. The girl had gotten all the attention at home. Why should things be any different here? Didn't men think about anything more than a pretty face? She gritted her teeth, determined not to say anything.

"Only joking, of course," Allyn said, glancing down to where Hierm and Oskar walked alongside the four riders.

"It's not a problem," Hierm replied with a smile. The boy had been chafing at Khalyndryn's unsolicited attentions. Likely, he would be grateful for her to fix her sights on someone else for a while.

Strange, Shanis mused, Khalyndryn's fawning over Hierm had not made her jealous. Annoyed, even amused in an unkind way, perhaps, but not envious in the least. Why should the girl's behavior toward Allyn affect her so?

"I'm sorry," Larris interjected. "I saw the two of you together when you came to our aid, and I just assumed you were together." He shrugged.

"It's all right," she assured him. "Many people think the same thing. We've been friends for a long time." She thought for a moment. How did she feel about Hierm? She had always taken for granted that he would be there for her, but he was just Hierm. Was there any more than that?

"If not you and Hierm, perhaps you and Oskar?" Larris' broad smile indicated that the question was not sincere.

Shanis laughed and shook her head.

"I'm not such a bad catch," Oskar objected, half-joking and half-defensive.

"Of course you aren't," Hierm retorted. "My mother says you sweep a floor better than any woman she's ever known."

Oskar gave Hierm a hard shove, and walked on in silence.

"Anyone special back home?" Larris probed.

"That's none of your business."

"No!" Oskar said. "She's available. That is, if you can get between her and her sword."

The burning sensation on her cheeks told Shanis that she was in the midst of one of her famous blushes. Everyone laughed.

"I notice you don't wear a sword," Larris said to Oskar. "What is your weapon of choice?"

"Books," Oskar responded. Larris cocked his head and looked quizzically at the stout youth. "Books are my weapons of choice. Knowledge is power, or so I read somewhere."

"I enjoy books as well," Larris agreed, "but they aren't much use in a scrape."

"I generally leave the fighting to Hierm and Shanis, but I suppose I can thump someone with a stick as well as the next person."

"That walking stick you carry," Allyn cut in, "do you know how to use it?"

"What do you mean?" Oskar asked, drawing his stick close to his chest.

"The staff can be a formidable weapon," Allyn said. "I thought all you herders knew how to use one."

"We're farmers," Oskar corrected, "not herders."

"If you say so," Allyn said in a voice that conveyed his complete lack of interest in the difference between the two. "I have some skill with the staff. I can teach you if you like."

"I'd like that." Oskar's face lit up. Doubtless this was, to his mind, another chapter in his adventure story.

"Tonight then, when we make camp." Allyn nodded and turned his attention back to the road ahead.

They rode on in silence for a time. What little conversation that took place was between Allyn and Khalyndryn. Allyn bantered playfully with the blonde girl. Khalyndryn giggled, and made nonsense comments. Shanis noted that Khalyndryn was quite at home playing the fool. She only hoped that the girl was not fool enough to let slip anything she shouldn't. Larris eventually spoke up.

"What are your plans?" he asked.

"What do you mean?" She tried to keep the defensiveness from her voice.

"Once we reach Apelmond, where to from there?" he said. "Hierm and Khalyndryn will marry. What of you and Oskar?"

"Back home I suppose." Shanis shrugged. She did not like being reminded that right now there was very little plan to her life.

"Home," he echoed. "Back to, where did you say you are from?"

"Grenhamsville," she said. Oskar had assured them that no one could possibly know the name of every village in Galdora, so they were safe in simply making up a name.

"A woman of your talent going back to simple town life? Difficult to imagine. Is there some pressing business calling you back?"

"Do you always ask so many questions?" She snapped irritably. What was it with the young man and his questions?

"Not usually, but it's a long way to Karkwall, and your sword might come in handy." Allyn turned an appraising glance in Larris' direction, but did not speak. "Oskar would be welcome as well."

"That would be interesting," Oskar perked up. "I've read about Karkwall. I'd love to see it."

"Have you done a great deal of reading?" Larris asked, blessedly turning his attention from Shanis.

"Hierm's father has a small library." Oskar said, not adding the fact that he read these books without the knowledge or permission of Lord Hiram.

"Books are hard to come by, and expensive as well," Larris said. "Quite generous of him to allow you to read them."

"Yes, Oskar," Hierm chided, "so kind of him to let you read them."

"Yes," Oskar mumbled, "he is an exceptional man."

"What is your favorite book?" If Larris noticed Oskar's discomfort, he did not show it.

"*Patrin's Conquests*," Oskar replied immediately.

"*Patrin's Conquests*? But we don't have," Laris said, "I mean, I didn't know that there were any copies in existence. At least, not in Galdora."

"I know of one. Lord Hiram," Oskar paused for a moment, realizing that he had unwittingly let slip another bit of information. "Hierm's father has a copy in fine condition.

"Truly?" Larris gaze bored into Oskar with an intensity that alarmed Shanis. "I have only heard tell of the book. What sorts of stories are in it?"

"It's fascinating reading," Oskar replied. Shanis rolled her eyes. She could tell from her friend's tone of voice that Oskar might be talking for a long time. "Heroes, battles, sorcerers, fantastic creatures, lost cities."

"You don't believe any of that foolishness, do you?" Allyn interrupted, an amused lilt to his voice.

"Why shouldn't I?" Oskar retorted.

"I fear that my friend is something of a cynic," Larris said smoothly. "He doesn't believe in anything beyond the tip of his arrow." He gave Allyn an unreadable look.

"I can appreciate that." Shanis ran her fingertips across the hilt of her sword. Allyn turned toward her and nodded, his eyes gleaming above his roguish half-grin. Shanis smiled back. From the edge of her vision, she caught Hierm staring at her. Her cheeks warmed. Freeze her fair complexion! She was blushing entirely too much today.

"Friend Oskar, we are surrounded by heathens," Larris moaned in mock-anguish. "They fail to realize that all legends contain within them a kernel of truth, sometimes more."

"I have said the very same thing many times," Oskar gushed. "Shanis, haven't I said that very thing?"

"What? I don't remember anything of the sort," she teased. "I thought it was Khalyndryn who always said that." The blonde girl ignored her jibe. Oskar gaped for a moment before realizing she jested. He shook his head, and looked back at Larris. "Have you ever read the story of the Glyphs of Riza?"

"I have indeed," Larris nodded. "Imagine, an entire system of writing created just so that a prince might woo a young lady with love letters written in their very own language."

"That is so romantic," Khalyndryn sighed, staring up at the pale sky, feathered with wisps of cloud.

"Not really," Oskar looked up at the blonde. "The love letters were a ruse. They were plotting together to assassinate her father."

"Oskar, you are horrid." Khalyndryn spurred her horse forward. She bounced awkwardly, clinging to the pommel of her saddle as her mount trotted away.

"Did it work?" Shanis asked, surprisingly curious about the story.

"The king, the girl's father, discovered their plot. Using her key to the code, he wrote a letter ostensibly from her, asking the prince to come right away."

"The letter led the prince into a system of caverns, where the king's daughter was waiting." Oskar picked up the narrative. "He sealed the entrance shut, entombing them for all eternity."

Shanis nodded approvingly. That was the sort of princess story that she could enjoy. Life did not come wrapped in a neat package; it was messy. Her life was certainly a mess.

"You mentioned lost cities. Any lost cities in *Patrin's Conquests*?" Larris leaned toward Oskar as he asked. Shanis thought she detected a bit of hopefulness in his voice.

"Several," the boy responded. "It's quite a long book, actually."

"You'll have to tell me of them," Larris said.

Oskar opened his mouth to reply, but Shanis had thought of a question of her own.

"Larris, in your reading, have you ever come across stories of furry manlike beasts with the head and claws of wild cats?"

The young man jerked his head around to stare at her. His eyes widened momentarily, but then his features smoothed.

"Not that I recall. Why do you ask?"

"No reason." Shanis did not entirely trust their new companion. He asked too many questions. Furthermore, she suspected that he knew more than he was letting on about the strange beasts. "Just something I've heard about."

"Grandmother's fireside tales," Allyn muttered. While he retained his calm exterior, his voice registered a note of concern.

"As I said earlier, my friend lacks imagination," Larris said. "I have read of many odd and frightful creatures, but none precisely like the ones you describe. Where did you hear tell of these particular beasts?"

"It was just as he said." Shanis nodded in Allyn's direction. "One of my grandmother's stories."

The blond youth rewarded her with a wink and she bit her cheeks to keep from smiling one of those idiotic girlish smiles. Why did he have such an effect on her?

"I have spent a great deal of time in the forests of Galdora and I can tell you that the next time I see such a creature will be the first." Allyn patted Khalyndryn on the shoulder as he spoke. The girl had trembled at the mention of their mysterious assailants.

"Fortunate that your work for Larris' father allows you so much time for adventures," Hierm noted with a touch of sarcasm in his voice.

"Larris' father is as generous an employer as your own father must be," Allyn said.

"How truly blessed we are," Hierm sighed and glanced at Larris, "to have such wonderful fathers."

A shame, Shanis thought, that the irony was lost on their new comrades. What was Lord Hiram doing right now? Had he sent men in search of Hierm? What must all their families think? She tried not to imagine her father returning from his haul to find her gone. To hear what she had done to the soldier.

"Allyn, I suppose every creature that walks this earth lives in the forests of Galdora?" Larris' jibe did not faze Allyn. "Have you ever been to the Ice Reaches?"

"What are the Ice Reaches?" Khalyndryn's voice quavered.

"The Ice Reaches lie somewhere among the highest peaks of the Walls of Stone." He turned his gaze to the west as if he could see those fabled mountains from here. "Evil creatures are purported to make their home there."

"Purported," Allyn emphasized, "not known."

"But as our friends are fond of saying," Shanis said, "every story contains a bit of truth, does it not?" She did not like Allyn questioning the existence of the creatures they had encountered, and took pleasure in disagreeing with him. In fairness to the young man, she hadn't actually told the story of their encounter. Nonetheless, it felt as if he were doubting her honesty.

"What of the wolfen?" Oskar inquired, obviously pleased at having discovered a kindred spirit.

"Ah, the wolfen." Larris smiled. "Beasts who are half-man, half-wolf. Another creature Allyn has never seen. Yet they are mentioned in countless stories. So many, in fact, that one would be a fool," he looked at Allyn and emphasized the word with raised voice, "not to consider the possibility that they are real."

"How improbable," Allyn intoned, "that two relatively ordinary young men happen to be so well-read. How truly fortunate we are."

"Yes, truly," Larris answered dryly.

Something passed between the two men. Shanis noted a tension that was not there before. She looked from one to the other. Allyn's partial smile was gone. He stared blankly in front of him. Larris, for his part, clutched his reins in a white-knuckled grip. They rode on in an uncomfortable silence.

Chapter 11

The sizzling meat popped and spattered grease into the campfire. Hungry flames leapt up to engulf the squirrel carcass. Shanis cursed and grabbed the skewer, lifting it high before it scorched. She turned the meat slowly, getting it just right before propping it back on the forked stick she had driven into the ground next to the fire ring. She checked the two others that were roasting, making sure they were not too close. Certain their dinner was now safe, she returned to skinning the last squirrel.

"I told them we needed to wait until we had some good coals to cook over," she muttered. "That's what I get for giving in to Khalyndryn's complaining."

"Smells good," Larris said, walking over to stand beside her. "Perhaps you should do all the cooking."

She rolled her eyes but did not reply to the young man's weak jest. Could he not leave her alone?

"Allyn says you're quite the huntress," Larris said, moving to sit facing her across the fire. "He says you move as quietly in the woods as he does. That is high praise from him, I promise you. He thinks everyone else sounds like a drunken bull moving through the forest."

"I'll be certain to thank him then," Shanis said. They had ridden with their new companions for two days now, and she was still uncomfortable with Larris. She had joined Allyn on his evening hunting excursions primarily to get away from Larris' prying questions. Allyn, by contrast, said little. And, truth be known, she had developed quite a fascination with the quiet young man. She admired his woodscraft, and he respected hers in turn. The few words he said to her were compliments regarding her tracking skills or her ability to move silently in the woods. This evening, he allowed her to use his bow, and she had surprised him by bringing down both squirrels with precise shots to the head, thus preserving the meaty parts. Her father had taught her well, though she certainly was nowhere near Allyn's equal.

She wondered what Larris would think if he knew that Shanis had tried to extend her trek through the forest with Allyn today, asking questions about plant names or pretending to not recognize a particular track, just to stay away from Larris as long as possible. Of course, a small part of her had also wanted to spend more time with Allyn.

"Why don't you go discuss books with Oskar?" she asked as she dragged her knife across the last squirrel's abdomen with unnecessary vigor. During their daily rides, Oskar and Larris had developed the beginnings of a friendship based on their mutual love of books, and they spoke of little else.

"You enjoy our tale swapping, do you?" Larris asked. His smile was flawless, and she hated him all the more for it. "I would be happy to share some more stories with you if you like."

"To be quite truthful," Shanis said, looking directly at him for the first time since he sat down, "I find almost every one of them most tedious."

"Tedious?" Larris' eyes opened wide as he spoke.

"Tedious," she said again. "Tiresome, monotonous, boring; shall I go on?"

"Forgive me," he said. "I was not aware that you were familiar with that word."

Shanis fixed him with what she hoped was a look of unadulterated disgust. She flipped over the squirrel carcass, scooped out the entrails with a deft twist of her knife, and tossed them at Larris. The gooey mass struck him on the chest, and slowly slid down the front of his silk doublet.

Larris looked down at the sticky heap of organs in surprise, but instead of being angry, he burst out laughing; a hearty, deep laugh that made him seem almost sincere. He plucked them off of his clothing with two fingers, and tossed them into the fire, where they crackled and hissed.

Shanis skewered the last tree rat, as her father called them, and positioned it over the fire. She sat down to keep watch on the meal, pointedly turning her attention away from Larris. It did no good.

The young man scooted up to sit on her right side. He drew his knees up to his chest and wrapped his arms around his legs, linking his fingers together. He sat that way, rocking back and forth, still smiling over the innards incident.

"You said you hated almost all of them."

Shanis took a deep breath, and breathed out slowly and noisily. "Some of them serve to pass the time," she admitted. Perhaps he would leave her alone if he got something positive out of her.

"Which ones?" he asked. He leaned toward her ever so slightly. She scooted away. If he noticed, he didn't let on. "Honestly, which ones do you like the most?"

"The ones where the pushy young man gets killed," she snapped. That gave him pause. He stared at her, mouth slightly agape, seemingly trying to decide if she was joking or not. Burn it all! Why did she feel guilty now? "You never answered my question," she said, trying to change the subject. "Why don't you go find Oskar?"

"Allyn took him into the forest to find a solid limb to make a quarterstaff."

"What's he going to do?" Shanis asked, looking at Larris with raised eyebrows. "String books along it and carry it over his shoulders like a yoke?"

Larris laughed and clasped her shoulder. Shanis laughed too, in spite of her discomfort.

"Allyn was showing him a few moves with his own staff. He thinks Oskar might be an apt pupil. Allyn says the lad has strong arms and quick wrists."

"Too bad his hands are so slow," Shanis deadpanned.

Larris laughed even harder at this.

Shanis stood and checked the meat before he could touch her shoulder again.

"Someone should tell the happy couple that it's almost time to eat," she said, looking around for Hierm and Khalyndryn. The young man was already chafing at having to pretend to be Khalyndryn's intended. For her part, Khalyndryn was taking full advantage, fawning over him worse than she ever had at home. Just then, the two of them walked up, arm-in-arm.

"Looking for us?" Khalyndryn cooed. She smiled sweetly, and batted her eyes at Larris, who bowed in an exaggerated, mocking fashion. The sarcasm was lost on Khalyndryn, who squeezed Hierm's arm in both hands and bounced excitedly on her toes. "Larris is such a gentleman, Hierm. He could teach you how to treat a lady."

Hierm grunted and shook loose of her grasp. He sat down next to Shanis and stared at the fire. Shanis wanted to laugh, but she was too worried that Khalyndryn might spoil their charade with her flirting.

"I think you should be more appreciative of your intended," Shanis said, looking Khalyndryn directly in the eye.

"I am not accustomed," Khalyndryn said, her voice lofty, "to taking suggestions from a servant girl." Folding her hands across her chest, she tossed her head and made a "humph" sound.

Before she realized what she was doing, Shanis went down one knee and felt her hand close around a large, smooth pebble. Its cool, unblemished surface felt just right in her hand. It would serve Khalyndryn right if Shanis bounced the stone off of her forehead. That, however, would be most un-servant like. Quickly gaining control of herself, she dropped the pebble and drew her knife from its belt sheath.

Khalyndryn gasped and took a small step backward. Her creamy complexion paled to a stark white. "You wouldn't," she whispered, slumping to the ground to sit next to Hierm. The concern in her green eyes made it sound more like a question than a statement.

"Wouldn't cut bread?" Shanis asked, trying to sound as innocent as possible. She picked up the small loaf of bread Larris had provided, and proceeded to cut off thick chunks and pass them out. Larris sliced up a hard cheese from his pack, and handed that around as well.

Oskar and Allyn soon returned from their trek into the forest, Oskar proudly sporting a length of wood for a new staff. Shanis smiled at the excitement evident in the youth's broad face. Growing up an aspiring scholar in a town where a young man was expected to learn to hunt, farm and fight had not earned him a great deal of respect from his peers. Likely, Oskar would take great pride in developing a fighting skill of his own.

"Sit beside me, Allyn," Khalyndryn said, patting the ground on her left. The blond woodsman shrugged and dropped to the ground.

"Can I help?" Oskar asked Shanis.

"Get the squirrels off the skewers. Start with the ones on the left. They've been over the fire the longest." Oskar complied, and soon, they were all feasting on bread, cheese, and roast squirrel.

"It's tough on the outside and raw on the inside," Khalyndryn complained, biting into a chunk of meat. Shanis was about to curse the girl roundly when Allyn intervened.

"You know the camp rule, don't you?" he asked. Seeing the blank expression on Khalyndryn's face, he continued. "Whoever complains about the cooking prepares the next day's meals."

"Oh," the girl said, turning to Shanis. "I'm sure you did the best you could." She returned to her meal, an obvious expression of distaste marring her lovely face. Around the fire, choked sounds of suppressed laughter sprang up. Even Hierm was fighting to keep his tight-lipped grin in place.

"I, for one," Larris said, regaining control of himself, "think this is fine cooking. You could apprentice in the kitchen of one of the larger houses or inns."

"What? Work in a kitchen?" Shanis sprang to her feet. "What are you saying? You think I can't handle a sword?"

Larris had gone too far this time, and he seemed to know it. "I did not say that," he said evenly. His bronze face was pale under the heat of her stare. "I was trying to pay you a compliment."

Shanis felt embarrassed, but she did not want to back down from the pushy young man. "I don't need your compliments, thank you very much." She stalked away as quickly as dignity would permit. Would she never learn to control her temper? No wonder Master Yurg had always been so hard on her.

Thoughts of Yurg led to thoughts of home, and with them, a wave of homesickness. Where was her father right now? Had he gone looking for her? Who was caring for her horse? Her eyes misted, and she stumbled in the fast-dimming light of evening. A hand caught her by the upper arm and lifted her up.

"It's all right," Hierm said, steadying her. His eyes searched hers. "What can I do?" He moved to put his arms around her, but she drew back quickly.

"You're betrothed, remember?" she whispered. "I'm fine. Just a little tired and homesick." She gave his hand a quick squeeze. "Thanks." She heard a rustling behind Hierm, turned and rolled her eyes as she saw Larris approaching. Silhouetted against the distant campfire, the young merchant looked vaguely wraithlike in the twilight. Or perhaps the sinister characterization was merely a product of her discomfort with him.

"May I speak with you?" he asked. "Please?"

Hierm looked from Shanis to Larris, then back at Shanis, his eyebrow arched. After a moment's thought, she nodded. Hierm threw a brief, challenging stare at Larris, holding his gaze for several heartbeats, before returning to the campfire.

"You have an interesting relationship with your employer," Larris mused. His expression betrayed nothing, but there was a touch of suspicion in his tone. Before Shanis could answer, he raised his hands in front of him, as if to ward her off. "I know. I've yet again managed to offend you." He took a deep breath, and looked up at the leafy branches that drooped just above their heads.

"What do you want to talk to me about?" she snapped. She didn't like being alone with Larris. She wasn't frightened of him, exactly. She was more concerned that she would let something important slip in the midst of his constant interrogation. She folded her hands across her chest, tapped her foot, and tried to imitate the face she had seen Mistress Anna make when Papa and Master Yurg came home after too long an evening in Master Serrill's common room.

"If we are going to be traveling together, you and I might as well find a way to get along with one another." He said it firmly, as if there were nothing else to discuss.

"I know Oskar likes traveling with you, as does Khalyndryn." She couldn't speak for Hierm, and her feelings were well known. She spoke slowly, careful not to speak in haste, as she often did. Near the campfire, a clacking sound arose: Allyn and Oskar practicing their quarterstaffs. "It's certainly safer for us all to be together," she added, thinking of the cat creatures. "Why isn't that enough?"

"Because I don't want any more evenings like this," he said. "We are traveling companions. What can I do, beyond what I have already done, to help us peacefully coexist?"

"Not speaking to one another comes immediately to mind," she said.

"No good," he replied, smiling, "I like to talk too much." He looked down at her waist, his eyes narrowing. She was about to smack the grin off of his face when he looked back up at her and grinned.

"How good are you with that sword of yours, anyway?" he asked slyly.

"Half again as good as you," she said, taking a step toward him. She was almost of a height with the tall young man, and she met his gaze resolutely.

"Perhaps I can persuade you otherwise," he said. He turned sideways and motioned back toward the campfire, moving into step behind her as she passed him by. Retrieving their swords, they squared off in the clearing. Allyn and Oskar broke from their practice, watching with interest.

They crossed blades, tentatively at first, then with greater intensity. Her earlier impression of Larris was correct; he was a fine swordsman. He flowed through the forms with the grace of a dancer, smiling broadly all the while. The smile only made her want to beat him all the more, and she poured everything into the attack. Her anger, her guilt, her homesickness, her loneliness, her suspicion, her fear, her hurts all flowed through her blade as it whistled its deadly song. Blows rained down in torrents upon Larris' defenses. No longer smiling, the boy gave ground grudgingly. Blow by blow, with all the precision of a blacksmith working a chunk of iron, she beat him back until Allyn stepped in.

"Hold!" the hunter called, pulling her away. "Put your sword away. I think I can find something more suitable."

Shanis was surprised to find that her anger was gone. She felt emptied, and in a strange way, cleansed. She had missed this. The sword had been a part of her life for so long that it felt like an important part of her.

The young woodsman vanished into the forest, returning a short while later with bundles of long, springy branches lashed together in bundles which roughly approximated the length and weight of practice swords. He had fashioned four of the makeshift swords: one each for Shanis, Larris, Hierm, and himself.

"A little safer," he explained, "though you can still leave a lovely bruise on your opponent."

Hierm initially declined to take part. Shanis tried to convince him, but to no avail. With a shrug, she turned to Allyn.

"What do you say, hunter boy? Do you want to try me?" she taunted, grinning broadly.

"Been dying to." With a wicked grin, he raised his "sword" to his forehead in a mock-salute, and assumed the ready position. Shanis dispensed with the niceties, and sent a lightning-quick thrust at his throat. Allyn deflected her attack with an economy of movement, and slashed back at her with a deft flick of the wrist. Shanis parried, and battered his defenses with a sweeping backhand.

The two were well-matched. Each had quick reflexes and moved well. Their reach was almost equal as well. They traded blows for what seemed like hours, laughing and playfully taunting one another all the while.

It did not take long before the clack of the imitation swords drew Hierm out of his shell. He joined in, squaring off first against Larris, then Allyn. Oskar and Khalyndryn enjoyed the display as well, alternately cheering and jeering the combatants. The duels continued late into the evening, long after they should have taken to bed. When fatigue finally overcame them, they lay around the fire, sharing wine from a skin Larris produced from his saddlebag. All of the previous tension had been wrung out of the small group of travelers.

"Fine blade work for a merchant's son and his hired hand," Larris said, offering his hand to Shanis. She stared at him for a moment before clasping it in hers.

"I suppose," she said, "we've found something in common."

Chapter 12

Shanis' horse pounded muddy footprints into a heavily-rutted street, fouled with manure and stagnant pools of rainwater. Houses and shops in various states of disrepair crowded the narrow thoroughfare. The smell of wood smoke hung heavy in the air, carrying on a struggle for dominance with the pungent aroma of horse dung. She crinkled her nose against the fetid odors. She was surprised at the size of the town. She had always believed her home must be the smallest place in the world, but it seemed to her that this hamlet would scarcely fit onto Galdora's green.

A short, fat man in a dirty, green tunic pushed a barrow of turnips down the street. He paused to scowl at the two young travelers before continuing down the way.

"A friendly sort, wouldn't you say?" Larris sounded amused, but his expression was grave.

Shanis would have preferred to avoid the place entirely, but Larris had insisted that they stop. She had racked her brain, but could not come up with an explanation to dissuade him that would not have raised his suspicions. She tried to convince herself that there was little to fear so far from Galdora. No one would recognize her. Still, a nagging fear bored a hole in the back of her consciousness, irrational though it might be. Would she ever be free of the feeling that she needed to hide from every stranger's gaze?

Oskar had gone with Allyn to purchase supplies, while Hierm was charged with purchasing two more horses for the group. Shanis' friend had initially balked, but Larris had assured him that the horses were not a gift. The horses would speed their journey, the young man had reasoned, and provide them with a means to carry the supplies they would purchase. Hierm's pride was not such that he could not see reason, though he was less than pleased with Khalyndryn accompanying him. Shanis had wanted to go with Hierm, arguing that she knew more about horses than her friend, but to no avail. Larris insisted on her coming with him.

"What makes you think the others will be able to find horses or supplies in this place?" Shanis asked.

"It is the last town of any size along the way to Lothan," the young man answered. "I told them to spare no expense."

All her life, Shanis had gotten her way, be it through fits of temper, or sheer determination. Larris, though, had a way of simply pronouncing his will, and assuming that it would be done. Strange, it seemed to work on her. She couldn't win an argument with him, which made her dislike him all the more.

She and Larris reined their horses in at the front of a small inn. A faded sign named it The Grinning Goat. As they mounted the rickety steps, Shanis looked with disdain upon the sagging roof and weather-stained walls badly in need of whitewash. She hoped the condition of the exterior was not an indicator of the quality of the fare served inside. Memories of evenings spent on the front steps of Master Serrill's inn, listening to the cheerful din of music and conversation, sent tremors of loneliness through her. Would she ever go home again?

The common room was dark and oddly cool for a warm summer day. On the far end of the room, a low fire smoldered and spat an occasional spark onto the dirty floor. A few patrons huddled over mugs of ale, their conversations merely a low whisper. A man in a greasy apron, eyes closed, reclined in a chair propped against the far wall. Larris selected a table near the door, and positioned himself with his back to the wall. Shanis sat down opposite him.

"Innkeeper," Larris called in an imperious tone, "two ales!"

The innkeeper's eyes popped open. The front legs of his chair crashed to the floor as Larris' shout jolted him from his slumber. Scowling, he made his way across the room to their table. He fixed them with a sour gaze.

"You have coin?" he grumbled, beefy arms folded across his chest above his paunchy stomach. Shanis cringed at his dirty hands and the black filth under his nails.

Larris jingled a fat purse at his waist. With a curt nod, the innkeeper turned and slowly made his way into a back room.

"Take your time about it," Larris mumbled, looking around the room with a pained expression.

"Do you treat everyone that way?" Shanis asked. Master Serrill would have shown this uppity lad the door, money or no. A rat-faced man at the end of the room apparently shared her opinion, glaring at the two of them over a cup of wine.

"I'm accustomed to having my instructions obeyed promptly. Besides, he should take pride in his work."

"How is he going to feel proud if you take away his dignity?" Shanis replied hotly. It felt good to give him the rough side of her tongue. "You treated him like he's nothing. Being a merchant's son doesn't make you a noble. Besides, I'll wager he's spat in your ale."

Larris winced, and opened his mouth to reply when the innkeeper returned. He plopped two frothy mugs of ale down onto the table, foam splashing onto Larris' tunic. Shanis smirked.

"Four coppers."

Larris reached into his money pouch, and withdrew a silver coin. He pressed it onto the table with two long, tanned fingers. The innkeeper reached for the coin, but Larris did not remove his hand. The man's eyes widened, and he regarded Shanis' companion with a questioning look.

"I would hear the news." Larris spared a glance at Shanis. "Please," he added. Shanis grinned at the way the boy's mouth twisted as it formed the last word.

The innkeeper rubbed his hands on his dirty apron. His eyes flitted from the coin to Larris' face, then back to the coin. "We don't get much news here, young sir."

"Four coppers, you said?" Larris dragged the coin back toward himself.

"Understand M'lord, this here is the middle of nowhere. We don't get much news here. Leastways, none that isn't as stale as Madrin's bread." The man tilted his head to his right, as if to indicate the direction of the baker's house, and smiled a broad, gap-toothed grin.

"Anything at all."

"Well, mostly the usual. There's talk of war with Kyrin, of course." The man scratched at his bald pate with beefy fingers.

"Any battles?"

"Not as I've heard. But things is pretty tense on the border, so they say."

"Has Lerryn done any recruiting in the area? I've heard that the prince has been traveling about raising troops for the army."

"No word of the prince hereabouts. But I did hear tell that there's some nobles camped just north of town. Don't know why they're here. We don't get many nobles pass this way."

"Interesting." Larris face indicated that the information was anything but. "Any other strange happenings?"

Shanis frowned. What was he talking about? The innkeeper apparently shared her confusion.

"Beggin' your pardon, young sir?"

"Oh, I don't know," Larris shrugged. "Anything odd, out of the ordinary going on?"

"Don't know about that." The innkeeper rubbed his ample girth. "The herders been saying that the wolves are coming down out of the mountains a bit further'n usual. I'd say that's about everything." He punctuated the statement with a firm nod.

"I thank you." Larris slid the coin across the table. It quickly vanished into the dirty apron pocket. Making an awkward bow, the man returned to his chair.

Larris looked into his mug of ale, as if searching for some impurity. With a shrug, he lifted it to his lips, and took a long pull. His eyebrows rose in surprise, and he nodded to Shanis. She took a sip, and found it surprisingly good, rich and dark, with a hint of honey.

She rocked back in her chair, and gazed intently at the young man seated across from her. She supposed he was handsome, in his own way. His long hair was wavy and brown where Allyn's was straight and blonde, his complexion bronze where Allyn's was fair. His brown eyes met her gaze, and he smiled. What was it about him that seemed so familiar? Had she met him before? She shook her head, and broke off her gaze.

She still didn't entirely trust him. What were all these questions? This need to know "the news"? He was always prying. Of course, she had to admit that their travels together had thus far not been entirely unpleasant. Having a horse to ride had certainly been a welcome change from walking, not to mention Oscar's floating contraption. She sat now, in a filthy tavern, gazing across a filthier table at this strange young man. He met her stare with an impudent grin.

"What are you smiling at?" she asked.

"Why don't you like me?" The expression on his face was earnest. "I want to know."

"What?" She wasn't sure how to answer the question. Obviously, she couldn't reveal the reason for her resistance to his constant questioning.

"You heard me. Why don't you like me?"

"What's there to like?" That was unkind. She felt a moment's regret as the young man's eyes fell, and he gazed into his mug of ale. "It's just that you ask so many questions. Why don't you just leave me alone?" Spoken aloud, her reasoning did not seem to her as solid as it once had.

"That's why you don't like me?"

"It's what I don't like about you," she said after a moment's pause. "Not the same."

"So there's a difference?" he said, tilting his head and frowning.

"Only a small one," she grumbled. Would he never stop pelting her with questions?

"Why shouldn't I ask you questions?" he asked.

"There you go again. Now you're asking me questions about asking me questions. Do you ever stop?" She was surprised to realize that she was laughing.

"I ask you questions because I want to know you better," he explained, gesturing with his mug. "Considering the time we've spent riding together, I don't know very much about you."

She took a long pull from her mug, using the time to think. Why did he want to know her better? Suspicion flared anew, but she quelled it. He seemed to mean it in a genuine way.

"I'd have to say, you know just as much about me as I know about you," she said.

"Fair enough. Ask me anything. I don't mind questions." He rocked back on the legs of his chair, tucked his hands behind his head. "You ask me a question, then I'll ask you a question."

"I don't want to know anything about you," she mumbled, taking another drink.

"Well, I want to know about you." The front legs of his chair dropped to the floor with a thump. He leaned forward, folding his hands together and propping his elbows on the table.

Silhouetted in front of the window, his appearance again struck Shanis as vaguely familiar. She shook the thought from her head. "Why do you want to know anything about me?"

"Aha! That was a question," he laughed. "I'll answer it, and then you'll have to answer one from me."

Shanis was about to protest when she felt an icy chill, harsher than the damp cold of the common room, envelop her body. She shuddered and drew her arms up against her chest.

"Something wrong?" Larris' face conveyed genuine concern as he reached across the table and placed his hand on her arm.

"Just a bit of a chill," she whispered through chattering teeth. She wanted to point out to him that he had just asked his question, but the tremors that ran through her seemed to have rattled her brain.

"You must be taking ill." Larris frowned deeply. "I'll tell the innkeeper to add a log to the fire." He made to rise from his seat but froze, eyes wide open, the blood draining from his face.

"What is it?" Shanis turned around to look.

Six armed men had entered the room and filed over to a large table near the fireplace. Three looked familiar. A reed-thin youth with an unruly shock of brown hair that obscured his eyes sat closest to the fire. A large, bulky boy bigger even than Oskar sat next to him. A lanky young man with long blond hair and a smile that displayed straight, white teeth sat next to the large youth. The three others made their way to the other side of the table. Her breath caught as she spied one of them. Pedric Karst!

She stood, ready to confront him, her chills forgotten. The sour-faced boy looked up, and their eyes met for a moment. Did he recognize her without red hair? A whispered warning from Larris drew her attention to the other two men at the table. One of the men, a gaunt, wrinkled man with strange purple eyes, she had never seen before. The other she knew.

She crumpled into her chair, the sound of Prince Lerryn's voice calling for ales all around echoing in her ears. She felt numb. Why was he here? How had he found her? Had he found her? What was he doing with Karst? Amidst the torrent of questions, one thought came through clearly. She leaned toward Larris.

"We need to leave," she whispered. "Now!"

Larris cocked an eye, then nodded his agreement. Slowly, calmly they stood, both of them keeping their backs toward Lerryn's table. She felt his arm encircle his waist, and he drew her close to him. Forcing herself to relax, she laid her head against his shoulder, and they walked casually out the door, like lovers on a stroll.

When they reached their horses, they unhitched them, and led them several paces down the road, so as not to mount up in front of the window of the common room.

"Allyn will take care of the others," Larris said softly as they mounted up. "No doubt he has seen."

Shame flooded through her. She hadn't even thought of her friends, only of herself. But would Lerryn even know the others? She was the one he was after. No doubt he would remember her; the girl with the sword. The girl who had killed his guard. She bit her lip. Perhaps neither he nor Karst had recognized her. Few people ever looked past her red hair and her sword.

An entirely different thought flashed through her mind, giving her pause. Larris had obviously recognized someone in the group that had entered the common room. He had reacted to them first. Was he running from someone too? She mulled things over as they made their way down the south road and out of town.

Rounding a bend, they came upon their companions waiting for them. Hierm had acquired two solid mounts. Everyone was mounted and ready to ride. Allyn exchanged glances with Larris, then turned to Shanis, motioning for her to take the lead. As she trotted her horse forward, she passed Hierm. The look in his eyes indicated that he too had seen Lerryn.

The whisper of a sword being drawn from its scabbard interrupted her thoughts. She felt the cold edge of Larris' blade pressed against her throat. She froze. What was he doing? From the corner of her eye, she could see that Allyn had drawn his bow. The archer had his bow drawn and an arrow aimed at the center of Hierm's chest. Obviously the two of them were considered the most dangerous of the group.

"Anyone moves," Allyn said calmly, almost cheerfully, "and your friends die."

His matter-of-fact tone chilled her. She looked back at Larris, who appeared equally determined.

"Why are you doing this?" she whispered through gritted teeth.

"You said that you didn't want to ask me any questions," he replied in even tones, "but now I have one for you. Why are you running from my brother?"

Chapter 13

Lerryn quaffed his ale in a few short gulps, and called for more. He wiped the foam from his mouth with the back of his sleeve, and took stock of his companions. Mattyas, or "Hair" as they called him, had proven to be a pleasant traveling companion, quick with an insult but quick to laugh at himself as well. Barlis, nicknamed "Bull", was equally amenable, though a bit on the quiet side, as was Edrin, the archer. Pedric Karst was another matter entirely.

"This place is filthy," the dark-haired boy muttered. "I am accustomed to better." He sat with his hands folded across his chest, staring down at the floor.

"And I am accustomed to young men who know their place," Xaver said, his face a cold mask.

"And I would like to enjoy my ale with none of your bickering, if you please," Lerryn said. He accepted a fresh mug from the innkeeper with a nod. He turned to chastise Karst, but stopped when he saw the strange look on the lad's face. "What is it?"

"I thought I knew that girl." Karst nodded toward the door. "Over there."

Lerryn turned to look, but saw only and empty table. The girl, whoever she was, had apparently left.

"You've never known a girl in your life," Hair chided, "except your mother perhaps."

"Take that back!" Karst leapt to his feet, his sword half drawn. "Right now."

"Sit down boy," Lerryn ordered, not bothering to rise.

Karst opened his mouth to reply, but closed it again as the innkeeper returned with ales for the rest of their party. Lerryn motioned for him to sit, which he did grudgingly.

Lerryn regarded Karst for a moment. The boy's pinched face and beady eyes were a perfect match for his personality, he mused.

"I am not accustomed," Karst grumbled, "to being spoken to in such a way by a commoner."

Lerryn had heard enough of Karst's foolishness.

"Master Karst, I have not shared with you the fact that I know precisely who your father is." He did not miss Karst's eyes flit down at the table for a moment before looking back at him in defiance. "You are the son of the chief pig farmer in a province of pig farmers. If you think that gains you any special favor from me, you are sadly mistaken."

Karst's face reddened, but he remained silent.

"Pedric Pig. I like it!" Bull said, clapping his huge hands. "We could call you Piggy for short."

"Lord Ham!" Hair laughed and smacked the table. Edrin joined in, and even Xaver cracked a smile. "Ham, Hair and Bull."

"My father is not a pig farmer," Karst whispered, still staring down at his drink.

"I suppose you are correct," Lerryn agreed. He knew somewhere in the back of his mind that he should be above goading the boy, but he couldn't help himself. He rocked back in his chair as he spoke. "Your father is a landowner. Tell me, what do his serfs raise on his land?"

"Corn, tomatoes." Karst frown deepened and he kept his gaze directed away from Lerryn.

"If you include the kitchen gardens, that is true. But what do they raise?" Lerryn asked.

"Pigs."

"And the tithes that your father claims from them, he is paid in what?"

"Pigs." Karst's voice grew more sullen.

"Need I say more?"

They sat in silence for a long time. Lerryn sipped his ale. It was dark and strong with a hint of honey. Not bad for a dingy inn in a dirty town. He was almost embarrassed that such a town could exist in his kingdom. Then again, such domestic issues were the king's domain. The First Prince was responsible for the military, and for justice. He hoped things were running smoothly in his absence.

"You still haven't told us where we're going." As usual, Karst's silence had not lasted long.

"We tell you what you need to know, Master Karst," Lerryn responded.

"One of us ought to know," Karst protested. Lerryn would not have thought it possible, but his expression turned even more sour.

"You think so, do you?" Lerryn snapped back. The boy always managed to raise his ire. He had done it again, cutting right to the heart of Lerryn's worries.

"This thing we're after," Karst probed, "it's one single thing, right?"

Lerryn nodded. What harm was there in revealing that small detail?

"So then, whatever it is, only one of us can use it." Karst's dark eyes narrowed, like a bird of prey spotting a potential kill.

"What makes you think someone is going to use it?" Lerryn retorted, knowing it was a weak response.

"You said we had to have it to save our country."

"That is true," Lerryn agreed. If only the boy knew how much truly depended upon the success of this quest.

"If either of you could use whatever it is, you wouldn't need the four of us. Obviously, one of us is going to have to use it." Karst propped an elbow on the table, resting his chin in a cupped hand and looking at Lerryn with an expectant smile.

"I was wrong about you, Master Karst," Xaver's dry voice interrupted. "I once thought you a great fool, but I was mistaken."

Karst's smile broadened in self-satisfaction.

"You are not a great fool, only an average fool."

Hair guffawed, choking on his ale. Bull slapped the coughing boy on the back. Hair regained his composure quickly under Xaver's purple-eyed stare.

"If one of us is to use this thing," Karst began again, "don't you think that person should at least know what it is? Unless, of course, you don't know which one of us it is."

Xaver's mouth twisted into a contemptuous snarl. He leaned toward Karst, eyes boring into the arrogant lad. "You go too far, boy. All of you get out. Wait by the horses." The four youths scrambled quickly to their feet, overturning chairs, and nearly upending the innkeeper on their way out.

Lerryn fumed inside. He was First Prince of Galdora, yet he did not intimidate the boys the way his vizier did. They had a healthy respect for him, he was certain.

Even Karst had learned to mind the sharper edge of his tongue. Yet they seemed to treat Lerryn more as first among equals, rather than someone whom they should fear.

"The prophecy has brought us together." Xaver turned to Lerryn. "Together! We must be united. We cannot be so without a leader. Stop drinking with these boys and start leading them."

"Do not tell me about the prophecy. I have seen no signs of your prophecy since this journey began." It was such a simple plan. Assemble the six, set off in the direction their research told them to go, and wait for the prophecy to take hold.

"The prophecy is in action," his Vizier protested. "Take the four boys. They fit perfectly." He paused for a moment. "Well, almost perfectly."

Xaver glared past Lerryn, as if he could see Karst through the wall. Lerryn shook his head. Perhaps Xaver could see through walls.

"Every day I look for signs," he argued, mindful of the need to keep his voice down. "I watch these boys, waiting for one of them to do something, I don't know, prophetic." He drank down the last of his ale, then relieved Xaver of his untouched tankard. "You aren't completely certain yourself. I've seen you at night, poring over the scrolls, looking for something you might have missed."

"The prophecy works in inexplicable ways. You mustn't lose faith. Something will happen when you least expect it, usually in the way you least expect."

"Something had better happen soon," Lerryn muttered sourly.

"Forgive me, M'lords. There's someone would like to have a word with you." The innkeeper approached their table warily, wringing his hands, and staring at Xaver as if he were a poisonous serpent. "It's the constable. Something terrible's happened. He's a hoping that you Lords might could help him." He backed away quickly, gesturing toward the door.

Lerryn rose from his chair slowly. He drained Xaver's tankard in a few greedy gulps, fished into his money pouch, and produced a heavy silver coin with his father's image imprinted on one side. He tossed it to the innkeeper.

"Our thanks for your hospitality. Lead us to this constable, and we shall see if we may be of some assistance."

"I thank you M'lord." The surprised innkeeper examined the coin with rheumy eyes. "Two of these in one day! Who'd have thought it?"

Lerryn frowned. Two in one day? Not likely. Perhaps he meant two silver coins in one day. Surely this pitiful place did not see much silver.

The innkeeper led them out into the street, where a heavyset man with bulging brown eyes waited. He pressed a giant hand against his ample girth and bowed deeply, displaying a bald spot peeking through his thin brown hair.

"M'lords, we have need of your assistance. Two men have been killed." The constable's eyes darted nervously from Lerryn to Xaver, then back to Lerryn.

"Constable, I can assure you that no one from our party was involved," Lerryn replied.

"I am sorry, M'lord, I did not make myself clear. Wild animals killed the men. Tore them up something terrible. Their family could scarcely recognize 'em."

"I fail to see how we may be of assistance," Xaver said. "We can hardly bring these men back to life."

The constable nervously rubbed his hands over his ample girth. He scraped the heel of his boot back and forth in the filth of the muddy street.

"They managed to bring down one of the animals before they were killed. Truth is, we've never seen the like. We had hoped that you, being travelers, might've seen one of these things before." He looked at Lerryn pleadingly, studiously avoiding Xaver's gaze.

"Very well," Lerryn agreed. He turned to find Hair waiting with his horse in hand. He mounted up and set off at a slow trot, following the relieved looking constable.

They came to a halt a few leagues west of town in a small patch of farmland. Rows of snap beans grew up the stalks of young corn, bright green in the summer sun. A woman stood at the edge of the field, sobbing over two figures wrapped in blood-soaked fabric. Two men, most likely neighbors, stood behind her, arms folded across their chests. Four small girls were being led away by two heavyset women, probably the men's wives.

Lerryn's heart groaned at the sight. He wished he had a bottle of wine, or something stronger.

"Her husband and her son," the constable explained.

Lerryn leapt down from his horse and walked over to the woman. He withdrew his money pouch and knelt down by the grief-stricken widow. "Mistress, I cannot hope to ease your pain, but perhaps this will ease your family's suffering a bit." He held the pouch out toward her. She looked up at him. Her eyes, red and swollen from crying, were a deep emerald green, and her hair was a lustrous brown. Had she been of noble birth, she would have married well. She shook her head, and drew slightly away from him. "Please take it," he said, this time pressing the bag of money into her hands.

Without a word, she accepted the gift, then threw her arms around him, and squeezed tightly. Silent tears dripped onto his shoulder. He awkwardly patted her back, but he had no words of comfort to offer.

The woman held on to him for a long time. She smelled vaguely of cinnamon, not altogether unpleasant. Certainly better than the scullery maids and serving girls he preferred. He stroked her hair, and noticed its softness. What sort of beast was he? The woman's husband lay dead not two paces from where they knelt! Slowly, reluctantly, he broke the embrace.

"My thanks," the widow whispered, and turned again to look upon the bodies of the deceased.

"Show me the animal," Lerryn said gruffly, trying to keep the emotion from his voice.

The Constable led him across the clearing. Xaver, Karst, and Edrin followed, along with the two farmers. A strange looking beast lay on the ground, its corpse feathered with arrows. Its fur was a glossy gray, tinged with silver. Its head was catlike, as were the wicked claws that extended from its all too human fingers and toes. Its body was vaguely human, though the short, muscular arms and legs added to the animal's beast-like quality.

"The oldest girl came out to bring them lunch. She saw it all," the Constable explained. "A pack of them came through the woods. They got enough arrows in this one to bring it down, but not the others. The critters tore through them like they was nothing." He shook his head. "The girl hid in the woods. She said the rest of 'em just kept on going. She said, if they was people, you'd think they had somewhere they had to be." He spat on the ground, and fixed Lerryn with a patient stare.

"I know what this is." Xaver pushed past Lerryn and knelt down to examine the beast. "This is a Halvalan snow cougar."

"Halvalan?" the Constable barked, "How'd a Halvalan anything get all the way down here?"

"It's rare, but they have been known to range widely. Unfortunate that the pack happened upon these men."

"That's not a cougar." Karst clammed up when Edrin slapped him on the back of the head.

"Don't contradict the priest." Edrin invoked the title Lerryn had instructed him to use for Xaver. "He's seen more than the rest of us put together."

Karst frowned and rubbed the back of his head, but said no more.

"What should we do with it, M'lord?"

Xaver looked at Lerryn for a moment, then turned to the constable.

"Burn it," Xaver said. "Burn it and bury the ashes deep." He turned and headed back to the horses, motioning for the others to join him.

Lerryn resisted the urge to say goodbye to the grieving woman. Hair and Bull hugged the girls, and mounted up. As they cantered forth from the clearing, Xaver drew his horse alongside that of Lerryn.

"Your Highness," he said, "I fear the frost creeps again."

Chapter 14

Oskar sat for a moment in stunned disbelief. His brother? Suddenly, things fell into place. He looked at Larris again, as if for the first time. Oskar had not seen Lerryn many times, but from what he remembered, the two certainly could be brothers. The tall, lean body, lightly tanned, skin, brown eyes and wavy brown hair all resembled Lerryn. If Larris was a prince, that would explain many things, including his breadth of knowledge, his access to so many books, and his general attitude of superiority.

Oskar looked at his companions. Hierm sat stone still, his eyes flitting back and forth between Larris, who held his sword at Shanis' throat, and Allyn, whose bow was drawn and aimed directly at Hierm. Shanis also sat still. Her angry eyes raged at Larris, and her face was flush. Not good, Oskar thought. If Shanis' temper got the better of her, she was prone to try something foolish.

What could he do? He was close enough to Allyn that he might be able to thump the boy with his staff before the archer could release his shot. But he liked Allyn! Allyn was his friend, had taught him to use his quarterstaff. At any rate, even if he managed to rescue Hierm, it would be a death sentence for Shanis. Larris would kill her. They had no choice.

"Wait! I'll tell you."

"Proceed." Larris' voice had grown even more imperious, if that was possible. He neither removed his eyes from Shanis' face, nor his sword from her throat.

Oskar quickly relayed the story. All of it. Khalyndryn sobbed quietly when he recounted the tale of her assault. For her part, Shanis' expression did not change when Oskar told the story of her killing the guard. Silence hung in the air for a few moments at the completion of his tale.

Allyn nodded to Larris, who turned and addressed Shanis and Hierm.

"I want your word, both of you," he said, his voice taut with tension, "that when Allyn and I put down our weapons, your swords will remain sheathed."

"Or else?" Shanis hissed.

"What choice do you have?" Oskar shouted. He had to make Shanis understand that this was not the time for her to lose her temper. Of course, holding back Shanis' temper was only a touch easier than holding back the sunrise.

"He's a prince," she said, her voice deathly quiet. "I killed one of his brother's personal soldiers. What do you think he's going to do to me?" Her eyes bored into Larris with hot fury.

"He could have already killed you if he wanted to," Oskar argued. Freeze it all! The girl was stubborn. "He hasn't given us any reason not to trust him so far. Trust him now."

"What possible reason is there to trust him?" she asked, her gaze never leaving the prince. "He lied to us. They lied to us."

"We lied too," Hierm said flatly.

"We had reason," Shanis said, her eyes flitting toward the ground for a split second.

"As did we," Allyn said. "I assure you. Give us your word, and we shall sort this all out."

At that, Shanis paused. She looked imploringly at Oskar. He nodded to her. He hoped she was seeing reason.

"All right," she whispered, "you have my word."

"Mine as well," Hierm agreed.

The tension left Larris' face. He smiled as he sheathed his sword. "First, let me tell you, I know Borram."

"You knew Borram," Allyn corrected with a smirk.

"A drunkard and a fool," Larris continued, ignoring his friend. "My brother kept him on as part of the guard as a favor to his father, who once performed a great service to the crown. I daresay you've done a greater service by ridding us of the sot."

Larris glanced over at Allyn for a brief instant. It seemed to Oskar that something was being communicated between the two. Suspicion rose inside of him.

"It isn't that simple, is it?" he asked. "There's something more. I can tell."

Larris met his gaze, and smiled a tight smile. "You are too smart for me by half, Oskar. My brother will doubtless be grateful to be rid of Borram. Unfortunately, the word of a commoner, even that of four commoners, does not change the fact that noble blood has been spilled."

"Borram could hardly be called noble," Allyn scoffed. "Unless that word has taken on a meaning with which I am unfamiliar." He cleared his throat and spat. "Of course," he added dryly, "I am not as well-read as you and our friend here."

"Borram's actions were not noble, but his family is," Larris continued. "If Allyn and I were to vouch for you, though, that should suffice."

"Would you do that for us," Khalyndryn asked hopefully.

"I would," Larris replied. Again he looked at Allyn. "I certainly would."

What is going on here? Oskar wondered. Something was very much amiss.

"You're running from him too!" Shanis shouted, a triumphant look on her face.

What was she talking about?

"I saw the way you looked at your brother," she said. "You didn't want to be seen any more than I did. Why not?"

"It's gone too far," Allyn muttered, shaking his head. "Much too far. We should never have let them join us."

"I trust them," Larris replied.

"We can't let them go running back to your brother," Allyn said. "What then?"

"They can't go running back to my brother," Larris said. "Whether he believes them or not, he'll have no choice. They need us."

"But do we need them?" Allyn asked.

"Perhaps we do." Larris turned to Oskar and his companions. "Allyn and I have embarked upon a quest. One that is vital to the future of our nation. If you will join us, and remain loyal to us throughout our quest, I will personally guarantee your freedom."

He drew his sword, and held it upright, with the blade in front of his face. "This I swear, upon my sword and upon the honor of my house." He kissed the blade. Shafts of sunlight flickering through the branches of the stately oaks lining the road shone on the young man's face, adding to the regal quality of the ancient oath. "This is my word and my bond. Will you join us?" He smiled at the four youths on horseback, the very image of royalty.

Oskar's heart pounded. This was what he had dreamed of all his life. He could join a prince on a quest. He could travel, have adventures.

"I'll do it," he blurted, perhaps with more enthusiasm than he had intended. He blushed as Shanis and Hierm stared at him angrily. Who cared what they thought? This was what he wanted. He swallowed the lump in his throat. His heart pounded so fiercely that his ears roared. "I will join you on your quest."

"I'll go as well," Khalyndryn sighed. "I don't know what use I'll be to you, but I don't suppose I have a choice."

"How can the two of you make such a promise?" Hierm asked, his voice heated. "Have you forgotten that two minutes ago they were prepared to kill us?"

"We didn't want to hurt you," Larris protested. "Our quest is too important to risk being found out. We needed to know what you were about."

"Can you truly do all that you promised?" Hierm asked. "Can you guarantee our safety? Our freedom?"

"A fair question," Larris agreed. "If it were not so important that I avoid my brother, I truly believe that we could ride into town right now, and my word, coupled with what we know about Borram, would more than suffice to gain your freedom. What I can guarantee you is, if we successfully complete this quest, my father will give me anything that I ask."

"If we complete this quest?" Shanis asked. "What kind of quest is this?"

"Swear first," Larris answered flatly. He met her frown with an implacable gaze.

"All right then," Shanis shot back. Oskar saw her fists close tightly around the reins, and for a moment feared that she might ride the young prince down. "I'll swear."

"I'll swear as well," Hierm added.

"Everyone off your horses," Allyn ordered crisply. He leapt down off of his own horse, and gathered the reins of the other mounts as Oskar and his comrades dismounted. "Kneel before your prince," he instructed.

None of them were accustomed to kneeling, and they did so awkwardly. Oskar dropped heavily onto one knee, cracking his kneecap on a sharp stone.

"Repeat after me," Larris said. "Upon my honor and upon my life...."

"On my honor and upon my life," Oskar's heart pounded as he spoke. His head was abuzz with realized fantasies, and wonderful disbelief.

"I swear to remain loyal to Prince Larris, and to the quest upon which he has embarked," Larris continued.

They repeated the pledge in unison. Oskar's voice quavered with excitement. Shanis veritably spat the words, a scowl of distaste twisting her face, while Hierm and Khalyndryn repeated them dully, as if not certain what to think.

After the words had been spoken, Larris extended his sword to Oskar. He did not know what he was supposed to do. Fearful of looking foolish, he went with his first instinct, and kissed the flat of the blade. The satisfied smile on Larris' face told him that he had done the right thing.

Larris went down the line, holding his sword out to each person. Khalyndryn kissed the blade, then Hierm. When he came to Shanis, she stared at the sword, face reddening. She slapped the blade away and leapt to her feet, muttering a curse.

"You have my word. That should be good enough for you." She whirled about, and stalked quickly over to Allyn. Snatching the reins of her horse from the blond youth, she led her mount a few paces away. She stood there with her back to the group, staring off into the dense tangle of forest.

Larris' eyes widened at Shanis' rebuke, obviously unprepared for such a reaction. He stared at her for a moment. He took a deep breath, and exhaled slowly, visibly gaining control of his emotions, then turned to face the three who remained kneeling before him.

"You may rise," he said. When they stood, he clasped hands with Hierm, then Khalyndryn. When he came to Oskar, the two clasped hands for a moment, then Larris yanked the larger boy toward him, hugging him roughly. "I am very glad you are joining us."

"So am I," Oskar replied hoarsely. He was stunned by the prince's display of emotion, and his apparent sincerity. How had he, and ordinary farm boy, befriended royalty? He could scarcely have dreamed a more unlikely scenario.

Larris walked over to where Shanis stood, and placed a hand on her shoulder. She did not look at him. Oskar saw the prince lean toward her, and whisper something into her ear that sounded like "Forgive me," but that couldn't be right. Princes didn't apologize. After a moment, he turned back to the group.

"Allyn and I have much to tell you. But first, let's ride," he said, grinning. "Come nightfall I want to be as far from my brother as possible."

Chapter 15

Aspin brought his horse to a halt at the Galsbur town green. It was a small place, and quaint in its own way. He looked across a central green to a sturdy, two-story log building. It had the look of an inn about it, albeit a small one. He took in the shops and the few small houses that surrounded the green. It should not be too difficult to find what, or should he say whom, he was looking for. To his right stood a large, white building toward the rear of which a wagon was being loaded. It had the look of a business. It was as good a place as any to start. Dismounting, he tied his horse to a post near the front door, brushed the dust from his plain, brown robe, and entered through the front door.

An attractive woman, just short of middle years, sat at a small table, polishing a ring with the hem of her dress. In doing so, she revealed a bit more calf than modesty permitted, but Aspin did not mind. She had long, pale blonde hair tied up in a bun. He could see just enough of her face to know that she was beautiful, or had been in her younger years.

"May I help you?" The woman did not look up from her jewelry.

"I certainly hope so, my good lady. I am seeking directions."

She raised her head and let out a small whimper. Her pale blue eyes widened, then seem to lose focus. The saikur's robe often had that effect on people. The woman cleared her throat, and stood slowly. "Directions to where?"

"I am looking for the home of Lord Yurg Van Sarten."

The woman's face turned a ghastly white, and she slumped awkwardly back into her chair. "Did you say, Lord Yurg?"

Aspin chuckled. It was just like Yurg to pretend to be a commoner. What story had he told these people? "Yes, Lord Yurg, my lady. It is my understanding that he lives in this village. Do you know of him?"

"Yes." Her voice was soft and her eyes had a distant look. "He is our swordmaster."

Aspin waited, but no more information was forthcoming. "And do you know where his home is?"

"I'm sorry." The woman stood slowly, and pointed with a shaking hand. "He lives that way. Between the sword yard and the smithy."

"You have my most sincere thanks, my lady. If I may trouble you for another moment." Aspen paused as the woman audibly sucked in her breath. "Was there a tournament here of late?"

The woman visibly relaxed. "Indeed there was. More than a week ago."

Aspin bit back a curse. "And Prince Lerryn was here?" He hoped that his anger was not evident in his voice.

"He certainly was. He left two days ago." The woman had regained some of her composure. "I had the good fortune of sitting next to him at the tournament."

"I must say that the fortune was his. I fear I did not get your name, Mistress."

"Oh! The name is Van Derin. Faun Van Derin." She blushed at the compliment.

"Again, you have my thanks, Mistress Van Derin. May the Gods smile on you this day." Aspin turned and left as quickly as dignity would permit. Outside, he made a right turn, and headed in the direction of Yurg's house at a fast walk.

Burn it all! He had missed it by days. Balric just had to go and catch fever along the way. And then the boy had the audacity to die on him. Aspin spat in the dust of the road. The boy had never been much of a disciple. An indifferent student, he was much more interested in late nights sipping ale in a common room. Learning about the common folk he called it. Next time, Aspin would choose his own disciple.

He passed the empty sword yard, and focused his gaze on the small house that lay next to it. He hoped that Yurg would be able to tell him what he needed to know. How many years had it been since he'd seen his old friend? He could not remember. How would Yurg look after all these years? Had he aged any better than Aspin had?

It was a peaceful day and few people were about. A gentle whisper of a breeze caressed the branches of the giant chanbor trees, the sound blending pleasantly with the gurgle of the nearby river. Only the steady ring of the blacksmith's hammer interrupted the melody.

Arriving at Yurg's home, Aspin rapped smartly on the front door. No response. Again he knocked. Still nothing. Nearby, the pace of the smith's hammer slowed.

"Yurg," he called out, "don't think you can hide all the wine before you let me in." He waited for a few moments and knocked again. The sounds of the smithy had died. "Yurg?" he called again. Still no answer. Turning to his right, he walked to the end of the small porch and peered around the side of the house. As he had noted earlier, the sword yard was empty. He hopped to the ground rather nimbly for a man of his years, if he did say so himself, and made his way around the house. Still he saw nothing.

As he completed his circuit, something on the ground caught his attention. He knelt down for a closer look, but was interrupted by a pair of dirty boots that interposed themselves into his line of sight. Aspin did not look up. He was not one to be intimidated. This country lout, whoever he was, had only succeeded in annoying him.

"Your boots could use some polishing, friend."

"Who are you?" The voice was firm, but Aspin detected no menace in it.

"My name is Aspin." With a sigh, he rose to his full height, and looked the man in the eye. "And you have just destroyed some tracks I was hoping to examine." He looked the fellow over. He was tall, of a height with Aspin. His leather apron, scarred forearms, and the hammer he clutched in one meaty fist named him the blacksmith. The man's gray eyes widened as he took in the brown robe and cloak.

"What do you want here?" The man's grip tightened around the hammer. Muscles bulged in powerful forearms.

"You have my name, friend. It is customary to return the courtesy." He was amused at how much simple courtesies could throw a person off-guard.

"Ham Lurel," the man said, "I'm the blacksmith."

"Yes," Aspin said, "I noticed your hammer."

The man scratched his head. If he blushed, Aspin could not tell. Working at the forge had flushed the smith's face an angry scarlet. "We look out for one another here. You have some business with Master Yurg?"

"As a matter of fact, I do. We are old friends."

"He never mentioned you," Lurel said.

Aspin was disappointed in the man. He gave him a condescending smile. Having a saikur for a friend was not something one mentioned in casual conversation. The man looked away for a moment. When he turned back, his expression was resolute. "We look out for one another around here."

"Glad to hear it. It happens that I am a bit concerned about your Master Yurg.

When did you last see him?"

Lurel's eyes narrowed. "Yesterday, seeker," he said, using the title that commoners often attached to those of Aspin's order. "Sometime early yesterday if I am remembering correct."

"You have not seen him at all today?" Aspin was puzzled by Yurg's absence, and more than a bit concerned.

"No." Lurel shook his head. "Of course, I've been focused on my work. But I haven't seen him come outside or anything."

"Is that unusual for him?" An icy ball formed in the pit of Aspin's stomach.

"It is." The smith paused. Cupping his chin in his hand, he gazed at the ground for a long moment. "Understand, now, things have not been usual around here for some time. Everything's been a mess since the prince announced that snow-blighted tournament." His lips pursed in a frown.

"I can imagine," Aspin replied. He could indeed imagine. A tiny little hamlet like this one would be turned on its ear by such an event. What was Lerryn up to? He hoped Yurg could tell him.

"You're worried about Master Yurg, aren't you?" The blacksmith calmly looked him in the eye.

"I am," Aspin confessed. He had not gotten a close look at the tracks around Yurg's house, but the first glance had chilled him to the marrow. "I think we should look inside."

Lurel nodded resolutely, and led the way to the porch.

"Master Yurg?" The blacksmith rapped on the door as he shouted. "Master Yurg, Mistress Anna," the pitch of his voice elevated, and a deep frown marred his face, "are you there?"

"I think we should go in," Aspin said. He tried not to think about the tracks he had glimpsed, nor what it would mean if he was right about what they represented.

Lurel tried the door. It was open. A foul odor assailed Aspin's nose almost instantly. He heard the blacksmith groan. Aspin pushed past the larger man, and was greeted by a horrendous sight.

Blood was spattered on the walls, and pooled in the floor around Yurg's lifeless body. He wore the tattered remains of a nightshirt. His body was shredded, rent open from throat to midriff in long, narrow slices, like the raking of claws. His sword lay a few paces away. Its shining, clean blade told Aspin that Yurg had not had the chance to put up a fight.

"They must have surprised you, my old friend," he whispered. "You probably thought you were safe in this sleepy town."

A door on the far side of the room led into the bedroom, where he found the remains of Yurg's wife Anna in a similar condition. She lay atop a blood-soaked bed, her knees drawn up to her chest, her arms shielding her face.

Aspin's eyes misted as he turned back toward the front of the house. Lurel slumped heavily against the door facing, still clutching his hammer in a trembling fist. Unshed tears clouded his vision as he stared at his dead friend.

"Do you know Colin Malan?" Aspin asked sharply. Lurel's head snapped up, and he nodded. "Bring him here right away. I need him."

He paced the floor, inspecting every inch. Much of the surface was covered in blood, but in several places he observed the same footprints he had seen outside. He shook his head. It was all happening so much faster than he had anticipated.

How had he let himself be caught unaware?

He retrieved two thick woolen blankets from the back room. He laid one over the remains of his old friend and covered Anna with the other. Someone else would have to take care of the burial. He would be leaving again soon.

It was not long before the door burst open. Colin Malan's hulking figure blotted out the sunlight as he passed through the doorway. He had changed little since Aspin had seen him last. His unkempt black beard and curly raven locks were sprinkled with a touch of silver, but he otherwise retained his youthful appearance. Aspin flinched as Malan slammed the door behind him.

"You let on that I know you? A seeker?" Thick forearm muscles rippled as he pointed an accusing finger at Aspin. "What would possess you to do such a thing?"

"It's too late for you to concern yourself with that. Look!" Aspin gestured at the lifeless bodies.

"Lurel told me," Colin said, shaking his head as he surveyed the scene. "What happened?"

"Ice cats." Aspin could not believe it. "A pack of them from what I can tell."

Colin shook his head. He squatted down next to Yurg's body, drawing back the blanket to peer underneath. He dropped the blanket with a sharp intake of breath.

"They gave Mistress Anna the same treatment," Aspin said. "She did not deserve to go like that."

"Freeze me!" Malan cursed, pounding his fist into a thigh as thick as a tree trunk." I had no idea. It's all too soon!"

A sudden thought struck Aspin.

"Why didn't they come after you, Colin?" He tensed as he waited for the answer. His palm itched, and he forced himself not to reach for his sword. Colin Malan was a dangerous man, and the wrong answer would force a confrontation that Aspin did not want. "Or, more to the point, why didn't they go after the girl?"

"She's gone." Colin looked up at him with defiance in his dark brown eyes. "Been gone for a while."

"Did she go with Lerryn?"

"No." The man rose up to his full height, and stared down his nose at Aspin, but the seeker was too angry to be intimidated.

"The cold take you and your reticence!" Aspin snapped. "Tell me what happened."

"I don't know." Colin turned away, his voice catching slightly. "When Lerryn allowed her to compete in the tournament, I knew the time had come and I knew better than to try and stand in her way, but I couldn't bear the thought of what she will have to do. I left town on a job for Van Derin." His voice grew husky. "I've had her since she was a baby."

"I know you love her," Aspin said. "You raised her, after all. But I need to know why she isn't with Lerryn."

"When I came home, they told me that she had disappeared before her final match. Her and some of her friends."

"How many friends?"

"Three."

Aspin cursed and shook his head. Too few!

"They found one of the White Fang dead. Another guard saw Shanis running away from the body. Rumor is, the guard was a drunkard and a womanizer. If he tried to have his way with my girl, he got what he deserved." Malan's mouth curled into a wicked grin, white teeth shining beneath his thick, black moustache.

"Did you try and track them?" Aspin was almost embarrassed at the look Malan gave him. "Allow me to re-phrase my question. Did you find any indications of where they might have gone?" Thoughts whirled rapidly through his mind. If the girl was with Lerryn, there would be reason to believe that things were happening as they should. But vanishing without a trace? Had the prophecy truly gone askew? Or had Aspin made a serious miscalculation?

"I didn't find anything at all. The families of the others were no help either. I had hoped she was hiding in the forest, waiting for Lerryn to leave, but she hasn't been back."

"Did Lerryn go back to Archstone?" Aspin asked.

"Strangest thing," Malan replied. "He sent the White Fang back to the city with most of the new recruits. But he and another man took a few of the boys and left on their own." Malan scratched his head. "I truly think she'll come back here. The girl who went with her wouldn't last very long in the woods. Who knows about the boys?"

"We have to find her. You can remain here and keep up the search. I'll head out after them."

A few minutes later, Aspin was back in the saddle. His hopes for a hot bath and soft bed would have to wait. Colin's descriptions of Shanis and her three companions were firmly etched in his mind. He had to find them.

As he left Galdora behind, a nagging thought played in the back of his mind. What if they had been wrong all along?

Chapter 16

Oskar hunched over the small campfire, trying vainly to absorb the scant warmth that it provided. Larris had permitted only a large enough fire for cooking. Oskar's stomach growled as he inhaled the aroma of roasted squirrel.

Perhaps Khalyndryn wouldn't want to eat hers. The girl had crinkled her nose in disgust at the sight of the carcasses roasting on spits. She sat in the doorway of her tent, eating some nuts that Allyn had packed for the trail. The others sat huddled about the fire, each quiet with their own thoughts.

"I suppose I've waited long enough," Larris announced, breaking the silence. "It's time to tell you about the quest."

Seated opposite the prince, Allyn shook his head, but said nothing. He had been even colder than usual, obviously unhappy with Larris' decision to include them on the quest.

"Ages ago, more than twenty grandfathers past, the forces of the Ice King invaded the nations of Gameryah. Historians call this invasion the Frostmarch. His minions ravaged much of Halvala, Kyrin, and Lothan, and threatened Riza, Cardith and Diyonus. It was only by the power of the Silver Serpent that they turned back the invasion. After the Frostmarch ended, the Silver Serpent vanished from the world."

Oskar's heart raced. This was a familiar story. To think that this quest, one in which he would take part, had something to do with this legendary tale was beyond belief. He glanced to Allyn, then Larris. He had heard bits and pieces of this story as a child, everyone had. He always considered it nothing more than that; a child's tale told by mothers to frighten the little ones.

"What happened to the Ice King?" Hierm asked, shifting uncomfortably.

"He was badly weakened and fled into the Ice Reaches. Prophecy says that one day, his power recovered, he will return." Larris paused to take a long pull from his water skin. "I believe that day is coming soon. I seek the Silver Serpent."

Everyone sat in silence, absorbing what they had learned. Hierm frowned, staring into the flames.

Shanis, elbows on knees, cupped her chin and looked directly at Larris for the first time since the incident on the road. "What sort of weapon is it?"

"No one knows," said Larris. "There is very little recorded about it. I believe it was created some time during the Godwars, but I can't say for certain. One legend, an old song, actually, holds that the gods concentrated the strengths of the greatest kings and queens of Gameryah inside it. All that is known for certain is that it is a weapon of supreme power. We must have it if we hope to defeat the Ice King." He picked up a stick and absently prodded the fire.

"Does he have a name, this Ice King?" Shanis leaned toward Larris, her gaze boring into him.

"Tichris," Oskar provided. "That's right, isn't it?"

"Freeze you for a fool!" Allyn shouted, leaping to his feet, Larris an instant behind him. "Never speak his name!" Allyn's angry whisper was like a knife in Oskar's gut. "Never!"

Oskar hung his head. He had only wanted to show them that he himself had some knowledge on the subject. He was accustomed to being the best-informed in his circle of friends. This mysterious quest had left him feeling as ignorant as Khalyndryn. He didn't look up when he felt a hand on his shoulder.

"It's all right," Larris said. "Likely it's little more than superstition, but it's a belief we've been raised with."

"You won't hear it again from my mouth," Oskar muttered, wishing he could have the words back.

"That name gives me the chills," Shanis said, clutching her arms to her sides. "Not only because we've heard it for so long. It's the very sound of it that seems to freeze your bones." She shivered as she spoke.

The ancient oaks that surrounded their campsite seemed to lean in on the small party. Oskar scooted closer to the fire, imagining frozen fiends creeping from every shadow.

"Any closer and you'll singe your eyebrows," Hierm teased. Oskar forced a smile, but did not move away from the fire's modest heat.

"What does he want?" Khalyndryn stood outside their little circle, and had interposed herself between Oskar and Larris. "The Ice King, I mean."

"What does anyone want?" Allyn removed a skewer from the fire and tested the meat with the edge of his knife. Finding it to his satisfaction, he handed it to Shanis. "Power, wealth, revenge." He offered one to Khalyndryn, who declined with a shake of her head. Oskar snapped it up greedily.

"I don't want any of those things," Khalyndryn said.

"Come now," Allyn fixed her with his half smile as he finished serving their dinner. "If you could choose your husband, what sort of man would he be?"

"I don't know." Khalyndryn's blushing face shone in the dim light. "Someone strong and handsome."

"And rich," Shanis said around a mouthful of roast squirrel.

"That isn't true," Khalyndryn protested. "I mean, it would be all right if he were rich," she smiled shyly at Larris. "But it isn't necessary. I mean, it's not the only thing that matters."

"Think back to your home," Allyn said. "Was there a particular young man who caught your fancy?"

Shanis snickered, and received a shove from Hierm for her trouble. Khalyndryn frowned at the pair, but said nothing.

"Was his one of the wealthier families, or one of the poorer?" Allyn continued.

Khalyndryn shrugged and looked away.

"No need to be embarrassed," Allyn continued. "You only want what everyone wants. And I think that if you are honest with yourself, you wish you could have taken your revenge against the man who assaulted you."

A single tear rolled down Khalyndryn's face. "I'm going to bed," she whispered, her voice thick with emotion. She rose gracefully, and walked back to her tent.

"My friend," Larris said, turning to Allyn, "sometimes I worry that your cold heart will freeze you solid."

"I understand people, nothing more." The archer shrugged and tossed the remains of his meal into the fire. "Beneath this thin façade of humanity, we are all animals. You just have to look deeper inside some of us, that is all."

Oskar took a large bite from his second squirrel, chewing the tough meat slowly and methodically. He wished for a squirrel stew, or perhaps some gravy, but the rich smoke brought out the gamy flavor in a way that made the meat quite savory. Allyn was wrong. The world was filled with kind, generous people who cared for others. People like Master Yurg or Ham Lurel.

The unexpected thought of home ached hollowly in the pit of his stomach. Allyn was correct about Khalyndryn, though it pained Oskar to admit it. He had always harbored a fantasy that she would someday lose interest in handsome, wealthy young men, and take a shine to a large, intelligent young man such as himself. Despite his secret hopes, Khalyndryn had always doted on Hierm. Until, that is, she had met Larris. The revelation that he was a prince had sealed the bargain. She had set her sights on the biggest prize of them all.

"I suppose I'll turn in myself." Larris added his skewer to the fire and made to stand.

"Sit down," Shanis commanded in a voice that made Larris' head jerk toward her in surprise. "I have a few more questions. The first of which is, why are you avoiding your brother? You conveniently neglected to explain that to us."

Larris glanced down at her, smirking. He returned to his seat slowly enough that Shanis shot him an impatient scowl. He looked up at the dark sky, seeming to choose his words.

"My brother is also searching for the Silver Serpent," he finally said, not looking at them.

"Why not join forces with him?" Hierm asked.

"Yes, Larris," Allyn said. "Why not run back to your dear brother and offer him our assistance?" The young man chuckled to himself as he plucked the last bits of meat from the carcass.

"My brother and I do not exactly see eye-to-eye on certain things," Larris said, frowning at Allyn. "His methods, for one. His vizier, for two."

"Make that his vizier for one, and his methods for two" Allyn corrected.

"What is a vizier?" Hierm's mouth twisted as he pronounced the odd word.

"Xaver is a sorcerer from the Isle of the Sky," Larris said. "He gave himself that odd name. I don't know why 'adviser' wasn't good enough for him. At any rate, he's a purple-eyed snake who has charmed my brother with his prophecies and visions."

"Purple eyes," Shanis said. "The ecclesiast at the tournament had purple eyes."

"Bah! That is just like him," Allyn said, a bitter look on his face. "I'm surprised the gods didn't strike him down on the spot." He pounded a clenched fist on his thigh.

"You mentioned his methods," Oskar said, not entirely certain he wanted to hear the answer. "What of them?"

"Xaver is a believer in the prophetic writings about the Serpent. His method, and that of my brother, is to first meet the conditions of the prophecy, whatever they might be. Second, to move south, which is where the prize is believed to lie, and wait for the prophecy to take command and guide them.

"Take command? You talk like the prophecy is some living thing." Hierm wore a confused expression. "As if it is going to take hold of us or something."

"Perhaps that was a poor choice of words," Larris replied. "My brother believes that the prophecies will come to fruition. His objective is to be the person of whom the prophecy speaks. By doing so, he believes that he cannot help but succeed." He shook his head as he spoke.

"How does your method differ from his?" Oskar asked. "Is it very different?"

"The war with the Ice King is a historical fact. The Silver Serpent is real. The best way to find it is through research. Allyn and I have done a great deal of traveling, studying both history and myth surrounding the serpent. We have amassed quite a bit of information on the subject."

"What have you found?" Oskar found himself sorely envying Larris' knowledge. Lord Hiram's collection, of which Oskar had availed himself as often as possible, was remarkable in its diversity, particularly for a village merchant. Unfortunately, the collection had great gaps in the topics that it covered.

"We know that the serpent lies to the west of Lothan," Larris counted on his fingers as he explained. "We have a rough map, with some clear landmarks, as well as some riddles that we hope to puzzle out along the way.

"There is a book in the Great Library in Karkwall that I would dearly love to get my hands on. I would have to reveal my identity in order to gain access. I don't know if it is worth the risk of my brother hearing of my whereabouts.

"The resting place of the Silver Serpent lies beyond the Ramsgate on the western border of Lothan. That we can find with ease. Somewhere in those mountains is Robrus' Pass. Given that Robrus was a famous king, though of a nation long gone, I hope we might find the location of the pass in the library in Karkwall, though the clues we have give us hope that we may find it on our own. Once we are through the pass, we must then search for the lost city of Murantha. At the present, we have little information on the city or how to find it."

Oskar felt the blood drain from his face. He rose to his feet. His legs were weak, and an icy tingle of disbelief swept through him. He swayed as he turned away from the fire.

"Are you all right?" Hierm sprang to his feet and laid a hand on Oskar's upper arm.

"I'm fine. Don't mind me. I'll be right back." He stumbled to his tent. Crawling inside, he quickly found his sack of belongings. Opening it, he rummaged through until he found his precious sheaf of papers. He withdrew them with care, and hurried back to the fireside. The others stared at him in curiosity but did not speak. He hastily removed the strings that held the bundle together, and withdrew the small piece of wood that served as both cover and protector of his bundle. It did not take him long to find what he was looking for. With shaking hands, he held it out to Larris.

"Is this what you're looking for?"

Chapter 17

Shanis had never felt as vulnerable as she did in this vast, open land, where anyone or anything could be hidden behind the next rise. In front of her, the road disappeared and reappeared as it rolled its way through the sparsely wooded hills of northern Lothan until it was swallowed by the morning mist. She missed the lush forests and tree-lined roadways of home.

"Does this whole country look like this?" she asked, looking around with barely concealed discomfort.

"Not all," Larris said. The western part of the country looks like this. It grows hillier closer to the mountains. To the south and east, the land is very different. It's all swamps and marsh."

"Will you take us to some cities?" Khalyndryn asked. "I've never been to a real city."

Allyn chuckled. Khalyndryn frowned at him before turning back to Larris with a beatific smile that turned Shanis' stomach. The prince rolled his eyes.

"Don't mind him," Larris said. "Karkwall, the capital, is the only true city in Lothan. The nation is so torn by civil war that a permanent settlement of any size is difficult to maintain. One side burns down whatever the other side builds."

"How long has it been like that?" Hierm asked. "The civil war, I mean."

Shanis laughed as Oskar opened his mouth to respond, only to have Larris cut him off.

"There has always been discord between the clans, but this particular war has lasted for forty years. Ever since Badla died."

"Who was he?" Hierm asked.

"She," Larris said, "was a warrior queen, the last to rule a united Lothan."

"I've never heard of a warrior queen," Shanis said. The discussion had suddenly turned interesting.

"She was a rare woman," Larris said. "Not content to sit on a throne and hand down orders, she remained in the field. Under her leadership, Lothan secured all of its outlying provinces. Any minor rebellions that broke out were quashed without mercy."

"What happened to her?" Khalyndryn asked.

"She was killed while fighting in the mountains. That's when the trouble started. They brought her body back to Karkwall, but the tribes could not agree upon where she should be buried. Her father was a Malgog from the eastern marshes. Her mother was Monaghan, a western highlander."

"What does it matter where she is buried?" Shanis asked. "It's just a body in the dirt."

"It matters to them. The Monaghan worship Dagdar, the god of the earth. Monaghan royalty is buried in the sacred grove just west of Karkwall. Malgog worship Boana, goddess of the water. Their kings and queens are laid to rest in the waters of a holy lake far south of the capital city."

I remember this story," Oskar interrupted. "The tribal leaders argued for so long that sorcery was used to preserve the body until a decision was made. The civil war began when someone stole the body. Each side accused the other. The rest, as we say, is history."

"What happened to her body?" Khalyndryn grimaced as she asked the question.

"It's still out there somewhere," Larris answered. "For forty years, the tribes have been stealing it from one another. Originally, the intent was to inter the body in the resting place of their choosing, but each tribe was on guard against that eventuality. Now, there is such great honor in being the chief of the clan that possesses the body that no one is truly interested in putting her mortal remains to rest. It has become something of a game to them."

"That's morbid," Hierm said. He thought for a moment. "Is it truly a good idea to travel through this place, what with the war and all?

"We will certainly need to keep our wits about us," Allyn said. "As long as we remain vigilant, we'll be safe."

For some reason, his self-assuredness allayed some of Shanis' concerns. She had another question on her mind. "Doesn't Lothan have a king?"

"Orbrad is the king, though one cannot truly say that he rules anything save Karkwall. His forces maintain some presence in the north between Karkwall and the border with Galdora," Larris said. "He was a Monaghan clan chief. When the civil war broke out, the saikurs, or seekers as you might know them, tried to solve the problem by marrying him off to Kalla, the daughter of a powerful Malgog chieftain. Their own clans remained loyal to them, as did most everyone in Karkwall. Everyone else viewed them as traitors. Kalla died of the wasting sickness soon after they married, which did not help matters. His current wife is an outlander. A Rizan, perhaps?"

Shanis' thoughts returned to the odd concept of a warrior queen. "Are women permitted to be warriors in Lothan?" Shanis asked, looking pointedly at Oskar. He had not mentioned this to her before.

Larris laughed. "Thinking about changing sides?" When Shanis did not respond, he continued. "It is not culturally prohibited, but it does not happen much anymore. The women generally try to stay pregnant."

"Which is the way things ought to be," Allyn said. He flashed a quick grin at Shanis to show that he was joking.

"Let me guess," Hierm said, "they're trying to replenish the population."

"That," said Larris, "and the fact that it's taboo to, shall we say, lay hands on a pregnant woman." After that proclamation, there seemed little to say. They rode on in silence.

Shanis tugged her cloak up around her neck and drew it tightly closed in the front. "It's cold."

"And damp," Khalyndryn added. "My hair must look a mess." She ran a hand gently over her tangled hair.

"It will warm up once the sun comes out and the fog burns off a bit," Larris said.

Allyn, riding slightly ahead of the others, raised his hand. "Riders," he whispered. He indicated a hill down the road and to the left. "Behind that rise."

"How many?" Larris asked.

"I saw movement," Allyn said, "but little more."

"Have they realized that we've stopped?" Larris looked very serious, but not alarmed or afraid.

"I don't think so, but if we sit here much longer they will." Allyn was equally calm.

"What if we attack them first?" Shanis asked, gripping the hilt of her sword. She let go suddenly. What was she becoming?

Allyn nodded at Shanis and reached for his bow.

"No," Larris ordered. "I would avoid conflict if possible. Perhaps they are hiding from us and mean us no harm, but we cannot be certain of that. We will try to avoid them."

Wordlessly, Allyn wheeled his horse to the right and led the group off the road. They wound their way between two small hills before turning south to move parallel to the road.

Shanis was startled by a loud curse from Allyn. She leaned to her right in order to see around the blond youth. A small cluster of riders was charging directly toward them.

"There are more behind us," Hierm called.

Over the muted sound of hoofbeats on the soft turf Shanis could hear the cries of their pursuers. To her chagrin, more shouts arose from her left. The first group Allyn had spotted must be in pursuit as well.

"Up the hill!" Larris shouted. He broke away from the group and plunged his mount up a steep embankment on their right. The others followed. Shanis leaned forward and gripped her horse's mane in one hand as they galloped up the precipitous slope. She hoped Oskar and Khalyndryn would be able to remain astride their mounts.

When they reached the wide, flat hilltop, they dismounted quickly. Oskar took charge of the horses, giving two over to Khalyndryn. Allyn held his bow at the ready. Larris unslung his own short bow and hastily strung it.

"Give it to her," Allyn ordered, inclining his head toward Shanis. "She's better than you."

To Shanis' surprise, Larris immediately handed her his bow and quiver before drawing his sword and moving to stand back-to-back with Allyn. Hierm, his sword at the ready, moved behind Shanis.

She quickly surveyed the scene. Groups of riders, about a half-dozen in each, approached from the east, the south, and the northwest.

Allyn took aim at the man who appeared to be the leader; a corpulent man with a massive red beard and a long tangle of coppery hair. Like the other riders, he was clad in a loose-fitting tunic, dark in color and decorated in an odd pattern of interlocking lines, and a deerskin cloak. What made him stand out was the high, conical headdress that he wore. It was made of some sort of hide, and decorated with red hawk feathers. Allyn let fly. The arrow sliced through the center of the headdress, sweeping it from the man's head, and burying itself in the shoulder of a trailing attacker.

The leader reined in his horse, and the others of his band did the same. They fanned out, encircling the base of the hill.

"You be a fine shot, boy!" the man called. His heavy accent made boy sound more like buy. "But even if the Malgog girl be as good as you, you can't take us all down."

Shanis frowned. "Malgog girl? What is he talking about?"

"Perhaps not," Allyn replied in his ever-calm voice, speaking loud enough for his words to carry "but I'll surely put the next one through your throat. That I can promise you."

The large man involuntarily put his hand to his neck for a brief moment.

"We can take them, Horgris." The man who had been shot rode up to the leader's side. He was lean, with greasy strawberry blond hair and a pockmarked face. The arrow had obviously not wounded him deeply. He, or someone, had pulled it out, though blood still stained the sleeve of his injured arm. He handed Horgris his headdress back.

"You want to be leading the charge then, Garmon?" Horgris asked. He donned his hat, and returned his attention to Allyn, whom he obviously took to be the leader. "You've got a strange crew with you boy. I see a Kyrinian boy," he pointed to Hierm, "and a Halvalan girl," he indicated Khalyndryn, "but it's the Malgog girl traveling through Monaghan territory that I be most concerned about."

Shanis was about to protest when Larris spoke up.

"We are Galdorans," he said.

"Mongrels, then," called one of the Monaghan. The laughter elicited by his comment died when Shanis trained her arrow upon the man.

"We have business with King Orbrad," Larris continued. The mention of Orbrad inspired more laughter.

"Lothan has no king." Horgris' face twisted as if the very title was distasteful to him.

"Be that as it may, we have business in Karkwall. There need be no bloodshed here today."

"You be right," Horgris replied. "There need be no bloodshed, provided you have protection on the road." He grinned, displaying a gapped smile.

Allyn cursed, and for a moment Shanis feared that he would loose another arrow, but he remained calm.

"That can be arranged," Larris said flatly.

"Good," said Horgris. "But you be leaving the Malgog girl with us."

"I have already told you...." Larris said

"I know what you be telling me, boy. The others I might believe, but that one," he pointed to Shanis, "be a black-headed Malgog if I ever be seein' one."

"She is not black-headed," Khalyndryn shouted. Releasing the reins she was holding, she grabbed Shanis by the back of the neck and pulled her head down. Shanis was too surprised to resist. "We colored her hair black. See where the red hair is growing…" her voice trailed away. Everyone stared at her in incredulity.

"Now things be getting stranger," Horgris said. "What do we be making of this?" He fixed Shanis with a look of puzzlement.

For the first time, Shanis noticed that to a man, the Monaghan had hair that was some shade of red. Burn it all! Now he probably thought she was one of them. She was about to roundly curse Khalyndryn's grandparents when the drumming of hoofbeats sounded from the south.

A column of riders materialized out of the fog. They were clad in capes and tunics of deep green, chain mail, and polished silver helms. They approached from the road, coming in behind Horgris.

The leader thrust his fist in the air, and the riders spread out, forming up in two rows of ten. The man removed his helmet, and surveyed the scene with a look of detached amusement.

"And what sorts of games are we playing today, Horgris?"

"This no be your concern, Martrin," Horgris replied. His voice oozed with contempt.

"What happens on the King's road is the King's business," the newcomer replied. He seemed unconcerned that Horgris' numbers were nearly the equal of his own.

"We be off the road," Garmon protested.

Horgris cuffed the skinny man absently with the back of a meaty fist, knocking him from his saddle. Garmon fell to the soft ground and lay there, rubbing his arm and scowling at Horgris.

"We be negotiating with these travelers," Horgris said. "Leave us to our business."

"Unless the rest of your clan is somewhere nearby, you haven't the men to stand against us," Martrin said.

"One Monaghan warrior do be worth five of Orbrad's armored jesters," Horgris retorted.

Martrin's complexion flushed until his neatly trimmed red beard seemed to fade into his face. He sat ramrod straight and his voice lost its amused edge.

"Perhaps we should put your theory to the test," he said, pushing his helmet back down onto his head. "Or mayhap you would like to try me man to man?" He placed his hand on the hilt of his sword.

"Ah Martrin," Horgris replied, hefting the sword he had not bothered to sheath when Allyn had shot at him earlier, "I always knew ye'd be dying young!"

A sudden chill ran through Shanis. An otherworldly scream pierced the air, and shouts of alarm rose up all around her. She whirled around to see a blur of silver fly across a nearby rise, and hurtle into the riders flanking the hill's western side. The cat creatures!

Horgris, his view obscured by the hill on which Shanis and her companions stood, kicked his horse into a gallop around the base of the hill. His men followed, all thoughts of Martrin apparently forgotten.

The cats tore through the surprised Monaghan, many of whom fled, or were thrown by their frightened mounts. The beasts surged up the hill, nine in all. Allyn dropped one immediately, a feathered shaft protruding from between its eyes. He was not as fortunate with his subsequent shots, but he and Shanis managed to slow their approach with several well-placed shots. Beside them, Larris and Hierm stood, swords at the ready.

With a roar, Horgris rounded the hill and charged up the slope in pursuit of the silvery creatures. Two of the cats turned to meet his charge. The Monaghan clan chief met the first with a vicious swipe of his sword that nearly cleaved the monster in two. The second beast hurtled into him, knocking him from the saddle. Horgris, still bellowing like a wounded bear, wrestled with the creature as they tumbled down the hill in a blur of red and gray.

Shanis lost sight of the combatants as Martrin and his squad galloped past them, meeting the final three beasts head-on. The eerie cries of the man-like monsters blended with the angry shouts and pained exclamations of the soldiers, the fearful whinnying of the horses, and the sickening sounds of swords meeting fur and bone, and claws rending flesh. Dropping the bow, she drew her sword, seeking comfort in its familiar weight and feel.

The fight raged on in a flurry of fog, fur, dirt, and blood. Soon, the sheer weight of numbers carried the day. Most of the beasts lay dead and the others had fled. Four of Martrin's men had also fallen, along with five of the Monaghan. Several of the soldiers nursed injuries. Of Horgris and the beast he had fought, there was no sign.

Larris walked over to one of the creatures and nudged at it with his boot. He turned back to Shanis.

"You asked me once about such creatures. They are called ice cats and they are minions of the Ice King. One of his many foul creations." He fixed her with a penetrating stare. "How is it that you know of them?"

"Two of them attacked our camp not long before we met you," Shanis said.

"People live their entire lives without ever seeing one of these, and you are attacked twice in a few weeks?" Larris shook his head. "The world is becoming a frightening place. We must succeed."

Martrin approached them warily, his sword still in his hand. "Dare I ask how you have knowledge of such creatures?"

Larris did not answer.

"You would do well to answer my questions," Martrin said. "Either way, you're likely going to the dungeon until this is all sorted out, but it will speak well of you if you cooperate.

Larris sighed deeply, reached into the collar of his shirt and withdrew a fat signet ring tied to a leather cord.

"My name is Larris Van Altman," he announced in a voice steeped in authority, "son of King Allar Van Altman, and the Second Prince of Galdora."

Shanis did not know if it was the name or the signet ring that affected the soldiers, but each snapped to attention as they were able. Martrin made a fist, brought it to his forehead, then snapped his arm down to his thigh in what Shanis surmised was a type of salute.

"Your Highness," Martrin said, "we must get you to the King."

Chapter 18

The giant towers interspersed along the massive stone wall surrounding Karkwall rose before them like sentinels in the morning mist. Oskar stood in his stirrups in an effort to see over the soldiers who rode in a square formation around him and his companions. This was his first visit to a city and he did not want to miss anything.

"Many of the great cities have an outer city," Larris explained. "People set up stands to hawk their wares outside the city gates, or camp outside the city looking for work. Enough of them put down roots and a sort of town grows up. Not here, though. At least, not anymore.

"Orbrad was so paranoid," he paused when Martrin cleared his throat loudly. "Excuse me. Orbrad, wisely fearing infiltration of his capital city, had the outer city razed. Residents had to either find a place to live within the city or leave. The land around the city was totally cleared of trees, rocks, anything that an attacker could use, and it is now regularly patrolled. For a league on every side, there is no cover. He may not control his own country, but his capital city is at least held firmly in his grasp."

"With all due respect, your highness," Martrin spoke in a slightly strained voice. "We have made great strides in taking control of the lands outside our city. The road we have traveled for the past four days is well patrolled." He turned his head to stare back at Larris. "Fortunately for you," he added with a smirk.

Allyn looked at Oskar and rolled his eyes. Oskar stifled a laugh. Expressions of humor were rare for Allyn. Larris ignored them both.

"Captain Martrin, you have my thanks for the timely intervention of you and your men, as well as the escort to Lothan. Your King will hear of your good work," Larris replied magnanimously.

"Your Highness is too kind," the soldier replied blandly. "But doing my duty to my country is all the thanks I need."

"Which are you, Captain?" Khalyndryn asked. "Which tribe, I mean."

Martrin took a deep breath and held it for several heartbeats before answering. "My grandparents were Monaghan. When the tribes rebelled, my father remained loyal to the crown. He is a soldier, like me."

"So your allegiance is to your king rather than to your tribe?" Oskar asked.

"My allegiance is to a united Lothan." Martrin turned and smiled. "Take that as you will." With a snap of the reins, he urged his horse forward, riding slightly ahead of the rest of the group.

They rode quietly for a while. Oskar took in the amazing sight that lay before them. As they drew closer to the city, he could appreciate the craftsmanship behind the mammoth city walls. What had appeared to be little more than great, grey, bulk was constructed of countless granite blocks, fitted together with such precision that he doubted one could slide a knife between any two of them.

Martrin led them around the long line of carts and wagons that waited outside the city gate. The gates themselves were huge, more than four times the height of a mounted man. They were constructed of heavy timbers, cross-braced, and bound in brass. Giant chains ran from the back center of each door to winches on either wall.

Two soldiers, clad in uniforms like those of Martrin and his men, each armed with a spear, stood at attention on either side of the gate. A number of others, Oskar guessed there were ten, were busy inspecting cargo, checking papers, and interrogating those waiting for entry. As they trotted by, one wagoner, a farmer by the look of him, scowled and spat a thick wad in the direction of their party.

"How crude," Khalyndryn said, frowning and leaning away, as if the phlegm might leap up onto her dress.

"I might feel the same way if I had to wait in that line," Hierm said.

Oskar expected their party to be halted at the gate, but as Martrin neared them, the sentinels at the gate clapped their fists to their hearts. Martrin returned the salute, and led them through the gates and into the city.

What he saw made him gasp in surprise. Nothing could have prepared him for this. Where the area outside the city walls had been stark and empty, the city pulsed with life. More people than Oskar had ever seen in one place moved shoulder-to-shoulder through the narrow thoroughfare. Peddlers sold their goods from carts on either side of the hard-packed dirt road.

The city had a haphazard feel to it. Houses were interspersed with taverns, inns, and shops with no apparent planning. All of the buildings were close together, some actually built against one another. Most were in a state of disrepair, and seemed to lean in toward the street, giving Oskar a vague feeling of having the breath squeezed from him.

Two women looked out of a second story window, waving and calling out to passers-by. Oskar noted with mild surprise that they were clad only in their underclothes, and had painted their faces in a most unseemly fashion. One of them saw him looking, and called down to him, suggesting something that he had thought was a physical impossibility. He heard Khalyndryn gasp, and Shanis chuckle wickedly. He surprised himself by shouting back an insultingly low price, which prompted the woman to bite her thumb.

"Oskar!" Shanis said, laughing. "If your mother could hear you right now."

"Sorry. Just excited to be in the city." And he was, in fact, almost giddy with joy at being in a real city. There was so much to see. There were more people and buildings in the area immediately surrounding him than in all of Galsbur, or so it seemed.

"Country oaf," one of the soldiers muttered. He spat on the ground and fixed his stare in the opposite direction.

Oskar ignored him. His eyes sought to drink it all in. To his left was a man dressed in the gaudiest clothing he had ever seen, juggling three colored balls, then four. He tried a fifth, but a stumbling, drunken fellow careened into him, sending the juggler and his balls tumbling into the roadway. The juggler's curses, though inventive, did not top those of the women at the brothel.

As they moved toward the center of town, the dirt road changed to cobblestone, and the buildings were in better condition as well. Larris explained that these sections of the city were organized into residential and business districts. Even the people were better dressed, and comported themselves in a calm, quiet manner that Oskar found quite boring. A few paused to give cursory bows in Martrin's direction. The soldier acknowledged each with a curt nod.

"How far do we have to go?" Khalyndryn asked, eyeing a tall man dressed in silks.

"There," Larris pointed ahead of them to a hill that rose out of the city's center. A crenellated wall of gray stone encircled the crest of the hill. Behind the wall rose the keep. Not an architectural marvel, it was a massive square structure with narrow windows. Atop it, the flag of Lothan, an orange fox against a field of dark green, rippled in the breeze.

Oskar trembled. He was going to see the inside of a real castle. He could scarcely believe his good fortune. Oh, the letter he would write to his family. His family. His heart sank. Doubtless they had given him up for dead by now. Perhaps he could send word to them without jeopardizing Shanis. They deserved to know that he was all right. All of their families should know that their children were safe. He resolved to speak with Allyn about it later.

Such was his fascination with the sights of Karkwall that it seemed mere moments before they arrived at the outer wall of the castle. It was much taller than it had appeared from a distance. The solid stone walls, eroded in places by time and weather, spoke of ancient strength. He craned his neck to look up at the battlements. Through the low embrasures he could just make out the figures of soldiers walking the wall.

They approached the outer gates, massive structures of wood bound with brass, set in an archway in the wall. They were met there by a squad of soldiers, each uniformed in the same fashion as Martrin and his men.

"State your business," one of the guards ordered.

"Martrin, a loyal soldier of Lothan, brings visitors to see His Royal Highness, King Orbrad."

Oskar's head swam. Him, a visitor to see the king? He sat very still, in hopes of not rousing himself from this most amazing of dreams.

The guard bowed to Martrin, then called for the gates to be opened. After a long moment, a loud creaking filled the air, and the gates slowly swung apart. At Martrin's signal, they proceeded through the gates, coming to a halt on the far side of the wall at a heavy iron portcullis. Behind them, the gates ground closed, leaving them shut inside the wall. Oskar looked around. The walls were a good fifteen paces thick. He noted that above them, a pattern of holes were spaced at regular intervals in the archway above them.

"Murder holes," Allyn explained. "Defenders use arrows, long spears, or even boiling oil to attack invaders from above." His smirk was incongruent with the horror he described.

"The walls are hollow, then?" Shanis asked, looking around.

"Not entirely, but tunnels run throughout them," Allyn said. "The keep is highly defensible."

Oskar shook his head, partly in amazement at the ingenuity, and partly at the grisly mental image of soldiers trapped inside the wall being skewered by invisible enemies.

Another group of guards waited on the opposite side of the portcullis. The earlier ritual was repeated, and the portcullis was raised. Martrin led them at a quick trot down a cobblestone street lined with fruit bearing trees.

They soon came to an inner wall, not as imposing as the outer wall, but sizeable none the less. A few paces short of the wall, the road divided. Oskar could see that it ran along the wall's face in either direction, and disappeared around the squat towers at each corner. Martrin led them to the right.

As they followed behind, Oskar took in the layout of the castle grounds. To his left, between the road and the heavy, angled batters that formed the foundation of the inner wall, lay an open, grassy area about ten paces across. To his right, between the road and the outer wall, a small orchard grew, and alongside that, a small garden. Both were tended by servants in green livery.

They turned left at the walls corner, revealing that the road and grassy swath encircled the inner wall. On this side, the area between inner and outer walls was occupied by crafters shops, a smithy, an armorer, a stable, and a corral. A mix of soldiers and liveried servants moved in and around the various buildings.

"Close your mouth before you draw flies." Larris drew his horse alongside Oskar's mount. "Servant's quarters and a small, spring-fed pond are on the opposite side. Barracks are on the far end, near the inner gate."

"It's amazing," said Oskar. "I never imagined it would be so," he searched for the right word, "so massive."

"It isn't the most beautiful castle I've ever seen, but it is well planned and easily defended," Larris said.

"I think it's the most beautiful thing I've ever seen," Khalyndryn said in whispered awe. Her eyes sparkled with childlike wonder.

It seemed only moments before they arrived at the inner gate. They dismounted and turned their horses over to a group of stable hands. Martrin's men departed for their barracks, while a detachment of foot soldiers escorted the remainder of their group through the gate and into a broad, grassy area, the "inner ward", Larris called it, that encircled the keep.

The massive doors of the main castle stood open. They entered into a dim hallway, illuminated by torchlight. Ornate tapestries depicting battle scenes were hung on either side of the hallway, doing little to detract from the austerity of the immense stone fortress.

A thin man with silvery hair and a pointed nose met them inside the doorway. He rubbed one hand absently across the breast of his silk doublet. The other hand cupped his clean-shaven face. He regarded them with a disapproving frown.

"Hmmm. This will not do at all. I say, it will not do." He turned and clapped twice. Two servants, one man, one woman, clad in the same green livery that Oskar had seen throughout the castle grounds, hurried to his side.

"Clean them up. Put them in some decent clothing. They are to be presented to His Majesty." He turned to walk away.

"Ah, Master…," Larris spoke up.

The man turned, the frown still etched upon his face.

"Bertram," the man said, looking disapprovingly at the travel-worn young man.

"Thank you. Master Bertram, our presence here at this time is, shall we say, a delicate issue. Your discretion in presenting us to His Majesty would be greatly appreciated."

Bertram's lips curled into a sneer. "If you will forgive me for asking, young man, who might you be to make such a request of the king's steward?"

Martrin stepped forward. "Forgive me, Master Bertram. May I present His Royal Highness, Prince Larris of Galdora?" The soldier did not try to hide his amusement as the steward's face fell in slack-jawed amazement.

"Please accept my most heartfelt apologies, Your Highness." Oskar was impressed at how quickly the man recovered his composure. "I will certainly address your situation with the utmost care. If you and your retinue will permit me to make you comfortable?" He motioned toward the servants, still waiting for them to follow.

"I will take my leave of you now, Your Highness." Martrin bowed deeply to

Larris.

"You have my thanks for your invaluable assistance, Captain Martrin," the prince replied. With a wave of his hand, he signaled for Oskar and the others to follow behind the servants into the heart of the castle.

Oskar waited outside the throne room with Larris, Hierm, and Allyn. The fancy clothes in which they had dressed him were comfortable, but felt awkward. Silks were for women. He hadn't minded the bath, though. He closed his eyes and remembered the exquisite feeling of hot water washing down his back, leaching away weeks of dirt, and with it, the aches and pains of travel. Washing in cold streams was no substitute for a hot bath.

Hierm had created quite a scene when one of the servants had tried to bathe him, yelling and jumping out of the tub, only to remember that he was naked, and jump back in with a splash that sent soapy water everywhere. The indignant servant had left in a huff, suds covering the entire front half of his body.

"Where are the women?" Bertram snapped at the servant girl who was hurrying toward them.

"A thousand pardons," she said. "We had trouble getting the redhead into a dress."

Oskar looked past her to see Khalyndryn and Shanis coming toward them. Khalyndryn looked positively regal. Her blonde hair was piled up on top of her head, and held in place with jeweled pins. Her dress was of deep blue silk, cut to accentuate all of her curves. She smiled with delight as first Allyn, then Larris greeted her with a bow and a kiss of the hand. Oskar and Hierm probably should have done the same, but they were distracted.

Shanis wore a dark green dress, cut high at the thigh and low at the chest. The black dye had been washed from her hair, which she now wore pulled back in an intricate series of braids interwoven with gold thread. She walked stiffly, as if she feared falling. Her angry countenance was as close to purple as Oskar had ever seen on a person.

"Don't either of you dare laugh," she growled. Her hand clutched at her waist, seeking the hilt of her absent sword.

"Shanis, you look exquisite." Larris swept past them. Dropping to one knee in front of Shanis, he reached for her hand.

"Stuff yourself, Larris." She snatched her hand back and folded her arms across her chest. She stood, tapping her foot and staring at the ceiling.

Bertram's eyes widened, and he made a squawking sound in his throat, which he attempted to cover with a cough. "Excuse me, Highness," he said. "His Majesty awaits." Larris and Allyn followed the steward through the open doors and into the throne room. Oskar and Khalyndryn entered next, followed by Hierm, then Shanis.

The throne room was immense, with ornately carved columns supporting a high vaulted ceiling. Colored floor tiles formed the flag of Lothan in the room's center. Set against the far wall was a dais of polished marble, topped by a massive throne of dark red wood, lacquered to a high sheen. Spread across the back wall, framing the throne, was a giant tapestry woven into a map of the lands between the ocean in the east and the Walls of Stone in the west. Oskar was amazed at the detail. There was Galdora, almost in the center!

"Kneel, you dolt," Bertram hissed in his ear. Oskar looked around and saw that on either side of him, the others had dropped to one knee, heads held low. Shanis dress had ridden well up her thigh and he could almost feel the heat from her blushing. He hastily took a knee, with Bertram dropping down alongside him.

"You may rise," said a bored voice. Oskar stood, along with the others. Smoothing his new doublet, he looked for the first time at the king of Lothan. He understood now how the ruler had escaped his notice. King Orbrad cut a wholly unimpressive figure. Just past middle years, the king was of average height, with plain brown hair that hung limply around his pale, round face. His body was thick around the middle, his arms and legs skinny. His robes were too big, the cuffs hanging down to his fingertips, and the unadorned golden crown atop his head appeared dangerously close to being too much for his thin neck to bear.

"Your Majesty," Bertram intoned, "may I present His Royal Highness, Prince Larris of Galdora."

Larris placed a hand across his stomach and genuflected. Orbrad's nod of the head was cursory at best.

"Shall we dispense with formalities, Larris?" Orbrad asked in his slightly nasal voice. "I find them most tiresome."

"And I, as well, Orbrad." Larris seemed unfazed by the presence of one who, at least technically, outranked him.

"What business do you have in my country that you could not forewarn me of your visit?" Orbrad asked, leaning forward and lacing his stubby fingers together in his lap.

"My apologies. No offense was intended," Larris said. "My business is only to pass through as quickly and quietly as possible. I saw no reason to trouble you."

"Your brother would not happen to be negotiating with one of the rebel tribes, would he?" Orbrad's voice grew more nasal as he spoke. "I am sure it would suit Galdora to have even more unrest in my poor kingdom than I already have."

"Not at all." Larris sounded as if he were trying to calm an unsettled mount. "I am on a task of my own. One that lies beyond the bounds of your kingdom."

"Larris," Orbrad said, "what business could you possibly have beyond my kingdom? There is nothing there, save mountains and wild men."

"I regret that I cannot disclose my plans. I respectfully ask that you accept my word that I have no intentions, neither good nor ill, with regard to your kingdom."

Orbrad stared at Larris for a long moment before sitting up and visibly relaxing. "I suppose I have no reason to disbelieve you."

Oskar felt himself relax as well. He had not realized how tense he had grown during the exchange.

"You must permit me to hold a banquet in your honor. Karkwall receives too few noble visitors. Once your arrival is announced, the palace will be teeming with bootlickers within the hour." Orbrad chuckled ruefully.

"I am truly grateful for the offer, but the situation is delicate," Larris said. "My father does not exactly know where I am right now. Neither does my brother. I would like to keep it that way."

Orbrad laughed again, a hard, snorting sound. "That explains why you wanted the throne room cleared before you came in. I wondered at that when Bertram told me." He paused for a moment, looking over the group. "I don't think I want to know what you young ones are about. Understand, however, hospitality is of the utmost importance in Karkwall. You come dangerously close to insulting me. Is there nothing I can do for you, aside from keeping your secret, that is?"

"I would be grateful if you would permit my man," Larris nodded at Oskar, "and I access to your library for the day. I'm something of a scholar, and have long wanted to visit it." Oskar's head swam. A royal library!

"My library?" Orbrad sounded scandalized. "Suit yourself. Bertram will show you all to your quarters, and see to it that you are fed." Larris bowed, and the others followed suit.

"Will you be sharing a room with your women?" Khalyndryn paled at Orbrad's question. Shanis actually smiled and stared at Larris with an expectant look.

"Ah, no," Larris mumbled. "They will require rooms of their own."

"See to it," the king said to Bertram. The steward bowed to his liege, then hastily led the group from the throne room.

"We're going to find it," Larris whispered to Oskar. "I can feel it!"

Chapter 19

"We are never going to find it," Larris said, closing the book with a cavernous thud.

Oskar fanned away the dust that rose from the ancient tome. "Don't give up. We haven't been looking very long, have we?"

"Since morning," the prince replied. "It's dark outside now." He gestured toward the library's only window, a small porthole set high in the wall.

Oskar was surprised to see the night sky. The time spent in the library had passed quickly. To be in a palace library, surrounded by more books than he ever imagined existed, was beyond his most far-fetched daydreams.

"Try this one." Oskar handed Larris a thick, leather-bound volume entitled The Wars of the Bogs.

"That isn't it," Larris said. "Robrus died long before any of those wars."

"Maybe the pass is mentioned." He was reaching, hoping, but he refused to surrender hope.

"The pass is in the mountains. The bog wars were fought in the south." Larris closed his eyes and buried his face in his hands. "I have a splitting headache."

"Out on the road, you told us that there was a book in this library that you would love to get your hands on. Which book is that?"

"It is called Robrus' Reign." Larris held up a dusty volume. "I located it right away, but it does not have what I am looking for."

"What do we have?" Oskar sat down next to Larris.

Larris sighed and dropped the book back onto the table. He swept the stack of bound volumes out of the way, and spread a roughly sketched map in front of them. "We know where the Ramsgate is." He pointed to the upper right corner of the page. "We know that somewhere beyond it is what was once called Robrus' Pass." His finger slid to the left across a blank portion of the map. "Once we find the pass, we know how to get to Murantha." His finger traced a path down the page, winding through a series of mountain peaks and ravines. Occasional landmarks were drawn in, with notes written to the side.

"Thanks to my map," Oskar could not resist commenting. He was still swelling with pride over his contribution to the quest. "You did a fine job copying it, by the way."

"So glad you approve," Larris replied dryly. A hint of a smile crept up the corner of his mouth.

"What do we know about Robrus' Pass?" Oskar pushed his chair back and propped his feet on the table, eliciting a hiss from the elderly librarian. He dropped his feet with a clump. The old man had left them alone some time earlier and Oskar had not noticed his return until now.

"Robrus led his army into the mountains west of Malgog lands to put down an incursion by a marauding force of mountain men. He pursued them for several days, chasing them deep into the mountains, until he found himself faced with an invading force of ice creatures and coldhearts.

"Coldhearts are what, exactly?" It always bothered him to admit that he did not know something, but his eagerness to learn almost always outweighed his reluctance.

"Men who have given themselves over to the Ice King. Something fundamental about them changes. I have heard that they gain strength and longer life, but they lose much of their humanity. Driven only by their primal urges, they are incapable of empathy, of love. And once they go over, they cannot go back. Their heart has turned cold."

Oskar thought about that for a moment. What would make anyone give himself to the cold? What good was a long life if you lived it under winter's shadow?

"As I was saying, Robrus and his forces were badly outnumbered. The Ice King's forces drove them into a narrow pass, where the coldhearts hurled stones and spears down upon them, keeping them moving. On a hill in the middle of the pass, more ice creatures waited.

"Robrus didn't hesitate. He led his men in a desperate charge. Most fell to arrows before they reached the top. Those who made it to the top engaged in ferocious hand-to-hand combat. The defenders finally broke under the desperate assault of Robrus' men, fleeing into the mountains.

"Of the men who began the campaign, only one in five lived through that battle. Short on food and supplies, they camped in the valley in which they had first encountered the ice minions. It is said that the valley was verdant, teeming with life. The deer were fat and lazy, and the stream that ran through the center was filled with silversides that practically jumped onto the hook. Some of the soldiers were so taken with the place that Robrus permitted them to remain behind. They founded a settlement and tended to the few wounded who remained."

"I take it the name of the settlement has been forgotten," Oskar said.

"It's been centuries," Larris said. "Even if we knew the name, by now it is likely to be known by another, if it exists at all." He rubbed his temples and groaned.

"Does the story mention any landmarks?"

"Only that when the sun sets, the mountain peaks around the pass glisten like a golden crown." Larris hung his head for a moment, then pounded his fist hard on the table. "Freeze it all! I will not let Lerryn beat me. I will not!"

Oskar looked up as four soldiers, swords at the ready, moved quickly and silently into the library. He looked behind him to see who they might be after.

Funny, he was certain that he and Larris had been alone all day, save for the librarian. He turned back around to find a sword leveled at his throat. Another soldier moved quickly behind him, and pressed the tip of his own sword into Oskar's back. Alongside him, Larris was in the same predicament.

"What are you about?" Larris showed no sign of fear, but instead sounded affronted.

"Do not speak," the soldier in front of Oskar ordered. "Slowly put your hands behind your back and fold your fingers together." Completely baffled, Oskar complied. The coarse rope bit into his wrists as the soldier cinched it tight. This had to be a mistake. Larris was a royal guest. He pitied these soldiers once King Orbrad found out they had arrested a Galdoran prince.

Guarded on all sides, they were led through the library and out a small door in the back, one so inconspicuous that neither of them had noticed it before. The door opened onto a dark, narrow corridor. Not bothering to light a torch, the soldier who had spoken to them, a thick man with hair the color of rust and a pitted face, turned right and led them into the darkness. The hallway had not been used in some time, Oskar thought, spitting out a mouthful of cobwebs. He crinkled his nostrils and tried not to breathe in the thick cloud of dust that had been stirred up by their passing.

The passageway ended at a stone staircase which they descended. The party wound their way down into the depths of the castle. The air grew cooler, and his boots slipped several times on the slick, wet steps. Oskar brushed against a wall, feeling damp moss climbing the cold rock face.

From the bottom of the stairs they moved through several twists and turns before coming to a halt before a heavy wooden door. Faint torchlight flickered through a small, grated window set at eye level in the door's center. Their guide rapped twice. After a moment, a face set in deep shadow against the faint light appeared. Another moment, and the door swung slowly inward. Oskar was dizzy with disbelief as they stepped through the doorway.

Sputtering torches set in brackets on the wall sprinkled flashes of firelight onto heavy iron cages that spanned the far side of the room. A dungeon!

"Are you men daft?" Larris said. "I am a prince of Galdora."

The soldier bringing up the rear cuffed Larris at the base of the skull with the hilt of his sword. The young prince stumbled forward. Unable to catch himself with his hands bound at his back, he fell heavily on his face. Two of their captors each took an elbow and dragged him toward a cell in the far right corner of the dungeon. Still guarded by two men and feeling a bit queasy, Oskar followed behind.

The man who had let them in now scurried ahead, a heavy key ring clinking in a thick fist. The jailer, Oskar assumed. He was a round man, with muscular arms and spindly legs. He opened a cell, and the soldiers tossed Larris inside. Someone gave Oskar a rough shove from behind and he stumbled over Larris' limp body, falling to one knee. He sucked in his breath sharply as he heard the door close behind him.

"Oskar," a voice whispered from behind him. "What's wrong with Larris?" He looked up to see the faint outline of Allyn coming toward them with Hierm following behind.

"They hit him," Oskar explained, as Hierm helped him to his feet and relieved him of his bonds. "He fell pretty hard."

"Will he be all right?" Oskar turned to see Khalyndryn and Shanis, mere shadows, in the next cell. They were pressed against the bars, straining to see.

"Don't ye be worryin' about yer lad." The jailer, a man as smelly as he was ugly, stood just outside the door to Oskar's cell, his arms folded across his chest. His smile revealed several stumps of teeth partially obscured by an oily moustache and beard. "The boy'll be awake in plenty of time to watch me have my way with both of ye girlies." He cackled a mad, mindless laugh.

Shanis cursed loudly and spat at the man, who stepped back a few paces and continued smiling.

"Don't ye be doin' that now. I'll have to be turnin' ye over to the boys in the other cells if ye can't mind your manners. They won't treat ye nice like I'll be doin'." With a chuckle, he turned and walked away.

Khalyndryn began to cry. Oskar walked over to her, and reached through the bars to take her hand. She drew back quickly.

"Do not put your hands on me," she sobbed. "Don't anyone touch me." She scurried into the back corner of her cell, where she dropped to the floor and sat with her knees against her chest, arms wrapped around her legs, trembling.

"Bad memories," Shanis explained with a nod in the girl's direction. She reached out and clasped Oskar's hand. "I'm so glad the two of you are all right."

"We are fine. How about you?" His head swam with disbelief. One moment he had been reveling in the joy of being a guest in a castle, the next, he was a prisoner in a dungeon.

"Oh, just lovely." Even in the darkness he stood close enough to see her roll her eyes. "I don't know which is worse: being in a dungeon, or being in a dress."

Oskar had to chuckle despite their plight. "I know you don't want to hear this, but that dress makes you look," he paused, "female." He flinched as Shanis punched at him through the bars. She didn't let go of his hand, though.

"Did they tell you why we're in here?"

Oskar shook his head. "They only told us not to speak."

"At first I thought it must be a mistake," Shanis said. "Now I wonder if perhaps someone from one of these warring tribes might have something to do with it. Perhaps they thought taking a royal hostage might somehow help their cause."

"How?" Oskar failed to see the logic.

"I don't know." She let go of his hand, and turned her back to him.

Oskar felt a hand on his shoulder. He turned to see that Larris had regained his feet, and apparently his senses.

"I wouldn't put it past Orbrad to allow guests to be whisked out from under his nose." Larris said. "But none of this makes sense."

The loud scrape of the dungeon door opening interrupted their conversation. It swung wide, illuminating the damp chamber. Two men approached, looking like dark, wavering specters in the flickering torchlight. One was the jailer. The other was King Orbrad.

"Orbrad," Larris said. "Open this door. I have business with this man." He fixed the jailer with a contemptuous scowl. "You won't mind if I dirty the floor of your cell with his blood?"

"Let you out?" Orbrad's detached grin did not match his cold voice. "Why, you only just arrived, Your Highness. Do you tire already of my hospitality?"

"Your guards dragged us down here, one of them dared strike me, and this vermin," he pointed to the jailer, "threatened the dignity of the young ladies in my charge. If you find humor in this situation, I fail to see it."

"The humor, my young friend, lies in the fact that you assume that all of this happened without my knowledge." Orbrad smiled like that cat that ate the cream. "My little birds have been singing in my ear, don't you know?"

Oskar's knees buckled. He grabbed a thick bar to support himself. Orbrad knew?

"I know what you are looking for." Orbrad reached beneath his cape and produced a rolled document. Oskar recognized their map. "This does not tell me a great deal. Not enough. I would know everything you have learned."

"I will tell you nothing," Larris said. "When my father finds out what you've done, you'll pay dearly."

"Thanks to your demand for secrecy your father does not know that you are here. Nor does anyone else, save a very few trusted members of my household and guard."

Oskar felt sick. The king was right. No one knew where they were. They were utterly at his mercy.

"You have tonight to consider the situation. If you are forthcoming, I promise you a quick death. If you are uncooperative, Moggs here," he clapped a hand on the jailer's shoulder, "will begin by questioning your women." The way his face contorted as he said the word 'questioning' indicated to Oskar that asking questions would be the last thing Moggs would do.

"It will be done in your presence, Highness. If watching them suffer does not move you, we will put every one of you to the question in the most painful of ways. I shall save you for last."

Allyn snarled with wild fury and leapt against the front of their cell. His curled fingers reached for Orbrad's throat. Moggs thrust his torch at one of the young man's forearms, and Allyn drew back.

Larris put a hand on his friend's chest, shoving him away from their captors. He set cold eyes upon the king of Lothan.

"I will see you dead, Orbrad. You have made the biggest mistake of your error-riddled rule. Enjoy the days you have left."

The rancor of the whispered words chilled Oskar. For a moment, he believed that Larris would do it. He didn't know how, but the words sounded more a vow than a threat.

Orbrad began to speak, but something stopped him. Likely he lacked the wit to compose a suitable response. He briefly met the young prince's gaze before turning away. As he exited the dungeon, he paused and looked back at them.

"I will give you the night to think on what we have discussed. Pleasant dreams."

Chapter 20

Aspin crinkled his nose in distaste as he mounted the steps of the inn. It was a dirty place, but there was no other in this small town. He paused in front of the door, arms folded across his chest, and turned to survey the surrounding area. The place was a cesspit. A single dirt road meandered through an ugly little town. Ramshackle buildings crowded together, giving the place an oppressive feel. He shook his head. All that beautiful, rolling farmland about, and they had chosen to build in the midst of the only dense forest for miles.

He turned about and strode into the smoky common room. He immediately spotted the innkeeper, a fat, balding man, dozing in a chair on the opposite side of the room. Aspin strode through the room and stopped in front of the man, who did not open his eyes.

"I require a room," Aspin said, "and a meal."

"I'm all filled up," the man said without opening his eyes. "A meal I can give you, but it'll be cold stew and day old bread."

Aspin put the ball of his foot on the front rung of the man's chair. He stomped down, slamming the chair to the floor, and nearly spilling the innkeeper from his seat.

The man bolted up with a curse, but the anger in his eyes instantly turned to fear.

"Forgive me, seeker," he said, bowing awkwardly. "I will find you a room."

"I thank you for your hospitality."

As the man scurried off, Aspin selected a chair in the corner near the fireplace. He tossed his saddlebags on the floor and sat down. As he took his seat, he drew the edge of his cloak back, exposing the hilt of his sword. No harm in having it within easy reach.

The sound of voices raised in anger penetrated the ceiling of the common room. A few moments later, a paunchy man with thinning ginger hair, dressed in cheap silks, thumped down the stairs. He was followed by a frightened-looking girl who could have seen no more than twelve summers.

"I'll not believe there's any seeker in this town until I see him myself," the man shouted. He took only a few steps into the common room before his eyes settled upon Aspin. He stepped backward toward the stairwell, visibly shaken. After a moment's hesitation, he nodded, placing his hand over his chest.

"My compliments, seeker," he stammered. "Forgive me for my outburst."

"No apology is necessary," Aspin lied. "I hope I did not inconvenience you and your daughter too greatly."

"My daughter?" The man shot an annoyed glance back over his shoulder at the young girl who cowered at the foot of the stairs. His face paled. "Oh, yes, my daughter. No inconvenience at all. We were leaving soon." He shuffled his feet nervously and looked around the room, as if seeking an escape route.

"You are taking to the road so late in the evening?" Aspin said. "Is that not dangerous?"

"We do not live far from here," the man mumbled, his face now white.

"I see," Aspin said. "In your haste, you seem to have forgotten your bags."

"We have no bags," the man's voice was barely perceptible. He turned and snatched the girl by the forearm, and led her roughly out the door.

Aspin closed his eyes and took a deep, calming breath. Was this world truly worth saving? If only he could pick and choose those who reaped the benefits of his work. He laughed to himself.

"Aspin," he whispered, "you may be getting old, but you don't have to sound like an old man."

"Don't know where he finds these girls," the innkeeper said. "Comes here from time-to-time with one of them. He's a wicked one, if you ask me." He stood with his hands on his hips, staring disapprovingly at the door.

"And yet, you accept his coin."

The innkeeper looked like a fish out of water. His mouth moved, but he made no sound. He stood like that for a moment, then coughed.

"I'll have that stew you mentioned, if you will be so kind as to warm it for me."

"Of course," the man said. "Ale? Wine?"

"Water will be fine." Aspin had little taste for ale, and had abstained from wine since Yurg's death. It was his way of remembering his old friend.

The innkeeper returned shortly with a bowl of thin stew, mostly potatoes and onions with a few scraps of some unidentifiable meat, along with a chunk of bread, and a cup of water.

"Thank you," Aspin said. "May I have a word?" He motioned to an empty chair on the opposite side of the table.

The innkeeper sat down cautiously. His hands kneaded a dirty cloth that he kept tucked in his apron. His eyes darted around the room as he sought any reason to excuse himself.

"I assume that most travelers in this area stop at your inn," Aspin said.

The man nodded.

Aspin held his breath for a moment. He had no choice but to ask the question. "I am looking for a group of young people. Two young men, two young women." He paused, trying to recall the description Malan had given him. "One of the young ladies is a striking young woman, tall with red hair. The other is blonde with blue eyes, a very pretty girl."

"Not seen the girls." The innkeeper shook his head. "I would remember either of those."

"How about the boys? One is a big fellow with brown hair, the other tall and blond with gray eyes."

The man shrugged. "Not as I remember."

Aspin wanted to curse. He had been certain he was headed in the right direction.

"We did have a tall girl come through her some time back, with some young lord or such," the innkeeper offered. "Pretty in her own way, but she had black hair."

Aspin continued fishing. "How about a group of six men traveling together? Most of them young. One an older man."

"Purple eyes?" The innkeeper leaned forward, his voice falling to a bare whisper. "Kind of pinched-looking face?"

"That's the one," Aspin said, keeping his voice calm.

"They came through here not too long ago. Had drinks, but didn't take rooms."

"No?"

"Constable came and got them. Some locals were killed by a strange animal."

Aspin leaned forward, intrigued by what he was hearing. Strange animals. Could it be?

"He asked the leader of the group to take a look," the man said. His tongue was unburdened now that it was obvious he had information in which Aspin was interested. "I hear he said it was a Halvalan snow cougar."

A cold lump formed in Aspin's stomach. Lerryn might or might not have seen such a beast, but Xaver knew very well that it was not a Halvalan anything.

"They had a sour-looking young boy with them, too. A contrary fellow with beady eyes. Didn't like him or that purple-eyed man at all. No sir."

"How long ago was this?" Aspin asked.

"Can't rightly say." The innkeeper scratched his head and looked up at the ceiling. "Several days. One day's the same as the next around here."

"You can't say how many days?" Freeze this backwoods lout. How could one be so ignorant?

"No, but the widow of the man who was killed could tell you. Seems a person would remember a thing like that."

Aspin stopped several paces from the small house, and called out a greeting. "Hello?" A woman living alone would likely be fearful of nighttime visitors. "Hello?"

"Who is there?" A gentle, distinctly feminine voice called out.

"My name is Aspin," he said. "I am a saikur, or a seeker you might call me. May I have a word with you?"

The door opened slightly, and a shadow appeared. Aspin stepped into the sliver of light that shone from the house. She regarded him for a moment, then nodded and opened the door.

The house was small but neat. The dirt floor was swept and the room was tidy. A delicious aroma wafted over him, and his stomach growled. Most undignified, he thought.

"Mother?" A tentative voice called from above.

Aspin looked up to see four small faces, all little girls, peering over the edge of the second-story loft.

"It's all right. Go back to bed," the woman said.

"Why is he dressed so funny?" the oldest girl asked.

"Hush now, Melina," she scolded, an amused smile illuminating her lovely face. "Go to sleep."

With a chorus of groans, the girls disappeared from sight.

"May I offer you something to eat?" the woman asked, gesturing to the rough-hewn table pushed against the far wall.

"That would be delightful," Aspin said with sincerity. "The fare at the Grinning Goat leaves much to be desired."

"My husband used to say that he wouldn't give Balman's food to the hogs. It might ruin the bacon," she forced a small laugh.

"I am sorry for your loss, mistress."

"My name is Marya," she said. Aspin took a seat on one of the benches on either side of the table, and in short order she sat a plate of chicken, beans, and bread in front of him along with a cup of water. "I am sorry I can't offer you anything else to drink." She sat down across from Aspin and folded her hands across her lap.

"This is fine. Your hospitality is most appreciated, I assure you."

"You're very polite for a seeker," she said, staring directly at him in a way that most people did not.

"And you are very blunt for a farm wife." Aspin cocked an eyebrow. "Have you known many seekers?"

Marya laughed. This time it was not forced, and the sound was like music. "You are not what I expected."

Aspin nodded. "I am not like most of my order. Perhaps it is because I came to it late." If she was interested in the story, she did not show it.

"So what business does a seeker have with me?"

Aspin admired her backbone. She was not the least bit intimidated by him or his station.

"I am certain that it is painful for you to discuss, but can you please tell me, on what day did your husband die?'

Marya's eyes dropped. She sat for a moment, seeming to gather herself. "My husband and my son," she said softly. "Six days ago they were killed."

"The men who came to identify the creature, did you happen to hear them say where they were going next?"

"South."

"Nothing else?" Aspin was disappointed.

"That's all." She looked back up at him, staring intensely. "The man who was the leader. The handsome one with brown, curly hair. Who is he?"

Sympathy welled up inside of Aspin. Surely Lerryn would not have taken advantage of this poor creature while her husband's body was still warm. "His name is Lerryn," he said.

"He is some sort of noble, isn't he?" There was something in her eyes that said she was not certain she wanted to know the answer to the question.

"He is." Aspin had to be careful here.

Marya looked up for a moment, here gaze suddenly far away. "Will he be coming back?" Her voice was soft, and her cheeks flushed pink as she asked the question.

"I cannot say."

"He seemed so sad. I can't explain it." She paused. "He was kind to me, but he seemed distant."

"He is a complicated man," Aspin replied truthfully, "but a good man. Shall I convey your greetings to him?"

"No." Marya shook her head. "He would not remember me."

Aspin was surprised to realize he had devoured all the food she had served him. The empty space the watery stew had left in his stomach was nearly filled.

"It is imperative that I find these men," he said. "Is there anything else you can tell me?"

"Nothing I can recall." She shook her head. "Is the man with the purple eyes a friend of yours as well?"

"We," Aspin paused, trying to decide how to answer, "are not friends."

Marya nodded, as if that were enough.

"How many were they traveling with?"

"Six, I think."

Aspin tensed for a moment. So that was their game. "I don't know the other four. It would help me if you could describe them for me."

She cupped her chin in her hand, her elbow now propped on the table. "One of them was a large boy. Another had the longest blond hair I've ever seen on a man. Another had brown hair and sort of a long nose." She paused for a moment.

"And the other," Aspin prompted.

"I didn't care for him at all. He had black hair down to his shoulders. His eyes were dark and cruel, and his face had a pinched look to it, as if he'd just smelled something foul."

Aspin nodded and rose from the table. "Mistress Marya, I thank you for the hospitality and the information." He fished into his money pouch and withdrew a fat, silver coin. "If you will permit me ."

"That is not necessary," Marya protested. "The man, Lerryn, gave me a very generous gift. My daughters and I are fine."

"I insist," Aspin said, and laid the coin on the table. He raised his hand as she opened her mouth to argue. "I know that a gift from a seeker always comes with strings attached. Think of it not as a gift, but as payment for the meal." When she made no further protest, he bowed and took his leave.

He took his time riding back to the inn. Enveloped in the cloak of darkness, he turned over in his mind the stories he had heard of strange creatures about. Most of them were farmers near the edge of the mountains losing livestock. The beasts were growing bolder. He hoped that things had not gone too far.

As he made his way into town, a faint sense of alarm sounded somewhere in the recesses of his mind. His military training took over, and he rolled from the saddle and dropped to the ground. He heard a hiss and a thud, and looked up to see a crossbow quarrel embedded in the side of a nearby building. He turned his head in time to see a figure vanish around the back of the smithy on the other side of the road.

Leaping to his feet, he drew his sword and gave chase, his mouth forming the words of a spell of shielding. Arriving behind the smithy, he was not surprised to find that the assailant had vanished into the forest. Footsteps sounded behind him, and he turned, sword upraised.

"I seen him," shouted a skinny man in ragged clothing. "I seen him running away."

"What did he look like?" Aspin stared at the man, who was perhaps the first person he had ever met who had only half his teeth, but had each tooth represented to some extent.

"I dunno," the man scratched at his thinning pate. His breath reeked of sour wine. "He had a dark cape, maybe gray. I couldn't see his face. He got away quick." The man pointed into the woods.

Aspin took a deep breath and held it for a moment. "Thank you for your help. If you will excuse me, perhaps I can learn something from his tracks."

The man stood there, a broken-toothed grin on his face. After a moment, Aspin realized what he was waiting for, and rewarded the man with a small copper coin. He bobbed his head in thanks, and hurried away.

The bright moonlight made it easy to locate the tracks in the damp earth. Aspin followed the heavy boot prints, widely spaced, toward the woods. He froze, staring at the ground. Looking all around to make sure no one was watching, he knelt where the outline of the assassin's boots vanished. A closer look confirmed what he thought he had seen. Where the footprints disappeared, perfectly aligned and in stride, were the clawed, padded tracks of a giant cat.

Chapter 21

Shanis clenched her chattering teeth and struggled to stay awake. Beside her, Khalyndryn slept fitfully, mumbling and groaning. The group had agreed that someone needed to keep watch, so she and Hierm had stayed awake. They didn't know what they could do without weapons, but, as Larris had pointed out, it was better than doing nothing. A shiver passed through her. This dress did nothing to keep the cold out. At the sound of her teeth chattering, Hierm reached through the bars and vigorously rubbed her shoulders, then her back.

"Shall I go lower?" he teased as his fingers reached the base of her spine.

"Rub Allyn's behind," she whispered, turning and playfully smacking at his hands.

"I thought that was your job," he said, a frown souring his face.

"What are you talking about?" Shanis stepped back, hoping that the darkness would conceal her discomfort.

"Just kidding," he said, but the playful lilt was now absent from his voice.

Shanis was content not to carry the discussion any further. Hierm had seemed increasingly distant since they met up with Allyn and Larris. It had not occurred to her that he might be jealous. Besides, there was nothing to be jealous of. Allyn was always flirting with Khalyndryn.

"If only your father could see us now," she said, trying to lighten the mood.

Hierm smiled and shook his head. "Likely he wouldn't be too surprised. It would break my mother's heart, though."

"She would not be the least bit surprised to find me here, though," she whispered. She noted that Hierm did not disagree. She thought about the life that he had left behind, and a wave of remorse swept through her. "I'm sorry about all of this, Hierm."

"What do you mean?" he asked.

"This all happened because of me." The longer they had sat in this cold, dark place, the greater her guilt had grown. "It's my fault."

"It's Borram's fault. He is the one who tried to hurt you and Khalyndryn," Hierm whispered, gripping the cold bars that separated their cells, and staring at her intently.

"I should have been the kind of person they wanted me to be," she said. "I should have given up the sword and found a husband."

"That isn't who you are." Hierm reached between the bars and took her hand. His presence was as comforting now as it had always been.

"I should have never entered that tournament."

"That's enough," Hierm said. "I still would have entered that tournament. I still would have lost to Karst, and Khalyndryn still would have followed me. The difference is, you would have been out in the crowd watching, probably with Oskar. And then, none of us could have gotten there in time to stop it."

Hierm was right, of course. If she had not fought in the tournament, she would have watched with Oskar. She would have gotten to Khalyndryn along with the two boys, too late to help. Her rage would have gotten the better of her, and she likely would have killed Borram, or at least tried to. The four of them still would have fled, with Khalyndryn even worse for the wear. Perhaps it was fated.

There was something else bothering her, though. An irrational thought that she needed to share with someone.

"Do you think everything is as it seems?" she asked. "Is it all for real?"

Hierm gripped the bars that divided their cells and gave them a tug. "Feels real to me."

"That's not what I mean," Shanis groaned. She should have discussed this with Oskar. Hierm was not slow, by any stretch, but he did not look beneath the surface of things the way Oskar did. "Do you think something is going on between Larris and Orbrad? Some hidden communication?" She lowered her voice so as not to awaken the others. "When they talk to each other, it seems so insincere, so false."

"Isn't that the way they all talk to each other?" her friend asked.

"It's more than that." She pounded her fist into her palm. "Think about it, though. Nothing has been as it seems. We lied to Larris and Allyn when we met them, and they lied to us. Larris is hiding from his family. Orbrad is pretending that he's some powerful king, when he barely controls his capitol city. He tells us we're his guests, then locks us down here."

"What is the point of all this?"

"I am just saying that if nothing else has been as it seems, why should this situation be any different?"

"Perhaps you should talk to Oskar about this," Hierm said. "But it seems to me that we should be concerning ourselves with what we know for certain. We need to get out of this dungeon. Worrying about anything else is a waste of time. Have you thought about that?"

Shanis nodded. The group had quickly given up on the possibilities of picking a lock or finding a hidden passage under a loose stone. Since then, she had managed to come up with only one plan. Looking around, she reassured herself that Moggs remained in his small room near the dungeon door, most likely asleep.

"Moggs is planning to, you know, have his way with Khalyndryn and me. Dressed like this, he won't consider me dangerous. If I can disable him, perhaps I can get us out of here."

"If no one else is in the dungeon. If he has his key ring with him," Hierm counted the ifs on his fingers, "if you can take care of him, that only gets us as far as the door. What about the guards on the other side?"

"Do you have a better idea?"

Before Hierm could reply, a loud knock sounded at the dungeon door. Shanis and her friend drew deeper into the shadows as around them, their companions were stirring. The knock came again, not loud, but insistent. Angry muttering came from Moggs' room, and after a few moments the fat jailer appeared, tugging on his clothing.

"I be coming." He slid open the peephole and peered through. "Wha' you be wantin'?"

"King's business," said a familiar voice.

Moggs stared for a moment longer, then, as if satisfied with what he saw, closed the peephole and unlocked the door. The door flew open, sending him stumbling backward. A guard burst in. Without a word, he delivered a vicious punch to Moggs' throat, followed by a solid kick to the side of the knee. Despite her surprise, Shanis noted that she, too, had planned to go for the knees. As Moggs fell to the floor, the guard doubled his fists, and struck the warden a crippling blow to the base of the skull. He quickly relieved the unconscious man of his keys, and hurried to their cells.

"Martrin," Shanis whispered in amazement as the soldier drew close enough for his features to become visible in the gloom. The captain nodded, and after a few failed attempts, located the proper keys and opened their doors in quick succession. Placing a finger to his lips, he tilted his head toward the dungeon door.

As they passed Moggs' supine form, Allyn paused to kick the man hard in the face. Shanis was surprised at this show of cruelty from the normally placid young woodsman. The guards were slumped on either side of the hall outside the dungeon door. Two empty wine cups lay on the ground nearby. Though the men were obviously unconscious, Shanis tiptoed around them, watching her steps carefully. When they came to the end of the entryway, they turned the corner to find Bertram, the king's steward, waiting for them.

"Your belongings," he said, and gestured grandly to a half-dozen bags lying on the floor behind him. Take one and follow me."

With a squeal of delight, Khalyndryn ran forward and squeezed his neck in a tight hug.

"Thank you Master Bertram," she said softly.

The man seemed taken aback by her display of affection. He put his arms around her and gave her a tentative pat on the back.

"You are quite welcome," he said. "Of course, Captain Martrin helped a bit, as well."

Larris stepped forward and opened his mouth to speak to the two men, but the soldier cut him off.

"There is no time for thanks," Martrin said. "Everyone grab your bag and move."

Shanis took a perverse pleasure in the look on Larris' face as he was brought up short by a commoner. She hastily found her belongings, and buckled her sword on over the ridiculous dress. Its weight upon her hip was reassuring. She squeezed the grip, finding a comfort in its solid feel.

Bertram led the way through the dank passages. After only a few turns, Shanis was thoroughly confused.

"This isn't the way we came down," she observed.

Bertram looked over his shoulder, looking mildly offended.

"Please," he said, "I am hardly so foolish as to try and take you back through the palace."

Shanis felt embarrassed at having spoken up.

"Besides, I have a greater sense of style than that," the steward continued.

"Might I remind you," Martrin called from the back of the group in a soft voice, "that we are trying to sneak out of the palace. Perhaps a bit of quiet is in order."

"Not that anyone will hear us down here," Bertram sighed, "but you are correct."

The passage made a sharp bend to the right. There, Bertram halted, raising his hand for the others to stop as well. He stepped to the wall and placed his hands across the ancient stone. Shanis thought that the man's long, dainty fingers, the nails so clean and neatly-trimmed, stood out in odd contrast to the moldy rocks of the wall. Bertram moved his hands round and round, seeming to caress the wall.

"Aha," he said, stepping back. He turned to the group. "You, the large boy," he said to Oskar, "push right here."

Oskar moved to the man's side, and placed both palms where Bertram indicated, against a large stone that was set in the wall at chest level. Shanis didn't see anything that would make this rock stand out among the others, but she assumed the steward knew what he was doing.

Oskar bent his knees, and braced himself. He glanced at Bertram, who nodded and waved his hand at him, a careless gesture as if he were ordering a servant. Oskar gave a great heave, and tumbled forward, falling to the ground in a heap as a section of the wall swung back as if on oiled hinges.

"That was unnecessary," Martrin said to Bertram.

"Couldn't help myself," the older man replied. "No hard feelings?" he asked, looking down at Oskar.

The red-faced boy shook his head and held his hand out for Bertram to help him up. When the steward grasped his hand, Oskar heaved, pulling the man down on top of him. Everyone laughed at the sight of the prim, proper man lying atop the big country boy.

"My goodness," Bertram said, with an amused lilt in his voice. "Had I but known, I would have led you to my chambers instead."

Oskar shoved the man off of him and lurched to his feet, sputtering incomprehensibly. He backed away from the older man, brushing at the front of his tunic as if to wipe away all memory of the embarrassing situation.

Bertram climbed to his feet, his expression impassive.

"Shall we?" he said, and led the way down the passage that the door had revealed.

The tunnel went on for some distance. It gradually sloped upward. As they moved forward, the air became less damp. The passageway came to an end at a blank wall. Handholds were hewn into the rock, vanishing into the darkness above.

"My work here is done," Bertram said, bowing ostentatiously. Everyone, including Oskar, thanked him profusely. He merely nodded in response, then turned toward Martrin, suddenly appearing very stiff and formal. Hands in front of his chest, he cupped his right fist in his left hand, and bowed to Martrin. The Captain repeated the gesture, and Bertram swept wraithlike down the hallway in the direction from which they had come.

Martrin pushed his way past Shanis and the others, stopping at the wall. He turned and passed the torch he had been carrying to Larris.

"Wait here until I call," he said. He turned, reached up, and grasped two of the handholds that were carved into the wall just above head level. He hooked the toe of his right boot into another depression, and began to climb.

Shanis watched him scale the wall until the darkness hid him from sight. No one spoke as they waited in the semi-darkness of the underground tunnel, their necks craned as their eyes fought to penetrate the darkness above. Finally, they heard what sounded like two sharp knocks on a wooden surface. After a moment, the knocks were answered by two muffled thumps. Another single, sharp rap, and then a faint sliver of light appeared high above them as a trapdoor was drawn open.

"You may come up, now," Martrin said quietly. Torchlight blossomed in the trapdoor, casting a faint glow on the walls above them. "Hurry."

Larris motioned for Khalyndryn to lead the way, with Shanis following behind.

Khalyndryn gave her pack over to Oskar, and grasped the handholds with shaking hands.

"You can do it," Oskar urged the girl.

Grimacing, Khalyndryn began to climb. She made her way up painstakingly, taking her time with each hand hold and toehold. Shanis unbuckled her sword, slung it over her shoulder, and fastened it. She took to the wall a few paces behind Khalyndryn. As they made their way up, she continued to encourage the girl. She hoped her voice did not betray the impatience that she felt. About halfway up, Khalyndryn halted.

"What if I fall?" the blonde girl whimpered. She started to turn her head back toward Shanis.

"Don't look down," Shanis snapped. "Keep your eyes on Captain Martrin."

Khalyndryn nodded, and continued her slow ascent. She finally reached the top of the wall, where Martrin and another man hauled her up through the trapdoor and into the darkness beyond. Shanis had almost reached the top when she heard a voice behind her.

"I can see up your dress," Hierm said.

Shanis raised a foot to kick at him, then thought the better of it. She looked down at him, and saw his eyes wide with surprise.

"I wouldn't really kick you, you mule," she said crossly. "I'd fall too."

"I know your temper," he said. She wished she could disagree with him.

Behind her friend, Shanis could make out the forms of Oskar and Allyn climbing up the wall. Oskar was breathing hard, but bearing up well under the combined weight of his own bundle and that of Khalyndryn. Behind him, Allyn wore a bored expression. Far below them, Larris stood, holding a torch. Suddenly, the flames of the torch took on a frightening clarity. The floor appeared to rush up to meet her, then fall away until Larris seemed a distant speck.

Shanis jerked her head around. She should have taken her own advice, and not looked back. She closed her eyes and breathed deeply.

"Are you alright?" Allyn called.

Shanis cursed softly to herself. Allyn was the last person in front of whom she wanted to make a fool of herself.

"I'm fine," she answered as nonchalantly as she could, and scaled the remainder of the wall as quickly as she dared. She refused Martrin's offered hand, instead pulling herself up and out of the opening in the ceiling.

She rolled away from the hole, and came up on the balls of her feet. A familiar aroma teased her olfactory senses. She looked down to see straw covering the floor. They were in a stable. The trapdoor was located in the center of an oversized stall. Nearby, Hierm was changing out of his palace finery and into his own clothes.

"Where's Khalyndryn?" she asked. Hierm tilted his head toward the adjacent stall. Shanis could see the top of Khalyndryn's blonde head just above the wall.

"Don't look!" Khalyndryn called through the wooden barrier.

"Mind the noise, girl," Martrin whispered harshly. He turned to Shanis. "Get changed. You'll also find a dark green, hooded cloak among your belongings. Put it on over your clothes."

Shanis turned to face Hierm, who had finished dressing and was donning his cloak.

"Screen me," she said. She moved to the end of the stall, positioned herself so that Hierm blocked the others' view of her, and began to undress.

"You're changing right here?" Hierm asked, his voice strained.

"Nobody's looking," she said. The truth was, she was still feeling embarrassed by her dizzy spell. On some level, she felt that if she acted as though she weren't bothered by changing clothes in front of the men, they wouldn't view her as a weak female, as they did Khalyndryn. Also, she couldn't wait another moment to get out of the ridiculous dress. Tugging on her own clothes, she was surprised to find that Bertram had seen to it that they were washed and mended. It was a relief to be back in her comfortable attire. Men's clothes or not, they were unquestionably better suited for hiking and riding than skirts would have been. She tugged the dark green cloak that had been provided for her, and found that the thick wool provided a welcome protection from the nighttime chill that she had been too nervous to notice before.

Soon, they had all changed and stood in the middle of the stable waiting for Khalyndryn. Hierm rapped on the door of the stall into which the girl had gone to change.

"I'm not coming out," the girl said. She sounded close to tears. Hierm peered over the side, and turned back quickly, a broad grin on his face.

"Miss Serrill," Larris said in a firm voice, moving up to stand alongside Hierm, "you are endangering the lives of everyone in this party. You will come out at once."

There was a moment of quiet, then a shuffling sound. Khalyndryn opened the stable door and stepped out, her blushing face shining red in the dim torchlight. Shanis gasped.

Khalyndryn was garbed in a fashion almost identical to Shanis. Her brown tunic and olive hose were obviously tailor-made to fit her. She held the dark green cloak in front of her face, and refused to speak.

"I suggested to Bertram that he have some clothing made for you," Martrin said. "Those skirts you were wearing would not have served you well in your travels. Now, put on your cloak. It is past time we should be leaving."

He led the way to the stable door. The man whom Shanis had seen through the trapdoor, one of Martrin's soldiers, kept watch in the doorway. The soldier nodded to Martrin, who led the group out into the darkened city streets.

"Where are we?" Larris asked, careful to keep his voice quiet.

"With all due respect, Highness," Martrin said, "the less I tell you, the better."

"The better for whom?" Larris asked.

"The order to which I belong is assisting you because of the nature of your quest," Martrin replied, "but our first loyalty is to our country." He stressed the word 'country'.

Shanis assumed that he meant country as opposed to king. She could not blame him for not supporting the duplicitous Orbrad.

The moon bathed the sleeping city in faint, silver light. There were no signs of life in this quarter of Karkwall. The streets were deserted, and not a light shone in any of the houses they passed. None the less, Martrin stayed out of the center of the road, keeping instead to the shadows and dark places.

Shanis looked around. Martrin had brought them out well beyond the castle keep. Its dark bulk rose up in the distance behind them, inky black in the faint moonlight. They turned a corner, and Shanis saw that they were not far from the city's outer wall.

They moved quietly, even Oskar managed to move carefully, making little sound in the stillness. From time to time she heard the approach of riders, most likely city guard on patrol. They ducked into shadowy recessed doorways whenever someone passed nearby.

They arrived at the back door of a large inn. Martrin knocked twice. The soft raps sounded like thunderclaps in the quiet night. The knock was returned by someone on the inside, but they did not go in. Instead, Martrin led them to the cellar door, which he opened hastily, and clambered inside. As his head sunk from view, he motioned for them to follow. They followed, one by one, with Hierm in the lead and Allyn bringing up the rear.

The cellar walls were lined with sacks of carrots and potatoes, along with shelves laden with bottles of wine and other provisions. Martrin stepped up to a narrow shelf, grasped it firmly, and gave it a tug. The shelf swung freely toward him, exposing another passage. Shanis shook her head. If she needed any proof that her way of viewing the world had changed, she need only point to the fact that she was already considering hidden doors and secret passageways commonplace.

The short tunnel led to a set of stone-lined steps that wound up into the darkness. Martrin pulled a torch from a bracket on the wall and led the way upward. Was a torch always kept burning in this tunnel, Shanis wondered, as she climbed the steps, or had someone provided it for them?

The stairway opened into a long, wide hallway. Shanis could not see the end of the hall in either direction. It vanished in the blend of torchlight and shadow. Martrin turned a sharp left and led them at a quick pace down the hall. They passed an occasional stairwell, but nothing else as they hurried along.

"We're inside the city wall, aren't we?" Oskar whispered.

"Yes," Martrin said. "We are on the highest level. It is all right to talk, by the way. Sound does not easily penetrate these walls, and the soldiers on duty in this particular area are, shall we say, sympathetic?"

"Are they part of your order?" Shanis asked.

Martrin seemed to consider this for a moment, then nodded.

"Why is this order of yours interested in helping us?" She wondered if she might be pushing the man too far, but after what she'd just been through, she really didn't care.

"There is a prophecy known to the tribes of Lothan that states that the bearer of the Silver Serpent will reunite the clans."

Larris began to protest, but Martrin raised his hand.

"Please, your Highness, you would dishonor the service that I've rendered you were you to deny what it is that you seek."

Larris closed his mouth, to Shanis' amusement. What a rare treat it was to see a royal brought up short.

"Orbrad did not merely wish to halt your search," Martrin continued. "He wanted your information. He would have tortured you until he extracted every last bit of knowledge pertaining to the Serpent."

"Why doesn't he search for it himself?" Shanis asked.

"Oh, he has been searching ever since he claimed the throne. Rather, trying to search. Those he sends keep vanishing without a trace. Also, you will be pleased to know that it appears your belongings had not yet been searched when Bertram recovered them. Orbrad is arrogant. Likely, he believed that he could inspect them at his leisure once he had you locked up."

"All of my papers were still there," said Oskar.

"As were mine," added Larris, "save what we left in the library."

Martrin looked back, eyes narrowed. "Was there anything of importance?"

"Nothing we can't live without," Larris said. "A rough map, a few notations. Without the key information that we are missing, the map is useless."

"Unless Orbrad already has that particular bit of information," Oskar said.

Shanis pondered the thought in silence. The hush that had fallen over the group indicated that the others were likely doing the same. What if they reached their destination only to find that Orbrad had gotten there first?

"Bertram has assured me that Orbrad knows very little beyond common myths and prophecies. He has no solid clues, and he is too distrustful of others to work together on the search."

"What is going to happen when Orbrad finds out that his pigeons have flown the coop?" Larris asked.

"He will rant and rave, as always. Your assessment of him yesterday was correct, Highness. He is more than a bit paranoid. He won't know who is responsible. Bertram and I are above suspicion, and we are very discreet." The corners of Martrin's mouth turned up in a wry smile. "The sleeping draught Bertram put in the guard's wine should wear off by morning. Moggs was so drunk that he'll likely believe that it was one of them who attacked him. I'm certain he didn't have time to recognize me. It should be quite a scene in the castle."

"Is Bertram one of your order?" Khalyndryn asked.

"Bertram is friendly to our order, but his reasons for helping us are more personal. His tastes in companionship are, shall we say, unconventional. He and Orbrad's nephew were quite close." He drew out the last two words for emphasis.

It took Shanis a moment to realize what he was talking about. She felt herself blushing furiously. The very idea!

"So what happened?" Khalyndryn asked, apparently not yet understanding what Martrin was telling them.

"Orbrad found out, and flew into a rage," Martrin said. "He caught them together, and defenestrated the boy."

"That is horrible!" Khalyndryn exclaimed. "I thought they only did that to bulls."

Larris and Allyn chuckled, and Oskar cleared his throat. Shanis remained quiet, as she had no more of an idea what the word meant than did her companion.

"Defenestrate means to throw someone out of a high window," Oskar said.

"You're lying!" Khalyndryn said, thrusting out her lower lip. "I don't know why you are always trying to make me feel so foolish. I do not appreciate it."

"I'm afraid he is telling the truth, my lady," Martrin said, suppressing a grin.

"Well, that is just beastly," Khalyndryn huffed. She settled into a quiet contemplation of what she had just been told. A few moments later, her alarmed squeak told Shanis that the girl had finally gotten the entire picture.

"So he helped us as a way of getting revenge against Orbrad?" Shanis asked. She did not blame him. From what little she had seen, Orbrad was a terrible man.

"That is part of it," Martrin agreed. "Also, he fancies your friend there." The soldier turned and nodded at Hierm, who looked back at him quizzically for a

DAVID DEBORD | 128

moment, then gasped and missed a step, nearly tumbling to the floor. The others kindly kept their laughter in check.

Martrin led them down a flight of stairs and along a narrow hallway that ended at a small, solid door.

"This is the outer wall," he said softly. "There should be only friendly eyes to see us, but we must move quickly none the less. Your escort is waiting for you, along with your horses." Not waiting for a reply, he turned and rapped twice on the door. When the knock was returned, he unbarred the door, and swung it open.

A soldier stood outside, apparently keeping watch. "All is clear, sir," he whispered, giving the fist-over-heart salute that Shanis had seen the previous day. Martrin returned the salute, and led them out into the darkness.

The wide swath of land cleared for defense made Shanis feel positively naked as they hurried toward a distant wooded area. She shifted the bundle on her shoulder to cover as much of her back as possible, certain that at any moment, arrows would come whistling down upon them.

It seemed an eternity, but the cleared ground finally ended, and she spotted a cluster of shadows waiting among the sparse trees and shrubs. As they drew closer, the shadows formed into the shapes of several mounted men, and several riderless horses. The riders fanned out and led them through the trees, which grew thicker the farther they rode.

When they were all safely inside the protective arms of the forest, they came to a halt. Martrin turned and addressed them.

"This is where I leave you. I cannot be away too long, or I risk rousing suspicion. Know that I wish you much luck." As they all thanked him, a large man on a heavy warhorse rode up alongside them.

"So these be the ones I'm a taking?" he growled.

Where had Shanis heard that voice before?

"Yes," Martrin said to the man. He turned back to Shanis and her companions. "I assume you all remember Horgris?"

Chapter 22

The moon was a small, silver orb balanced on the tip of a distant mountain peak when Horgris led them into a large encampment. Groups were gathered around several bonfires in the midst of an open area surrounded by huts and tents. Shanis heard laughter, shouts and raucous voices belting out songs that were unfamiliar to her ear. As they drew closer, she could see that the people were obviously Monaghan. All had red hair of varying shades and were garbed in the same rough animal skins and dark, cross-hatched tunics as their leader.

They dismounted in front of the largest hut. A youth with a pitifully sparse beard took their horses. A young woman about Shanis' age stepped out of the hut. Horgris spoke to her quietly, then motioned for Larris to follow him inside.

"Come with me," the girl said. Without waiting for a reply, she led them over to the nearest fire. The people there eyed them curiously, but did not cease their merry-making. Chunks of meat roasted on skewers, and the girl pointed to them. "Eat," she instructed, and walked away.

"Nice to make your acquaintance," Allyn said with a smirk. The girl ignored him. He turned and said to no one in particular, "Where can a man get ale around here?" Almost immediately someone put a tankard in his hand. Soon, Shanis, Oskar, and Hierm were all holding large, frothy mugs. Khalyndryn declined the ale, but accepted a cup of wine.

Shanis took a sip of hers. It was warm and on the bitter side, but not all bad. She sat down next to Allyn. The ground was soft and damp, but it felt good after a night and day in the saddle. "What do you think they're talking about in there?" She gestured with her mug toward the hut into which Horgris and Larris had disappeared.

Allyn shrugged. "Something boring, no doubt." He took a long pull of his ale and stared at the fire.

Hierm sat down on her left and handed her a skewer of meat. She looked at it for a moment. "Any idea what it is?"

Hierm shook his head, and gingerly tore off a chunk of the hot meat. He blew on it a few times, then put it in his mouth. He frowned as he chewed. "It's a bit tough, but not bad. I don't recognize the flavor."

"It's snake," Allyn said.

Hierm choked and coughed, spitting the bite onto the ground in front of him.

"Only joking." Allyn took another drink. His expression was stoic as he stared into the flames.

Shanis laughed. She looked at Hierm, who was on his feet, brushing the dirt off of his hose. "It's all right Hierm. Sit down."

Hierm looked at her, then at Allyn. "No thank you." He picked up his mug of ale and stalked away into the crowd.

"No sense of humor, that one," Allyn said, still staring straight ahead. "Has he always been like that?"

"In the last two days we've been waylaid by bandits, attacked by monsters, arrested, put in a dungeon, then rescued, only to be told that the bandits who accosted us are our friends," Shanis said. "Surely you can forgive him if he's not feeling himself."

"I doubt he has ever had much of a sense of humor," Allyn said. "He seems touchy."

"You would have to know his family to understand." She had sometimes tried to imagine being raised by Lord Hiram and Mistress Faun, but the thought was too terrible to entertain.

Allyn seemed content to let the conversation end there, so Shanis returned her attention to the meat. She took a bite of the still-hot chunk, and chewed. "So what is this, anyway?"

"Highland rat," Allyn said.

"Very funny," she said, still chewing.

Allyn turned to look her in the eye. "I am not joking."

Shanis punched him in the shoulder, and took satisfaction in the tiny wince he made. "I can't tell when you're lying and when you're telling the truth. Should I be worried?"

"Everyone lies," Allyn said. He stood and walked away, leaving his half-full mug of ale behind.

What had she said? First Hierm, now Allyn. Perhaps she should find Oskar and offend him. She looked around, but did not see him. As she was about to take another bite of the rat, or whatever it was, a chorus of giggles rang out behind her. She turned to look.

Khalyndryn stood a few paces away, her back to Shanis, surrounded by a small group of girls a few years her junior. She had changed back into her dress.

"She thinks she's a boy," Khalyndryn said, loud enough for Shanis to hear. "She wears boy's clothes, she fights with the boys. My mother says she'll make someone a good husband one day." The girls laughed again.

Shanis felt her face heat. It was just like at home. Khalyndryn had not been too intolerable while they were on the road. Get her back to a semblance of civilization, and she was right back to her old tricks, holding court with a bunch of little girls who treated her like a princess.

"Do you think you could teach me how to make my hair silky like yours?" one of the girls asked. "I be trying to catch Granlor's eye, but he no seems to notice me."

"Well, I don't know that your hair could look like mine," Khalyndryn said, "but we will see what we can do."

Shanis could listen to no more. She lurched to her feet, feeling dizzy. The ale was stronger than what they brewed at home. She wandered off through crowd, trying not to bump into anyone. She didn't see Oskar anywhere. All the strange faces seemed to blur together.

"Here gal," someone grasped her elbow, "dance with me." Her ale fell to the ground and she staggered a bit as a young man pulled her toward a group of people who were hopping around in pairs to the beat of a primitive sounding drum.

She looked up at the young man. He was fairly handsome, though he could stand a bath. His beard was not too bushy, he had a pleasant smile, and he wasn't angry with her: three points in his favor. Not quite believing what she was doing, she put her hands on his shoulders.

"I don't dance very well," she said.

"This one be simple," he said. "You know how to use that sword you wear?"

Shanis nodded. What did her sword have to do with anything?

"Get up on the balls of your feet like you be dueling. Then, we hop around in a circle, and spin as we go. You understand, no?"

Shanis nodded, though she was not entirely certain she understood. Ordinarily she would not even consider dancing, but the ale had relaxed, if not emboldened her.

He led her in among the group of dancers, put his hands on her waist, and said, "Come now. Hop."

Following his lead, she rose up on the balls of her feet and started bouncing. They spun to the left, all the while following the other dancers in a circle around the bonfire. By the second turn, she realized she was actually enjoying herself. The ale must have seriously affected her judgment.

"My name be Granlor," her partner said. "What be yours?"

Where had she heard that name? Her thoughts were fuzzy. "Shanis," she said.

"What clan be you?"

"Umm, I'm Galdoran." Was everyone going to think she was Monaghan?

Granlor cocked his head and fixed her with an odd look, but did not say anything.

Another turn around the fire, and the drummer shouted, "And back".

Granlor spun her in the other direction, and the dancers reversed their circle. "Keep you from getting too dizzy."

"Too late," she said. Her head swam, though the sensation was not entirely unpleasant.

"Would you be wanting to sit down?" She nodded, and he led her away from the fire. They sat down beside another pair who appeared wearied from dancing. Granlor introduced them as Jamnir and Calia.

"Have a drink," Jamnir said, offering her a big earthenware jug. His hair was dark auburn, almost brown.

She took a sip and her mouth was immediately assaulted by the foulest taste she could ever imagine. She spewed it on the ground. "That is the vilest stuff I've ever tasted."

The others laughed as Jamnir took the jug back from her.

"It be called skok", Granlor said. "Has a flavor all its own, it does. No everyone can handle it." He smiled and patted her on the shoulder.

. "It took me by surprise, that's all." In her condition, Shanis was not about to refuse a challenge. "Let me have another taste." She took another drink, a small one, and held it in her mouth. The second drink wasn't as bad as the first, though it certainly didn't taste good. It had an earthy taste, as if the water had been filtered through peat. She swished it around her mouth and swallowed. It burned all the way down, warming her entire body, but she managed to keep a straight face.

"Skok be the only thing good that come from Malgog." Granlor gritted his teeth as he made the concession. Jamnir grudgingly added his agreement.

"What he be doing with her?" a girl's voice cried. "That girl in the boy's clothes?"

Shanis turned and saw Khalyndryn standing with one of the girls she had been talking with earlier. Now she remembered. Granlor was the man whose attention this girl had been trying to attract. The girl whirled and stalked away, with Khalyndryn hurrying behind her.

"Rinala," Khalyndryn called as she hurried away. "Wait for me. I am sure it's just a misunderstanding."

"She never be giving up," Granlor said, shaking his head. "I be no interested. She be too much trouble for me, that one." He took another drink of skok.

"Trouble in what way?" Shanis asked. Her throat was a touch raw from the skok.

"It no be her that's trouble," Calia said, an odd tone in her voice, "so much as it be her father."

"Let us no talk about that," Granlor said, taking Shanis' hand. "You be wanting to take a walk?"

Shanis thought she knew what he meant by 'a walk', and she wasn't interested. "Actually, is there somewhere I can go? I don't feel well."

"I'll take you to the pits," Granlor said, rising.

"No, let me take her." Calia gently took Shanis hand from Granlor and led her away.

"Thank you," Shanis whispered when they were out of earshot. "Granlor seems nice enough, but I wanted to get away."

"We girls must be looking out for each other, no?" She was pretty, with broad, pleasant features and blonde streaks in her light red hair. "Granlor no be too bad, but he do move quickly sometimes."

Shanis spied Allyn seated nearby, chatting with a plump young woman. He was even smiling. "Granlor isn't the only one who moves quickly," she said, hurrying past before he noticed her.

"Why so sour? Oh, I see." Calia shook her head. "You do fancy him."

"No I don't." She didn't want to think about Allyn.

"I no be asking a question," Calia said. "You no be worrying. Sometimes it be taking them a while to know what be good for them."

Shanis decided to change the subject. "How long have you lived here?"

"A long time," Calia said, "It be several moons that we be in this place."

"That doesn't seem like a very long time."

"In Monaghan, we no be staying in one place for too long. But this place be close enough to Karkwall that the Malgog," her facial features tightened as she said the name, "stay away."

"I have lived in the same place all of my life." The words seemed to constrict her throat as she realized that the statement was no longer true. Could she truly say she had a home anymore? Between the homesickness and the drink, she felt like she could cry.

"We hope to be staying here for a while." Calia seemed not to notice Shanis' sadness. "Over there, they be building a stone meetinghouse. We no have many permanent buildings."

Shanis looked in the direction the girl indicated but paid little attention to the waist-high stone wall that would someday be the meetinghouse. Instead, she stared in utter disbelief as she watched Rinala lead Hierm into a nearby hut and draw a heavy skin across the doorway.

"What be wrong?" Calia asked.

"I have to go." Shanis pushed the girl away, not too roughly, she hoped, and hurried blindly away from the huts. Away from Hierm. Tears filled her eyes. Where was Oskar? She needed a friend.

A cool mist had descended upon the camp as full night came upon them, and she wandered half-blinded by fog, smoke, drink, and tears. She wanted to go home. She missed her father. She missed Yurg and Anna. She missed Seventhday market, sword practice, her horse, and lying on the big rock by the river.

"Shanis, are you all right?" Someone grabbed her by the arm and turned her about.

"Larris." The stream of tears became a torrent. Some remote part of her brain now resented Larris even more for having seen her like this, but she couldn't stop crying. She laid her head on his shoulder and let her weight sag against his chest. He put his arms around her and held her up. He was stronger than she had realized.

"Did someone hurt you?" His voice was gentle, yet a note of menace lay underneath.

She shook her head. She didn't know how to explain. Her sobbing had abated, and he wiped her cheeks with his sleeve. He was sort of handsome.

"Am I pretty?" she asked. Where had that come from?

"Yes," he said, looking her in the eye. "Perhaps the prettiest girl I have ever seen."

She stared at him for a long time, waiting for him to laugh, or add on an insult, but he did neither. The drink must have been in control of her tongue, because the next thing she heard herself say was, "Will you kiss me?"

Larris' eyes widened for a moment, then he smiled. He moved his hands to her face, cupping her cheeks, and leaned toward her.

Then he stopped.

"What's wrong?" she asked.

"I want to kiss you," he said, moving his hands to her shoulders and stepping back a bit. "But only when it's you who wants to kiss me."

"I don't understand." First Allyn, then Hierm, now Larris. Was something wrong with her?

"Lerryn would take advantage of a girl who is too much in her cups, but I will not."

Shanis could swear she saw regret in his face.

"Horgris has provided quarters for the night," he said. "Let's take you there."

She wanted to protest that she was not drunk, but suddenly there was only one thing she could say.

"Larris, I'm going to be sick."

Chapter 23

"Your Majesty, I present Prince Lerryn of Galdora!"

Lerryn was impressed that so small a man as Bertram could muster such volume. He stepped through the doorway into the throne room. The small cluster of petitioners and bootlickers parted, allowing him a clear path to the throne. He ignored the expressions on their faces, all various levels of wonder or suspicion, and focused on Orbrad.

The king of Lothan looked like death. His face was ghastly white and his hands trembled as they clutched the arms of the throne.

"You did not forewarn him that I was here, did you?" Lerryn whispered to the steward.

"I thought he would enjoy the surprise," Bertram replied without moving his lips, which were frozen in a polite smile.

Lerryn chuckled. He halted several paces from the throne and made a formal bow, though not too deep.

"What are you doing in my kingdom?" Orbrad snapped, still gripping his throne as if it was going to run away.

"And a good day to you as well, Orbrad. Are you ill? You look like a dead goat." If Orbrad was going to dispense with the niceties, he could do the same.

"You have not answered my question, Highness." Orbrad replied in his nasal voice.

Did the poor man actually believe he sounded threatening? How pathetic.

"Your Majesty, I apologize for intruding upon you," Lerryn said. "My retinue and I are merely passing through your kingdom. I thought it would be rude of me not to make my presence known."

"Why does everyone want to pass through my kingdom?" Orbrad threw up his hands in exasperation. He suddenly dropped his hands to his side, and his face turned red. He cleared his throat. "Never mind," he said, before Lerryn could ask what he meant. "I won't bother asking your business. How long do you plan to stay?"

"We are dirty and road-weary," Lerryn replied. "I would be most grateful if I could beg the hospitality of your castle for one night."

"I suppose that will not be too great an inconvenience." Orbrad appeared to relax a little. "Anything else?"

"My throat is dry from the dust of the trail. A bit of wine would not go unappreciated."

"Yes, I've heard that you like your wine," Orbrad said with a sneer. "Bertram, see to it."

The little steward bowed much more deeply than necessary, then turned and led Lerryn from the room. When they were again in the hall, Bertram signaled for the guards to close the massive doors. He turned to Lerryn and smiled.

"He must be in a good mood today. I presumed he would throw you in the dungeon." Without another word, he hurried down the hall, motioning for Lerryn to follow.

Lerryn scratched his head, then followed the sound of the little man's footsteps as they receded into the depths of Karkwall Castle.

Lerryn stared out the window of his chamber at the keep below. He watched soldiers going about their duties and servants working the small gardens inside the walls. What must it be like to live under a constant siege mentality? For his nation, the threat of war with Kyrin was always a possibility, but it was not an immediate threat such as that under which these people lived. What would happen if the clans united under a single leader? How long could Orbrad hold this castle against a siege? How many would even remain loyal? In Lerryn's experience, most commoners had little taste for war, and wanted only to live as ordinary a life as possible. They would support whichever leader seemed to offer that hope.

An ordinary life. How he envied the common folk. Ironic that so many of them likely harbored the same envy for him and his life. Perhaps one of them would trade with him one day He chuckled at the thought.

"Honestly, Highness! Talking to yourself is one thing. But a man who goes around laughing for no apparent reason will, at best, be thought a fool."

Lerryn turned away from the window. How did Xaver always manage to enter a room without his hearing? His vizier sat in an overstuffed chair against the far wall looking pleased with himself. Above him hung a tapestry showing a battle between Tichris and the kings of the east.

"Did anyone ever tell you that you look like the Ice King?" Lerryn asked.

"That is not amusing, Highness." Xaver's expression was blank, cold.

"It is to me." Lerryn sat down at the small table near the window, and poured a cup of red wine. He took a sip and held it in his mouth for a moment. It was a bit on the sour side, but it was wine. He swallowed, feeling it warm his throat ever so slightly on the way down. "What have you learned?"

Xaver chuckled. "Most of the rumors are the usual castle fare, but there is one rumor that is on everyone's lips."

Lerryn took another drink of wine and waited. "Are you going to tell me, or not?"

"Sorry. This one is so rich, it is worth waiting for. Apparently, you are being held in the dungeon."

"What?" Lerryn put down his cup, and leaned forward, propping his elbows on the table.

"Everyone," Xaver said in a low, conspiratorial voice, "and I do mean everyone, is whispering that the Prince of Galdora is being held in the dungeon."

"Foolishness," Lerryn scoffed. "Orbrad must have arrested some pretender to the throne of Lothan. You know how facts become distorted when whispered in the halls and under the sheets."

Xaver shook his head. "Everyone is saying exactly the same thing. The Prince of Galdora and his five traveling companions are in the dungeon. That is very specific and quite a coincidence."

Lerryn stood and walked over to the corner where he had left his sword leaning against the wall, picked it up and belted it on. The feel of its weight around his middle, and the solidity of the hilt in his palm was comforting. He did his best thinking with a sword in his hand and a horse beneath him. The horse was not an option at the moment, so the sword would have to do.

"Do you think Orbrad is planning something?"

"I would not put anything past that buffoon," Xaver said, folding his long, pale hands across his lap, "but I doubt it. Everyone is talking about it. Even Orbrad can keep a secret better than that. Also, it's being talked about as if it has already happened."

"So, either everyone in the castle is grossly misinformed, or Larris has sneaked away from Archstone, gathered five companions, ridden to Karkwall, and offended the king."

They both laughed.

"There is another possibility." Xaver looked directly at him. His purple eyes seemed to bore into Lerryn.

Lerryn stared back, uncomprehending. Then it dawned on him. "The prophecy," he whispered.

"Precisely. The ice cat was evidence that the prophecy is in motion. This is further proof."

"So, the prophecy is warning us that Orbrad is going to arrest us?"

"It could mean many things. When the Silver Serpent is yours, you will be the most powerful ruler in the east, perhaps in the world. Kings will fear you, even hate you. The rumor may be a foreshadowing of how you will be perceived in the new world we create."

"We are not going to create a new world," Lerryn said. I want to end the threat of Kyrin, and I want the nations of the east to no longer view Galdora as a bastard land. Nothing more or less." He wondered if his words sounded as foolishly altruistic to Xaver as they did to his own ears.

"A poor choice of words on my part," Xaver said. "In any event, we should be alert for what the prophecy has to tell us. This evening's banquet should be interesting."

Chapter 24

There it is. The Ramsgate." Larris pointed toward a narrow gap between two mountains.

Shanis shielded her eyes against the brightness of the afternoon sun and squinted, trying to ignore her headache. It was altogether a disappointment. She was not sure what she had expected, but for so storied a locale, at least according to Oskar, she thought it should have been grander. The pass was merely a narrow cleft in the rock. She could see only a few paces in before the way vanished in shadow. She would be surprised if they could get the horses through.

Larris seemed to read her thoughts. "Horgris assured me it is passable. We might have to unload the horses, though. It will be difficult, but not impossible."

Hierm groaned. Shanis took a small measure of satisfaction in the fact that he seemed to be feeling as poorly as she.

"Why do they call it the Ramsgate?" she asked.

"Because it is so narrow that common wisdom said that only a single ram could pass through at a time." Larris scratched his head and stared down at the narrow defile. "Of course, old stories tend to be exaggerated. At least I hope so."

"I read a different version," Oskar said, drawing his mount even with theirs. "I heard that the mountains here are so impassable that even the rams have to use this pass to get through."

"Either way, let's be at it," Allyn said. "The day is wasting." He put heels to his horse and set off down the slope at a steady pace.

Reaching the pass, they dismounted. Allyn handed his reins over to Oskar and went ahead of the group to scout. He returned soon thereafter, his expression unreadable, as usual.

"It's a winding path, narrow in parts. We will definitely have to carry our bags."

Shanis set to unloading her horse with a detached, sick feeling. Her stomach roiled and her head felt as if a horse has stepped on it. She fumbled with the buckle on one of her saddlebags, and cursed.

"Need any help?" Hierm asked. He did not quite meet her eye as he spoke, and he was obviously staying out of easy hitting or kicking range.

She gave him what she hoped was a withering stare, and returned to the task at hand. Finally loosing the bags, she hooked them together and slung them over her shoulder. Taking her horses' reins in her left hand and gripping the pommel of her sword in her right, she started toward the cleft between the mountains.

"Shanis," Larris said, "wait for the rest of us." He smiled expectantly, as if last night's offer of a kiss was going to be renewed now that she was sober.

She ignored him. She gave her horse a tug and tried to move faster. They could catch up with her later. The morning's ride had been unbearable. She did not want to speak to any of them, Oskar included. In fairness, he hadn't done anything wrong, but it was obvious that he was dying for someone to explain to him what was going on between the rest of the group, and she neither wanted to talk, nor hear about it.

The pathway curved to the left and the light dimmed as the cleft above her narrowed. Another turn back to the right and now the way was not much wider than what her horse could fit through. She came to a place where the path widened and ran straight ahead for some fifty or more paces ahead. A chill passed through her and she paused, drawing her cloak tight around her neck.

She stood in a rocky fissure, the walls of which ran far above her, broken up by occasional stone outcroppings. The mountain peaks blocked most of the sunlight, casting the pathway in dusky shadow. Something caught her eye, and she stepped back to get a better view.

Above a ledge, about thirty paces up, she could just discern the outline of a cave. Despite the dim light, she could see that its shape was unusual. The opening was a smooth, even arch, so unlike the rough stone all around. More than that, the cave seemed to beckon to her. She felt herself drawn toward it.

She examined the rocky face beneath the cave, looking for handholds. She had never climbed like this before, Galsbur being in the midst of rolling farmland and dense forest. She immediately noticed several likely-looking outcroppings and some wide cracks where she might wedge a boot.

"Should I try it?" she asked no one in particular, staring back up at the shadowed entry. If her horse had an opinion, he kept it to himself.

Down the passageway, from the direction she had come, she heard the clatter of horseshoes on stone, and the soft murmur of distant voices. That fixed it. Anything that would buy her some time away from her so-called friends was a welcome diversion. She selected her first hand- and footholds, and began to scale the rock.

The climb was surprisingly easy and she reached the small ledge in front of the cave only a bit winded. She caught a whiff of smoke and noticed a flicker of light deep in the cavern. Drawing her sword, she stepped inside.

"Your blade is needed not." The voice was thin, cracked with age, but resilient, like old leather. "Come in."

Shanis lowered her sword, but did not sheathe it. She walked slowly. As her eyes adjusted to the gloom she could see that the walls and floor of the cave were perfectly smooth. As she moved deeper, she could make out a small figure sitting on the opposite side of a small fire.

The woman was unbelievably old. Her face was deeply lined, with bags under her sunken, yellowed eyes. Her matted, silver hair hung limply around her face. She was garbed in a coarse, dark robe. She beckoned to Shanis with a long, gnarled finger.

"Who are you?" Shanis asked, stepping into the firelight, and finally sliding her sword back into its scabbard.

"Questions you have, but my name be not one of them. Call me Hyda, if you must." The woman's words sounded mysterious, but she uttered them matter-of-factly. "Sit down."

Shanis eased down onto the cold, stone floor, and sat cross-legged. She noticed that her headache was gone, though her mind was far from clear. The same feeling of being drawn up to the cave now seemed to work at her tongue. She did have questions, and for some irrational reason, she believed that this old woman could answer them. A small voice in the back of her mind urged caution, but it was suppressed by the greater desire to unburden herself to this crone.

"What is the Silver Serpent?" she blurted. Why could she not seem to hold her tongue?

"What you seek." The old woman replied.

"Yes, I know," she said, her frustration rising. "But what is it?"

"That which you must find." The woman looked Shanis directly in the eye. There was no humor there, no suggestion that the woman was toying with her.

Shanis took a deep breath. Above all, there was one question to which she wanted to know the answer. A doubt that had lingered in her mind from the day of the tournament. A simple phrasing at the end of a note. She bit her lip. Did she truly want to know the answer?

"My father," she paused, not certain how to ask the question. "Is he truly my father?"

The crone rose and moved slowly around the fire toward Shanis. She leaned down and extended a withered hand.

Shanis winced at the black earth under the woman's yellow fingernails. Rough skin brushed her cheek as the old woman cupped her face. "Girl, you do ask all the wrong questions."

Shanis drew back from the distasteful touch. "Why don't you tell me what I need to know, then?" She wondered for a fleeting moment at the wisdom of offending her host, but the woman did not seem to care. She turned and shuffled back into the depths of the cave, vanishing into the darkness.

Shanis looked around, but could see little in the smoky darkness. Discomfort and an odd fear itched at the back of her neck, but curiosity and the inexplicable belief that she was supposed to be here kept her anchored fast.

The woman returned carrying an earthenware bowl filled nearly to the brim with liquid. Water, Shanis guessed. She carefully placed the bowl on the ground, then looked up at Shanis.

"Give me a hair." She held her hand out, palm up, above the fire.

Shanis hesitated for a moment, then, as if in a dream, plucked a long hair from her head. She handed it to Hyda, who held it over the low flame. Shanis saw a small spark. She twisted up her face as the odor of burning hair filled her nostrils.

Hyda held the burning hair in her upturned palm until it burned out. She reached across the fire, holding her hand in front of Shanis' face.

"Spit."

Shanis looked down at the small bits of ash in Hyda's hand. She frowned, then shrugged, and spat into the creased palm.

Hyda rubbed the saliva in a circular pattern, smearing the bit of ash. She then scooped a handful of water, and held it up.

"Breathe your life into it," she said, her voice hoarse. "Blow on it."

A pleasant feeling of dizziness spun in Shanis' mind as she leaned forward again, and blew gently. Her vision narrowed, and she seemed to shoot forward until her consciousness was but a mere speck floating above the rippling sea in Hyda's palm. A faint mist rose up, enveloping her in its delicate arms. She felt herself borne up, enshrouded in gray vapor.

"Your path is not your own." Hyda's words rolled across the water, breaking over her in thunderous waves. "Many are the claims on your life, and either way you go, you do good for the one and ill for the other." A long pause. "Your companions, all needed to complete your task, but one is not true."

Shanis felt her brow crease, as if she were far removed from her body. She understood what the woman meant about her path not being her own. But, one of her companions would be untrue? Could she mean Hierm and that girl? It couldn't be. The thought dissolved in the mist, and she lay back in the warmth of what felt like the most pleasant of dreams.

"What you seek, you may find, but only if you do not look for it. Your way is perilous."

The sudden absence of Hyda's voice was a shock. When the words came again, they were a tremulous, frightened whisper.

"Prevail you must. Hold fast girl. With all you have and all that you are, hold fast." The last two words were sobbed more than spoken.

The sound of Hyda's voice fled, and with it the comfort of the warm mist. Shanis drifted alone in cold, blackness. She had only a moment to feel fright, before her awareness dimmed, and she faded into comforting slumber.

Chapter 25

"Your Royal Majesty, noble guests, I present His Royal Highness, Prince Lerryn of Galdora." The herald, a paunchy, florid-faced man in a garish green and orange silk doublet, bowed, and gestured for Lerryn to enter the great hall.

Lerryn scarcely noticed the surprised expressions on the faces of the minor nobles gathered around the single, giant table that stretched the length of the hall. He brushed past the chubby man and slowly made his way down the wide, stone staircase. He forced a smile and hoped that he did not look as surly as he felt. Xaver had insisted he forego the wine until dinner. His Vizier was correct, as usual. It wouldn't do for Lerryn to meet foreign nobility, even ones as insignificant as these, reeking of drink. He was nonetheless displeased with the entire situation.

He surveyed the hall. It was wrought of the same gray stone as the rest of the palace. Dark, dingy walls rose high above them, narrowing to meet in an architecturally unimpressive vaulted ceiling. Faded banners hung from the rafters. On the far end of the room, spread across the back wall, hung a giant tapestry, depicting a great battle from ages past. Remnants of the great nation Lothan had once been. Slivers of evening light shone through narrow windows in the ceiling, casting a bluish hue upon the sad scene.

He heard the hushed whispers of the nobility as he moved along the massive table. Orbrad sat at the head with his wife, Queen Agnes to his right. The pale, black-haired young woman was Orbrad's third wife. An odd coincidence all three had proved to be barren. She smiled and nodded to him.

Lerryn noted, with some annoyance, that the seat of honor, the one to the queen's right, had not been reserved for him. His annoyance burst into scarcely-contained rage when he saw who occupied that seat.

The white-haired man rose belatedly, stretching to his full height, just slightly taller than the Galdoran prince. He regarded Lerryn with intense, brown eyes set above a slightly crooked nose.

"Your Highness, I believe you are acquainted with His Excellency, Count Nadrin of Kyrin?" Orbrad made no effort to keep the amusement from his voice.

"Forgive me, Highness," Nadrin said, "I did not intend to usurp your place at the table. I was merely conversing with Her Majesty. Please." Bowing politely, he motioned to the seat he had just vacated.

"You are too kind," Lerryn said. He bowed politely to Orbrad, then kissed Agnes' hand. "Your Majesty, you are most radiant this evening." The queen blushed and giggled. She nodded to her husband, who motioned for all to be seated.

Lerryn settled into his chair, and immediately reached for his wine glass. He cocked an eyebrow. Real crystal. He swirled the burgundy liquid, enjoying its rich bouquet.

"It is from Diyonus," Orbrad said. "The finest vintage I have in my cellar."

"I am humbled that you thought me worthy." Lerryn took a sip and held it in his mouth a moment before swallowing. "Exquisite."

"I am gratified that you find it so. It is not often we receive two esteemed guests in one day." The king of Lothan gestured to Nadrin, who smiled and bowed his head.

"What brings you this far south, Nadrin?" Lerryn attempted to sound casual. He took another sip of the wine, forcing himself not to gulp it down.

"You know, just keeping up relations with a friendly nation." Nadrin smiled. His eyes said that they both knew he was lying.

"I did not realize your nations had reached a different status in your relations."

"I admit that we have not always seen eye-to-eye," Orbrad interrupted. "Nadrin has pointed out, however, that we have some mutual interests." The two men openly exchanged knowing grins, enjoying whatever was their shared joke.

Lerryn's fists clenched. He caught himself before he shattered his goblet, forced down his anger and took another drink.

"Perhaps it is you who should explain why you are here," Nadrin said. "I suggested to His Majesty that I would be concerned if Galdoran princes were suddenly wandering through my kingdom."

"How many Galdoran princes have you seen around here, Nadrin?" Lerryn asked.

A fit of coughing suddenly racked Orbrad's chest. The pudgy monarch spewed wine across the table as he hacked. Agnes clapped him on the back in a most undignified manner.

"Are you all right?" Nadrin asked in a condescending voice.

"Quite," Orbrad choked. He cleared his throat with a loud rasp, and signaled for more wine. "The count here has pointed out to me that each of our nations has claims on certain ancestral lands that are occupied by Galdora."

"Gentlemen, Galdora consists entirely of your ancestral lands, as you call them. I can assure you that my father will not be handing our country back over to the two of you." Lerryn drained his glass and held it out to be refilled as the servant arrived to attend to Orbrad.

"With all due respect, Highness, that has never been our desire." Nadrin leaned forward, plaintive palms upraised in front of him. He was obviously putting on a show for everyone within earshot. Down the table, guests lowered their voices and turned their heads to listen. "There are certain lands that are of great historical and religious significance to us. Kyrin would compensate Galdora for the land in question. We seek a peaceful resolution to this issue."

"Count Nadrin, I am a soldier, not a diplomat. I feel confident, though, in saying that you can tell your king there is no issue. The borders of Galdora were established centuries ago. They are not flexible, and neither is my father."

"That is precisely the problem." Nadrin spoke in a soothing voice, so unlike his normal manner. "Kyrin is willing to negotiate on this matter. Galdora is not."

"You wish to negotiate the annexation of the richest farmland in our kingdom."

"Burn you, boy!" Nadrin slammed his fist down hard, nearly upsetting his untouched wine glass. "Kyrinians bled for that land before your bastard nation every existed."

"No need to raise your voice, Your Grace." Lerryn smiled, pleased that he had gotten the better of the verbal joust. He looked down the length of the table, enjoying the disapproving expressions on the faces of those who had been listening. On the far end of the hall, he could barely see Xaver. His vizier was seated near the foot of the table, along with Pedric Karst, whose nobility, though tenuous, had merited him a seat in the great hall. The remaining members of Lerryn's party were taking their meals in their rooms. He would have gladly exchanged places with any of them.

"There are our concerns to deal with, as well," Orbrad spoke up. "There are lands in the southern reaches of your realm that are traditional Lothan clanholds."

"Your Majesty, you cannot control your own kingdom, much less any portion of Galdora."

Next to Lerryn, Queen Agnes gasped and sat upright.

"You dare speak so to us when you are a guest at our table? It is most unseemly, Highness." The woman was positively quaking with rage. She clutched her crystal goblet in a small, trembling hand. A bit of wine had sloshed over the side, staining the sleeve of her pale green silk dress.

"No matter, my dear." Orbrad placed a hand on hers. "Perhaps what Lothan needs is a cause behind which to unite our warring factions." He fixed Lerryn with a meaningful stare.

Lerryn was about to ask where Orbrad had suddenly acquired some sand, though he knew the reason was sitting across the table, when shouting erupted from the other end of the great hall. He closed his eyes, not needing to look to know the source: Karst. He took a deep breath before standing.

Karst was facing off across the table with a tall, fair-skinned man with a neatly-trimmed auburn beard. The man, though dressed in doublet and hose with the traditional clan sash running across his chest from left shoulder to right hip, was obviously a soldier: Lerryn could tell by his bearing and economy of movement. Karst was good with the sword, no doubt, but the boy just might have poured himself too strong a drink this time.

"Captain Martrin!" Orbrad shouted. "What is all of this? At my table, no less!"

"Forgive me, Your Majesty," Martrin said loudly, not taking his eyes from Karst. "Your young guest seems to have forgotten his manners."

"Must be catching," Nadrin mumbled.

"Do you accept or not?" Karst called. Around him, the dinner guests moved away from the pair. "Prove that I am as misguided as you say."

I ought to let him kill the boy and be done with it. Larris entertained the thought for only a fleeting moment. The prophecy would not permit it. They had to be six, and like it or not, Karst was one of them. He hurried to Karst's side, and grabbed the youth by the shoulder, yanking him away from the table.

"Captain Martrin, I apologize for the behavior of this young man. He is inexperienced at court. I would consider it a personal favor if you allow us to forget this unfortunate event entirely." It galled him to make nice in front of all these people, but he could not take the chance of losing Karst, and this Martrin fellow did not deserve to bear the brunt of the boy's foolishness.

The soldier continued to stare at Karst. "If he withdraws the challenge, Highness, I will not hold him to it. But only because it is you who asks."

"Withdraw the challenge," Lerryn said through gritted teeth.

"I will not."

Lerryn smacked him on the base of the skull with his open palm.

Karst turned and glared, rubbing the back of his head. "What did you do that for? I am within my rights." He drew back a step, but the look in his eyes was defiant.

Lerryn leaned toward him, his nose nearly touching Karst's. He whispered, in his iciest voice, "Withdraw it now." He tensed, waiting for an answer. It was reckless of him to give Karst such an order in this setting. What if the boy defied him in front of everyone? With any other person, it would have been unthinkable, but Karst was foolish enough to do it. What would he do? Kill the boy and bring the quest to an end? To the ice with Karst!

Karst glared for a moment longer, then turned back to face Martrin. He visibly gathered himself before speaking.

"Because my liege orders it, I withdraw my challenge."

Lerryn relaxed when he saw Martrin nod his acceptance. He did not think he'd ever heard so sour a voice, but the words were enough. He turned back to face the head of the table, where Orbrad stood, arms folded across his chest. Next to him, Nadrin stood grinning. Lerryn ignored the Kyrinian's amusement.

"Your Majesty, I apologize for disrupting your fine banquet. I regret that I must beg your leave to take my young charge back to our rooms for the evening. I thank you for the hospitality of your table." He bowed deeply. To his right, Karst grudgingly followed suit.

"We regret that His Highness must take his leave," Orbrad lied without conviction, bowing perfunctorily before motioning for everyone to take their seats. Stealing glances toward Lerryn and Karst, the dinner guests returned to their meals.

Lerryn shoved Karst toward the door. He turned and spotted Xaver rising to leave, and shook his head. Xaver frowned, then nodded and settled back into his chair. Perhaps he could glean some useful information. Lerryn was finished for the night. After he chastised Karst, he would return to his quarters and drink himself to sleep.

"Wake up Highness." Xaver hurried through the door, bumping against the frame as he entered. "We must leave."

"I'm awake." Lerryn slipped his feet off of the table, and sat up. The bottle of wine sat untouched in front of him. "What's the hurry?"

"The rumor I heard earlier. I believe the prophecy was trying to warn us of Orbrad's duplicity." He sat down across from Lerryn, noticed the full wine bottle, and raised his eyebrows before continuing. "Obviously, Nadrin has Orbrad's ear, and is trying to form an alliance against Galdora. Karst's very public scene could give Orbrad an excuse to arrest us."

"I interpret it differently," Lerryn said. "I think the prophecy was warning us that we would be arrested if Karst slew that Martrin fellow. Besides, if we were incarcerated, couldn't you do something?"

Xaver sighed and looked up at the ceiling. He laced his long, pale fingers together and rested them on his chest.

"I can do some small things, but neither magic nor sorcery is what it once was. The feats of the past are just that: in the past. Even in my lifetime I have felt the power, for lack of a better term, dwindle. I could open a cell, yes. Perhaps I could do away with a few guards. But get us out of a dungeon, through a palace, and out of a hostile city? That is beyond my capabilities."

"So you think we should go now?"

"Regrettably, yes. The banquet will be breaking up within the hour. The meal is over, but the wine is still flowing. I suggest that we gather the other four and go."

Lerryn stared at the ceiling, mulling over what Xaver had said. It was all so frustratingly nebulous, just like the prophecy. All he could do was go with his gut instinct.

"I won't run out like a beaten dog," he said finally. "I will not give Nadrin the satisfaction." He paused, waiting for Xaver to protest, but not a word came. That was a surprise. "Your advice is sound, but my instinct tells me to wait until morning, then move on. If we light out like thieves in the night, that will confirm in Orbrad's mind that our intentions are dishonorable."

"Very well. I can cast a ward on the door to our chambers. It will give us warning if someone comes for us during the night. For now, that is the most I can do."

"No arguments, Xaver? I expected at least a small objection or two."

Xaver rose from his chair and headed for the door. "No, Highness. I fear that when you are sober, you actually make sense from time-to-time." He twisted the corner of his mouth into an almost-smile, bowed, and slipped quietly from the room.

Lerryn looked at the closed door for a surprised moment, then smiled. "Don't grow accustomed to it."

Chapter 26

"Shanis, wake up."

The voice was so distant she could scarcely make it out. Dark. Everything was dark. She seemed to float, cold and sluggish in thick, black, air.

"Come now. Wake up."

Was that Larris? She felt pressure on her shoulder. Someone was shaking her. Slowly, consciousness clawed its way back to the fore. She was lying face down on the cave floor. Dust clung to her cheek, and her front felt like ice. She rolled onto her back, and opened her eyes. Larris was leaning over her, so close she could feel his breath on her cheek. Worry radiated from his deep, brown eyes. Over his shoulder, she saw Hierm looking equally concerned.

"Where's Allyn?" she mumbled.

"He's down with Oskar and Khalyndryn," Larris said. "Can you sit up?" He slipped a hand behind her, and gently helped her sit up. He was stronger than she had realized.

She looked around, and felt her body go cold. The cave was nothing like she remembered. The floor was dusty and uneven. The ceiling was low and jagged. There was no sign of Hyda. There was no fire, nor any remnants. Everything was different.

She rubbed her temples, squeezing her eyes closed. She opened them to find that things still had not returned to the way she had expected to find them. Had any of it even happened?

"I can stand," she said, though she was not certain of the veracity of that statement. She tried to get her feet under her, wobbled a bit, and felt Larris' arm around her waist. A moment later, Hierm was on her other side, clutching her right arm, trying to help support her. She waited for the ground to stop moving beneath her feet, then rose to her full height, banging her head on the low ceiling.

"Perhaps you should sit back down." Larris placed his other hand on her shoulder and tried to push her back down.

"I'll be fine. It's just that the ceiling wasn't this low when I came in earlier."

"What?" The prince frowned and cocked his head.

"Never mind. How did you find me?"

"We almost didn't. We looked up and down the pass for you. Finally, Khalyndryn spotted this cave. The light was such that it was almost invisible. Why did you climb up here, anyway?"

"I'll explain later." She turned to Hierm. "I'm surprised you were able to make the climb, what with your headache and all."

"Don't worry about me," Hierm mumbled, blushing and looking away.

So it was true. Her anger at him returned in a flash, searing the cobwebs from her mind. She was about to say something cruel when a thought struck her. Why was she so angry with him? He had always carried a torch for her, while she repaid him with friendship. Close friendship, but nothing more. What did she care what he did with other girls? She had much more in common with Allyn. The remnants of her upset crumbled to dust. Allyn had not been concerned enough about her to come up here looking for her. Even Larris had shown more concern than he had. She hated men!

"I feel well enough to climb back down," she announced. "Let's get moving."

The setting sun cast long shadows in the rocky gray landscape. They settled in for the night under a deep overhang about ten paces above the path. Toward the back, they found a small pool of water, a seep spring, Oskar had called it, which had collected in an indentation in the rock. After tending the horses, they secured them in a nearby patch of coarse grass and scrub fir trees. They settled in for the night around a tiny cook fire and dined on fruit and dried meat, courtesy of Horgris and his clan.

Larris amused them with a story about a one-armed juggler and a queen's chambermaid. Some parts were naughty enough to make even her blush, and she was grateful that no one could see her well in the dim firelight. She was surprised that a prince would know, much less tell, such a bawdy story. It was good to laugh together and forget the peril they had been in just days past.

"Quiet." Allyn whispered, raising his hands. "I hear something." He crawled to the ledge and looked back and forth. "It sounds like men; lots of them. Somewhere to the west."

"Oskar, douse the fire," Larris instructed. He picked up his bow and quiver, which lay nearby, and crept to Allyn's side. "Do you want me to go with you?"

Allyn shook his head. "I'll take Shanis. She moves quietly, and she's better with the bow."

"So you keep reminding me," Larris said. He sounded annoyed, but in the silver moonlight, Shanis saw a grin on the young man's face. He handed the bow and quiver to Shanis. "Leave your sword here. It will just get in the way."

She nodded, ducking her head down and slipping the strap of the quiver over her shoulder. She felt his hand on her arm, and she looked up.

"Be very careful," Larris said. "We lost you once today, and I didn't like it."

The warmth in his brown eyes disarmed her. When had he ceased to be annoying? She nodded, uncertain how to reply, and followed Allyn into the semi-darkness.

"Who are they?" Shanis whispered. They had gone west, following the same path on which they had been traveling earlier in the day, until it made a sharp turn to the south. There, the right side of the trail opened up into a sheer ledge, dropping down to another pathway about fifty paces below. A band of men, at least a hundred in all, garbed in a motley assortment of furs, leathers, and various mismatched bits of chain mail and armor plates, sat in small clusters. Some ate. Most sipped from wineskins and talked in loud voices. Some distance away from the group, and directly beneath Shanis and Allyn, three men who appeared to be in charge were engaged in an animated conversation.

"Mercenaries of some sort," Allyn whispered, his voice scarcely audible. "From where, I don't know." He turned an ear toward the men below them.

They lay face down on the trail, their heads hanging slightly over the ledge. In the faint light, there was little chance of them being spotted, provided they did not draw attention to themselves. Shanis strained to hear the snatches of conversation that drifted up to them.

"We need to stop fer' the night. We been walking since before first light." A skinny man with long, greasy hair and a wicked scar running down his right cheek stood with his thumbs hooked into his belt. "These men ain't the kind to be takin' much orders, anyhow."

"They will follow orders or they will die where they stand." The man who spoke was a tall, lean fellow. Everything about him, from the way he spoke to the way carried himself, spoke of grace and danger. Just looking at him gave Shanis a chill. He lowered his voice, his words sounding almost like a cat purring. "We have a rendezvous three days hence. I will not be late. Our master does not abide failure."

"Y'see, that's the whole problem there," the third man, a short, rat-faced fellow, spoke up. "None of us is the kind of men who hold to having a master. We's in this for the gold, which we ain't seen a spot of yet."

The tall man lashed out, cracking the speaker across the bridge of the nose with the back of his left fist. Rat Face dropped to his knees with a whimper, blood streaming between his fingers as he pressed his hands to his face. All heads turned toward the sound, turning away just as quickly. The scar-faced man took a step back, his mouth hanging slack-jawed.

"Give the order to march, and cut the throat of the first man who even so much as grumbles. You are men without a country. Were it not for the grace of the master, you would all be long dead, frozen in the mountain passes to which you were exiled. Betray him, and you die. But I promise you, the lands of the east are fat and lazy. Serve him faithfully, and you will have all the gold you desire."

Chapter 27

"You cannot abandon the quest." Allyn sat cross-legged in front of the fire they had rekindled. He and Shanis had waited until they were certain that the mercenaries were gone before reporting back to the others. "It is too important, and you've put too much of yourself into it to just pack up and go home."

"I have just learned that the lands of the east are imperiled by an army of unknown origin. I have a duty to my father and to my country to warn them of this danger. How can I ignore that? We must go back." Larris paced to and fro across the mouth of the sheltered overhang in which they were encamped.

Oskar lay on his side, propped up on an elbow, half-listening to the argument. In his mind, he replayed what Allyn and Shanis had told them, turning the information over, trying to make sense of it. The apparent leader, the one Shanis had said gave her the chills, had called the others "men without a country." The nations of the east had long held to a practice of banishing their most hardened criminals to the mountains to fend for themselves against wild animals, bitter winters, and other perils that some said existed only in grandmother's tales. It sounded to him as though someone had organized the survivors into some sort of raiding party. It wouldn't have been a difficult sell to convince such hard cases as these to plunder the very countries that had sent them away.

"What would you tell them?" Allyn's voice had lost some of its usual serenity. "That a hundred or so poorly-armed mercenaries, operating from an unknown location in the mountains are going to raid some town somewhere in the east? How does that information do anyone any good?"

"I believe you underestimate the threat, my friend. They were on their way to meet up with someone else. Obviously the group you saw was not their entire force." Larris held up his hand as Allyn opened his mouth to interrupt. "And the leader spoke of 'the lands of the east'. That sounds to me like a more grandiose plan than merely raiding a few villages."

"Let us say, for argument's sake, that you are correct," Allyn said. "The fact remains that we have nothing to tell, save a vague threat from a force of unknown size. Your father could not act upon what information we have, except to put his commanders on alert, which he has already done thanks to Kyrin." He stopped speaking, his eyes darting to Oskar, then back to Larris, who waved the comment away.

"It's all right," Larris said. "We haven't any secrets from them anymore."

Oskar doubted that, but it still felt good to hear. He cleared his throat, drawing everyone's attention to himself.

"It seems to me that, even if we did have information that was of some value, we would have a hard time getting back to Galdora at all, much less in time to tell anyone of the threat. Your brother is somewhere behind us. And don't forget that we're supposed to be in the dungeon in Karkwall right now. Martrin and Horgris only helped us because we were looking for the Silver Serpent. What will we say to Horgris when we come riding back into his camp after being gone only a few days? 'Sorry, we couldn't find it. Pass the ale?'"

Shanis chuckled and elbowed Hierm in the ribs. "I'll just bet you'd like to go back to Horgris' camp, wouldn't you?"

Hierm tensed for a moment. Then, seeing her smile, he relaxed. "Don't remind me," he said, an embarrassed grin on his face. "I never drank that much before and I don't intend to again."

"Don't be like that, friend Hierm," Allyn said. "Once Larris sees reason and we get back on our quest, I am sure we will find time to build up your tolerance of strong drink. Oh, don't look at me like that Larris," he said, staring up at the annoyed-looking young man. "You know that wherever you lead, I follow, but I believe Oskar is correct. Going back is not an option."

Larris sat down next to Shanis, on the side opposite Hierm. He laced his fingers together and hooked his hands behind his neck. He sat that way, staring at the fire.

"Truth be told, I am almost convinced that we should continue on our quest, but I don't feel right about it."

"I have a thought, if I may," Khalyndryn said in a soft, hesitating voice.

"That would be a first," Shanis jibed.

"Let us hear what she has to say," Larris said, grinning at Shanis' insult.

"What if you are right, and this is one small piece of a big army?" she said. "You told us that you must find the Silver Serpent in order to counter some unknown threat to the kingdom. What if this army is that threat? If we don't find it, do they win?"

Oskar smacked himself in the forehead, and turned to stare across the fire at Larris, who looked equally amazed. Everyone sat in silent amazement. Shanis was in such shock that Oskar believed he could knock her over with a stick.

"I'm sorry, was that a foolish idea?" Khalyndryn looked embarrassed that she had spoken up.

"Far from it," Larris said. "My dear, you have convinced me. In the morning, we move on. We must succeed in our quest. I truly believe that the fate of our kingdom rests on our shoulders."

Shanis hated drawing a middle watch; it always left her feeling groggy the next morning. She preferred waking up extra early for the last watch, rather than having her sleep broken into pieces. She drew her cloak tighter around her, and pulled her knees to her chest. The moon had long since departed, leaving only a faint glow above the dagger peaks of the surrounding mountains.

Hyda's words weighed heavy on her heart. Which of her companions could be a traitor? It was difficult to believe it of any of them. She evaluated each of them, trying to be objective.

Hierm? Two days before, she would have said "never", but now she was not so sure. She could not rid herself of the memory of her best friend vanishing into the hut with that *girl*. With a shake of the head, she rattled the thought out of her mind, but the bitterness remained. How could he have done that? Another thought occurred to her. Was it possible that the betrayal had already occurred? Could Hyda have been making reference to Hierm's betrayal of their friendship?

She dismissed the idea almost as soon as it entered her mind. The old woman had clearly indicated that the betrayal would take place in the future. Even more than that, she knew intuitively that it was wrong.

Besides, she wasn't being entirely fair to Hierm. Yes, she knew that he had feelings for her, but had she reciprocated those feelings? Not really. In fact, how did she feel about Hierm? Did she want anything more than friendship from him? Was it possible that she took some sort of perverse pleasure from the situation—enjoying the admiration, but keeping him at a safe distance? It couldn't be. Girls like Khalyndryn kept boys on a string, not her. Or did she? A weight hung like a stone in the pit of her stomach, and she hastily moved her thoughts along.

Oskar? Could he betray them? Objectively, she could imagine him getting swept up in the excitement of the adventure, and making an honest mistake. Shanis believed him to be naïve enough to allow himself to be manipulated under the right circumstances.

Larris was a possibility. His quest was of the utmost importance to him. Would he let anyone stand in the way? He was, after all, nobility, and nobles were not famous for caring one whit for regular folk. Then again, Larris had not thus far conformed to her notions of royalty. He did not treat the others as if he was their better. He also impressed Shanis as being an honorable person.

What about Allyn? He was an enigma: fiercely loyal to Larris, but in a manner that seemed to say that their relationship was one of near-equals. He did not, however, seem the sort to act completely independently.

She put off Khalyndryn until last. Though Shanis was convinced that Khalyndryn would not betray the group out of malice, the fact remained that the girl could be a fool at times. She was definitely the most vulnerable member of their little party. Would she be the one?

"Talking to yourself?" Oskar emerged from the darkness of the cave and sat down next to her. He reached over and laid a tentative hand on her shoulder. "Sorry if I'm disturbing you. I couldn't sleep." He stretched his legs out straight in front of him, toes pointed forward, arched his back, and groaned deeply. "Even with a blanket under you, the rocks just seem to suck the warmth right out of you."

"You don't have to tell me," Shanis said. "My backside feels like ice. Don't say anything." She frowned comically, then scooted up against him and laid her head on his shoulder. She felt his arm around her as he gave her a squeeze. If she ever had a brother, she would want him to be like Oskar.

"What happened in the cave?" His voice was nonchalant as he stared up at the sky. "You didn't tell us everything. I know you well enough to know that something is wrong." He let the statement hang there between them. Unusual, as Oskar was seldom comfortable with silence for any length of time.

She wanted to tell him, to unburden herself. But what if it had not really happened? Perhaps the fatigue and the strain had been too much, and the old woman and her prophecy had been a hallucination?

"There was a woman." The story poured forth despite her reservations. Hyda's advice that they must all remain together if they were to succeed. Her apparent distress at what she saw in her scrying. The exhortation that they, that she, must succeed. She held back the detail that one of her companions was untrue. It didn't seem right to burden Oskar with it. Even if he was not the one, he would drive himself mad with worry that it would be him. What was more, she could not see him keeping it to himself for long. If the group were to remain united through the quest, they could not afford the suspicion that such a revelation would raise.

Oskar just listened. When she had finished, he pulled her close, giving her a hard squeeze. "Did she say anything at all about what frightened her, or why it's so important that we succeed?"

"No. She was looking down into the bowl, and all of a sudden her eyes got big, and she looked like she had seen a ghost. She told me that we had to succeed, that I must hold fast."

"And then what?"

"And then I fell asleep, I guess." She wasn't sure she wanted to tell him this next bit. "When I woke up, everything was different. The cave was smaller, and it was empty. No fire, no old woman, nothing."

"Maybe she carried you to another cave," he said with little conviction.

"It was the only cave in that cliff face," she argued. "I wonder if I dreamed it all."

"You didn't dream it," he said. "I can tell by the way you're reacting just to the memory. It was real. It happened."

"So what do we do now?"

"The only thing we can do." He looked out at the dark sky. "We keep going."

Lerryn slept fitfully, his dreams confused and unsettling. In one, he was trapped at the bottom of a well, struggling to climb out, but his fingers could find no purchase on the slick, smooth stone, and he kept sliding back to the bottom. He was cold and soaked to the bone. Far above him, Orbrad, Nadrin, and Xaver laughed and poured wine down onto his head.

In another dream, one which he remembered with vivid clarity, he knelt before a small fire in a tiny cave as a shriveled old woman told his fortune. She gazed long into a smoking bowl of liquid, then raised her head and fixed him with dead eyes.

You know not where you go. Blind, you are. Blind. With that, she tipped the bowl into the fire. Sparks peppered his face, and thick white smoke burned his eyes and filled his nose. A scream filled his ears. It sounded like his own voice.

He sat up, gasping for air. He took a moment to orient himself to his surroundings, then slipped from his bed. Out of habit, he reached for the bottle of wine. The memory of the well dream still fresh in his mind, he drew his hand back, and moved to the window.

Leaning against the sill, he looked out over the fortified keep of Karkwall castle, and down at the sleeping city. Only the occasional flicker of light broke the perfect blanket of darkness. He thought he could see movement on one of the streets. His night vision had always been excellent.

"I am not blind," he whispered, "I just need to know where to go next." He looked up to the heavens, as if the answer lay there. A sparse array of stars was visible through the ever-present curtain of mist, and a hint of the new day glowed a faint gray upon the lip of the horizon. Like a beacon from the gods, a star suddenly caught fire and coursed across the sky, hurtling toward the morning light. It took only a moment for the firestar to burn away, ending its brief trek across the dome of the universe. But its fiery imprint was etched upon Lerryn's mind, and he had his answer. "We shall go east."

Chapter 28

The oppressive crush of the mountain peaks opened onto a lush, green valley. A precarious trail ran down the rocky slope, where it met a narrow dirt path. Shanis' eyes followed the dirt walk up a gentle slope to where it vanished among a cluster of small buildings. Most were small houses with stone foundations and wooden roofs. Some houses had small kitchen gardens, all healthy and heavy with produce. A few people moved about, busy with their daily regimen. It had been a week since they had seen other people and looking down upon the scene from afar gave her the disconcerting sense of being somehow removed from reality.

The village disappeared over a hill. In the distance beyond, the valley sloped upward again to meet the encircling arms of the mountain range. The peaks continued on as far as she could see. She sighed. So they wouldn't be leaving the mountains anytime soon. She heard bleating and looked down to see an old man walking behind four goats.

The man looked up at the same time, and stopped short. He stared, mouth hanging open. Finally, he spoke.

"Hello?" he squeaked. He raised his hand, palm open, in cautious greeting, then let it fall limp at his side. A short, wiry fellow, his gaunt face was partially obscured by a gray beard, peppered with bits of black. His hair he wore short and parted in the middle. He was garbed in deerskin leggings and tunic, and a homespun cloak dyed a hideous shade of red.

Shanis raised her hand, and was about to call down to him when she heard a light scraping of footfalls on stone. She glanced back to see Allyn coming up behind her.

"I didn't find anything down the path I scouted. I see you had better luck." His eyes took in the village. As he moved to her side, Shanis elbowed him and nodded down at the man who still stared up at them.

Nonplussed, Allyn greeted the man. "Good day to you sir! We are travelers seeking accommodations. Is there an inn about?"

"An inn?" He cackled, closing his eyes, head tossed back. "An inn!" The fellow collected himself, and opened his eyes. "We have no inn here, young sir, but we can find a place for you and your woman to stay." He motioned for them to come down.

"I'm not his woman," Shanis shouted. She immediately felt foolish. The man did not care what her relationship to Allyn was or was not.

He shrugged, as if confirming her thought. "We will feed you and give you a place to stay. Have you any wine?" His face took on an expression of childlike hopefulness.

"Our companions have wine. We will be glad to share it with you." Allyn said.

"Oh no!" he said. "We must trade. We must trade." He made a strange crossing motion with his hands. "Come down, bring your companions, and we will trade with them."

Shanis found herself wanting to be anywhere but with this strange, manic little man. Something about him made her feel very uncomfortable. Perhaps it was his odd voice or his eccentric manner. Either way, he and his village suddenly seemed very sinister.

"Let's not go down there," she said softly, her mouth frozen in a false smile. "Just ask for directions, or something."

"No," Allyn said. "We need vegetables, fruit if they have any. We need to sleep in a warm, dry place for at least one night. Why would you not want to go?" His brow furrowed and he cocked his head as he looked at her.

"I don't know." The feeling of discomfort was gone. She looked down upon the little goat herder, still gazing innocently up at them, his head tilted to the side like a puppy, and wondered why he had given her a moment's pause. In this desolate place, he might never have seen an outsider. Perhaps fatigue was clouding her judgment. "Don't mind me."

Allyn nodded and turned back to the little man. "What is this place?"

"It is called Thandryll."

The knock came again. Oskar rolled over onto his stomach, and raised his head. Foggy, his awareness returned slowly. He felt as if he had slept for weeks. He looked down and was surprised to find that he was lying on a bed. After all these weeks of sleeping on the ground, a real bed. He sighed contentedly and flopped back into the straw tick mattress, closing his eyes.

This time the knock was accompanied by a shout. "Oskar! Time to wake up."

He heard the sound of a door scraping across the floorboards, light footfalls, then he felt the covers stripped off of him. He groaned, turned his head, and opened his eyes. Allyn leaned over him, grinning.

"Is the roof afire?" Oskar grumbled. Allyn frowned and shook his head. "Then there's no need for me to get up."

"Fine by me," Allyn said, "but you'll miss the feast."

That got Oskar's attention. He sat up too fast, and his head swam. He squeezed his eyes closed and pressed his hands to his temples. "How long have I been asleep?"

"Since we arrived this morning. I fear your snoring will become part of the local folklore when we leave. People kept coming to the window to listen."

"So what is this place like?" As the cobwebs of sleepiness were cleared away, he recalled their arrival in the small village. The villagers crowded around them, all of them small and pale, talking in strange, high-pitched voices. They spoke the same language as Oskar and his friends, but in a stiff, almost formal manner. Even in the short walk through the village, he noticed that sometimes, in place of words, they communicated with strange, hooting sounds. The experience was so surreal as to contribute to his sense of tired confusion.

"It is all right," Allyn said, sitting down on the bed. "The people have an odd manner of speaking, and they insist on 'trading' with us, whatever that means to them. Larris has been meeting with the leader of their village, trying to understand something of their customs. We don't want to offend them if we can help it."

"In that case," Oskar said as his stomach growled, "we don't want to offend them by showing up late for the meal."

Allyn led him to a large, low-lying, round structure at the end of the village. The walls, built stockade-style with vertical logs, were only shoulder high, surmounted by a humped thatch roof. Smoke rose from a hole in the center. They arrived at a small, square door. Allyn drew back the hide draped over the entryway, and motioned for him to enter.

Oskar froze as he stepped inside. The floor sloped downward at a sharp angle, gradually smoothing out into a broad, shallow depression, more than fifty paces across. The floor was covered with furs, and people were seated all around, eating, drinking, and quietly conversing. Near the fire in the room's center, a scrawny man beat out a gentle rhythm on a small drum. In the sparse firelight he could just make out his friends sitting in a cluster near the fireplace along with a local man and woman.

He took his time weaving between the clusters of people. His mother had always said he had all the grace of a drunken bull. Fatigue and inadequate light did not help matters. As he picked his way through, he realized that people were staring at him, and whispering. It's my imagination, he thought, but the deeper he went into the room, the more obvious it became. Some folks were actually gawking. Joining the others, he sank to the floor next to Hierm, who was chewing on a generous hunk of deer meat on a skewer. Allyn took a seat to Oskar's right, next to the villagers.

"Why are people staring at me?" he asked the others. "Did they do that to any you?"

"You must forgive us, I pray," the man seated next to Larris said, leaning forward and fixing Oskar with an overeager smile. "We have never seen anyone as large as you before. All of you are taller than anyone in our village, but you are...."

"Large." Oskar completed the sentence for him as he reached for a chunk of meat from the platter of meat, vegetables, cheese, and bread that sat on the floor in the midst of the group. "Do you not have many travelers pass this way?" A slip of a girl dressed in a loose-fitting homespun robe belted with a strip of rawhide knelt down beside him and held out a bottle of wine and an empty cup. Oskar took the bottle from her and turned back to the conversation.

"You are the third to visit us in my lifetime. The others were wanderers. Half-mad mountain men, to be perfectly frank."

Seated next to the speaker, Larris nodded knowingly. Apparently they had already had this discussion. "This place is quite far from civilization," the prince said.

"I suppose." The man shrugged, taking a sip of his wine.

Oskar took a long pull from his bottle. The wine was sour and weak, but it had a hint of some unusual flavor, like green apples. He swished the drink around his mouth and mulled over the idea of living somewhere so remote that you were virtually cut off from the rest of the world. He swallowed, the wine stinging his throat as it went down.

"Oskar, this is Malram, the chief councilor of Thandryll." Larris indicated the man with whom Oskar had been talking. "And this is his wife Ramilla."

Ramilla was a tiny, kind-faced woman with gray-streaked light brown hair, which she wore in a bun. She nodded politely when Larris introduced her. Her husband's hair was of similar color, and he wore it in a ponytail. His neatly-trimmed beard was generously sprinkled with gray.

Oskar felt a soft touch on his shoulder. He jerked his head to the side and was startled to see that the young girl who had brought his wine was stroking his arm. His first instinct was to jerk away, but he did not want to seem rude. Also, seated at close quarters as they were, he couldn't have moved very far in any event. He looked at her face, eyes glistening with...he didn't know what. Some sort of worship, he supposed. No girl had ever looked at him that way. In his fantasies, it had felt a great deal more comfortable than he felt right now. Besides, she was so young.

"I see my wife fancies you," Malram said with a smile.

"Your wife?" Khalyndryn, seated next to Larris, leaned across the prince to speak to the councilor. "I thought Ramilla was your wife."

"I have four wives. Some have more, but I fear I am too old to be, shall we say, a satisfactory husband to any more. Lilan is the youngest of my wives. I fear her needs are quite great." He smiled indulgently at the little girl the way a man would smile at a favorite dog.

"You are very strong," Lilan said in a high, almost birdlike voice. She squeezed his arm and her smile grew wider.

If anyone in Oskar's party was as taken aback as he was, they didn't say so. He shook his head. This was crazy.

"Isn't she awfully young to be married?" Shanis asked.

"I am seventeen winters this turn," the girl said. "I hope to give my husband a child soon."

Shanis screwed her mouth into a grimace. Appearances notwithstanding, she and Lilan were the same age. Doubtless, Shanis was trying not to imagine having a husband and children.

Oskar grinned at his friend's discomfort. Lilan, mistaking his smile for encouragement, pressed her body against him, and laid her head on his shoulder.

"A new baby would truly be a blessing to our community," Malram said. "Perhaps our new friend could help us in that respect? He is obviously of solid stock."

Oskar coughed and held a fist to his mouth, hoping to hide his blushing. He had read about such a thing once, but thought it little more than a fanciful legend. This man truly wanted him to get a child on his wife? Surely this was some elaborate joke that the fellow had conspired with his friends to play at his expense.

"If not Oskar, perhaps Hierm could oblige you," Allyn said, his voice dry, and his eyes dull over the top of his upraised wine cup.

For an instant, Oskar thought Hierm was going to jump on Allyn, but he merely smirked and stared intently at the fire in the center of the room. Next to him, Shanis cleared her throat and frowned at Allyn. This was a change. Apparently, Shanis was the only one permitted to needle Hierm about his indiscretion back at Horgris' camp.

"If I have given offense in some way, friend Oskar, please accept my apology." Malram formed a diamond shape with his thumbs and index fingers, and bowed, touching the tips of his fingers to his forehead.

"No offense was taken, I assure you," Larris said, covering for Oskar's obvious disconcertment. "Being married to more than one woman is not something that is part of our culture. We are simply unaccustomed to it."

"It is of necessity, truly," Malram said. "We have many more women than men. Being isolated as we are, it is not as if we can marry off our young women to men of other villages. And if we do not reproduce," he held his hands open, palms up, and shrugged.

Oskar was about to ask about the dearth of males in the village, but Khalyndryn spoke first.

"Where are the old people?" she asked.

"I beg your pardon?" Malram said. He had an odd look on his face, as if he had been affronted in some way. Next to him, his wife Ramilla stared down into her wine cup, looking sick.

"Men aren't the only thing you don't have many of," she said. She swept her hand in a circle. "Look around. You are one of the oldest people in this room. Where are your elders?"

"Khalyndryn," Larris said carefully, "perhaps that is not a subject that is proper for us to discuss. We are outsiders."

"It is all right." Malram had regained his serenity. "Life is difficult here. The winters are long and bitter. The growing season is short. Food is always scarce. Sadly, our life expectancy is obviously much shorter than that to which you are accustomed."

"I am sorry. I did not intend to bring up such a painful subject." Khalyndryn actually looked sincere. She reached across Larris' lap and laid a hand on Malram's arm.

"Your apologies are unnecessary, I assure you. You are correct that I am one of the oldest in our village. I sometimes wonder how many more winters I will see. It is a difficult thing to reflect upon one's mortality." He stared despondently down at the ground for the briefest of moments, then looked up, forcing a smile. "Enough somber talk." He stood, and clapped his hands three times. The soft murmur of voices faded away, and he moved to the fireside to address the crowd.

"My friends, it is our privilege to welcome our esteemed guests to Thandryll." He motioned for them to rise, then bowed deeply. They were greeted not by polite applause, but by odd hooting sounds, as if a flock of owls had settled in the rafters. "Let us entertain them with words and music."

The drummer, who had been tapping out a gentle rhythm while they ate, accelerated his pace, striking a primal beat. Everyone clapped along, and Oskar found himself tapping his foot in time to the music. Many of the young girls moved to the center of the room, and began whirling about the fire. They spun one way, then the other, arms outstretched, heads thrown back so that their unbound hair flew about them. At various places around the room, young men stood and stomped out a muted back beat on the earthen floor. One by one, more girls joined the circle until the area around the fire became so full that Oskar wondered how they avoided crashing into one another. Lilan's gaze flashed from the dancers to Oskar, then back to the dancers. With a flash of regret on her face, she rose to her feet and joined the other girls around the fire.

Despite the raucous atmosphere, Oskar noted with interest that the girls' faces remained solemn as they danced. Lilan turned round and round, like the others her head was thrown so far back that he could see her serious expression and closed eyes. The way she held her arms out, her throat exposed, reminded him of a sacrifice. A vision came to him unbidden of her lying spread-eagle on a stone altar, a knife held above her throat by an unseen hand. The image settled onto him like a dark cloud, and he turned his thoughts and his gaze to his bottle of wine.

"Are you going to share any of that?" Shanis asked, holding out a cup. Her back remained turned toward the dancers. Such things had never been of much interest to her.

"Why don't you join in the dancing?" Oskar poured generously, laughing at the sour expression on her face.

"Tell you what," Shanis said, ignoring her wine. "I will take that challenge if you'll take Lilan up on her offer."

Oskar choked on the sour wine, and spat it on the ground. "What are you talking about? I barely know her." He wiped his mouth with the back of his sleeve.

The others made no attempt to conceal their amusement.

"She is a lovely girl, Oskar," Allyn said, laying a hand on his shoulder. "In any event, perhaps it is time you became a man."

Larris had the grace to shake his head at Allyn, but Oskar could see the twinkle in the young prince's eyes. Hierm was keeping quiet, while Khalyndryn was doing her best to look offended, but Oskar could see the amusement in her eyes as well. Become a man. Who was Allyn to say that he was not a man? He was tired of being laughed at. Everyone complimented him for his knowledge, yet treated him like a fool. It's because I'm big. If I were some slender, pasty-faced fellow, they'd treat me like I knew something. I'm tired of being mocked.

"How do you know I'm not already a man?" He regretted the comment almost immediately. Rather than shocking or silencing the others, it made them laugh aloud. All of them. He looked down at his wine cup and tried to pretend that his face was not burning. "I'm just saying you don't know," he muttered.

He was spared Allyn's reply when Malram stood and clapped his hands thrice again. The sharp, staccato sound caught everyone's attention. The drumming and dancing ceased, and the hooting started up again. Malram raised his hands and looked around the room, waiting for quiet.

"My friends," he said, as the sounds faded away, "may we enjoy the words of Barthomes." The hooting erupted again, filling the domed gathering place with its otherworldly sound. A tiny man stood and daintily picked his path to where Malram stood. They greeted one another by making the odd triangular shape on their foreheads, and bowing.

Barthomes' hair was snow white, but otherwise he appeared to be several winters younger than Malram. He stretched his hand out in a grand, sweeping gesture, and the room fell silent as frozen night.

"And how shall I entertain our guests this evening?" he asked the room. His voice was deep and rich. Oskar wondered at the plotting of the Gods, that such a small body should contain so large a voice. "A poem, perhaps? A story from ages ago?"

"Raw Bruce!" someone shouted, eliciting more hoots.

"Yes!" another cried. The hooting started up, but was quickly overwhelmed by eerie chants of "Raw Bruce! Raw Bruce!"

Oskar looked around the room, and was frightened by what he saw. The looks on the local's faces could only be described as zealous. This must be quite a story, he thought. The whispered chant, the semi-darkness, and the wine he had drunk gave the scene a surreal air. He glanced at Shanis, and was not altogether pleased to see that she too appeared uncomfortable.

"Very well," Barthomes replied. "Raw Bruce it shall be." He lowered his head, his hands together in a gesture like supplication. He stood there for so long that Oskar was wondering if the man had forgotten the words. But finally he lifted his head and stared not so much at, but through the audience. His face had taken on a wooden quality, as if it were a mask, hiding something sinister. He opened his mouth, and the words flowed forth in a rich cadence that seemed almost ritualistic in its ebb and flow.

"We live our days like dying flame,
but none will remember our name,

lest we rise up and defeat fate,
and become one anointed great.
So open your ears.
My tongue I will loose.
As I tell you the tale
of the brave man Raw Bruce."

The chanting resumed. "Raw Bruce! Raw Bruce! Raw Bruce!" It ceased, as if on cue, as Barthomes began the next stanza.

"All vested in green his warriors they came.
But our brave Raw Bruce had no thought of fame.
For down from the hills, and cold mountain peaks,
came minions of ice. Midst their angry shrieks,
Raw Bruce he did turn, and urge his men on,
knowing full well they would not see the dawn."

He spread his arms and lowered his head again. This time, there was no chanting. Everyone waited, anticipating the rest of the story.

He is quite the showman, Oskar thought. The others in his party were as enraptured as he, wondering how the story would end. They all gazed intently at Barthomes, their wine forgotten. Even Khalyndryn, who rarely showed interest in old tales, was paying attention.

The story continued, and Oskar was spellbound. The beauty of Barthomes' voice, and the hypnotic cadence of his retelling captivated the audience. Oskar listened eagerly as Raw Bruce led his forces in a reckless charge into the left flank of the Ice King's army. The creatures of ice, and coldheart soldiers were caught off-guard by the aggressive tactic, and Raw Bruce's charge ripped through their lines. Not slowing, they fought their way through the reserve forces, paying a dear price. Raw Bruce himself led the way. The powerful warrior, half again taller and broader of shoulder than his biggest soldier, fought with a broadsword in each hand, and cold blood flew wherever he led. Oskar supposed the man's size, and perhaps his prowess had been exaggerated over time, but the thought was merely a minor one in the back of his consciousness, and did not detract from the tale.

Raw Bruce and his men fled into a narrow pass, leaving behind one of every three men lying dead or wounded on the field of battle. Their enemies, surprised by the fury of Raw Bruce's attack, were slow to pursue. Just over a rise and around a bend in the pass, the heroic leader placed himself and a company of his most loyal foot soldiers directly in the path of the assault. The remainder of his forces he sent up onto the ridges on either side. Moving with haste, they got into position before the bulk of the Ice King's forces engaged them.

Bravely, Raw Bruce and his finest held the line in ferocious hand-to-hand, and hand-to-claw combat, standing against overwhelming odds until all of the forces of ice were backed up in the pass. That was when the archers opened up from above, raining death upon the coldhearts and ice beasts. Other soldiers hurled boulders and logs down onto their enemies. The ice creatures tried to climb the walls, but were summarily brought down by the arrow fire that raked the sheer stone walls. As the rear elements of the Ice King's army faltered, Raw Bruce and his men fell back. The front ranks, now reduced to the wildest and most ferocious of the coldheart warriors, charged recklessly after them, to be met by the cavalry Raw Bruce had held in reserve just out of sight. Their resolve broken, the minions of ice fled from the pass, harried by the cavalry and peppered by missile fire all the way out. They poured out through the valley, their numbers reduced by more than half, and scattered into the mountains.

> *"And so, my dear friends, this story now ends,*
> *but remember you ev'ry word.*
> *His men he did save, for Raw Bruce was brave,*
> *and cunning as the fox on his standard."*

Oskar frowned. Suddenly, the tale sounded familiar, as if he had heard it long ago. What was it that caught his attention?

> *"And remember with pride, that here many men died,*
> *their blood crimson on the green grass.*
> *For our homes we have wrought, on the site where they fought,*
> *in the shadow of brave Raw Bruce Pass."*

Oskar's stomach lurched, and he staggered to his feet, scarcely hearing the hoots of approval raining down upon Barthomes. He felt cold inside, but he trembled with excitement. His head was dizzy with the thrill of discovery, a feeling he had not felt since he had learned that he possessed the map to the lost city of Murantha. He had to be right!

"Are you all right?" Larris asked. He clambered to his feet and grabbed hold of Oskar's arm, as if to steady him.

"I'm fine," Oskar said. He was surprised that Larris had not made the connection. Perhaps the prince had imbibed a bit too heavily. "Come outside with me for a moment. I want to talk with you."

Larris frowned, looking Oskar in the eye. With a shrug, he turned to Malram, who made his strange, fingers-in-a-diamond bow, and indicated that the two might take their leave.

Outside, Larris stepped in front of Oskar and grabbed his shoulders. "What is this about? Are you ill? Is it Allyn? He doesn't mean anything by his jests. He is just so dry that people take him the wrong way. What are you looking at?"

Oskar drew away from Larris, and turned slowly about, admiring how the setting sun shone golden on the knife tips of the mountain peaks. This had to be the place!

"I'm marveling at how the setting sun makes the peaks encircling the valley look like a golden crown." He paused, waiting for Larris to react. It was only a moment.

"A golden crown. Raw Bruce. Robrus. Oskar, this is it. You did it again." He wrapped an arm around Oskar's neck and jumped up and down. "I was so discouraged, so distracted by the army we saw, it did not even occur to me." He laughed.

"Stories change over time," he said, his words coming faster, "and so do names. Barthomes' account of the battle is the reverse of how I have always read it, though his version makes more sense. The valley. Robrus' Pass. These are the descendants of those soldiers. They've been cut off for so long from the rest of the world for generations. That is why they seem so small, so unhealthy. No wonder Malram wanted you to mate with Lilan. A robust fellow like yourself would add strong blood to their lines. Oskar, how did I not realize it?"

"It was not until he mentioned the fox standard that I connected the two stories," Oskar explained. "Then he said 'Raw Bruce's Pass', and it sounded so much like Robrus' Pass that I knew it had to be true." He realized, as he stared at the overjoyed Larris, that his feelings of resentment had abated. Some might think him a great oaf, but he knew better. Twice now, he had come through. He just stood there for a moment, enjoying the heady feeling of vindication, but eagerness to explore quickly got the better of him. "Should we tell the others?"

"Not yet. Let's find the pass first, just to be certain. It must be on the far end of the valley, over that rise."

Chapter 29

After stopping for Larris to retrieve his sword, and Oskar his staff, they hastened through the deserted village. Oskar wanted to bounce like a little boy at play. Pride swelled within him so strong he felt he would rupture. Not only was he along on a grand adventure, he was a real part of it. Not just some tagger-along.

They moved quickly through the deserted village. Everyone had apparently gone to the gathering. The clustered houses gave way to a gently sloping field, beyond which the mountains closed in. Cresting the hill, they scanned the rocky slopes until Larris spotted something.

"Over there." He indicated a place where the shadows deepened from gray to black. As they approached, it resolved into a narrow crevasse, sloping upward. Without hesitation, they headed in.

The sharp rock dug into the soles of his boots as he clambered over the rubble from erosion and rockslides that cluttered the path. He laid his hand against the cold, firmness of the stone that walled them in. He imagined he could actually feel that ancient strength of the mountains. How much had these fractured old stones seen?

Side-by-side they picked their way up the gentle slope. Cresting the rise, they looked out upon the beauty of the mountain peaks, aglow in the shimmering light of the cradle moon. Oskar held his breath, awestruck by the spectacle. The mountains before them were not as tall as the ones through which they had come. There was no sign of snow on any of them. Everything seemed to slope downward from here. It was as if he was standing on the highest spot in the world.

"We're on the divide," Larris said, his voice made soft by the wonderment which mirrored that which Oskar felt. "You know what lies beyond those peaks?"

"The Lands West," Oskar breathed. "Wild men, barren wastes, and parched deserts. Do you know anyone who has been there?"

"No," Larris replied, still gazing ahead. "A lord from the eastern part of the kingdom tried it once. I fear he had more gold than sense."

"Does that not go without saying when speaking of a noble?" Oskar jibed.

Larris gave him a withering stare before continuing. "At any rate, he came to court with some outlandish story about black gold, and petitioned my father to finance his expedition. My father refused, of course. Somehow, the fool raised enough to buy and crew three ships. He set sail for the Boot."

Oskar shook his head. The very idea of sailing around the Boot! "I suppose he was never heard from again."

Larris' grin was all the answer he needed.

"Did you hear something?" Larris cocked his head and turned an ear toward the pathway.

Oskar strained to listen. A whisper of wind, the rustle of scrub brush, and then the distinctive clink of metal on stone. He tightened his grip on his staff and looked around. He saw nothing.

Larris eased his sword from its scabbard. Holding it at the ready, he crept forward. Oskar followed, hoping he would not stumble. His father had always called him "Oxfoot" for his clumsiness.

The sound came again, sharp in the stillness of the evening, this time followed by an odd, groaning sound. Oskar's first thought, though, was of the ice cats, as if one might be wearing armor or carrying a sword. He chastised himself and focused on picking his way quietly across the broken rocks, ignoring the tightness in his throat and the cool sweat that was beading on the back of his neck.

A few paces down the slope the pathway made a hard bend to the left. Larris pressed his back against the inner wall, scooted up to the bend, and peered around.

Oskar could barely see his friend in the deepening shadows. He moved cautiously up behind Larris, resisting the urge to ask him what he saw. He did not have to wait long.

After only a moment's pause, Larris stepped around the corner, motioning for Oskar to follow. Rounding the corner, he saw a man lying chained to a wide, flat rock in the center of the path. They moved to either side of him.

The fellow was obviously one of the villagers. He had the look about him, and was garbed in the same fashion as the others they had met. His graying hair and beard told him to be of late middle-years. Sweat beaded on his forehead, his eyes were open wide, and his breath came in gasps.

"Are you hurt?" Oskar asked, not knowing what to say. The man shook his head and continued his labored breathing. "We'll get you out of here." He glanced up to see Larris examining the shackle that bound one of the man's wrists, and shaking his head.

"You," the man gasped, "you must go." He swallowed loudly, and took a deep breath. "Golorak. He comes. You must go!"

"What is a golorak?" Larris asked, leaning over the captive.

"Golorak! You must go now!"

Oskar opened his mouth to speak, but a scratching sound drew his attention. He turned to see a bizarre shape appear in the dim light. It was the height of a draft horse, and three times the breadth at the chest. Moonlight glowed faint off the scaly hide covering its muscular form. Its shape was vaguely like that of a bull, but sleeker, with massive hind legs and a long, thick tail. Shadows rippled across its powerful haunches, and the long, sharp claws that tipped all four feet shone like daggers. The beast had no visible neck. Its wide head and bulging eyes reminded Oskar of a frog. Its gaze locked upon them, and it hissed angrily, opening its mouth to reveal rows of razor teeth.

Oskar could not move, could not breathe. Twice now, he had encountered ice cats. In both cases, the attacks had come swiftly, and ended just as fast. There had been no time to be afraid. Now, the golorak's measured approach froze his very soul.

Larris raised his sword and took a step backward. "Oskar," he said softly. "Run. Don't look back."

"I don't think I can." Oskar said truthfully. His eyes remained locked on the golorak. He had no doubt that the creature would catch him before he had run twenty paces.

"You must finish it, Oskar," Larris said firmly. "Finish the quest. You can do it. Run back to the village. I'll slow it down as much as I can."

The full realization of what he was saying struck Oskar like a hammer. He took an involuntary step backward, more out of surprise than any desire to flee. "No. I won't do it."

"One of us has to live, Oskar. They can't do it without at least one of us. They don't have the knowledge." Without warning, Larris darted toward the beast, his sword raised, his defiant roar rising above the terrified shrieks of the chained man.

Oskar tried to run, but he could not take his eyes away from the scene before him. The golorak paused only a moment before charging. Larris darted to his left, just avoiding the wicked claws. He struck hard with his sword, slicing the beast across the haunch, but his blade had no visible effect. The golorak hissed, whirled and charged again. Larris' blade bounced off the beast's hide, and its claws slashed his shoulder. He cried out in pain, but gritted his teeth and kept his sword in front of him.

Oskar had never felt so powerless. The staff in his hands would be useless, and Larris would never survive long enough for him to go for help. In fact, it was highly doubtful that Larris could last long enough for him to escape with his life. In that moment, there was nothing more he wanted than to save his friend. Everything he had ever wished for, all his hopes and dreams fell away. He stood alone with his own complete and utter helplessness, and his all-consuming need. He was nothing. He surrendered.

An icy fire swept through him. His body seemed to draw it in from all around him. Up from the ground it raged. His skin seemed to absorb it from the very air. It roiled through him, up through his legs, down his arms, and whirling in the center of his chest.

Something leapt forth from within him. He grunted as a blinding white light shot forth from his extended fist that still clenched his staff out in front of him. The beam struck the golorak in mid-leap, ripping through it at an angle from behind its left shoulder. The creature uttered nary a sound as its head and leg were severed from its body, the remains falling heavily at Larris' feet. The prince stared blankly at the lifeless form, blood soaking his sleeve, his sword still held aloft.

Oskar's body tingled all over, but all strength had left him. His legs were like water. He dropped limply to his knees, and knelt there, staring straight ahead.

"What happened?" Larris asked, looking at Oskar with a baffled expression.

Oskar did not know precisely what had happened. Whatever it was, he wasn't ready to share it. "It was lightning," he said, hoping Larris would take the uncertainty in his voice for shock or weariness.

"Lightning," Larris echoed, looking up at the cloudless sky. "Amazing."

"It was, Master," the man on the rocks groaned, straining to rise. "I seen it. A flash of white light. Cut the golorak clean in two. Nothing can harm the golorak."

"Something or someone must be looking out for us," Larris said, though the flat tone of his voice indicated that he did not believe it. His eyes vainly scanned the surrounding cliffs, as if he could see anything in the impending darkness. "At any rate, we must get you off of this rock, assuming you have no further objections.

"No, Master, I do not object."

"Who are you and why are you chained to this rock?"

"I'm Kelrom. The golorak, it feeds on, rather fed on us. Every new moon, we gave a sacrifice, and it lets the village be."

"I see," Larris replied sardonically. "I suppose that explains the lack of elders in your village."

"And the lack of men," Oskar said, using his staff to help himself to his feet. "One man can impregnate several women. As long as they keep a few healthy young men, they can maintain their population. It must be how they survived with so few resources." The shock of whatever it was he had just done was forgotten as he fit the pieces of the puzzle together. "The infirm, the weak, likely even anyone with a serious injury, anyone expendable.

Kelrom nodded. "You have the right of it, young sir. We knew not what else to do. It is the way it has always been done."

"I cannot even begin to fathom it," Larris said. "I assume there is someone in the village who can unlock these?"

The sound of voices reverberated down the passageway, along with that of feet scrabbling on loose rock. "Here they come," Oskar said, looking back.

Soon, torchlight flickered on the walls of the passage. Allyn and Shanis appeared at the head of a column of villagers. Shanis ran to Oskar's side.

"What happened to the two of you? You disappear, and then next thing we know, someone comes rushing in telling us there's some strange light up on the hill." She paused, noticing Larris' injury. "What happened?"

"It looks worse than it is," Larris said.

Shanis frowned, but before she could argue with him, she caught sight of Kelrom. "Who is that?"

"It's a long story," Oskar said. He had not regained his strength, and he was feeling woozy. He placed a hand on Shanis' shoulder to steady himself. She touched a warm, dry palm to his forehead.

"You're all clammy." She took hold of his hand. "Oskar, you're like ice. Are you hurt too?"

Oskar put his hand to his head and leaned against his staff, trying to explain what happened. Where should he begin? Should he tell her about…whatever it was he had done?

"The golorak!" Someone shouted. "They have slain the golorak. Kelrom is still alive!"

A woman shrieked and fell to her knees, covering her eyes. Others groaned, or cried out. It almost seemed as if they were somehow angry.

Larris and Allyn appeared at their side, along with Malram. The villager wore a tight-lipped frown.

"I do not understand what has happened here," he said.

Larris quickly recounted how they had found Kelrom, then were attacked. He did not offer any explanation as to how they had slain the golorak, but Malram did not let the omission pass.

"But how did you slay the golorak? No weapon can pierce its hide. Our ancestors tried."

"Lightning struck it," Oskar said.

"Lightning?" Malram looked up at the clear sky, just as Larris had done. "I suppose that would explain the bright light Lilan saw when she went out looking for you." He looked directly at Oskar as he said the last.

"That was no lightning I saw," Lilan piped up from behind her husband. "The light came up from behind the hills. It was the brightest I have ever seen."

"I only saw a flash of light. My attention was on the beast that was about to kill me," Larris said, turning to cock an eyebrow at Oskar. The others followed suit.

"If it wasn't lightning, then I have no idea what it was," Oskar said. There was an element of truth to his statement. He had no idea what the light was. That it somehow came from him was not a detail he intended to share.

"They called down lightning on it," someone in the crowd murmured. The villagers who had followed Malram gravitated toward the remains of the beast that had held them in terror for countless grandfathers past. Slowly, curiosity overcame fear, and soon they were huddled around the remains of the golorak.

"What about Kelrom?" Oskar asked, embarrassed that he had forgotten the poor fellow.

"Ah, yes." Malram appeared uncertain what to do.

"For the god's sake, let the man loose!" Shanis scolded. "There's no monster anymore." She spoke slowly and loudly as if she were speaking to someone thick-skulled and hard of hearing. "You no longer have to feed your people to it."

"I beg your pardon," Malram replied tersely, the glare in his eyes belying his apology. "This is all a shock to me. If you will now excuse me." He turned and stalked over to the sacrificial stone. Fishing a key from inside his robe, he freed Kelrom, who sat up slowly and began rubbing his wrists.

Oskar still felt wrung-out, but he wanted a closer look at the creature that had nearly claimed their lives. Still using his staff for support, he picked his way over to the crowd that encircled the beast. They gave way, awestruck by the slayers of their nemesis.

He knelt down alongside the bulk of the creature. Full night was upon them, but the moonlight and torchlight blended to cast the creature in a wavering golden light. He lay a hand on the smooth, reptilian scales. Unlike the ice cats, it was not cold to the touch, though the warmth of its body was scant. His eyes moved to the wound in front of the shoulder, where the lightning, or whatever it had been, had sliced through the golorak. He sucked in his breath at the sight. It was cut through as cleanly as a baker would slice a loaf of bread. *What did I do?*

A chill breeze swept through the assembled group. He rose and shrugged his cloak up around his shoulders. Larris, Hierm, Allyn and Shanis were engaged nearby in quiet conversation.

"Where's Khalyndryn?" he asked, sidling up alongside Allyn.

"Left her in the village," Shanis replied, her expression unreadable. "Larris was just telling us how the two of you came to be out here in the first place."

"I should like to hear that explanation as well." Malram stood with his arms folded across his chest. The other villagers were clustered behind him, most staring with expressions of disapproval or outright anger.

"Why are you looking at us like that?" Shanis snapped, stepping toward the group. "You live in this valley, feeding your people to this creature. Now it's dead, and you're angry with us?" Larris grabbed her forearm, but she pulled away. "No! I've been chased from my home, attacked by the gods-only-know-what kind of monsters, been thrown into a dungeon. I'll take no more!" She stalked toward the knot of villagers, her eyes wide with anger. Oskar had seen that look before, and he feared for Malram.

Shanis stood nose-to-forehead with the village leader and poked a finger into his chest. "You will take a civil tone with us," she said, her voice icy calm. "We will not be interfered with, nor will we abide another moment of your sour looks and suspicious questions. You owe us a debt of gratitude. Do you understand?" The last came out as little more than a whisper, but it was clearly audible in the stillness.

The villagers fell back a pace, but to Oskar's surprise, Malram did not back down. He met her stare, his mouth working, but producing no sound. Oskar's heart was racing, and he counted twenty beats as he waited for one of them to break the silence. He was not afraid. He and his companions could dispatch these frail little people with ease. Freeze me! What am I thinking? He turned to Larris and gestured for the prince to do something, but he hesitated before stepping in.

"Master Malram, it was not our intention to abuse your hospitality. We have been through a number of hardships of late, and I fear our nerves are stretched thin." He glanced at Shanis, who thankfully remained silent. "On behalf of myself and my party, I apologize."

Shanis locked eyes with Larris, and they stared at one another nearly as long as she and Malram had. Oskar felt his heart lift when finally, she nodded her head. "I apologize for shouting at you," she said to Malram, taking a step back and lowering her head. "I am tired, and I was frightened for my friends."

Malram's frown made a deep, v-shaped furrow across his forehead. "I fear that my tone of voice did not help matters," he said. "Please hear me. I must know what you were doing out here tonight. I must know why all of you are here. I must."

The hesitation Larris had shown earlier was gone. Without so much as a glance toward any of his comrades, he sprang up on top of the stone where Kelrom had been chained. Facing the villagers, he drew the leather cord from his shirt, and held up his signet ring.

"I realize that this symbol will mean nothing to you, nor will the name of my country, but it is the symbol of my house and my birthright. I am the Second Prince of the nation of Galdora. The frost creeps forward again. We have twice been attacked by minions of the Ice King." A collective gasp went up from the listeners. "For my kingdom, my bloodline, and for the good of all those who walk under the heat of the sun, I seek the Silver Serpent."

Shrieks rose anew from the villagers, even louder than when they had discovered the slain golorak. Malram raised his hands to the sky and dropped to his knees. In groups of two and three, the villagers, many of them weeping, approached the stone. They prostrated themselves before Larris, softly chanting, "Bringer of heat. Bringer of heat."

Someone grabbed Oskar's forearm, and he turned to see Hierm standing next to him, looking baffled.

"I thought Larris was crazy for telling them," he whispered. "Now look at them. What does this mean?"

The chant continued. "Bringer of heat. Bringer of heat."

"I don't know," Oskar replied. "But at least it doesn't appear we'll have to fight them." He looked over Hierm's shoulder to see Khalyndryn round the bend, followed by more villagers. She frowned at the strange sight, but surprisingly had the good sense to remain quiet. Allyn walked over to meet her, taking her by the elbow and guiding her over the loose rocks with the aid of his torch, to stand by Hierm and Oskar.

"Where is Shanis?" she asked.

"Over there." Allyn tilted his head in Shanis' direction.

She stood only a few paces from Malram, arms folded, and foot tapping like an impatient mother. She stared up at Larris with a mix of disgust and wonder painted on her face. One corner of her mouth was tilted up in the beginnings of a smile.

Larris surveyed the scene as the newly-arriving villagers joined the ranks of their brethren, falling prostrate to the ground and joining in the chant. He cocked an eyebrow at Allyn, who shrugged and shook his head. Larris turned back to Malram, who had finally risen to his feet.

Bringer of heat.

"My friends," Malram said, his tone now changed from annoyance to wonderment, "I ask that you return with us to the village. Tomorrow, we must trade."

Chapter 30

"Our clan chief's hut be there," the young man said, indicating the largest of the primitive-looking structures that encircled the floor of the tiny canyon. "I will notify him of your arrival."

"And to whom do I owe thanks for guiding me?" Aspin asked, reining his horse in and looking around for a place to tie off the reins.

The fellow's eyes narrowed, and he cocked his head to the side.

"What is your name, young man?" Aspin spoke loudly and slowly, as if speaking to a dullard. Despite his weariness, he knew that he should not treat the lad so, after all he had saved Aspin at least two days of riding and what would likely have been a dull, if not outright unpleasant visit to Karkwall. The party he had described to Aspin had to be the Malan girl and her friends. Who the other two with them were, he could not deduce.

"Oh. My name be Jamnir. At your service, Saikur." He thumped his fist to his chest and bowed, keeping his eyes on Aspin as if to see what else he might do to unintentionally give offense.

Aspin looked down at the Monaghan scout. His bright red whiskers scarcely covered his cheeks. "Jamnir, I wish to thank you for guiding me to your encampment. I shall commend you to your clan chief. What is his name?"

"Horgris, sir. His name be Horgris." Jamnir's features relaxed, obviously relieved that he had not drawn the ire of a Saikur. "If you be allowing me, I'll see your horse be tended to."

"I would be most appreciative," Aspin said, slipping out of the saddle and stepping down onto the spongy turf. He passed the reins to Jamnir before freeing his saddlebags and slinging them over his shoulder. "Lead the way."

Jamnir hastily turned Aspin's mount, as well as his own, over to a young lad of no more than ten summers, unless Aspin missed his guess. They walked over to the hut that Jamnir had indicated. As they approached, he heard shouts from within."

"You'll be telling me now, girl!" A voice like low thunder rolled through the damp morning mist. "I'll be knowing it, or you'll be marrying the first goat-herder I be setting my eyes on!"

"I will not!" a strident, female voice shrieked. "I will be telling you when I be ready, and not a moment sooner!"

"If it be Granlor, just tell me." The rough voice had softened a bit, but not much.

"It not be Granlor. Just leave me be!" A pretty, round-faced girl with auburn hair burst through the doorway, jostling Jamnir as she stalked past. A moment later, a large, heavyset man clad in the traditional Monaghan garb, emerged.

"Rinala!" he shouted, though he made no move to follow her. "Fool girl," he muttered. He turned toward Aspin, his brown eyes locking in on him with the challenging gaze of a cornered wolf. "Who this be?"

Jamnir's eyes darted from Horgris to Aspin and back to Horgris again. He swallowed, and took a deep breath. "Ah, Horgris, this be a saikur.

"My name is Aspin. This young man was good enough to guide me to your camp. I believe you can help me locate some people I am looking for. I realize that this is probably not the ideal time for you to receive a visitor."

"Ah, it be no matter." Horgris waved a beefy hand at him, and turned back toward the hut. "Come inside. Do you drink skok, or be you weak in the gut?"

Aspin smirked. It was refreshing to be around someone who was neither intimidated by the Saikur cloak, nor openly hostile toward him. This Horgris fellow would be interesting.

He entered the hut, ducking slightly as he passed through the doorway. A fat-burning lamp cast the room in a smoky, yellow haze. Save the small table where the lamp rested alongside a jug and a few mismatched mugs, the only furnishings were a few blankets on the floor.

Horgris motioned for him to sit, before filling two mugs. He drained one and refilled it before passing the second to Aspin, and taking a seat on one of the blankets.

"My daughter Rinala," he said, shaking his head, "gone and got herself with child."

"I am sorry to hear that," Aspin said levelly, taking a sip of skok. Vile stuff, really, but he needed information, and did not wish to offend his host. At least not until he had learned all he could.

"Bah!" Horgris made a dismissive gesture. "I no care about that. But she'll no tell me who the father be. I want the boy, whoever he be, to live up to his responsibilities, that be all." He took a gulp of skok, closing his eyes and smiling as he swallowed.

"I am certain she will tell you when she is ready," Aspin said. In Monaghan culture, it was incumbent upon the host to initiate business discussions. For Aspin to broach the subject of the Malan girl before Horgris inquired as to the reason for his visit would be the height of rudeness.

"No doubt," Horgris grumbled, staring down into his mug. "I be a grandfather soon. Hard to believe." He snapped his head up. "I no look like a grandfather, do I?"

"Not at all," Aspin replied truthfully. The man, despite his girth, was obviously robust. He exuded strength.

"You be a good liar. I like that." Horgris laughed, a sonorous sound, and raised his cup. "To the seeds of my planting!"

Aspin raised his mug, and recited a blessing remembered from a lifetime ago. "May your descendants be as plentiful as the stars of night." He took a healthy swallow, squeezing his eyes closed and willing himself not to shudder as the drink scorched his throat.

"May they be so, but no time soon, yes?" Horgris took another drink. "Very well. Now you will be telling me what you be doing here."

"I am searching for the daughter of a friend," Aspin began, grateful that Horgris seemed one to appreciate directness. "A young woman, a girl really, taller than you, red hair, gray eyes. She dresses like a boy, and carries a sword. I understand from young Jamnir that someone meeting her description passed through here not long ago." He took another sip of skok, thankful for its warmth in this cold, damp place.

"Ah yes. That one, she be traveling with Prince Larris."

Aspin choked, spewing his drink all over the front of his cloak. A series of racking coughs cleared the drink from his windpipe.

"You be all right?" Horgris asked, looking perplexed.

"Fine," he wheezed. A fine thing for a Saikur to let himself show surprise like that. What was Larris doing down here? And how in the god's names had the Malan girl gotten mixed up with him? "Just haven't had skok in quite some time. Went down the wrong way."

"Ah." Neither the utterance nor the look on Horgris' face indicated whether or not he believed the explanation. "Why you be looking for the girl?"

Many of Aspin's order might have taken the opportunity to educate Horgris as to the impropriety of questioning a Saikur's motives. He chose not to do so. For one, arrogant people annoyed him. For another, he suspected that such a comment might elicit a half-hearted apology from Horgris, but the clan chief would likely deny having any further knowledge of the Malan girl. He decided to lie instead.

"The girl set off adventuring. She has always wanted to be a soldier, which a woman cannot be in Galdora. She spirited away three other youngsters from her village. Her father is an old friend, and he asked me to bring her home."

"Finding lost children no seem like important enough business to be troubling one of your lot." Horgris put his cup down, and folded his arms across his chest, resting them on his paunch. "And how she come to travel with a prince of Galdora if she be no more than a runaway?" He sat, waiting for an explanation.

"I owe her father a debt," Aspin said. "As for the latter, I was hoping you could tell me. Did Larris say where they were going, or what they were doing?" He took another drink, hoping the Monaghan would be forthcoming with something helpful.

Horgris sat in quiet contemplation for a long while, his drink forgotten. Finally, he sighed and looked Aspin directly in the eye. "You be a seeker, so I no can think of a reason not to tell you. But first you answer me this, and answer true.

The girl you seek have the look of a Monaghan about her, but she be having the eyes of a Malgog. Do she truly be Galdoran?"

"I know for a fact that she was born and lived her life in Galdora," Aspin said. He could tell by Horgris' frown that this answer would not suffice. "Her father was born a Malgog. I did not know her mother." It was almost the truth.

Horgris raised his eyebrows and leaned forward. Whatever he was thinking, he did not share. "Very well, seeker. I can tell you what your Galdoran, Malgog, maybe Monaghan girl be about, and where she be headed. I sent them to the Ramsgate. They be in search of the Silver Serpent."

Aspin was grateful that he had not been taking a drink when Horgris said that, else he might have choked again. Pieces rapidly fell into place, and others began to organize themselves in at least a remotely sensible fashion. Lerryn's sword tournament held in the middle of nowhere suddenly made a certain amount of sense. But how had the girl ended up with Larris? Were the princes working together? And if so, did that mean that Larris was under Xaver's sway? That was unfair. He had nothing more than an instinctive dislike of Lerryn's vizier upon which to ground his suspicions. His mind was abuzz with possibilities.

"I see that be meaningful to you," Horgris observed, grinning like the cat that got the cream. "I be thinking it might be important."

Aspin couldn't resist taking the man down a peg. "Horgris, are you a member of the order?" The smile fell from the man's face instantly, and he gaped at the Saikur. "You had to be. Why else would you have aided them? What I don't understand is why you did not go after it yourself."

Horgris picked his cup back up, but did not drink. "Boys from the clan, they go in search of it from time-to-time. Foolishness, mostly. We can no spare the men, what with the Malgog raiding us all the time." Aspin noted that he did not mention the Monaghan raiding the Malgog. "Besides, we no know where to look. One legend say it be in a lost city beyond the Ramsgate, another say it be carried away to," his eyes flitted toward Aspin, then away again, "to another place."

He was going to say Vatania, Aspin thought. "But Larris believes he knows where to find it?"

Horgris nodded. "He be looking for Robrus' Pass. Says if he be able to find it, he be able to find the city. I tell him the location of the pass be lost to memory, but I send him to the Ramsgate. Wasting his time if you be asking me."

Aspin's thoughts raced again. He had never put much store in prophecy, dismissing it as the ravings of madmen. However, this was too much of a coincidence to ignore. If the bearer of the Silver Serpent was to be the one to reunite the clans, then would not the reverse be true as well? Would the one chosen to reunite the clans be fated to bear the Serpent? And what became of his plan if the wrong person discovered it? It was too much to worry over. He could only control his own actions, and right now, he needed to find the girl.

"What be on your mind, seeker? I know how you and yours be doing your business. Things be not so simple as you make them seem. Tell me I be wrong."

How much should he tell? "The frost creeps again." He expected to see surprise on Horgris' face, but the man simply nodded. "That does not surprise you?"

"We be attacked by ice cats the first time I be meeting up with Larris and that girl. First ones I ever be seeing in my lifetime. And I hear tell the wolves and pumas be ranging far out of their territory. Something be pushing them out; something they be afraid of."

"Have you heard anything else? Anything that might be of importance?"

"One of my scouts come across a mountain man, half-wild he be. Said he seen an army moving through the passes far west of here. My scout say he no see any sign this way, and he doubt there be an army, but he believe the man be telling the truth as he be seeing it. A man live alone in the mountains, perhaps fifty men be seeming an army to him. Still, it be strange."

"Strange indeed." Aspin took another swallow of skok, now so immersed in thought as to be blissfully oblivious to the taste. Perhaps fifty men, and perhaps not. "Can you direct me to this Ramsgate?"

Chapter 31

"Your Highness, might we have leave to walk around the city?" Hair, flanked by Bull and Edrin, stood on the opposite side of the table, eyes wide with excitement.

Lerryn sometimes forgot that even a city of moderate size, like Brisacea, was far beyond the realm of these country boys' experience.

"You may, but do not wander far, and be back here before sunset. I don't want to have to go looking for you." He fished into his belt pouch and withdrew a few coins. He inspected them, culling the golds, and handing the rest to Hair. "Enough to enjoy yourself, but not enough to get into too much trouble, I suppose."

"Thank you, Highness!" Hair exclaimed, bowing. Bull and Edrin murmured their agreement, and made awkward bows. They turned and hurried toward the door. Pedric Karst, who had been sitting nearby with his feet propped on a table, stood and made to follow them.

"Not you, Master Karst." Lerryn gritted his teeth as Karst turned, his ordinarily sour expression now curdled. "Have you forgotten the last city we visited?"

"It wasn't my fault," Karst complained, folding his hands across his chest. "He provoked me. I was only protecting my honor."

Lerryn did not bother to reply. They had discussed the matter on the evening in question, and he was not interested in repeating the lesson. Until the boy demonstrated that he could conduct himself as a proper guest, Lerryn would not chance letting him roam. He stood, pushing his chair back, drained the last dregs of his wine, and fixed Karst with a broad smile that he knew would infuriate the lad to no end.

"You will be coming with me. Did you leave your sword with the steward, as I instructed?" Karst nodded, still frowning. "Very well." Lerryn stepped out the door and onto the street.

Foot traffic was light this morning, and the city was devoid of beggars, one of the details of Diyonan life that Lerryn appreciated. The morning sun sparkled on the white paving stones flecked with bits of gray, and shone on the solidly-constructed shops and homes, all set well back from the road and at a comfortable distance apart. Uniformly built from the same white with which the street was paved, all of Brisacea seemed to shine against the verdant backdrop of the valley in which the city nestled.

Most of the structures were topped by roof gardens, where people conducted business over glasses of rich Diyonan port, or sat enjoying the unseasonably cool summer morning. Several people raised hands or glasses as they passed by. Lerryn nodded and smiled in return. Walking at his side, Karst kept his gaze on the ground in front of him.

"I understand why people hate me," the young man suddenly said. "I have a strong sense of pride, and I give and take offense easily. I don't suppose any of you would understand how it feels to be raised by a pig farmer. No matter how high my father's station rises, he will always be a pig farmer in the eyes of the nobility. I traveled so far to be a part of your tournament in hopes that no one would know anything about me. I wanted to advance on my own merit without anyone knowing from whence I had come."

Lerryn felt a slight pang of guilt, knowing that he was the one who had brought the Karst family's livelihood to light. That fact notwithstanding, he would not permit the youth to wallow in self-pity.

"Do you know that you are more than a pig farmer?"

"I suppose," Karst said, still looking down.

"You suppose," Lerryn echoed. "I advise you to stop trying to convince everyone else what you are and are not. Instead, try convincing yourself."

Karst cast a sideways glance at him. "I am not certain I understand."

Lerryn clapped a hand on the lad's shoulder as they walked. "When you truly know your own value, it will no longer matter what anyone else thinks of you. Remember that." Karst had no reply, and they continued on in silence until they arrived at their destination.

They proceeded along a narrow stone walk lined with short evergreen shrubs. A houseman stood outside the front door holding a ceremonial spear. He was dressed in traditional Diyonan fashion. His shirt, tunic and hose were white. Over this he wore a red surcote with his house symbol, a cluster of yellow grapes, emblazoned on the chest. The surcote, which looked to Lerryn like nothing more than a blanket with a hole cut in the center for the head, hung to the man's knees and was belted with a twist of gold rope. The guard greeted him with an expectant look.

"Lerryn of Galdora to see the master of the house, if you please." He handed his invitation to the guard, who held it aloft, letting it unroll only far enough for him to see his lord's signature and seal. "He received my request last evening, and was gracious enough to reply almost immediately."

"I shall announce you at once." The man frowned. "Forgive me, but how shall I announce you. I do not know your title."

"Forgive me," Lerryn answered, deciding to have a bit of fun with the fellow. "You may announce me as 'Sir' if you so desire. 'Lerryn Van Altman, First Prince of the Sword to His Highness, King Allar of Galdora' is such a mouthful." Karst snickered as the man's face blanched. Lerryn smiled to put the man at ease.

"Very well, Your Highness," he whispered, his voice suddenly hoarse, before turning and opening the front door. Clearing his throat, he straightened, and pounded the butt of his spear on the ground three times. "Sir Lerryn of Galdora to see the master," he called out.

In the span of two heartbeats, Antonn appeared from behind the door. The wizened little man was garbed much like his guard, save for his surcote which was white. He smiled an easy smile. His teeth were as white as his closely-cropped hair, and shone against his leathery skin. He raised his clenched fists to his chin, bowed, and rapped his knuckles together three times.

Lerryn returned the gesture, bringing his knuckles together twice, all the while inwardly bemoaning the Diyonan's overvaluing of ritual. As he stood, he turned and gestured to Karst, who stepped forward and perfectly imitated the ritual greeting. Realizing he had not instructed Karst on how to properly greet someone, he flashed three fingers at the youth, who thankfully understood, and rapped his knuckles three times. He should have taught the boy. Too much wine early in the day, Xaver would have said.

"Ministrar Antonn, may I present Master Pedric Karst, son of the Duke of Kurnsbur."

"I bid you both welcome," Antonn said, smiling. "My wine is your wine. My bread is your bread."

"May your vintage be as fine as your hospitality," Lerryn responded.

"Do come in." Antonn led them down a narrow hallway to a winding iron staircase at the back of the house. They mounted the stairs and climbed to a small room with a finely-wrought door of iron and glass set in one wall, which opened onto the roof garden. A flower-lined walkway led to a small table laden with wine and bread, and surrounded by chairs of woven reed, appointed with red cushions. Beyond the flowers on either side were a variety of vegetable plants, ornamental shrubs, and small fruit trees, planted with an eye to aesthetics rather than practicality.

Antonn motioned for his guests to sit. He then broke the bread, giving a large piece to each of them. "Heart and life," he intoned, and took a bite.

"Heart and life," Lerryn replied slowly, giving Karst the opportunity to join in. He took a bite of the bread. It was typical Diyonan: chewy, with herbs sprinkled into the flour to give it a unique, almost minty flavor. Waiting for Antonn to take the first sip, he raised his glass and took a drink of the orange-tinted drink, schooling himself not to drain the cup. Diyonus might be a mere shade of what she had once been, but her vineyards still produced the finest wine in Gameryah.

"You honor my house with your presence, Your Highness," Antonn said. "I must confess my surprise both at your presence in our city, and that you wanted to see me. How may I be of service?"

"I asked about, as we traveled," Lerryn said, "as to whom I might go to hear old stories. It is my understanding that you are Diyonus' foremost collector of ancient lore."

"Foremost in the western region, perhaps," Antonn replied. He neither smiled nor attempted to look abashed. It was the simple truth. "I cannot help you with anything that has happened over the course of the last twenty-five or so imperators. Prior to that, perhaps I can. Is there a particular story you are seeking?"

"The Silver Serpent." If the name affected Antonn in any meaningful way, he did not show it. "I am familiar with the basic story of its crafting and use. The prophecies are also well-known to me. What I would like to know is if there are any stories of what happened to the serpent after the Ice King was defeated."

"An odd request," Antonn said. He took another drink before answering. "As I recall, most of the stories tell of it being secreted away in a city called Murantha, somewhere in the mountains west of Lothan." He rubbed his chin thoughtfully, and his eyes lost focus as he gazed upward.

From where he sat, Lerryn could look directly across the table and out across the city. It was truly a picturesque scene, the sparkling white buildings and shining roads set in a series of progressively smaller circles, glowing bright among the verdant hills. At Brisacea's center stood a monument to Rantor, god of the sun. The once-magnificent statue, as tall as ten men, now showed signs of its age. His body was pockmarked with gaps where stone had fallen away, and the stone was discolored due to the ravages of time. The spikes radiating from his head, symbolizing sunbeams, were broken and eroded. In his left hand he held a bowl from which a reluctant flame smoked and sputtered. Standing in the midst of beautifully tended lawn and ringed by late blooming flowers, he looked more like a beggar than the chief deity of a proud nation.

"He once inspired awe and reverence," Antonn said, following Lerryn's line of sight. "It is said that he glowed as if plated with gold, and neither scratch nor stain marred his surface for generations."

"I am told he was made and maintained by magic. But now sorcery wanes, and magic fails as often as it succeeds." Larris said, remembering what Xaver had told him many times. "That, of course, is another conversation entirely."

"Sorcery and magic," Antonn replied, shaking his head, "are little more than legend, I fear. As to your question, there is one story that comes to mind as something that might be of use to you. I mention it only because I have heard so many versions of it, each only slightly different than the next, that I believe there must be some truth to it.

"It seems to have its roots around the time of the reign of Imperator Buratell, the second woman to guide the Council of the Nine. By our calendar, that would place it about four-hundred."

"Forgive me Ministrar," Karst interjected in a surprisingly respectful tone. "I am not familiar with your calendar. What does the date mean?"

"You may call me Antonn, Master Karst, and there is naught to forgive. Our nation was once ruled by a series of self-styled noblemen, who ruled by force of arms rather than wisdom. After the revolution, the Council of the Nine was formed, and an imperator selected to lead them. A new calendar was created, counting forward from the date of the founding of the new government. Each summer marks a new year. It is now, by our calendar, the year seven-hundred sixteen."

"Thank you." Karst returned to his wine.

"The story is of a Malgog clan chief who vanished as a young man, returning six years later with a talisman he claimed to have found in the mountains. He carried it into the next battle, and his clan was victorious. Under his guidance, his clan prospered, and eventually came to adopt the image of the talisman as their clan symbol: a serpent. The clan chief died an old man, and took the serpent with him to his grave. Admittedly, the story does not call it the Silver Serpent, but the coincidence is intriguing."

Larris thought it was more than coincidence. It is the prophecy. The star guided me to this place so that I might hear this story. "Can you tell me where to find this particular clan?"

"Certainly. In fact, it is not far. Only a few days ride from here." He pushed back from the table, stood, and smoothed his surcote. "If you will excuse me, I will prepare a map for you." He bowed slightly, and took his leave.

"So they don't do the thing with their fists when they leave a place?" Karst asked.

"Strictly a greeting." He drained his glass, enjoying the rich flavor. "You understood the knuckles?"

"I assume it reflects social standing. The lower your rank, the more times you pound your fists together."

Lerryn nodded, pleased at the way Karst had presented himself thus far. His spirits were lifted by the new light that had been shed on the mystery. Perhaps this was the clue they had been searching for.

"The wine is excellent as well. I have had Diyonan wine only twice before, and neither were this good. And the color is unusual as well. What gives it the orange tint?"

"Movanan Orange," Lerryn replied. "It is only produced in one valley in central Diyonus. Its making is a closely guarded secret. Some believe that it has something to do with the soil in which the grapes are grown." He chuckled. "My father claims that they let their vats rust. Of course, he has little taste for wine." He wondered if Karst would ask where Lerryn had gotten his taste for wine, but Antonn chose that moment to return.

"I believe this will be of help to you," he said, proffering a rolled parchment. "Of course, given the situation in Lothan, there is no telling if the village remains." He shrugged, nothing more to say.

"Please accept my heartfelt thanks for your assistance," Lerryn said. He imagined he felt a tingle as his fingers closed around the map. "I am sure this will be of great assistance. I regret I must take now leave of your hospitality."

"You have been a blessing to my house, Highness. Allow me to show you out, and we shall say our goodbyes."

The late morning sun shone brightly on the freshly-painted picture of a golden goblet and bunch of grapes hanging in front of The Vintner's Cup. As they approached the front steps, Larris took Karst by the elbow and pulled him past their inn. Continuing his unusually good behavior, the boy kept his mouth shut until they had passed on by.

"What is it?" he whispered, keeping his eyes to the fore.

"Two men, one on either side of the porch. Both were outside Antonn's house when we left. Also, another man has been following us the entire time. I know you don't have your sword, but do you have a knife?"

"In my boot. I can use it too." Karst did not sound the least bit afraid. In fact, there was an eagerness in his voice that reminded Lerryn all too much of his own youth. "Do you think there are more?"

"I would be surprised if there is not at least one more waiting somewhere ahead of us." His battle instinct took over, and he formulated a semblance of a plan. "How well can you throw that knife of yours? The truth, now."

"Very well. Just give me a target. Once I've lost my knife, though, I don't know how much use I'll be to you."

"I'll give you mine." Hastily, keeping watch for any threat that might be coming from in front of them, he outlined his plan, if it could be called that. Karst whispered that he understood.

Up ahead, two men leaned against a cart laden with vegetables. To the untrained eye, they might appear inconspicuous. Lerryn noticed any number of things wrong, though: spotless cloaks, clean hands, fine boots, not to mention the poorly-concealed sword under the first man's cape. He cleared his throat, the signal to begin.

Karst pretended to stumble. He dropped to one knee, rubbing his ankle. Without warning, he slipped the knife from his boot, whirled, and slung it at the fellow Larris had described; a broad shouldered man with curly blond hair and a mustache that reached almost to his ears. Taken completely by surprise, the man stopped short, the hilt of Karst's knife blossoming in his throat. Lerryn handed his heavy belt knife to the young man, as they sprinted back the way they had come.

The men he had seen lounging on the porch of the Vintner's Cup had followed as well, and they both struggled to free their swords. Lerryn made a beeline for the one on the right, while Karst dashed directly toward the other. His target had just raised his sword to strike when Lerryn leapt into the air. Drawing his knees to his chest and twisting to his left, he kicked out. His right foot drove hard into the man's throat, his left taking him full in the chest. The fellow made a gurgling shriek as he tumbled backward.

Lerryn fell headfirst, rolling on his forearms and springing to his feet behind the second assailant, whom Karst had distracted by circling, knife drawn, just out of sword reach. Foregoing style, Lerryn stepped up behind the man and drove a vicious kick between his legs. As the fellow crumpled to the ground, Karst relieved him of his sword and his life in short order. Lerryn took up the other man's sword, and turned to face what he hoped would be the final two assailants, the men who had been lounging by the produce cart.

The brigands were almost upon them. The one on the left was a short, thick fellow with trunk-like arms and a scar running from above his left ear down to the corner of his mouth. The sun glinted off of his shaven head. He raised his sword high above his head as he charged in. Lerryn ducked inside his downstroke and ran him through the gut. The goon's eyes went wide, and he made a gurgling sound as his sword dropped from his limp fingers. As life faded from his eyes, Lerryn put his foot on the dying man's chest and pushed him off of his sword.

He turned to see Karst driving the other attacker back. He was obviously the superior swordsman, and he was toying with the fellow. Blood ran freely from cuts on the assailant's forearms, cheek, chest, and thigh.

"Finish him!" Larris shouted. Karst's eyes tightened, the only indication he had heard. A feint high, a slash low, and it was over. The last of the attackers lay in the roadway, entrails spilling from a gaping wound in his midsection.

"Will there be a constable coming after us?" Karst asked, kneeling to wipe the sword on the man's cloak.

"Diyonus has a city watch," Lerryn replied, scanning the crowd for potential threats. Fortunately, the few who had not already scattered were studiously ignoring the scene. "If I do not miss my guess, they will allow enough time to just miss catching us." He stood and indicated with a jerk of his head that Karst should follow him. They set off at a quick jog back to The Vintner's Cup.

Arriving at the inn, he was surprised as he entered the door, to see Xaver sitting at a table in the common room, a full cup of wine before him. The far end of the common room, the one closest to the fireplace, was crowded with a cluster of morning patrons who did not wish to sit near Lerryn's vizier. Before Lerryn could speak, he stood and moved in close.

"I see there is no need to inform you that someone is after us." He glanced down at Lerryn's blood-spattered tunic. "Two armed men were waiting in our room. I was able to summon enough power to quickly disable them. The only useful information I could draw from them was the name Antonn."

"He moves fast. We left his home not long ago, and were waylaid in the street." A question gnawed at the back of his mind. "Two men were waiting on the porch here. I noticed them right away. How is it that you were unaware of them?"

"I don't know what you're implying, Highness, but I resent your tone. As I was dealing with the intruders, the boys arrived. I instructed them to load everything on the horses while I did my delving. I must have been upstairs when you passed by, as I have only been in the common room a few minutes."

"Not implying, just asking," Lerryn said with a sigh. He snatched up Xaver's wine cup and drained it in three large swallows. Even cheap Diyonan wine was palatable. "I'll settle with the innkeeper, and we'll go. I hope he will be discreet after we leave."

"I have dealt with the innkeeper." Xaver forced a smile. "No worries there."

Lerryn's stomach went cold. "He was an innocent. What did you do?"

"I paid him, Lerryn. Paid him well, and promised to remember him on our next visit." He shook his head. "Truly, I do not understand your paranoia."

"Perhaps it has something to do with the fact that a friendly little old scholar just sent assassins after me. I mean to have some answers."

Antonn's house guard was visibly taken aback by Lerryn's reappearance. He hesitated before taking a tentative step forward, holding his spear diagonally across his chest, attempting to bar the way. Without breaking stride, Lerryn batted the sword down and punched the fellow hard in the jaw. He fell to the ground with a surprised grunt, clutching his face, his spear clattering to the ground. Lerryn kicked the door open and stalked inside.

"It was locked?" Xaver asked, glancing at the shattered door facing.

"I have no idea." He looked around for Antonn. The man had broken bread with him! It was unforgivable. Toward the far end of the hall that bisected the first floor of the house, a servant poked his head out of a doorway. Blanching at the sight of six armed strangers stalking toward him, he jerked his head back and slammed the door.

"Bull. Edrin." Lerryn motioned toward the door. Bull hooked the short-handled warhammer he had been learning to use back onto his belt and hurried down the hall. Edrin, looking uncomfortable with his bow strapped onto his back instead of in his hand, followed close behind, a broad-bladed hunting knife clenched in a white-knuckled grip.

"Do you think there are more guards, highness?" Hair asked, with neither eagerness nor trepidation in his voice.

"Not likely." Between himself, Karst, and Xaver, he suspected Antonn's personal security force had been utterly demolished. He heard footfalls and a crash behind a door to his left. He tried it and found it unlocked. He pushed through, dimly aware of the others following behind him.

It was a private office. A small table with quill, ink and parchment sat in the center of the room. A padded chair similar to those on the roof garden lay upended behind it. Directly across the room, a small, half-filled bookshelf sat beneath a tall, narrow window. The sash was closed. Someone was still inside. He took in the details as he surveyed the space. Paintings of landscapes, mostly vineyards and pastoral scenes, were hung head-high at precise intervals around the room. Finding the room empty, he came to the obvious conclusion.

Turning back to the door through which they had entered, which now stood almost flush against the inner wall, he leapt forward and threw his shoulder into it with all his might. The impact stung his shoulder, but the surprised cry of pain from behind the door was more than satisfying.

Antonn stumbled out, falling to his knees on the hard, tile floor. He pressed his hands against his side, probably clutching a broken rib or two. Blood dripped from his nose and mouth, staining the golden grapes on his surcote. Karst pushed past Lerryn, grabbed the man by the forehead, hooking his fingers into his eye sockets, and yanked his head back to expose his throat.

"Karst! You've killed enough today. Let him be." He paused for effect. "For now." Karst hesitated for two heartbeats before letting go. Sheathing his sword, he stepped back to stand next to Hair, arms folded across his chest, his ever-present pout firmly in place.

"I'll tell you nothing," Antonn said through swelling lips. "The watch will be here soon, and they'll take you to the nearest garrison. You will regret this."

Lerryn smacked him on the ear. "Xaver, can you persuade this gentleman to answer my questions?" Antonn made a sound like a stuck pig, and scrabbled on all fours toward the window. Without looking down at the man, Lerryn stamped down on his right hand, eliciting a higher-pitched squeal. "Gentlemen, will you please hold our friend, here?" Karst and Hair hauled Antonn to his feet, and bent his arms behind him, arching his back so that his stomach thrust forward.

Xaver moved to stand in front of Antonn. He placed his hands on the man's temples and began muttering in a deep, choppy voice. It was Colquahil, the language of the Gods. It sounded like someone being punched repeatedly in the gut. With each throaty exhalation, the room seemed to grow warmer. Antonn's face turned deathly white, and his knees shook. Gradually, his eyes turned glassy, until there seemed a coating of ice across his vision. He stared blindly back at Xaver, panting and trembling.

"You may ask your questions now, Highness." Xaver continued to hold Antonn's head. "But do not take too long. Twice in one day is as much as I can manage."

"Why did you send your guards after us?" Lerryn asked, beginning with the obvious.

"You seek the Silver Serpent." Antonn's voice was a loud whisper, without inflection. "It is best if you die."

"But you don't believe in sorcery or magic," Lerryn protested, dimly aware of the irony of the statement given Antonn's present circumstances. "Why would it matter to you?"

"Does not matter. The Lothans believe in it. Cannot have them united. The barbarians might turn their attentions on us if they were ever to stop fighting one another. Must do what is best for the realm."

"How many men did you send after us, and how many more have you told?" Escape would be difficult if there were others sounding the alarm as they spoke.

There was a brief pause before Antonn answered. "I sent seven of my household guard after you. Kevrann remained at the door. The other two have liberty today. I told no one else of you and your dealings. I did not think it necessary." A string of spittle, tinted pink by blood, hung from the corner of his mouth.

Lerryn was grateful that Antonn's force had been neutralized. He would have to kill the man, of course, and probably the rest of the household staff. He could not have the Diyonan army tailing him back into Lothan, and murdering a ministrar would do just that.

Edrin appeared in the doorway. "Highness, we rounded up the household staff and closed them up in a room across the hall. Bull is guarding the door."

Lerryn nodded, not turning away from Antonn. "The story you told me and the map you gave me. Are they false?"

"No," Antonn's voice carried a slight touch of insistence despite Xaver's delving. "I saw no point in lying to you. My guard would have recovered the map from you when they killed you."

"Highness, you must hurry." Xaver's voice had lost much of its serenity. "I cannot do this much longer."

"I am finished with him." He drew his sword, and placed it against Antonn's chest. No point in making a bigger mess than necessary. Xaver released the man, and he went limp in the two young men's grip.

"Do not kill him," Hair protested. "Tie him up. Tie them all up and lock them in the cellar. We can get away before they are discovered."

"Don't listen to him, Highness," Karst snapped. "He does not have the stomach for killing like we do. Get out of here, Hair. I don't need your help to hold him. He's near-unconscious anyway."

"Let a man face me with sword in hand and I have plenty of stomach, but this is not right. He is an old, unarmed man." His voice softened. "Please, Highness," he entreated, "I beg you, do not do this."

Lerryn paused. Killing Antonn was the practical thing to do. He did not relish the idea of chancing the man getting word to the local army detachment before they could see their way clear of the border. But Hair was correct. Running an old man through was distasteful at best. Also, the fact that Karst thought the man should be killed made the idea that much less appealing. He needed to act. Indecisiveness was the death of a commander.

"It does not matter anymore," Xaver said, stepping forward. He pulled up one of Antonn's eyelids and examining his pupil. "I could not control the delving. I was tired from earlier, and I was careless with my incantation."

"What are you saying?" Lerryn asked, his sword still pressed to Antonn's chest.

"In simple terms, the part of his mind that is aware is permanently detached from his body. He will remain in this state until his body expires. I apologize for my failing." His clinically detached tone did not convey any sense of regret.

"Very well," Lerryn said, sheathing his sword. "Hair, you and Karst take him down to the cellar. Edrin, you and Bull take the others down there as well, and tie them up. Our innkeeper can send someone to 'discover' them in three days."

"Won't they send someone after us then?" Karst asked, glowering over the missed opportunity to kill Antonn. "Will three days be enough time?"

"I don't think you need to concern yourself about it. They don't know where we are going, and Antonn certainly won't be telling them anything. Be about your business quickly. I mean to ride within the hour."

Chapter 32

The cliff dropped away before her, looking like the end of the world. A thin veil of mist, hanging just below the edge of the precipice, obscured her vision. There must be water down there. Of the lost city of Murantha, or even the far side of the gap, there was no sign. She sighed and grasped her sword hilt for comfort. Her clothing felt heavy in the moist air, and she had pulled her hair up to keep it from clinging to the back of her neck.

Not for the first time, she turned and surveyed the rugged mountains above her. Rocks of the same varying shades of gray she had been looking at for weeks, scattered patches of scrub pine, sheer cliffs as far as she could see. No signs of human habitation, present or past. The scuffle of footfalls on loose rock told her that Hierm had finished scouting farther down the way. She cocked her head as he approached.

"Nothing," he said, shaking his head. "It's a sheer drop-off not much farther down. Nowhere to go." He folded his arms across his chest and looked out at the fog. He had always been a serious young man, but he had lost his youthful optimism. "Do you think Larris and Oskar truly have any idea where we are going?"

"They can't be wrong," Shanis said, mostly believing what she was saying. "Their maps and landmarks have gotten us this far. It would be too great a coincidence for all of them to match something along the way."

They made their way over to where the others waited. Larris was shaking his head.

"When the Thandrylls wanted to trade with us, I truly believed that the trades would somehow aid us in finding the city." He chuckled. "And then, when they told us to keep them secret until the time came, I was certain. Foolishness." He slipped his hand into his belt pouch and fished out a very large, very tarnished coin. He held it up close to his eyes and turned it over slowly. "There is nothing helpful here. I have looked it over twice now." He looked at the others. "Anyone else receive something helpful?"

They all shook their heads and murmured in the negative and, one by one, shared with the others what they had received in the Thandryll's odd trading ritual. Khalyndryn had been given a kerchief, Oskar a plain, brown cloak, and Hierm a woman's circlet of woven vines. Shanis had traded an ornate pearl button the she had saved from the dress Bertram had given her in Karkwall, and received a pendant on a silver chain in return. The pendant was a flat, silver circle on which was engraved a stream winding down between two hills, and pooling at the base. She liked it, and was, in fact, wearing it.

"At least all of you were given something." Allyn said. "I didn't get a thing."

"They didn't trade with you?" Shanis asked, remembering the stone Allyn had given to the Thandrylls. It was pale green with dark blue stripes running through it. Just the right size to fit in your palm, it had been worn smooth from who-knew-how-many years lying in the streambed where he had found it as a boy. It was the only thing he had ever said about his childhood, and she was still surprised that he had parted with a remembrance of his childhood.

"Oh, they traded with me," he said, his upper lip curling into a sneer. "They taught me a dance. Right foot, left hand, right hand, left. Right foot, left hand, right hand, left." He acted out the dance, stomping his feet and waving his arms in such an exaggerated fashion that Shanis had to laugh. It was so unlike his unusual demeanor.

She was about to remark when she espied Oskar out of the corner of her eye. He was gaping at Allyn. He turned to look at Larris, and as he did, the corners of his mouth turned up into a smile. Larris was smiling back, his eyes gleaming.

"It can't be," Oskar said, still grinning.

"It must be." Larris was actually bobbing up and down on the balls of his feet. "Can you think of another answer?"

Without waiting for Oskar's reply, he hurried to the edge of the cliff, sighting his location against a distant peak. "About here?" He shifted a half-pace to his right.

"That looks about right to me." Oskar held up his thumb and closed one eye, lining Larris up with the landmark. "Try right there."

"Would one of you care to tell us what you're talking about?" Shanis asked. She had known Oskar long enough to be accustomed to his reticence when he thought he knew something no one else new, but it still rankled her. This time, her patience was stretched thin.

Larris lay on his stomach and reached down over the edge of the cliff. A few moments, and his facial features relaxed into a smile of contentment. "It's there," he announced. With extreme caution, he brought his right foot down over the edge.

Oskar hurried over beside him and grabbed his right arm. "Be careful. Go slowly."

"There's the right foot," Larris said. His face was pale, and a sheen of sweat covered his brow, but his smile remained firmly in place. "Now the left hand." Trembling a bit, he brought his left hand down. "It's right here. You cannot even see it until you are right on it, it's so small. It's carved at a downward angle so you can hook your fingers into it. Ah, there's the left foot." His head sank a bit lower. "You can let go now." Oskar released his grip, and Larris sank out of sight.

Shanis and the others walked over to the ledge and looked down at Larris. He was descending by way of hand and footholds in the cliff face. The holds were invisible from above, but he was having no trouble finding them as he descended at a steady pace.

"Coded handholds," Oskar said. "Ancients used them as a system of defense. If you did not know the correct pattern, you would find yourself halfway down the cliff with nowhere to go."

"But where is the city?" Hierm's frown made him look like his father.

"It's here!" Larris cried from down below. He was barely in sight now, the inward slope of the cliff, so subtle as to have been unnoticeable before, obscured their line of sight. "It's beautiful! Everyone come down! Bring water and torches.

And some food."

"The city," Oskar's knowing smile reminded Shanis of Master Yurg, "is carved into the cliff."

"But we didn't see anything when we scouted," Allyn protested.

"You would have had to be on the other side of the canyon in order to see it. They built the city beneath an overhang set so far back that you cannot see it from above or from the side." He smiled. "Your dance reminded me of the coded handholds. Once I came to that conclusion, it was obvious."

"Happy I could help," Allyn muttered. "Let's get what we need from the horses. Hierm, help me?" Hierm nodded and the two headed back up the trail to where their horses were tethered.

"I'll stay here," Khalyndryn said, staring into the emptiness. "Climbing out of the dungeon in Karkwall was quite enough for me. I can wait with the horses."

"Larris said that everyone should come down," Oskar protested. "I think you should go."

"He's right." Shanis was letting Khalyndryn grate on her again. "There is no telling what might happen to you if you are alone up here."

"No." Khalyndryn folded her arms across her chest and looked Shanis in the eye. "I will not go."

"You will go if I have to throw you over the cliff." Khalyndryn shook her head. Shanis leaned in toward her, hands on hips, bending down until their noses nearly touched. "I killed a man to save you!" Her voice rose. "Yet no matter where we go, what we do, you never change! You are the same childish girl you've always been."

"I have no purpose!" Khalyndryn's shout froze the words in Shanis' throat. "Everyone else can ride, fight, track, or hunt." She looked at Oskar. "Think! What use am I? If I go down there I'll fall, or I'll get lost, or I'll touch something I shouldn't. I'll do something to ruin it all." She did not back down one step. She kept her chin up and continued to meet her eye. "I will take my chances with whatever may or may not be up here. Can you truly tell me that my presence down there would serve any purpose at all?"

Hierm and Allyn had run back when the shouting started. They now stood at the mouth of the trail where it wound back into the rock, staring at the two girls. Oskar remained rooted to his spot near where Larris had descended, saying nothing, but watching them.

Shanis was taken aback. Khalyndryn had just given voice to Shanis' own thoughts. She took a deep breath, regaining a bit of composure, and buying herself a moment to think.

"My father," she began, "always taught me that everyone has a purpose. He said that those who never find it are either too lazy or too afraid. Which one are you?"

"I never liked you, Shanis. You are the most spoiled, selfish person I have ever met." Nearby, Hierm coughed and turned away. "You never had to do anything the other girls had to do. You never lived by any rules. And when the time came to be an adult, you threw a tantrum because you wanted to keep playing at swords like the boys. Killing that guard was probably the first selfless thing you ever did. I am grateful, but do not expect me to fall down and kiss your boots. You forget. I chose to come with you for reasons of my own. You were going to leave me. You,

Oskar and Hierm all had your own reasons for leaving, and they had nothing to do with me.

"I don't like you," she repeated. "But I liked and respected your father. He was a strong, humble person who could have done more with his life than raise a spoiled daughter and haul goods for Lord Hiram. Did you know that he and I used to talk while he loaded the wagons?"

Tears welled in Shanis' eyes, and her throat was tight and sore. She turned her back on Khalyndryn, but she could not walk away. Somehow, she knew she needed to hear what the girl had to say.

"He listened to me, and he always gave me good advice. I'll wager I talked to him more than you did. You would have thought Master Yurg was your father, you spent so much time at the sword." Khalyndryn's voice was tinged with bitterness. "If Colin believes that everyone has a purpose, then I will listen to him." She emphasized the last word. "I'll be back."

Shanis turned around to see Khalyndryn push her way past Hierm and Allyn, heading toward the horses. Allyn followed behind. Hierm took a step toward her, but she waved him away. He shrugged and went to join Allyn.

She felt a firm hand on her arm, turned and fell onto Oskar's shoulder. "Is that what everyone thinks of me?" The tears flowed unabated as she allowed him to support her weight. She rarely permitted herself to cry, and never to break down. She wrapped her arms around his shoulders and squeezed tight, trying to reign in her sadness, her fatigue, her frustration. "Is that what you all think?"

"No," Oskar whispered, stroking her hair. She could hear the lie in his voice, and couldn't say anything. He pushed away from her, cupped her chin in his hand, and raised her face to look at him. "You just said that everyone has a purpose. That goes for you as well. You cannot change anything that is past: only what lies ahead of you."

"Aren't you coming?" Larris called.

She drew away. Khalyndryn and the others would soon be back, and she would not let them see her cry. "Thank you," she mumbled. "I'll see you down there." She pressed the back of her sleeve to her eyes, letting the rough cloth soak up the tears. Using less caution than she should have, she found the first foothold and began her descent. Her anger and confusion lent her a touch of recklessness as she scrambled down the cliff face.

She had never thought of herself as a selfish person. True, she had pursued swordsmanship with single-minded purpose. She wanted to be the best she could be, in order to make her father proud. He began teaching her the sword when she was small, and he carefully supervised her until she was ready for the swordmaster's tutelage. She still remembered the way he smiled when she mastered a new skill. The special pride he took whenever she bested one of the boys. She knew no other way to please him, and the thought of giving up the sword was more than she could bear. Khalyndryn could not possibly understand the way the sword connected her and her father. As for the thought of Colin engaging in serious conversations with the girl, it felt like such a violation.

"You might try looking down just about now." Larris sounded as if he were directly beneath her. "Slow down!"

She cast her eyes downward just as her right foot struck solid ground. She tumbled backward, and felt strong arms envelop her.

"Not enough warning, I suppose. Sorry." He held on longer than necessary, supporting her weight, his arms across her breasts. Shanis felt his breath on her neck, warm and damp. After he neither raised her up nor let go, she cleared her throat in a loud rasp. She imagined she could feel reluctance as he released her. She straightened, strangely feeling the absence of his embrace.

"So, where...." She stopped abruptly when she saw the city.

Murantha lay in the shelter of a massive rock overhang, recessed so deep into the stone face that it was no wonder they had been unable to see it. This place was wrought by no human hand. It seemed to have flowed out of the native stone in one single piece. It was a mound of domed structures, each with a rounded door set in the front, connected by a series of serpentine paths that wound from building to building. Coming toward them from the center was a walkway hewn into the rock. It too curved like the belly of a snake in the dust. A ceremonial well lay near the place where the path curled up into the city. The morning sun glinted on the surface of the water that filled it near to the rim.

Behind her, someone dropped to the ground with a grunt, but her attention was on what she saw above the city.

Glittering in the morning sun, a giant serpent wound its way across the cliff above Murantha. It was rendered in amazing detail: its scales glittered, whether from the stone from which it was hewn or some form of sorcery, she could not say, but it was marvelous. She barely noticed the others as they gathered around her and Larris. Her eyes followed its sinuous length. It was the most beautiful thing she had ever seen, and it seemed to beckon to her.

"We found it," Oskar whispered, breaking the silence. "I never truly believed that we would. Even as we made the journey, it all seemed a grandmother's tale."

"As if we would wake up and find ourselves back home," she said in an equally soft voice.

"Well, we are awake," Larris said, "and this is Murantha." He turned to face the others, and took a few backward steps toward the city. "My friends, you have been faithful to your oath, and our quest nears its end. Let us complete our task. Let's find the Silver Serpent."

They approached the city warily, each moving at a slower pace than usual. The path beneath their feet was carved like the scales of a serpent, and wound snake-like toward the city. The stone beneath her looked brand-new.

"It looks as if no one has ever walked here before," she said, watching mesmerized as her boots trod on the stuff of legend.

"Precious few, at any rate," Larris said. "Murantha has been legend for so long, that few believe it exists. I'll wager it was created for no purpose other than to house the serpent. Likely no one lived here. It certainly does not appear that the surrounding land could sustain a population." He looked around, his eyes still wide with childlike wonder.

"You hope we're the first," Hierm added. Larris arched an eyebrow at him, and then gave a curt nod.

The pathway split, wrapping around both sides of the well. Shanis looked down at its sparkling surface, and wondered how deep it was. She stopped and knelt alongside it, gazing into its depths. The blackness beneath the surface was total, and seemed to draw her in. Her head swam, and she jerked back, springing to her feet.

"Are you all right?" Hierm asked, taking her by the forearm. His blue-gray eyes stared into hers with concern.

"Just dizzy," she said with forced cheerfulness. "A lot of excitement for one morning." She pulled away from his grasp, sidled past Larris, who was also looking at her with consternation, and continued along the path. "Well, Your Highness, where do we start?"

"At the bottom, I suppose," Larris said, quickening his pace to walk beside her. The path was just wide enough for the two of them to walk abreast.

"You suppose?" Larris had never said that he knew where to find the serpent, but she had assumed that once they found the city, he would lead them directly to it. In retrospect, that had been a foolish assumption, considering he had admitted that he did not even know what it was.

"I got us here, did I not? Well, Oskar and I got us here. We will find it." His voice exuded confidence.

"Do you practice talking like that?" she asked. Behind her, she heard Allyn snigger. Larris frowned at her.

"Don't look at me that way," she continued. "You know exactly what I mean. Like a general leading his troops into battle. I assume you weren't born talking like that. It must be intentional."

Larris smiled and shook his head. "This will go faster if we divide up. Oskar and Hierm, begin with the doorway farthest to your left, and work your way to the top. Allyn, you and Khalyndryn take the far right, Shanis and I will begin with the three in the middle."

Before she could so much as make a wise comment about Larris taking charge, the others had headed in opposite directions, eager to begin the search. She stood with hands on hips, and surveyed the city from up close.

There were five of the dome-like structures arrayed in a line before them. Curving stairways wound up between each of them, and swept up each side of the cavern, leading to the second level, where there were four such edifices. The stairs snaked their way progressively upward to a level of three, then two and finally to a lone dome at the top.

"Waiting for something?" Larris kidded before leading the way through the arched doorway of the center room. Shanis followed behind him, ducking beneath the low arch.

The room, which Shanis had thought would be round from looking at it from the outside, was oval, and sunk deep into the cliff face. The faint glow of sunlight through the doorway intruded only so far into the blackness beyond. She heard a scraping sound, and a yellow-orange glow blossomed in Larris' hand.

"What is that?" she asked.

"Firestick," he replied. Moving forward, he raised his hand to let the light shine on the domed ceiling above. Something was carved in the surface, but Shanis paid little mind.

"I thought only thieves used firesticks!" she said.

Larris looked at her and smiled. "Come now, do you think we royals let the thieves have all the fun? Seriously, though. They aren't as volatile as they once were. They're quite safe. Want to hold it?" He held the firestick, about the thickness of her middle finger and the length of her palm, toward her.

"No, thank you," she said. Larris' reassurances notwithstanding, she did not trust the firestick's reputation. Her eyes took in the round room, twenty paces across, with its perfectly smooth floor, and no visible seam where the curving walls met the level floor. It was empty. She looked back up at the ceiling. "What is all that?" She gestured at the markings that spiraled down from the center. They almost looked like writing, but not quite. Some of the images were tiny pictures: birds, trees, stars, and people. Others were squares with differing numbers of dots inside. These, she intuited represented numbers.

"Glyphs," Larris said, lifting the firestick above his head. "An ancient form of writing. What I would give to be able to record these and decipher them at my leisure." He touched the wall, letting his hand linger. "What stories might they tell?"

"Let's hope they're not telling us that another golorak is coming up through that hole," Shanis said. She indicated a spot just a few paces in front of him where another ceremonial well lay.

"Thank you for the warning," he said. "My father always said my eyes were so far in the clouds that I couldn't see what was right in front of my face. Or in this case, my feet." He lowered the firestick to reveal a well of about half the diameter of the one they had seen outside. A serpent was carved into the stone around the well; its eye glinted with silver flecks of some stone that had been embedded in the figure. The light of the firestick revealed that, unlike the well outside, this one was empty and no more than a few hands deep. "I'll wager there's one of these in every room."

His prediction was borne out as they continued their explorations. Every room they entered was approximately the same size and shape, with what appeared to Shanis to be the same writing winding its way down the ceiling. And in the center of each room was the same ceremonial well, with the engraved serpent coiled around the outside. The sameness did not end there. Each room was void of any signs of human habitation, or even passage.

They had dutifully examined every room, searching for nooks, crannies, hidden passages, anything that might conceal their objective. They even sifted through the dust at the bottom of each well, but found them all to be equally empty. By the time they reached the top of the city, the others were waiting there with discouraged looks on their faces, and an air of defeat about them.

"Nothing," Oskar said, looking out at the canyon.

Khalyndryn pointedly looked away from Shanis, who was more than happy to ignore her as well.

"This can't be it," Shanis protested. "It's too empty, too clean." Oskar met her gaze with a blank stare. Hierm and Allyn looked at one another and shook their heads. She turned back to Larris. "Can't you feel it, Larris? It feels false. This is not real." Frustration welled within her. She could not find the words to describe what she felt, but she knew she was right.

"Looks real to me," Allyn muttered. He slipped a knife from his belt, and began trimming his nails.

"Never mind," Shanis said.

"No," Larris said, taking hold of her upper arm. "Say more." The keen interest in his brown eyes persuaded her to try again.

"I don't know," she said, feeling frustrated. "I'm hungry. Let's sit down and eat."

They circled around the well and sat down. Shanis chewed on a piece of jerked venison and contemplated their situation. What should they do? She gazed down into the well. Once again, the waters seemed to pull her down, drawing her in. She gazed at her reflection, and saw someone she scarcely recognized.

She had lost weight since they had left home. Her cheekbones were more prominent. She looked older, more serious. She leaned closer, watching the image grow larger, until she was nose-to-nose with her reflecxtion.

"Shanis, what are you doing?"

Someone grabbed her shoulder and yanked her back. She sat upright, wiped her face with her sleeve, and looked around at the ring of incredulous faces.

Larris took his hand from her shoulder and frowned, but said nothing. His brown eyes held a mix of concern and curiosity.

"Don't mind me," she said. "It's the well. It feels like it's pulling me down. It's foolish, I know. Just a feeling." She sat back and turned her attention to her meal, still aware of a tugging sensation that seemed to draw her toward the water. She took a bite and slowly chewed on the dried meat. What was it about the well? The water!

"Where is this water coming from?" The others looked at her quizzically. "We've seen very little water for days. And this," she slapped the ground with her palm, "is solid rock. Where did this water come from?"

"There's nothing to feed an underground river in these parts," Oskar mused. "Especially not at this elevation."

"No rain to speak of," Allyn added. "You can see that by vegetation, or lack thereof. Just some scrub and stunted trees. Nothing that requires much moisture."

Larris dipped a hand into the well and scooped out a palmful of water. He took a long look, then passed his palm under his nose, then nodded.

"It's clean and cold," he said, letting it spill back down. He hesitated for a moment, and then touched two wet fingers to the tip of his tongue. He frowned and leaned down close to the water, inhaling deeply. "I'm hesitant to drink it, but it seems fresh." He looked up at Shanis. "I believe you are on to something."

She stood and took a step back, bumping her leg against Hierm. He clambered to his feet to stand alongside her.

"The well is the only thing that is different," she said, puzzling it out as she spoke. "That is what I was trying to say earlier. There is a sameness to everything over there," she gestured toward the city. "It's all the same shape, the same carvings, the same stone. The serpents around the doors are plain. Here," she pointed to the well, "the serpent twists and coils. You can see the scales. It's done in as much detail as the one in the cliff."

She narrowed her eyes and gazed intently now at the serpent that encircled the well. The sensation of being pulled along was stronger. She relaxed and imagined that her gaze was being drawn forward by the unseen force. She followed the body of the serpent around until she focused in on the serpent's eye. Unlike the rest of the carving, which was rendered in lifelike detail, the eye was plain and round, too large for the head, and totally unlike a snake's hooded orb.

Larris saw what she was looking at. He reached down and probed the carved socket with gentle fingertips. His brow creased and he narrowed an eye, setting his jaw in contemplation. His brown eyes still locked on the serpent's eye, he drew his hand away, and reached into his belt pouch. He spoke softly to himself as he fished around for something.

"My gift," he said. "My trade. I wondered why they would give me such a thing. Where is it?"

Shanis and Hierm exchanged puzzled glances. Khalyndryn appeared thoroughly confused, Allyn merely bored. Only Oskar appeared to know what the prince was thinking. He smiled and nodded, still gnawing on his piece of jerked meat.

"Where is it?" Larris whispered. "Ah!" From his belt pouch he drew out the old coin the Thandrylls had given him as a "trade". He turned it over in his palm, then held it between his thumb and forefinger, feeling the tarnished surface. "I shall look the fool if I'm wrong," he said, but his eyes were alive with confidence. With that, he laid the coin over the eye socket. A quarter-turn and it slid neatly into the hole.

Nothing happened.

Shanis watched as the grin drained from Larris' face. His jaw went slack, and the glint in his eyes dimmed. She felt sorry for him, kneeling there, crestfallen.

Whoosh!

Larris fell back on his behind, startled by the sudden noise. Shanis backed up a step as well. The surface roiled as fat air bubbles burst to the surface. A circle appeared in the midst of the water, expanded into a turbulent whirlpool. Everyone crowded around the well, watching as the water drained away to reveal a series of handholds, much like those down which they had descended the cliff face. Larris looked down into the well, then lifted his head, smiling.

"Who's first?"

Chapter 33

Shanis held back, letting the others make their way down the tunnel first. She still hesitated at the thought of responding to the beckoning tug from down below. Even now that she had solved the mystery, it still drew her downward. She took a long look.

"Are you coming?" Hierm's voice echoed from the well.

"All right." Gingerly, she lowered her left foot into the well until it found purchase. Keeping her palms firmly on the ground, she stepped down with her right. The footholds were damp, but not particularly slippery. Another step down and she spotted the first handhold. She hooked the fingertips of her left hand into it and continued her slow descent, all the while mindful of the pulling sensation that sought to drag her down. The cold rock sucked the warmth from her hands, and the dark blanketed her. She heard the scraping sound of a firestick, and soon a yellow glow shone up from below.

Her foot hit solid rock and she looked down to see a stone grate, cut through with narrow slits. A thin trickle of water flowed from a small spout about chest-high and disappeared through the floor. She knelt and tried to peer through one of the slits, but only blackness lay beneath. Her heart fluttered at the thought of infinite emptiness that her imagination conjured. She was suddenly aware that the sensation no longer seemed to be drawing her down, but instead seemed to be over her right shoulder. She looked back to see her companions standing in the mouth of an arched tunnel, staring at her. She was about to say something acerbic, but one look at the tunnel rendered her speechless.

The passageway was about ten paces wide, flat at the bottom, and rose at a gentle angle before narrowing at the top, to meet at a sharp point. Where the tunnel opened into the well, a groove ran all the way around, where the wall that sealed the tunnel had locked into place. She looked down to see where it had receded into the floor. She pushed between Hierm and Khalyndryn, and stepped into the passage. An odd decorative pattern was carved into the apex of the ceiling. Long, cylindrical segments with spikes jutting from either side were evenly spaced as far as she could see. The appearance was familiar, but she could not place it.

"It's the backbone," Larris said, walking up beside her. "And these," he reached out and touched one of the vertical protrusions that formed arches every ten paces are so, "are the ribs." His voice was soft and reverent as he spoke. "We are in the belly of the snake."

Shanis knelt and touched the smooth black floor, inlaid with shiny stones carved in the shape of scales. A quick glance revealed that the walls between the ribs were the same.

"You were right, Shanis," Khalyndryn said, sidling up to her. Her voice was tentative, and she looked as if she would flee if Shanis so much as blinked in her direction. "The city up above was false. This is the real thing."

Shanis stood, and met the girl's worried frown with a long, level stare. Perhaps it was only wishful thinking, yet she believed she saw, not an apology in Khalyndryn's eyes, but a sincere desire for things to be right between them.

"Thank you," she replied. Gods, that was painful! Resisting the urge to add something cutting, she turned away as the broad, shining smile she had hated since childhood bloomed on Khalyndryn's face.

"Well done," Larris whispered, clasping her shoulder in his strong hand.

"Don't patronize me," she shot back, pulling free of his grasp. "Let's see where this tunnel leads before Oskar fouls his breeches."

"Wait a moment!" Oskar protested, but nervous laughter from the rest of the group drowned him out.

She snatched the firestick from Larris and led the way down the tunnel.

The passage gently wound back-and-forth like a serpent slithering across the ground. Allyn cautioned them to watch for traps or side tunnels, but they saw neither. After what seemed like an hour, but surely was not, they finally came to a place where the tunnel split into two passages.

"It seems the serpent has two heads," Oskar quipped.

Shanis opened her mouth to ask in what direction Larris wished to proceed, but a deep roar startled her into silence. The sound came again, this time so powerful that she feared it would shake the walls down upon them. She saw Larris and Oskar exchange frightened glances.

"What was that?" Khalyndryn whispered, her voice quavering. Giant cracks were appearing in the brave façade she had adopted that morning, and the scared town girl was emerging. She clutched an annoyed-looking Hierm's upper arm in both hands.

"Golorak." Oskar sounded as if he had swallowed a frog.

"But you killed it!" Khalyndryn protested.

"I suppose there is more than one," Larris said. The pallor of his face was evident even in the uneven light, but his voice was surprisingly calm. "We did not expect it to be easy, did we?"

Shanis found herself grudgingly admiring his composure. She remembered his tale of their fight with the beast, and how his sword had bounced off its tough hide. What would they do if it found them? What could they do?

"Which tunnel did the sound come from?" Hierm asked, stepping toward the passage on the right and inclining an ear. The ensuing discussion yielded no agreement. Oskar and Larris thought the sound had come from the tunnel on the left, Allyn and Khalyndryn insisted that it came from the tunnel on the right, while Hierm and Shanis agreed that it sounded as if it had come from behind them, though that was impossible.

"Why couldn't it come from behind us?" Khalyndryn asked.

"If it is even half the size of the one we saw, it would never fit down the tunnel," Oskar replied. His voice had regained some of its strength, as if the realization reassured him.

While the others continued to discuss their plight, Shanis closed her eyes and willed the sound away. Just as she had done so many times at sword practice, she turned her focus inward. No distractions, no physical sensation. She sought the calming oneness with the blade. Within her consciousness she created the image of a shining sword. Her thoughts followed its razor edge down to the shining, perfect tip. Her flesh was steel, and she was one with the blade. The voices around her melted away, and the orange flickers of firelight upon her eyelids faded. At that moment, she felt perfect peace.

What to do when the wrong choice might mean death?

She remembered her father teaching her woodscraft. He took her into the forest and got her thoroughly lost. "Trust your instincts," he said. "You can feel the path, if you will allow yourself to. It will call out to you, but you must let it." Wrapped in the oneness, she felt no pang of homesickness at the memory.

She opened herself to the beckoning of the pathway that had guided her as a small child. A skill she had seldom had need to use. She felt something. It was the same tugging sensation that had drawn them into the well. It called out to her. It took her hand in a gentle grip and drew her forward.

She visualized the two passages. The tunnel on the left exuded a feeling of warmth and light. The passage to the right poured forth an icy cold like a gushing mountain stream. She shivered within her void, and her bones seemed to freeze in a way they had not since the last time they had encountered the ice cats. Her eyes snapped open.

"We must go that way," she said, indicating the tunnel on the left. The sensation was so strong now, her certainty firm. She did not know what lay at the end, but she knew their path lay to the left. "The golorak is down the other tunnel," she added.

"How do you know?" Allyn stepped directly in front of her, his right hand on his sword hilt, his left thumb hooked in his belt. "It is our life if you are wrong."

"I know," she averred. She met his challenging stare with what she hoped was a look of firm resolve. She had no doubt that she was correct, but she had serious doubts about her ability to convince the others. "I feel it."

"You feel it," Allyn echoed.

Larris put his hand on Allyn's chest and interposed himself between the two.

Anger flashed in Allyn's eyes for an instant, and then he returned to his usual calm exterior.

Larris appraised her for a long, uncomfortable second, before nodding his assent. "We take the passage on the left, and may the gods smile upon us."

"Wait!" Khalyndryn called out, recovering some of her earlier salt. "She feels it? Shanis has never felt anything in her life, save anger. She doesn't know which way we should go."

"So," Larris said, "it is your opinion that we should take the tunnel on the right?" He waited as Khalyndryn gaped at them for a heartbeat before shaking her head. "You prefer the path to the left?" Khalyndryn only shrugged. "Well then, seeing how as it makes no difference to you." Leaving the statement hanging, he turned and led the group down the passage Shanis had chosen.

She felt gratified that he had taken her side and her advice. It was good to be trusted for something other than hunting and fighting. It also pleased her to see someone else take Khalyndryn down a peg. She suppressed a smile. She was not one to act the fool over a prince. He was just seeing good sense, that was all.

They followed the tunnel at a steady pace. She kept glancing back over her shoulder, expecting to see the golorak, though she knew the passage was too small. She wondered how far they had come. She imagined they were deep in the mountains, Murantha left far behind. She spared a thought for their horses, hoping the mounts were safe.

Her thoughts snapped back to her immediate surroundings when the golorak bellowed again. Thankfully, the sound clearly came from behind them. She felt relieved until she heard the second cry. It was a golorak, but its cry was slightly higher-pitched. She imagined it was a female. Worse, it came from in front of them.

"Two of them," Allyn muttered. They walked side-by-side a few paces behind Larris. When the first golorak answered, he fished a bowstring from his belt pouch and strung his bow with dexterous fingers. Shanis imagined that the bow would do them little good, but it likely made him feel better.

"If they are a mating pair," Oskar said to no one in particular, "then there might be younglings. And if the younglings are small enough to pass through the tunnel..."

"Shut up, Oskar," she said. Not looking back to see if she had hurt his feelings, she gripped her sword hilt and quickened her pace to catch up with Larris. Always better to meet a problem head on, so Master Yurg always said. Of course, Master Yurg never had a golorak for a problem.

The tunnel wound downward at a gentle angle, and the air grew damp and distinctly chilly. The tunnel narrowed to the point that she and Larris were almost touching as they walked together. Though she understood that a narrow passageway made them safer from the golorak, or should she say, goloraks, she still sensed the oppressive weight of the stone above and around her.

Their path continued to carry them downward and she felt a slight breeze on her face as she walked. Larris paused, taking her by the arm to hold her back, and raised his torch high. Ahead of them, the blackness gave way to a gray, arching space. The tunnel had come to an end.

"Oh, my," she whispered. The tunnel opened onto an expansive underground cavern. Unlike everything they had seen since the discovery of the city, the cavern appeared natural. Massive stalactites dangled from a ceiling so far above them that she could not guess the height. The walls were jagged, and fell into a bottomless blackness that made her stomach tremble when she tried to fathom its depths.

A faint hissing sound caught her attention. All around the cavern, as far as she could see, tiny streams no broader than arms width, poured forth from the stone, tumbling down the rocky faces into the silence below.

The others crowded up to the edge of the precipice, all wanting to witness the marvel. For a moment she feared they would push her over the edge.

"Gently," she said in a firm voice as Oskar shoved against her from behind. She felt Larris' arm around her waist, and for once she did not mind.

"Look at the lights," Khalyndryn said, awestruck. They all raised their heads to follow her gaze.

Far above them, six small openings had been bored in the rock. They formed a diamond shape, and were spaced too evenly and aligned too perfectly to have been formed naturally. Shafts of sunlight streamed through.

Each shaft of light shone on a stalactite, and she could see that they were imbued with sparkling crystalline rock. She followed the cascade of light as the beams tumbled down, dancing on the shining stones, dividing like channels of a river, and flowing back together at the tip of a thick bole of stone that hung down to eye level and shone against the far wall in a tight circle.

"There it is! There it is!" Larris' voice danced with childlike joy. His arm still around her waist, he turned and crushed her in a tight embrace.

She was too surprised to resist. She was about to ask what he was talking about when she heard Oskar cry out.

"You're right! I couldn't see it before. The stalactite was in the way. Everyone duck down and look."

She gently freed herself from Larris' clutches, and dropped to her knees next to Oskar. "What is all this fuss about?" He pointed across the chasm, and she was surprised to see another tunnel, the twin of the one they were in, illuminated in the shaft of light. The giant stalactite in the center of the cavern had blocked their view.

She needed only a moment's glance to know that this was the source of the pulling sensation. It seemed to glow from within, with a pulsating blue light. What was more, it seemed to her to be crackling with energy. She could neither understand nor express the feeling, but when she gazed upon it, it felt as though lightning shot through her.

"How do we get across?" Allyn asked. For once, there was no trace of skepticism in his voice, only eagerness.

She studied the rocky face of the opposite wall, and her eyes quickly picked out a line of shadow running horizontally from the floor of the tunnel into the darkness to the right. Before she could call it to his attention, Allyn pointed into the distance.

"The ledge runs to a bridge. Or what's left of one. I can see it from here. There was a bridge spanning the chasm. The middle has fallen away, but there are stone footings still in place."

She strained to see the bridge, but all she could make out was a dark blob. She had not realized how good Allyn's eyes were.

"There's a ledge on this side as well, see it?"

"Yes, we see it." Larris' voice was tinged with impatience. He was likely frustrated at being unable to make out the bridge in the distance.

"If you follow it out, you can see where the bridge was on this side. There is a bit more of it left over here. If we can make our way over to it, I think I can get a rope around one of those footings, and we can climb across."

"Climb across that?" Khalyndryn gasped. "I don't think I can do it. I'm not strong enough."

Oskar looked as if he were about to join the protest when another roar from a golorak shook the tunnel floor.

"That was right underneath us," Hierm whispered, his voice almost inaudible over the ringing in Shanis' ears.

Larris did not have to give the order to move. Allyn moved to the edge of the tunnel, took a moment to scrutinize the ledge, then extinguished the firestick and dropped it to the floor.

"I have more," he explained. "If we give our eyes time to adjust, there is enough light to make our way across." The others followed suit, extinguishing their lights. By then, Allyn was already several paces out onto the ledge. His body was pressed flat against the rock, which was not exactly smooth, but appeared to be blessedly free of any large protrusions. "There is a groove cut into the rock at shoulder level," he called back. "Hook your fingertips into it. It helps."

"I'll go next," Oskar said, his voice choked with fear, "before I change my mind." He adjusted his staff, which he wore slung across his back with a length of leather Allyn had given him. He looked back at Shanis, winked, and stepped out onto the ledge.

The golorak roared again, so close that Shanis thought she must be standing on top of it. The sound startled Oskar who whirled his head around to look back at them. For a moment she feared he would lose his balance, but he held steady, and continued his trek. Khalyndryn needed no further encouragement to mount the ledge and begin her trek across.

"Follow her and stay close," Larris said to Hierm. "Try to keep her calm and don't let her go too fast." Hierm nodded and followed Larris' instructions.

Her curiosity getting the better of her, Shanis lay down flat on her stomach and hung her chin over the ledge. A faint animal scent wafted up, foul and unfamiliar. As her eyes adjusted to the gloom beneath the ledge, they focused on another tunnel directly beneath the one through which they had passed. This one was three times the width, and was rough and round, like a burrow. She heard a wet, snuffling sound, and the scratching of claws on stone. She did not need to see the frog-like face and razor teeth to know that the golorak was there.

She sprang to her feet and snatched Larris by the forearm, dragging him toward the ledge. "There's a tunnel right below us. It's right there!" She did not have to explain what "it" was. He hurried to the side, and gestured for her to go first.

Trying not to think about the emptiness beneath her, she put her left foot onto the ledge. Making sure she had firm footing, she reached up and hooked the fingers of her left hand into the groove. She held her breath, brought her right foot onto the ledge, and grabbed the handhold with her right hand.

The ledge was just wide enough for the ball of her foot. She was sickeningly aware of her heels hanging out in space, and the narrow pathway prevented her from centering her weight above it. The sword strapped to her back made her situation more precarious. She dug her fingers into the groove and suddenly was struck with a feeling of gratitude that she did not have Oskar's large behind to further unbalance her. The absurdity of the thought and the tension of the situation were nearly her undoing. She lost her focus for a moment, and with it her balance.

"What are you doing?" Larris whispered. He waited at the edge of the tunnel for her to move so he could mount the ledge.

Down below, the golorak made a grumbling sound that put Shanis in mind of an empty stomach. Not liking the images that thought conjured, she began to move along the ledge. Her first steps were cautious. She slid her left foot out as far as she dared, then moved her left hand forward. Her right hand followed, then she shifted some of her weight to her hands as she slid her right foot up to meet her left.

That's one. Only a hundred or so more to go.

Her second step was a bit more confident, and her third even more so. She heard a scuffing sound behind her, and knew that Larris was out on the ledge.

The golorak roared again, nearly startling her off the ledge. She looked back to see the beast snap at Larris' heels. With its flat face and virtual absence of neck, the golorak had no hope of reaching the young man. A wave of relief passed through Shanis as the creature turned back into the tunnel. The feeling was short lived, as the golorak thrust its hindquarters out of the tunnel, and whipped its thick, muscular tail at Larris.

It struck the wall with a violent slap, spraying shards of stone over Shanis and Larris. Slivers of rock cut her face and hands. The golorak bellowed, and struck again. Shanis screamed and turned her head as another wave of sharp fragments sliced into the back of her neck.

She tore forward across the ledge, thinking of nothing except getting away. She took reckless chances, actually lifting her feet off the ledge to take longer strides, and letting go of the handholds so she could reach farther forward. But no matter how fast she moved, she felt as if she were standing still. She imagined the ledge tilting upward, sliding her back into the golorak's gaping maw.

"Shanis, slow down!" Larris called. "He can't get to you!" He shouted something else, but it was overwhelmed by another roar. All the while, the creature continued to pound the rock with his tail.

Shanis was aware of blood oozing onto her fingertips from the cuts opened by the flying stone. Her grip was less sure, and she was about to slow her pace when it happened.

Her left foot came down on a sliver of rock, probably dislodged by the golorak. It was not large, but enough to turn her ankle. Her left leg buckled, and her right foot slipped free. She screamed, her feet scrabbling for purchase against the rough stone as she dangled from bloody fingertips over a black abyss.

Her right instep caught a rough protrusion, and she pushed up, at the same time pulling with slippery fingers. She could almost get her left foot onto the ledge. She was frighteningly mindful of the pulling sensation that drew her toward the tunnel on the other side of the cavern. She fought to ignore it as she struggled to regain the ledge.

Nearly there. Her left hand began to slip. Almost! Her toe touched the ledge.

The rock beneath her right foot broke away, and her weight fell heavy onto her hands. Her left hand lost its purchase, and she knew she was going to die.

And then Larris was there. He gripped the back of her belt through a handful of cloak, and pulled her up. He could not lift her all the way onto the ledge by himself, but his added strength was enough to help her regain her grip, and get her feet back onto the ledge.

She looked at him, all six of him refracted in her frightened tears, and could not speak. She felt his hand on her shoulder, comforting her.

"You are all right," he said. "You are the bravest woman I have ever known. Lead us across this ledge and away from that smelly animal."

In that moment, she understood why a man would die for his ruler. In her moment of weakness, Larris had affirmed and inspired her with a few simple words. In the back of her mind, she knew he said those things to calm and encourage her, but in that moment she believed them to be true.

With her resolve firmed, she resumed her trek. She narrowed her focus on the ledge in front of her, and repeated her calming exercise, this time with her eyes open. Now it came easier. She formed the blade in her subconscious and imagined her senses to be the keen edge. All else was gone: the golorak, her fear, the tugging sensation.

In what seemed like seconds she felt hands on her, and looked up to see Hierm pulling her onto the remains of the old bridge. She fell into his arms as she stepped forward, and then felt Oskar wrap his bearlike arms around her from behind. They were squeezing the breath out of her, but she did not care. She felt a hand on her cheek and opened her eyes to see Khalyndryn weeping openly. She reached out and pulled the girl to her. Soon, the four villagers were in a tight circle, hugging and crying, a world away from home.

She broke the embrace with reluctance at the sound of Allyn clearing his throat. He stood at the edge of the chasm, having managed to lasso one of the square stone footings on the other side and had secured the other end rope to a nearby boulder.

"We need to get across right away," he snapped. "Who knows what might come out of that tunnel?"

In her relief at making it across the ledge, she had not noticed the gaping passageway that opened onto the bridge.

"I'll go first in case it doesn't hold," Larris said, striding to the jagged edge of the broken stone bridge.

Allyn nodded and picked up another rope lying at his feet, and cinched it around Larris' waist. He showed Shanis and the others how to hold it, and instructed them to keep tension on it, and to play the rope out as Larris climbed across. "If his rope doesn't hold, it's up to us." He tied the other end to the boulder for good measure, then signaled for Larris to cross.

Shanis and the others watched in silence as Larris took hold of the rope in both hands, hooked his ankles around it, and began to make his way, feet-first across the chasm. It seemed an eternity, but soon he was standing on the other side, untying the rope from his waist.

"Send Oskar next," he called. "While we still have enough hands on that side to support his weight."

Oskar was trembling visibly as Allyn secured the rope around his midriff. The archer joked that he hoped there would be enough rope left after spanning Oskar's middle, but Oskar was too nervous to laugh. Nonetheless, he too made it across without incident.

Khalyndryn was next, and Shanis was surprised at how nimbly she made her way across. It was decided that Hierm, the heaviest of the remaining three, would go next, followed by Shanis, then Allyn.

Hierm made his way, hand-over-hand, with ease, and was almost all the way across when the golorak came.

The deep, throaty roar burst forth from the passageway in a primordial challenge. It crept forward, its belly low to the ground. Muscled haunches rippled in the firelight, and its bulbous eyes glowed silver. Shanis had never seen anything so frightening.

In a flash, Allyn fired off an arrow that clipped the golorak in the middle of its forehead and bounced harmlessly away. It roared again, and continued to slink forward. Another arrow just missed its eye, and it shook its head and took another step forward. Then it stopped.

Emerging from the tunnel, its eyes caught sight of two firesticks Allyn had wedged into cracks on either side of the tunnel. It flinched and drew back, baring its teeth.

"Come on while there's time!" Larris called. "You'll have to do it without the safety rope."

"Go," Allyn ordered her. "I'll be right behind you."

Shanis hurried to the edge and began the traverse. She resisted the urge to go too fast, having learned her lesson on the ledge. The ropes cut into her already damaged hands, and her sore ankle screamed in pain as she scooted across the rope. She tried not to think of the unrelenting nothingness that reached up for her. She kept her eyes focused on her companions who waited on the other side, shouting encouragement to her.

She heard the golorak rumble, and stole a glance back. The creature had moved out of the tunnel, and was tensed to spring.

Standing at the very edge of the precipice, Allyn held his bow, an arrow nocked, in his left hand. In his right he held a firestick. Calmly, he struck the firestick against the bottom of his boot. Flame blossomed, and he touched it to the arrow, which instantly caught fire. *Pitch covered!* she thought.

Silently, the golorak bounded forward. In a quick, fluid motion, Allyn took aim and let fly. The arrow took the monster full in the left eye, and it let out a deafening cry of pain and rage. It stumbled and fell. Rising, it turned and fled, bellowing all the while.

Shanis cheered, and she heard the others join in. With renewed spirits, she made her way across.

Allyn waited for her to reach the far side before he mounted the rope. He was the most agile of them all, and in no time he was halfway across.

We made it, Shanis thought. She was about to voice her thought when a flash of movement caught her eye. She looked up to see the golorak come hurtling out of the tunnel, sprinting toward the broken bridge.

Allyn's back was toward the creature, but the look on the other's faces must have told him what was happening. He scooted across the rope, hands and feet flying.

Shanis watched in fear as he drew closer, all the while mindful of the dizzying rate at which the golorak was eating up the intervening distance. Could it jump so far?

Allyn was no more than twenty paces away when the golorak slid to a halt at the edge of the broken bridge, its claws grinding into the stone as it stopped.

Shanis could have sworn the creature looked right at her with its good eye as it raised a clawed foreleg and smashed down, crushing rock and cleaving the rope in two.

Chapter 34

Shanis cried out in alarm as Allyn fell. Upside down, his legs still wrapped around the rope, he swung down toward the wall below Shanis. His rope ran out of slack, and he nearly lost his grip, the jolt causing him to slip almost to the end. Before he could recover, he hit the wall hard. His legs came free, and he flipped in midair. Somehow he managed to hold on.

"He's like a cat," Hierm marveled.

Allyn looked up at them, blood pouring down his face. "Pull me up," he croaked. "I don't know how long I can hold on."

They immediately set to hauling at the rope, aided by Larris and Oskar. Allyn grunted as he banged against the rock. He used his feet to try and keep himself from the rock. Soon, he lay on his back, breathing heavily. Against his faint protests, Larris checked him for broken bones. When he was finished, he shook his head to indicate that he found none.

Shanis turned her attention away from Allyn and looked around. This side of the cleft was similar to that from which they had come. Another ledge ran along the stone wall to the glowing cave. From somewhere far away, she heard the faint call of a golorak. It was answered moments later by another, more distant than the first. Then another.

"This place is like a warren for those frost-blighted things," Hierm muttered. He looked at the cave entrance, the blue light pulsing faintly. "What do you think we'll find in there?" He turned to face her.

She was surprised to realize how much older he looked. So much had happened to them on this journey that she had not noticed the effect on her friend. He was leaner, more serious-looking. In fact, he looked like his father.

"What is it?" he asked.

"Just thinking about how far we've come," she said. "We've been through so much, and now here we are." It defied belief.

"I know," he said. "I can't believe it either." His eyes clouded as he looked at their destination. "Whatever it is, I hope it will protect us from the goloraks." He shook his head. "I never thought anything would frighten me more than an ice cat."

"The gods willing, we won't encounter any more of them," Larris said, walking up next to them. Behind him, Allyn was on his feet, though he was visibly fatigued. "Allyn insists he's ready to move on." He shook his head to indicate that he did not agree with his friend's assessment.

Shanis led the way across. Khalyndryn followed, with Hierm close behind. They were concerned that Khalyndryn was growing fatigued, but she was holding up well.

This time, the climb across the ledge was blessedly uneventful. She heard a few distant golorak calls, but nothing more. She was concerned about Allyn, but dared not steal a glance back until she reached the other end.

The ledge terminated on a broad shelf in front of a yawing cave. The blue light flickered with an eerie glow. She turned and offered her hand to Khalyndryn, who clasped it with cold, moist fingers. Stepping onto the shelf, she offered a thin smile of thanks before turning away.

The strain was wearing on her. She looked back to see Allyn making his way across. Blood still trickled from facial cuts he had sustained when he crashed into the rock. His face was a grim mask of determination. Larris was behind him, holding fast to the wall with his right hand. His left was on the small of Allyn's back, steadying him. It was only then that Shanis noticed how wobbly Allyn's legs were. She admired his resolve, and respected Larris for his concern for his friend. All in all, she supposed the prince was not so bad.

Oskar brought up the rear. His face was pale, and he gripped the wall so hard that his knuckles seemed to glow. His breath came in gasps.

"You're almost there," Shanis called to him. "Just a bit farther."

Soon, they all were gathered in front of the tunnel. They stood in silence for a moment, looking from one face to another. The gravity of the moment rendered them speechless. She supposed that it was possible that this tunnel would lead them to another dead end, like the city up above, but somehow she knew that it would not. This was it. They had arrived.

Larris stood with his back to the others, gazing down the tunnel. She wondered if he was savoring the moment. Or perhaps he feared what he might find. Or what he might not find. He turned to face them, smiling. He started to speak, but Shanis cut him off.

"You are not going to give us another one of your 'Larris speeches', are you?"

"Actually, yes I was." He looked a touch abashed, but it lasted only a moment. "Instead, I'll simply say, thank you for seeing this through with me."

Shanis did not have time to feel guilty. Larris turned, drew his sword, and led the way down the passage. Blue light danced around him, and the edges of his form seemed to waver. Suppressing a wave of fear, she gripped her sword hilt and followed. Allyn took up his bow, which he had not unstrung since shooting the golorak, and fell in alongside her, with the others close behind.

She felt the mystical pull again, now almost irresistible. She felt like she should lean backward in order to keep from falling over forward.

Her thoughts swam. What would it mean to find the Silver Serpent? What would it mean to them? To the world? Her mind was abuzz with possibilities. What if the power was so great that Larris could not control it? What if, in a moment of weakness, he used it for ill? Could they even take it? Could they touch it? Would it hurt them?

Her knees gave just a bit, and she caught herself. Performing her focusing exercise, she pushed the thoughts away, and steeled herself against whatever seemed to be dragging her forward.

Why is it only pulling me? Looking around at the others, she saw that only Oskar's face showed evidence of strain, though they all looked serious.

"Do you feel that?" she whispered to Oskar, who nodded his head. She noted his pale, sweaty face.

"What is that?" Larris halted and turned to face them. His face was taut, whether with excitement or annoyance at the distraction, she could not tell.

"It's pulling me," she said. "It's as if invisible arms are drawing me forward. It's almost tangible. You don't feel it?" She looked around, generalizing the question to all of her companions. All, save Oskar, shook their heads.

"I don't feel anything but afraid," Khalyndryn said.

Ordinarily that statement would have annoyed Shanis, but she had to admit she admired Khalyndryn, just a touch, for going on in the face of her fears, especially after the golorak. Her attention moved to Oskar. Why would only the two of them feel it?

"Well," Larris said, "whatever the reason you are feeling it, let us hope that it is drawing us toward something good." He did not need to say what that something was. "I can't believe otherwise." He motioned for them to continue, and led the way.

Shanis took the final steps down the passageway as if she was walking naked in snow. Her body tingled, and she shivered. Numbness engulfed her and she heard a faint humming sound that grew louder with each step.

They reached an arched doorway. Carved into the stone all around it were serpents coiled around bolts of lightning. It looked powerful and deadly. Larris paused to look at the carvings before entering the room.

The humming burst into a crescendo as Shanis stepped over the threshold. Blue light flowed around her, rippling across her in soft waves of bright blue, almost white, and in troughs of a deep cerulean.

The chamber was round, arching up to a dome high above. A circle of columns carved like impossibly twisting serpents held up the ceiling in the room's center. The walls, ceiling and floors were dark, polished stone.

Larris pointed toward the columns. Shanis followed the line of his finger and saw a dark figure kneeling among them. Moving closer, they saw that it was a statue.

It was a warrior clad in ancient armor. The figure was rendered in lifelike detail. Veins bulged in his powerful forearms, and his muscles seemed to ripple in the flowing light. His long, braided hair lay across his broad, powerful back. He was down on one knee, his head bowed low. A stone sword lay on his upraised palms, as if it was an offering to the gods.

The sword, too, appeared breathtakingly real. Above the round pommel, a serpent coiled around the hilt, its gaping mouth and needle-like fangs formed the guard. As they drew closer, Shanis could make out another serpent, twin to the one carved in the cliff face above the city, etched into the blade.

"It looks razor sharp," Hierm whispered. Oskar, who had been reaching out to touch the sword, snatched his hand back.

"This is the place," Larris said. "We've found it." He dropped to his knees before the stone figure, and gazed at its face, his expression unreadable. "We are here," he whispered. "Reveal your secrets. Where is the serpent? What is it?" They waited as if they expected the stone to speak.

After a few moments, Oskar cleared his throat. "Perhaps the answer lies back there."

Arrayed along the back wall, thirty paces away, six stone coffins lay in silent repose. Larris sprang to his feet and they hurried to the one in the center. They were surprised to discover that these were the source of the blue light.

"Seastone," Larris said. "Father gave two of his finest stallions and a small chest of gold and jewels for a piece of stone that was only large enough to make Mother a ring and a set of earrings. I'll wager there is not this much seastone in all of Gameryah combined." He trailed his fingers across the surface, the stone rippling like water. "I can't believe I didn't notice them before."

"What? Who is in here?" Oskar asked. "I think I see some writing."

"Yes," Larris said, moving his hand toward the head. "You can just make it out. It is in Elevated. I know very few words, but this one," he pointed to a word, "is 'Cardith'. And this says 'ruler'." He ran his fingers over the ornate, curved text, that looked to Shanis more like a tangle of rope than writing. He paused, sucking in his breath. "Frostmarch." The word sent a chill through the room. "I believe," he said, straightening, "that this is the tomb of Sarala, who ruled Cardith during the Frostmarch."

"But she fell in battle," Oskar protested. "They carried her body home, and it lies in a crypt beneath the temple of Vesala."

"Have you looked inside the crypt of late?" Allyn said.

Oskar scowled but did not reply.

They waited while Larris made a brief inspection of the other tombs. "This is amazing," he said, stepping away from the last one. "The rulers of the six nations at the end of the Godwars and the beginning of the Frostmarch are entombed here."

"So the Serpent lies with one of them?" Allyn asked.

"We shall find out," he said. "Help me with this." Allyn, Hierm and Oskar helped him lift the lid from the sarcophagus farthest to the left. "It's quite light," he said as they laid it to the side with care.

Shanis sidled up to Hierm, who stood with the others peering into the coffin. Khalyndryn joined them after a brief hesitation. The contents of the vault were illuminated in the blue glow.

A dry, brittle skeleton, its rib cage collapsed under the weight of tarnished chain mail, lay grinning up at them. A gold circlet with an onyx raven set in its center hung askew across its forehead. Its hands were folded across its chest, and it held a short sword, its blade worn and the leather wrappings around the hilt crumbling from dry rot.

"Adar, King of Kyrin," Larris announced. "But I don't see anything here that could possibly be the Silver Serpent."

Disappointed, they replaced the lid and moved on to the next crypt. Riljin, King of Halvala, wore a moldy bearskin over his chain mail, and was buried with his battle axe, Wulfbane. Mardid of Lothan wore a leather jerkin over his cross-hatched clan garb, and was laid to rest with his round, bronze shield and a broken sword.

"It was broken in the battle of Storlom," Larris explained. "He fought on with only the hilt and the hands-length of blade you see there. He slew the commander of the forces of ice, a shifter named Crattas, but he suffered a mortal blow in the fight."

Hollac of Riza was buried with his war hammer. Oskar commented on the man's stature, having read that Hollac was a mountain of a man. His remains, however, proved him to be unremarkable in both height and breadth.

Sarala, and Damenn, Primor of the Council of Diyonus, were buried without weapons, neither being warriors. Sarala wore the crown of Cardith and a silken dress. Damenn was outfitted in the traditional Diyonan robe and tabard. Around his neck hung the thick golden chains that indicated his station as the head of the Diyonan council.

When the last coffin was sealed, they stood in silence. It put Shanis in the mind of a mourning circle back home. Somehow, it seemed wrong to speak at this moment. After what seemed to her to be a suitable length of time, she spoke up.

"Where is it?" There was no need to say what it was. "There was neither silver nor anything that looked like a serpent in any of these." She gestured toward the coffins.

"It is here," Larris said. "Is that feeling of yours telling you anything?"

Shanis shook her head. "It is so powerful that it seems to be everywhere. All I can say is that it is centered on this room."

"Everyone spread out," Larris said, obviously disappointed. "Look everywhere. It must be something so obvious that we missed it."

Shanis moved to the wall behind the crypts. Running her fingers across the smooth stone, she felt for…she didn't know what. A door, a hidden switch like in the stories. Something caught her eye. A crack, no, a tiny seam, running on a perfectly plumb line down to the floor. She followed it with her fingers. The stones were fitted together so perfectly that she could scarcely feel it. Just overhead, it cut across horizontally for two arms lengths, then back down to the floor.

A doorway! She had turned to announce her find to the others, when Larris cried out.

"Right under our feet! I've found it!" He stood staring at the floor just outside the columns that encircled the kneeling warrior.

The others hurried to his side. Beneath their feet, a serpent, rendered in silver tile, coiled around the columns. Everyone dropped to the floor and began running their fingers across it.

"It appears to be only a design," Shanis said, the doorway temporarily forgotten, "just a pattern in the tile."

"We were so distracted by the statue and the crypts that we walked right over it," Larris said, ignoring her. "I told you it would be something obvious. Didn't I?" He was on his hands and knees, following the glittering scales with his hands.

"Larris, this is perfectly smooth," Allyn protested. "It's naught but a picture."

"There must be something," Larris muttered. "Here. The eyes are slightly recessed. Remember the eye of the serpent at the well? It was the key to opening up the passage."

The eyes were two perfect circles of glittering green stone. From her vantage point, they looked like part of the tile to Shanis.

"I wonder what will happen if I do this." Larris placed his index and middle fingers on the eyes and pressed.

Green light flared and a loud hiss filled the room. Larris leapt to his feet and drew his sword. The others backed away, drawing their weapons as well. Khalyndryn moved behind Oskar, the person closest to her, who was fumbling with his staff, which he wore strapped across his back.

The silver tile rippled and bubbled as the serpent took form. Silver scales coalesced on a body as thick as Shanis' thigh. The tail pulled loose from the floor, then the head. Green light danced in its eyes, and it turned and fixed its gaze on her. With another loud hiss, it opened its mouth, baring crystal fangs. It struck.

She spun to the side and heard the jaws snap closed just inches from her heart.

She swung her sword, but the serpent dodged the awkward stroke. She backpedaled, and ran squarely into one of the coffins.

Its body now fully free of the floor, the serpent pursued her, fangs bared. An arrow bounced harmlessly off the glittering scales of its head. It paused to turn its head and hiss at Allyn.

She resisted the urge to hide behind the coffin. I need room to move. She danced to her right as the creature struck again. She heard the seastone shatter and Larris cry out. She turned to see him attack the serpent from behind. With a shout of rage, he brought his blade down hard across its neck. Green sparks flew, but the serpent was unfazed. With a whip of its tail, it caught Larris in the side, sending him crashing into the wall, where he fell hard, his sword clattering to the floor.

Allyn loosed two more arrows in quick succession. Both caught the snake in the head, but had as little effect as the first. It turned its attention to him for only a moment, before turning back toward Shanis. It hurtled toward her, its metallic scales clicking on the stone floor.

Shanis raised her sword again, and when the serpent struck, she beat its attack to the side and danced away.

Hierm joined the fray, hacking at the tail. It spared him not so much as a glance. Larris, having regained his feet and sword, joined him in his desperate rear assault. The serpent whipped its tail at them, but they were ready. They dodged it and resumed hacking. Now the serpent spun and darted toward them. They moved apart, and the beast went for Larris.

"Go for its tail!" Allyn shouted, dashing in to attack again. "I think I knocked a scale loose!"

Shanis saw a flash of green light, and aimed her sword at it. This time, she could swear she felt the blade bite into the scales. She danced away as the snake came about, and she saw a sliver of green light shining through the silver skin.

"It can be hurt!" Larris shouted.

But would it be enough?

"The door is closing!" Khalyndryn screamed.

Shanis turned to see a wall of stone slide into place, sealing off the tunnel from which they had come. Khalyndryn was trying in vain to raise the stone. Next to her, Oskar stood stock-still, staring at the serpent. He was holding his staff out in front of him, and moving his lips. What was he doing? Silver light flashed in the corner of her eye, and she looked back to see glittering fangs lash out at her. She fended off the attack with her sword and danced away.

Her arms burned, and her step was slowing. The long day of climbing had worn her down, and now the fight was sapping the last of her strength. Another arrow found its mark, this time on the injured tail. Green sparks flew, and its venomous hiss burned their ears. It reared to strike at her again.

Larris and Hierm moved in from either side, this time attacking the creature's middle. It was waiting for them. A whip of its tail caught Hierm across the temple and he crumpled to the floor. With lightning speed it struck back at Larris, who could not move fast enough. Shanis saw a rip in his sleeve and blood running down his arm, purple in the blue light.

There was no time to ask if he was all right. The serpent came after her, striking with fury, driving her backward. No swordsman had ever kept her on such a defensive. She was fighting off its attack, but just barely. Allyn loosed another arrow, but the serpent was ignoring them, its full attention on her. It struck again, this time low, and she jumped back. She came down on something soft, and tumbled to her backside, her sword flying free from her grasp.

She had stumbled over Hierm's unconscious form. She scrambled backward on hands and feet, the serpent's gaping jaws seemingly right above her. Before it could strike, Larris struck it with a broad, reckless swing, his wounded left arm hanging limp at his side. The blow must have done some damage, because the snake now directed all its fury at the young prince. It caught Larris' ankles with its tail, sending him stumbling backward. It struck, its jaws clamping down on his sword, shattering the blade. Before Shanis could get to her feet, it had Larris in its coils, crushing the life from him.

Allyn came sprinting from the corner of her vision. He leapt onto the back of the beast, wrapping an arm around its neck, and tried to gouge its eyes with his hunting knife. The serpent shook free of him, and he fell winded to the ground.

Everything seemed to slow. She heard Khalyndryn screaming. She saw Oskar, crying out in fright, beating at the beast with his staff. She saw Hierm and Allyn lying on the floor, the latter struggling to get to his feet. She saw Larris, his face purple, pummeling the snake with his fists. What she did not see was her sword,

I need a weapon. She turned and her eyes fell on the statue in the center of the room, and the stone sword lying across his upraised palms. Three steps and she was there. She heard Larris cry out as her hand closed around the hilt.

Chapter 35

Aspin sighed as he looked at the precarious switchback running down the side of the cliff. He had been traveling blind in the days since leaving the Ramsgate. He had no idea where the girl was, and signs were few in this rocky land. He had seen evidence of the passing of a great number of people, but they were too many and headed in the wrong direction. He wondered what they were about, and it concerned him more than a little, but his task was too important for him to allow himself to be diverted. He supposed he could try and send a message, but it was risky this close to the Ice Reaches. He preferred to pass across this country like a shadow. He hoped that he was heading in the right direction, but hope was all he had. That, and the bond he shared with his quarry.

He checked the sun where it hung high above the distant, snow-tipped peaks. Time was difficult to estimate in the mountains, but he could make a general estimate. This would be as good a time as any to rest.

He turned to retrieve his water skin when he felt a tremor. It was as if the world had shifted ever so slightly. He froze, fearing that the ledge was about to give way beneath him. He felt it again, and realized that it was not a physical tremor, but a wave of energy that seemed to come from beyond the snow-capped peaks. The direction in which he was headed. He waited.

It struck him. A blinding wave of pure energy. His mind screamed in exquisite agony, and he crumpled to the ground.

Lerryn tensed as they approached the village. Several dirty men with shaggy black beards and unkempt hair stood outside the log stockade, spears held in white knuckled grips. They eyed him with looks varying from caution to outright hostility.

"Do not draw your weapons unless I give the command," he instructed his comrades. Nearby, a group of indecently-dressed women farmed a muddy patch of garden. They pretended to ignore the newcomers, but eyed the group with sidelong glances.

They reined in at a safe distance from the gate and, in accordance with Malgog custom, waited to be greeted. The men continued to stare. Several heartbeats later, one sauntered into the village, returning with a wizened old man, his long hair and beard showing only faint signs of what had undoubtedly been hair as black as the others. He wore baggy pants and tunic, typical of Malgog. As a sign of his office, he wore a string of swamp lizard claws around his neck. Lerryn counted nine claws. This man had led the village for more than thirty-six springs.

Leaning heavily on his staff, the man made his way over to Lerryn. "You may dismount," he said, his deep voice incongruous with his frail body.

Lerryn climbed down, and made a show of slowly removing his sword belt and laying it on the ground in front of him.

"My name is Lerryn Van Altman, First Prince of the Sword of Galdora. I offer you this gift." He reached into his tunic and withdrew the pouch he had secreted there earlier.

The old man cackled, showing a full mouth of ragged, yellow teeth. "And what use have we of your money in this place, young Highness? The Malgog have no commerce anymore."

"You misunderstand, Esteemed One." He loosened the drawstring and opened the bag. "I offer you herbs from my homeland. Ground and used in a poultice, they help prevent wounds from becoming infected. Brewed in a tea, they have, shall we say, certain other benefits for an older gentleman." He raised his eyebrows

"And what might those be?" The man's eyes said that he already knew the answer.

"Let us just say, your wife will be very pleased if you accept this gift."

The man laughed again. "My wife is less than twenty springs old, Highness. I daresay she will not be pleased. I, however, gladly accept your gift." He nodded to one of the armed villagers who hurried over to accept Larris' gift. "As you obviously know our customs, you are aware that now is the time that you should state your business."

"Esteemed One, I am in search of an ancient relic," Larris said. "I have traveled far."

"I know where Archstone is," the old man interrupted. "What relic do you seek?"

"The relic I seek is a remnant of the war of the Frostmarch." Lerryn held his breath, hoping the response would be the one for which he longed. He breathed a sigh of relief when the man smiled.

"A pilgrim are you?" The old man sounded delighted. "You have come to see our relic. Yes, come this way." He turned and headed into the village.

Lerryn signaled for Karst to follow him. The others could wait with the horses. Inside the rough stockade was a cluster of stick and mud huts. A pig scurried underfoot, and ran away squealing. He wondered if Karst was feeling at home.

"An important relic it is, but no one remembers that it was brought here."

Lerryn's heart danced. The prophecy had led them to this place. Soon, he would lay his hands on the Silver Serpent. So great was his excitement that he scarcely heard the old man continue.

"We once had a small temple to house the relic, but with the clan wars, it was not safe. You understand, no? It has been many years since we had a pilgrim. Perhaps this is a good omen for us. This way! It is in the cave."

Lerryn's excitement grew as he caught sight of a small cave set in the side of a hill. An old woman sat in front of it tending a smoky fire. She wore a dress of animal skins and a necklace of bones. Of course they would have a witch guarding a relic of such power. The woman looked up, her eyes wide in surprise.

"We have a pilgrim," he said. "A pilgrim!"

If the witch was impressed, she did not show it. "You may leave your offering on the altar," she said in a raspy voice, indicating a flat stone at the center of the cave entrance. The old man turned to Lerryn and gestured for him to enter the cave.

Lerryn fished a gold coin from his belt pouch and dropped it onto the altar. He was certain that he could have come up with something more useful to these people than gold they would likely never get to spend, but he would not wait a moment longer than necessary. The moment was at hand.

The old man, who still had not told them his name, drew a flaming brand from the campfire and joined them. "It is just a ways back." He led the way into the darkness.

The cave bent to the left, and as they turned the corner, the light glinted off of a metallic surface. Lerryn's heart raced.

The torch cast a faint circle of light around and in front of them. The flickering glow fell upon a battered bronze breastplate.

"The breastplate of Karnis the Good, greatest Malgog hero of the Frostmarch. The forces of ice pinned the Lothan army against a sheer cliff, threatening to overwhelm them. King Mardid looked at this breastplate, and saw a vision of how to defeat the enemy. Karnis and his clansmen scaled the cliff in the dark of night, and assaulted the enemy's right flank. Only Karnis survived, but their attack opened the way for the Lothans to fight their way free. They say the tears Karnis wept for his fallen clansmen fell upon this breastplate and gave it the power to meet one's need in his most desperate hour. Is your need great?"

Lerryn felt the bile rise in his throat. He forced himself to stand straight, though his knees felt like they would buckle. He could not believe it. The disappointment was almost more than he could bear.

"That cannot be." Karst shut up when Lerryn cuffed him on the back of the head. His dark eyes fixed Lerryn with an evil glare.

An anguished scream from behind them saved Lerryn the trouble of speaking an insincere word of thanks. He spun around, drew his sword, and sprinted back to the mouth of the cave, Karst right behind him.

Emerging in the gray light, he almost fell across the witch woman, who lay writhing on the ground. She held her hands pressed to her temples and her lips were drawn back in an agonized grimace. Bloody scratches marred her cheeks where she had clawed her face. A frightened villager knelt beside her, looking at Lerryn with uncertain eyes.

"Highness!"

Lerryn turned to see Bull beckoning to him. He sprinted over to his party, and stopped short when he saw Xaver on the ground, in a similar condition to that of the witch woman. His vizier's eyes were opened wide, and his breath came in labored gasps. Lerryn dropped to his knees next to Xaver. He had seen his share of battlefield injuries, but never anything like this invisible malady.

"What is it? What can I do for you?" The others stood in a semi-circle behind them, leaning over to stare at the struggling man.

"Found it," Xaver gasped, "Found it."

"No, we did not," Lerryn said. The admission seemed to burn his tongue. "It was just an old piece of armor."

"No!" Xaver grabbed Lerryn's tunic with both hands. "Someone else." He closed his eyes and fell back to the ground, squeezing his eyes shut. "Another."

Lerryn did not want to believe what he was hearing. How could Xaver know? He was dimly aware that Karst had detached from their group and mounted his horse. As the sound of hooves pounding the soft turf rang in his ear, Xaver opened his eyes again.

"Lerryn," he wailed. "We were wrong!"

"With all due respect, Prelate, Aspin must be reined in. For too long he has gone his own way, doing the gods know what. And now, when he is needed, we cannot find him."

Denrill inspected the back of his hands and waited to be certain Taggian had finished his diatribe. All due respect? That would be something new from Taggian. After an adequate silence he spoke.

"And that, Proctor Taggian," Denrill explained with more patience than he felt he owed the insufferable man, "is precisely why I cannot 'rein him in.'"

"You could contact him."

"I am perfectly aware of the capabilities of aciash smoke. You have seen me use it. Are you suggesting that senility is encroaching upon my faculties?" Taggian shook his head, but the expression on his face indicated that he at least suspected the prelate was losing his mind. "Excellent. Now that we have established that I am not mentally impaired, I shall remind you of the potential danger of sending such a message, depending upon Aspin's location when the message is received."

"So he is in a precarious location?" Taggian moved to the window and looked out over the Vatanian cityscape. The man fancied himself clever, but he had no subtlety. That he had risen to proctor was, in Denrill's estimation, an indictment of the entire order of saikurs.

"I have already told you," Denrill said, his voice clearly indicating his fatigue, "that I do not know where he is. I can assure you, and those whom you purport to represent," he added, ignoring Taggian's frown, "that his task is of critical importance."

"Permission to sit?" His attention to protocol was belied by the fact that he was already settling into the chair opposite Denrill's desk when the prelate flicked his hand toward the seat. "Prelate, I understand that you have heard rumors from the west of, shall we say, curious activity." No one within the order had thus far been willing to consider the possibility of a second frostmarch. "But we have a situation between Kyrin and Galdora, a situation in which Aspin is uniquely qualified to intervene."

"Proctor, we have more pressing issues than another round of the constant friction between Nadrin and the Van Altmans."

"Both princes of Galdora are missing. You cannot convince me that Nadrin had nothing to do with it. Nor can you convince the King, for that matter. Kyrinian troops are massing on Galdora's northwest border. War could break out at any moment." Taggian rearranged his robes, shifted in his seat, and leaned toward Denrill. "We need Aspin. Your trust in him, though I am certain that it is well-founded, has become a source of concern for many of the order."

Denrill slapped the tarwood desk with the flat of his palm. "You forget yourself, Proctor. I will execute my duties as I see fit, and at this moment, I see fit to permit Aspin to continue his work."

"But Prelate, the Kyrinian situation is urgent."

"You are correct, Taggian. It therefore requires the attention of one of our most experienced and influential Saikurs." The look on the other man's face said that he already knew who that someone would be. "I have your orders here, Proctor." Denrill drew a stack of folded and sealed parchments from his desk and handed them to the confused-looking Taggian.

"What are the others for?" he asked, shuffling through them and looking increasingly ill as he read each name.

"It seems that a number of urgent situations have come to my attention in the last few days. If you will do me the kindness of delivering these orders. I believe these are all men with whom you work closely?" These orders would scatter nine of Taggian's most ardent supporters, and Denrill's most vocal detractors, across Gameryah for three moons or more. It would not quash their dissent, but it would buy him time and a measure of blessed peace.

His satisfaction was short-lived. A humming sensation filled the room. He turned toward the window and was struck full in the face by a wave of energy that knocked him backward. He crashed into his desk and fell to the floor. He sat there, the wind knocked out of him.

Taggian appeared at his side. The proctor looked like he was about to vomit. He bent down and took Denrill by the upper arm, and carefully helped him to his feet.

"Are you in need of attention, Prelate?" he asked. "I will send for a mender." Denrill couldn't tell whether the frown on Taggian's face was out of concern for his health, or out of fear of the strange phenomenon they had just experienced.

Before Denrill could answer, the door flew open and Almate bustled into the room. A large patch of ink stained the front of his robe. Obviously, he had been taken by surprise as well. "Prelate, are you all right?" So great was the clerk's worry that he did not even acknowledge that he had burst into a meeting of two superiors.

"We are both fine," Taggian answered for the two of them. "You may go now."

"My Lord?" Almate turned his attention to Denrill.

"I am fine, Almate. Thank you for your concern." When his secretary did not leave, he paused and stared. The soft lines of his florid face seemed to fade away against his rust-colored hair. "Is there something else?"

"What was that, my Lord?" Almate looked as if he were going to sick up.

"We shall certainly find out. You are dismissed." Denrill inclined his head toward the door. Without waiting for Almate to leave, he turned and straightened his desk. "You are both excused, Taggian."

"But Prelate, I...."

"I am sorry. Did I mumble?" The scuffling sound of the proctor's hurried departure soothed his frayed nerves a touch. Only when he heard the door close did he cease the pretense of working, and let the papers fall from his hands. Placing his palms flat on the smooth wood of his desk, he leaned forward heavily, and took a deep breath.

"Aspin," he whispered, "where are you?"

The sweet scent of amalino root filled Eramon's nose as he sprinkled it into the brazier. He watched as the blue smoke drifted up, wending its way up the steeply angled ceiling and spiraling out through the hole in the center. Behind the brazier hung a curtain of deepest crimson, dividing the Hall of Sacrifice from the Sanctus, the ceremonial abode of Arscla, the god of fire. He knew that it was all superstition, but he loved being a priest. The ornate temple, the fine robes, and the theatrical elements of the ritual appealed to him. What was more, in a city of this size a priest of Arscla was always well-fed, and had no shortage of altar boys from which to choose, though some of the more provincial clergy preferred beggar girls or orphans.

He turned to address the single worshipper, a merchant from the look of him, who knelt on a cushion in the center of the floor. *Why did they always choose the center?* Eramon wondered. Why not one of the cushions to the right, left, or the back? For that matter, why did they keep so many kneeling cushions in the hall? Kyrinians were not known for their devotion.

"You may approach the Sanctus," he intoned, holding his hands out to receive the sacrifice. "Sacrifice" was perhaps no longer the most precise word. The temple had long ago done away with the practice of animal sacrifice, though some of the rural priests still held to the old ways.

The merchant proffered his offering: a square of raw meat, rolled in spices. The sacrifices were prepared early in the morning by novices, and sold to worshipers for two silver crowns. It made for a tidy profit for the temple, but the adherents had no other choice. Their own meat offerings were, by temple decree, unclean and unworthy for sacrifice. Eramon took the piece of meat and turned back to the brazier, his mouth watering at the thought of the tasty meal it would make after it had been roasted. Unless, of course, the worshiper spent too long at the altar and the meat burned. Hoping that would not happen, he skewered the offering and laid it across the brazier, where it began to crackle and smoke, emitting a most pleasing aroma.

"Almighty and most munificent Arscla," Eramon intoned, raising the offering high. "A humble worshiper approaches your altar." When the merchant remained rooted to the floor, he cleared his throat and inclined his head toward the waist-high wooden rail, two spans wide, that stood just in front of the brazier. "The unworthy one bows humbly before your divine and magnificent presence."

The paunchy fellow scurried forward, red coloring his cheeks. He snatched the round, flat silk hat from his head to reveal a thinning pate of short, black hair. He tucked the cap into his finely-tooled leather belt. He dropped awkwardly to his knees, propped his elbows on the rail, and opened his hands, palms up.

"Holy Arscla," Eramon continued, "hear the prayers of this, your faithful servant. May this humble sacrifice be pleasing in your sight." With more drama than was strictly necessary, he dropped the offering into the fire. It cracked and sizzled, sending a column of fragrant white smoke drifting upward.

"Most gracious and, um, munifical Arscla." The man had no gift for language. "My enemies are many."

The man ceased his prayer when a column of brilliant orange flame, as wide as the brazier, shot upward, pouring out of the hole in the ceiling with an angry roar. Heat seared Eramon's face, and the entire Sanctus shone with an unearthly brilliance. The chamber was alive with an energy he had never felt.

"What is happening?" Eramon whispered. He wanted to run, but his legs would not respond to his mind's commands. He scarcely noticed Arscla's lone adherent jostle him in his hurry to escape the searing pillar.

With an audible rip, the curtain was split asunder, revealing the faceless statue that represented the fire god. Reflecting the firelight, it almost seemed alive.

Chapter 36

Shanis' hand tingled as her fingers closed around the hilt of the stone sword. Fire coursed through her veins. She felt powerful. She whipped the sword, light as a feather, around and held it out in front of her. What she saw made her gasp.

Sparks ran up and down the edge of the blade, and within its black stone depths, tiny lights like stars whirled. Faster they spun, until the entire surface of the blade was streaked with silver light. And then the sword began to change.

Beginning at the tip, the light coalesced into solid metal, the brightest silver she had ever seen. As the stars continued to whirl, the band of silver crept downward, turning the blade to something like steel. Against the silver background, the outline of the serpent shone in dancing red fire. It seemed an eternity, but somehow she knew it had taken only a matter of heartbeats.

A mist rose all around, dimming the glow and obscuring her friends from view. *What is happening?* The statue from which she had taken the sword spun, slowly first then faster, and began to sink. The floor started to tilt down toward the disappearing statue, and soon there was a gaping hole in the center of the room. She shifted her weight to try and maintain her balance, but despite the sloping floor, it felt as if she was standing on level ground.

The serpent drew back before her, hissing and swaying from side-to-side. Suddenly the creature was no longer so anxious for her blood. It did not snap at her, but continued to draw back. It swayed hypnotically, and its hisses almost sounded like words.

Sssselfisshh. Cannot be the one. Ssselfisshh. Its eyes burned a brilliant emerald flame in the midst of the cool fog. They drew Shanis in, muddling her thoughts. *You have drawn it. Only by your death may you let it go.* It continued to undulate, swaying before her, just out of reach of the sword.

The thickening soup of fog dampened the shouts of her friends. Larris' voice came faint to her ears. "Kill it Shanis! Kill it!" She willed her feet to move, and again noticed the strange sensation of walking on soft, level ground. She took a tentative step toward the serpent, then another. Her legs felt like stone.

The serpent glided to its left. As she turned to follow, she caught sight of a thin band of light forming a square in the wall behind the creature, its intense glow shining through the fog. The serpent slithered backward, sliding closer to the light. Shanis followed. As the creature neared the wall, she noticed that the seam in the stone she had discovered had opened up into a doorway.

"There's a way out!" she shouted. "Follow my voice until you see the light." The serpent was blocking the way. She had to drive it away so the others could escape. Without further thought, she leapt forward, swinging with all her might. The sword seemed to sing as it whistled through the air, narrowly missing the serpent. She was amazed that the weapon seemed to have no weight at all. She whipped a backhand stroke that narrowly missed severing the snake's foul head, and was forced to leap aside as it struck hard at her chest. She felt a burning sensation over her heart, and for a moment thought she had been struck, but a quick glance told her otherwise.

The creature drew back again, and hissed. *Ssselfisssh you are. The Sssilver Ssserpent mussst be wielded by one who isss willing to sssacrifice. You think only of yoursssself. You cannot be the one.*

She was stunned. The sword was the Silver Serpent? Then she remembered what the beast had said before. *Only by death may you let it go.* She had drawn the Silver Serpent and could not let it go? But it was to have been Larris who drew it. She did not want this. The fate of Galdora rode on her shoulders? No! She wanted to be a soldier. Nothing more. Nothing less.

You sssee? The beast seemed to read her thoughts. *You have never cared about otherss. You cannot do what mussst be done.* It began its swaying again, its eyes drawing her in. *You have alwaysss thought of yoursssself firssst.*

"Why are you saying that? You don't know me!" The angry words she had exchanged with Khalyndryn now came back to her in a rush. Each word now hit her like a hammer. She was selfish. Memories came firing back, distant images from childhood. She was a spoiled brat. She was demanding and indulged beyond reason. She recalled fits she had thrown over the littlest thing.

"Don't talk to it! Kill it!" Larris shouted. Shanis couldn't see him, but somehow she knew that he was scrabbling along the sharply tilting floor. She wanted to protect him, to protect all of her friends, but her mind was a morass of confused thoughts.

Put down the Ssserpent, and I ssshall end your sssufering. Let it go, and sssomeone worthy ssshall bear it. It isss the leassst you can do after the life you have lived.

"Oskar's slipping!" Khalyndryn cried. "I can't hold him! Shanis, you have to make it stop!"

A stray tear rolled down Shanis' cheek. She didn't know how the creature knew, but it was correct. She was a selfish person. The least she could do was make this sacrifice. She relaxed her grip on the hilt and let the sword point dip.

"No Shanis!" Larris was at her side, and he leapt at the serpent, wrapping his arms and legs around the writhing silver body. It thrashed about, slamming Larris into the wall. He lost his grip and fell hard to the floor, but immediately tried to regain his feet. Blood still flowed from his wounded arm, soaking his shredded tunic.

Shanis was still aware of everything around her. Somehow she knew that

Hierm had regained consciousness, and Allyn had recovered his feet as well. The two were working their way toward her. She saw Oskar, unconscious, sliding toward the gaping hole in floor. Khalyndryn lay flat on her stomach, holding his cloak with one hand, and gripping a handful of hair in the other. Her jaws were clenched tight and her eyes wide as she tried in vain to dig her toes into the stone floor.

"I have to end this," Shanis whispered. She let her sword arm fall to her side. The burning in her chest intensified. The serpent saw her lower her guard, and hesitated.

In that pause, Larris voice came to her calm and clear. "Shanis, a selfish person would not be willing to give her life for her friends." The serpent hissed with fury, turned and snapped at Larris, who leapt back. "Kill it."

New memories flooded Shanis. She remembered taking care of her father and their home, tending to her horse with the utmost attention to its needs, helping Mistress Anna in the garden, a thousand small acts of kindness and concern. She was no monster. The monster was in front of her. It looked at her, and drew back. It was afraid of her! That was why it was trying to break her down, to make her question herself. But a part of her still doubted herself. Who was she to be a savior?

"Shanis," Khalyndryn called out, "you saved my life!"

That sealed it. The beast bared its fangs to strike, but before it could move, Shanis brought her sword to bear, slashing the snake across the throat. The Silver Serpent slashed through shining scales, sending gouts of green fire pouring forth. The wounded creature made a strangled hiss, and fled through the doorway. She knew she had to follow. She had to kill it. She sprinted up the sloping tunnel, following the flashes of green and silver. As she sprinted, the floor beneath her vanished, and the dark stone walls melted away. She was running through dark clouds, flying. And she was gaining. The serpent looked back at her, its green eyes still burning. Hot fire still leaked from the wound, burning holes in the clouds upon which they ran. Shanis leapt over one of the holes and looked down to see light shining through. Far below she could make out snow-capped mountain peaks. Another leap, and she could almost reach out and touch the tail of the fleeing beast.

Help us! The words were faint, like a shout's last faded echo. They came again. Help us. It was Larris. They needed her. But she had to kill the snake. She did not know how she knew, but it had to die. She was almost there. She would kill it quickly, and then go back for her friends. And then Khalyndryn screamed, a long, shrill wail that faded into hollow nothingness. The snake's words assaulted her again.

Ssselfishhh.

She reached back with her mind, searching for the tunnel from which they had come. She found it quickly, and her consciousness raced down the cold stone, and burst into the chamber. She felt through the room, her mind brushing across the ancient tombs, now grinding slowly down the sloping floor. She found Larris and encircled his waist with, a thought was the only way she could describe it, and drew him forth. She found Allyn and Hierm in short order, and began searching for Oskar and Khalyndryn. She soon found the room empty. Here emotions were distant, but a cold fear swelled inside her. She followed the sloping floor to the hole where the statue had been. She swept down, down, down and found emptiness.

The farther she searched, the duller the sensations became. Until she felt nothing. She tried to reach farther but could not. They were gone.

She screamed in anger and frustration. She yanked her three friends toward her as she pursued the snake with the intention of venting her rage upon it. She wanted to cry, but tears could come later. Her eyes searched the cloudy skies ahead and saw a flash of green. It was outdistancing her again. Larris and the others were slowing her down. She skipped over another hole in the clouds and saw the highlands of Monaghan beneath her. Spotting a wide, flat hilltop, she laid her friends down on the spongy turf and continued her pursuit.

They flew across the sky. The dark clouds began to clear, and down below the hilly land gave way to damp marsh and tree-choked swampland. The beast before her continued to bleed green fire, and where the fire fell to the ground, chaos erupted. Green fire splashed down on wet ground, and warriors rose up, some red-haired, some black. They hacked at each other with great broadswords while the trees burned all around them. The creature turned to the northeast, where the countryside was lush and green. Blood fell on the ground, and a dark-haired young man on horseback sprang up, leading a band of mounted raiders through a village of screaming people. The young man swung his sword, and an old man went down. And all around them the village burned. Back to the west, toward the mountains. Blood now flowed freely from the beast's wounded neck, and where it splashed onto the ground, a great army rose up, moving northwest, moving toward home. This had to end.

Shanis reached out with her thoughts, like she had done before. Tendrils of her will stretched out, wrapping around the snake, and solidifying into thick ropes of power as they encircled the silvery coils. The snake hissed and snapped at the bonds, but for every one it severed, she ensnared it with another. It turned to fight.

Shanis faced the beast high above a broad expanse of lush farmland. A silvery band of river wended its way across the green stand. She swung the Silver Serpent with all her might, cleaving through the metallic scales. Green fire erupted from the gash, scalding her. She gritted her teeth and swung again and again. The sword struck home, and with each blow, energy ran up the blade and surged through her. She had never felt such power, such intense exultation. Holding the hilt in one hand now, she continued to hew great chunks from the twisting creature. The beast's bloody fire rained down on the ground below, and a great mass of black-clad soldiers formed ranks facing south and west.

Her blade cut deep into the body of the beast, and suddenly the snake lashed out at her throat. Unable to get her sword into position, she instinctively threw her left hand up. A crystal fang pierced the center of her palm, and she screamed as blistering cold pain froze her hand, doing battle with the hot power that flowed through her. She backed away and held up her hand.

Blood flowed from the hole in her palm, but where her blood struck the ground, the soldiers melted away. The snake struck again, but she dodged to the side, striking it another vicious blow. It twisted and writhed in agony, but it would not die.

The energy now flowed up the sword in a torrent, and she felt like she would burst if she could not let it out. That was the answer. She stepped back and pointed the Silver Serpent at the oncoming beast. She focused every thought, every scrap of her will, and sent it hurtling through the sword and into the snake, and with it she sent the power.

A shaft of the purest white light, brighter than any sun, burst forth from the Silver Serpent. She felt the accumulated energy pour from her body like floodwaters through a tiny channel. It was ecstasy. The beam of light struck the snake full in the chest. Tiny lines of white energy crackled as it enveloped the surface of its writhing body. The snake managed one faint hiss, and the green light began to fade as the power of the Silver Serpent enveloped it, growing ever brighter. With a flash, it was gone, the afterimage of the great snake burned into Shanis' vision. The power continued to drain from her body. With the last of her will, she reached out for Hierm, Allyn and Larris. Larris! She fixed her thoughts on the hilltop where the three young men stood in bewildered silence. Focused. Focused.

She was a leaf falling to the ground. Drifting, falling, swinging to and fro on the crest of the wind. Settling gently to the ground. She felt soft, damp earth against her back, and saw Larris' brown eyes looking down at her, and she drifted into darkness.

And Gameryah was rent by blood and fire. Blades showered blue sparks into the night sky, and fires blazed on the horizon. Leaders rose and were struck down in the batting of an eyelash, and the carrion birds whirled in a smoke filled sky. And three words were upon every tongue....
"The Silver Serpent".

End of book one of The Absent Gods.

KEEPER
OF THE
MISTS

To my mother, Barbara, in thanks for all the stories you read to me.

Chapter 1

"You cannot find me now, Harvin." Jayla giggled and pressed her body deeper into the farthest recess of the tiny cave hidden behind a stand of brush. The cool stone surface leached the warmth from her hands and her belly as she lay in the dark, listening for the sound of her brother's approach.

At six summers, she was still small enough to wriggle in and out of tight places where Harvin, nearly nine, and big for his age, could not fit. When chores were done each day they would spend hours exploring the warren of rock ledges, chimneys and tunnels they called "the castle." Neither of them had ever seen an actual castle, but they agreed that a real one could be no more majestic, and certainly no more fun than this, their special place. Hidden by thick stands of blue-gray panon trees and dense tangles of briar, the network of caves, crevasses, and passages wended its way down the steep side of Marlat Mountain. One could climb down if he or she was very careful, though incaution could lead to broken bones, or worse. It was a much faster way down, however, than the meandering switchbacks of the old mountain road the grownups traversed.

One of these days Jayla was going to surprise Mama and Papa when they took the cart to Galsbur. She would clamber down through the castle and be waiting for them when they finally reached the bottom. She would lean against a tree, looking bored, and when they finally arrived, she would say, "Hello Mama and Papa. What took you so long?" Mama and Papa would want to know how she reached the bottom first, but she would tell them it was magic, and they would laugh.

Harvin was taking his time about finding her. He was bigger, stronger, and faster than her, but he was a daydreamer. He had been known to let the smallest thing distract him—a colorful bird or an oddly shaped rock—and forget all about their game. Where was he? She did not want to wait all day for him to remember to look for her.

Careful to remain quiet, she slid toward the front of the cave and, squinting against the afternoon sunlight, she saw nothing but forest. The snows take him! She had not spoken aloud, but she immediately clapped a hand over her mouth. Mama would punish her for even thinking such a foul oath, but it would be just like her brother to leave her hiding in a cave all afternoon. He had done it before.

When she was certain she had given him sufficient time to discover her hiding place, she crawled out of the cave and began her climb back up to the top of the castle, where the dakel bushes lined the road and hid their secret place from passers-by. The going was more difficult on the way up, but she had made this climb countless times, and she raced up the rocky face like a squirrel dashing up a tree.

She had almost reached the top when she heard hoof beats and men's voices. Lots of them. She slowed down, wary of what might wait at the top. Few people lived in their tiny village among the foothills of western Galdora. She was taken by the conviction that these were strangers, and therefore to be looked upon with suspicion.

"Nothin' but a farming town. And not even a town at that. More like a village. Told us we would have all the loot we could carry home. All the women, too. But what do we get?" The speaker cleared his throat and spat. "Farmers. No gold, no silver. Not even a copper among them. Bah!" Several other voices muttered in general agreement.

"But there was women, wasn't there, Garge?" The second voice was soft, and oily, putting Jayla in mind of the squishy brown newts that lived under rocks in mountain streams. "Healthy farm women and a few young girls, too. Can't complain about that now, can you?" Someone barked a sharp, mirthless laugh.

Jayla did not know what the men were talking about, but it frightened her. She stayed very still, her feet and legs braced in the sides of the cleft in the rock face. She was getting tired and her arms burned, but she was not about to move. She closed her eyes, and whispered a prayer to the forest fairies, asking them to lead the bad men away. Harvin did not believe in the little people of the forest, but Jayla did.

"Not hardly enough to go around." Garge was closer now. "Though we made a fair job of sharing them around like good little boys, didna' we? I tell you, Tarn, there'd better be sweeter pickings when we come down outta' these hills, or some of the boys just might up and leave this outfit."

Other voices chimed in, most echoing Garge's sentiments, others disagreeing.

"You can't do that. You made a blood pledge. Do you think they'll let you out of it just like that? You know what they do to deserters. Besides, every farming village we raid brings us that much closer to the cities. And in cities there will be gold."

The voices began to fade.

"I declare, there had better be gold, or blood pledge or not, I'll walk away."

When she could hear them no more, she counted all her fingers and toes twice before climbing the rest of the way to the top. Trembling from fright and fatigue, she crawled beneath the shelter of a dakel bush, careful to avoid the thorns, and sat clutching her knees to her chest, and rocking to and fro. Silent tears ran down her chin, dripping onto her plain woolen dress. Where were Mama and Papa and Harvin? She wanted to know what had happened, but she was too afraid. She hurt all over and she wanted to go home.

Something scraped on the dirt road. Someone was walking toward her hiding place. Her heartbeat pounded out an angry rhythm in her ears, and she felt as if the whole world could hear her.

"Jayla? Are you here?"

"Harvin?" she called back, her voice thick with emotion. "Is it really you?"

"Where are you?" The panic in his voice was plain, and it frightened her all the more. "I can't see you. Are you all right?"

"I'm in the bush, over here." She was still afraid to come out, so she waited as he crawled to her. It was a relief when his broad, freckled face finally peeked out through the wall of greenery. She wrapped her arms around his neck and tried to squeeze some courage into her heart.

It did not work.

"Jayla, you must listen to me." He gently untangled himself from her embrace and held her at arm's length so he could look her in the eye. "Something very bad has happened. You cannot go back to the village. Mama and Papa say that you must climb down the castle as fast as you can."

"Wait! How do they know about the castle? Did you tell them?" The surprise had momentarily driven all thoughts of the bad men from her mind.

"That does not matter now. You must climb to the bottom and then go east. Do not walk. Run. Do you know which way is east?"

She nodded. In the morning, east was toward the rising sun. In the late afternoon, the shadows pointed east. At mid-day, or if there was no sun, you just put your back to the mossy side of the tree and turned left.

"Good. Go east as fast as you can until you come to a village. Keep to the forest and hide if you hear anyone coming. Do you understand?"

"I want to go home." She hated the way her voice sounded right now—like a little baby, but she did not care. Hot tears streamed down her cheeks and she tasted the salt in the corners of her mouth. "I want Mama and Papa."

"We will come for you." Harvin's voice was soft, but insistent. "We will come east, too, and we'll find you. But you have to get away as fast as you can. Promise me you will."

"But what will you do?"

"Promise me!" He gripped her shoulders and gave her a shake.

She nodded, and Harvin seemed to accept that as her oath. "Time to be going then. Come on." He crawled out the way he had come. She bit her lip as he vanished into the foliage.

"You there. Stop!" The man's voice froze her heart. Who was out there? More bad men? She heard a rapid scuffling and she knew Harvin was running away. Booted feet pounded the dirt, chasing after him. She had to help him!

She crawled out of the bush, thorns raking across her back as she went. At the edge of the bush, she thrust her head out and looked up and down the road. To her right, she saw a tall, lean man with silvery hair and a gray cape dashing down the road.

"You leave him alone!" She screamed as loud as her little lungs would permit. She regretted it almost immediately.

The man stopped in his tracks and whirled about with catlike grace. His eyes narrowed as his gaze met hers, and then his whole body seemed to ripple.

Jayla gasped as he changed before her eyes. In a span of two heartbeats the man had transformed into a creature from her worst nightmares. He stood as tall as a man, but his muscled body was covered in sleek gray fur. His hands were tipped with wicked black claws, and his head was that of a cat, something like the puma that Papa had killed last winter, but she was sure that no puma's eyes had ever shone with the cunning malevolence with which this beast gazed at her. It threw back its head and screamed a primordial cry, dropped down to all fours, and took off up the road toward her.

Survival instinct took over, forcing her paralyzed limbs to move. She scrambled back through the bush, ignoring the scrapes she received. Reaching the ledge, she dropped feet-first down into the crevasse. There was precious little slope, and she had to use her feet and hands as brakes to keep her from plummeting to the bottom. The stone was mostly smooth, but her hands found every imperfection as she slid down, and soon they were slick with blood.

She hit the first ledge hard, the pain shooting up through her legs and into her back. She was too afraid to permit so much as a whimper to escape her lips. She ducked down into the little tunnel on her right and crawled to the next chimney. She heard a scrabbling sound like claws on rock somewhere far above.

The monster was still chasing her.

She slid down the next chimney in the same manner she had done the first. Her hands were now numb to the pain, or perhaps her whole self was numb. She did not care. She no longer thought of Mama, Papa, or Harvin. She only wanted to get away.

At the bottom of the next chimney, she wriggled beneath a low-hanging rock, coming out at a ledge above a precipitous drop off. She hoped the monster would be too large to force itself through the tight space through which she had just come, but she would not wait around to find out.

She took a deep breath and looked out at the gap that lay before her. She could not climb around it—the sheer rock face to her right offered no handholds. The only way across was a thick vine that spanned a gap thirty paces wide. To cross it, she had to stand on the vine and scoot across sideways, keeping her hands against the wall for balance. Lean too far, though…

She shook the frightening thought out of her head. Harvin had done it once, but she had never tried. If Mama knew of Harvin's reckless indifference to his own safety, she would have taken a stick to him. Now Jayla would have to cross it. She took a deep breath. This was going to be the scariest thing she had ever done.

Gingerly she stepped out onto the vine, and was pleased to discover that it supported her weight with ease. She placed one hand against the rock wall and found her center of balance, just the way she had seen Harvin do it. Holding her breath, she slid her right foot onto the vine. It continued to hold her. As quickly as she dared, she scooted across the vine, letting out a small moan each time it swayed beneath her feet.

She heard the monster sliding down the chimney, and she started to cry, but she kept moving.

Don't look down. Don't look down.

She remembered Harvin saying that same thing over and over as he made the crossing, so she took his advice and kept her eyes on the rock. So surprised was she when her foot touched solid ground that she almost lost her balance, but caught herself just in time.

She could still hear snarling and scraping as the monster climbed down. He was not moving as fast as she, but he was coming fast enough. If only there was something she could do.

She spotted a broken stone with a sharp edge, snatched it up, and began hacking at the vine where it met the ledge on her side. She was strong for her age, thanks to hard work and lots of climbing, but the vine was tough. She struck it again and again, feeling each blow all the way up to her shoulder.

She had cut almost one-third of the way through when she heard the creature's ragged breathing. It was close. Reluctantly forsaking her task, she scooted away on her backside, squeezing into a narrow fissure. Surely the thing would be much too big to get to her back here.

The beast appeared on the other side of the gap. It stood on its hindquarters and peered down over the ledge.

And then it looked up.

Its eyes fell upon her. It dropped down again on all fours, and tensed to jump, but seemed to think the better of it. It took a long look at the intervening gap, its silver-flecked eyes taking in every detail. Making its decision, it bared its glistening fangs in a sinister mockery of a grin, and once again stood on two legs.

As Jayla sat mesmerized in horror, its form blurred again, and once more a man stood before her.

"I did not mean to frighten you. I was afraid you would fall over the edge, and my cat form is much faster than my normal shape." He smiled. Perhaps his intention was to reassure her, but the shadow of the beast was on his face and in his eyes, and he looked every bit as deadly as he had moments before. "Just stay there and I will come and help you back across. You have nothing to fear."

As the man-beast crossed the vine, Jayla tried to press deeper into her hiding place, her hand gripping the sharp stone, seeking comfort in it, but it was no good. She could not get away.

Her pursuer was much heavier than either her or Harvin, and the further he moved out onto the vine, the farther it sagged. Soon his bottom half had sunk out of her field of vision.

There was a loud crack, and the vine gave a little. He gritted his teeth and snarled like the cat he had been, his fingers splaying out against the rocks. Jayla imagined she could see claws sprouting from their tips. But the vine held, and the man-cat thing crept toward her, slower this time.

The vine gave again, dipping the beast lower. She realized it had not noticed the cut she had made in the vine. As this thought occurred to her, the vine gave way again.

Please fall. Please fall.

But the vine continued to hold. He was now ten paces from the edge. As he looked up at her, his mouth twisted into a depraved grin and he made a noise in his throat that sounded nauseatingly like purring. He took another step across the space that measured the moments of the rest of her life.

She tore her eyes away from his and looked at the place where she had cut the vine. With the added weight, the vine had almost broken in two! Not pausing to think about it, Jayla squirmed out of the narrow cleft and dashed to the cliff's edge. Startled by her sudden movement, the beast froze for a moment.

That was all Jayla needed.

She raised her sharp stone above her head.

"No!" The man beast realized what she was doing a moment too late.

She brought the stone down with all of her might.

Crack!

The vine snapped clean in two. The man-cat monster, whatever he was, seemed to freeze in mid-air for a moment, the malice in his eyes having given way to disbelief.

Then he fell.

He clawed at the cliff face as he plummeted to the ground far below. Down, down he fell, screaming with insane rage, until he finally struck with a wet sound.

And then it was quiet.

Jayla sat there for a long time, wondering what she should do next. She wanted to climb back up and find Mama, Papa, and Harvin. She knew other paths up, so the broken vine was not an impediment. But what if she reached the top only to learn that her family had already left? In any case, she did not know if she had enough strength left to make the climb.

She did not want to climb down. The monster thing was down there. But he was dead, wasn't he? She peered down over the cliff, and her eyes fell upon the tangled remains of his body lying broken on the ground. He was definitely dead. Still, she would keep her distance. She never wanted to be near one of those things again.

Her mind was made up. Mama and Papa wanted her to go east, and they had promised they would come for her, so that was what she would do. She would make her way east as fast as she could, and one day, she would find her family again.

Chapter 2

The world was tilting, spinning. Shanis' memory shattered into miniscule fragments; images she could not understand dancing through her consciousness like fireflies, always evading her grasp. She bolted upright, her heart racing, and gasped for breath. She felt a strong hand grip her own.

"Relax. You are safe." The calm soothing voice was familiar, and in her state of delirium it seemed to hold a mystical power of command. Her breathing eased, and her confused eyes took in her surroundings.

She was in a hut. Its walls were supported by rough posts, the gray, peeling bark still clinging to them in places. The walls were of woven branches, with gray-green moss stuffed into the largest holes to help keep the weather out. Something dark and solid, probably deer hide, formed the outer layer.

She lay atop a thick, soft bear skin, and her legs were tangled in a rough blanket. A smoky peat fire in a stone ring at the center of the hut provided a faint light. The room began to seem familiar, as if she had been here before, but the haze of smoke made her feel as if she was still dreaming.

Her thoughts returned to the dream in which she had just been immersed.

She walked at the head of a solemn procession, followed by attendants dressed in fine clothes, but of a style she had never seen. A young man, tall and muscular, but with a stern face, looked at her through tear-filled eyes. She forced herself to look away from him, and instead focused ahead, where a man in a dark robe stood behind an altar, upon which lay a stone sword...

"You are finally awake, then?" Larris knelt beside her. His eyes were bleary and his hair disheveled as if he had not slept in days. "I am glad. You gave us quite a fright in more ways than I care to count." He smoothed her hair with an air of familiarity that seemed inappropriate, but strangely, she did not mind. Perhaps it was the fatigue.

It was coming back to her now. She and her friends had fled their village, met up with Larris and Allyn on their journey, and gone with them in search of the Silver Serpent. They had journeyed into the mountains and...

"Where?" Her own voice sounded strange in her ear. "How did I get here?" The questions died on her lips. There were too many things she wanted to ask, so much she did not understand, and the whirlwind of confused thoughts was more than her weary mind could bear. She fell back onto the bearskin and closed her eyes. "I don't remember..."

"Shanis, I need you to think." Larris sounded uncomfortable. "Tell me, exactly how much do you remember?"

She tried to recall the events of the previous days. Of course, she had no idea how long she had been in this hut. How long ago had her most recent memory been?

"I remember the golorak." She shuddered at the mental image of the grotesque creature that had nearly killed them in the caverns beneath the mountains. She felt his hand on her forearm, and she did not pull away. "We found the chamber. Then the snake came alive and I lost my sword. I was so scared and confused; I tried to grab the stone sword from the statue. Everything is fuzzy after that. Mostly I remember strange dreams of flying through the air and fighting a giant serpent. All my dreams have been odd."

"It was not a dream." Larris spoke softly, but his grip on her tightened. "You did fight the snake. The stone sword became a real sword, and you used it against the snake. You hurt it and it tried to flee, so you followed it out through a tunnel and," his voice grew hoarse, and he seemed to choke on the next words, "and into the sky. Somehow you took us up with you. When the fight was over, we were lying on a hill in Lothan. Horgris found us the next day. This is the encampment of the Hawk Hill clan—his clan."

She grew increasingly numb with each word. It was impossible, but in the depths of her soul she knew it to be true. Her old obstinate nature welled up within her, and she sat up, her ire rising.

"That is the most ridiculous heap of goat dung I have ever heard." She looked him in the eye, and he met her gaze with a level stare. As desperately as she wanted to cling to her disbelief, she could not deny it. Her anger fled as quickly as it had come and, to her horror, she began to cry, the firelight sparkling like diamonds through her tears. "How can it be?"

"That stone sword is the reason." Larris looked up at the ceiling, then back at her. "It is the Silver Serpent."

"No," she gasped. "It was for you, not me. You have to take it." She realized she was babbling and clammed up. Her thoughts now spun so fast she was surprised Larris could not hear the buzzing they seemed to create in her mind.

"I cannot take it. I tried. When you came down from… the sky, you dropped it on the ground. I tried to pick it up and it felt like my entire body was afire and frozen at the same time. I was certain it had burned my hand off, but there was nothing. Hierm tried as well, but the same thing happened to him. Allyn refused to even attempt it. Finally, we used our swords to push it onto my cloak. Once it was covered, we were able to bundle it up and carry it away, but no one can actually touch it. A few of Horgris' men have also tried and failed. They finally gave up."

He inclined his head toward the far wall. The sword leaned there, the firelight dancing on the image of the serpent etched in the blade, seeming to bring it life. The jeweled eye sparkled back at her in sinister silence. Larris clasped her hand in both of his. "For good or ill, I fear you are now the bearer of the Silver Serpent."

She did not know what to say. It was all too much to take. She shook her head. "There must be some way to give it up. It can't be me."

"It has marked you. Look here." Gently he grasped the low neckline of her loose-fitting tunic and slid it down to uncover her chest just above her left breast. It was a measure of her stupefied state that she permitted him to do so.

A silver serpent, the twin of the one she had seen carved in the rock above the lost city of Murantha, shone on her chest. Instinctively, she tried to wipe it away, and then claw it away, but to no avail. It felt like stone affixed to her skin. Larris pulled her hands away. Her first instinct was to fight him, but then her whole body sagged. She let her head fall against his chest, and she cried tears of confused despair.

Her entire world had changed. Who was she? What was she? Had this somehow altered her very nature? Was she still the farm girl whose father had taught her to use the sword? Was she even human anymore? Suddenly, she wanted nothing more than to be back at home with her father and her friends.

Her friends.

She pushed away from Larris. "Where are the others?"

"Hierm is nearby, sleeping in one of the huts. He offered to take a turn sitting with you, but I didn't mind." He shrugged and looked away.

"Allyn is out hunting. He has not been himself for some time, but he's been especially out of sorts ever since…" He neither finished the sentence, nor mentioned their other companions.

"What about Oskar and Khalyndryn? Where are…" Another memory formed in her mind. She did not want to believe it, but the look on his face confirmed it. "They fell, didn't they? They fell and I could not reach them." The tears came anew. Larris pulled her close. "We have to go back for them," she said with little conviction.

"You know we cannot," he said. "Once we made our way back, how would we find them again? Who knows where that chasm ended, or where they might have gone by the time we got there? That is, if they…"

"Don't say it." He was probably right, but to speak of it made her feel as if she was giving up what little hope remained. "They have to be alive." She sat for a long time in the silence, grieving for lost friends and the loss of her life as she knew it. "What do we do next?"

"Go back to Galdora I suppose. Prophecy holds that the Silver Serpent is crucial to the crown in some way. Until we know what that means, I would keep you close by my side."

"Only until then?" She jerked away from him, not sure why his words angered her. Perhaps it was because suddenly her life seemed to no longer be her own. "Have you forgotten the other prophecy? Didn't Martrin say that whoever bears the Silver Serpent will reunite the clans? Won't they try to keep me here when they find out?"

"Shanis, I…"

"I am right, aren't I?" She did not wait for his reply. "Well I have something to say to you and everyone else. I might have been branded like an animal, but I am not your cow to be herded along wherever you please. I will do exactly what I want, when I want to do it, and no one will stop me." She clambered to her feet, slower than she had intended, but determined not to let Larris see any weakness in her. "Where are my clothes?"

He pointed to a neatly folded pile next to the sword.

"Thank you. Now get out."

Larris stalked to the doorway, turned and folded his arms across his chest. He looked as if he were about to argue, but he changed his mind. He gave her a curt nod and pushed his way through the thick skins that hung from the door frame.

Getting dressed was no easy task. She was still weak, and she felt like she might faint when she leaned over to lace her boots. She had been provided a basin of tepid water. She scrubbed her face, determined to erase all signs of the tears she had shed. She hated crying, and she hoped she never did it again. Her hair was a tangled mess, but she combed it out the best she could and tied it back.

Finally, she took a long look at the sword. Her sword. The thing that now apparently marked her new identity and her new purpose in the world. At least until she could figure out a way to get rid of the thing.

Forcing herself to ignore her fears, she picked it up. She touched it gingerly at first, but when she was certain that it was not going to burn her arm or carry her up into the clouds, she took a firm grip and held it out in the dim light so she could examine it more closely.

It was beautiful. The craftsmanship was exquisite, and the etched serpent seemed to writhe as the light played along its scales. The hilt, shaped like the open mouth of a fanged serpent, was deadly looking. She noted how light the sword felt. That could not be right. This sword was a hand longer than the one her father had gifted her, yet she could easily wield it with one hand. She chuckled. If the thing could make her fly and fight giant snakes in the sky, she supposed making itself almost weightless was a relatively small matter.

She was pleased to see that someone had provided her with a simple scabbard and a shoulder harness. She slid the blade home and slung the strap over her shoulder. Taking a deep breath, she steeled herself before striding forth from her dim, smoky hut and into the damp morning air. It was time to face the world.

The cool autumn mist clung to her face, teasing her senses into wakefulness. She inhaled the cool mountain air and felt life returning to her sleep-fogged mind and weary body. Her eyes took in the haunting, lonely beauty of the fog-shrouded hills. They looked like she felt: desolate and somehow private, as if the fog hid their true nature from prying eyes.

She wended her way through the waking encampment. Smoke from cook fires hung low in the moist air, snaking through the gaggle of huts like ethereal serpents. A chill ran down her spine. She did not want to think about serpents of any kind.

A few of the Monaghan acknowledged her with a nod or curt greeting, but most just stared. She heard their whispers as she walked past. "That be her. She be the one."

"Shanis. Over here!" Hierm's voice was blessedly familiar. He hurried over to her, his damp, white-blond hair plastered to his face. He clutched her in a bear hug, and she returned the embrace with gratitude. "I'm so happy you're all right." He looked her over, as if trying to convince himself that she truly was well. A frown suddenly marred his face. "Did Larris tell you what happened?"

"Yes. I don't know what I'm going to do now. Larris wants me to stay close to him because he thinks I'll be important to Galdora's future. But I just don't know. I thought I was trapped back home, but now I wonder if my life will ever be my own." She pulled away from him, keeping her head up and her gaze level. She was disconsolate, but felt herself already growing impatient with her feeling of helplessness. She would not be ordered around.

"There you do be, girl." Horgris lumbered up to her, his eyes shining and his face more open and friendly than she had ever seen it. The remains of his breakfast clung to his beard, and he held a half-full tankard of ale in one hand. He smiled and clapped her on the back. "Good to see you awake, it do be. Wondered if we ever would, that we did. Come with me and we will talk." Having nowhere else to go, Shanis followed, taking Hierm along with her.

When they reached his hut, Horgris went on in without any formality. Shanis assumed she was invited, so she followed him inside. They settled down on bearskin rugs laid out around the fire ring. Horgris stoked the fire, added a chunk of peat and blew on the coals until it caught. She watched the heavy, pungent smoke spiral up to the smoke hole in the ceiling and out into the foggy morning sky.

"I don't need to be telling you how surprised we all be. What with you being the one. We kept council about it over the whole night, arguing and such." He took a swig of ale and wiped the foam away with a hairy forearm. "They don't all be liking it, but here be the way it is. If you be willing to lead us, we be willing to follow." He placed his mug of ale on the ground and stared at her, waiting for a reply.

"I don't know what to say. Lead you?" She had been prepared for him to make demands, even threats if she did not take up the Silver Serpent and follow them, or perhaps find a way to give it over to them. But to lead? Lead them where? She shifted uncomfortably and looked at Hierm, who only shrugged and moved his head side-to-side in a non-committal way. She looked again at Horgris and wondered how he felt about giving his allegiance to a young outlander girl. What must it cost him to even make this offer to her?"

"I never expected to find the Silver Serpent, much less bear it, so I was not at all prepared for what I woke to find. One thing I can tell you, though, is that I am no leader. I never have been."

Horgris laughed.

"You don't need to be worryin' about that now. You are destined to lead, and the power of the serpent will guide us. And whatever you don't be knowing, I can help." He raised his hand to silence the protest that was forming on her lips. "Hear me out before you be arguing with me.

"When I was a boy the fightin' be not going on for so very long. I remember me Pap tellin' me about how it was before. You know we used to have games? Every year the clans would gather for games and feasting. We did no fight with the Malgog, either. They no be our favorites, but we were at peace. It was a place our children could be growing old." He paused and stared into the fire, as if his memories were visible within its light. "My daughter be expecting my first grandchild. I would see that child grow up in a different world than that which I do know. You can change that."

"I cannot change anything." How could he believe her capable of such things? She was a farm girl. "I have never done anything right in my life." Hierm laid a hand on her arm, but she shrugged it off. She did not know why she was unburdening herself to Horgris, but now she had started and would not stop until she had her say. "I am the most selfish person you will ever know. I spent my life believing I should have whatever I wanted. The only thing I am good at is using a sword, and you have plenty of those. I am no good to you or anyone else."

"Stop it, girl." Horgris winced. "You be making my head hurt something fearful. Let me say this. It takes character to be admittin' your faults, but I'll wager you be no as bad as you be thinkin' you are. You did no have to take part in the quest, but you did, and you fought for your friends. I also hear tell of that other thing you did. I don't know what it be meaning, but it took courage. In any happenstance, the prophecy say you be the one to bring us back together, and if I believed nothing else, I believe that. We need someone to reunite us, girl, and you be the one. Help us. Please."

Shanis sat dumbstruck. He wanted an answer. Needed one. But what could she say? No matter what she decided, it would be wrong. Larris was convinced that she was critical to the safety of their homeland, and did she not owe something to the place from which she came? But what of these people? Horgris' words had touched her heart in a way she would not have thought possible from the brutish chieftain. Lothan had suffered for so long. What would her answer be?

She was saved the trouble of giving a reply when a familiar young girl burst through the draped hide doorway.

"Be it true? Do he really be here?" The girl's eyes fell upon Hierm and she let out a cry that was at once both joyous and despondent. Hierm had scarcely reached his feet when she hurled herself into his arms and began sobbing.

"Rinala!" Horgris bellowed. "What be the meaning of this?" He lurched heavily to his feet and stared at the two with a look of utter confusion and helplessness that was entirely out of place on this forceful man. "What you be doing, girl?"

Shanis looked at the young woman, then back to Horgris, and she understood.

Rinala finally loosened her grip on Hierm, who was staring at her in astonishment. Tears flowed freely down her lightly tanned cheeks, and her smile brightened the dim, smoky room. She took his hand and laid it on her rounded belly. "I am only a few moons, but I will give you a son. The bone woman told me so."

"A son?" Hierm's face went ashen. "What do you mean?"

"You be the only man I am ever laying with. No one before you. No one after. I will give you a strong son, I promise. And I will be a good wife to you."

Hierm's lips were moving but he made no sound. Horgris bellowed so loudly that Shanis reached for her sword, but there was no need.

"My boy!" Horgris thumped him on the back so hard that he took a step forward. "A pleasure to welcome you to the family it will be. This girl been no telling me who it was, but now I be seeing why. Fearful for your life, she was." He pumped his fists and laughed. "Wait until the other chiefs be hearing that me daughter be marrying one of the Six! Good blood, I tell ye, and a good omen." His celebration finished, he wrapped his arms around his daughter and the still-dumbstruck Hierm. "I am proud of ye, Rinala. You done good."

Suddenly remembering Shanis, he smiled at her. "Do think about what I have said. We'll be talking more later, girl. I do have a wedding to arrange."

Chapter 3

The wedding took place three days later. In accordance with Monaghan tradition it was held on a hilltop and in the moonlight. Hierm, though stunned by Rinala's revelation, was determined to do what he believed was the right thing. Horgris' enthusiasm at having a member of "The Six," as he called it, had rubbed off on his clansmen. Hierm was suddenly a well-loved member of the community, never without a companion or a mug of ale. He wandered the camp dazed by shock and strong drink in equal measure.

Shanis worried about what would happen to her friend. He was now an expectant father and about to become a husband, married to a young woman from another country and culture. On the other hand, honesty compelled her to admit that she rather enjoyed the thought of Mistress Faun being introduced to her new daughter by marriage. The mere thought of Hierm bringing the young clanswoman into the Van Derin home made her laugh. If Faun had felt Shanis did not know her place as a woman, she had a hard row to hoe with Rinala, who was strong-willed even for a Monaghan woman.

She was also grateful that the wedding had somewhat distracted Horgris from pressing her for a decision. He had not entirely left her alone, occasionally making mention of their previous conversation, but he had, for the most part, left her to make her mind up. She assumed that, once the wedding was over, she would have to make her decision.

Larris sidled up to her as they joined the crowd of Monaghan circled around the crest of the hill. He had surprised her by also not insisting on a decision. She knew he wanted her to go back to Galdora. That possibility had upset her more and more over the past few days, because she had gradually come to the disconcerting realization that if it was her Larris wanted, and not just the Silver Serpent, she probably would go with him. When had her feelings for him changed? In any case, she was much too proud to say anything to him.

"Does the moon look brighter to you?" He stared up at the silver orb.

"Is this a joke, or a poor attempt at being romantic?" Strange. She craved his company, but still took great pleasure in needling him.

"I'm serious. At first I thought it was my imagination, but I've noticed it for several days now. It's brighter and seems closer. I thought perhaps the air here is clearer than other places I've traveled, but we've passed through this territory before. I don't know, what do you think?" He scratched his head and continued to gaze at the sky in a manner, in Shanis' estimation, unbecoming of a royal.

"I don't know. Truthfully, I haven't thought of much besides myself and that ice forsaken sword. When that hasn't been on my mind, I've been busy trying to talk Hierm out of this wedding." She turned her eyes toward the sky. "I suppose it does seem brighter, now that you mention it." He was right. The moon did look different. Larger, brighter, more real. Strange.

"You are not the only one who does not want this marriage to take place. Rinala has no shortage of admirers, and several young men sound almost mutinous over the clan chief's daughter marrying an outlander." He fell silent for a moment.

"Does it bother you so much?" Larris' voice was light, but his expression grave. "Hierm's marriage, I mean." He turned to stare at her in that way he had of seeming to delve into her thoughts. She was finding it less annoying than she once had. Her verbal jousts with Larris were a fresh return to normalcy, an opportunity to forget about the sudden, drastic change in her life. "Or is it the entire concept of marriage to which you are opposed? The mighty warrior girl needs no man, and such."

"Oaf!" She shoved him away. "What bothers me is that my friend is about to marry a girl he has known for three days. How can that possibly be a good thing?"

"Three days, plus one evening," Larris added, grinning wickedly. He took a step back as if to avoid another push. "I am only joking. I can understand your concern. Among the nobility, our marriages are arranged for us and, more often than not, both parties are at least... content with the arrangement."

"Are they truly, or is that merely the face they put on for others to see?"

"I don't know," he confessed, "but I admire that Hierm is willing to stand behind his convictions. There's precious little honor among the nobility, I fear. All the court intrigue, the manipulation, the games that are played in the name of power. I find a bit of old-fashioned morality refreshing, if you want to know the truth."

"Give me a sword any day. There's no deceit in that. Just two people and two blades." It was perhaps the most pompous thing she had ever said. It sounded like something Master Yurg would say, or perhaps a storyteller. She hoped Larris would let it pass, but he did not.

"No deceit in swords? Hmmm." He rubbed his chin and frowned in an exaggerated look of thoughtfulness. "Though you are probably correct in the main, I think I still might be inclined to disagree."

"So would Hierm." She thought of Pedric Karst and the tournament they had not finished. She wondered what had become of Karst. The last time she had seen him, he was with Lerryn's party, and she had been convinced they were after her. But there had been no repeat encounter, thank the gods. Most likely Karst was now studying at the Prince's Academy, preparing to be an officer in the Galdoran army. A shame. She would have loved to cross swords with him. Such an eventuality was now highly unlikely.

"Truly? You will have to tell me about it sometime." The high-pitched trilling of pipes and the gentle thrumming of a hide drum interrupted their conversation.

The clan elders strode single-file up the hill, the light of the torches they bore casting eerie shadows on their weighty expressions. The onlookers parted to let them pass. They took up places in a semi-circle near the apex of the hill. Arborator Bomar, clan priest to the god Dagdar, came next. He was clad in the traditional clan garb, but wore a thick silver chain around his neck to denote his office. Hanging from the chain was a cylindrical pendant, which Shanis had been told contained soil from Amangdar, the sacred burial ground of the Monaghan. His snowy hair showed only traces of the red it had once been. Unlike the other clansmen, he was clean-shaven, revealing a round, kindly face that appeared misplaced on his short, powerful body.

Hierm strode to the top of the hill to stand beside the arborator. Granlor, the young man for whom Rinala once had eyes, stood at Hierm's right as his second. Hierm had wanted Shanis to stand with him, but like so many other traditions, she was excluded because she was female. A pity Oskar was not with them. He could have stood with Hierm. Her throat knotted at the thought of her lost friends, and she feared she would cry. Seeing the look on her face, Larris slipped his arm around her shoulders and smiled. He thinks I'm emotional because it's a marriage ritual!

"I wish Oskar could be here," she whispered, her voice thick. Larris' gaze dropped a little and his features sagged. He nodded and drew her closer to his side. She took a deep breath and forced her thoughts back to the moment at hand.

Rinala looked positively radiant as she came up the hill. Shanis had only seen her dressed in ordinary clothing and usually dirty from whatever daily tasks she had performed. In general, Monaghan women tended to be sturdy and handsome, but tonight Rinala was beautiful. She was garbed in an ornate silk dress, obviously old, but well-cared for. Perhaps it was an heirloom from a more peaceful time. Her hair was woven in a complex web of tiny braids, and mossflower adorned her head like a fine dusting of snow in early winter.

Horgris escorted her, wearing his clan garb, which looked to have actually been washed for the occasion, as no food or drink stains were evident, along with his tall, hawk-feathered hat. She noted with detached amusement that a few additional feathers had been strategically placed to cover the hole Allyn's arrow had made in it months ago. The clan chieftain smiled and walked with a jovial bounce to his step, clearly enjoying the attention the moment brought. Considering he had intended to kill her the first time they met, she rather liked the man. He was a ferocious warrior to be sure, but a good and decent leader as well as a doting father. Miliana, his wife, followed behind, dressed in a simple gown. It was obvious where Rinala had gotten her lithe build and good looks. The only things she appeared to have inherited from Horgris were his coppery hair and, if the whisperings were true, his prodigious temper.

The wedding party reached the top, and all turned to face the arborator. Shanis noticed that Rinala and Horgris were bound together at the wrist with a strip of fabric. A hush grew over those assembled as the ceremony began.

"In the sight of Dagdar, who brings life to the earth, and upon whose benevolent hands we stand, may these two who stand before us be blessed upon their path. May their household be blessed with a solid foundation, strong walls, and a warm fire. May the fruits they bear be abundant, and may they remain united in marriage, in service to their clan and to their god.

"Hierm Van Derin, of the clan Van Derin of Galsbur. You stand before this assemblage to make your pledge to Rinala ni Miliana, of the Hawk Hill clan of Monaghan. Do you pledge upon your honor and your life to be a husband to her, to provide for her with the toil of your labor, to protect her with the might of your sword, and to love her with the strength of your heart?"

Hierm knelt and scooped up a handful of dirt. Rising, he held his clenched fist before him. "In the sight of Dagdar who brings life to the earth, I so pledge." He opened his hand and let the soil fall to the ground.

Granlor handed him something. It was the ancient wreath he had been given by the Thandrylls. A soft murmur ran through the onlookers as he placed it on Rinala's head. Shanis had paid no attention to it when he received it in the Thandryll's trading ritual, but now she took a closer look. It was masterfully woven, the twisted coils of ancient vine were shaped into the semblance of flowers: daisies, mossflower and moonblooms. Had human hands truly woven such a creation? The gray-brown vines were smooth and shiny with age, and glistened in the combined light of the torches and the full moon. Rinala's eyes shone as she saw the gift her new husband had bestowed upon her. Horgris nodded in approval.

"Rinala ni Miliana of the Hawk Hill clan of Monaghan. You stand before this assemblage to make your pledge to Hierm Van Derin of the clan Van Derin of Galsbur. Do you pledge upon your honor and your life to be a wife to him, to bless him with the fruit of your loins, to serve him with the work of your hands." Many people chuckled at that, including Horgris. "And to love him with the strength of your heart?"

Rinala repeated the ritual just as Hierm had, scooping up soil, making her pledge, and sprinkling the soil onto the ground. For her part, she placed around Hierm's neck a braided leather hawk claw necklace. The process was awkward with her left arm still bound to her father, but she managed. She stepped back, beaming up at Hierm, who smiled in return.

He does seem happy. Perhaps he really does care for her. Shanis marveled at the realization. She had assumed that he was only doing this out of a sense of duty and obligation, but Hierm appeared happy. He had been such a brooding young man under his father's constant disapproving gaze and his mother's suffocating control, that she had forgotten what it was like to see him relaxed and at peace. The thought warmed her heart. Without realizing what she was doing, she slipped her arm around Larris' waist and pulled him close.

"Do you, Horgris ni Lamana, Chieftain of the Hawk Hill clan of Monaghan," Bomar continued, "grant your blessing upon this marriage and accept Hierm Van Derin of the clan Van Derin of Galsbur into your hearth and home?"

"That I do," Horgris said, his voice strangely soft. He kissed his daughter gently on the forehead, and stood smiling as Bomar untied the cloth that bound him to his child. He stepped back and took Miliana's hand. The two watched, Miliana tearfully, as Bomar now bound Rinala to Hierm.

"In the sight of Dagdar," the arborater boomed, "I declare you are husband and wife. May the road before you be smooth, the rain be gentle, and may the earth always be soft beneath your feet."

At that proclamation, the pipes sang out and the drums struck up a joyous beat. The onlookers roared as they moved apart, creating a path down which the new husband and wife descended the hill. They pelted Hierm and Rinala with chunks of the gray-green moss that grew in the lower branches of nearby trees. Well wishes from the women and bawdy suggestions from the men chased the couple down the hill where a blazing bonfire, food and drink awaited them.

Chapter 4

The new couple was the center of a loud and ebullient celebration, with everyone wanting to give blessings, advice, or both. Shanis was finally able to draw Hierm aside. He had abstained from drinking, but was in a fine mood. His face had a relaxed quality that made him look like the Hierm she remembered from their early childhood. No longer did he appear weary from the strain of their adventure. The fatigue and worry had made him look too much like his father for Shanis' comfort. Now he seemed renewed.

"Are you all right?" Shanis asked. It seemed impossible that marriage to an almost-complete stranger could have such an effect on him. "You seem happy, but I just wonder."

"Yes. I am happy." He said the words as if they came as a surprise to him. "I was shocked and frightened at first, but the thought of being a father and a husband appeals to me. I want to be the sort of father I did not have. And Rinala is a kind, beautiful girl. She also has a temper, but that just makes her more interesting. In many ways she reminds me of you." He glanced away for a moment. "I'm sorry. That was an odd thing to say, wasn't it?"

"I am flattered." Shanis squeezed his hand. "Truly I am. We were always close, but it never seemed exactly right between the two of us, did it?"

"No, it didn't." He shook his head and looked back at the cluster of well-wishers that encircled Rinala. "But with Rinala, it's almost as if this is my destiny. Ever since we left home I've felt that something was directing our lives—some force beyond our control. This marriage feels like a part of it."

He shrugged. This was not the sort of conversation in which Hierm normally took part. This was more Oskar's domain. Each thought of her missing friends was another dagger to her heart. Hierm's sudden downcast look matched her feeling. "I had better get back. It would not do to make Rinala jealous on her wedding night."

"Good luck." She turned to find Larris standing behind her. "Spying on me?" She smiled to make certain he knew she was joking. "How are you enjoying the festivities?"

"This is my first Monaghan wedding. It is quite interesting. Not so liturgical as that to which I'm accustomed, but it has its own beauty." He held out his hand to her. "Would you care to dance?"

Shanis protested that she could not dance, but he would not hear of it, reminding her of their last visit to Horgris' village. He seemed to have forgotten that the evening of which he spoke had not ended so happily. But, despite her reservations, he was soon leading her through an ancient promenade. He danced like he fought—with confidence and practiced grace.

She found herself drawn more and more to this young man, and she stared into his brown eyes, as if trying to read his intentions. He had definitely seemed interested in her when they first met, but she worried that her almost-constant rejections had dampened his spirits. Foolishness! He still paid plenty of attention to her. It was up to her to decide what she wanted.

The drummers now struck a faster beat, and they flew into a raucous, foot-stomping Monaghan traditional dance. Neither of them was familiar with it, but they made a good approximation of the steps, which mostly involved stomping, clapping and turning while working your way around the bonfire. Partners switched several times during the dance, but she found herself back with Larris at the end.

Horgris interrupted the dancing to make a speech, in which he praised his daughter, mostly due to her fine bloodline and upbringing. This part of his speech drew loud laughter and derisive comments at the appropriate times. He went on to praise his new son by marriage and proclaim his blessing upon the union. He then grew very serious.

"It be Monaghan tradition that the father must be givin' his daughter a marriage gift. Were times bein' as they once were, I would be proud to grant you a piece of land to call yer own. It is my vow," he continued, turning to look across the crowd directly at Shanis, "that things be changin' in my lifetime. I pledge to you that, in my lifetime, I be makin' good on yer gift."

The clansmen and women cheered, but only Shanis and Horgris knew what had passed between them, though she supposed a few of the elders also knew what he was suggesting. How dare he? It was her decision to make, and she would not be guilted into making it one way or the other. She turned and stalked away.

"Where are you going? It's almost over." Larris hurried up and fell in step with her. "Rinala's brothers kidnap her and Hierm has to fight them to get her back. It's not as serious as it sounds, but it should be fun. What's wrong?"

"I can't take it any longer. You are all pulling me in too many directions." She stopped walking and turned to face him. "You want me to go to back Galdora. Horgris wants me to stay here and unite Lothan. As usual, no one seems to care what I want."

"All right. What do you want, Shanis?" Larris moved closer, their faces almost touching, and lowered his voice to little more than a whisper. "Tell me you don't want to go to Galdora with me, and I will accept that. Reluctantly, to be sure, but I will accept it."

How could such a simple question confuse her so? Was he asking her to go to Galdora for the good of the realm, or was it because he wanted them to be together? There was a world of difference between the two, but her pride had kept her from asking. Now was the time.

Shouts arose from the far side of the camp. Hoofbeats thudded in the soft earth. Not many riders. She suddenly remembered her sword back in the hut. "I'll be back." She left Larris standing alone in the dark as she sprinted away.

"I'll find you later," Larris called out, his voice a blend of annoyance and amusement.

Her feet slipped on the damp loam, and she stumbled on protruding rocks. The cries had died down, and there were no sounds of fighting. She slowed and looked back, but she could see little in the foggy air, save the glow of the bonfire and dark shadows moving around it. She hurriedly retrieved her sword and made her way back.

Most of the villagers were clustered near the fire, and she had to force her way through the crowd in order to find out what was happening. Breaking through the throng, she came upon a group of elders tending to a dozen or more newcomers. All were injured, some more serious than others. One was dead. Blood, looking slick and black in the firelight, soaked his tunic and obscured his tartan so she could not tell if these people were of Horgris' clan.

"They set upon us without warning. We been trying to skirt around them, but their outriders spotted us and chased us down," one of the men was explaining to Horgris while Amia, the bone woman of the Hawk Hill clan, tended to his wounded shoulder. "We be havin' no chance except to flee. Dagrim put arrows in a couple and I took a few down me'self. They finally leave us be when it be plain we no be coming back their way." His voice broke a bit as he spoke. "Little Lissie, she been hurt something fierce."

"Ye no be worryin about her," Horgris said in his gruff voice. "We be takin' care of her." Shanis could see the lie in his eyes. "You say the Three Oaks be doing this? We no be havin' trouble with them for a long time." His voice heated. "Why they be this way to you? Do you be knowin?"

"They thought we be spies or the like," the man said, grimacing as Amia bound his wound. "They no be lettin' anybody close to their camp. They do have Badla."

The murmur that had filled the crowd erupted in cries of surprise, anger and, in some cases, joy.

"Badla! We be takin' her from them for sure!" Granlor raised his fist in the air. "Honor to the Hawk Hill! Honor to Monaghan!" Other young men joined their voices to his. Chants of "Badla! Badla!" rang through the hills.

Shanis turned away, disgusted by the hunger for pride in the face of so much hurt. Vengeance she could understand, but to be so easily distracted by the opportunity to steal a corpse?

Her thoughts were distracted as her eyes fell on a little girl who lay gasping for breath in her mother's arms. Blood soaked the blankets in which she was wrapped and smeared her face. Her mother looked up at Shanis with eyes as dead as her daughter was soon likely to be. This must be Lissie.

"She did take an arrow." Her mother spoke in a vacant tone that matched the look in her eyes. "We did remove it out, but her body be so... small. She be only six summers old. Why my little girl?"

Rinala, who was attempting to comfort the woman, looked up at Shanis with tearful eyes aglow with unrecognizable thoughts.

"You be the one," Rinala said. "You able to be helpin' her." While Shanis stood dumbstruck, trying to find the words to protest, Rinala lifted the little girl from her mother's arms and thrust her upon Shanis. "Use the Silver Serpent. You can do it." Others heard Rinala's words, and gathered around.

"Yes!" someone cried. "You be havin' the power. You save Lissie then you be punishin' the Three Oaks!" A few shouted curses at the Three Oaks, while the rest pressed in on Shanis, speaking to her in urgent tones, begging her to believe in the power she supposedly possessed.

What could she say? She looked down at the little girl, who gazed up at her with big, green eyes. The courage she saw there broke her heart. She wished she could help, but she didn't know how. She wanted to shout at them, to tell them that she neither knew what the power was, nor how it worked. She could not even remember using it the first time. But when she looked around at their desperate, pleading faces, she knew she could not disappoint them.

How did magic work? How did sorcery work? Kneeling down beside the little girl and taking her hand, she closed her eyes and fixed her mind on the sword strapped to her back. She imagined power flowing out from the blade, through her body and into the little girl. She opened her eyes and looked down at the child.

Nothing.

Her vision misted, her throat pinched, and she sagged under the twin burdens of expectation and despair. She could not do it. She didn't know how. She was helpless.

I give up.

The serpent on her chest suddenly burned with an intensity that made her gasp. Her back stiffened straight as a post as something she could only call power surged like an avalanche through her body. It raged down her arms and into Lissie. The little girl uttered a small cry, and her eyes widened in surprise, but not pain.

Shanis could not see what was happening, but she felt it. She felt the little girl's body mending, the wound closing up. Her heartbeat strengthened and steadied, as did her breathing. With a contented sigh, Lissie curled up against Shanis and closed her eyes.

"Lissie!" Her mother wailed and she snatched the girl away, but her despair turned to joy as she realized that her daughter had not died, but was sleeping peacefully. The woman stripped away Lissie's bloody clothes to expose the girl's fully healed body. She held her daughter in her arms, stood, and turned for all the others to see. They were too amazed to cheer, or even smile. Lissie awoke and vehemently protested her state of undress and the effect of the chill night air. Still laughing, her mother held her tight as someone led them to a nearby hut.

And now Shanis remembered. She could recall the moment of absolute surrender in which she pushed her own limitations aside and let the power of the Silver Serpent take her over. She remembered the battle with the serpent, and the words it had spoken to her. Most of all, she remembered the torrent of power that surged through her then just as it did now.

"Girl! Help me now!" someone shouted.

"No! Me next!" cried another.

She could not.

Right now she was struggling to control the storm that raged within her. Her body felt as if it would explode as the force grew within her. She imagined herself swelling from the sheer volume of power. She focused her mind on the serpent on her chest. Stop! No more! The flow cut off, but the power still stormed within her. Crying out in agony, she fell to her hands and knees, clawing at the turf. She was aware of Larris at her side, asking if he could help. Hierm was there as well, and Rinala. Allyn was nearby, but he cringed and drew away at the sight of her struggles.

She had to do something with all of this power. She could no longer contain it. Her thoughts turned to the sword. It seemed to beckon to her, and she willed the power into the weapon. The sword drank it up. She could feel it draining from her body as it filled the ancient blade. Finally, the weapon could take no more. Energy still surged within her, but now she could contain it.

"Help me stand," she whispered to Larris. He took her by the arm and aided her as she rose. She chose the person who appeared to be the most badly hurt and laid her hands on his temples.

"I have only done this once before, so I make no promises." She closed her eyes and allowed the power to flow forth through her fingertips and into the man. This time, she was ready for the shock as it poured forth, and she barely flinched. She felt the healing energy flow into him, finding and mending his wounds. It was as if some unseen force controlled the energy. She was simply the vessel that carried the power. When she finished, the man smiled and thanked her profusely. Too tired to do more than nod, she moved on to the next person.

Larris and Hierm remained by her side as she tended to more of the injured. By the time she had healed the fourth person, she was completely spent. The energy that had surged within her was gone. The serpent on her breast pulsed and tingled, wanting to unleash another torrent, but she was too weak to manage it. If another such flow of power entered her body, she would be unable to control it, and she was certain it would destroy her. She forced herself to stand up straight, but Larris read the look in her eyes.

"She has done all that she can," he told Horgris, his arm now wrapped protectively around her. "She needs rest."

"Aye," Horgris replied. "You done well, girl. But if you going to be a leader, you no let them see you be weak. Can you be walking on your own?" She wanted to tell him that she was not going to lead anyone, but she lacked the energy to argue, so she merely nodded her head. Larris let go of her arm, but he did not move away.

"My kinsmen," Horgris shouted. "Today be a blessed day. Not only do my daughter be getting' married, but today we be seein' the miraculous power of the Silver Serpent, and she who do bear it. Glory to the Hawk Hill! Glory to Monaghan! Glory to Lothan!"

Cheers exploded and shouts of Hawk Hill! Monaghan!, and even a few of Shanis! rang out. The crowd parted for her and, with the last of her energy, she made her way back to her hut.

She did not bother to undress, but fell heavily onto the thick bearskin sleeping mat. Larris covered her and extinguished the light. She did not know if he planned to stay with her or not, but she hoped he did.

Sleep devoured her, filling her head with dreams she did not comprehend. When she woke the next morning, she had come to a decision.

Chapter 5

Oskar had sometimes tried to imagine what death was like. This was definitely not it. It was cold, wet and utterly devoid of light. And he hurt all over. The next life was supposed to be a pleasant reward for a life well-lived, but this was dreadful.

Wait a moment! Cold, dark, painful. He was in the underworld! He had never truly believed all his mother's warnings that his sharp tongue and irreverent attitude were offensive to the gods. Perhaps she had been right. All the misdeeds he had ever done came rushing back. What was he going to do? What if this was how he was to spend eternity?

He realized his arms were bound. He struggled to move, but he could not get loose. Something was crawling on him. He felt its cold tongue on his face. He thrashed and twisted, trying to break free. What was it going to do to him? He tried to scream, but no sound would come.

"Oskar. Oskar." It whispered his name, and he imagined a dark wraith ready to take him in its chill embrace. He tried to turn his head, to shake loose from its cold kiss. "Wake up. You're safe."

He would not believe its lies. He flailed about, and a groan escaped his lips.

"Open your eyes. You are all right. I'm here with you." A red-orange glow filled his field of vision. The beast stopped licking his face, and the air around him grew warmer. So the beast was trying a new tactic—trying to entice him with warmth and light.

"Please come back to me. Just wake up. Open your eyes." The voice was feminine, enticing. He felt a light pressure on his chest. It was touching him, but the feeling was not so disconcerting this time. Perhaps he would open his eyes just long enough to see what torture eternity held in store for him. He had to find out sooner or later.

Opening his eyes was no mean feat. It was like loading heavy sacks onto a wagon. Finally, with significant effort, he parted the lids enough to see smoky light shining on a rough stone ceiling. Someone was leaning over him. Someone familiar.

"Thank the gods you're awake. I don't know how long you've been unconscious, but it seems like days. I tried to keep you warm, but everything got so wet when we fell."

The person kept talking, but Oskar was not listening. He was trying to remember.

Falling, falling, falling.

He remembered falling, but not from where, or how it had happened.

He searched his mind and recalled the golorak coming after them. The chamber with the seastone coffins. The battle with the serpent. He had raised his staff and tried to do whatever it was he had done back in Thandryll.

And then nothing.

He forced his eyes to open wider and tried to sit up, but a wave of nausea swept over him and he fell back. He groaned again and wished that he could have been dead after all. Being alive was not worth this misery.

"Once I was certain you were not going to die, I did a bit of exploring. Really, I just felt my way around. I didn't want to use what few firesticks we had. I found bits of wood and such, and I finally was able to make a fire. Can you believe it? Me! I made a fire the way Shanis does it. It isn't much, but it gives a little light and warmth. I had to use some of your parchment, Oskar, but I made certain it had no writing on it. I hope that is all right. I needed something dry to burn."

He finally realized who was speaking. No one else could talk for so long without need of someone else taking part in the conversation.

"Khalyndryn?" he croaked. "Where are we? Where are the others?" His mind no longer moved like cold molasses, and thoughts coursed through his mind. Where were Shanis, Hierm, Larris and Allyn? Had they survived the battle with the serpent? They had heard the bellows of more than one golorak. Were more lurking somewhere nearby?

"I don't know," she said, though she did not indicate which question she was answering. "Do you remember the fight?"

He nodded.

"Shanis took the stone sword off of the statue in the center of the room, and something happened. It looked like the statue turned into a real sword, and she started fighting the serpent with it. But when she took the sword, the statue sank out of sight, and the floor started sloping down toward the hole where the statue had been. You fainted, or something, and I tried to hold on to you. But we fell."

Khalyndryn had tried to save him? He remembered a little bit more now. He was holding out his staff, trying to call down the lightning again, but when Shanis touched the sword, a blinding flash of agony burst in his mind. Somehow, the sword had done it to him.

"I have no idea what happened to the others." Her voice was rife with sadness. "I hope they are alive, but I do not know. We fell into deep water and we were carried a long way. I don't know how I found you, but we drifted together, and I was able to keep your head above water. You float on your back quite well, by the way."

"Thanks," he grumbled, trying again to sit up and managing to prop up on an elbow. "So, where are we now?"

"When the water was shallow enough, I managed to drag you onto this ledge. Our packs held up very well, being oilcloth and all. Our spare cloaks were dry, as were our food and firesticks. I only wish we had more. What we have will not last very long, I fear. We left so many of our belongings up on the mountain above Murantha that there just is not much left. I found one other pack. I think it is Allyn's. That gave us a little more food and a spare cloak.

At the mention of food Oskar's stomach rumbled. He suddenly felt as if he had not eaten in weeks. "Can you spare a little for me?"

"I think so," Khalyndryn said. "I haven't had an appetite. I did manage to warm some water. No tea, unfortunately, but warm water takes the chill off."

Oskar ate a small piece of cheese and a hard crust of stale bread, washing it down with a cup of hot water. He still felt worse than he'd ever felt in his life, but he was alive and, hopefully, so were his friends.

"What should we do now?" He was surprised to hear himself asking Khalyndryn such a question, but he was not in any condition to make a decision on his own. "We can't stay in the dark forever."

"This ledge follows the stream. I suppose we should go in that direction." She sighed and looked away into the darkness. "The gods willing, we'll find a way out." She did not remark on what would happen if they did not find an escape before their food ran out.

For a fleeting moment, Oskar imagined wandering alone in this abysmal darkness, buried beneath earth and stone, far from sun and sky. He shuddered.

"I hope you aren't taking a chill." Khalyndryn misunderstood the reason for his trembling and scooted up against him to try and add her warmth to his. The feel of her touch was like a shock, but in a good way. How many times in his life had he admired her from afar, knowing she had eyes only for the most handsome young men?

"I know it's cold and damp down here, but I did the best I could for you."

He placed his finger on her lips, surprised at himself that he would touch her in such a familiar way.

"Thank you, Khalyndryn, for taking care of me. I would not have survived if you had not been here for me."

Her smile warmed his spirit as her body warmed his flesh. She had never been strong or independent, but she had certainly been self-reliant while looking out for him.

Much too soon, she pulled away from him and stood up, hastily brushing nonexistent dirt off of her clothing. "I suppose we should gather our things and start walking."

They wandered for what seemed like days, feeling their way along the cold, smooth passage. They saved their meager supply of wood for the occasional fire, so they might have a little extra warmth when they stopped to sleep. They lay on spare cloaks when they slept, but the stone floor leached the heat from their bodies.

The ledge on which they walked narrowed in places, or even disappeared entirely, and they found themselves slogging knee deep through the dark, icy water. It sapped the feeling from Oskar's legs and feet, and drained him of what little warmth and energy he had. They were forced to stop all too frequently, always at his behest. He still did not feel right. Every time they paused, he found himself wanting to lie down and never get back up again. But every time he faltered, Khalyndryn would get him moving again.

"Come on Oskar!" Her voice cracked like a whip. "Get up and move. You are not going to curl up and die on me down here after I've worked so hard to keep you going."

And they would go on. Step by mind-numbing step, neither of them giving voice to what they both wondered—would they ever again ever see a glimmer of light, a reason for hope?

The longer they remained in this black prison, the further his spirits fell. One time, half-conscious, he staggered into the water and felt something long and slimy slither past his leg. He shouted and scrambled away, sputtering and shaking. After that he clung to the wall, fearful that something might reach out and grab him.

He tried not to voice his fears, but from time to time he would let slip a comment about the hopelessness of their situation.

"We will get there, don't you worry." Her voice never wavered, and she gave no indication that she might entertain even the slightest possibility that she might be wrong. To drive her point home, she seized him by the front of his damp cloak and yanked him forward. Either she had grown stronger or he was still very weak, because she guided him around like a cow led to milking, and she kept him going that way until they reached the end of the passage.

The tunnel finally ended in a blank wall where the stream formed a deep pool. They felt around for any opening at all. They searched about for the faintest light, or breath of fresh, dry air, but they found nothing.

They lit a fire and repeated their search by its faint light. Finally they took flaming brands and worked their way back up the tunnel in case they had missed a side passage or egress, but they soon gave up. They returned to their campfire too disheartened to speak.

They would die here.

Oskar had neither the energy nor the desire to retrace their steps, and their food would not hold out much longer. They shared a silent meal and fell asleep by the dying embers of their tiny fire. As his eyes closed, he wondered if he should bother to wake again.

"I see light! Oskar, I see light!"

Khalyndryn's voice roused him from his slumber, and he returned to consciousness like a swimmer coming up for air. Slowly, slowly, then gasping for breath. The meaning of her words finally broke through the haze of sleep, and he bolted up, afraid to believe what he had heard. Surely it had been a dream.

Khalyndryn took him by the arm and led him to the water's edge.

"Look down there under the water. You can just see it. It must have been after dark when we reached this spot. I suppose it's morning now. That has to be light from outside!"

He lay down on his stomach and peered down into the dark pool.

He saw it—a shaft of light far beneath the surface. It was the first cause for hope since he had awakened in this dark, dank place, but he could not permit himself to feel optimistic. It might be an opening to the outside, but what if it was too small to get through? What would they do then? Might it not be better to die in the dark than to die so close to freedom?

"We'll just have to swim down to it and see where it takes us." Khalyndryn's voice trembled with excitement. "We did it! We found the way out!"

He did not have the heart to voice his concerns to her. Instead, he began stuffing his things into his pack in preparation for a swim.

Chapter 6

"What do you mean you are staying here? Are you out of your mind?" Larris threw his hands up and looked up at the sky as if searching for a source of help there. They had taken a walk away from camp in order to speak privately. "We need to understand more about the sword. What you are able to do with it, it makes no sense."

"What do you mean?"

Larris turned and took her hands in his. "Almost nothing is known for certain about the Silver Serpent, but I collected legends, stories, and songs. A common thread was that the gods somehow put the best qualities of the kings and queens of Gameryah into the Serpent: wisdom, courage, strength, integrity. The conclusion was that the Silver Serpent gave those attributes to the bearer. But the reality is nothing like that." He sighed. "In any case, you are a Galdoran. The prophecies say that the Silver Serpent will save the royal family. My family!"

"I know what you've told me the prophecies say. The prophecies also say the bearer can unite the clans in Lothan." She already knew how this argument would likely play out, but her mind was made up.

"Those are different prophecies." He frowned. "I have read them, and I am uncertain about their reliability."

"Well, I haven't read any of them. It occurs to me that I have been doing a remarkable amount of listening to other people, and it's time for me to make my own decisions." She touched a finger to his lips before he could interrupt her again. His eyes flared. This was probably the first time someone had done that to the prince. "Please, just listen to me. I held that little girl in my arms, looked into her eyes, and I realized that if there is any chance at all that I can stop the clan wars, I have to try. What is happening here is too terrible to just turn away from them when there is a chance I can help."

"Your heart is in the right place, but what can you truly do? You aren't a clan leader. You aren't a Lothan at all. Why would they listen to you?" He had regained control of his temper and was now speaking calmly.

"Because I have this." She pointed to the serpent on her chest. "But most of all because the prophecy says I'm going to." She folded her arms across her chest and waited for him to argue, but he just stood there. Might there be a chance he would listen to her?

"I could use some help. I don't know how to lead people. I need you." That was as close as she was going to come to opening her heart to him, until he did some opening of his own. "Will you help me?"

Larris stared at her, his expression blank. For a moment, she feared that he was not going to say anything at all, but finally he broke the silence.

"You should begin with this clan. They have witnessed your power firsthand, and right now there is no one here more beloved than you. Besides that, Horgris has already pledged his support. Capitalize on that. Get them behind you today. Right now."

"All right." She had asked for his help, but she was a bit taken aback by his quick turnaround. "How do I begin?"

"The people need not only a person to follow, but a vision in which to believe. What is your vision?"

"Well, I...."

"No! That will never do. You must know your vision and believe in it. You must be ready to speak from your heart any time someone asks. Tell me, from your heart, what will you do to change the lives of this clan?"

"I would heal their broken country. Give their children the chance to grow up. Their grandchildren could know peace and prosperity. I would bind Lothan's wounds and make her strong." She didn't know where that had come from, but it was what she felt.

"That's a good start." He suddenly reminded her of Master Yurg criticizing her sword technique. "But tell them what you will do. Not what you hope to do, or want to do. They must know that you will do what you say." His brown eyes burned with intensity.

"I can do that."

"Very well. Now, tell me how you are going to do it."

"What? I don't know. I suppose I will stop the fighting and start rebuilding."

"You cannot suppose anything. Tell me, without pausing, stammering, or showing the least bit of doubt, what specifically you plan to do. Even if you're not completely certain. Go ahead." He sat down on a nearby stump and stared up at her with an expectant look.

"We will start with the Monaghan." Larris had annoyed her, so her words were firm, even harsh. "We will march up to the holds of each clan one at a time. I will heal their wounded, show them the sword and the serpent, and then I will tell them that the time of clan war is at an end. I will call them to unite, and then I will move on to the Malgog."

Larris just stared at her, the morning sunlight framing his face in golden light. Finally, he smiled. "It's a start," he said. "Your plan will likely change as you go, but it is enough to get the people behind you. Listen to those you trust behind closed doors, but always be strong in front of the clan. Do not let people know that I am advising you. The last thing you want is for them to believe that you are somehow under the control of the Galdoran crown." His eyes softened. "In fact, I should probably leave for that very reason."

He let his gaze fall to the ground, and her heart fell along with it. He was going to leave her? Oskar was gone, Hierm was married and now Larris was going to leave. She didn't want him to go, not only because she was lonely and in need of his counsel, but she was finally able to admit to herself that she wanted him there. But the frost would take her before she spoke first.

"But I don't want to go." He sat there, staring at the ground. "I should be back in Galdora. It was childish of me to leave without telling my father, and I am probably needed, but I don't want to leave."

"Then why don't you stay?" She tried to keep her voice casual.

"Because a royal cannot wed a commoner," he said quietly, his voice strained as if the words pained him. "And I would never treat you the way Lerryn treats women."

She could not believe what he was saying. Her eyes burned, but she was determined not to cry. Her throat choked off the words she wanted to say.

Larris rose, came to her, and caught her in a crushing embrace. She wrapped her arms around his neck. Before she knew what was happening, his lips were on hers, their bodies pressed together. Too soon he broke the kiss and pressed his cheek against hers.

"I am sorry. I know I should not have done that." His breath was warm in her ear. "You must know I would never shame you."

"Stay with me." Her voice was almost a sob. "All the rest we can figure out, but please stay with me. I need you here. I want you here."

The space between her declaration and his reply seemed interminable. They stood there, locked in their embrace, and she hoped it would not end. She felt a warmth she had not felt since she left home, a feeling of belonging, of being home. What if he said no?

"All right. I will stay for as long as I can. If you are certain you want me?" He drew back to look her in the eye. Their noses were almost touching. She was surprised to see a touch of fear in his eyes.

"You be out here, girl?" Horgris' voice boomed from somewhere nearby. She pushed away from Larris and wiped her face. A moment later, the big man appeared through the trees. "Apologies," he said when he noticed Larris' annoyed expression. "I know we already been talking about this, but the elders be wanting to speak to you. After last night, they be hoping to convince you...."

"There is no need to convince me," she said, grateful for the distraction from Larris. She had wanted him to admit that he cared for her, but now she was even more confused. What sort of future could they have? "I have made up my mind. I would like to speak to the entire clan if I may."

Horgris smiled. "That be the spirit! You be doin' the right thing girl. You'll never regret the decision you make, and you always have Horgris to support ye." He beckoned for them to follow him back to the camp. He led them through the shady patch of forest, and as she stepped out into the daylight, it seemed to her as if she were stepping into a new world.

She stood atop the hill where Hierm and Rinala had wed only the night before. The clanspeople were gathered round. She felt sick; her heart pounded, her stomach was icy and sour, and her hands were clammy. What was she doing? She was a farm girl from a village in Galdora. Who was she to presume she could unite a nation? The very thought was absurd.

And then her eyes fell upon Lissie, the little girl she had somehow healed. She smiled up at Shanis with total adoration. This was why Shanis had to do what she was going to do. By no choice of her own, she was destined to heal, and she would begin by healing this land and its people. She had agonized much of the night over what she would say, and the talk with Larris had fueled her desire and focused her thoughts. The words seemed to come unbidden.

"I am Shanis Malan," she began. "I bear the Silver Serpent." Cheers erupted all around her. "And I have been so marked." She pulled her tunic down far enough to reveal the silver marking on her chest. "As you know, I have been granted the power to heal." A few cheers again, but most people were listening closely to what she said.

"In the short time I have spent among you, I have grown to admire and appreciate your courage, your strength and your kindness. My heart weeps at the suffering of such a proud people and a noble land. Monaghan deserves better." Loud shouts of agreement answered this statement. "Lothan deserves better." More cheers, though less enthusiastic. "I would heal your people, and I would heal your land. Lothan must again be united and stand as a proud, powerful nation. I would do this so that ones such as these," She picked up Lissie and held her up for all to see," may grow old. That your grandchildren and their grandchildren might prosper."

They were quiet now. Some were frowning at her, suspicious of her message.

"I do not promise you peace. At least not yet." Sadly, that drew nods of approval. "Nor do I demand that you come to me on bended knee. I offer to you my sword and my service. The power of the Silver Serpent can both heal and destroy. It is my most fervent hope that this power be used only to heal, but if it must be used to break those who oppose peace, so be it. In any case, I promise you this: the days of interminable clan war are at an end."

Utter silence met her proclamation. Some looked at her in confusion, while a few smiling women wept silent tears of hopefulness and thanks. A few young men stared down at the ground or shook their head. But many were nodding.

"I call upon those who will join me to come forth and make yourselves known."

This was the moment. Horgris stood in the back. He could not be the first to come forward. As clan leader he could not seem to be in her thrall, nor could he give the appearance of guiding the clan down this path. Someone else had to be the first to come forward.

"I will follow you." Granlor stepped out of the crowd. Unsheathing his sword, he knelt before her, the point of the blade on the ground, his hand resting on the hilt. She had asked them to join her, not follow her, but that is precisely what he had just pledged to do. Two more young men came forward, close friends of Granlor's, and joined him.

And then there were others: a few older men, one of the leading women, and then Hierm and Rinala together. The sight of Hierm kneeling before her moved her deeply and strengthened her resolve. Next came Horgris, along with men she knew to be members of the Order of the Fox, a semi-secret society dedicated to the re-unification of Lothan. And when Horgris came forth, it was as if the dam had burst. Soon, she was ringed by members of the Hawk Hill Clan, all kneeling before her. Larris and Allyn stood over to the side, Larris smiling and Allyn looking at her dispassionately. Seeing the two of them side-by-side now, it was strange to remember that she had once preferred the standoffish archer to the gregarious prince.

Only a small knot of young people remained standing. Six young men and three young women, led by Arlus, a broad-chested young clansman with flowing auburn hair and a sparse beard that scarcely covered his face. He scowled at her, his face filled with contempt.

Horgris looked up and noticed those who had not joined them. "We would be having this unanimous. No division among the Hawk Hill. Join us, men of Monaghan."

Arlus shook his head. "She be an outlander and a woman at that. You hear her words. She be wanting peace with the Malgog, with the other clans. She would break bread with those who spill our blood. The Hawk Hill cowers before no one!" His companions nodded. "We be proud warriors of Monaghan, born to fight and die for clan and honor, no to be making nice with our enemies."

"Lothan has more enemies than it can count." Shanis wondered how Larris would receive what she was about to say. "Her borders are threatened by greedy neighbors who see the lack of unity as weakness. Every year her borders shrink." The elders gathered around her murmured in general agreement.

"And there are others. I have seen with my own eyes the creatures of the Ice King. I was there when brave men of the Hawk Hill clan slew such beasts."

Horgris stood up, fished around inside his tunic, and withdrew the silver-gray paw of an ice cat. He held it up for all to see. The people gradually stood again, and they stared at the paw in fascination. Had he never displayed it before?

"Grandmother's tales," Arlus scoffed. "Next you be scarin' us with tales of boggarts and buggins. I be saying it again. I will no bend knee to no outlander woman, and I will no make peace with the Malgog. Not ever." He turned and strode down the hill, the others following behind.

"Your clan be seeing it different, Arlus!" Horgris shouted.

"It be no clan of mine." He stripped off his tartan and hurled it to the ground. "We be of the clanless. And Hawk Hill be our enemy." The others followed his example, leaving their clan garb lying in the dirt as they departed.

Horgris looked as if he would go after them, but then he turned back to face Shanis.

"The Hawk Hill clan do pledge its swords and its honor to the cause of unity. May the bearer of the Silver Serpent be leading us to a united Lothan."

As the clan cheered, the men raised their swords in celebration. Shanis drew the Silver Serpent and raised it overhead. The morning light shimmered golden on the blade. Was she bringing a shining light to this dark land, or was she starting a fire that would burn out of control? Time would tell.

Chapter 7

Aspin stoked the cookfire and set a pot of water on to boil. He had found a most satisfactory campsite at the edge of a deep pool nestled in a tiny valley. The autumn sun, cheery and warm, shone through a stand of birch trees. It was a fine morning.

It would have been even finer were he not completely baffled as to where to go next. He had pursued the Malan girl past the Ramsgate, but not long afterward, the sorcerous blast had happened. How long he had lain unconscious there was no way to know, but by the time he awoke, the world was somehow different. The sky was a richer hue of blue, the clouds thicker and puffier. All the life surrounding him seemed more vital. The entire world was… more alive.

What was even more puzzling was what he had come to think of as a magical residue arching across the sky back toward Lothan. It was as if some powerful work of sorcery had taken place somewhere far above. He could not say for certain, but he could sense that the trail started in the mountains and ended back to the east. With nothing else to go by, he had changed his course and headed in that direction.

He checked the lines he had set out the previous night and was pleased to find he had hooked two fat silver-sides. His water was boiling by the time he finished cleaning the fish. He skewered them and set them to broil. He sprinkled some tea leaves into the pot—a fine Diyonan leaf. He inhaled the sharp aroma and smiled. With a full belly and a few cups of tea in him, he would almost feel human. He would get back on the trail and hope he was moving in the right direction. He should probably report back to the prelate, but he was too stubborn to do so until he could tell him something definitive. He sighed as unwelcome thoughts of the citadel intruded on his peaceful morning.

Something caught his eye, chasing those thoughts from his mind as quickly as they had come. The surface of the pond rippled. What could it be? He strode to the edge and peered down, but he saw nothing. A fish? Or just his imagination?

He was about to turn away when he caught sight of bubbles floating up to the surface. A shadow appeared deep down in the water, growing larger and taking shape as it rose. Then a head broke the surface. It was a young man, his brown hair plastered to his face, sputtering and gasping as he treaded water. Behind him, a young woman surfaced, also sucking in air in huge gulps as she swam awkwardly for the shore.

Aspin prided himself on seldom being taken by surprise, but he was positively baffled as to how and why two young people could suddenly appear out of a mountain pond in which he was certain they had not been before. This was most unexpected, and it piqued his curiosity.

The boy shook the water from his eyes and searched out his companion. He took her by the arm and together they hauled themselves, weighed down by their sodden clothes, to shore. Once on dry land, they each dropped the bags they carried, and slumped to the ground.

The boy was the first to catch his breath, open his eyes. He looked up at the sky and let out a whoop of delight, raising his fists in triumph. The girl sat up, smiled, and hugged him, both of them laughing joyfully.

They still had not noticed him, so he waited until the laughter died down a bit before making his presence known.

"Good morning," he said. The pair started, scrambled to their feet, and gaped at him. "My name is Aspin. I am a saikur, or a seeker, if you prefer." They continued to stare, so he went on. "You are welcome to share breakfast with me. I have fresh fish and hot tea."

He turned his back to them and strode back to the fire, where he fished two extra tin cups from his pack, along with his tea strainer. He had poured three piping cups by the time the two joined him by the fire.

They accepted the tea with quiet thanks. The girl drank it down so quickly that Aspin feared she would scald herself. The young man drank his slowly with his eyes closed, savoring the drink. His big hands dwarfed the cup, and he held it close to his chest as if to hoard its warmth. They did not seem eager to talk, but Aspin was a patient man and comfortable with silence. It was not long before the young man spoke.

"My name is Oskar. This is Khalyndryn." He paused, seeming unsure how to continue. "We are lost." He looked down at the fire, seeming to have nothing more to add.

Aspin's heart hammered in his chest like an invader seeking to batter down a city gate. These two were part of the Malan girl's party. This proved he was at least headed in the right direction. But where were the other members of the party? And most important, where was the girl? Was Oskar being reticent, or had he simply had no reason to mention the others?

"I must confess my curiosity about how the two of you came to be in this pond."

Khalyndryn flashed a look of warning at Oskar. He grimaced as he spoke. "We were in the mountains, got lost, and fell into a river. It carried us to this place, and we found our way out."

So he was being reticent. Perhaps if Aspin took him by surprise, he could jar the truth from the boy.

"Tell me, Oskar. Where are Shanis Malan, Prince Larris and the others?" He smiled politely and lifted his cup to his lips, enjoying the boy's startled expression. Khalyndryn sat up straight and glanced at her friend.

"Understand," Aspin continued, "I mean them no harm. I have, in fact, been sent by Shanis Malan's father to find her." It was almost the truth, but it would suffice.

"You know Andric Malan?" Oskar asked, taking a sip of his tea and trying unsuccessfully to look casual.

"Colin Malan," Aspin corrected. "And yes, I know him. Clever of you, though."

"When did he send you?" Khalyndryn's voice was sharp with suspicion.

"I visited your village some weeks ago—just a few days after you left, in fact. I spoke first with Mistress Van Derin, and then your village blacksmith, before speaking with Colin. He apprised me of the circumstances surrounding your departure."

"You met Hierm's mother?" The corners of Oskar's mouth turned up in a wry smile, and he chuckled. "No doubt the pleasure was all hers."

"Did you see my parents?" Khalyndryn interrupted. "Master and Mistress Serrill. My father is the innkeeper in town. If you stayed in town, I suppose you took a room at the inn. It is the only one, after all."

"I fear I did not stay the night." Aspin needed to be cautious here. He had not yet won their trust, and the news that he had left town upon discovering Yurg had been murdered would likely unsettle them. "But Colin did indicate that no one believes your virtue has been tainted in any way. They know the truth about what happened, and they are anxious for your safe return. Colin urged me to begin my search immediately, as he is very concerned about his daughter, as well."

"Why did he not come after her himself?" There was suspicion in Oskar's eyes, if not his voice.

If the lad was intimidated by Aspin, or by saikurs in general, it did not show. He seemed astute, but there was something more about him that Aspin could not quite identify. Oskar had an air about him that drew Aspin's attention. He did not yet know what it was, but it would come to him in time.

"No one was certain of the direction in which you had gone, how far you might have traveled, or when, if at all, you planned to return. Given the circumstances, Colin thought it likely you had not gone far. He assumed that Shanis would return once she was certain Lerryn had gone. He wanted to be there when she came home. He planned to continue making inquiries and searching the forests close to your home."

"Why are we important enough for a seeker to take the time looking for us?"

'You are not, but Shanis is. And I consider her father a friend." No harm in that lie. He respected Colin Malan, even if he had no regard for him beyond that.

"I began by following Lerryn's path, on a hunch more than anything else, but neither of us dreamed you would have ventured such a great distance."

Khalyndryn hung her head, gazed into her cup, and said nothing. Colin had described her as a delicate girl, like a flower, but she had an underlying hardness Aspin had not expected. She was lean and serious looking. Obviously, the months of travel had toughened her. Had it hardened her as well?

"You have not answered my question. Can you tell me where Shanis is? It is important to her father, to me, and to her own safety that I find her."

"We don't know where she is." Oskar met his eye with a resolute stare that held no lie. "We have not seen her in days… weeks. We seem to have lost track of time. No sunrises or sunsets underground."

"Tell me this, then," Aspin said, keeping his annoyance in check. He had hoped these two would prove the key to finding the girl. Perhaps they still would. "Did you find the Silver Serpent?"

Had the situation not been so grave, he would have found their reactions amusing. Khalyndryn gasped and dropped her cup. She sprang to her feet and wiped her cloak with her hands, despite the fact that she was still soaked from her swim. Oskar gaped, his eyes bugged out like a bullfrog.

"H—how did you know?" Oskar stammered.

"That does not matter right now." Aspin's voice was harsher than he had intended, but he was wearying of their reticence. "Do the two of you have any idea of the importance of the Silver Serpent?"

"Larris said that the fate of Galdora hinged on the Silver Serpent" Oskar shrugged.

"The fate of the royal family," Khalyndryn corrected. "He didn't actually say that Galdora itself was in danger."

"That is true." Oskar glanced at her. "But we have to consider the army Shanis and Allyn saw headed toward Galdora. Larris thought they might be a threat."

"It was not an army."

"It wasn't exactly a handful either," Oskar protested. "And Shanis said that they mentioned meeting up with others." The two of them had forgotten Aspin in their bickering. "In any case, Larris was sure it was a major force."

"Peace! Both of you." Aspin's head was abuzz with this new information. "What are the two of you talking about?" If troops of any size were massing near the borders of Lothan and Galdora, the Gates would have to know about it. Or perhaps they were already aware. It was the price he paid for cutting off communication for so long. "What army?"

The youths stared at each other until Khalyndryn finally nodded at Oskar. "Go on. You tell it. Be sure to tell him about the ice cats and the Thandrylls too."

Aspin buried his head in his hands and groaned. "My young friends, I fear that I will need more tea before I am ready to hear your tale. Would you care for some fresh fish?"

By the time they had finished off the last of the fish and a second pot of tea, Oskar and Khalyndryn had told Aspin their story. It was fascinating, almost beyond belief, that they had come to be here. The things these simple village youth had seen, particularly beyond the Ramsgate, fascinated him. The village of Thandryll definitely merited study, but not by him and certainly not at this time.

"What do you think?" Oskar asked. "Khalyndryn and I do not really know what to do next. Of course, an hour ago we thought we were going to die under the mountains, so we haven't exactly had time to give it any real thought. I suppose we should look for Shanis and Hierm, but we don't know where we are, and even if we could find our way back to Murantha, we have almost no provisions. Besides, I doubt they would still be there. They might even have gone looking for us."

"What do I think?" Aspin echoed. "I think it is an ineluctable conclusion that the sword Shanis took from the statue is the Silver Serpent. That would explain the transformation Khalyndryn observed. It is obviously an artifact of tremendous sorcerous power, which would explain the blast that struck me down. It is the residue across the sky that puzzles me. I think we should follow it." He realized he had said "we" rather than "I." He had not yet invited them to join him. Of course, lacking supplies, they had little choice but to rely on his aid. If either of them noticed his choice of words, neither said so.

"Residue across the sky?" Oskar frowned.

"Sorcerous power leaves its mark behind. The greater the act, the more substantial the residual effect." With his index finger, he drew a line across the sky from west to east. "Something happened very recently. It makes no sense, but it seems to have begun in the mountains and continued... across the sky, ending somewhere east of where we sit. Whatever it was, it was so powerful that it rendered me unconscious for some time, though I do not know how long."

A look passed between Oskar and Khalyndryn that they did not bother to hide.

"Excuse me, but what exactly is sorcerous power? I've heard it talked about, but what is it? Magic?" Khalyndryn was obviously trying to redirect the subject, but Aspin let it pass. What had he said that had drawn such a reaction? Given enough time, he would find out.

"They are not precisely the same thing. They both come from the same source, through different pathways, if you will. Sorcerous power is the channeling of the life force that the gods imbued in the earth at the time of creation. The sorcerer acts as a vector for that power, drawing it in and directing it outward. A bit like a funnel. Magic is an appeal to one or more of the gods, asking that the gods perform a certain action."

"The person does not perform the magic?" She cocked her head as she waited for the answer.

"The person in question says the spell and, if done properly, the god performs the action."

"So, it is like a prayer?" Oskar scooted closer to Aspin, very interested in the conversation.

"It is more like a formula. If one says the correct words, in the proper manner, some reactions are automatic. It is almost as if magic is an unlocking of the rules that govern the universe. Strictly speaking, one is making an appeal to the gods, but it is unlikely that the god is even aware of that request, or making a conscious decision to fulfill that request."

A contemplative silence fell over them. The wind rustled in the treetops, and somewhere far away a hawk sounded its hunting cry. Despite his impatience, instinct told Aspin this was an important conversation. There was something about Oskar. The boy was important.

"What can you do with sorcery and magic?" The young man seemed very interested. "I have read that sorcerers accomplished great feats in the past, but that now they can do comparatively little."

"That is true. There are various theories as to why this is the case, but most believe that, just as strength and vitality leave our bodies as we age, the world's life force has diminished over time. No one can say for certain." Indeed, it was a quandary that vexed scholars. Saikurs today could not do one quarter of what their predecessors had been able to do centuries ago. They still knew the theories and the spells, but their effects were nowhere near as powerful as what was described in the records of previous saikurs.

"As far as what one might do with the power, that would depend on the amount of force available, and the person's ability to channel and direct that force. Just as some men are stronger, faster, brighter, or more talented than others, sorcerers have different capacities to take the power in. Our gifts with that power differ as well. Of the sorcerers with which I am acquainted, most use the power as a weapon, either for defense or attack. Some can touch the mind of another. Others can commune with animals. Rare sorcerers can shape metal or stone, and can imbue their creations with life force that keeps those creations whole, invulnerable to the elements. Magical abilities are much more varied. Some discover magical abilities on their own, while others study a particular branch of magic, seeking to master the particular spells of that discipline."

"Fascinating!" Oskar truly seemed to mean it. "How do you know...." He stopped in mid-sentence. "Nevermind. We are grateful for your help. If you do not think we will be too much of a burden, we will travel with you."

"You shall not be a burden at all. I would be glad for the company." He was surprised to realize that he meant it, though only a little bit. He preferred solitude, but he enjoyed talking with this bright, inquisitive young man. And the girl was not nearly as foolish as he had been led to believe. "With luck, we will find your friends soon."

Chapter 8

Lerryn reined his horse in at the edge of a murky, green lake. His eyes scanned the ominous, black clouds drawn across the sky like a thick blanket. They would need to find cover, and quickly. He raised his hand, signaling the others to halt.

"We will make camp here. Edrin and Hair, find a good place to make camp among the trees. If the storm that is coming is half as strong as I suspect, our tents will not be enough." The two dismounted and led their horses into the forest of red cypress that ringed the lake. The massive trees, their trunks two warhorses thick, with heavy, low-slung branches, would provide a measure of protection against the heaviest rain.

"Bull, take the horses back into the trees and tend to them." He dismounted and handed the reins to the muscular, barrel-chested youth. Bull made a cursory bow and accepted Kreege's reins. Lerryn grinned as he watched the lad walk away. His shoulders were so big and his neck so thick that when the young man attempted a bow, it looked like his head was bobbing in and out of his chest.

When the young men had gone, he helped Xaver dismount. His vizier had nearly recovered from whatever had struck him down days before, but he was still weak. The pace they set was tiring him out as well. They rose early, pushed their mounts as hard as they dared, and typically waited until near dark before making camp. Xaver was convinced that the Silver Serpent had been found, and that its recovery was the source of the sorcerous wave that had rendered him unconscious.

They walked together along the edge of the lake, scanning the area for potential threats. Marauding bands of Malgogs were common to this area. He did not truly expect to come across anyone, though. It seemed that every Malgog in Lothan was on the move. They had been forced to hide from five separate clans, all traveling to some unknown destination deep in the heart of Lothan.

Xaver's eyes were on the western skyline, which was now a roiling black cauldron on this stormy evening.

"Do you still feel it?" Lerryn asked. "The resonance, or whatever it is you call it?" Xaver insisted he could feel what he called the echo of a massive use of sorcery somewhere beyond Karkwall to the west. If he was correct, it meant that Lerryn and his party had gone in completely the wrong direction on their search for the Silver Serpent.

"Yes, but it is fading. Every day it grows weaker, but it is still there. I am certain we are headed in the right direction… this time." His voice was weak and despondent. The quest was his long before Lerryn became involved. A bleakness had set in, as though Xaver was now without purpose.

"Do you have any further thoughts as to why the clans are moving?" Lerryn grabbed Xaver's arm and pulled him back just before his booted foot trod upon a marsh frog. The speckled brown creature hissed and sprang into the water with a loud plop. "Have a care. Their meat is delicious, but they spit poison. Deadly if it gets into your eyes."

"In that case, I suppose I should keep my eyes on the path, rather than the sky." Xaver grimaced. "I am not ready just yet to pass on to the next world." He grinned, his white teeth seeming to glow in the dusky light. "As far as the clans are concerned, I do not know. Some of their witches might practice sorcery at some level, in which case they would have felt what I did. It is possible that they have interpreted this event in such a way as to cause this mass migration."

"Could the Monaghan be launching a massed invasion of Malgog lands?" Lerryn asked. In his mind, war was much easier to understand than sorcery. "I know it would be unlikely. The Monaghan fight one another as often as they fight the Malgog. But what if they had a unified purpose? A campaign of genocide, perhaps?"

"Were that the case," Xaver's tone was skeptical, "I would imagine that the women and children might move east, but the clansmen would be moving to meet the threat. I have never known of a Lothan clansmen of either tribe to run from a fight, but the women take up arms only in the most desperate of times."

"True," Lerryn said. They had circled about a quarter of the way around the lake.

He was satisfied that the thick tangles of vegetation hid no human threat, at least not in the immediate vicinity. The two retraced their steps back to where they left the other members of their party.

"Suppose you are correct, and the Silver Serpent has been found by the Monaghan?" The words were bitter on his lips. He despised the thought of his prize in the hands of the barbaric hillmen. It belonged to him...to Galdora! "Could that be a reason for what we have witnessed?"

"Their prophecies connect the Silver Serpent with the reunification of their lands, so it is possible. If that is the case, we have to consider what threat a united Lothan with the power of the Serpent behind it might pose to Galdora, or to the rest of Gameryah for that matter. We do not know the exact nature of its power, but we can be sure it is prodigious."

Lerryn pondered the thought. He was so frustrated by his own personal failure that he had not considered the likelihood of another nation bearing the weapon. Galdora existed under the constant threat of a superior Kyrinian force. What if an army from the south, aided by a weapon of legendary power, were to ally with Galdora's enemy? His nation would truly sit between the hammer and the anvil then. His eyes caught movement up ahead, and he saw Hair hurrying toward them. He would have to learn the boy's name one of these days. He and Xaver stepped up their pace as the long-haired youth hurried toward them.

"Highness, we found a small village nearby. Few people remain. Only some elders and a mute. They invited us to stay with them if we like." His tight grimace and narrowed eyes said that he was not comfortable with the thought for some reason. Odd, the lad was usually quite gregarious.

"There is something you are not telling us. What is the matter?" Out of the corner of his eye he caught a flicker of distant lightning. The cool breeze was fast becoming a strong wind, and he smelled the rain, heavy in the air. He would much prefer to pass this night indoors.

"I don't know." Hair looked down at the ground, scuffing at the mud with the toe of his boot. "It was an uncomfortable place— all dark and muddy. The mute was a strange one, and one of the other men was... I don't know how to say it." He bit his lip and looked away.

"Come now. Out with it, before we are caught in the storm. Did someone threaten you? Did you spot anything that might pose a danger to us?"

"I don't like little people." Hair would not meet Lerryn's eye. "A showman once passed through our town when I was small, and he had with him a man only about three feet tall. He did flips and handstands, but he was ugly and told very crude jokes. He gave me the creeps." He stopped and clamped his mouth shut. If it were not so close to dark, Lerryn was certain he'd see the young man's face the brightest shade of red it had ever been.

"I understand completely," he said, clapping a hand on Hair's shoulder. "If this little man gives you any trouble, I shall cut off your legs at the knee so that the two of you can see eye-to-eye. Will that be of comfort to you?"

Hair grinned and shook his head.

"Would it not be easier, highness, to simply find a stump or large stone upon which the man might stand?" Xaver mused. "I would hate to see you nick the blade of your sword." Lerryn and Hair stopped to stare at the vizier.

"Why, Xaver my friend, I do believe you just made an attempt at humor."

Lerryn gaped in mock-incredulity. "Truly this is a momentous occasion."

"I forgot myself for a moment, Highness. I am surprised that I could make a jest at all, so saddened am I at the absence of our friend Master Karst." The irony that dripped from his voice deprived his words of their humorous effect. Karst had ridden away the moment they discovered their quest had failed. No one had seen him since, and no one missed him.

They collected their horses and made their way to the Malgog village, which was no more than a league from where they had stopped. It was located on high ground among a soupy patch of stingreeds and swamp moss, and surrounded by a stockade of sharpened cane pole. They waited outside the gates for someone to invite them in.

It was the mute who finally came to greet them. He was, as Hair had described him, strange. He was as tall as Lerryn, but he leaned to his left as he walked, giving him the appearance of being shorter than he was. His right arm and leg were muscular, but his left side was shriveled and weak. His left leg was skinny, twisted inward, and shorter by a hand than the right. His tiny left arm he held clutched to his side, his pitiful three-fingered hand grasping something Lerryn could not quite see.

Even the left side of his face had not been spared of the defect from which he suffered. The left corner of his mouth drooped, and his left eye wandered. Bits of moss and twigs clung to his close-cropped black curls. He was clean shaven, unlike most Malgog men. When Lerryn went through the ritual introduction and stating of business, the man merely grunted and motioned with his good hand for them to follow, before hobbling back through the gate.

The village itself was much as Hair had described it: small, muddy, and unattractive. Malgog architecture was limited only by imagination and the available supply of sticks and mud. Their dwellings looked like inverted bird nests on poles, caked with mud and packed with vegetation, giving the impression of hillocks floating above the soggy earth. Their common buildings adhered to no set pattern, and usually conformed to the shape of whatever dry land they were built upon. The central gathering place in this village was a multi-leveled treehouse set in the branches of a huge red cypress that rose majestically above the surrounding settlement.

Leaving their horses with two elders who were as silent as the mute, they climbed up a rope ladder and onto a solid deck of black oak, the dark, jagged grain giving it a sinister look. They were sheltered by a canopy of woven reeds. Smoky torches cast an unsteady light upon those gathered. Lerryn crinkled his nose at the foul smell that emanated from the torches. It was necessary in a land where it was said the insects could suck a man dry in a night, and leave him a bag of bones in the morning. He grinned at the memory of the old grandmother's tale.

"Thank you, Haffun. That will be all." An old man in the typical baggy Malgog clothing dismissed the mute and turned to greet them. "Welcome to our village," he said, bowing low. "Your young companion has already identified you to us. We are humbled to welcome such esteemed guests. His eyes included Xaver in the compliment. "My name is Jakway. I speak for what remains of the Gray Lake Clan. May I invite you inside for food and shelter from the storm?"

"We would be most grateful for your kind and generous hospitality." Lerryn led the group into a room that was actually a small cave carved out of the giant trunk of the red cypress where it grew up through the deck. Two others waited at a round table that took up most of the space. Tapers set in carved niches cast a peaceful glow around the room. They waited as Jakway made introductions.

"This is Maralla." He indicated a lean old woman with black-streaked silver hair and a kind smile that dampened the effect of her homely face. She nodded politely. "And this is Heztus." Heztus was the dwarf of whom Hair had spoken.

"I'd stand up and bow to you, but I'm no taller standing than I am sitting." The fellow was much younger than the others, no more than thirty summers. His black hair was done in about two-dozen narrow braids. Snake bones at the end of each braid clacked together when he turned his head. His beard and moustache were neatly trimmed, contrary to Malgog fashion. "Please, sit down and be at ease. Our table is your table. And don't tell me my hospitality is greater than my stature, because that's not much of a compliment, is it now?

"Actually I was racking my brain to think of another ritual reply, but I fear my knowledge of your customs is limited." Lerryn held out his hand, and Bull passed him a full wineskin he had brought from among their supplies on Lerryn's orders. "I hope this will be a satisfactory guest gift. We have recently come from Diyonus, and I still have half a skin of Monavan Orange that I would be delighted to share."

The dwarf looked pleasantly surprised, and he stood up in his chair to get a better look. He grinned at the sight of the wineskin and nodded.

"A princely gift indeed," he said. "I fear we have no clan chief or other person of worth with us to formally accept your gift, but I hope you will allow one so lowly as myself to serve in his stead."

"Of course." Lerryn handed the wine to the dwarf with only a mild pang of regret. Monavan Orange was the finest in the world. He motioned for the others to take their seats.

No sooner had they sat down when Heztus clapped twice, and a cluster of old men and women tottered in with plates of food. The dishes were mostly foreign to him, but the aromas were enticing, and his mouth watered in anticipation. Bull's stomach rumbled, the sound filling the confined space. Everyone shared a good laugh at the abashed-looking young man's expense. Lerryn reflected again on Bull's good nature, so contrary to his brawn and rough exterior.

Unlike formal meals, the bowls were passed around the table and everyone served himself. First came a dish of fish and swamp peppers that numbed his tongue, followed by a soup of sweet vegetables in a thin, red broth. The next bowl was filled with crispy fried frog legs. Lerryn had eaten frog legs before, and found them tasty, so he helped himself to several. The others were obviously uncertain what they were about to eat, but took some out of politeness. Mashed tubers with butter, tiny black beans, and a salad of swamp lettuce and carrots rounded out the meal. The Diyonusan wine was an odd companion to the Malgog fare, but it was a most satisfying repast.

When the food and polite conversation had dwindled, Lerryn asked the question that had been gnawing at him.

"Forgive me, but where is the rest of your village? There can't be more than twenty of you, and this village could comfortably be home to two-hundred. The buildings appear to be in good repair, so they cannot have been uninhabited for very long."

"Two days." Heztus' voice was slurred by wine. "They left two days ago. Those of us they believed would be unable to make the journey, they left behind. So here we are: the elders, the cripple and the dwarf."

"Of course, Heztus is a capable guide and traveler. In his case, the others find his company…' Maralla smiled as she searched for the word.

"Tedious?" Heztus offered.

"Infuriating is closer to the truth." Maralla continued to smile at him. "You can't resist demonstrating your superior intelligence every chance you get."

"I don't do it on purpose." Heztus put his hand on his chest and adopted a wounded expression. "My superior intellect simply flows out of me at all times. They should accept it rather than flee from it."

"Where did they go?" Lerryn asked. "We passed several clans headed toward central Lothan, but we cannot fathom what might be there for them."

"Something happened six days ago. Something momentous." Maralla spoke slowly, her eyes flitting to the other Malgog at the table. "Not everyone could feel it, or understand it, but for those of us who are attuned to such things, it caused a powerful disturbance.'

"We are aware." Xaver's eyes met Maralla's and something seemed to pass between them. Finally they nodded, both apparently satisfied.

"Two days later, word reached us that the Silver Serpent has come again into the world. The bearer is uniting the clans of Malgog and will once again unify Lothan. The clans are called to Calmut."

"What is Calmut?" Lerryn hated feeling ignorant, but his desire to understand what was happening outweighed his ego.

"It is where the new leader will be chosen. 'Tis very strange, but the bone women tell us that the serpent is raised in the east. A great warrior there is uniting the Malgog, and he vows that the Monaghan shall be brought to their knees."

"But the disturbance…"

"Was in the west," the woman added. "The serpent has been raised there by the Monaghan." She grimaced like she had just swallowed something bitter. "Two people claim to bear the serpent. The choice must be made at Calmut."

Chapter 9

The highlands were never going to end. The hills rose all around them like an endless sea of green. Oskar sighed as he stared out in to the sameness through which he had spent the better part of the last two days hiking. From atop Aspin's stallion, Khalyndryn gave him a sympathetic nod and reached down to pat him hard on the head.

"There's a good boy. You can do it."

"I am not your dog," he muttered. Then he looked up at her and saw her grinning. He laughed and gave her hand a squeeze. Such a casual act was a measure of how their friendship had grown in such a short time. She was no longer the self-important girl who had left the village. Needless to say, he liked her much better this way.

Winding around what seemed like the thousandth hill, they disturbed a fox, which darted away in a blur of orange. The horse shied, but Aspin calmed him with a word. Oskar wondered if it was magic, or simply good training.

The saikur was an enigma. He rarely spoke unless spoken to. He also had a way of sometimes answering questions without actually giving any specific information, or so it seemed to Oskar. The man was unfailingly polite and serene to the point of annoyance. He seemed to harbor no ill intent toward Shanis, but Oskar felt that

Aspin had not sufficiently explained his reasons for wanting to find her.

A faint rustling sound caught his ear. As they drew closer he recognized it as the sound of falling water. It was a pleasant, peaceful sound, though it reminded him of that dark underground stream in and along which they had spent too much of their time.

At the juncture where twin hills met, a tiny waterfall snaked between the rises, tumbling down into a peaceful pond. Its smooth jade surface beckoned to Oskar, as it apparently did to Khalyndryn. With a squeal of delight she slid down from her mount, handed him the reins, and hurried over to kneel in the soft grass at the water's edge.

Something about the pond struck Oskar as unnatural. The surface seemed especially smooth despite the water splashing down from above. The surrounding vegetation was unlike any he had ever seen, and it gave the place an alien quality that unsettled him.

Khalyndryn waved to him, holding a finger to her lips. When she had his attention, she pointed to a thick stand of aquatic plants on the far end of the pool where a scaly green snout poked out.

Careful not to make a sound, he guided the horse over to where she sat. They watched as the animal swam toward them. It reached the shallows and stood a few paces away, water dripping from its emerald body.

"It's a little horse," she whispered. And it was, after a fashion. The size of a small dog, it resembled a horse, but with green scales and a spiny fin along its neck where the mane should be. As it moved closer, it lifted a leg out of the water, revealing a webbed foot tipped with three black claws. Khalyndryn reached out a hand to it and made kissing sounds. The creature's eyes narrowed and it hissed. She jerked her hand back and the beast leapt at her. Khalyndryn screamed as it went for her throat with its razor teeth and needle-like claws.

Some invisible force struck the creature and sent it hurtling across the pond where it slammed into the bank and fell limp at the water's edge.

Oskar shuddered. He felt like someone had first dunked him in an icy river and then set him afire. He put his arm around Khalyndryn. She was trembling, and her face was white as a sheet. He leaned against her, letting her bear some of his weight. He was suddenly weak in the knees and did not understand why. The creature had surprised him, certainly, but that was all. It was nothing to make him feel ill.

"What was that thing?" Khalyndryn did not sound nearly as frightened as Oskar would have expected. "It was so cute, but it was mean." She said the last with wonder and a note of judgment. Oskar was surprised at her calm. This was not her usual reaction to danger. "I was foolish to get close to it without knowing if it was dangerous."

"That you were." Aspin squatted down next to them. "The buggan is small, but it can do you serious harm. Those claws and fangs can be deadly if they get your throat, or some other vulnerable spot. Fortunately for you, I was here." It was not arrogance on his part—simply a statement of fact.

"You did that?" Khalyndryn pointed at the stunned creature. "Did you have to hurt it? You knocked it all the way over there." The buggan was coming to. It raised its head and looked around, still hissing. "I've heard stories of buggans, but I never believed they were real." She frowned as if a thought had occurred to her, and grew quiet.

"I assure you, I had no intention of doing anything more than deflect it away from you." Aspin crinkled his brow. "I do not understand what happened. I cannot remember the last time I underestimated my power like that. I have not done that since I was a disciple." He leaned down to look Oskar in the eye. "Are you all right?"

"I am all right." The quaver in Oskar's voice betrayed him. He felt like he was going to sick up. "I was just frightened for Khalyndryn is all. That thing gave me a scare when it leapt at her."

"Of course." Aspin's eyes bored into him like a hawk circling its prey. After staring at Oskar for a few moments longer, he rose to his feet. "Follow me," he ordered, pacing over to a level space a few paces away. Oskar, still woozy, followed behind.

"Sit down here in front of me." Aspin sat cross-legged on the ground. He watched impassively as Oskar did as he was instructed. "Look me in the eye and hold my gaze; do not look away."

Oskar again did as he was told. As he looked at Aspin, the saikur's pupils seemed to expand into pools of inky blackness, filling Oskar's vision until they were all he could see. He was in a whirlpool, being drawn into the darkness.

"Take a deep breath, and exhale slowly." Aspin's voice softened. "Now take another deep breath; hold it." A lengthy pause. "Now release it slowly and let your shoulders fall as you breathe out." Oskar felt himself drifting away, his eyes still locked on Aspin's. "Now, tell me about the moment Shanis Malan took up the serpent."

"I don't remember." Oskar's voice seemed to come from far away. He wondered why Aspin was asking him this right now, but he was too detached to care. "She grabbed it, and I don't remember anything else."

"How did you feel in the moment she touched it?" Apsin's voice was so calm, so inviting, that Oskar found himself dying to give him an answer. His mind swam back to the cavern. He saw the flowing blue light of the seastone coffins. He saw the statue. He watched Shanis, desperately trying to fend off the attack of the giant snake, reach for the stone sword. Her fingers closed on the hilt.

"I felt cold all over, and then hot at the same time. It was like a shock. And then everything went black." Something told him that the memory was significant, but he could not concern himself with that right now.

"Tell me about the moment after the lightning struck the golorak. How did you feel?"

"I felt hot and cold and I don't know what else." Oskar clammed up. He was still trapped in the saikur's gaze, but now he was trying to resist. Something inside him did not want to remember this. He tried to shake free from Aspin's gaze, but he was held fast.

"It was not lightning that killed the golorak, was it Oskar?" There was no accusation in Aspin's voice. He was inviting Oskar to unburden himself. Perhaps he could tell Aspin. Maybe it would be all right.

"Who slew the golorak?" The question hung in the silence. Oskar fought the urge to fill the silence, but the longing to tell the truth was too strong.

"I did." He heard Khalyndryn gasp at his revelation. "I don't know what I did, but I know I killed it."

The words startled him out of the semi-trance in which Aspin had put him. His mind seemed to float upward toward full consciousness.

"I held out my staff and a bar of light shot out of it. It sliced right through the golorak. I don't know how it happened. I really don't."

Aspin smiled and nodded. "Tell me how you felt the moment before it happened. Try and remember precisely what you thought, what you felt, anything you can recall."

"I watched Larris trying to fight it." As if the revelation had unlocked a door in his mind, everything came back to him clearly. "His sword just bounced off its hide. All I had was my staff, and I knew I couldn't do anything to help. He told me to finish the quest without him. He was ready to die and I couldn't help him. My friend was about to be killed before my eyes and there was nothing I could do about it."

He hung his head. The memory was powerful and painful. His voice was thick as he spoke. "Something inside of me just gave up."

Aspin looked... pleased, as if this was the answer he had been hoping for.

"In order to channel life force, one must step aside, so to speak, and allow it to flow through. You cannot force it to happen; you must allow it to happen. For most of us, the first time we do it requires total and complete surrender, which is what happened to you. The ability has always been there within you, but you were not in a situation desperate enough for complete and utter surrender of control."

Aspin sounded triumphant, and his smile was broad and happy. It looked out of place on his face, which, with its raptor-like eyes and hooked nose, made him look more like an angry eagle than a man.

"And that is why you could not do it again in the chamber. You did not know that you had to surrender to the power. You were trying to make it happen, weren't you? You wanted to slay the serpent the way you slew the golorak."

Dumbstruck, Oskar could only nod his head. He knew what Aspin was saying, but it could not be true. Him? It was unthinkable.

"I don't understand," Khalyndryn whispered. "Aspin, what are you trying to tell us?"

"I am saying that your friend Oskar is a sorcerer."

Chapter 10

Jayla was tired and hungry, and she didn't want to hide in the bushes anymore. Her escape from the shape-changing cat man had left her terrified. She had spent the last two days going east as fast as she could. She had found the wagon track that villagers sometimes used, but every time she heard a strange noise she would scurry into the bushes and wait until she was certain it was safe. Her hands and knees, already banged up from her flight down the rocks, were now covered with fresh scrapes. She hurt all over, and she wanted to sleep, but nerves and hunger kept her from sleeping more than an hour or two at a time.

Food was a problem. There were all kinds of berries along the way, but Papa had taught her that many could kill you or make you sick. She did not know which ones were which, so she had only eaten the fat, black grapes with the tough, bitter skin and mushy sweet insides. She had eaten them husks and all, sometimes swallowing the seeds by accident. She ate whenever she found them, which was not often enough. She had come across a walnut tree, but the branches were bare and nearly all the walnuts on the ground were rotten. She ate the ones that were not too bad, but her stomach cried for more.

Now she was hunkered down beneath an itchy, sticky evergreen bush, watching the rider come down the track toward her. His was a tall, graceful mount with long, lean legs and sleek coat, so unlike the short, broad-chested work horses with which she was familiar. As horse and rider drew closer, she got her first good look at the man, and what she saw made her draw in her breath in surprise.

He was the biggest man she had ever seen. Papa was tall and strong from hard work. This man was as tall as Papa, and he was big all over. His arms were like other men's legs. She wondered how long it took his wife to sew his clothes. Mama always complained about having to sew such long tunics for Papa. How would she feel about sewing for this man? His chest was as wide as Jayla was tall. His bushy black beard and dark curly hair made him look like a wild man. Suddenly, he snapped his head around to look directly at her hiding place. His black eyes narrowed, then relaxed. He could not possibly have seen her, not from so far away. Could he? She held as still as she could as he trotted toward her.

He reined his horse in and dismounted just a few steps away. He tied the horse off to a nearby tree and let it crop at a clump of grass on the edge of the path while he dug through his saddlebag. He pulled out a bundle and sat down right next to her hiding place, where he unwrapped a loaf of bread. It looked delicious, and she hoped her empty belly would not growl and give her away. He tore off a small piece and ate it slowly, staring up into the branches of a nearby tree.

"You can come out, little one. It is all right." His voice was surprisingly gentle, nothing like his outward appearance. "I won't hurt you. I imagine you are hungry. I have bread, cheese and dried meat."

Could she trust this man? He did not seem to be like the bad men at her village, but how could she know for sure? He was coming from the east, which was the way she was headed. Maybe he was from one of the villages there. Maybe he could help her find Mama and Papa and Harvin.

But she was so afraid. What if he really was a bad man? She thought for a moment more. She probably could not run away from him right now if she wanted to. He was big and strong and there weren't any good places to hide around here; just trees and bushes. There was no point in hiding. If he wanted to catch her, he would. Slowly, her heart pounding, she crawled out.

He smiled and held out the bread. Jayla snatched it from his hand without so much as a thank-you and took a huge bite. Mama would have scolded her for her bad manners, but she was so hungry and the man didn't seem to mind. He nodded and unfolded another cloth that held the cheese and meat he had promised. He placed it on the ground between them, taking a small piece of jerked meat for himself. After she had eaten most of the bread and cheese, he offered her a waterskin. This time she remembered to thank him when she accepted it from his hand.

"What's your name?" She was uncomfortable with the lengthy silence and her own lack of courtesy.

"Colin," he said simply.

"I'm Jayla. What are you doing out here in the forest?" Mama had told her before that it was not polite to ask questions, but Jayla was inquisitive by nature, and grownups usually laughed at her interrogations. She didn't know why they found her questions funny, but they did.

"Actually, I am looking for my little girl." He frowned and glanced down at the ground for a moment.

"Is she lost?" Jayla, too, was lost, and she felt sorry for any little girl who found herself in the same situation. It was scary.

"I don't think so." That was a funny answer. "She left with some friends of hers. I keep hoping she will come back home, but I don't know if she will."

"Her mother must be very worried about her. Is she little, like me?"

"Her mother died a long time ago." He looked very sad now. "And no, my daughter is not so young as you. She is more than fifteen summers. I suppose she is a young lady now, but to me she will always be my little girl." He turned his gaze toward Jayla. "You are not from my village, and you are a long way from anywhere else. May I ask what you are doing hiding in the forest?"

She hung her head. It made her unhappy to think about what had happened, but this man was sad, too. Maybe, if he knew her story, he wouldn't feel so bad about losing his little girl. Besides, he might know how to find her family. Before long she had poured out her story. Anger flashed in his eyes when she told him about the bad men, but when she described the man who turned into a cat monster, his eyes grew big and he sprang to his feet, his hand on his sword.

"You are not safe in these woods." He reached down and picking her up like she weighed nothing. "But you will be safe in my village. Will you tell your story to the people there?" She nodded. "That's a brave girl. Have you ridden before?" She nodded again, and he hastily untied his horse and mounted, plopping her down in front of him. As the horse cantered back up the trail, a thought struck her.

"Colin, can I stay at your house? I mean, since your little girl isn't home right now, maybe there is room for me. Only until we find my family." She couldn't see his face, but his voice sounded funny, like he had something in his throat.

"I suppose you can, little one. At least until we find your family."

Chapter 11

"Close your eyes. Take a deep breath and exhale slowly." Aspin's voice flowed through him like a lazy river. "Be aware of the life force that is alive in your body. Feel it in your fingertips and the tips of your toes." Oskar's fingers and toes began to tingle. Was he feeling the energy, or was it merely the suggestion in Aspin's words?

"Imagine the energy flowing up through your arms and legs, along your spine, and finally pouring into your mind. Feel it flow throughout your body."

He tingled all over, like he was being pricked by a thousand hot needles and pelted with drops of icy rain. The feeling took his breath away.

"Feel it now gathering in the middle of your body, just below the center of your chest. Do you feel it?"

"Yes," Oskar whispered. He could somehow see it—a silver orb the size of his two fists spinning inside of him, its glowing surface surging, ebbing, and pulsing like a living creature.

"Now slowly open your eyes. Good. Now hold out your hand, palm up."

Oskar followed Aspin's directions without question. This was the step at which he always failed. He could sense the power, but could not make it flow. He kept his eyes on the center of his palm, partly because he knew that was the next step, but mostly because if he looked up, he was certain he would see his own lack of confidence mirrored in the seeker's eyes. If Aspin did not believe in him, he could never believe in himself.

"Concentrate on a spot in the center of your palm." Aspin's voice continued to wash over him. "Now be aware of a channel flowing between your center of energy and the spot in your palm."

Oskar focused his thoughts and concentrated. He tried to create a pipeline of sorts running from his center outward to his hand. He could actually see it grow, creeping slowly outward.

And then it stopped.

He wrinkled his brow and tried to force it to keep growing, but he could not do it.

"The connection is already there, Oskar." Aspin's voice was serene, but firm. "You need not recreate it. Simply be aware of its presence."

This was impossible. That time he channeled and killed the golorak had been a fluke. He let his shoulders sag and, with a discouraged sigh, gave up.

And suddenly it was there!

The power surged through him. His arm felt like it was on fire. The sensation made him gasp.

"Good." Aspin's eyes twinkled, but he otherwise remained calm. "Now I want you to raise your hand in the air. You are in control of the power. The channel is now closed, but you may open it again any time you wish. Focus again on the center of your palm and, in one controlled burst, release the power out into the air."

Suddenly fearful, Oskar raised his hand and envisioned the center of his palm opening. A white bar of light shot straight up into the sky. He was so amazed that, for a moment, he forgot to make it stop. Regaining control of his thoughts, he commanded the power to cease. The bar of light vanished, leaving its golden imprint burned into his vision. He sat in silence, his heart racing. He had done it!

"Excellent!" Aspin gave Oskar's shoulder a squeeze. "A bit more intense than I had planned, but very well done. I sense great power in you. You will require training, of course, but I believe you are capable of great things."

"You were wonderful!" Khalyndryn wrapped her arms around him from behind and hugged him tight. "I am so proud of you. I cannot wait to find the others and tell them what you have done. They are going to be amazed."

Oskar did not know what to say. In a matter of seconds, he had just received the highest praise of his life. He was not sure which was more gratifying: Aspin's prediction, or Khalyndryn's declaration that she was proud of him. So much of this journey had been like a dream. Bigger, in fact, than his most far-fetched daydreams. And now, to discover within himself a legendary power. It was just too much to believe. He figured he might as well enjoy it before he awoke.

"So, what comes next?"

"Next we will teach you to gather the power in from outside of yourself and to safely release it again. But no more tonight. You have already exceeded my expectations."

Oskar grinned. He was so excited that he scarcely noticed Khalyndryn's arms still around him. It was not too long ago that the very thought of her embrace would have sent shivers down his spine and given him an upset stomach.

Now that he came to think about it, he was, in fact, shivering. He was freezing. He wrapped his arms around himself and drew his legs to his chest, his body shaking.

"Are you ill?" Khalyndryn held him tighter, but he could not feel her warmth.

"That happens quite often when you first touch the power," Aspin said. "It is normal, and it will diminish as you grow accustomed to sorcery. For now, you might wish to put on a heavier cloak, if you have one, and sit close to the fire. It would not hurt for Khalyndryn to remain close to you as well." Aspin winked and Oskar felt his face grow hot. He wondered if she noticed, but it appeared she had not, for she was already rummaging through his pack where he kept the brown cloak the Thandrylls had given him. She draped it around his shoulders over the top of his lighter cloak, sat down next to him, and leaned against him.

Aspin did a double-take when he saw Oskar's brown cloak, but he did not say anything. Oskar looked down at it and realized that it was nearly the twin of Aspin's saikur cloak, save for the fact that Oskar's cloak was made for someone half a head shorter and half again as broad of shoulder as Aspin. Before he could say anything about it, he heard the sound of riders approaching, and climbed heavily to his feet.

Aspin raised his hand, signaling them to be quiet. He moved quickly to where his sword leaned against a tree and belted it on. Oskar picked up his staff and moved to stand next to Aspin. He looked back at Khalyndryn, and inclined his head toward the tent, indicating that she should go inside. She shook her head. The fool girl! Not knowing who these passers-by were, it would simplify things greatly if they did not have a beautiful girl drawing the attention of any unsavory men who might be in the group.

He thrust his finger toward the tent, and mouthed the words "Now! I mean it!" To his surprise, she retreated to the tent without further argument.

Men appeared all around them at the edges of the clearing in which they were camped. Swords gleamed in the twilight, and he saw at least two bows drawn. Aspin whispered something too soft to hear, and Oskar's skin tingled.

"You need not hide from us." Aspin's voice rang with authority. "We will do you no harm provided you have come in peace."

Angry murmurs sounded from all around, but one warrior sheathed his sword and stepped out of the woods, chuckling as he came. His scarlet beard was twined in a mass of tiny braids, as was his hair. His clan garb was similar to that of Horgris' clan, save the sash he wore across his chest, which was stitched with a chain of blue stags, and his headdress, which was adorned with a pair of antlers.

"You do be a brazen one, me friend," he said, walking toward them. "The light be bad. Had I been knowin' we had a seeker and disciple here, I would no have been so concerned about the lights in the sky."

Aspin glanced at Oskar before turning back to the newcomers. "I apologize for the disturbance. I was giving my young pupil a lesson."

"It be of no moment." The man stopped suddenly, a confused look on his face.

"My apologies." Aspin whispered and flicked his fingers. "I had to protect us until I was certain of your intentions."

Oskar felt that they still did not know the man's intentions, but he would have to rely on Aspin's judgment. Had it been up to him, whatever barrier Aspin had conjured would have remained up for a while longer.

"Come and sit by our fire. I have no skok to offer you, but I have wine."

"Wine do be most welcome." The man hunkered down next to their small fire. "My name be Culmatan of the Blue Stag Clan."

"I am Aspin. I am a saikur, as you have already noted." The two nodded to one another. Apparently no further formalities were required, and Oskar did not merit an introduction. "Oskar, will you please retrieve the wineskin from my tent?"

Obviously Aspin did not want Khalyndryn coming out, or he would have called for her to bring it out. When Oskar slipped inside the tent, she was sitting near the doorway holding a knife, but she appeared calm. She gave him an inquiring look, and he shrugged as he retrieved the wineskin. "I think it's going to be all right," he whispered, "but stay here for now." She nodded and relaxed the grip on her knife.

Back at the fire, the two men were engaged in quiet conversation. Culmatan's clansmen had stepped out of the trees and stood around the clearing. They had put away their weapons, but none of them looked comfortable.

"So your bone woman has been in contact with the Malgog?" Aspin was asking, surprise in his voice. "That seems unusual."

"No so unusual as all that." Culmatan tilted his hand from side-to-side. "The bone women, they no hold to the clan wars in the same way we do. They be loyal in their own way, but they say they be holdin' to a united Lothan, even though that do be a memory, at least for now." There was a distant look in his gray-green eyes as he accepted the wineskin from Aspin. He took a long drink and handed it back, nodding in approval. "That be no so bad for wine."

"So what do the bone women tell you?" Aspin took a drink and handed the skin back to Culmatan.

"They say someone be claiming to raise the Silver Serpent. There be rumors he use the power to heal many in one of the clans. I don' know which one. Maybe Bannif or Circle of Oaks, I no be sure."

Oskar took note of the man's use of the word he. Did Shanis no longer have the sword? Most likely she had given it to Larris. He was the one who was searching for it after all. What if she still had it, and the man was simply assuming that the bearer was a man? Some things never changed for Shanis. He smiled at the thought.

"The Malgog, though, they be tellin' us that someone be raisin' the serpent in the east. Whoever it is, he be stirring things up there. Been raidin' the borderlands near Diyonus and Galdora. Some of the young 'uns be flocking to his banner, but most of the clans no be sure what to think, so they do stay away. And then, when they hear of one in the west, they make their decision."

"What decision is that?" Aspin's look was intense and his voice sharp. Clearly the news of two people claiming to possess the Silver Serpent had taken him by surprise.

Culmatan's mouth twisted into a sour grimace. He spat on the ground between his feet. "Bah! They say a choice must be made. They call us to gather at Calmut." He shook his head. "Couldna' have come at a worse time. The Three Oaks have Badla, and they be close by. We be headed to raid them when the word come to us."

"Must you go to this Calmut place? Is it required?" Aspin asked. Oskar was surprised. He had always assumed that seekers knew almost everything. Apparently, there were gaps even in Aspin's knowledge.

"Aye. That we must. Honor requires it. 'Tis a place we all hold sacred. When the bone women do call us to Calmut, we must go or be cursed." He took another swig of wine and belched.

Oskar could not hold his tongue. "So the Monaghan and the Malgog will be at this place together? Is that a good idea?" Aspin looked annoyed at the interruption, but Oskar did not care. Culmatan might think he was Aspin's disciple, whatever that meant, but he was not under the man's command. Of course, he would need to be careful not to offend Aspin if he was going to continue his lessons.

"The peace of Calmut rules there. We can no lift so much as a finger while we be there. No against one another, nor against the ice-encrusted Malgog." He let out a stream of vile oaths that made Oskar's ears turn red. Aspin cleared his throat, and the clansman regained his composure. "Forgive me, Seeker. I forget myself."

"It is of no moment." Aspin waved his hand as if to brush the apology aside. "Pray tell, what happens when you reach Calmut? I assume you will confer with the other clan leaders and the bone women and choose which person to follow."

"It be something like that," Culmatan averred. "We must confer, aye, but there be more to the decision. Otherwise the Malgog most likely follow the man from the east and we follow the one from the west."

"So your clan will follow the bearer of the serpent?" Oskar's heart was pounding. He remembered from his talks with Larris that part of the serpent prophecies, at least the Lothan prophecies, was that the recovery of the Silver Serpent would signal the reunification of the clans, while a different, more obscure, prophecy spoke of the bearer actually leading the reunified nation. If that person was either Shanis or Larris, he was very interested in how things would unfold.

"If I be satisfied that this man do bear the true Silver Serpent, then I will follow. I be a member of the Order of the Fox, but I no suppose you know what that do mean." Oskar nodded that he understood. Culmatan raised his eyebrows in surprise and continued.

"I be certain that all of my clansmen who be members of the order will follow. Most of my clan be followin' as well by my say-so. The rest, who knows?" He shrugged and raised his hands. "If enough men no follow, we just trade one kind of war for another. I be hoping, though, that what we do at Calmut be enough."

"You said there was more to the decision." Aspin had forgotten the wine, and now he gazed intently at Culmatan. "What more is there?"

"Calmut do be a... special place. I can no tell you very much, but I can tell you this. When the two who claim to be bearers of the Silver Serpent do come to Calmut, they will be submitting themselves to the Keeper of the Mists. One will be chosen, one will no come back again."

"What happens to the one who does not come back?" Oskar could hear the tremor of fear in his voice.

"I can no say. I only know that, of those who entered and did no come back, not one has been seen again."

Chapter 12

"The Three Oaks be just up ahead." Granlor reined in his horse and looked back over his shoulder at them. "I think their outriders be seeing me. Maybe they come, maybe not."

"They saw you." Allyn fixed him with a disapproving stare. Granlor grimaced, but did not reply. The two had been scouting together since they left the Hawk Hill settlement. Granlor was good, but Allyn was better, and Allyn let the young clansman know it every chance he got. He had changed so much from the young woodsman who had taken pleasure in tracking and hunting with Shanis not so long ago. "And now they will be coming."

"No need. We will go to them." Shanis hoped the tension she felt did not show. Speaking to the Hawk Hill clansmen had been difficult enough, but they had already witnessed her power and thus had reason to believe in her. The Three Oaks clansmen knew nothing of her. It would not be easy. "We mean them no harm, so there is no reason for them to fear us."

Horgris, riding to her left, leaned in close. "The outlanders should be movin' to the back. You, at least, look like a Monaghan. They'll no believe any of it if they see the prince or his man." He glanced over his shoulder. "And that be true of you as well, husband of me daughter."

Hierm grimaced and gave Shanis an apologetic look which she returned with a smile and a shrug. It comforted her to have friends close by, but she was not about to interfere with Hierm's new family. According to Monaghan tradition, Hierm must treat Horgris as he would his own father. If only they knew how well Hierm got along with Lord Hiram.

"It will be as you say, father of my wife." Hierm wheeled his mount and rode toward the back of the clan, out of sight.

"Larris, will you and Allyn please join the rear clutch?" Larris did not answer, but he complied with her request, Allyn following behind. Allyn still rarely spoke directly to her and, at times, he seemed almost pained by her presence. Twice, she had tried to engage him in a private conversation, but each time he had remembered some errand or other and hurried away from her.

"I think only a small contingent should approach them," she continued. "We will look less like we are about to attack if only a few ride up, as opposed to bringing an entire raiding party down on them."

"It no matter now." Garmon, the oily little man who served as Horgris' tracker and messenger pointed ahead of them. A long line of men emerged from the woods. More than fifty clansmen armed with shortbows stood with arrows nocked and ready. A cluster of men on horseback rode out of the center. The man in front held their banner: three golden acorns on a field of dark green.

The riders drew to a halt halfway between the two lines. Shanis did not hesitate, but rode out to meet them. Her heart was in her throat as she approached.

Horgris cursed and hastily called out five names. He and the five he had called brought their horses up behind Shanis. The groups were of the same size, seven Hawk Hill and seven Three Oaks. She assumed there was some matter of honor involved. She would have to learn some of these traditions before she made too great a fool of herself.

When the two parties met, a man with a yellow-streaked gray beard and a headdress with oak branches jutting out like horns brought his horse forward a pace and looked first at her, then at Horgris with unmasked disdain.

"Gerrilaw." Horgris gave him a curt nod.

"Horgris." The other man inclined his head a fraction. "Before you be telling me your business, mayhap you be telling me when you did become a jokester. Or do you be meaning to insult my clan?"

"There be no insult here." Horgris' face was already flushed, and it appeared to be a struggle for him to remain polite. Obviously, most of his diplomatic expertise involved hacking at another man with his sword until the fellow saw things his way. "This be..."

"You be bringin' a woman as part of your seven!" A young man, his blond hair twisted into a knot with oak branches crossed through it, stood in his stirrups and pointed at her. "You be sayin' one of us be half a man?"

"Peace, Gendram." Gerrilaw motioned for the young man to sit.

"But Father, he…"

"You be calmin' yourself, my son, or I be sending you back to help your mother tend the young ones." Gerrilaw never took his eyes from Horgris, but the rebuke stung Gendram, who sat down hard in his saddle, shame evident in his reddening face. "We be talking about this insult later, Horgris. Now you tell me where he be."

"Where who be?" Horgris sounded both impatient and confused.

"The snow take you, Horgris! The bone woman been telling us that you got a man in yer clan be claiming to bear the Silver Serpent. They say he healed a girl who…" His voiced trailed away. Shanis assumed he was remembering that it was his own clan that had done the girl harm in the first place.

Hot anger raged inside of her. No matter where she went, people underestimated her, even ignored her, because she was a woman. Now she bore a talisman of prodigious power and she still gained neither respect nor regard. She reached back over her shoulder, took hold of the hilt, and drew the sword. It slid free with a serpentine hiss.

"I bear the Silver Serpent," she said in as loud a voice as she could manage without shouting, holding the blade aloft. The Three Oaks men drew back and gaped at the blade glinting in the sun. "And I bear its mark." She pulled down the neck of her tunic to reveal the serpent on her chest. She lowered the blade, but kept it out in plain sight.

"And who do you be?" Gerrilaw's voice was hoarse from shock.

"My name is Shanis Malan." She felt as though she should say more, but now did not seem the time to make her speech about the end of the clan wars.

"A woman," Gerrilaw replied. He did not sound scornful this time, but neither did he sound pleased. "And you claim that this be the Silver Serpent."

"No," she said. Horgris started to say something, but she spoke over him. "I claim nothing. This is the Silver Serpent. I have come to demonstrate its power, that you might know I am the one."

"This can no be." Gendram had forgotten his father's instruction to calm himself. "A woman must no bear the serpent. A woman can no lead the clans. Father, this be a waste of our time. Tell these Hawk Hills to leave us be and take their girl with them."

This time, Gerrilaw did not reprove his son. Instead, he turned and fixed Shanis with an expectant stare, waiting for her to continue.

"Have you forgotten whose corpse you carry so proudly?" Angry mutters from both sides told her they did not care for her choice of words, but she did not care. "Yes, we have heard. Your clan attacked innocent people, and nearly killed a little girl, because you thought they wanted to steal the dead body of the last warrior to lead a united Lothan." She raised her voice so the Three Oaks men who waited in a line behind their leader could hear her.

"And who is this leader, whom you all revere? Who is this great warrior, over whose memory you have shattered your kingdom?" Stone silence was her only reply, but she did not need their admission to know her words had struck home.

"Badla. A warrior queen. Did you hear that? Queen! A woman. Do you still believe a woman is too weak to lead? Because if you do, feel free to hand her body over to a clan who remembers her greatness, and still reveres her as a fighter and a leader. She deserves better than to be carried by those who are ashamed of her simply because she is a woman."

"You go too far, girl!" Gerrilaw gritted his yellow teeth.

"I will go much farther than this before I am finished." Once again her anger was getting the better of her. She could almost see Master Yurg shaking his head. "Your world is about to change, Gerrilaw. The sooner you accept that fact, the better it will be for you and your clan. Too many people have died fighting over a woman who is not coming back. The time has come to join together to fight as one. This," she hefted her sword again, "is the herald."

"If that do be the Silver Serpent, then we just take it from her and wield it ourselves." Gendram spurred his horse forward.

"Take it." Shanis reversed her grip on the sword and held it out hilt-first for the young clansman to take. The jeweled serpent's eye sparkled in the sun.

Gendram hesitated. He had thought to intimidate her, and her reaction was not what he expected. His eyes moved from Shanis to the sword, over to his father, and then back to the sword. His expression said he was weighing the possibility that this was a trick against the probability that he would look like a fool if he did not follow through on his words. He reached for the sword, but paused just before his fingertips touched the hilt.

"I wouldna' do it were I you," Horgris said. "No one be able to touch it but her. Many did try and all did fail. It do burn and freeze your hand at the same time. I no think you should, but you may try it if you like. We will no stop you."

Gendram remained frozen for an interminable instant before Gerrilaw waved him away. "Follow me," he said to Shanis. "We be seeing what you do be about."

The Three Oaks village looked much like that of the Hawk Hill. The structures were solid, but lacked an air of permanence. She wondered if the Lothans would ever live in true towns and cities again. As they rode, everyone they passed stopped and stared. What she saw in their eyes broke her heart. Despair and hopelessness lay heavy upon these people. But in a few eyes that met her own, she thought she saw a glimmer of hope. If some believed, then others could as well.

A group of older men were gathered in a round dirt area at the village's center. She dismounted and handed the reins over to Garmon, who scowled but said nothing. He had not liked her since their first encounter on the road so many months ago. She reflected that he really should not direct his anger toward her—it had been Allyn who put an arrow through Garmon's hat. Of course, he did not like Allyn either. She was not certain the man liked anyone very much.

"This woman claim to be the one." Gerrilaw climbed down from his mount. "What say the council?" The men exchanged looks, clearly unsettled by the revelation that the bearer was not a man.

"Can you be proving it?" A short, fat man, who was missing his front teeth, asked. "We hear you be doing remarkable things. Can you be showing us some demonstration of your power?" The others nodded. And the clan circled around, though they kept their distance.

Shanis was hardly confident in her abilities. Since the episode at Hawk Hill, she had practiced drawing the power from the sword and putting it back until she could do it almost all the time. Still, almost was a far cry from always, as Master Yurg used to say. She unsheathed the sword and held it out in front of her with both hands. She did not need to touch the sword to draw on it, but she hoped the sight of it would have an effect on the onlookers.

She was not disappointed. Many people gasped and backed away. Though the prophecy did not speak of what the serpent looked like, the sword was obviously something special. The fat man stepped forward for a closer look. His eyes followed the blade to its tip, then back down to the hilt and rested on the sparkling jewels. He gave an approving smile, satisfied with what he saw.

Gendram would not be persuaded so easily. "A fancy sword be no proof. Anyone can be carryin' a blade. Show us what you can do."

What would satisfy them? Something impressive. Her eyes fell upon a cluster of trees topping a nearby hill. Could she channel enough power to blow up the hilltop? That would show them something. She took a breath and prepared to draw the power when she realized the trees were oaks. Considering this was the Three Oaks clan she was trying to impress, destroying their namesake trees might be a grave insult.

A few of the onlookers were already growing impatient. A couple of the young men started to laugh. She needed to do something now. Her eyes fell on a boy only a few summers younger than her. His spine was twisted and he stood hunched over.

Can I do it?

Refusing to entertain thoughts of failure, she strode toward him, sheathing the sword as she walked. She took a long look at the faces of the laughing men, fixing every detail in her mind. One of them, a handsome fellow of below-average height, leered at her as she met his eye. The anger did not distract her, but fueled her determination.

The misshapen boy's jaw dropped when he realized she was coming to him, but he did not try to back away. A heavyset woman, probably his mother, started to protest, but her husband silenced her with a touch and a shake of his head.

She lifted the boy's chin so their eyes met, and she saw fear there. "It's all right," she whispered. Between practice with the power and the time she spent reflecting on her healing of the Hawk Hill girl, she had come to the conclusion that the power was not something she could pull into herself. She had to allow it to flow.

Focusing her thoughts, she opened herself to the energy, and felt it surge into her like a raging torrent. She directed the flow down her arms, through her hands, and into the young man. He gasped and jerked when the power poured into him. His mother whimpered and reached out for him, but her husband held her back.

Trying to repeat what she had done to the injured Hawk Hill girl, Shanis let her mind follow the flow of the power down his twisted spine. The power soaked into the muscles and tendons, loosening and stretching them. She felt him go limp, but she held him up with the energy of the serpent. The power encased his spine, turning and reshaping the bones. The boy grunted with each pop as the vertebra moved into place.

Finally, she was finished.

"Stand." She felt the muscles draw tight again, pulling him up to his feet. When she took her hands from his head, he looked down at his feet and then around at his clansmen, who were in an uproar. He took one tentative step, then another, and then hopped up and down. His mother burst into tears and embraced her son. His father dropped to his knee in front of Shanis.

"Thank you," he said. "You be the one. I do pledge to you my faithful service for all of my days." His wife and son joined him on their knees in front of Shanis. "I do pledge my family to your service as well."

"I accept your pledge." It felt inadequate, but she could think of nothing more to say. "Please stand," she added.

The young man was the first to rise. "My name be Olphair," he said. "I can no thank you enough for what you do for me. However I can repay you, I will."

"No thanks are necessary." The joy in his eyes was all the thanks she needed. This was what she was meant to do—make people whole again. Make a nation strong again.

A commotion arose behind her. While many of the villagers had dropped to a knee, bowing to her, Gendram had moved to stand with the elders, waving his arms and shouting.

"What is she going to do. Heal the Malgog into submission? A leader can no be a healer. A Monaghan leader must be a fighter. Must be one who can lead the clans to victory by the strength of the sword. Can this girl be doing that?" Many appeared to agree with him.

Too many.

"Gendram!" She shouted so that all could hear her. "I challenge you to prove yourself by strength of arms." She had no idea whether this was appropriate, but she remembered it from one of Oskar's stories, though it had not been a story of Lothan. She hoped he accepted. Right now, there was nothing she wanted more than to knock some sense into Gendram, and prove to everyone there that a woman could fight if she must.

Gendram stared dumbstruck at her. Many of the young men urged him on, but he stood rooted to the ground.

"You have been challenged." Gerrilaw looked gravely at his son. "Honor do require that you be answering that challenge."

"I can no fight someone with a magic sword," Gendram sputtered. "It do no be a fair fight."

Shanis unslung her sword and sheath and handed it to Olphair. "Hold it by the strap and do not touch the hilt." He accepted the sword from her, though he looked at it as if it were a live viper, and not a thing of steel.

"If someone will lend me a sword, I believe that will put us on even terms." She walked directly toward Gendram, forcing herself to keep a check on her anger. Now was not the time to lose her temper. She stopped less than a pace from the young Monaghan. He was only a hair taller than her, and she could look him in the eye with ease.

"I will no fight a woman," he protested.

"Does someone have a skirt for Gendram to wear?" she called out. His face reddened as laughter rang out all around. She did not push it farther. She remembered Pedric Karst and the way he had baited Natin by doing insult to their entire village. Most likely, she had already made a lifelong enemy of Gendram, but she was here to heal, not to divide. She would not offend the Three Oaks. "I know this is a proud clan of strong warriors," she said, turning around to address all of those assembled. "If this man will not cross blades with me, perhaps someone else will?" No one stepped forward.

"I will try you, girl." Gendram drew his sword. "And may Dagdar guide my blade and have mercy on your soul."

Granlor hurried over to her. For a moment, she thought he was going to try to interfere, but he offered her his sword.

"I hope you do know what you be doing."

She tested the sword weight and balance and found it satisfactory. It was longer and heavier than the sword she had grown up using, but she was as tall and strong as most men, and it was not too much for her. She took a couple of practice cuts before making ready. She glanced at Horgris and saw a concerned look in his eyes. His clan had thrown their lot in with her, but they had never seen her fight. She would not let them down.

She nodded to Gendram, who raised his sword and leapt forward, a ferocious roar rising from his lips.

She turned his first stroke with ease and countered with a slash that he beat away almost contemptuously. He drove forward, hacking at her like a woodsman at his work. She kept her thoughts and feelings focused on the blade, just as Master Yurg had taught her. She turned away each stroke, giving ground as Gendram came at her. Many of the onlookers interpreted her retreat as a sign that she was in trouble, and cheered Gendram on. Gerrilaw and some of the others, however, were already looking worried.

Gendram's attack slowed, and his technique became sloppy. He had expended too much of his energy in his aggressive attack. Sweat poured from his brow, and he was breathing through his mouth.

Now it was her turn.

She sprang forward, striking first high, then low. His defense was clumsy and, when she gave a thrust to his midsection, he scarcely turned it aside. Two overhand strokes in quick succession drew his guard up high. She feinted low, and struck high. Slowed by fatigue, he could not get his blade up in time, and she sliced open his left cheek.

Spewing vile curses, he swung at her head with a broad, reckless swipe that she easily ducked. She pivoted and swept her foot out, catching his ankle and dropping him to the ground. He landed hard on his back and his sword fell from his grip. He looked up at her, wondering what she would do next.

She did not know why she did it, but she tossed Granlor's sword aside, and beckoned for Gendram to come at her again.

He clambered to his feet, teeth gritted and hands curled like claws. He did not come charging at her like before, but circled, standing on the balls of his feet, tensed to spring. She took a similar stance, and they moved in lock-step, each looking for an opening.

The Three Oaks shouted encouragement to both combatants. Her skill with the blade had swayed a few more supporters to her cause. Gendram struck at her face, but she twisted to the side, making him miss. She repaid him with a kick to the shin and a jab to the jaw that did no damage. He grabbed her wrist, but she twisted her arm and jerked back, pulling free. Gendram struck her hard in the ribs with his left hand. She grunted and grasped his tunic, yanking him toward her as she drove her forehead into his nose. The sound was sickening and her forehead stung from the blow. He staggered backward, blood pouring from his ruined nose. He ignored the injury and kept his hands at the ready.

Shanis feinted with her left hand, then followed with a kick aimed at his knee. He managed to grab her ankle, but before he could pull her off balance, she sprang up and kicked him square in the chin with the heel of her free foot.

Gendram wobbled, took a step backward, and crumpled to the ground.

The onlookers cheered. She knelt and laid her hands on his head. After healing Olphair, it was a simple task to repair Gendram's nose and bring him back to consciousness.

He sat up shivering, eyes wide. He looked at her with a blank expression on his face. Finally he nodded.

"So that be it, then." She stood and offered her hand, which he clasped, and she heaved him to his feet. Loud enough for those around them to hear, he said, "I do believe you be the one, and I do accept you as leader." He did not take a knee as others had done, but the words were more than she had hoped for.

A long journey lay before her, but she had taken another step.

Chapter 13

"Are you certain this is the way we must go?" Lerryn gazed at the tangle of vines and creepers that blocked their way. They had been fighting through the growth for what seemed like half the day.

"Please." Heztus sneered. "I am the guide, remember?" The dwarf turned and hacked at the thick foliage with a long, flat knife that looked like a short sword in his hand. Two swings and the vines came down, revealing an overgrown pathway. "And here we are. Follow me, but not too closely. There are certain stinging vines you don't want to touch. They are rare, but sometimes we find them in this area. I shall warn you if I see any." He started forward again, continuing his battle with the dense vegetation. "By the way, if you should see any snakes, don't pick them up, all right?"

Lerryn chuckled and followed behind the dwarf. He held Kreege's reins in one hand and his long knife in the other. He still could not believe he had agreed to let the little man join them. Then again, the fellow knew the shortest, safest route to Calmut, or at least he said that he did. If that was where the Silver Serpent was headed, Lerryn wanted to be there.

He was not certain how the Malgog would receive an outlander in one of their most sacred places, but he was determined to go regardless. He stole a glance behind them to confirm that the others were still following behind. Xaver looked disgusted by the mud and the mess, while the three young men wore dazed, wearied expressions. He wondered at how their worlds had changed since they entered his tournament. When this was all over and they were students at the Academy, they were going to find themselves blessedly bored.

"Are you sure our horses will be able to make it through?" Hair called to Heztus. The way had grown ever more precarious, and some of the paths they had most recently trod were quagmires the consistency of thick porridge.

"Young man, if I am going to have to answer each of your questions three times or more, it is going to make for some exceedingly boring conversation."

Lerryn could not resist the opportunity to needle Heztus. "I suppose this is a bad time to ask you if you are certain that moving due north is the best plan, given that Calmut lies northwest of your village?"

Heztus looked back, rolled his eyes at the prince, and muttered something about "swimming in quakewater" before returning to the task of hacking his way down the path with renewed vigor. Doubtless, he was taking out his frustrations on the surrounding plant life.

Lerryn laughed. He rather enjoyed Heztus' good-natured insolence, so unlike Pedric Karst's sour disposition. It occurred to him that, once again, they were a group of six. Perhaps this time the six would bring them luck.

The sun had disappeared behind the trees when they stopped to make camp on a sand bar in the middle of a blackwater swamp where a lone cypress spread its limbs across the width of the bar and out into the water. They tied their mounts in the shelter of the tree and tended to them before settling down for the evening.

Heztus lit a smoky fire to keep the insects away, and they dined on dried meat and some tasty raw tubers the dwarf had brought along. Heztus and Hair each took turns teaching the others drinking songs of their respective countries while they passed around a skin of the sourest wine Lerryn had tasted in years, though he drank his share. By the time they turned in, the wine was gone and Lerryn was feeling better than he had in some time. All in all, it had been a good day. He did not know what lay ahead of them, but he finally knew where he was going, and that was a good feeling.

A frightened cry jolted him from sleep. He bolted up, his hand instinctively going to his sword. The cry came again. Rather, it was a pained scream.

"Bull!" Lerryn shouted. "What is happening?" The young man had taken the first watch, all the while insisting that it was folly to believe they might be attacked here in the middle of the swamp.

A torch blossomed in the darkness and Heztus scrambled out from under a low branch. "Leeches! Huge, poisonous leeches. Do not let them spit in your eyes."

"I've got to help Bull. Where is he?

"He's already dead. I'm going to get the horses. The leeches consume flesh of any kind." He scurried off into the darkness, and Lerryn followed.

The news about Bull pained him, but he was a trained warrior and had lost men before. There would be time enough for grief later. He grabbed a flaming brand from the fire and followed the dwarf. Up ahead, one of the horses whinnied in fright, and then another. He heard men shouting, and suddenly an intense white light blossomed up above them, bathing the sand bar in an ethereal glow.

Two of the horses were on the ground, twitching in their death throes. Black, pulsing masses like creeping sacks of mud crept toward the remaining men and horses.

Xaver held one hand aloft, keeping the light burning in the sky. With the other hand, he pointed one-by-one at the slugs. Each time he pointed a finger, one of the slugs burst into blue flame. The fire did not deter the other slugs. They gave the fires a wide berth, but kept coming. Edrin was putting arrows in the air as fast as he could, but his and Xaver's combined efforts would not be enough. There were too many of the things. Hair stood holding the reins of the horses that remained alive. He looked to be on the verge of panic. Heztus had bound a strip of cloth around his eyes and was trying to fend off a slug half his size with a torch and short sword.

Ignoring the dwarf's earlier warnings, Lerryn leapt into the fray, cleaving a slug in two, then turned to look for another victim. Two more of the slimy monstrosities oozed toward him. Shielding his eyes with his left arm, he dashed toward them. He heard a wet hiss, and felt something spatter all over his forearm. It seared his flesh and he cried out in anger. Before one of the slugs could spit at him again, he leapt over them, twisted in midair, and came down behind them. With a vicious stroke, he cleaved them both in two.

"Follow me!" Heztus, the cloth now stripped from his eyes, darted past him. Keeping the light aloft, Xaver brushed by with the others close behind. Lerryn relieved Hair of Kreege's reins and took the rear.

It was like one of his worst nightmares come to life as he stumbled through the darkness. Creepers reached out to ensnare his legs, and with every step, the sand gave way beneath his feet, making him feel that he was running in place. Another slug slid out of the undergrowth, and he skewered it on his sword.

Suddenly, he was out of the sand and on firm ground. He heard a cry up ahead and saw Edrin clutching his arm. Lerryn slashed the slug that had spat poison at Edrin, and then helped the young man along. The slugs were slow, but they were everywhere.

They ran for a league or more through mud, sand, and water before Heztus finally called them to a stop.

"We are well clear of the swamp." He dropped to the ground and sat with his forehead in his palms. "I do not know what to say. I have never seen them out this late in the year, and at no time in memory have they come up out of the water after their prey. I do not understand."

"Much has changed in the world in a very short time." Xaver was examining Edrin's arm. "There is no blame to be placed here. Right now, I could use your assistance in tending to this boy's arm."

Heztus told Xaver which herbs made the best poultice to counter the effects of the poison on the skin.

"His Highness will need a poultice as well." Heztus indicated Lerryn's injured forearm. In the fight and flight, he had completely forgotten about the injury.

"Am I poisoned? It hurts, but otherwise I feel strong."

"It only burns the skin," Heztus explained. "If it gets in your eyes, it can blind you. If you are bitten, however, you will die very quickly. That is what happened to your man."

"We should go back for Bull's body when it is daylight," Hair said, "and give him a proper burial."

"He is gone." Heztus looked at the young man with genuine regret. "I am sorry, boy. There is no delicate way to tell you this, and even if there were, I doubt I would bother. The leeches were dragging his body into the water to feed. I imagine he and the horses will be nothing but bone by morning."

Hair shuddered, but accepted the dwarf's words.

Lerryn could think of nothing to say that would bring comfort to the others. He was angry at the needless loss of life, but he held no animosity toward the dwarf. It was an unfortunate tragedy, nothing more. His mood was now black as the mud beneath his boots. Somehow he would make things right.

Chapter 14

Karst had never seen so pitiful a group of people as those who stood before him right now. They were all that remained in this mudhole the Malgog called a village. Most of their number had already fled his coming. The cowards. These had not even bothered to put up a fight when he and his men rode into the village, but instead looked up at him in resignation and waited for him to state his business. It was getting too easy.

"You follow me now." He called out so that anyone who might be hiding in one of the mud huts would hear him. "I am the bearer of the Silver Serpent." He pushed back the sleeve of his tunic and raised his arm, revealing the silver armband that snaked around his wrist and forearm. He felt a thrill of delight. This was his favorite part.

"Behold my power!" He pointed at a nearby hut, and it erupted in flame.

"Grandfather!" A woman ran screaming toward the burning dwelling, but by the time she got there, the flames had already reduced it to cinders. Power was a marvelous thing and could be an effective tool in the proper circumstances.

"Get her away from there." Padin and Danlar obeyed instantly, taking the woman by the elbows and dragging her away. He paid no attention to where they were going with her. Instead, he turned to continue addressing the villagers.

"My terms are simple. You will give me and my men a tithe from your stores and a portion of any coin or other valuables you might have. You will swear fealty to me, and all able-bodied men will join me on my quest to unite the clans of Malgog. The rest of you will remain here, continue on with your lives, and await my return."

"Do we have a choice?" A wizened old man looked up at him, the defiance in his tone matched by that in his eyes.

"As a matter of fact, you do." He guided his horse over to where the man stood. Too stupid to know what was about to happen to him, the old man stared up at him, unafraid. In one swift movement, Karst drew his sword and slashed him through the heart. He heard gasps and a few moans, but everyone was too shocked to scream. He once again addressed the villagers.

"Your other choice is death."

Feeling that was as strong an ending as he was likely to have, he dismounted, gave his horse over to one of his men, and made his way to the central hut.

Malaithus waited inside.

"Another fine job, Lord Pedric. Your father will be pleased to hear of your progress."

"I expect he will." Karst dropped into a chair facing Malaithus. "That was nicely done with the hut."

Malaithus waved the compliment away. "It is a simple thing, and they never take notice of me, dressed as I am. They think it is all your doing."

"Yes, they do." Karst propped his feet up on the table and rocked back in his chair, folding his hands across his chest. He was not sure what to make of Malaithus. The man had found him in a tavern, drowning his frustrations after abandoning Lerryn and his failed quest. He came bearing a message from Karst's father. Duke Rimmic Karst had grand plans for his son, and Malaithus was to serve and advise Pedric as he put those plans into action.

He remembered the letter from his father.

The forces of ice have captured the Silver Serpent. Someone must fulfill the prophecy and unite the clans to oppose the next frostmarch. You must be that someone. It was your destiny to bear the serpent. You must reclaim that destiny. If they will not bend to your will, you must bend them.

The next thing Karst knew, he was wearing a snake-shaped silver armband and traveling from village to village in northeastern Malgog, proclaiming himself as the bearer of the serpent and calling upon them to follow him.

The first village had been a challenge. They had scoffed at his claim, until he and

Malaithus had given them a display of power. After that, the demonstration was always the first response to any hint of resistance.

Not everyone had to be bent to his will. Many had flocked to his banner, mostly young men eager for adventure, or bitter older men who wanted payment for what they believed were the wrongs life had done them. Some were violent by nature and viewed following Karst as an opportunity to oppress and abuse others without fear of retribution. His ranks quickly swelled, and he had taken to sending small raiding parties into Diyonus where they raided farms, vineyards and villages. This not only afforded them more provisions, but sated the appetites of the more unsavory of his men.

Of late he was finding the villages almost deserted. No one told him why, and he did not ask. He refused to appear ignorant in front of these primitives. His men believed the able-bodied villagers were fleeing in fright, and that explanation was good enough for Karst.

He now had a respectable force at his back, and virtually all of western Lothan had sworn fealty to him. The Mud Snake clan had forsaken their chieftain and elders, and had sent emissaries to Karst, pledging their support and acknowledging him as the bearer of the Silver Serpent. Padin and Danlar were Mud Snakes, and bloodthirsty raiders. They sometimes went a touch farther in their depredations than Karst would have preferred, but he appreciated their enthusiasm. They were eager for Karst to lead an invasion of the lands of the Black Mangrove clan. That would come in good time, but right now, Pedric Karst was the lord of what amounted to a small nation.

"Something is on your mind." Malaithus interrupted his thoughts. "What is it?"

"How does my father know the fate of the Silver Serpent, and why does he want me to be the one who unites Malgog?" There. It was out, and the snows take him if Malaithus did not like the question.

"I wondered when you would ask." Malaithus chuckled, and the sound was like a gurgle deep in his throat. He stretched, yawned, and shifted in his seat before answering. "Let us say I have a special window into certain events. I may not say more, but the time will come when I can tell you all."

Karst thought about that. A window into events. Was it Xaver? Malaithus was a sorcerer. Perhaps the two were in league. It was the only explanation that made sense. He smiled at the thought of that drunken fool Lerryn being too blind to see that his most trusted adviser was the spy in his midst.

"As for why he chose you, I think that should be obvious. Malgog borders your family's duchy of Kurnsbur. With a Karst in control of those lands, King Allar can no longer dismiss Kurnsbur and Duke Rimmic as inconsequential. It might even mean an Earldom and a favorable marriage for you."

And no one could ever call me a pig farmer again. Though he enjoyed the thought of his family gaining power and honor, something bothered him.

"So, this is not truly about making ready for the next frostmarch?"

Malaithus met his gaze with a level stare of his own.

"Does it matter, Lord Pedric? Given the choice, would you choose any other path? What difference does it make if the fear of another frostmarch is merely a tool to aid you in conquest? The end result is the same, is it not?"

Behind him, someone cleared his throat. Karst turned to see Padin standing in the doorway.

"My Lord Karst." The young Malgog stood straight, trying to look like a proper soldier. "There is a bone woman here who begs an audience with you. Will you see her?"

An old woman bustled through the door, shoving Padin aside. Padin looked at her in bemused surprise and did not try to stop her.

"I don't beg nothing of nobody." She scowled at Padin, as if daring him to interfere. Satisfied, she gave him a curt not and joined Karst and Malaithus at the table.

"I have a message for you," she said without preamble. "You have been summoned."

Karst exchanged glances with Malaithus, who looked as baffled as he felt.

"I have been summoned," he repeated, recovering from the surprise and gathering his thoughts." Very well. By whom, and to where?"

"Another claims to bear the Silver Serpent. The clans call the both of you to meet at Calmut, where you will face the Keeper of the Mists. There will the choice be made, and there the clans will swear their allegiance to the true bearer."

"It is a lie!" Malaithus' face tightened. "The Silver Serpent is in the possession of the ice."

The old woman moved her head from side to side, as if to say, perhaps, but perhaps not. "All the same, you have been summoned."

"But I already have the allegiance of every village in eastern Malgog from the border of Galdora down to the lands of the Black Mangrove clan."

The woman laughed.

"The clans have gone, boy. Haven't you noticed? Save the Mud Snakes, they have all gone to Calmut. You have the allegiance of a few villagers—the old and the infirm, and an army of troublemakers, but you do not have the clans. Go to Calmut, submit to the Keeper of the Mists and, if you are the bearer, then you will truly rule the clans."

"What is this Keeper of the Mists?" Karst was annoyed at being called boy, and his voice was harsh.

"It is a myth. A product of superstition." Malaithus scowled at the bone woman while he spoke to Karst. "They gather in a ruined city. The leaders enter a cave, inhale some steam, come back out, and do whatever it was they were already planning on doing long before they arrived at Calmut."

Now he addressed the bone woman. "Tell your sisters to pass this message along to the clan chiefs; the bearer will not lower himself to participate in your demeaning, primitive rituals. They will bend knee to him or pay the price."

The woman was unfazed. She turned to look at Karst. Her eyes bored into him, making him feel dizzy.

"Does he speak for you, or have you a mind of your own?"

"You tell them this." He bolted up out of the chair, sending it clattering to the floor. "You tell them Pedric Karst is no man's lapdog. Pedric Karst does not come when an old woman calls." He gripped the table, his body quivering with rage. "Now get out of here."

The woman looked from him to Malaithus and back again. One corner of her thin, dry mouth turned up in a sneer.

"So be it then, bearer. The call comes only once. The clans gather in Calmut should you come to your senses." She strode from the room with the same sense of determination with which she had entered.

Karst watched her go, rage boiling in him like a seething cauldron. With great effort, he regained control of his emotions.

"So much for the foolishness of old women. If the clans have gone to Calmut, this is the perfect time to move our forces south."

Chapter 15

"**There be riders** ahead." The Blue Stag outrider brought his horse to a halt. "It do look like a full clan, maybe two."

"Do they be moving in the direction of Calmut?" Culmatan took off his headdress and ran a hand through his braided hair. "Most likely they be meaning us no more harm than we be meaning them, no?"

"That do seem to be the way of it." The rider squinted at the distant riders. "I do see some Hawk Hill down there, if I no be mistaken."

"Hawk Hill is Horgris' clan, is it not?" Aspin asked. Culmatan nodded. "Horgris and I are on good terms. I think I should like to ride on ahead and speak with him. Oskar, you and Khalyndryn have met Horgris and his clansmen. Would you care to join me?"

"I suppose." Oskar shrugged. He had no particular desire to see Horgris again, but it might make for a nice change of scenery after traveling with the Blue Stags for three days. They were a standoffish lot, perhaps because he was traveling with a seeker. In any case, he was going to stay close to Aspin. Khalyndryn, who was mounted up behind him, agreed as well.

"I be going with you, then." Culmatan settled his headdress back on his head and put his heels to his horse. "I must give them my greetings and speak of the news."

The four of them followed the outrider along the dirt road that twisted through a thin scattering of trees. The highlands were starting to level out a bit as they made their way down out of Monaghan territory. They emerged from the sparse forest at the top of a long, sloping hill.

A long line of clansmen and women stretched out below them. As they trotted their mounts down the hill, a few of the Hawk Hill men broke off from the main body and rode out to meet them. They made no effort to hide their suspicion of Culmatan, but Aspin's presence piqued their curiosity. After questioning the seeker, the men escorted them to the front of the Hawk Hill column.

As they drew close, Oskar spotted Horgris riding in the lead alongside a tall red-haired clanswoman. There was something familiar about her. Suddenly, he realized who it was.

"Shanis!" Oskar cried. "Shanis!" He spurred his horse to a gallop, and almost fell from his saddle as he bounced along.

"Careful! Don't take me down with you." Khalyndryn clung to him as they rode along. "Is it really Shanis?"

"Yes. She's with Horgris."

Up ahead, Shanis heard her name and turned around. Her eyes fell on Oskar and Khalyndryn and she immediately turned her horse and galloped toward them. Two more riders followed, and now Oskar recognized Larris and Hierm.

It was a joyful reunion. In his eagerness to dismount, Oskar tangled his foot in the stirrup and landed flat on his back. Laughing uproariously, Larris and Hierm piled on him. When they unpiled, he was surprised and pleased to see Khalyndryn and Shanis hugging. Not to be left out, he rushed over and caught them both up in a crushing embrace.

"I am so sorry." Shanis' voice was pleading. "I tried, but I couldn't save you. And I didn't mean to leave you. I still don't know how we got out of the mountains. The sword brought us here."

"What happened to you?" Larris asked. "How did you get here?"

"It is a long story best told over several ales. I imagine you have much to tell us as well."

"That we do." Larris grinned at Hierm, who looked abashed. Seeing Oskar's confused expression, Larris clapped a hand on his back. "Don't mind us. Come and let Hierm introduce you to his wife."

Oskar was amazed by all that had changed in such a short period of time. Shanis had the power of sorcery as well, it seemed, though unlike Oskar, she actually had an idea of how to use it, at least in the aspect of healing. And the path she had chosen was a daunting one, but he admired her for her choice. He had always been able to look past her faults, but this act of selfless surrender for the good of a nation not her own was remarkable. He tried to imagine her leading an army, but could not form the image in his mind.

Truth be told, he had not given much thought to the future of anyone other than himself. In a very general way, he had assumed Shanis would find a way to use that sword of hers, perhaps working for Lord Hiram guarding his wagons or some such thing. He had never truly believed she would become a real soldier, though even now he would not say that to her face. It was just too much to believe.

He caught a glimpse of Larris across the fire. He was so happy to see his friend again. The evening had been consumed by catching one another up on happenings, but he looked forward to renewing their conversations about books and history and the like. He had already made up his mind that the best way he could help Shanis would be to research serpent lore and Lothan history and tradition. How exactly to go about that he was not entirely certain, but it seemed like putting his scholarly gifts to work to help his friend was the wise course.

Larris had an odd expression on his face that had nothing to do with the wine. He and Shanis kept exchanging glances when they thought no one was looking. Had Shanis finally come around? The young royal's regard for her had been obvious to anyone with eyes, but she had either ignored or rejected all of his overtures. Of course, that relationship would be fraught with difficulties, but who was to say what could or could not happen anymore? It was not too long ago he had been a starry-eyed farm boy. And now he was… something more, though what exactly his path would be was still to be determined.

"You are awfully quiet, Khalyndryn." Hierm lay propped on one elbow next to his wife Rinala. His marriage was not as improbable as Shanis bearing the Silver Serpent, but it was very much a surprise. What was more, he truly seemed to care for the girl, which was a feat since they had known one another such a short time.

"I'm just enjoying listening to the stories. It is all so hard to believe." A few of the young women whom she had befriended in their previous visit with the Hawk Hill clan had sought her out when they learned of her arrival, but she had politely declined their invitation to walk about, choosing instead to remain with her friends.

Since then, she and Rinala had engaged in quiet conversation while listening to the stories.

"Where did Allyn go?" Oskar had noted Allyn's absence and thought it strange.

"He went out." Larris let his gaze fall. "He spends little time around people anymore. I fear that our experience has affected him in some way I do not understand." His eyes held a sadness Oskar had never before seen in the young man. "I regret bringing him with us."

"You did not force him to go with you." Shanis took Larris' hand and gave it a squeeze. "He wanted to. He did it because he is your friend."

"He was my friend, you mean. He hardly speaks to me anymore, and he never wants to be around us. You saw how uncomfortable he was tonight. He didn't even finish one drink before he left." He lay down on his back with his head in Shanis' lap. If the subject at hand was not so somber, Oskar would have laughed at the sight, especially when Shanis began stroking Larris' hair. "In any case, he came because of our friendship, which is precisely why it is my fault."

"I have come to understand," Khalyndryn said, her voice grave, "that acts of friendship are gifts given without price or obligation. I was the reason we left our village in the first place." Her pained expression made Oskar's heart ache. "For a long time I felt guilty about that. But when Oskar and I were lost under the mountains, and all I could think of was keeping him alive, I realized that I was doing it because I wanted to. I was never much of a friend to anyone before, and it felt good to be needed, and to do something to help a friend. As difficult and frightening as it was, I still count it among my fondest memories." A stray tear trickled down her cheek. "None of this makes much sense, I suppose. What I'm trying to say is, if you don't accept someone's gift of friendship, you are robbing them of something very precious."

"I think that be one of the wisest things anyone ever be saying," Rinala whispered, reaching out to take Khalyndryn's hand. Even Shanis appeared moved by her words, and she gave Larris a sad smile.

"I would not trade it either." Shanis looked around at her friends. "This is what we were all meant to do, isn't it? Me, Oskar, Hierm…"

"I still do not know what is intended for me." Khalyndryn forced a laugh. "Perhaps I'll be a guide through underground caverns."

"If it makes you feel any better, I spent most of my childhood and youth fully convinced that my destiny was to bear the Silver Serpent and save my people." Larris made a mocking face at Shanis that elicited laughter from everyone gathered around the fire.

"Shanis, I've been wondering," Oskar said, "how you will learn to use this power you have."

"I don't know." She shrugged. "I suppose I shall just keep figuring it out on my own. It's worked so far, and I don't know any other way to do it."

"Aspin, the seeker, has been teaching me. I believe he would be willing to help you if you like. He was actually searching for you when he found us."

"Was he?" Shanis sat up straight, her voice cold and her expression uncertain. She glanced down at Larris, who looked thoughtful. "Did he happen to say why?"

The memory struck Oskar like a blow to the head, and he could not believe he had forgotten to say something before now. "Actually, he says he knows your father." Her eyes widened when he mentioned Colin. "He came to our village, and your father asked him to help search for us. Your father believed we had not gone far and would return soon, but he asked Aspin to look for us as well."

"That does not make sense." Larris sat up. "What reason did he give for coming to your village in the first place? And why would he travel so far? In fact, how did he know where to look for us?"

The same questions had occurred to Oskar, and Aspin's answers had been sorely lacking in detail, but he had not wanted to offend the saikur by pressing him too hard, especially now that they were traveling companions. Now Oskar's training in sorcery added another layer of complication.

"The only thing he told us was that Shanis is important somehow. I don't know any more than that, but if you were to ask him, I think he would tell us the truth."

"I don't like it." Larris stood and began pacing back and forth. "You should watch yourself around him, Shanis."

"So now you're giving me orders?" She grinned and gestured for him to sit back down, but he shook his head.

"I am serious. He had better have some very good reasons for pursuing us like he did. And even if he does have reasons, I won't trust him until he proves himself."

Allyn chose that moment to reappear. No one noticed his silent approach, and they all looked up, startled, when he interrupted their conversation.

"Oskar, may I have a word with you?" His tone was cordial, but his face was set in a mask of discomfort, as if being close to his friends made him ill.

When they were out of earshot of the others, Allyn finally spoke.

"Can you feel it? The magic, I mean. Can you feel the way it pulses and pounds? It's like my head is the anvil and..." He pressed his hands to his temples and groaned. The groan soon increased in pitch until it became a snarl of pain and frustration.

"I don't feel it." Oskar took a step back. "Well, not really. I do seem to... sense something when I'm near the sword, but that is all." What was Allyn trying to tell him? Was Allyn a sorcerer too? Or was it as Larris had said? Had the entire adventure damaged the young man in some way?

"I cannot stand to be close to her for very long. She must think I hate her. Larris looks at me like I am mad. They don't understand. But if they knew..." He sucked in his breath and stared up at the moon. "I am not going crazy, Oskar."

"No one believes that." In spite of his words, he could not help but wonder if, in fact, Allyn was losing his mind. Why had the sword affected him that way, but had not done the same to anyone else in their group?

"My ears are sharper than you think. I know what Larris says about me. He suspects I have been damaged in some way." His expression suddenly changed. Terror filled his eyes, and his breath came in gasps. He grasped Oskar's shoulders with trembling hands. "I have been damaged, Oskar." His voice was strident and filled with desperation. "I am trying to get out. Help me get out!"

"But Shanis can heal people now. Let her try and help you. Better yet, there is a seeker with me..."

Allyn snarled and struck him across the jaw, sending him stumbling back. "Tell no one!" The fear was gone from his voice, and he now spoke in a tone like a primordial growl. "Do not betray me, friend. I only need more time!" He turned his back and dashed away into the night.

Chapter 16

"Do you think we have done enough?" Hiram Van Derin's voice had an odd ring to it. Deferring to his hired man was obviously uncomfortable for him. "I wonder at the wisdom of remaining here at all, so far from the larger towns and the military outposts. Perhaps I should send more riders for help?"

"To whom would you send them?" Colin's attention was still focused on the boys who were feathering shafts under the close supervision of Nelrid Hendon. Galsbur had no fletcher, and most of the locals were self-reliant enough to make the few arrows they needed for hunting. Nelrid had a particular aptitude for the task, so Colin had set him to training some of the boys who were too young to fight. "We have sent men everywhere I know to send them. In any event, much help is not likely to arrive ahead of the enemy."

"Bah! It chills me when you talk like that." Hiram scuffed the ground with the heel of his boot and stared down. "An army marching toward Galsbur. Who would have believed it?"

"Believe it," Colin said. "Everyone who has fled from them tells the same story: wild ones, exiles, and mercenaries led by coldhearts and shifters." He found it difficult not to shiver at the thought of the latter.

"I'll believe in shifters when I see them," Hiram said in an overloud voice, glancing toward the boys who had ceased their work on the arrows and were listening intently. "No need to frighten them with grandmother's tales come-to-life," he said in a softer voice. "It will be trouble enough without them fearing the monsters of their nightmares."

"Perhaps." Colin had never truly understood children. Consequently, he raised Shanis like he would a young man. There had been other compelling reasons for such an upbringing, but it had left him woefully lacking in empathy for young people. "But what happens when they finally see one face-to-face?"

"Likely the enemy will put enough fear in them that not much will scare 'em any worse." Nelrid left his charges and joined the conversation. "I've only been in two battles in my life. Soiled myself the first time, but the second time I just didn't think about nothing but fighting. War is frightening enough all by itself, don't you think?"

Colin nodded, his eyes still on the young men who were now back at work. How many of them would live to see next year? Or even next week?

"The shafts aren't going to be dried properly. You know that, don't you?" Nelrid indicated the arrows on which the young men were working. "Not enough time to do an adequate job of it."

"All you can do is your best," Colin assured him. "I am certain that your worst arrow is a far better one than I could ever make."

"That's kind of you to say." An embarrassed grin seeped across Nelrid's face. "So tell me, Malan, where did you see fighting?"

Colin was spared the difficult answer by Faun Van Derin, who chose that exact moment to intrude, along with her elder son, Laman, who stood behind her, his angular face and intense eyes the mirror of his father.

"We are going now, Hiram." Faun's face, usually so severe, drooped like a sodden sheet on the line, and her voice was gentle, almost pleading. "I truly wish you would let me remain behind with you. It will be so dangerous here."

Colin glanced at the cluster of mounted escorts, the carriage, and the heavily laden wagon containing so many of Faun's prized possessions, and knew her words to be false, though the feelings behind them actually seemed sincere. Hiram probably knew it as well. He loved the woman, but he was no lackwit.

"Which is precisely why you must go, my dear." Hiram took her by the hand and pulled her close to him. "I could not bear the thought of you in harm's way. Besides, your regard for our capital city is no secret." His smile did not reach his eyes, but Faun beamed at him.

"At least let me stay with you, Father," Laman said. "I know I am not much with a sword, but I can do my part. I am not afraid."

"I know you are not afraid." Hiram took his eldest son by the shoulder and fixed him with a grave look. "That is precisely why I trust you to see your mother safely away, and to defend her if the need should arise. Should anything happen to me, you will be the man in the family." He looked up at the sky. "Besides," his voice grew hoarse, "I might have already lost one son. I do not intend to lose another."

Faun gave a little cry and fell against her husband's chest. Hiram enveloped her in his arms and pulled her close, pressing his face into her silken hair. It was the most affection Colin had ever seen between the two of them.

"He is all right." Hiram whispered and stroked her head. "Hierm can take care of himself. Wherever he is, it must be safer than home right now."

"I just want him to come back to us." Her voice was muffled as she pressed her face into his chest. "You don't truly believe we've lost him?"

"No," he soothed, "but I'll not take any chances with Laman. The two of you had better get going now." With obvious reluctance, he drew away from his wife, clasped hands with his son, and escorted them to the waiting carriage.

Colin turned away, looking up at the sky. He tried not to think about Shanis. There was naught that he could do, and ruminating on it did not make things any better. He was certain she was alive, though. Most likely her destiny had finally caught up with her no matter his wishes. But enough of such thoughts. He had a responsibility to these people to keep them alive if at all possible.

A rustling in the nearby trees drew his attention, and one of the local youth who had been dispatched as a scout appeared from the foliage. Behind him walked a man and woman with their young son.

"These folks have just found their way here," he said. "They say trouble's not too far behind." He shook his head. "Still can't believe it."

"Nor can I." Colin turned his attention to the new arrivals. "You did well to make it here in one piece. I daresay you'll find a few of your townspeople among us. I'll show you to the inn. You'll be fed and given some clean clothes, and then we'll see about a place for you to stay."

"I intend to work for my keep, Sir," the man said. "We don't want nothing just given to us."

"When the invaders arrive, there will be plenty of work for you to do, I assure you."

Colin led them into town and across the green, which was now populated by tents and temporary shelters for those who had fled from the invaders, as well as some locals who had reluctantly abandoned their outlying farms for the relative safety of town.

They passed Mardin Clehn and his sons, who were sharpening stakes to be set in the ground to build a defensive wall. Mardin nodded, but did not greet Colin. The

Clehns seemed to blame Shanis for Oskar's decision to leave town. If they had taken any time at all to get to know their eldest son, they would have known the wanderlust was strong in him.

The front porch of the inn was crowded with people exchanging gossip, which they called "news." A few children played in the grass nearby, kicking around a rag ball. Though they were engaged in common, everyday activities, there was an eerie quiet about the scene. Everyone was afraid.

"Papa! Mama!" A familiar voice shrieked. "Harvin! It is really you!"

"Jayla?" the woman whispered, her face pale and her eyes wide with disbelief. She turned around and was nearly bowled over as Jayla leapt into her arms. She swept the little girl up and held her close, as if fearful she would get away again. "I can't believe it."

Almost instantly, the family was locked together in a knot, squeezing each other tight. Jayla told them of her escape, and how Colin had found and looked after her. Her parents sobbed and laughed and recounted how they had searched for her near their town until they dared not wait any longer.

Colin chose that moment to slip quietly away. He did not wish to intrude upon their joy, and he had things to which he must attend. While he was pleased to see the family reunited, it also served to remind him of his own broken family. First his wife, then Shanis. Now Jayla would no longer brighten his home with her smiles and laughter. Sadly, he was growing accustomed to losing girls.

Chapter 17

Aspin was far enough now from the encampment that he could be reasonably assured of privacy. He found an open spot in a dense stand of the stunted, twisted oaks that choked the roadways of central Lothan. He cleared a space for a fire, scooping out a trench to contain the flames, crumpled dry leaves, added bits of twigs and tinder, and continued adding increasingly larger sticks until it was time to cheat. He whispered, and then a cheery flame engulfed the wood.

He could not suppress a grin. Not only had his sorcerous abilities grown stronger, but his magic was more consistent now, and the responses to his spells were more immediate, effective, and dependable. He had pondered the source, but had drawn no firm conclusion.

He took a pinch of ground aciash root from the soft leather pouch at his belt and sprinkled it over the flames. The result was immediate. Thick, white smoke smelling vaguely of pine and cedar roiled upward in a dense, twisting pillar. But when the smoke reached head-high, it ceased climbing, and held there, boiling in an angry mass.

A figure appeared in the smoke: first a vague outline, then a solid shape. It was one of the younger men—one who had followed the clerical path. Aspin had never bothered to learn his name. He looked at Aspin beneath lowered eyelids, as if he was half-asleep.

"May I help you?"

"You may bring the prelate immediately."

The man's eyes snapped open. "Aspin," he whispered. "Wait. I shall fetch him straightaway." The young man vanished from the smoke and was soon replaced by Denrill. The prelate's expression was one of relief mixed with a strong dose of

"I shall not ask where you have been," he said. "The foremost question in my mind at the moment is, do you have the Malan girl?"

"I am with her," Aspin said. It was the truth. He could not honestly say he had the girl, she was not the sort one could control with ease, but he was certainly with her." We are in central Lothan, moving toward the Malgog border."

"What? Your orders were to bring her to us so we could prepare her! She cannot possibly be ready. Doubtless Colin and Yurg taught her to fight, but there is so much more she must learn before she can lead." Denrill clenched his fist as if he were going to shake it at Aspin. "Why," he asked, his puffed chest deflating like a stuck bladder, "would you deviate from a plan that has been so long in the making?"

"I did not deviate from it, Denrill." Aspin was perhaps the only saikur who dared address the prelate by his first name. "She chose this path before I found her, and she will not be deterred." In truth, he had failed to even engage her in anything other than casual conversation. She would not talk with him alone, and abruptly ended the conversation any time he tried to discuss her plans.

"I don't understand any of this." Denrill's voice was tight with exasperation. "You are telling me that she had already set off to reunite the clans when you found her?"

"That is... accurate, though it is an oversimplification," Aspin took a bit of perverse pleasure in Denrill's frustration. "There is too much for me to tell you at this time. Suffice it to say I am with her, and she has chosen her path—one for which she is woefully unprepared, but I assure you, I will do all I can to help her succeed."

"I hope the time will come soon that you can explain this all to me. I assume you experienced the recent event?"

"The event?"

"Freeze you, Aspin! Do not toy with me. I am speaking of the wave of sorcerous energy that, according to our reports, shook all of Gameryah. I assume you did not miss that? Some of us felt it, even at this great distance."

"Certainly not, Prelate. In fact, I was so close to the source that it rendered me unconscious for the better part of a day or more."

"So you know the cause?" Denrill's voice grew soft and he leaned forward, as if Aspin could whisper in the ear of the smoky spectre that hung before him.

"I assume it happened when Shanis Malan took up the Silver Serpent."

The reply had the expected effect. Denrill, who was taking a sip of wine, choked and began hacking. Aspin reached out to clap him on the back before remembering it was only Denrill's image in the smoke. Denrill glared at Aspin while he recovered his breath.

"I declare," Denrill wheezed, "I have half a mind to send as many men as it takes to drag you back here and have you horsewhipped. To the ice with you and your arrogance! You will tell me what I need to know and tell me quickly before your smoke dissipates."

Aspin gave a quick recounting of his pursuit of the Malan girl, her connection with Larris Van Altman, and her recovery of the Silver Serpent. He also told Denrill of Prince Lerryn's similar, albeit failed, search.

"That allays one of my concerns," Denrill said. "You cannot imagine the uproar over both princes of Galdora vanishing during a time of war."

"A time of war?" Aspin sat up straight.

"I see it is my turn to surprise you." Denrill paused, savoring Aspin's surprise. "The news is not good. Kyrin has invaded Galdora. They have not penetrated deep, but are holding the territory they have taken. Much of northeast Galdora is now under Kyrinian control."

Aspin cursed, but did not interrupt the prelate.

"The duchy of Kurnsbur in southeastern Galdora has declared its independence. We have little information at the moment, but the Duke of Kurnsbur is somehow connected to a group of marauding Malgogs who are terrorizing eastern Lothan. The Diyonans have mobilized to protect their border and are threatening to take a hand. And surprise of surprises, what passes for the Lothan army has moved across the border into Galdora. They are doing little more than burning a few barns, but it is the first time Orbrad has shown any sand. The Galdorans are occupied on the Kyrininan front, and are unable to deal with Kurnsbur or the Lothans. King Allar needs his best captain in the field, yet Lerryn is off on a failed treasure hunt."

"I fear I can only add worse news." Aspin grimaced. "I have reason to believe a large force is moving out of the mountains and into western Galdora. I found signs of its passing through the mountains, and Prince Larris confirms that he and his companions actually saw one detachment of the same army. We do not know for certain that they are headed to Galdora, but that is the direction in which they traveled."

"I do not know where I need you the most," Denrill said. "No one is better qualified than you to intercede between Kyrin and Galdora. Do not bother to argue." Denrill held up his hand to quell Aspin's protest. "But if the Malan girl can unite the clans, perhaps that will take some of the pressure off of the south and we can focus on Kyrin."

"As well as whoever or whatever is coming in from the southwest," Aspin added.

"Yes. And that as well." Denrill's eyes took on a faraway cast, but he quickly recovered. "Send Larris home. I don't know what help he will be, but it is something. He needs to be in Archstone right now. We need to find Lerryn. Let us hope your paths cross again."

"Larris will not want to leave. He appears to be quite taken with Shanis Malan."

"His nation is being invaded from all sides. He will see reason." Denrill stood, the top half of his head vanishing from the block of smoke. It would have been amusing were the circumstances not so dire. "The clans must be reunited. See to it that it happens with all due haste."

"I will, as always, do all that I can," Aspin said.

"Aspin." Denrill's voice was like stone. "Be assured, if you ever again wait this long to report to me, you will surrender your cloak. Am I understood?"

"Perfectly." He did not go on because, just then, a commotion was rising from the direction of the camp, drawing his attention. "I must go, Prelate. Forgive me." Without waiting to be dismissed, he sprang to his feet, kicked dirt over the small fire, and dashed back to the encampment.

He had not gone far when a group of riders galloped past him, steel bared and eyes aflame. As he hurried on, he passed more armed men, all running around and shouting confused questions.

Someone kicked the anthill, Aspin mused.

A group of men ringed Shanis' tent, but they made way for him as he strode into their midst. He ducked inside to see Khalyndryn covered in blood, lying on a blanket. Her tunic had been ripped open at the chest. An arrow shaft had pierced her just above the breast. He had seen more than his share of battle wounds, and this was a grave injury.

Rinala looked up from where she knelt, cleaning the flesh around the arrow, and shook her head. The meaning was clear. Her mother and sister were there as well, each holding one of Khalyndryn's hands.

"It did pierce her heart," Rinala whispered. "She did live only a short while. We have no told Shanis yet. She is no in her right mind, I think."

Shanis sat cross-legged a few paces away, with Larris on her right and Hierm on her left. Her ashen face glowed in the dim light. "I couldn't find it," she mumbled. "I tried and it just wouldn't come. Why couldn't I find it?"

Larris caught sight of Aspin. "We were attacked," he explained. "Raided would be more accurate. Arlus has apparently been gathering other disenchanted young men to join him. One of them managed to slip in among us, and when the raid began, he used the moment of confusion to take a shot at Shanis. Khalyndryn saw him and put herself in the arrow's path." He looked at Shanis, who continued to stare straight ahead.

"I couldn't heal her," she whispered. "Sometimes the power just flows through me, but this time..." She shrugged and then her entire body sagged, and she let her head fall onto Larris' shoulder. "Do you know what she said to me? She was lying there in my lap, and there was blood and that... arrow just sticking out of her, and she said, 'I finally found my purpose.' Like saving me from that arrow was her entire reason for being born. And now, when I think about the way I've treated her all these years..."

"You must be strong," Larris said. "You are going to rule the clans, and a ruler may only show weakness in private."

"We're private enough at the moment," Hierm said. "It is only us and my... family." Rinala turned and gave him a wan smile. "I am not quite accustomed to having new relations," he whispered. "So strange."

Aspin knelt in front of Shanis, drawing her gaze to his. "Listen to me. Healing is a difficult thing to master. It requires knowledge and experience that you do not yet have. You cannot do it alone. Please let me help you." Aspin had rarely said 'please' to anyone, but it was imperative that he make a connection with this girl.

She stared into his eyes, that implacable gaze so reminiscent of her father. "For right now, you must help Khalyndryn, if you can." Her voice was desolate, as if she already knew his efforts would be futile. "We will talk later."

"I am sorry, but she can no longer be helped. She is gone." He expected Shanis to break into grief-racked sobs, fall back onto Larris' shoulder, but instead she met his gaze with a blank stare, her eyes void of emotion. "There is, however, something you and Larris must know. I have word from..."

"Not now! I can't..." She sprang to her feet. "Later." She waved away the protest that was forming on his lips. "Larris, I need you." She took the prince by the hand and led him out of the tent.

Aspin watched her go, resisting the urge to follow her. He had never been one to mourn the dead. People lived and people died, and the world did not stop for every minor tragedy. The snows take Shanis and her Malan stubbornness! Of course, she came by it honest, but that did not help matters right now. He needed to tell them about his conversation with Denrill, and he needed to find a way to persuade Larris to return home. That was obviously not going to be easy.

Chapter 18

"Are we almost out of the swamp?" Lerryn scraped the last of the gooey, black mud from the bottom of his boot. The last rays of the setting sun had disappeared over the horizon, and they would soon have to bed down for the night. He would prefer to do it outside this accursed bog, if at all possible. They had not encountered anything else as bad as the leeches, but the need to constantly be on watch during the day for quakewater, poisonous reptiles, and the myriad of other potential perils had put him in a foul temper, and lack of sleep thanks to the biting insects had only made it worse.

"What is that you say?" Heztus looked up at him, mock surprise painted across his face. "Surely you are not in a hurry to leave the hospitality of my lovely home."

"If it is all the same with you, I will be pleased to reach dry land, as it were. I feel damp all the way through. Dry land, a fire, and a bottle of wine will suit me nicely."

"Good news then, Highness. The road to Calmut is just beyond that thicket. We will not precisely be out of the swamp, but the land here is a mix of lakes and swamplands, and not so dangerous as that through which we have just passed. And the road is, as you say, dry. A good place to pass the night. After that, Calmut is not too far."

"That is good news," Hair said. "I..." He stopped as Heztus held up a hand.

The dwarf cocked his ear and frowned in concentration. "Riders are coming."

Lerryn rested his hand on the hilt of his sword. Hair and Edrin moved to flank him while Xaver and Heztus stepped back. As they watched, a squad of Monaghan riders appeared around the corner, reining in at a distance and frowning at Lerryn's party.

"Good evening," Lerryn greeted them in a firm but courteous voice. No reason to be impolite, after all. "Do you travel to Calmut?"

"Aye," the man in the lead replied. He was a long, angular fellow with a braided, red beard. "We be escorting the bearer of the Silver Serpent." His back straightened a little as he said the last, and his voice resonated with pride.

"Do you, now?" Lerryn's emotions were a mix of curiosity, jealousy, and suspicion. He wanted to see this person who had claimed what should have been his. "I should like to meet him." At that, the Monaghan men smirked. "Did I say something amusing?"

"You be seeing for yourself." Another of the men, a young fellow with scarcely any chin whiskers of which to speak, grinned at him. "You come with us." His voice gave the words a sense of both invitation and command. In any case, Lerryn was not about to pass up the opportunity to meet the man who had claimed his prize.

The warriors led them into a crowded encampment. It appeared that the Monaghan had brought everyone: men, women, children, even their elders. Most paid Lerryn and his party no mind, but a few spared curious glances for them as they passed through, doubtless most of them staring at the dwarf Heztus, who ignored them all.

Lerryn took everything in, his eyes searching for the bearer of the serpent. His gaze fell upon a young man seated by a campfire. Lerryn froze at the sight of him.

"Larris," he whispered. What in the gods' names? "Larris!" He shouted. His brother jerked his head around and his face fell as he stared at Lerryn with a stupefied expression. He mumbled something to the person seated next to him, a familiar-looking young woman with red hair. The two of them stood, Larris looking sheepish, and the young woman looking defiant.

"Brother," Larris greeted him, standing up much straighter than courtesy dictated.

"Brother." He folded his arms across his chest and waited for Larris to explain himself. Larris appeared to be using the same strategy, because they waited in silence for one another for an uncomfortably long time. Xaver joined them and stood off to the side, his expression of mild amusement out of place on his normally serious face.

The girl ran out of patience before either of them did. "This is ridiculous. Larris, if you're not going to explain things to him, then I will."

Lerryn remembered her now. The Malan girl, Shanis, the one who should have faced Karst in the finals of the tournament. The girl who, by rights, had not been defeated.

"The Victor," Xaver murmured. He cleared his throat and raised his voice. "Tell us girl, where is the Silver Serpent?"

She answered him with a defiant grimace, reached over her shoulder, and drew a gleaming sword. The image of a serpent was etched in the blade, and the hilt and guard were crafted in the shape of a coiled, open-mouthed serpent.

Just by looking at it, Lerryn could feel its magnificence. It should have been his. "How?" he whispered, involuntarily reaching out for it.

"I wouldn't." The girl sounded friendly, and not the least bit defensive. "You're welcome to try, but so far no one but me has been able to hold it."

Lerryn pulled his hand back and looked over the group that had now assembled. "Royal Blood," he said, looking at Larris. "The Victor." That would be Shanis. Behind her, a broad-shouldered youth rose to his feet. "The Bull." Another young man rose and strode over to stand next to Shanis. It was the Van Derin boy, a fair-haired youth with deep blue eyes. "The Eyes of Sky." He looked around. "I suppose Allyn is here somewhere?"

"And he would be the Archer," Xaver said. "But where is the Golden Mane?"

"What are you talking about?" Shanis' face flushed.

"He is talking about the prophecy." Larris' words came slowly, like the first raindrops in a summer storm. "Despite my skepticism, if not outright disbelief, it seems we have inadvertently managed to fulfill the prophecy." He turned to Lerryn. "Our friend, Khalyndryn, must have been the Golden Mane. She died today."

Lerryn supposed he should offer words of sympathy, but he did not care. He had failed.

"Highness," Xaver began, "I suppose we can take some consolation in the fact that we were correct, at least about the Six."

"But we were the wrong Six." Lerryn shook his head and then looked again at Larris. "I do not suppose you would care to tell me why you chose to embark upon my quest?"

Larris' eyes flitted toward Xaver, then hardened.

"Allyn and I embarked upon our own quest because, as you know, I do not trust Xaver. And, forgive me brother, I had concerns about you bearing the Silver Serpent, considering your…"

"You did not want it in the hands of a drunkard." Icy fury swept over Lerryn, but it melted almost instantly because he knew his brother's words were true. He wanted to protest that he was gaining control over his need for wine, but he knew how pitiful that would sound. Though the words pained him, he knew Larris was right.

"That is not the word I would have chosen. You are far from a drunkard, Lerryn, but you cannot be counted upon to be sober when you are needed the most."

"Says the boy who ran away from home to go on an adventure."

"Says the man who succeeded," Shanis snapped. Her eyes blazed and she looked like she was about to strike Lerryn. "You should have stayed home and let him go on the quest."

"Let it go," Larris said, touching Shanis' arm in a familiar way.

The gesture did not go unnoticed. There was obviously something between the two of them. His noble brother had fallen for a commoner? Their father would be apoplectic.

"As I was about to say, I wanted to find the serpent first. I did not, however, believe in the prophecy. I gathered all the stories and legends I could find, and we set out on our search. Along the way, we joined with Shanis and her companions, and became the Six without ever realizing it. Every time we seemed on the verge of failure, providence nudged us back onto the path. The prophecy was real after all."

"A small comfort to me." Lerryn's mouth was dry. He wanted wine, but he would not give in to the urge, at least not where the others could see him. "So where does this leave us?"

He directed the next question to Shanis. "The prophecy says the Silver Serpent will save the royal line of Galdora. You are a subject of Galdora, yet your current path indicates that you plan to forsake your country in an attempt to become leader of this…" He could not properly call the clans of Malgog and Monaghan a 'nation,' at least not in any true sense of the word.

"There is more than one prophecy." She sounded uncertain for the first time. "The finding of the Silver Serpent also heralds the reuniting of the clans. Too many here have died. Someone must bring them together."

"There is more." A man in a brown robe spoke up from where he sat in deep shadow just beyond the firelight.

Lerryn searched him out. A saikur! How had he not noticed the man until now? He truly was slipping.

"My name is Aspin. As you have doubtless noticed, I am a saikur. I must say, Highness, it is providential that we meet at this time. There is news of which all of you are unaware. I was just about to apprise the others of this when you arrived."

"What do you mean?" Suspicion crept into Lerryn's mind. Saikurs were often of great service, it was true, but they always had their own agendas.

"There are many things of which you are not aware. Please sit down." Aspin motioned for everyone to return to the campfire.

Lerryn motioned for Xaver to join the group at the fireside and instructed the remainder of his company to find a place to bed down for the night. He moved closer to the fire but did not take a seat. Instead, he stood waiting impatiently for Aspin's news.

"I have received word from my prelate, and the news is grave. Your nation is at war. Kyrin has invaded from the north. Meanwhile, Orbrad is making noise along the border, and at least one of your southern duchies is in full revolt. This rebellion might or might not be connected to a pretender in the east who claims to be the true bearer of the Silver Serpent." He paused to let the news sink in.

Lerryn's neck grew hot. Though a matter of concern, war with Kyrin was not a surprise. That particular threat was what had led him to seek out the Silver Serpent in the first place. His stomach sank as he thought again of his failure, but he pushed the thought away. He had more pressing matters now. A rebellion in the southwest? It was unthinkable.

"There is more," Aspin said. "The western border of your kingdom, it is rumored, is also under attack."

"The army we saw in the mountains," Larris breathed. "I'll wager that is who it is." He turned to Lerryn. "While we were in the mountains, we came upon a sizable force of armed men. They did not appear to be particularly well-organized, but there were plenty of them. We debated whether or not we should try to head back to the east and deliver a warning, but... we decided to continue on our quest." He stole a quick glance at Shanis before looking back at Lerryn.

"We have no reliable information,"Aspin said, "but if the rumors are true, the army is headed directly toward Galsbur." This elicited surprised comments from Shanis, the Van Derin lad, and the large boy who had not yet been introduced.

Aspin looked meaningfully from Lerryn to Larris. "I am sure you both understand that this is not a good time for Galdora to be without both of its princes.

Lerryn clenched his fists, drew in a breath, then relaxed. It was a simple exercise that at least permitted him to appear as if his emotions were under his control. "I shall return to Galdora on the morrow. Larris, you shall come with me." He turned to Hierm. "Master Van Derin, I remember you from the tournament. You are a fine swordsman and, if you wish it, I can offer you a place at the academy. In any case, you shall return with me as well."

Shanis and Larris exchanged glances. Lerryn gave it no mind. Obviously, his brother fancied the girl, but that did not matter. Larris had a higher calling upon his life that superseded the desires of the flesh. He was a prince of Galdora, and he would fulfill the obligations of his station.

"And you, Miss Malan. I thank you for recovering the Silver Serpent. As you know, it is prophesied that the serpent and the fate of Galdora are bound together. You shall return with me as well. I know it is unorthodox, but you may have your place at my academy until we determine how and when the Serpent shall come into play."

"She no be going anywhere." Horgris, the clan chief had joined them. Lerryn had met him years before, and he had changed little. He was still a bear of a man. He stood with his hand on the pommel of his sword. "She do be our leader, and she be leading us to Calmut."

"She is a subject of Galdora." It was only with great difficulty that Lerryn kept his temper in check. "She is my subject. Her liege demands her obeisance."

Shanis sprang to her feet and moved to face him. She was tall for a woman, and Lerryn needed only to look down slightly to meet her eye. She stood nose-to-nose with him, glaring at him with an intensity that caught him off guard.

"I am my own person. I go where I choose, and I do as I please."

"And what will you do if I insist?" Lerryn's voice was soft, but she could not miss his meaning. He was suddenly itching for a fight, and this jumped-up girl would do for the moment.

"You no want to try and take her out of here against her will." Horgris sounded like a father counseling an impudent child. "Fine soldier you may be, Your Highness, but you no can best my entire clan."

He was right. Lerryn took another calming breath and forced himself to speak in a reasonable tone, despite his urge to strike her down for her temerity. "Your home is under attack. Your nation is threatened from all sides, and you hold its salvation in your hand. What shall you do? Hide in the jungle and pretend to be a clanswoman?"

For a moment he thought, even hoped, she might draw her sword. Instead, she flashed him a look of pure hatred and stalked off into the forest.

"I will go after her," Larris said. He vanished just as quickly without sparing a glance at Lerryn.

Lerryn turned to Aspin. "Can you not talk sense into her, Saikur? She is obviously too stubborn to listen to me."

"Even if I could, I am not certain which is the most sensible path. The Silver Serpent..."

"Belongs in Galdora. The prophecies say..."

"The prophecies are vague. And of all the prophecies, only one suggests a connection with Galdora. In fact, it actually says that the Silver Serpent...."

"Will mend the broken crown of Galdora. I am familiar with that passage. In any case, our nation is broken. We must have the Serpent."

"And what of our own prophecies?" Horgris growled. "Those of Lothan. We do have been at war for all my life. Galdora, what, a few days? Our prophecies do say the Silver Serpent be going to heal us all. Will bind us together as one. Do my people no deserve peace as much as yours?"

"She is a subject of the crown."

"And she be of our blood." Horgris rose to his feet, quaking with anger. Was everyone going to confront Lerryn today? "And if things do go as I expect, very soon she may wear a crown of her own."

"Your Highness," Xaver interjected. "Forgive me, but unless you intend to capture the girl and take her back in chains, the only thing that matters is what she believes. Perhaps your brother can convince her. He seems to have, shall we say, forged a special connection with her."

Lerryn did not like it. His instinct was to use the power of his station, and force of arms, if necessary, to get what he wanted. But, in this instance, Xaver spoke sense. He looked down at Van Derin and the other boy, who met his gaze with uncertain looks

"Tell Allyn, Shanis, and my brother that all members of Larris' party who remain loyal subjects of Galdora will leave with me in the morning. I shall leave each of you to the consequences of your choice."

He motioned to Xaver, and together they left the gathering. Finding the spot where Hair, Edrin, and Heztus had made camp, he accepted a cup of wine and a bit of bread and cheese before retiring to his tent. He had a long, sleepless night ahead of him.

Chapter 19

"What are you going to do?" There was no challenge in Larris' voice, only sympathy.

"I don't know," she sighed. "It seems that whatever I choose, it will be wrong." Shanis sat on a fallen log, her head resting in her hands. She had been so certain that reuniting the clans of Lothan was the proper things to do, but now she was not certain. Galdora obviously need her. But how could she leave now? Forgetting for a moment that she had vowed to bring the clans together, there remained the fact that so many people were suffering in Lothan. Children were dying. How could she not try to stop it if she had the power?

Larris sat down next to her and put his arm around her. His soothing presence relaxed her.

"What about you? Are you going to go with your brother?" She braced herself for the answer she knew was coming.

"I have no choice. As prince, I am honor- and duty-bound to serve my king and country. I am ashamed of the way I left, and I will not add to my disgrace by failing to be there when my country needs me the most."

Shanis had expected nothing less, though it pained her to think of him leaving her now. She felt tired, confused, and so very alone. All of her life, she had been surrounded by friends and family upon whom she could rely. But she had left her father and Master Yurg behind, and was now losing her friends one after the other. Hierm was married, Oskar spent most of his time with Aspin, Allyn had become a recluse, and Khalyndryn was dead. Larris was all she had left, and now he was leaving her.

"You could come with me," he whispered.

She tried to imagine going back to Galdora with Larris. Before all of this started, she would have loved nothing more than to gain a spot at the academy. Now, that seemed such a childish dream. She realized she had been playing at the sword all her life. Now she was part of something real. And what sort of life could she and Larris have anyway? She was a commoner.

Putting aside her selfish desires, how could she abandon the Lothans? They had followed her based on her promise that she would make them whole again. They were willing to make her their leader. Would it matter to them that the only home she had ever known was in danger, when danger was all they had known their entire lives? She certainly could not tell them she was abandoning them in order to be with Larris.

A memory came unbidden to the forefront of her thoughts, and she remembered the words whispered to her by the serpent as it fought her. It had tried to break her will by making her question herself. Selfish, it had called her, and it had replayed for her a lifetime of choices that benefited none but herself. And how had she defeated it? By affirming to herself that what she now did was not done out of a selfish desire for power, but from a desire to help others, and to do the right thing.

"I am not selfish," she whispered. "Larris, I started out on this course knowing that I was doing the right thing for the right reasons. That has not changed. But if I go with you, I could not be certain if my decision was made out of a desire to help those in Galdora who are in danger, or out of a selfish desire to be with you.

"I have to finish what I have begun here. It is the only way I can know for certain I am acting selflessly. I might regret my choice, but I know in my heart that there is no selfishness in it." She stood, took his hand, and pulled him up next to her. "I don't know much about the power, but I am almost certain that it will never answer to my selfish whims. That probably makes no sense to you, but I need you to trust me."

Larris enfolded her in his arms and drew her close. She laid her head on his shoulder, allowing herself a moment of weakness. A solitary tear fell from her cheek and melted into his cloak. For just a moment, she wanted him to argue with her—to convince her she was wrong. Make her go along with him. It would be so much easier than the path she had chosen. But that was precisely why she could not go with him.

"I cannot fault your decision." His voice was choked with pain. "My heart tells me to stay with you, but what I want and what is right are seldom one and the same."

They stood there in the darkness for a long time, holding each other close, and dreading sunrise.

"You will be safer with your family." Hierm saw skepticism in Rinala's eyes, if not outright defiance, and he hurried on before she had the chance to interrupt. "I do not know what dangers we will meet on the road, and I have no idea when I might see combat." It had all happened so fast. A few hours earlier, they were on their way to Calmut with Shanis, all thoughts of Galdora and the life he had left behind were buried in the deepest parts of his mind. Now he was on his way home. Not just home, but to the prince's academy, then to the army. After that, who knew?

"What do you be talking about?" Rinala stood with her hands on her hips, staring at him as if he were a fool on a festival day.

"You cannot go with me. You are with child. It would be wrong to take you into the middle of a war." He secretly thought it would be a relief to be away from Rinala for a short while, at least. His marriage was another thing that had happened too fast. He was unaccustomed to the constant close presence of another person in his life. He no longer enjoyed any sort of privacy. Besides, the girl was mule headed, outspoken, and much too certain of the value of her own opinions. Then again, he sort of liked those things about her. She reminded him of Shanis. In fact, he had grown quite fond of Rinala. Still....

"Oh, do that be so?" He had heard this tone of voice from women before. It usually preceded bouts of screaming and hurling breakable objects. "You no want me to ride into a war zone? And what do you think I been doing all of my life, Hierm Van Derin?"

She had a point. The girl lived in a society that was constantly at war. And if he should leave her behind, she would still be a woman with child traveling into dangerous territory.

"Don't you want to be with your mother and your family when our child comes?"

"You do be my family now." She moved in close until their bodies almost touched, her expression softening as she reached up to stroke his cheek. She really was quite lovely, if a bit rough around the edges. "A woman of Monaghan do make her home at the side of her husband, wherever that be." Tears glowed in her eyes, and he could see that an unasked question waited there. He rarely understood women, but this time he thought he knew what she was thinking.

"I do want you to come with me." It was an easy admission to make, though he was surprised to realize how much he meant it. "I want to be there when our child is born..."

"You mean when your son do be born!" Horgris, apparently considering this to be sufficient notice of his presence and intent to enter their tent, stepped inside. Another man might have at least apologized for the interruption, but that was not the way of Hierm's new father in-law. Hierm still found his presence intimidating.

"I tried to get her to stay with you," Hierm said. The big clan chief surely would not want his daughter to stray so far from home, especially when he was so eagerly anticipating the birth of his first grandchild.

"No. There be none of that now. Rinala do be a clan chief's daughter, and she know her duty. She do be a strong girl, and you will be needing her at your side." His voice grew husky and he grimaced. "That do be our way."

He did not know what to say. Rinala fell into her father's arms, sobbing. Hierm felt like he was intruding on a private moment between father and daughter. Finally they broke the embrace, and Horgris held her at arm's length.

"You do bring my grandson back to see me soon as you can. And remember how proud your mother and I do be of you. Always."

Rinala smiled and nodded. She gave her father's hand a squeeze and said, "We do be having things to get ready, but I will come to see you and mother shortly."

Horgris nodded and took his leave.

Rinala turned, grabbed Hierm by the back of the neck, pulled his head down, and kissed him soundly. When she let him go, he felt dizzy, but pleasantly warm. She was something.

"I can no wait to see your home and meet your family." Her voice trembled and her eyes sparkled with excitement.

Hierm's stomach sank like a stone dropped into a well. What, he wondered, was his mother going to think of his new bride.

Chapter 20

"Shanis, you must come now!" Larris' voice quavered and his face was pale. He trembled as he reached out to take her hand. "It's…" Words failed him, and his face twisted in… pain, nausea, she did not know what. He let his hand fall to his side, and he turned and hurried away. Surprised and confused, she dropped the last of her breakfast of bread and cheese onto the ground and hurried along behind him.

A crowd milled around an unfamiliar tent. A worried-looking Hierm was there, along with Rinala. Prince Lerryn stood in the center of the group, his arms folded across his chest, looking as though he might, at any moment, cut off someone's head. His traveling companions stood behind him, all save the purple-eyed man whom Larris had told her was a sorcerer and Lerryn's adviser. She could not remember his name, but she recalled his unsettling eyes and aloof manner.

"This is Xaver's tent," Larris said, his voice hoarse. "I think you should see this, but I warn you, it is a grim sight. Steel yourself before you go inside."

Granlor stood at the front of the tent, his expression grave. As Shanis approached, he drew the flap aside and stepped out of the way. The smell that emanated from the tent told her what she would find before she even looked inside: blood and death.

Xaver lay sprawled on the floor, his arms and legs askew like a grotesque parody of a discarded rag doll. His clothing was shredded and his body torn. It was the most revolting thing she had ever seen. His throat was ripped open in an uneven gash, and deep cuts crisscrossed his chest. His palms were sliced as well. All around him was blood: on the floor, on the walls of the tent, on the upended chair. It was positively horrific. She stepped back from the tent, marshalling all her willpower to keep from retching. It was important that she appear strong and resolute in front of the Lothans.

"We think he knew his attacker," Larris said. "Xaver always took... steps to protect himself and his tent at night. He also was capable of defending himself with sorcery if need be, but obviously..." No further explanation was needed.

"So Xaver must have been comfortable enough with whoever it was to let him come close enough to..." she swallowed the bile rising in her throat, "...to kill him. But who could it have been? He knew so few people in the camp."

"We will find the murderer," Lerryn said, pushing through the throng of Monaghan milling about, "and I will deal with him personally. You and your... people will not interfere. I want your word."

"You no be giving orders here!" Granlor stepped toward Lerryn, his hand on his sword. Before the prince could reply, the sound of hoofbeats broke the silence, and shouts arose from all around.

"They be back!"

"They have someone!"

"We be catchin' him!"

A shiver ran down Shanis' back. If the killer had truly been caught, might she now be asked to administer justice? Despite Lerryn's vow to see to the killer himself, he held no power here. Did the Lothans already view her as a leader? Would it fall to her to decide how they would deal with the perpetrator? This was much more complicated than healing, or even fighting. This would involve her deciding someone's life based solely on her judgment. Could she do it?

The crowd gave way as the riders, led by Aspin, cantered up to where she stood. They dismounted and handed their horses over to three young men who led the mounts away. Now she could see whom they had captured.

Allyn, bound and gagged, sat astride a horse, with a Monaghan clansman on either side, half supporting him, half holding him in place. His eyes were wild with crazed fury, and he snarled and twisted against his ropes and his captors. His clothing was caked with dried blood, and spatters of blood marred his battered face and pale hair.

"He killed Hamor!" one of the warriors shouted. "Put an arrow right through his heart, he did. Had it no been for the thick forest, I do think he would have killed more of us before the seeker be puttin' up his magic shield or whatever it was." He shivered at the thought. "He is no one of the clan, so we be bringin' him to you for justice, my lady."

Shanis' heart fell. This was going to be complicated no matter what she decided. Allyn was Lerryn's subject, and Larris' friend. He was her friend, for that matter, and Oskar's. If his captors were to be believed, he had killed Lerryn's vizier, which gave Lerryn the right to dispense justice upon him, but he had also killed a Monaghan, and this was not Galdora.

"It cannot be," Larris whispered, moving toward his friend. "Allyn, tell me what has happened." He reached out to his friend, but Allyn twisted away, still snarling like a feral beast. The Monaghan men wrestled him down from atop the horse and frog-marched him to where Shanis stood. As one warrior knelt to bind Allyn's feet, Lerryn stepped forward, his fists clenched.

"No, brother!" Larris shouted, stepping in front of the larger man and trying to push him back. Lerryn stood stock-still, gazing with hate-filled eyes at Allyn. "Think!" Larris pleaded. "You have known Allyn for nearly all of his life. There must be an explanation!"

"I thought I knew Allyn. We shall hear what he has to say, and then I shall kill him."

"Doesn't seem to have much to say, other than growling." Heztus was trimming his fingernails with his dagger. "I doubt you will learn anything from him. He looks insane to me."

"Perhaps I can help with that." Aspin strode through the crowd. Those who had pressed in close now gave way to him as if touching a seeker was taboo. Oskar, looking like he was about to sick up, followed a few paces behind. Shanis felt for Oskar. He and Allyn had been close. She also did not like that he spent so much time in Aspin's company. He even wore the brown cloak the Thandrylls had given him, making him look like a young seeker himself.

"Hold him tight," Aspin instructed the men who were struggling to keep Allyn from squirming loose, though, bound as he was, he would not go far in any case. "Oskar, do you remember the calming spell I taught you?"

"What?" Oskar looked like he had been wakened from a nightmare. "Oh, yes I do."

"Very good. I want you to use that spell to settle him down so I can question him. Do not stop the spell until I say so. Do you understand?"

"Yes, Saikur," Oskar said, more formally than Shanis had ever heard him speak. He positioned himself directly in front of Allyn and began whispering. Shanis did not recognize the words, but she felt their power. The air around them grew warm, and the serpent mark on her breast burned. Oskar continued the spell and, as his voice grew softer, Allyn's struggles diminished. Finally, he stood calmly, almost in a daze.

Aspin touched Oskar's shoulder, and the young man stepped to the side, still whispering his spell. The seeker took Allyn's head in his hands and gazed into his eyes. His incantation was harsher, more guttural than Oskar's, delivered at a primordial cadence that made Shanis want to squirm away. All around them, everyone had gone silent, watching in rapt attention.

Aspin's raptor-like eyes widened, and sweat beaded on his forehead. "Speak your name," he whispered.

"Which name shall I speak?" The voice that came from Allyn's mouth was not his own but was instead a low, throaty snarl. "Mine or that of the other?"

"Speak your name," Aspin commanded with greater force.

"I shall not," the voice growled. "If you harm this body, you harm only the boy."

"There are other ways of doing harm." Aspin took a deep breath and Shanis felt him drawing power into himself. It was as if a strong wind blew at her back, flowing toward the seeker. As the drawing grew stronger, the air crackled with energy as life force gathered all around.

Shanis was sweating profusely, and her skin tingled. She looked around and saw that no one else seemed to be affected. Just when she thought the very air would shatter from the sheer force of the gathered power, Aspin ceased drawing in. His eyes bulged and his gaze intensified.

"It hurts! Take it away!" Allyn screamed, and this time it was his own voice. "Larris! Make him take it away!"

Larris took a step toward him, but Shanis held him back.

"Tell me your name," Aspin ordered.

"My name is Allyn," he sobbed. "Please kill me. I am evil and should die. Kill me!" He wailed in agony.

"I shall not kill this boy, thereby setting you free. Tell me your name."

"Take it away!" The sinister voice was back. "Take it away and I will tell you my name."

Aspin did not relent, but continued to bear down on Allyn, his eyes burning with intensity.

"Aaaaah!" The voice was weakening. "My name," it croaked, "is Takkas."

"Takkas, by your name you will obey me!"

"I will." The coarse voice sounded resentful, but cowed.

"When did you take possession of the boy?"

"Time holds no meaning for me. I possessed a human named Moggs. I grew weary of him and left his body."

"In the dungeon at Karkwall," Shanis whispered. "All this time Allyn has been under this... thing's control?"

"The boy is stubborn. Even now I reside within him, but I cannot always control him."

"Why did you kill Xaver?" Aspin quavered, but Shanis could tell by his demeanor and posture that it was not from fear, but rage.

"The boy went to him for help in getting rid of me. I regained control of him in time to kill the sorcerer before he discovered the truth."

"Why did Tichris unleash you upon the world?" At the sound of the ice king's name, a collective shiver ran through those assembled.

"You know nothing. Tichris is nothing."

Angry mutters ran through the crowd. Shanis heard whispers of, "Seeker's tricks," and "Devil boy."

"Release me and I will spare the boy. But if you force me from him, I shall destroy him."

"You have not the power," Aspin said. "You gave me your name."

"But what shall you do with me? I am a mere shadow and mist. I shall fly away on the wind. Or perhaps I will take control of this boy," Allyn's eyes locked on Oskar, who blanched but did not falter in his incantation. "He has power and I have knowledge. I shall claim his body and then I shall destroy you. Or better, I shall claim his body and destroy these others. And when you kill me, I shall fly away again."

There was a commotion on the other side of the circle and Magla, the bone woman of the Blue Stag clan, scurried forward, clutching a bleached skull.

"Your Honor," she whispered to Aspin, and held up the skull. Aspin looked startled, but then he smiled and nodded to the woman.

Magla grasped the top of the skull and twisted. A circle of bone popped out like a cork, and she held the grinning skull directly in front of Allyn's face. He shied away, and Takkas' voice became high-pitched as he blathered incoherently.

"Takkas," Aspin said, his voice filled with an air of command that would have been the envy of any king. "In the names of the seven gods, I abjure your control over this man and order you by your own name to come forth."

Allyn and Takkas screamed. Allyn's features blurred, and then it was as if he was being split in two. A corporeal form of roiling gray mist was rent, bit by bit, from his body. Shanis could feel the agony as Takkas was drawn out with excruciating slowness. With a final shriek of rage, Takkas burst forth, floating above Allyn's body which had gone limp. His smoky form was that of a muscular man with the head of a cat. He laid his head back and screamed like a mountain lion. The men holding Allyn leapt back, letting him fall unconscious to the ground.

"By the earth of Dagdar I summon you," Magla spoke. Takkas' smoky form wavered for a heartbeat, and then broke apart and was sucked into the skull, which Magla hastily capped with the circle of bone.

Aspin staggered to the side, and Oskar hastily moved to steady him. Shanis suddenly found herself supporting Aspin on his other side, and together she and Oskar guided him to a stump where he sat down heavily and let his head rest in his hands.

She was overwhelmed by the feat this man had just performed, and the power it had required. There was no longer any doubt. She had to let him teach her.

"What was that?" she whispered.

"A cogarra," Aspin said. "It is a spirit creature of the ice king. There are blessed few in recorded history. They can possess a man almost at will. One who is predisposed to violence or inflicting pain upon others is easily taken. A strong person like Allyn can fight it, but he will always lose in the end. Now we know why he has been keeping his distance since my arrival. I had no idea that was what was wrong with him, but I sensed its presence almost as soon as I delved into his mind."

"And that thing is trapped inside the skull?"

"It is," Aspin replied. "I do not know what we shall do with it, but at least Takkas is contained for the time being." He drew long, controlled breaths, visibly weary. "Allyn will need sleep, and he may be confused when he wakes, but he should make a full recovery."

"Perhaps..." Shanis bit her lip. "Perhaps when you are rested, you can begin teaching me?"

For a moment, the weariness drained from Aspin's face, and he smiled. "I shall be delighted," he said. "But first, as you say, I must rest, or I will be no good to anyone." He laid a hand on Oskar's shoulder, and the young man helped the seeker walk on shaky legs back to his tent.

Shanis felt a pang of jealousy at the sight. Oskar had changed. Aspin had claimed some part of her friend, and there was now a subtle distance between them. A feeling of remorse bit at the back of her throat, and she suddenly longed for everything to be as it had been. She wanted them all to be farm children again. The cares she had once thought so great seemed small compared to what she now faced. She missed...

She cut off that line of thinking with a firm shake of her head and returned her attention to Allyn, who still lay unconscious. Larris knelt beside him, holding his friend's head in his lap, his face awash in disbelief. Lerryn stood over them for what seemed no more than a heartbeat's time, then spun on his heel and strode away.

"I cannot believe we could spend so much time with him and not..." Larris' voice trailed away.

"We knew something was wrong," Shanis whispered. "He was not himself."

"Truth be told, I thought he was jealous of you and me. I never dreamed he was... possessed."

"It does not matter now," she said. "The demon is gone now."

Someone nearby cleared his throat. It was Heztus, the Malgog dwarf who accompanied Lerryn. "I have some herbs in my pouch that will let him sleep, and keep away dark dreams. I can fetch them if you like."

"My thanks," Larris said, nodding to the dwarf, who gave a quick bow and hurried away.

They laid Allyn on a soft bed of furs in Larris' tent. Heztus appeared soon thereafter with a pot of boiling water. He rummaged in his pouch and drew out a pinch of some tiny, green leaves. He crushed them and let them fall into the water. They gave off a minty aroma. He held the pot close to Allyn's head and fanned the smoke toward his face.

"With some herbs," he explained in a soft voice, "I would make a tent over the patient's head in order to concentrate the vapor. This herb is much more delicate." He cupped his hand and appeared to scoop a handful of vapor into Allyn's nose and then fanned the mist toward his mouth, and then hastily drew the pot away.

Allyn snorted and, for a moment, his entire body quaked. Just as suddenly as the tremors had started, they ceased. His body relaxed, and his breathing became deep and regular, and his face relaxed in a peaceful mask of sleep.

"He should sleep all day and through the night, and his dreams will not trouble him." Heztus bowed again, and before they could thank him, he disappeared from the tent.

Shanis gave Larris' shoulder a squeeze, and he smiled a tired smile. "You stay with Allyn," she whispered. "I have some thinking to do."

Chapter 21

The air in the tent reeked of stale wine, dirt, and sweat. Lerryn lay sprawled on the ground, an empty bottle lying next to his open hand. The bedding that had been set out for him lay ignored in the corner.

Shanis grimaced at the sight. Larris had told her about his brother's... problem, but she had never known a drunkard before. Jamin Rhys back home had come home one night too drunk to walk straight, and his wife had dunked his head in the rain barrel until he begged for forgiveness. The women in Galsbur tolerated the occasional overindulgence on the part of their menfolk, but that was all. In any case, a man too deep into his cups would be hard pressed to keep up with the hard life of a Galsburan farmer.

She sighed as she looked down at the prince of Galdora. By all counts, his drinking notwithstanding, he was a great warrior and leader of men. No matter how desperately Shanis wanted to go back to Galsbur, to stand beside her father and defend her home, she knew in her heart she could not. Her destiny lay here. Someone else had to defend her homeland.

She had thought on it all morning. She could return home and possibly help save the people of her village. At worst, she could heal the injured during the battle to come. Or, she could remain here and possibly heal a nation. If she could stop the clan war, how many more lives would be saved? It was the right thing to do. It was the unselfish thing to do.

Now she needed Lerryn.

"Wake up!" She nudged him with her foot. He groaned, but did not otherwise stir. "Get up!" She put her foot on his shoulder and pushed with all her strength.

With unexpected speed and strength, Lerryn grasped her ankle and yanked, dropping her hard onto her backside.

"What do you want?" he grumbled, sitting up slowly and casting a bleary gaze on her. "I was trying to sleep, in case you had not noticed."

"I need you. Your people need you. Have you forgotten the war?"

"They don't need me." He shielded his eyes from the paltry sliver of sunlight that trickled into the tent. "I have made a botch of everything. I am an utter failure."

"Stop feeling sorry for yourself." She had a vague idea that speaking in this manner to a royal was a bad idea, if not outright dangerous, but her temper and Lerryn's current state combined to embolden her. Besides, something told her that what he needed right now was not sympathy. "Yes, you failed in your quest. Yes, you allowed drink to take over your life. Now, what do you plan to do about it?"

"Do about it?" He regarded her in slack-jawed amazement, as if she was a raving lunatic. "What can I do about it? Xaver is dead. You have the Serpent. It is over."

"Nothing is over. Well, Xaver's life is…" She winced. Her mouth sometimes ran faster than her thoughts. "What you can do about it is stand up and fight. I have always heard that you are a fearsome warrior, no matter the drink. There are men outside waiting for you to lead them in defense of our homeland. Forget what is past. Lead them today." She felt as if she was babbling, but something seemed to have gotten through to him. He now wore a thoughtful expression as he fingered the stubble on his cheek. A glimmer of hope sparked inside her, but it was immediately snuffed out as Lerryn sighed and let his chin drop to his chest.

"I need a drink," he muttered, feeling for the wine bottle that he obviously did not know was empty.

Shanis wanted to throttle him. This was her prince? Her supposed liege? She reached for him to give him a good shake, but as she touched him, something deep within her… spoke to her. Her skin tingled, and she suddenly saw Lerryn as if through a tunnel of fog. Everything in her field of vision was cloudy except his face.

Guided by this unseen… instinct, or whatever it was, she placed her trembling hands on his temples. He tried to pull away, but a torrent of icy cold rolled through her, coursing down her arms and into Lerryn. He gasped and went rigid.

Shanis felt the connection between the two of them. Her consciousness flowed into him, and she was suddenly aware of his body. All of his physical hurts, his inner workings, even an awareness of his very thoughts, was open to her. It was the deepest connection to another human being she had ever felt, almost indecent in its intimacy. She knew she should probably be frightened, but overwhelmed as she was by the force that guided her, she simply allowed it to be.

Lerryn seemed… sour on the inside, as if something were fouling his body. The power gathered in his center and slowly expanded, an irresistible wall of something beyond understanding. Lerryn groaned and twisted, but he did not resist. Cold sweat dripped from every pore in his body; his eyes and nose ran, and the air was suddenly filled with the foul odor of his bladder and bowels letting loose.

Shanis was dimly aware of a frightened part of herself that screamed for her to let go of this power before she killed him, but a deep, abiding sense of peace calmed her fear, assuring her that all was well.

Now something else oozed forth from him—a viscous, yellow substance that stank like nothing Shanis had ever smelled. She grimaced, but still did not draw away.

She sensed that something important remained yet to be done.

She let her thoughts flow again, searching his entire being. His body felt... purified. The foulness was gone, yet something about him remained incomplete. The body was whole, but the spirit was broken.

There was something there. Rather, there was an absence of something. In a way which thoroughly baffled her, she understood Lerryn completely, yet his inner self was beyond her comprehension. What she did understand, however, was that in the midst of his soul was a void. It spun like a whirlpool, draining him of his spirit. She could not even fathom what this was, much less what to do about it, but that was a good thing, because the force that had been guiding her simply took over.

The power poured into the void, spinning counter to its relentless depletion of Lerryn's very soul. Lerryn grabbed her wrists and thrashed about in silent agony, but she held on. The power seemed to solidify, filling the empty space. Gradually, the spinning slowed, and finally ceased.

And somehow, she knew Lerryn had been made whole.

Shanis released him and backed away. She knelt there, afraid to move further, afraid to break the silence.

Lerryn did not open his eyes. He inhaled deeply, like a released prisoner breathing the air of freedom for the first time. A trace of a smile grew on his face as he exhaled.

"If you would be so kind as to bring me water and soapstone," he finally said, his eyes still closed, "I should like to make myself presentable before my departure."

"Of course." Standing, she turned and pushed back the tent flap. Clean air filled her nostrils, and the midday sun seemed somehow brighter.

"Shanis!" Lerryn spoke in a firm voice.

She jumped, startled at hearing him call her by her first name. She turned to face him. His eyes were open now, and they radiated strength and something more profound.

"Yes, Highness?"

"I don't know what you did, but thank you."

It was a somber farewell as Lerryn's party departed for Galdora. Rinala exchanged tearful hugs with her family, and even Horgris looked as if he might cry, though he maintained his gruff exterior. Hierm sat astride his horse, looking as perplexed as he had almost every moment since his marriage. He had shared with Shanis his worries about how Mistress Faun would receive her daughter-in-law. She wished she could be there to see it. Faun was going to be irate. The thought raised her spirits and helped numb the pain of Larris' departure. He bade her goodbye with a long, passionate kiss. She had never let him kiss her in front of the others before, and her friends wisely pretended not to notice. Allyn was pale and visibly weak after his ordeal, but he managed one of his roguish smiles as he said his goodbyes. For the first time in months, she saw flashes of the young man she had met so long ago, and was glad. Hair and Edrin, the only remaining members of Lerryn's original six, were returning with him as well.

Oscar had chosen to stay behind, more so that he could continue studying with Aspin than out of any desire to stay with Shanis, she suspected. Heztus had chosen to join them on the journey to Calmut where, she supposed, he would rejoin his clan.

Hierm had promised to get word to Shanis' father, as well as Oskar's and

Khalyndryn's families. Her heart fell as she thought about Khalyndryn. Shanis was certain the Serrils would blame her for taking their daughter away. She hoped her own father, at least, would forgive her for the choices she had made.

Lerryn sat his horse with poise and dignity, exuding a powerful sense of strength and self-assuredness. The healing she had performed upon him seemed to have done more than merely sober him up. She did not know how to explain it, but she had filled a hole in his spirit, and the result was what she saw before her now. Their eyes met. Lerryn gave her a military salute, touched his heels to his horse's flanks, and led his party away.

Shanis watched until they vanished behind the trees, wondering if she would ever see any of them again.

Chapter 22

Karst hated these meetings with his father. The man treated him as if he were still a child, and not the feared leader he was fast becoming in eastern Lothan. As disenchanted Malgogs continued to swell his ranks, and frightened villagers bent the knee, his plan gained momentum. He hated having to slow down for anyone, especially for Rimmic Karst.

The guards outside his father's tent were both familiar to him, having watched him grow up. They bowed to him, though not as respectfully as he thought he deserved. Karst ignored them, pushed back the flap, and entered the tent, followed by Jakom, a disgruntled Malgog whom he had appointed his bodyguard.

Duke Rimmic Karst sat poring over a map spread out on a table in the center of his tent. Without looking up, he motioned for his son to take a seat. After a long wait, he finally raised his head.

"You have not reported to me in some time," Rimmic said, before returning his attention to the map, "which is why I felt it necessary to come to you. I expect that you will not let it happen again."

Jakom tensed and inhaled sharply at what he obviously perceived to be an insult to his leader. A dismissive wave from Karst settled him.

"I have sent messengers every week, Father. If some did not get through…" He shrugged. It was a lie, but he did not care if his father believed it or not. He would need his father a while longer yet, but not forever.

"So give me the report now," his father said, finally giving him his full attention. His stare was as hard as granite.

"I estimate that we control half of the Malgog lands- the equivalent of the eastern quarter of Lothan." Of course, that control had not been too difficult to achieve, as most of the able-bodied Malgog had gone to some place called Calmut.

"And the Diyonan border?"

"Stable at the moment. We have had a few skirmishes, but nothing to speak of. Now that they know we are here to stay, and have no intention of leaving, they seem content to let us do as we please, provided we do not cross into their lands. They patrol the border, but no longer cross over into our territory."

"That is satisfactory for our purposes," Rimmic said. "And the river?"

"We control almost all of the Igiranin." Karst continued on as his father arched an eyebrow at the word 'almost.' "As we go farther south, and thus closer to the sea, the way grows more difficult. It is a dense jungle, and we are finding it nearly impossible to root out the Malgog there. They know the land better than we do. They can hide with ease and ambush us without warning."

"Then do not try to root them out. Bring them into the fold instead."

Pedric frowned. "It amounts to the same thing."

"It most certainly does not." Rimmic folded his fingers together and looked at his son with an expression of exaggerated patience. "It is the difference between taming an animal and breaking it. Until you understand that, you will not be an effective leader."

Karst bit his lip, reminding himself again that he needed his father's support and resources. The lectures and chastisements would not be forever. He did, however, regret letting Jakom come along. Letting one of his followers witness him being lectured by his father did not strengthen his standing. Of course, Jakom had been one of his first volunteers, and the man was one of his most devoted followers.

"I suppose we could build rafts and send men downriver to negotiate with the Malgog who live there. Perhaps we could purchase right of passage on the river and then proceed from there. I will need gold for that, though."

"Gold? Bah! Think, boy! What use do the Malgog have for gold? Their cities are abandoned and fallen to ruin. They have no commerce, save barter. Give them the things they need: food, tools, blankets. Show them that their lives will be better if they are with us than against us."

"And if that is not successful?" Karst understood the wisdom in his father's advice, but he could not bring himself to admit it.

"Unless you make a complete botch of it, I have every confidence that our efforts will bear fruit. I realize some of your followers are... zealous, and follow us only because we offer them an opportunity to exercise their more... animalistic tendencies at times. They will not do for this job, so choose your envoys with care. Once the river is ours to safely travel, we can establish ourselves and work on extending our control. Now, how stands the west?"

"We have met with little resistance. So many of the clans have traveled to this Calmut that few remain to resist us. We could march all the way to Calmut virtually unopposed if we wished, but what would be the point? We have what we want: firm control of the Igiranin River and the land surrounding it." In fact, Karst now controlled an area larger than his home duchy of Kurnsbur. "We do not have sufficient manpower to risk overextending ourselves, so I have chosen the most defensible positions and established a western border of sorts. Of late, I have been focusing on maintaining order and making incursions to the south."

"The incursions shall cease," his father said, "in favor of negotiations. You were wise, however, to establish a definite, sound border. We have all the land we need, save the southern stretch of the river. Access to the sea will be important for commerce."

Karst hated that a compliment from his father lifted his spirits. So much of his life he had received nothing but criticism from the man, and he had not entirely broken the habit of trying to please him.

"At long last, Kurnsbur shall once again be a free land." Rimmic stared off into the distance, as if seeing that land before his eyes. "As it should be."

Karst was about to take his leave when Rimmic's eyes refocused, and his gaze snapped back to Karst.

"One other thing." He took a folded piece of parchment from the table and handed it to his son. Karst noted the family seal stamped into a wax circle. "Give these instructions to Malaithus. He is to be High Priest of Kurnsbur. Along with restoring order, we shall be instituting a new religion."

"What? You want to bring the Galdoran way of worship into…"

"Wrong. The people of Kurnsbur once worshiped Arthos, the god of the hunt. We shall reinstate that worship. You have in your hand instructions for basic prayers, rituals, and items for worship. Begin with those most loyal to you, and proceed from there." He paused, looking Karst in the eye. "It is of the utmost importance that you do this. Do you understand?"

"I understand." In fact, Karst did not understand at all. Well, he understood what he was to do, but the point of it was beyond him. He supposed it did not matter. Let the people mumble a few prayers and sacrifice the occasional animal. He had greater concerns. "Is that all?"

"That is all. You are dismissed."

Karst bowed, hoping his father did not notice his reddened cheeks. Dismissing him like a common servant! He maintained his composure as he left the tent, returned to his horse, and rode away. His time would come.

Chapter 23

"Tell me again about the way in which you heal people." Aspin was supposed to be teaching Shanis about sorcery and magic, but it seemed he was spending more time trying to understand her than teach her.

"I do not know how I do it," she said. "Sometimes it does not work." She paused, thinking. "The times it does work, I sort of reach my mind into the sword, and it is like a channel opens. What is inside the sword flows through me and into the person I am healing. Sometimes I know exactly what needs to be done, although I don't know how I know that, and I guide the power. Other times, the sword seems to know what to do on its own, and I am merely the vessel. That is what happened with Lerryn. I don't think I had anything to do with it at all, save being the one who transferred the power into him."

"And what do you actually do to someone when you heal him or her?"

"I don't know how to explain it exactly. I search them, understand them somehow, and the power… does what it needs to do."

"No, that is not how it works." Aspin shook his head. "You describe opening a channel; that is how sorcery works. The sorcerer opens himself to the power drawn from the life force all around him. Power flows through him, and he redirects and releases it."

"So, you are saying the Silver Serpent is a vessel for sorcerous power?"

"In principle, there is no such thing as sorcerous power. We are merely vectors for the energy that exists in all life." He raised his hand to cut off her protest. "I understand your question, though. I first believed the sword to be such a repository, but what you have told me indicates that I am mistaken. The sorcerer merely gathers life force and exerts it against an object. It can move things, even destroy them, but it cannot heal."

"But you can heal. I saw you."

"Yes, but healing is done by magic, not by sorcery. It is a thing of the gods."

"I thought it was all the same."

Aspin sighed. "I am sorry. I am usually a much more patient teacher." Sitting on the other side of the fire, Oskar snickered, but the saikur ignored him. "I grow frustrated when I am unable to comprehend something." He also had been teaching Oskar for some time now, and he occasionally forgot what he had taught Oskar, but had not yet taught Shanis. More than once he had chastised her for forgetting something he believed he had already told her, only to realize he had taught it to Oscar. Rather than being put out, however, it seemed to be of comfort to her to realize that seekers, as she still called them, were not as perfect as many made them out to be.

"All magic is prayer. You do know what prayer is?" Shanis rolled her eyes, so he continued. "A spell is merely a personal plea to the gods, which the gods answer. The result is what we call magic." He raised his hand again, cutting off another potential interruption. "There are many ways to draw the gods' attention: prayers, sacrifices, rituals. You make your request and the gods grant it. Only their power and... tractability limit what can be done. But gods are whimsical beings, oh yes. Priests might pray all day and not get an answer, while someone else says a short prayer and gets an immediate response."

"So how can you make sure your magic works? If it is all subject to their whims?"

"That truly is the question, is it not? Somewhere along the way, no one can say how long ago, someone noticed certain prayers, always said with precisely the same words and in the exact same way, always drew a like response. Some wise cleric wrote the prayers down and they became the first magic spells. Over time, our knowledge of spells has increased. Some saikurs devote their entire lives to gathering spells from other lands and cultures. So you see, magic is essentially nothing more than reciting a prayer which we know will get a response.

"Why do some prayers always get a response?" Shanis was an inquisitive student, though she argued more frequently than he would have liked.

"As to that, we can only speculate. But I feel confident of the answer. Imagine you are a god. You have access to the prayers of all of your adherents. In fact, you hear every prayer uttered by each and every one of your worshipers." He smiled as Shanis shuddered at the thought. "Exactly. You would spend all of your time answering prayers. It would consume every moment of your existence and you likely still could not answer all of them. But you cannot simply ignore prayers, or your worshipers lose faith in you, and a god's worshipers are his power."

Shanis exchanged glances with Oskar, who made a placating gesture and inclined his head toward Aspin. Her inquisitiveness had the unfortunate effect of drawing Aspin off of the subject at hand if he and Oskar did not rein her in.

"That is another lesson for another time," Aspin said. "At any rate, it is believed that the gods have, if you will, effectively closed their ears to most prayers. In the case of certain spells, though, it appears that humans have found the precise wording and cadence to speak to the gods on a subconscious level. That is why a spell must be spoken perfectly, not only in wording, but in pacing, pitch, and cadence. Of course, one cannot perform great feats through spells; for that you need to draw the immediate attention of the god. But the properly trained magician can work wonders. You see, while sorcery is truly little more than hurling energy at a target, to do magic is to do the work of a god. That is why sorcery can only destroy, but magic can make whole."

"You told me before that not everyone has the ability to be a sorcerer. Can anyone be a magician?"

"Theoretically, yes. Anyone with a disciplined mind who can learn and perfectly recite the spell can perform magic."

"But I don't know any spells," she protested. "How did I heal when I don't know magic?"

"Could you have learned some sort of healing spell when you were very young and, buried it in your memory?" Oskar suggested, though he sounded doubtful. "Or perhaps there are spells stored inside the sword?"

"That is not possible." Aspin shook his head. "Power, raw energy, those can be stored if you have the proper vessel. Spells are words, not powers to be stored. Shanis is drawing power in the manner of a sorcerer, but the power she is drawing works in the manner of magic. It is most confounding."

"If healing is of the gods, and the sword allows me to heal, then might it be possible that the gods made the sword for that purpose?"

"I cannot say," Aspin replied truthfully. "I simply do not know."

They made camp early that evening. Heztus had advised Shanis that the land ahead was marshy, and adequate places for an encampment would be difficult to find until they reached Calmut. The distance was not far, he assured her, but the going would be slow.

She could not decide if this was good news. On the one hand, she was eager to get to Calmut and face whatever challenge lay ahead. On the other hand, everything had happened too fast. She now wondered if her vows to unite the clans and stop the killing were merely another product of her rash nature. She still knew little about what she could do, and absolutely nothing about why she was able to do it. What if she was not ready for the challenge she would face at Calmut?

Her slumber was fitful, as it so often had been. The darkness pressed in upon her, embracing her in its sinister arms and dragging her down into disturbing dreams. She struggled against its irresistible force, fighting to escape its clutches.

The dreams carried her along dark tunnels of stone that seemed vaguely familiar. She was dressed in fine silks and escorted by a grave-faced young man who would not meet her eye. In a room of pulsating blue light, she knelt before a stone altar. She mouthed words, and she could almost understand what she was saying, but the meaning slipped away. She raised her head and all was pain. She felt her sword ripped away from her...

No! That was not part of the dream! She sat bolt upright, her eyes searching the darkness. Silhouetted against a faint slice of starlit forest, a figure loomed above her, a knife clutched in his upraised hand. She cried out and twisted to the side as he struck. The knife pierced the blanket where her head had lain only a moment before. Her legs were tangled in her blanket, but she struck out with her fist, catching her assailant in the temple. He grunted and stumbled back a few steps before regaining his balance. She frantically struggled to extricate herself from her tangled bedding, all the while waiting for him to strike again with the knife.

Instead, the man ducked down, grabbed something, and sprang from the tent. She finally pulled the last of her blankets away and leapt to her feet. She was now aware of noises outside of her tent: sounds of combat, cries of alarm, orders being shouted, and the clatter of hoofbeats.

She reached for her sword, which she kept by her bedside, but she could not find it. Kicking aside the blankets she had flung on the floor, she searched with her hands across the dark floor – nothing. As her eyes adjusted to the dim light, a feeling of cold resignation spread through her. The light streaming through the slice in the canvas at the back of her tent revealed what she feared to be true. The man had stolen the Silver Serpent.

She freed her belt knife from its sheath and hurtled through the hole in her tent. She was determined that someone would pay.

The night air was cool on her sweaty skin. Her bare feet seemed scarcely to touch the ground as she dashed into the middle of camp. Already the fighting seemed to have abated, and the faint sound of receding hoofbeats told her she was too late.

"Do Shanis be all right?" Horgris called from somewhere up ahead.

"I'm fine," she called back, not trying to keep the bitterness from her voice. She let her hands fall to her sides as she moved toward the sound of his voice. The big Monaghan chief emerged from the darkness, followed by a cluster of angry-looking warriors.

"Who was it?" she snapped.

"It was Arlus and some of the others who abandoned us when we did make you leader," Horgris growled, his head swiveling as if he might spot some new foe upon which to vent his rage.

"Clanless," Granlor muttered. He spat on the ground as if to get the foul taste of the word out of his mouth.

"How did they get through?" Shanis demanded.

"No one did get through." Granlor frowned and cocked his head. "They did try to get to our horses down on the far end of the camp, but they no succeeded."

"One man got through," she said. "The attack was a diversion. He came into my tent."

"But he no hurt you, did he?" Horgris stepped closer and peered intently at her.

"No," she said, "I am fine. But he stole my sword."

Chapter 24

Her frustration grew with every day they spent in pursuit. Three days, she thought, wasted. The Hawk Hill and Three Oaks clans had each provided one of their finest trackers: Granlor from Hawk Hill, and Gendram from Three Oaks. Heztus, Aspin, and Oskar had come along as well. They were six again, for good or ill, and she hoped that number would again lead them along the proper path.

Unable to track in the dark, they had been forced to give their quarry a night's head start, though travel in this tangled land was so difficult that Arlus and his followers could not have gained much of a lead. Nonetheless, she feared they were not gaining much ground at all.

The trail they followed divided, with some of their quarry heading north in the direction of Galdora, and the remainder turning east. Though reluctant to split up their group of six, she set Granlor and Gendram to following the northern trail, while she, Oskar, Aspin, and Heztus continued east. She was pleased to discover that Heztus was as good a tracker as she was, perhaps better, given his familiarity with the land.

She believed they were on the right track. The men who had headed north had made no effort to hide their passage. The trail she followed was not so obvious. Already they had come across places where the men had either ridden up streams, or dismounted and changed direction, leading their horses across hard-packed ground in order to throw off pursuit. They had also laid false trails and sometimes simply erased their tracks. She did not mind. She was certain that the time the men had spent trying to hide their passage far exceeded the time it took her and Heztus to pick up the path again whenever it vanished.

She had to recover the sword. It would be of no use to anyone other than her, but she needed it not only for the power it provided, but because of what it symbolized. Now, she had only the serpent branded over her breast to identify her as the one chosen to unite the clans; that would not convince anyone.

"Where do you think they are taking it?" Oskar asked.

"To the pretender, most likely," Aspin said. "What better way to prop up a false claim than to carry with him the very proof people expect?"

"I suppose the pretender could wear it, as long as he is careful not to touch the hilt," Oskar mused. "Perhaps that would be enough. He only needs people to believe he is the rightful one. In any case, keeping it away from Shanis helps the pretender's cause."

"I must confess, I never thought someone would try to take it." Shanis still could not believe it was gone. A part of her wondered if she ought not be relieved? No sword, no burden. She could return home to be with her father, and perhaps with Larris. But she knew that to be her own selfish nature rearing its ugly head. And even if she was tempted to give up and go home, her anger at the thieves' temerity and her desire for retribution overwhelmed any desire she had to go her own way.

Oskar turned to Heztus. "You are a Malgog. Do you know anything about this pretender?"

"A man. An outlander like yourself," Heztus said. "He has gained many followers among my people. At first it was discontented young men, troublemakers mostly. As he grew in power, some villages bent knee for safety's sake. Others actually believe he is the one. Of course, with most of Malgog headed to Calmut, he has faced little resistance. He now controls nearly all the eastern portion of the kingdom—everything north of the Black Mangrove Clan's lands from the Igiranin River east to the Diyonan border. Of course, that tells you nothing about the man, only the circumstance. In any case, he seems to draw the vilest and most sadistic to his cause. I have no sympathy for the traitors who have bent knee to him."

"People are starved for peace," Shanis muttered. "I cannot fault them for that."

"But if he gets the Silver Serpent, he could cement his hold on the east." Heztus said. "Does that not bother you? Your destiny is to unite the clans"

Shanis sighed. "I don't care about destiny. The only reason I haven't thrown that frost-blighted sword into the nearest lake and gone my own way is that I want to put an end to the suffering." She turned to meet Heztus' eye. "If this pretender, whoever he is, helps bring peace, it would not be the worst thing to ever happen to the Malgog, would it?"

Heztus hesitated. "Of course not, but in order to bring peace to the rest of the land, the clans must believe that you are the chosen one. Without the sword..."

"But they have to believe her!" Oskar clenched the reins of his horse in a white-knuckled grip. "Clan chiefs have seen her with the sword. They know who she is and what she is."

"But others have not seen her." Aspin's voice was serene, but his eyes were flinty. "And there is little, if any trust in Lothan. If Shanis appears in Calmut without the Silver Serpent, the kingdom could remain fragmented. In fact, the east might be the only stable region in the entire realm."

"I fear that it could be worse," Heztus said. "We Malgog have fought one another just as fiercely as we have fought the Monaghan, and the same is true of them. Now, the Monaghan appear to be uniting behind Shanis. If the Malgog unite under this pretender…"

"It will no longer be skirmishes between clans, but an all-out war between two tribes," Aspin finished. "Meanwhile, Orbrad sits back and watches his kingdom bleed." His face was unreadable, but cold certainty filled his voice. "You have a good mind, Heztus. I am glad you have come with us."

The dwarf said nothing, but Shanis thought she saw a shadow of a smile on his face.

Shanis bit her lip, feeling her frustration turn to rage. It roiled inside her. How had she come to this point? All her life, she had wanted to be a soldier, to use the sword as she had been taught. But seeing the effects of war upon the clans of Lothan had changed that. She did not want to fight; she wanted to heal. And now, despite her best efforts, she found herself far from home in vain pursuit of the one thing that might help her fulfill what she now believed to be her destiny. But even if she did manage to recover the sword, she still did not know how to use it. Not properly, anyway. What if she did recover the sword, only to fail when called upon to use it?

"I should have gone home," she muttered.

"Shanis…" Oskar began.

"I should have gone home to help protect our families. I am neither a healer nor a leader. I am a fighter, though the thought of war turns my stomach. At home, at least, there is a clear right and wrong. Our families are in danger, and here we are riding through the gods-know-where, chasing after a sword I'm not sure I can use. I should let this pretender unite the clans. The end result would be the same, would it not? That is all that matters."

A reflective silence hung in the air as everyone took in her words.

"You truly mean it, don't you?" Heztus looked taken aback. "You don't want to conquer Lothan."

"Of course not." Shanis could not keep a touch of scorn from her voice. "All of this… everything happened by accident. I am no one special, and I have no great ambition in life, save to never again have to look upon the face of a dying child."

"So tell me who you were before you became the great hope of Lothan." This was the most interest Heztus had shown in her since they had met.

Shanis smiled despite herself. "A farm girl who wanted to be a soldier."

"You have come to the right place, then. There is plenty of fighting to be done here, and sometimes the women even fight."

"I have done very little fighting since I left home, yet I already want no more of it. Learning the sword, dueling, I realize now it was all a game to me. A duel was a contest of skill rather than preparation for harming another person."

"Putting a blade through someone is much more personal." Aspin looked away as soon as he said the words, but there was something in his face that led Shanis to believe that perhaps the seeker's comment went much deeper than the subject at hand.

"Well, there's no putting the milk back into the goat." Heztus regarded her with keen interest. "You have come too far to turn away now. You realize that, do you not?"

Shanis nodded. "I tend to say what is on my mind…"

"And only later does she actually think about whether or not what is on her mind is a good idea or bad," Oskar added.

She did not have to look at Oskar to know he was smiling. She could hear it in his voice. A touch of her friend's banter was a welcome comfort in this desolate place.

"If you are not abandoning us," Heztus said, "then what is your plan for bringing us together?"

"Nothing firm," she admitted. Since leaving home, everything that had happened to her had happened by chance. She had taken for granted, she supposed, that everything would continue to do so. The theft of the sword had taught her differently. "I need to understand your people before I can help them." Out of the corner of her eye, she thought she saw Aspin nod in approval. "Can you teach me about them?"

Heztus chuckled. "How much time do you have?"

"As much time as it takes."

Chapter 25

"My Lord," Danlar said. "There are some Monaghan here who wish to see you."

"Monaghan?" Karst sat up straight. "What do they want with me?"

"They say they come in peace. They have encamped at a respectable distance, no effort to hide their presence, and sent only three men. They are all unarmed except for… well, you will have to see."

"Fine. Bring them to me." Karst waved him out and exhaled deeply. What could Monaghan want from him? His efforts to gain control of the last remaining stretch of river had not been entirely rebuffed, but neither had they been particularly successful. The Black Mangrove clan, which made its home in the southern salt swamps seemed to prefer isolation. Karst's promises, sent through envoys, of peace and prosperity had made little impression upon them. They also seemed to place little value on material possessions, so trade or bribery was ineffective. They wanted nothing more than to be left to their own devices. Perhaps his father was wrong, and they would have to resort to force. If so, it would be a difficult, if not impossible, task to root out those human swamp rats.

He gazed out through the open window at the ruins of what had once been a Malgog city called Salgo. He had taken for his headquarters one of the few structures that remained standing. Located near the westernmost edge of the territory that was now under his control, Salgo had become his center of operations. He had put many of his new subjects to work clearing away two generations worth of uncontrolled jungle growth. Soon they would begin rebuilding the crumbling wall that had once surrounded this place. What better way to solidify his control than to set up a permanent capital? When the wall was rebuilt, this place would be as defensible a location as he could want.

He caught sight of the Monaghan men approaching under close guard. They did not wear the odd clothing with criss-crossed lines that identified their respective clans, and their beards had been trimmed short in the Galdoran style. As they entered the room, their eyes fell on Karst, and each gave a bob of the head that passed for a bow, but only barely. No more respect than what was necessary to meet the requirements of basic courtesy. He gritted his teeth, but returned the nods with one even less perceptible.

"Your Lordship." The speaker was a tall young man. His golden hair did not quite hide the scar that ran from mouth to earlobe on the left side of his face. "My name be Arlus. Once of the Monaghan, but now clanless. We be bringing you a gift." He produced a long, narrow object wrapped in a saddle blanket.

"What is that?" His voice was more severe than he intended. He did not care about being rude to these men, but he did not like sounding as though he had been taken by surprise.

The man tugged back the edge of the blanket to reveal an exquisite sword hilt. It resembled the head of a snake. A shaft of sunlight twinkled in its sinister jeweled eyes.

"This do be the Silver Serpent. We did steal it right out from under her nose."

Karst reached out to touch the hilt, but Arlus' words suddenly registered. "Did you say her?"

"Aye. Disgraceful how our clans have taken to following an outlander woman. Shanis Malan be her name."

The name was familiar. Where had he heard it before? And then it struck him. The girl from the tournament back in Galdora! The one who had shown him such disrespect, and whose disappearing act just before the final match had deprived him of a portion of the glory that was rightfully his. How had he forgotten that name even for a moment?

Karst's head swam. He could not keep his thoughts in the moment. Images burst forth one after the other. The image of the big, red-haired girl was as clear as if it had been only days since she had confronted him when he had beaten that fool farm boy in a fair fight. She had the audacity to want to fight him. He could not forget the challenging looks she had thrown his way throughout the tournament. And then she had fled before he could put her in her place.

"My Lord? Are you well?" Danlar reached out a hand as if to steady him.

"I am fine." Karst pushed the man's hand away. "I know this Shanis Malan." He turned his attention back to Arlus. "And she claims to be the bearer of the Silver Serpent?"

"Aye. She did arrive at the Hawk Hill settlement with this sword and a mark upon her breast. They believe she do be the one."

"And you do not?"

Arlus shook his head. "She do have the mark, and she did heal some, but we hear she do have a seeker with her. Could he not have done the magic? Maybe she do his bidding. And if she do be the one, how is it that we took the sword so easily?"

Karst had little idea what a seeker could or could not do, but he kept his silence. Arlus' objections, whether true or not, could be very useful.

"What exactly do you want from me?"

"I did hope you were a Lothan, but no matter. We do want to join you. We will no be ruled by an outlander girl, and certainly no by a seeker's puppet. I do no believe that the clans will accept her without the sword. If you go to Calmut bearing the Silver Serpent, and she do arrive with no more than a mark on her chest and a seeker pulling her strings…"

"What happens at Calmut?" He hated asking the question. He never liked revealing that he did not know something, but curiosity got the better of him.

"It do be where kings are crowned. They do submit to the Keeper of the Mists, and be accepted or no."

"So if this Keeper of the Mists accepts Shanis Malan, what happens then?" His heart was racing now.

Arlus shrugged. "Most will follow her, but some are no superstitious enough to believe in the clan witches' tales. We will no follow her."

Karst nodded. Yes! This could be the answer. He could get his revenge against Shanis Malan and gain control of all Lothan in one blow.

"Danlar, how far is it to Calmut from here?"

"A day's hard ride, perhaps. But, meaning no disrespect, your father said…"

"Well, you have given disrespect whether you intended to or not. My father is not here. In any case, he would not want me to pass upon the opportunity to take control of all of Lothan. Give me that." He reached for the sword.

"I would no…" Arlus said, stepping back.

Fire and ice filled his veins the moment his hand closed around the hilt. He gasped and staggered back, releasing his grip on the sword.

"I did try to warn you," Arlus said. "One can no touch it, save the girl. Anyone else tries to take hold of it, and…" He held his hands out, palms upraised.

"What good is it to me, then?" he snapped. "It is useless to me if I cannot even hold it."

"I would not say that, M'Lord." He had not noticed Malaithus join their group. "It is still a symbol of power— your power if you are the one who bears it. You may leave it in its scabbard and wear it slung over your shoulder where everyone can see and recognize it. The girl can hardly call herself the bearer of the Silver Serpent when you possess it."

"I suppose that is something." Karst pursed his lips. "Why are you smiling?"

Malaithus was grinning like a wolf in the sheepfold. "I was thinking. I have traveled far and wide, and learned many a story and song, and I have heard tell of many a magical artifact that will answer only to its rightful owner… until," his eyes gleamed, "that owner dies."

Karst grinned. "I think we should find out if you are correct, Malaithus." He now lifted the sword by its sheath and slung it across his back. It felt almost weightless, or perhaps it was buoyed by his happiness. "You will guide me to this place?"

Arlus nodded.

"Very well. Danlar, assemble my guard. We are going to Calmut."

Chapter 26

"Do you think we are safe in returning to the road?" Allyn whispered, peering off into the foggy hills. His personality had been slowly coming to the fore since he had been cleansed of the spirit that possessed him, but he was still decidedly jumpy and much more suspicious than he had been before.

"I believe so." Lerryn stroked his chin. "We are well past Karkwall, and rumors of raiding parties notwithstanding, I doubt Orbrad has extended his reach much beyond what it once was. Likely he raised his gates and armed his city walls the moment word reached him that the bearer was gathering the clans." The troops' absence, as well as that of the clans who had gone to the gathering, had made for a fast return trip. Nonetheless, he had insisted on giving Karkwall a wide berth as they made their way back to Galdora.

The muted thuds of hoofbeats on soft earth drew his attention as Hair came riding out of the forest up ahead, where he had been scouting. His eyes were wide and his face strained.

"Highness, there are soldiers ahead."

"How many?" Lerryn was already considering their options. They were too small a group to make fighting a prudent choice, though a part of him itched for combat. Since Shanis had... cleansed him, he supposed it should be called, all of his instincts were sharper, his mind clearer. He was eager to face an opponent and see what this newly-whole body could do.

"Forty that I saw, but they likely..."

"Have already sent out scouts," Larris interjected. He rode behind Lerryn, along with Hierm, Edrin, and Rinala."

"You do not think we can slip around them?" Lerryn asked, turning his attention to his brother.

"Considering one of them just spotted us, I would say no." Larris indicated with a nod of his head a lone figure approaching them on horseback.

Before anyone else could react, Allyn had drawn back his bow and was taking aim.

"Stop!" Lerryn shouted. "I know this man!" He put heels to his horse and trotted toward the rider, who raised a hand in greeting. When they met, they clasped hands.

"Korlan, what are you doing here?" Lerryn was stunned to see one of the White Fang, his elite unit, in northern Lothan.

"Looking for you, Highness. Your father sent us personally. Told us not to come back at all if we did not find you." He then spotted Larris and his eyes widened. "And Prince Larris! This is most unexpected."

"Our father did not send anyone looking for me?" Larris' voice was unreadable.

"We... we did not know you were missing. You have not been at court, but your father told everyone you were away on his orders."

"Doubtless he did not want it known that both princes of Galdora had disappeared. I can think of a few relatives who might have tried to take advantage of that situation." Lerryn still felt foolish to have gone off on his quest, and Larris had admitted to feeling the same way. "What can you tell me of the situation at home?"

"Captain Tabars is the only one who knows the full of it. Let us join him, and I shall tell you what I can as we ride." Korlan led them on a winding route down through the forested hills, talking as they rode. "Kyrin has invaded in the northeast. They control two duchies and the war stands at a stalemate. It is taking all we have to fight on that front, since no other nations have come to our aid."

"So we have heard." Lerryn muttered.

In the southeast, Duke Rimmic has declared Kurnsbur to be its own nation. He has..."

"Rimmic Karst?" Lerryn could not believe what he was hearing. Aspin had told him about a revolt in a southern duchy, but if he had mentioned Karst, it had slipped

Lerryn's wine-addled brain.

"Karst?" Hierm frowned. "Do you mean…"

"Pedric Karst's father. I curse the day I ever met that useless boy." If Lerryn had been eager for a fight earlier, now he truly wanted to take out his frustrations on someone. "So, the Duke of Swine is founding a nation of pigs. Doubtless they shall become the leading nation in Gameryah, what with the lack of adequate farmland and trade routes."

"Your father apparently feels the same way. He is content to let Rimmic play king until the other wars are over."

They topped a rise and below them saw a cluster of riders. In the center rode a blocky soldier with dark hair sprinkled with gray. He wore three silver bands around his forearm.

"Tabars!" Lerryn called. The man looked up at him and, for a moment did not seem to recognize him. Then a broad grin split his face and he hailed his prince. The other soldiers recognized Lerryn as well, and a cry went up that drew the men who had been scouting back from the forest.

Lerryn rode to his officer's side, where they clasped hands in greeting. Tabars stared into Lerryn's eyes, his brow furrowed. "Is something amiss?"

"No, Highness, but you look different somehow. I can't put a finger on it."

Lerryn knew exactly what the difference was, and he was pleased to hear it, but he was not going to proclaim before these men that a girl from Galsbur had cleansed him of drink. Let them discover on their own that he no longer had a taste for the stuff. In fact, the mere thought of wine, ale, or anything stronger, turned his stomach. He wondered if he would be able to take so much as a swallow again, but he doubted it.

Tabars then caught sight of Larris. "Your Highness." He inclined his head in respect.

"You need not be any more formal with me than with Lerryn." Larris rode forward and clasped hands with Tabars. Tabars remembered Hierm, Edrin, and Hair from the tournament in Galsbur. He raised his eyebrows when Larris introduced Rinala as Van Derin's wife, but he greeted her with as much courtesy as a career soldier could muster. Soon they were on the road north to Galdora. They set a fast pace, having sufficient remounts so as not to overtax their horses.

"Korlan has told me of the situations in the northeast and southeast," Lerryn said. "What of the west?"

"His Majesty sent us to find you as soon as word reached Archstone about the force moving in from the west, thus little was known at the time we left. We do not know their numbers, or how well armed they might be. Some of the rumors claim they are accompanied by shifters and ice cats, but that is just backwoods superstition."

Lerryn and his brother exchanged tight glances, but let Tabars keep talking.

"They do not appear to be a proper army, but more of a large marauding force. They are moving in from the mountains, sacking mining towns and fur trader's encampments. Their progress is slow, but they are moving in a direct line toward Galdora. Specifically toward Galsbur." His eyes flitted to Van Derin, who said nothing, but made no effort to hide the fact that he was hanging on every word. "Your father cannot spare many troops from the war with Kyrin. He sent a small force as soon as he heard the news, and will send more as he is able. Our orders are to find you and accompany you to the western front, where you will take command of the defenses."

"Why can the king no spare more troops for my husband's home?" Rinala demanded. Rather than being offended, Lerryn rather found the girl's aggressive demeanor amusing.

"The duchies in the northeast are perhaps the richest farmland in all of Gameryah, with few natural barriers to aid its defense," Larris explained.

"And Galsbur is just a name on a map." Hierm's voice was bitter. "We are expendable." No one disagreed with him.

They traveled unmolested across the countryside, stopping where opportunity arose to graze the horses, or to buy or trade for feed for them. It seemed Lerryn had been correct in his assessment of the state of things in Lothan, and southern Galdora was much the same. People were keeping to their homes and going about their business. Larris observed that even this was a bad thing. Commerce, he said, was critical to the kingdom's well-being, and the empty roads indicated that goods were not flowing from place-to-place as they should. The young man would make a fine ruler someday. By contrast, Lerryn lived for the moment, and the immediate resolution of conflict. Larris saw the breadth and depth of things. He was wise in ways Lerryn had no desire to be.

On the third morning after meeting up with Tabars and the men, just as they were ready to depart, Lerryn called everyone together. His heart was pounding. The decision to which he had come had not been an easy one to make, but he knew it was the right thing to do.

"We shall part company today. Larris, you will take Van Derin, his wife, Hair, and Edrin north to Archstone." The protests began at once.

"But brother, I…"

"But my home…"

"We want to stay with you, Highness!"

"Enough!" Lerryn shouted. "I will hear not a word." He was a bit surprised that they all obeyed immediately—even Larris. "You three," he looked at Van Derin, Edrin, and Hair, "are not yet soldiers. Two of you took an oath to enter my service and train at my academy. You will better serve the kingdom when you are trained soldiers.

"Van Derin, you have taken no oath, but your liege commands your obedience. I understand you want to fight for your home, but you now have a family of your own to care for. Take your wife and unborn child to safety. Larris will see to it that she has safe quarters and is cared for." Lerryn realized that, in a way, he envied Van Derin. He regretted that he would never know the love of a family of his own. An image came unbidden to his mind of eyes that sparkled like emeralds. He forced it from his thoughts. Now would be the hardest part. He took Larris by the arm and pulled him close so they would not be heard.

"Father needs you. The kingdom needs you. I am a soldier. I am of no use for any other purpose." He waved off his brother's protest and continued. "If you come with me, you will be another sword and nothing more. You are worth more than your sword. You will be a great ruler."

"What do you mean?" Realization dawned on Larris' face, and he was momentarily rendered speechless.

Lerryn seized the opportunity. He raised his voice so that all could hear. "I, Lerryn Van Altman, First Prince of the Sword to King Allar Van Altman of Galdora, declare before these witnesses that I hereby abdicate my birthright to my brother, Larris Van Altman."

Shocked silence hung like fog in the air. He did not wait for them to argue.

"Captain Tabars, do you witness this?" Tabars, rendered dumbstruck, merely nodded. Lerryn shook his head. "You must speak."

"I do witness this." Tabars' voice was dull and his expression sullen.

Lerryn now turned to the tall soldier with a pockmarked face who stood alongside Tabars. "Squad leader Khattre, do you witness?"

Khattre's face was beet red, and his eyes watery. "I do witness this."

"Hierm Van Derin, do you witness?"

The young man flinched as his name was called, but he immediately recovered from his surprise. "I... do witness, Highness."

"Make your mark on this," Lerryn drew from beneath his cloak the document he had prepared the night before, "and you shall no longer have to address me with that title." He drew his dagger, and each witness pricked his finger and signed in blood. He was pleasantly surprised and pleased to see that each knew how to sign his own name. When they were finished, he handed the parchment to Larris and dropped to one knee.

"All hail Larris, First Prince of the Sword!" Everyone present, save Rinala, dropped to one knee, and bowed. Each soldier placed his right fist over his heart.

"You may rise." Larris' voice was as bitter as Lerryn had ever heard. He turned to Lerryn. "Come with me. We shall speak of this."

Lerryn's first instinct was to chastise his younger brother for addressing him in such a manner, but then he remembered he was no longer a prince, and Larris was now his liege. In other circumstances this would have taken some growing accustomed to, but in this case, it did not matter. They moved away from the others so they could talk without being overheard.

"Congratulations, Brother." Larris scowled down at the document. "I would not have thought you clever enough to think of this. Selfish enough, certainly, but not clever enough. Of course, now that your mind is no longer muzzy with drink, who knows what you are capable of?"

Lerryn's face burned and he clenched his fists. He forced himself to relax. He had been prepared for Larris' anger, but not to be accused of doing this for himself. Did Larris not see that this was best for the kingdom? Lerryn would never be fit to rule. He was fit only to kill and to die.

"This document binds me tighter than any chains ever could. I am now the sole heir. I could not risk my life if I wanted to. If I die, our house dies." Larris looked up at the sky, his lips compressed and his eyes searching. He took a long, deep breath and exhaled. Lerryn was painfully aware that every eye was on them, and everyone was straining to hear any part of what they were saying. Finally, Larris continued. "Very well. I can do nothing else. I appoint you," he spoke in a loud, clear voice, "to the rank of general, and order you to fulfill your King's command by leading the defense of our western border."

"I hear and understand, Highness." Lerryn thumped his fist to his chest three times, followed by a bow.

Larris did not return the bow. He returned, mounted up in silence, and rode away at a trot. Edrin and Hair followed behind him. Rinala handed the reins of her horse to Van Derin and stalked over to Lerryn.

"You are no a prince now, so I can speak to you as I like." Of course, a man's standing had never stopped the girl from speaking her mind before now. "You know he loves Shanis, and now he can no ever marry her. Either you did think of that, or you did no. In any case, he is right. You do be a selfish man." She turned on her heel and stalked back to her husband, who stood looking abashed. Neither of them looked at Lerryn as they mounted and rode to catch up with Larris.

Lerryn shook his head. She was correct. He had thought of Larris' feelings for Shanis Malan. That union could never have come to be, and the sooner Larris saw that, the better for the kingdom. He did not relish hurting his brother, but he had no doubt he had done the right thing. He had not, however, anticipated the sudden field commission Larris had given him. Another thing that did not matter. He would not be a general for long. He sighed and turned to address his men.

"I know that every man here will follow me into battle without question. I have witnessed your bravery many times before. The battle to which we now ride is, perhaps, the most hopeless we have ever faced. Our numbers are few, but our hearts are strong, and our cause is noble. I ask that you ride with me one last time. I ask this not as the man who was once your prince, or as your general, but as a brother in arms who will lay down his life for you, and for his king."

Khattre was the first to draw his sword and raise it in the air. In a heartbeat, forty-nine blades, including Lerryn's, glittered in the sun.

"White Fang!" Lerryn shouted. "We ride!"

Chapter 27

The trail breaks up here." Heztus knelt and carefully inspected the ground. "It is as if the entire party scattered in different directions." He snapped his head up, his eyes scanning the surrounding forest.

"Ambush!" he shouted.

Shanis rolled out of the saddle as an arrow whistled through the air where she had sat only a moment before. Flat on the damp earth she looked around for her attackers. She saw flashes of color moving through the dense greenery. Their assailants were well-hidden.

A whisper of chill air passed over her, and suddenly the arrows were falling to the ground as if striking an invisible wall. Aspin raised his hand, and a flash of light burst forth. A surprised cry rang out, then fell silent as suddenly as it had arisen. Another flash, this time in a different direction, and another cry. Now the attackers were falling, the sounds of them crashing through the brush receding.

Shanis clambered to her feet and freed her bow from where it was tied to her horse's saddle. She strung it with practiced ease and sprang into the saddle. She urged her horse forward, determined to catch the attackers. Aspin was right behind her, while Oskar helped Heztus up onto his horse.

The going was slower than she would have liked. The ground grew soggier the farther they rode, and the undergrowth thicker. Soon they would have to dismount and lead their mounts or risk a horse breaking its leg. Up ahead, angry shouts pierced the forest. They burst forth into a clearing and immediately reined in.

Dark clad men, some armed with spears, others with bows, ringed the clearing.

The men they had been pursuing had dismounted and stood with their arms outstretched as they were relieved of their mounts and weapons. A rustle behind her caught her attention. She glanced back to see that they were now surrounded.

"We might as well join them," Aspin said, sliding out of his saddle. Taking care to make no sudden movement that could be interpreted as having ill intent, Shanis dismounted. Oskar jumped heavily to the ground. He offered a hand to Heztus, who ignored him and sprang down with ease.

Shanis took a long look at their captors. Though they were dressed alike, all in plain black clothing, they were clearly a mix of Monaghan and Malgog. Of course, Heztus was the only Malgog she had actually met, but these men fit the description: darker of hair and eye than their Monaghan cousins, their hair adorned with bones, claws, and teeth, but otherwise they were similar in build and facial features. Her eyes fell upon the biggest man in the group, and she had the sudden feeling that she had met him before. Then it struck her. Give the man a bath, comb out his hair, and trim his beard, and he would look very much like her father.

An angular fellow with a bushy beard and long hair stepped forward, interrupting her thoughts. He gripped his spear tightly, every vein on his lean forearms standing out in the mid-day sun that glistened on his sweaty skin.

"I am Ibram of the Gray Moss clan and an appointed guardian. Why are you breaking the peace?"

"They have stolen something that belongs to me." Her stare burned into the men who had ambushed them. She did not know their names, but she recognized them as some of the Monaghan who had broken away. "A sword."

"We no have any sword, save our own." One of the men whom they had been pursuing sneered as he spoke.

"It makes no nevermind to me," Ibram said. "You will not be breaking the peace of Calmut."

"Calmut!" Heztus muttered. "I've never approached it from the north before, so I had no idea. Stupid!"

"If you are coming in, you are almost out of time. The supposed bearer of the Serpent has not yet arrived. The elders are breaking the call on the morrow."

Shanis gasped. She was almost too late! And she still did not have the sword. She looked around at her companions. Oskar shook his head, but Aspin nodded.

"You must follow where your destiny leads and trust that all will be well." His voice was calm and reassuring.

Oskar swallowed hard and added, "It has all worked out so far. It will again. We should go in."

"All right." Shanis turned to Ibram. "We will enter."

"Ye will enter with no weapons," Ibram continued. "All of the Monaghan can enter." It took Shanis a moment to realize he was including her among that group. "And the dwarf as well. The seeker and this outlander must stay out."

Shanis felt the blood drain from her face. She had been nervous about going to Calmut and facing this Keeper of the Mists, whoever he was, but had not anticipated going alone. First she had lost Larris, Allyn, Khalyndryn, and Hierm, and now Oskar. She would be without any of their original group. Even Aspin's presence would have been some comfort. In fact, the seeker's wisdom and experience would have been much appreciated.

Heztus must have noticed the expression on her face. He stepped forward and offered his elbow as if he were escorting her into a ballroom. "My lady?"

The comical expression on his face broke the tension, and she laid her hand on his arm and followed the Monaghans, who were filing through an opening in the line of guards. She looked back at Oskar, who mouthed "Good luck," and at Aspin, who merely nodded, his face a mask of serenity. His steadiness gave her strength, and she turned to face what lay ahead.

The guards escorted them through a maze of crumbled stone buildings around and inside of which Monaghan and Malgog alike had set up camps. She could tell that this had once been a city of respectable size, though not as large as Karkwall, which was the only true city she had ever visited.

"So the entire nation is gathered here?" She wondered how an entire nation's worth of people could assemble in one city.

"No one in Karkwall considers her or himself part of a clan any longer, so they will stay put. Many from the eastern clans have aligned themselves with the imposter and will not be here. The Black Mangrove clan from the salt swamps keeps to itself. If they are represented at all, it will be a handful. I am told that the Mud Snakes have lost most of their number to the imposter. Many Malgog will stay put, because our settlements in the swamps are well-hidden and easily defensible. The Monaghan will be here in force, as they have no permanent homes any longer. The lands to the south and west, where the ground is more open and level than that through which we approached will be packed with people waiting to hear the news. There is clean water aplenty, but they cannot stay too long before food and sanitation become concerns. That is one of the reasons the elders will not wait much longer."

Shanis would never have even considered such details. She would have worried about conflicts breaking out, but had not thought about the mundane aspects of everyday life.

"That is a lot of people." She thought that she should have something more profound to say, and felt foolish.

"There are not that many of us, and not even as many as there were a few generations ago. There are twelve clans in all, none of great size. Swamps and hills do not provide the sort of arable land that allows a nation to thrive. Then, of course, there is the fact that we have been trying to kill one another for generations."

"I want to put a stop to that."

Heztus looked up at her, his expression now serious. "Forgive me, but why does an outlander, one who has obviously spent a good part of her life learning how to kill people, care if we live or die?"

"Why do I care? Because I cannot bear the sight of children suffering." She bit her lip. "My mother died when I was a baby, and I was raised like a boy, and a spoiled one at that. I don't know why my father raised me as he did, though I am certain he had his reasons. Ever since I left home, it seems, no matter what I do, my destiny has taken control of my life. That bothered me at first. I was a selfish person who wanted what she wanted and, when it seemed like outside forces were controlling me, I felt enslaved.

"Now I realize that my destiny, or the prophecy, or whatever it was that was guiding my steps, was merely showing me a part of myself that I did not know existed." She looked down at Heztus, meeting his gaze. "This clan war is an abomination, and I am the person to end it. I will end it because I must, and because I want to."

"If words would be enough to bring us together again, I believe you would succeed. For what little it is worth, you have my support."

His words moved her. The whirlwind that had swept her life in this new and unexpected direction kept her mind overwhelmed with thoughts of what she must do. Often she felt less than human, like a piece in the gods' game. Heztus' simple declaration affirmed that what she hoped to do could make a very real difference in the lives of suffering people.

"Thank you."

"Shanis! It do be you!" Horgris drew annoyed glances as he pushed his way to her. "Do you have it?"

She shook her head.

"It no matter now. Time, it do be almost up. The clan leaders do be gathering in the circle as we speak. Follow me." He glanced down at Heztus. "You come, too. If the leaders do see that she is presented by Monaghan and Malgog, it will be well for her."

Heztus shrugged and followed behind them.

The circle was a ring of stones, each a span wide and the height of two men, with just enough space between each to allow someone to walk between them. The clan chiefs sat upon a circle of smaller stones around a pool of undulating liquid earth—quakewater, the Lothans called it. It was shady here, but the cool air seemed scarcely to touch her. She felt hot and itchy all over and impatient for… whatever was about to happen.

She scanned the faces. Gerrilaw, the leader of the Three Oaks, met her eye and nodded. The other clan chiefs regarded her with varying degrees of suspicion in their eyes. One man stood out. His silver-sprinkled hair and leathery skin spoke of advancing age, but he exuded strength. His icy blue eyes shone with intensity, but his face gave little away, save a hint of cool disinterest.

"Krion, leader of the Black Mangrove clan," Heztus whispered. "He and his people rarely leave their clanhold. He will not be easy to sway, but if you can bring him over to your side, it will go far."

Silence fell upon the clearing in which the circle lay. Beyond the ring of stones, the Lothans were gathering. Malgog and Monaghan stood shoulder to shoulder, all feuds cast aside as they waited for… her.

Horgris broke the silence. "I, Horgris, chief of the Hawk Hill clan, do bring before you Shanis Malan, bearer of the Silver Serpent, she who be prophesied to unite the clans of Lothan."

He glanced at Heztus, who repeated the ritual words, naming himself son of the clan chief of the Red Water clan.

Horgris guided her into the circle of chieftains. A narrow footpath led to a small circle of solid ground in the middle of the quakewater. Refusing to let apprehension show on her face, Shanis strode across the footpath as Horgris took his seat among the chieftains. When she reached her destination, she was uncertain which direction she should face, so she settled on Krion. If he held as much sway as Heztus believed, she might as well start making an impression.

"By what right do you claim to be the bearer?" A Malgog chieftain asked in a level tone that suggested neither judgment nor suspicion.

"I recovered the Silver Serpent from its resting place in the mountains." She hoped her answer was proper. The only preparation she had been given during the trek to Calmut was to tell the truth. "I have used its power, and I bear its mark." She pulled down the neck of her loose-fitting tunic to display the silver mark on her breast. "I have witnessed the suffering this clan war has…"

She fell silent as Krion raised his hand. He nodded to Gerrilaw, who cleared his throat. "We did no ask your reasons for wanting to unite us. We ask only by what right you make your claim." The other chieftains nodded in agreement.

"Ye have the hair of a Monagahan," another Malgog chieftain spoke, "the eyes of a Malgog, and the tongue of an outlander. Who are you in truth?"

"I was raised in Galdora. My father is Colin Malan. He has never spoken to me of his home or family, but now that I have met the Malgog, I wonder if he might be of your blood. I never knew my mother, but I am told she looked much like me, except not so… large." Her height and strength had often been a source of embarrassment growing up, but the clan chieftains merely nodded.

"My son presented you," the chieftain continued. So this was Heztus' father, Jayan. Shanis could now see that he and Heztus had the same eyes, though this man was tall and muscular like most of the Malgog she had seen. She wondered how Jayan felt about his dwarf son. "So he believes in you, but I am not certain. A woman, and an outlander at that, the bearer of the serpent?" He shook his head.

"Man or woman, Lothan, or outlander. The prophecies no say anything about those things," Horgris protested. "Besides, the Keeper will choose her or no. She do have been spoken for and shown us her mark." Quiet muttering, both within the circle and without, rose up in response to his words.

"What of this other claimant?" Culmatan of the Blue Stag spoke up. "He has no come to make his claim."

"Yes he has." A new voice rang out. Shanis turned around to see Pedric Karst stride into circle.

Chapter 28

"They are coming in force!" Dannil's sweaty face was flushed from exertion. "Moving through the forest," he gasped, leaning against the table in the common room of the inn where Colin and Lord Hiram waited to receive reports and send instructions. "They are over near the Clehn farm."

"We will hold them, just as we have done every other time. That position is well-defended." In fact, Colin doubted they could continue to do so, but there was nothing to be gained by voicing that thought.

When attempts to parley with the invaders, or even communicate, with the enemy were rebuffed, the Galsburans had not wasted a moment. They sent messages to the king, prepared their defenses, and began harrying the oncoming army. The king had sent a single squad of foot soldiers. Their sergeant had not believed Colin's report of a large marauding force, and had set out with his small contingent of men to engage the enemy.

They had not returned.

For weeks now the Galsburans and the refugees from the frontier settlements had engaged in a campaign of delaying tactics against the force that moved inexorably toward Galsbur. They had taken the fight to their enemy, sending skilled woodsmen out to kill their scouts and conduct minor raids. Of course, such actions would have little impact on a force of any size, and the Galsburans had lost skilled woodsmen.

The enemy had now reached the banks of the Vulltu River at the westernmost edge of Galsburan farming land. Colin and his men had turned away several attempts to cross, but those had not been serious attempts. The enemy was probing their defenses. Soon, the real attempt would come, and Colin had no idea if they could turn back the tide.

"Colin!" Natin Marwel came dashing up. Having lost his hand the previous year, the young man was unable to fight, but he had a good mind, sharp eyes, and was a fast runner, so Colin had put him to work scouting and carrying messages. "They are crossing at the White Run!" A favorite fishing spot for catching silversides and redeyes, the White Run was a rocky stretch of water just north of Galsbur. The river widened at this stretch, and was thus shallower than the southern stretch, but was also perilous due to the fast-running whitewater that gave the spot its name.

"Tell me what you saw."

"There are about fifty of them fording the stream. They are raining down arrows on us from the opposite bank, trying to cover the crossing, but the range is too far."

"How many archers?"

"Ten or twelve, though they are putting enough arrows into the air for twice as many."

"It is a diversion," Colin said. "The true attack is the one by the Clehn farm."

"Are you certain?" Lord Hiram scowled. He had an annoying habit of questioning nearly everything Colin said, but to his credit, he seldom argued once Colin explained his thinking.

"I am. They are not sending enough men across at the White Run to make any difference even if they did make it to our side of the river. They hope to make us divide our forces so that their crossing at the Clehn farm is easier, that is all." He turned back to Natin. "Go back to the White Run. Stay out of range of their arrows. I shall need you to report back here if it looks like their crossing has even a chance of succeeding. Do you understand?"

"I do." Natin turned on his heel and dashed away.

"I am going to the Clehn farm." Colin told Hiram. "You have a dozen men at your disposal should you need to send them to White Run or anywhere else for that matter. Send a runner to me if you need more." Hiram nodded and Colin left the room.

A dark mass moved like an oncoming storm cloud through the forest on the other side of the river. The defenders of Galsbur waited behind the hastily constructed defenses of earth and sharpened stakes. A buzzing like angry hornets filled the air as a few nervous men loosed arrows at their enemy, their shots falling well short of their marks.

"Hold until I give the command!" Colin shouted down from his perch in the lower limb of a chanbor tree. They could not afford to expend arrows through futile volleys. Others down the line echoed his command, and soon an expectant silence fell over the defenders.

The shadow moved forward, and as it came into range, Colin saw that something was wrong. The line was too high, too uniform to be a mass of men.

"Hold!" he commanded. He needed to understand what he was seeing. And as they came into clear sight, his stomach fell.

"What is that?" someone muttered.

The defenders had constructed large wooden shields three yards high and two yards wide. It looked like a stockade wall was moving in their direction. Colin gritted his teeth. The enemy had to know that these oversized shields would do little good once the men were down in the river. What were they planning? The answer came as soon as the line of attackers reached the opposite riverbank.

The wall of shields stopped on the bank and came together into a solid wall. The soldiers on either end fell back, forming a box to protect their flanks. Unable to wait any longer, some of the Galsburans released their arrows, then others followed suit. The ragged wave whispered through the air with deadly intent, but most of the arrows bounced harmlessly off of the wooden wall, or off the upraised shields the soldiers farther back held above their heads for added protection. Scattered cries indicated that a precious few had found their marks.

"Hold until I give the command!" Colin shouted again. Lack of discipline was the bane of any militia, and this gathering of farmers could scarcely even be called that. He hoped they would stand their ground when they closed with the enemy. The attackers would have to ford the river, climb the bank, and break through their defenses. If the Galsburans held fast, they could break this attack.

A rhythmic beating sound arose from across the river, followed by another, and then another. Then the men were banging on their shields and crying out. The Galsburans did not answer the cry, but stood resolute.

From the back of its ranks, the enemy sent a volley of arrows at them. The defenders huddled down behind their defenses and weathered the assault. Colin did not know if anyone had been hit, so loud was the noise from across the river. The cacophony rose to a tumult, yet still the men did not charge down into the water and attempt a crossing. And then Colin realized the purpose of the noise. The first noise he had heard was the sound of axes biting into trees. He scanned the opposite bank, his heart pounding. And then he saw it.

A flash of movement. A glint of light on steel. A hollow thump. They were bringing down the trees! All along the opposite bank, boxed in by the protective wooden walls, groups of men were relentlessly hacking away at the tallest chanbor trees. If those fell...

He barked out a series of commands, indicated the locations, and young men with slings sent clay jugs filled with redroot sap hurtling across the river. Highly flammable, redroot sap was not as viscous as most resins. Most of the jugs found their marks, shattering against the chanbor trees and spilling their contents onto the surprised men below. Fire arrows followed, and some found their marks, setting the resin aflame. Tongues of fire raced down the tree, igniting the men upon whom the liquid had fallen. They screamed and fell back, but were quickly replaced by fresh men, and the work began again in earnest.

Colin groaned. The sap was difficult to come by, and their supply was limited. They certainly did not have enough to burn every man who picked up an axe.

A cry went up as the first tree fell. Then another came down. In a matter of moments, four of the statuesque trees crashed onto their defensive positions. The huge trees, with no low-hanging limbs, were now bridges not only across the river, but over the Galsburans' defensive lines.

Quick as a flash, a furry gray form shot across the nearest bridge. An ice cat! Arrows sang through the air, but the creature was too fast. In an instant it was among the surprised defenders, biting and tearing at them. As Colin clambered down from his perch, he saw more ice cats dashing across the bridges. Warriors followed behind them, their faces painted blue and white, roaring out their battle cries. The defenders who were not occupied fighting the ice cats let loose a barrage of arrows and rocks, toppling the warriors in the front, but they kept coming across the tree bridges.

Colin reached the ground as the archers on the far side of the river sent a barrage of arrows into the defenders. Many found their targets. As the defenders fell wounded or took cover from the deadly rain, more warriors poured across the bridges.

And now the attackers were putting their wooden shield wall to a new use. Under the covering fire of their archers, the warriors dropped them into the river and began lashing them together, creating a floating bridge across the river. A handful of men fell to Galsburan arrows, but the invaders' numbers were too great.

"Retreat!" Colin shouted, brandishing his sword and sword breaker. "Back to the town!"

A warrior in blue face paint charged him, jagged teeth bared in a predatory grin. Colin turned the man's sword with ease and opened his throat with a tight slash. He kicked the dying man's body into the path of another charging warrior, who stumbled and fell. Colin ran him through, wrenched his sword from the body, and charged at the nearest cluster of enemies. Strange how the old battle reflexes come back so quickly, he mused.

All around him the Galsburans had taken up the call to retreat. To their credit, they fell back not in a panicked flight, but in the way they had been trained, weaving their way between the hidden pits and traps they had laid out well in advance, occasionally stopping to shoot down an attacker. Fortunately for them, the pursuit was minimal. The invaders were concentrating on clearing the defensive positions on the riverbank, and allowed the villagers to flee.

Colin fought his way clear and dashed after his comrades. The battle madness was upon him, and part of him wanted to stand and fight until they cut him down. The rational side of his mind reminded him that his leadership would be needed long after this first failed engagement.

A sound of unsurpassed wildness caused him to stumble, but he kept his footing and looked back over his shoulder to see an ice cat hurtling after him. The sweat that soaked his body seemed to freeze. He could never outrun the beast. It would catch up with him long before he reached the next line of defense.

Something whizzed past his head, hissing like an airborne serpent, and the ice cat snarled in pain and rage as an arrow blossomed above its left foreleg, but the wound served only to slow the creature, and not much at that. Another arrow missed its target, but a third caught it in its hindquarters.

Colin stole another glance behind him. It was still coming, and though its movement was obviously hindered, it was closing the distance fast. He scanned the ground in front of him. The defenses were a good four rods away—too far, but just ahead... He had to risk it. If it did not work, well, he was going to have to turn and fight in any case, so why not?

He sprinted four more steps, stumbled, and staggered to his left. He kept moving in that direction as he drew his sword and turned to face the creature's charge. Its eyes and teeth shone in the sun as it charged its prey.

And then the ground fell out from under it.

In a half a heartbeat, the roar of angry surprise turned to a feral cry of pain, and then fell silent. Colin did not spare a second glance at the creature that now lay impaled on the sharpened stakes, but hurried to safety before another monster from grandmothers' tales could chase him down.

Behind the safety of the wall they had constructed to protect the town, he sank to one knee and inspected his wounds. A few superficial cuts, nothing more. They could wait.

He rose to his feet and assessed their situation. Defenders, mostly young men with bows, lined the walls, ready for the next assault. A good twenty Galsburans were being treated for minor wounds. He hoped they had not lost too many men in the fight at the river, but he would not know until he took full stock of their defenses.

Suddenly feeling more tired than he could remember ever having felt before, he made his way back to the inn where Lord Hiram waited. The firstman fixed him with a grave look as he entered.

"Well?" He looked far older than his years. His face was taut, and his hands trembled.

Colin shook his head. "Too many of them. We bled them a little, but had no hope of holding them back."

"Do we have any idea of their numbers?" Hiram offered him a bottle of wine, from which Colin took a long drink before answering.

"Several hundred, I think." That was more than twice their number.

Hiram grunted and sat down heavily. He propped his elbows on the table and buried his face in his hands. "Who are they?" he asked, not for the first time. "What do they want here?"

"They are no nation of which I have any knowledge." He hesitated. "They have ice cats with them."

"What?" Hiram gaped at him. They had heard these rumors from the refugees from the frontier settlement that had been raided, but few of them had believed the tales. "But ice cats are just..."

"They are real. One almost killed me."

"The snows blind me! I just can't believe it. If they are real, what other tales might be true?" If Hiram's hands had trembled before, now they quaked. "Have I done the wrong thing? Should we all have fled to safety?"

"Everyone here chose to stay. They wanted to fight, in full knowledge that the worst might happen."

"What do we do, then?"

Colin moved to the window and stared out upon the town green where the wounded had been moved. All of the young women with children had fled to safety, at least he hoped they had made it to safety, but most of the women who were past childbearing years had remained behind. He watched as Marra Hendon bandaged Ham Lurel's wounded forearm. What was it about a home that made someone willing to die for it? There was dirt aplenty in Gameryah. They could plant their crops elsewhere. Why remain here, fighting a losing battle, all the while hoping for aid that might not come?

He almost laughed at his own cynicism. His wife had always chided him for his outlook on the world. He knew the answer to his question. In fact there were two. The practical answer was that the western frontier of Galdora was one of the rare places in which a man could be free from indenture. There was nowhere else these people could go where they would not live in near-slavery. The other answer, the true answer, his wife would have said, is that there was power in home. It was that same power that made him long, on occasion, for the black water and tangled swamps of his youth.

"We keep fighting," he finally said. "We hold them off as long as it takes for help to arrive. This is their home. They will do what it takes."

"It is your home too, Colin." Hiram's voice was surprisingly gentle. He rose from his chair and joined Colin at the window. "One day soon, our children will return to us. Let us make sure there is a home for them to return to."

Chapter 29

"I am the bearer of the Silver Serpent." Karst's voice was a viper's hiss. "I have come to be recognized as such and to claim my rightful place."

The clan chiefs exchanged dark glances.

"You no be presented?" Culmatan frowned. "This is no proper."

A young Malgog warrior stepped forward. "I, Padin of the Mud Snake clan, do bring before you Lord Pedric Karst, bearer of the Silver Serpent, he who is prophesied to unite the clans of Lothan." He grinned and stepped back behind Karst, who turned to glare at Shanis.

Her heart was in her throat. Karst was the imposter? How could he be? And then her eyes fell upon her sword. He wore it slung across his back, its hilt glittering in the sunlight. All thoughts of bringing peace to the Lothans vanished. Right now, the only thing she wanted was to snatch her sword away from Karst and run him through.

Someone coughed. She looked to see Horgris frowning at her. With a slight jerk of his head, he indicated that she should direct her attention to the chieftains, rather than to Karst.

The chieftains looked displeased. They all turned to stare at Krion, who in turn stared at Karst. Krion scratched his beard, cocked his head, and then gave a thoughtful nod. Apparently Karst's presentation was acceptable.

"By what right do you claim to be the bearer?" The same Malgog chieftain who had asked her the ritual question now posed it to Karst.

"I bear the Silver Serpent." He inclined his head toward the sword slung across his back. "I am the one." He held up his right arm, around which a serpentine band of silver coiled. "I already control most of western Lothan. Malgog and Monaghan recognize me as the true bearer, and flock to my banner."

Shanis was about to challenge him, but warning looks, this time from Horgris and Culmatan, froze the words before they passed her lips. It was plain to see that the chiefs were not pleased with Karst's words. Perhaps the wise course was to remain silent and let him continue giving offense.

Tell him to draw the sword, she thought. Then you'll see. Horgris knew! So did Culmatan and Gerrilaw! Why didn't they say anything?

"You be an outlander as well." The Monaghan chief who spoke was one whom she did not recognize.

Karst nodded, but did not elaborate. His usual sour frown was fully in place, and there was an air of impatience about him as he waited for the chieftains to deliberate.

"He could be of our blood from old." Padin, the young Mud Snake warrior, interjected. "He has the look about him."

"You are not to speak!" The eldest Malgog chieftain stood, shaking with rage. "Ye will not disgrace me like this."

"You are the disgrace, Father," Padin snapped. "Lord Karst makes us strong again, yet you abandon the clan."

"My clan abandoned me," the man rasped. "They have all forsaken their rightful leader."

"Peace, Labar," Horgris said. He signaled to someone outside the circle. Two warriors stepped forward and dragged Padin bodily from the circle. "We do have two outlanders. We can no exclude one but no the other."

What was Horgris doing? He knew Shanis was the true bearer, and he also knew Karst could not draw the Silver Serpent. Why did he not say so? She tried to catch his eye again, but he kept his gaze on Krion.

Finally, Jayan stood. An eager silence hung in the air as they waited for him to speak. "Both shall submit to the Keeper of the Mists."

One by one, each clan chief showed his agreement by standing, until only Krion remained. The chieftain of the Black Mangrove looked from Shanis to Karst and back to Shanis. Finally he nodded and stood.

Shanis felt as if she had been doused with cold water. So it was really going to happen. She was going to face the Keeper of the Mists, whatever it was. But Karst was going too! Again she wondered at the Monaghan chieftains' failure to disprove Karst's claim by simply challenging him to draw the sword.

The chieftains remained standing as Jayan approached Karst.

"You will remove the sword. It will be in the circle should you return."

If Karst was troubled by the suggestion that he might not return, he did not let it show. He unslung the sheath, careful to hold it only by the strap, and carried it to the center of the circle where Shanis stood. His eyes burned into hers with the same intensity as they had when the two of them had nearly come to blows over Natin's injury.

Shanis returned the glare double. Anger surged within her, and it felt like an old friend. How long had it been since she had let her temper run unchecked? She wanted to pummel Karst in front of all of these people. That would show them who was the imposter. She clenched her fists.

And then she remembered.

If an opponent can make you angry, he can kill you just as easily.

Master Yurg had understood her weakness better than anyone. If she gave in to her rage now, no telling what might happen. She had to remain calm. She forced herself to remain under control.

Karst saw the tension leaving her body and smirked. He took a step closer, doubtless thinking she was frightened, but Horgris stepped between them, turning her around and guiding her away.

"You do be chosen to submit to the Keeper of the Mists," he intoned. "Turn to the north." Shanis had no idea which way was north in this circle, but she quickly took note of the angle of the sun and turned around.

And the world went black.

She gasped. Someone had covered her head. Strong hands pressed her arms against her sides.

"It will be all right." Hogris' whisper was so quiet that no one could hear it but her. "Trust me."

He led her along a winding path. The air grew cooler and she no longer felt the sun on her arms. All was quiet, save the sound of muted footfalls on soft earth. They finally halted and Horgris uncovered her head.

She and Karst stood before an ancient tree. Knots in the shape of grotesque faces bulged from its twisted limbs. Two standing stones, like smaller versions of those that formed the circle, stood before the tree. Between them, the light danced on a curtain of mist. It undulated like a living curtain.

Krion moved to stand before them. "The way forward is there." His voice was deep and rich. "Ye will speak no words before you pass between the stones. The way back will show itself to you, if you are found worthy." He stepped back and motioned for them to continue.

It was too late to turn back now. Steady steps carried her to the standing stones, where the curtain of mist shimmered. It seemed so substantial that she wondered if she could truly pass through it. Only one way to find out.

She took a deep breath and stepped into the mist.

Chapter 30

"You inside! Open the gate! Open up in the name of the King!"

Confused faces peered cautiously over the makeshift stockade wall, speaking in low tones to one another. Lerryn caught the words "soldiers" and "help." One man finally mustered the courage to rise up and take a good look at the mounted force that waited outside.

"It can't be! Did the king send you?"

"Don't stand there gaping like a frost fool! It will soon be sunrise. Open the gate before I tear it down myself." Tabars had grown surlier each day as they taxed themselves and their horses to get to Galsbur before it was too late. Lerryn's abdication of his title had not set well with Tabars either, not that it made a difference. What was done was done.

The gate swung open and Lerryn led the way in. The faces that gazed at them in the waning moonlight showed both surprise and relief. Some grinned openly at the new arrivals. Clearly they had not been expecting relief of any kind.

"I would speak with the man who is in charge of your defenses. Take me there."

"Yes sir. This…" The speaker glanced up at Lerryn and was momentarily struck dumb. He regained his wits and dropped to a knee. "Your Highness! I remember your face from the tournament. Sorry we did not recognize you at first."

"We have no time for that. Show me the way."

"Yes, Highness. The inn. It is this way."

"I remember the way." Lerryn had stayed at the inn the previous year while holding his tournament in Galsbur. He winced at the memory. All that work for nothing. And yet another thing that no longer mattered.

Two men sat in the common room. He recognized Hiram Van Derin, who was the town's firstman and Hierm's father. The other, a physically imposing man with shaggy dark hair and beard, was unfamiliar to him. They both sprang to their feet as Lerryn stepped inside.

"Your Highness," Van Derin gasped. He bowed and then motioned for Lerryn to take a seat. "May I offer you a glass of wine?"

Lerryn's stomach wrenched at the very thought, and he gagged, though he thought he covered his reaction well. He was growing accustomed to these strong physical reactions to the sight, smell, or sometimes even suggestion of drink. How had that girl done this to him?

"Water or tea if you have it." Travel weary, he sank into the chair Hiram offered him. Hiram fetched him a cup of tea, and stood expectantly. Finally, Lerryn realized the men were waiting for his leave to sit. He motioned for them to join him at the table. Hiram introduced the other man as Colin.

"What can you tell me of the situation here?" Lerryn asked.

"It is grave, Highness. They outnumber us, and refuse to tell us who they are or what they want." Hiram glanced at the big man, who took up the explanation.

"We face what appears to be a marauding force of several hundred. They are well-armed, and fight reasonably well together, but lack the discipline of a proper army. No cavalry, no siege engines... not yet anyway."

Lerryn took a sip of the piping hot tea. It was dark and bitter, but it seemed to sharpen his thoughts at the first swallow. "From what I gather, you have been holding them off for some time."

"As soon as our attempts to parley failed, we began doing what we could to slow them down. Once they crossed the river, they have tried us each day. Yesterday, they almost breached our walls. We have bled them, but not enough. Every man we lose, however, deals us a great blow."

"What are our numbers?"

"Near two hundred healthy men and boys. Another thirty or so who are wounded, but can fight in a pinch. Fifty eight either dead or too hurt to fight."

"Add to that number forty-nine mounted fighting men; the best in Galdora. And subtract from theirs the three scouts we rode down on the way in."

The big man nodded grimly. He was clearly pondering the same question that troubled Lerryn. Would it be enough?

"His Royal Majesty sent word to you? Orders? Promises of reinforcements?"

"He sent us one squad," Colin growled. "And the ice-encrusted sergeant was too great a fool to believe us when we said it was an army we faced, and not a band of highwaymen. He went off in search of them several days ago. We can only assume he failed."

Lerryn contemplated this over another swallow of tea. The situation in the north must truly be dire if his father could send only a token force to aid these people. Then again, his own unit represented little more than a token response to so vast an enemy.

"Highness, if I may ask, why here?" Weariness dripped from Hiram's every word. "What does an enemy gain from attacking a farming town like ours?"

"I suppose they had to make their attack somewhere. Most likely this is a mercenary force hired by the Kyrinians in an effort to distract us from the war in the north." Seeing their confused looks, he explained the situation to them. They had neither heard about Kyrin's invasion, nor the rebellion in Kurnsbur.

"There is something I neglected to mention." Colin folded his hands and leaned closer to Lerryn. "There are ice cats with them."

Lerryn choked on his tea. He spat it back into the cup and glared at the man. "How many?" he rasped, coughing the liquid out of his windpipe.

"I personally saw eight of them on the day they crossed the river. We killed four.

The others have not been seen again." He gazed up at the ceiling as if coming to a decision. "There are refugees from the mountain villages among us. When they first began arriving, a little girl told me a story that I dismissed at the time, but upon seeing the ice cats, I am wondering if it is true." He leveled his gaze at Lerryn. "I believe they have a shifter among them as well."

Lerryn did not want to believe it, but if there truly were ice cats in the invading force, it was not so far-fetched to believe there would also be shifters.

"Find Captain Tabars," he said to Colin. "He will be waiting outside. Take him and my squad leaders around your defensive perimeter and let them assess the situation. Tell them everything you have told me and answer any questions they might have. They are good soldiers, the best, in fact."

The big man rose from his chair, gave a perfunctory bow, and left the room.

"I should tell you," he said to Hiram, "that I have seen your son, and he is well. He wanted to come here to join in the defense of your village, but I did not permit it. As we speak, he rides with my brother to Archstone to enroll in the academy."

"That is welcome news, Highness. Thank you." Tears welled in Hiram's eyes, but his countenance brightened, and he sat up straighter. "His mother and brother have gone to Archstone. Perhaps they shall find one another."

"When this is over, you can go there yourself and organize a reunion." Lerryn doubted any of them would live that long, but one could hope. "Oh, and congratulations are in order. You are to be a grandfather." He resisted the urge to laugh at Hiram's flummoxed expression. "He is married to a Lothan girl, a Monaghan to be exact, and she is with child." Hiram continued to stare at him. "He married well, she is the daughter of a clan chief, and I am told she can put an arrow through a deer's heart at forty paces, and skin it as well as any hunter."

Stunned silence filled the room as Hiram gaped at Lerryn. Then he burst into a fit of laughter. He slumped back in his chair, the tears now trailing down his cheeks. When he recovered himself, he sat up and wiped his face.

"Forgive me, my Lord, but I wish I could be there when my wife meets her new daughter."

Lerryn had to laugh as well. He remembered Faun Van Derin well and could imagine how she would receive Rinala. Now that he thought about it, it seemed that everyone who knew Mistress Van Derin had made a similar comment. "You are not the first person to make that observation."

"Have you news of Colin's daughter, Shanis, and the others who left our village?"

"That is Shanis Malan's father?" Lerryn wondered how much to tell either of the men about what the girl was doing in Lothan, and how she came to be there, but that decision could wait until after the battle. "She is well. Last I saw her, she was in Lothan with the other young man from your village. I believe his name is Oskar."

Hiram nodded. "And what of Khalyndryn Serrill. A pretty blond girl."

"The news is not good." Lerryn saw no need in softening the blow. This was not the girl's father. "She was killed. An accident," he added. He saw no harm in the small lie.

"A shame. Her family also fled, so there is no one to whom we need to break the news just yet. Colin will want to know of his daughter, as will Oskar's father. I shall let them know."

Lerryn glanced out the window. The first brush of dawn was painted low upon the horizon, a dusty orange trimming the horizon.

A shout arose outside, followed by other cries of warning.

"Attack! Attack!"

Lerryn sprang to his feet, his fingers searching out the comfort of his sword hilt. Not sparing a glance at Hiram, he dashed out the door.

Chapter 31

Shanis expected the sheet of mist to be damp and chilly, but instead it felt like a warm bath. It wrapped her up and drew her in with unseen hands. She seemed to drift forward, enveloped in an ever-darkening cloud.

As gray surrendered to black, she once again felt the earth beneath her feet. The sensation of drifting dissolved, and she took a tentative step forward. The spongy ground gave a little as she put her weight down, but it held her. She took another tentative step, wondering where she was and what might be hiding in the blackness.

Moving one cautious step at a time, she discerned a faint glow up ahead. She could now see that she was inside an earthen tunnel. Thick, gnarled roots, worn smooth with age, formed the walls and ceilings, and held the black earth at bay. At least she hoped they were holding it back.

A crystalline sphere filled with a glowing yellow substance sat atop a cracked stone pedestal. Approaching it with caution, she peered down into the sphere, where the shining substance whirled about inside the container. It put her to mind of thousands of fireflies dancing within the sphere. The thought warmed her heart and gave her comfort.

Behind the pedestal, the tunnel branched off in three different directions: one leading upward, one going straight ahead, and one descending. She took a long look at each one in turn. There was nothing to indicate which was the proper path. Next she examined the pedestal itself, but found nothing on the aging stone cylinder to give her guidance. She examined the walls, ceiling, and even the floor of the tunnel, but found nothing but unrelenting earth and roots. No symbols, no writing, not even a footprint in the soft earth.

She looked around again, suddenly remembering that Karst should be here too, but she did not see him. Beyond the circle of golden light, there was nothing but unrelenting darkness and silence. Why wasn't he right behind her?

"So," she said aloud, unable to abide the silence any longer. "I suppose it is up to me." Her words were braver than she felt, and they rang out in the stillness. She looked again at the tunnels. They appeared to be identical, save the direction in which each led. The tunnel on the left sloped upward, while the one in the center ran on a level with the passage in which she now stood, and the one on the right disappeared down into the darkness.

"Which one? Which one?" Her whisper sounded like shouts. She narrowed her eyes and thought of what each direction might symbolize. She dismissed the upward-leading tunnel as the way of a coward who sought only to escape from destiny. But what of the other two? The tunnel in the center might symbolize staying the course, or it could represent someone who was unwilling to change.

She reflected on her life since leaving home. Nothing had remained the same. Every time she came close to something she desired, it was snatched away. She still resented it, but she now accepted that her destiny was not her own. And she held in her heart the hope that someday things would be as they should. Perhaps the time would come that the gods, or whoever was pulling at the strings of her destiny, would release her, and let her live her life. But for now, change was her reality. Her life must change. The Monaghan and Malgog must change. The world must change.

It was possible that the tunnel on the right, the one leading down into the darkness, symbolized someone who would sink to any depths to get what they wanted, but she did not think so. To her, it was the only courageous choice; the only choice for one who was willing to embrace any path upon which the gods placed her. And had she not already experienced the depths of pain and despair in this quest? Losing Khalyndryn, almost losing Allyn, witnessing the tragic lives of the Lothans. She supposed being brought low was sometimes a part of following one's destiny.

Her decision made, she entered the tunnel on the right and began her descent into darkness.

Pedric Karst wanted out of this place. Each step was a labor as he tugged his boots from the muck that was the floor. Cold, slimy water dripped down from the ceiling. He raised the hood of his cloak, but it was a poor barrier against the persistent dampness. All about him was filth. Serpentine roots coiled up the tunnel walls, glistening in the pulsing red light that oozed forth from the crystal vase that sat on the stone pedestal.

He had no idea how long he had been standing here, staring at the three tunnels, trying to choose his path. His search had provided no clues as to the proper choice. Obviously, each tunnel held symbolic meaning, thus the three directions. He gazed at each in turn, imagining himself passing through each.

And suddenly he understood.

The way down was a way of subservience, the path of the lowly. The way ahead was the path of one who was content with his station, and sought to climb no higher. He was neither of those things. He would rise high. A warm sense of self-assuredness now flowing through his bones, he chose the tunnel on the left, and began his ascent.

The passage spiraled down into the blackness, but the air remained warm and dry as Shanis descended, feeling as if some invisible force was drawing her ever forward. After what seemed an eternity, she emerged in a gloomy chamber that somehow was familiar. The floor was smooth stone, as if hewn by a master craftsman, and the walls arched up in uniform perfection. An ancient woman, her face lined and cracked, sat behind a small fire. Shanis knew her at once. This was the old woman whom she had encountered in a mountain cave during the search for the Silver Serpent.

"Hyda?" she gasped.

"I do be the Keeper of the Mists." Her voice creaked like a rusty hinge. "That do be the only name by which you shall call me."

Shanis noted that the woman did not explicitly deny the name by which Shanis had called her.

As she drew closer, she noticed subtle differences in the woman from her memory and the one who now sat before her. The lined face and silver hair were the same, but where Hyda's eyes had been yellow, her hair unkempt, and her clothing ragged, the Keeper's eyes sparkled like precious gems, her hair was a silken cascade, and her robes a snowy white. Still, it was the same woman.

The old woman set a stone bowl filled with water into the midst of the flames.

Shanis sat down and reached up to pluck a hair from her head, just as the old woman had asked her to do at their previous encounter.

"No!" The woman seized her hand and pulled it toward her, stretching Shanis' arm over the bowl. She pushed back the sleeve of Shanis' tunic, baring her fair skin. "Blood," she whispered. The Keeper drew a small knife from inside the sleeve of her robe and pricked Shanis' wrist. The blood glistened like the ruby eyes of the Silver Serpent. Shanis watched impassively as it trailed down her wrist and dripped into the bowl.

Steam billowed up, angry orange like sunset after a storm. The Keeper released her hand.

"Now, you shall submit to the mists." She placed a gentle hand on the back of Shanis' head and drew her face down toward the bowl of water. The steam wrapped around her, and she was falling... falling... falling...

Chapter 32

"Their main force is in sight, Highness." Colin grimaced, his fingers working as if seeking someone to throttle. "We shan't hold them long. Our supply of arrows is almost exhausted. All we have left are shafts sharpened and scorched at the tips." He bit his lip, putting Lerryn in mind of Colin's daughter Shanis. It was the first time he had noticed a resemblance between the two of them. "They must know we are on our last legs."

Lerryn was careful not to allow concern to show on his face or in his voice. "I do not think they know about my men, however. Surprise is in our favor. Perhaps we can hold them long enough for you and your men to flee into the forest."

"We will stand and fight, and perhaps die, but we will not flee." Determination glowed in Colin's dark eyes, and he threw Lerryn a challenging look, as if daring him to order the men to make their escape.

"Very well." He had suspected that would be the answer, and he admired the townspeople for their resolve. "See to it that your men hold their fire when we charge. We do not need to be struck by our own arrows." Colin's impatient nod was little more than a jerk of his head. "Another thing, Colin. There is too much to tell at the moment, but I want you to know that your daughter is well."

Colin gaped, stupefied by the words. He recovered from the surprise and bowed. "Thank you, Highness." The display of respect did not suit the man at all, which made Lerryn appreciate it all the more. "Forgive me, but, is she in Lothan?"

Lerryn nodded, wondering how Colin had known this. Having no time to spare for such puzzles, he turned and barked a series of clipped orders to his men. One of the soldiers brought Kreege to him, and he mounted up. His men formed up behind the makeshift gate.

For a moment, Lerryn considered making a final speech by which he could be remembered, should anyone survive to tell of this battle, but he discarded the thought as quickly as it had come. He was here to fight and die. Words would only delay that purpose, and the longer they waited, the greater the likelihood the enemy would spot them, and they would lose the element of surprise.

He signaled to Colin, who instructed his men to loose one volley on his command, and then hold. The order came, arrows sang through the morning sky, the gate was flung open, and the White Fang rode forth for the last time.

Up ahead, the enemy soldiers ducked beneath upraised shields, or just ducked, as arrows rained down. Lerryn and his men were almost upon the enemy before someone raised a warning cry.

There were defensive measures infantry could take against mounted men, but the marauding army had taken none of them. The head of the White Fang charge ran down the first men who tried to stand before them. Riders on either side broke off from the formation, sweeping around the flanks, looking for targets for their short bows. Lerryn and those supporting him went after anyone who looked like he was giving orders. Lerryn opened the throat of a man who was trying to regroup his confused troops. Tabars split another man's skull just as the fellow called for his men to rally.

All around him, warriors began a clumsy retreat. Lerryn did not waste his effort on those who were fleeing, unless they ran in front of Kreege, in which case they found themselves trampled beneath the warhorse's hooves. Instead, he concentrated on disposing of those who offered the most resistance, reasoning that breaking their will first, or simply breaking them, might cause even more men to flee.

A burly man with one eye thrust a spear at Lerryn's head. He batted the spear aside, slashed the man across his good eye, and wheeled around, looking for his next victim.

His battle senses had never been so clear. He supposed he had the Malan girl to thank for that. A shame this would be the last time he would get to use them. He spotted a cluster of men trying to drag Khattre from his saddle. The squad leader fought with sword and dagger to good effect, but there were too many of them for one man to hold off for long. Lerryn charged them, running down two and killing a third with a deft stroke of his sword. Khattre used the distraction to dispatch another attacker, and the two of them broke free.

Lerryn scanned the battlefield. His men were doing their job well. Only two of the White Fang lay among the dead that littered the open ground. All about him, his men were hacking or shooting down the enemy with reckless abandon.

But there were too many.

Despite their efforts, the marauders were regrouping, and finally using their numbers to their advantage. They attacked the riders in groups, seeking to encircle them and drag them from their mounts. At Lerryn's command, Khattre blew the rally order on his warhorn, and the riders began to fight their way free from the throng. Some had charged too deep into the ranks and were pulled down before they could break loose.

Another horn sounded in the distance, so shrill that it pained the ears. Lerryn saw the fleeing invaders slow, and then, one-by-one, turn and reluctantly head back toward the fray.

A tall warrior clad all in gray strode behind them. Flanked on either side by three ice cats, he held a sword in his right hand, and a crescent-shaped moon knife in his left. His form seemed to ripple as approached.

A shifter!

"You and Tabars take the lead!" Lerryn shouted to Khattre. He put heels to Kreege and charged.

The shifter saw Lerryn coming and ran to meet him. Meanwhile, the ice cats broke away from their master, charging into battle.

As the intervening space narrowed, Lerryn took in every detail of the creature:

the catlike eyes, its predatory face that shifted back and forth from flesh to fur, the bared fangs.

And then he was on it.

The shifter sprang aside, deftly avoiding Kreege's charge. Its sword whispered in a deadly arc, and Lerryn deflected it with a desperate parry. As he wheeled Kreege for another charge, the shifter sprang forward. The thing could leap like a mountain lion, and it cleared Kreege's hind quarters in one bound, slashing at Lerryn with its moon knife.

Lerryn twisted away from the strike and felt the blade skitter across his chain mail. Alarmed by the creature's attack, Kreege kicked out and struck the shifter a solid blow to the chest. The shifter cried out in a feral shriek of rage as it leapt back and crouched to spring again.

Knowing the beast was too quick for him to fight from the saddle, Lerryn leapt down, ducking behind Kreege as the shifter hurtled through the air where Lerryn had sat astride his mount an instant before. Sword in one hand, dagger in the other, he turned to face the creature.

The shifter sprang forward and thrust its sword at Lerryn's chest. He had known the thing was quick, yet had underestimated just how quick it was. He used his dagger to turn his opponent's thrust, pivoted out of the way, and struck back, but the shifter danced out of reach, its fangs bared in mocking laughter.

It went on that way for what felt like an eternity: thrust, slash, dance away. Lerryn had taken several superficial wounds and had inflicted none on the beast. He was breathing from his mouth, but the shifter seemed fresh. Lerryn would not last much longer.

The shifter attacked again, slashing at Lerryn's thigh. This time he did not try to parry the blow, but charged in at the moment the shifter committed to the attack. He felt the blade slice into his leg, but his timing was perfect. He caught the shifter off-balance. It raised its moon knife an instant too late, deflecting Lerryn's strike instead of blocking it, and the stroke that was intended for the shifter's neck banged off the creature's temple, denting its helm and sending it reeling back.

Abandoning his weapons, Lerryn dove onto the beast and bore it to the ground. Shifters were lightning-fast, but not as strong as a man, and this one was stunned from the blow to the head. He pushed the creature's arms apart as they fell. When they hit the ground, he shifted forward, pinning its arms. It thrashed and snarled, but could not break free. Mustering his remaining strength, he struck the shifter on the jaw. Its eyes clouded, and its form began to waver. He struck it again and felt the fight go out of the beast.

The battle fury full upon him and rage coursing through his veins, he wrapped his hands around the shifter's throat. He felt the flesh change to fur and the chest cavity narrow as it reverted to its true form. It struggled weakly for a moment, and then the life left its eyes.

Lerryn staggered to his feet and looked around, too weary to care if he was in danger. The attackers had rallied, and the battle had shifted to the walls. The bodies littering the field testified that his men had done their job well, but what remained of his force was now pressed back against the wall, fighting for their lives against the teeming mass of humanity that surged forward. Desperate townspeople manned the walls, struggling to keep the attackers at bay. They had to realize that hope was rapidly fading, yet they fought on. Where there was breath, a little hope remained.

He retrieved his sword, but forsook his dagger in favor of the shifter's moon knife. In a different time and place he would have admired the craftsmanship of this rare treasure from beyond the Claws, but there was no time. He was only one wounded man, but he would fight until the end. His eyes fell on two ice cats savaging a fallen soldier. Fury renewed his strength, and he charged.

If it is my day to die, I shall make it a day to remember.

The walls were holding. Colin was surprised they had held out for this long, but the attackers' lack of discipline, plus the heavy bite the White Fang had taken out of the enemy, was working to the Galsburans' advantage. Furthermore, the determination that came with fighting for home and family, and the reality that they all would surely die should they not emerge victorious, had strengthened their resolve. He now dared to hope that a few of them might survive this day.

He had only just permitted himself to entertain this thought when a cry of alarm arose from the eastern side of the town—the side opposite the mountains and farthest from the attack. A modest contingent of guards was keeping watch on that side.

He dashed toward the sound and caught sight of an ice cat as it pounced onto one of the few defenders who had maintained his post. The man's surprised shout was cut off in a strangled cry of pain as the cat ripped his throat open. As the remaining guards closed with the cat, another of the creatures clambered across the wall, sprang to the ground, and dashed away toward the town's center.

Colin had feared that a detachment of the enemy might try to circle away from the main attack and slip over the wall at a more vulnerable spot, but he had counted on the guards spotting the attack and sounding the warning in time for him to send support troops. These ice cats could move like the wind and melt into shadows when it suited them.

"Reserves to the east wall!" Hiram had been holding a few youths in reserve. They would make little difference if a larger force crossed the wall, but against two ice cats they could be of help, provided they kept their nerve.

Hiram came dashing out of the inn, his sword at the ready. He immediately spotted the ice cat, which had veered toward the very center of the green, putting the surprised firstman right in its path.

So fast was its attack that Hiram had time only to brace himself before the cat was upon him. Hiram went down in a blur of gray, his sword falling uselessly to the ground. The cat opened his throat with a single swipe and continued on its way.

Colin had never heard of an ice cat fighting with such precision. His question was immediately answered when the beast stopped just short of the sacred oak. Its form blurred, and suddenly a man stood in its place. The shifter raised its hand and fire burst forth, engulfing the sacred oak around which the town green was centered.

The shock caused Colin to stumble as he ran. A mage shifter? Here? Any remaining doubt he had that this was more than a marauding army was now gone.

The oak showed no damage from the burst of fire, but the ancient symbols carved into its trunk now glowed like iron in a forge. The mage shifter sent another burst at the tree, with no more discernible effect than the first blast.

And then Colin was on him.

The creature moved in a blur, dancing aside as Colin's sword sliced through empty air. He kicked out, and his foot met bone. The mage snarled as its leg went out from under it and it fell heavily to the ground. Colin stabbed at it, but it scrambled out of the way again. Colin pressed the attack, knowing he had no chance if the mage could gather its power.

The mage slipped a long knife from its belt, but Colin's ferocious stroke battered it from the creature's grip. His back stroke bit into the mage's chest, but not deep enough. The creature was wearing some sort of mail beneath his robes. It wasn't enough to completely stop his sword, but it prevented the stroke from being a killing blow. Colin yanked his blade free, but now the mage was on him, its fingers clutching at his throat. Colin lifted the mage bodily and slammed it to the ground, but it held on, pulling him down on top of it.

The hands gripping his throat suddenly felt like ice. It was gathering its power. Colin battered the creature's hands away and raised his fist to pound it into unconsciousness.

And he froze.

The shifter had him by the wrist, and the feeling was like an icy mountain river in the dead of winter pouring through his body. He could not resist. Somewhere nearby, he was aware of people running toward him, but he could not call out, could not turn to see who was coming to his aid. He could do nothing but stare into its eyes.

"Where is the girl?" The mage's voice was a primordial growl. "We can no longer see her. Our eyes grow cloudy and our senses dull. Where is she?"

Colin did not know the girl of whom it spoke, but his lips could not form the words. He tried to answer, but only a low groan rose from his throat.

The creature placed his other hand on Colin's temple. Colin's memories seemed to fly backward in a blur too fast to follow. Shanis swam to the surface, and the visions slowed. He relived their last argument in agonizing slowness, wishing he had taken her in his arms and held her close. And then the visions blurred again, this time moving forward, stopping at the moment just prior to the battle, when Lerryn had told him that Shanis was in Lothan.

The mage shifter snarled and pushed Colin off of him. The icy feeling that had engulfed him immediately melted, and Colin drew his knife, but the creature was now running away, this time toward the front gate. He scarcely had the energy to pursue it, but he forced his legs to move.

Up ahead, the mage shifted back into the form of an ice cat and dashed toward the gate. It was going to take the men at the gate from behind and let the attackers in. Colin shouted a warning, but the defenders could not hear him over the tumult of battle.

But the cat did not attack. It took the gate in one leap, bounding over the sharpened stakes and disappearing from sight. Its cry rang out above the din, startling the defenders who had not noticed it. Even the attackers trying to cross the wall seemed to freeze for a moment at the sound. Colin kept running, the creature's cries growing ever more strident, but receding fast. It seemed to be running away.

He reached the wall, sagged against it, and slid slowly to the ground. He had no strength left to fight. The mage power had drained him. His vision clouded, and sounds faded. He sucked in ragged breaths, filling his lungs with sweet air, and waited to fade into unconsciousness.

But he did not.

Gradually, his strength returned, and he was finally able to regain his feet. His head felt like it would split in two, but he otherwise felt strong and well. He scanned the walls and was surprised to see puzzled-looking defenders standing all along the line, weapons hanging loosely at their sides. Natin Marwell stood on a mound of earth a few paces away, staring out across the wall. Despite having only one hand, he had joined the defense of the town when it looked like the walls would be breached. His face was battered and filthy, and blood stained his long knife. He caught sight of Colin and shook his head.

"They left. That thing jumped over the gate and started roaring at them. Some of them seemed to understand, and they started calling for a retreat. Next thing I knew, they were all disappearing into the forest." He brushed a sleeve across his face, smearing the dirt and sweat. "A few of them made it across, and we killed them. But then there was the fire on the green, and I suppose we were distracted, because more of them came across. And then they were gone. Why did they leave?"

"I don't know for certain, but I suspect our defenses finally proved to be too much for them." Colin suspected he did, in fact, know why the enemy had called off the attack, but he saw no reason to tell the townsfolk. They had fought bravely. Let them feel they had won the victory. "But I don't think they will be back."

Chapter 33

Shanis drifted in clouds of gray vapor, her body without substance, a mere consciousness within the shifting mists. Shadows drifted toward her, little more than dark outlines within the endless grayness.

The mists swirled and then opened to reveal a forest. She floated among the tree limbs. Looking down, she saw a young man and young woman clutched in a tight embrace. Her heart lurched. It was her and Larris on their last night together. She watched as Larris wiped the tears from her cheeks. She tried to turn away, to flee from the agonizing scene, but the mists held her fast, forcing her to live that painful night again. When it was over, and the two of them had gone their separate ways, the mists spun again.

As if an invisible hand was drawing back a curtain, the mists parted again to reveal a new scene. She held Khalyndryn in her lap as the girl gasped for breath, an arrow lodged firmly in her chest. Blood oozed from the side of her mouth. She looked up at Shanis with fading eyes and whispered, "I finally found my purpose."

She cried out in anger and pain as the mist engulfed her. Wrapped in their cocoon, she was powerless to escape as it carried her deeper into the past.

Now she saw her father kneeling at the bedside of a beautiful auburn-haired woman. Mistress Anna stood at the foot of the bed, holding a baby wrapped in swaddling. Colin's eyes glistened with unshed tears as the woman stroked his cheek.

"Now, do no be like that." The woman's voice was weak. "We do have us a beautiful little girl. You must take good care of her and teach her right. She will be someone very special someday."

"You are someone special." Colin could scarcely speak, so choked with emotion was his voice. "I don't want to lose you. You are my treasure."

"Now," the woman whispered, "you do be sweet to say so." Shanis cried insubstantial tears as her mother closed her eyes and passed away.

What was this cruelty? Why was she being forced to witness these excruciating scenes? Was it a test of her ability to endure pain? If so, she would not relent. She was made of stronger stuff than that.

The visions continued.

She watched Aspin draw a metal band from his wrist and hurl it to the ground. A dark-skinned soldier scowled and fingered a fox medallion underneath his cloak as he watched an aging priest place a crown on a young man's head. An old Malgog dashed into a burning hut and staggered out moments later carrying a squalling baby.

And then the mist spiraled like a whirlpool, sucking her down into the midst of a high mountain range. Their snow-capped peaks seemed to reach up toward her like icy claws, threatening to snatch her, but she plummeted down through them and into the very rock of which they were formed.

Now she drifted in pulsating ripples of blue light. In fact, she was the light, ebbing and flowing in the darkness, filling every space with her power.

Five men and one woman stood in a semi-circle, all bathed in blue light. Behind each stood a priest chanting words Shanis could not quite discern. The woman, a tall, blonde wearing a golden tiara stepped forward to face a young man who could only be her son. He wept openly, but his mother laid a hand on his shoulder and spoke to him in reassuring tones. The young man nodded and raised... a stone sword? He placed the tip against her heart, his hands shaking so that he could scarcely hold it in place. He hesitated, but she nodded and spoke to him again. He bit his lip, took a deep breath, and thrust. Her expression barely changed as the sword pierced her heart. As she crumpled to the floor, her son dropped to his knees, letting the stone sword, which now glimmered as if dusted with stars, fall from a limp hand.

Next, a lean man wearing a golden circlet with a raven set in its center stepped forward. A weeping girl picked up the stone sword and placed it against his chest, but froze. He whispered words of comfort to her. Then, placing one hand over hers, and gripping the cross-guard with the other, he forced the sword into his own heart.

She watched as the ritual was repeated four more times. Each person stepped forward to be killed by a reluctant young person who appeared to be her or his son or daughter. Each time, the stone sword shone brighter.

When the last person had fallen, the priests stepped forward, each continuing his chant. As one, they took hold of the sword and raised it into the air. Six tiny sparks of light whirled in the air above the sword, growing brighter as they circled one another. The light grew to the intensity of a tiny sun until, with a flash, it shot down into the sword, which burned brightly for a moment, then fell to the ground amidst the ashes of what, moments before, had been six priests, where it glistened in the blue light. The serpents on its blade looked alive, and the ruby eyes on the stylized hilt flashed dark red.

Shanis gasped as she realized she had just witnessed the creation of the Silver Serpent.

Before she could wonder at what she had just seen, the mist carried her up into the sky. Far below, she and Pedric Karst faced one another, each backed by an army of Lothans, but behind Karst's army loomed a dark specter, its sinister form growing ever larger as it rose above the horizon. As it grew, it formed into a vaguely human shape that towered over the army. Power emanated from it in dark waves, and wherever it stepped, the land was made barren. She turned to see a figure standing above the mountains behind her own army. Snow and ice raged within it, and whatever it touched froze and shattered.

She saw herself raise a sword and cleave the land between her and Karst. Where she smote the ground, a river grew between them, pushing the armies apart. She broke the sword over her knee, tossed it into the river, and turned to face the thing in the mountains.

It looked down upon her with eyes of ice, reached out a hand, and all was black.

Chapter 34

"Have you any food, my lords?" The dirty-faced woman grasped at Larris' leg as he rode by. "We are starving." Others took up the cry, and the crowd began to press in on the riders. Allyn rapped the woman across the knuckles with the flat of his sword, and she sprang back with a cry of pain, sticking her fingers in her mouth. She fixed them with a reproachful stare, and others muttered their disapproval, but they now gave way as Allyn rode to the front of the group and led them down the road to the gates of Archstone.

"Swords out," Larris instructed, keeping his voice low, "but do not use them. We only want the people to leave us alone until we reach the city."

"Forgive me, Highness, but could we not give them what food we have? Surely we will not need these meager rations when we are inside the city." Hair frowned down at two skinny children sitting in the dirt staring up at them, too weary to even play. His shoulders sagged as he looked into their hopeless faces, and he thought he understood a little better why Shanis had made the choice to remain in Lothan.

"We no have enough food to feed all of the people. Look at all of them." Rinala made a sweeping gesture that took in the veritable city of humanity that had sprung up outside Archstone in the form of tents, lean-tos, and shacks as refugees had poured into the capital from the north and the west. "At the first sign of food, they will tear each other apart to get it, and maybe do tear us apart, too. And even if they did no do that, how would we choose who do get fed and who continues to starve?"

Larris continued to be impressed by Hierm's wife. She was perceptive, and had a greater breadth of knowledge about the world than he had expected from a Monaghan tribeswoman, whom he had always imagined to be fairly primitive.

"Your wife is a wise woman, Van Derin, even if she does interrupt on occasion." After parting ways with Lerryn, he had explained to the others the need for him to adopt a more formal way of interacting with them. Once inside Archstone, it would not do for the first prince to interact with commoners as if they were his equals. Everyone had understood and all, save Rinala, had complied.

He did not truly mind. The closer they drew to the capital, the heavier the duties of his new rank seemed to weigh upon him. He was going to miss the easy interaction and camaraderie of the trail. That was far from the only thing he would miss, but he shoved those feelings as far from his conscious mind as he could. Freeze Lerryn for doing this to him!

"I am no wise." Rinala shook her head. "I have known too many hungry people, that do be all." The melancholy in her voice was matched by her downcast expression.

The sun shone brightly on the city walls, atop which bright banners snapped smartly in the crisp breeze against a clear blue sky. He wondered how such a beauty could hang above a scene of such sadness, as if the gods were taunting the wretched and downtrodden.

The city gate, colossal double doors of iron-bound wood, loomed before them.

Sentries manned the gate towers on either side, their bearing alert and suspicious. Larris felt their gaze upon him, and was painfully aware that one false move, or an impulsive decision by an archer on the gates, could spell doom for him or one or more of his party.

A contingent of guards stood sentry outside the gates. They waited until Larris and the others had reined in before one guard approached them.

"Name yourself and your business." His bored expression indicated that he did not particularly care who they were or what their business was; he would hear what they had to say, and then turn them away.

Larris drew from within his cloak the document naming him First Prince of the Sword. He unrolled it far enough to reveal Lerryn's seal and signature, and held it up for all the guards to see.

"We are on the prince's business. We will require an escort to the palace."

The guard frowned. "Does that document state that all of you must go to the palace? If you are merely delivering a message, there is no need for all of you to enter the city."

"Can you even read?" Allyn interrupted, his voice dripping with scorn.

The guard's face reddened, and he took a step toward Allyn, his hand on the pommel of his sword. "You can watch your tongue or you will enter the city in chains. These gates are closed by order of the king himself, and none may enter, save they have a very good reason."

A second guard joined them, holding out his hand to Larris. "I have my letters, M'lord. Let me see that paper."

This would not do at all. Larris had hoped the seal would be enough to gain him entry to the city without questions being asked or his identity being revealed. That was no longer a possibility, but he positively could not have news of Lerryn's abdication whispered about the city before he could deliver the news to his father.

"Enough of this!" He threw back the hood of his cloak, and then stripped the glove from his left hand. He held up his hand, displaying his signet ring that was the sign of his office. "I am Prince Larris Van Altman. You will escort us to the palace immediately, and you will speak of this to no one." He knew the latter command was futile. Soldiers gossiped as much as any chamber maid.

That did it. The guards babbled apologies and explanations as they scrambled to open the gates.

"I thank you for your assistance." Now that these men were compliant, there was no need to browbeat them. You never knew when the loyalty of even the most ordinary man might prove to be useful. "I shall commend you to my father for the seriousness with which you have taken the responsibility of guarding these gates." The relief in their faces was almost comical.

They passed through the main gate and into the barbican. An aging man, uniformed, but armed with a quill, recorded their names in a ledger. He frowned at the name Van Derin and turned back several pages in his records with trembling, liver-spotted hands.

"Are you any relation to a Mistress Faun Van Derin and Laman Van Derin?"

"They are my mother and brother. Why do you ask?" Hierm squeezed Rinala's hand.

"They took up residence in the city prior to the King's closing of the gates. I remember your mother asking to be notified if word came of her other son. I assume she meant you."

"And what of my father, Hiram Van Derin?"

The guard took a second look at his book. "I fear I have no record of anyone by that name entering the city, at least not in recent weeks." His mouth crinkled in a poor attempt at a sympathetic frown. "I can have one of my men escort you to your mother if you like."

"That is a fine idea." Larris turned to Hierm. "You should see your mother and let her meet your wife. I shall send for you soon."

Rinala and Hierm bade them goodbye. Next, Larris had Edrin and Hair, or Mattyas, as the young man would be called upon entering the academy, taken to the nearby barracks to be fed and outfitted for service. Finally, he took a deep breath and looked at Allyn.

"I suppose it is time, Your Royal Highness." Allyn made a mocking bow.

"That it is." Larris signaled for the guards to lead the way, and they trotted out into the city. In the distance, the spires of the royal palace were just visible. He frowned. He remembered all the times he had rued his position as second prince, wishing he could one day be king. And now he was first prince, and it was the last thing he wanted.

"Are you unwell? You look as if you have eaten a dozen green apples." Allyn's sardonic grin was back—a sure sign he was recovering.

"I am all right." It was a lie, but what did it matter? Right now, he could see no way to redirect the course of his life. The path the gods had laid out before him was not of his choosing, but he must follow it, at least for now. "I was just thinking that nothing is ever going to be the same again."

Chapter 35

"Oskar, you are not concentrating! You have parried that stroke hundreds of times before." The anger fled Aspin's face as quickly as it had come. His expression softened, and he laced his fingers over the end of his staff and leaned on it, staring through the trees in the direction of Calmut.

"It has been three days and still nothing." Oskar spun his staff as he, too, gazed into the distance. He had almost forgotten what the sun looked like, so cloudy had it been since the day Shanis entered Calmut. Dense clouds blanketed the sky above them, hanging precariously low like a hammer about to fall.

He was not sure what he hoped to see as he stared toward the ruined city. Shanis emerging from the forest with an army of Lothans at her heels? Shanis walking along, having failed in her quest, but ready to return to their old life, to be his friend again? He dismissed that thought. There was no returning home for him, whatever path Shanis took. Though he felt a touch of homesickness, village life had never been for him. He had gotten his first taste of the larger world, and though it had sometimes been bitter, it had whetted his appetite. He wanted more.

"Regardless," Aspin reproved, "you must always concentrate on the task at hand. Push your worries to the back of your mind and focus your thoughts."

"What if I can't do that?"

"Then one day someone will kill you." Aspin's voice was conversational, but his face mirrored the gravity of his words. "Your heart is your strength, but if you cannot master it, it will be your undoing."

"You sound like Master Yurg," Oskar grinned at the memory of the old swordmaster chastising Shanis and Hierm, but his heart fell. He still could not believe the man was gone. Shanis and Hierm had been closer to Yurg, and thus had taken the news much harder than he, but Oskar had admired the man, and keenly felt his absence at moments such as this.

"Yurg was a good man. One of the finest you or I will ever meet. And he would not want you to let Shanis distract you from what you must do."

Aspin had never explained exactly how he had known Yurg, but this was not the time to ask. Besides, he doubted Aspin would answer him.

"I want to help her." Oskar's throat tightened as he spoke. "I could not help Allyn. He asked me to help him, but I thought what happened to us in the mountains had addled his mind, so I did nothing. I slept through the raid when Shanis' sword was stolen. My home is being attacked and I sit here playing with sticks, pretending I shall be a saikur some day."

Aspin's eyes, so like a bird of prey, bore into Oskar, and he smiled.

"Your story is not yet written. You are strong of mind, body, and heart, and I have no doubt you will be a saikur one day, provided you can learn to believe in yourself as others believe in you."

"No one believes in me." Oskar kicked at a pebble. He was being childish, but just now it felt good to indulge his emotions a little bit. "I was always the odd one: in my family, in town, among my friends…"

A cry rang out, followed by what sounded like a multitude of voices calling out as one. A column of silver-gray mist shot up toward the sky from the direction of Calmut. Straight up it climbed, spinning like a maelstrom, until it met the low-hanging clouds. Flecks of silver spread across the cloud cover, setting the blanket of gray to sparkling. All around them, guards dropped their weapons and dashed toward the column to see what was the cause.

Oskar hesitated only a moment. "The winter take me if I am going to stand here a moment longer!" Clutching his staff, he dashed off behind the guards. He did not know what he would find when he got there, but no longer would he sit passively by and wait. If Shanis should have need of him, he was going to be there for her.

The chamber was empty. The fire was reduced to cold ash, and the bowl was dry. All about her was black, save the faint light of the passage in front of her.

The way out.

She tried to stand and found herself weak as a newborn babe. She took several deep breaths and gathered herself for the effort. She forced herself to her feet, head spinning, and staggered on unsure legs to the arched tunnel that she somehow knew would take her back to Calmut.

Warm, fresh air with the scent of rain and earth clinging to it welcomed her as she stepped out of the chamber and into the tunnel. It seemed to renew her strength and steady her steps as she began her ascent.

She had taken only a few steps when someone called out. She froze. The sound came again, a cry of pure despair that pierced her soul. And it was coming from behind her. She turned back to the chamber from which she had just come, and stopped short.

The cavern floor was now a morass of black mud and filthy water. Water dripped from the walls, and moss dangled from the ceiling. The fire was burning again, a sick, smoky green, and in its glow Pedric Karst writhed, his face twisted in agony. Though she detested the young man, she could not leave him writhing in the filth.

Returning to the cavern, she slogged through the thick mud and grabbed Karst by the wrist.

"Get up Karst! It is time to go. Come with me. I'll help you up and we'll get out of here." She would rather have asked Mistress Faun for dancing lessons than speak to Karst in such a friendly, encouraging manner, but she knew she was doing the right thing. He was her enemy. She could leave him here to die, but there would be no honor in it. Master Yurg would never have approved.

Karst looked up at her with blank eyes. Blood oozed from deep scratches where he had clawed at his own face. He gaped at her, slack-jawed and bewildered. For a moment she wondered if he had lost his mind, but finally he spoke.

"Not you." His voice was a groan of abiding agony. "Anyone but you."

"There is no one else but me. Come with me or die here. Your choice."

Where her kindness had met with rejection, her blatant disregard for his well-being prodded him to action. He permitted her to help him to his feet, but refused further assistance until he stumbled and fell flat on his face in the mud. Grimacing, she grabbed him by the belt and collar, hauled him up to all fours, and half-led, half-dragged him through the mud and up the tunnel. The way grew steeper, and Karst could bear little of his own weight.

As their climb grew more difficult, he grew more and more surly, muttering deprecations under his breath in a hollow voice. By the time her eyes fell upon the dancing silver mist curtain that she hoped marked the way out, she was ruing her decision to help him at all. She released her grip on Karst and he dropped like a sack of grain.

"The way out is there," she said. "Stand up and walk out on your own like a man."

"What does a girl know of being a man?" A drop of his characteristic venom returned to his speech.

"More than you do. If it were not for me, you would still be down there wallowing in the mud, and crying like a newborn. Now stand up!"

Karst raised his hand as if to shield himself from her words. He gaped at her for a moment, and then life slowly returned to his eyes. His flinty stare was soon back. He took a deep breath, shuddering as he let it out, and then rose on unsteady legs. He braced himself against the wall and closed his eyes. He was a muddy, bloody mess.

"Why do you care what happens to me?" She could not tell if it was suspicion or hatred that marred his face. Probably a healthy dose of each.

Shanis did not have to mull the question over. There was only one honest answer.

"I don't." She turned her back on him and passed through the mist.

Chapter 36

A clamor arose from the throng pressing toward the center of Calmut. Oskar whispered one of the few spells he had mastered, and a sliver of air snaked through the mass of bodies. Another word and it pushed apart, shoving people to one side or the other and opening a path through a wall of startled onlookers. He was too focused on his destination to be amused at the confused and even angry expressions that turned his way as he lumbered by.

"Very good!" Aspin shouted from behind him. "Not as discreet as one might like, but nicely done."

He stopped at the edge of a stone circle that seemed to mark a line that the clanspeople dared not cross. Inside, the chieftains sat around a pool of quakewater from which the silver mist poured on its way to the sky.

The mist dissipated, and a figure gradually appeared. No. Two figures came forth! Shanis and Karst both stood before the chieftains, but the two could not look more different. Shanis stood confidently, a hint of her old temper flaring in her eyes. Karst was caked in mud, and his face was cut, but his glare was as defiant as ever.

A hush fell over those assembled, broken only by confused whispers. Perhaps they had expected only one of the two to return. The chieftains exchanged long looks, but no one seemed willing to be the first to speak.

Oskar wanted to ask them what they were waiting for, but knew it would be foolish to say anything just now. He was not even supposed to be here.

After what seemed an eternity, a Malgog chief addressed Shanis and Karst. "You have submitted to the Keeper of the Mists, and you both have returned. What words have you for us?"

"I am the one." Karst stepped forward. Despite his present state, he held his chin high. "A walk through the mud in the darkness did nothing to change that. I am the same man I was when I entered."

Several of the chieftains exchanged whispers behind their hands, disapproval clearly evident in their eyes. This was obviously not the reply they had been expecting. Horgris rocked back and forth, tapping his toe and chewing his lip. He appeared torn between the desire to speak and the need to give no hint of partiality.

Culmatan finally broke the silence. "We do be asking what did the Keeper show you?"

Karst flinched at the question, and his complexion grew even paler, but he did not waver. "She showed me that, without me, you will surely die." He let that sink in, looking around at each leader in turn, and then extending his gaze to the masses that pressed in close to hear his words. "All of you. I am your only hope."

His words had no visible effect on the chieftains, but a ripple of whispers flowed through the throng of Lothans who watched the proceedings. Oskar ignored them. He was waiting for Shanis to speak. In fact, he was surprised she had held her tongue for this long.

Culmatan turned to Shanis. "And tell us what the Keeper did show you."

Keep your temper, Shanis. Just hold on to your temper. Don't do anything to give offense. Oskar tried to send his thoughts across the intervening space, though he knew it to be foolish. Karst had not made a good showing so far, and Oskar sensed that Shanis could persuade the Lothans to accept her if she could just present herself as a calm, confident leader.

Shanis' expression was unreadable. She took her time in answering Culmatan's question. "She showed me things about my past that are not for you to know."

Oskar grimaced, wondering how best to get himself and Shanis out of here alive should she let loose with one of her tirades in the midst of all of these people. He saw no way out through this mass of humanity. He supposed he would have to use the air spell again.

"A few of the things she showed me I do not yet fully understand. But I can tell you this much with certainty." Shanis took a step forward, ignoring Karst's offended stare. "Your greatest threat is no longer your neighboring clan. I have seen the shadow of a grave danger rising in the east, and the frost is marching in the west. Clan war ends today, whether you wish it or not. Unite now, or Lothan shall be crushed between the hammer and the anvil."

These words should have offended at least some of the Lothans, Oskar was sure, but to a man, Shanis' words had silenced them.

"Many here have seen me heal your injured. The power of the Silver Serpent can work through me to mend the direst of wounds, but it is foolishness to heal one person at a time, only to watch you cut them down again. No one has been spared in your foolish wars. Women, children, and elders all suffer and die along with your young men. I have seen your suffering. I have seen the remnants of once proud cities now fallen to ruin." She paused again, letting the words sink in. No one was paying any attention to Karst now.

"I did not come to Calmut to convince anyone that I am the rightful bearer of the Silver Serpent. I did not come here to claim the right to lead you in battle." She let the words hang in the ringing silence. "I came to Calmut to heal a nation."

Oskar's blood sang, and he found himself drawn in by her words as much as everyone around him. He had never heard Shanis talk this way. Where had it come from? Then he remembered all the evenings she and Larris spent alone, deep in quiet conversation. Perhaps the young prince had given her lessons in how to inspire one's followers. Whatever he had done, it had wrought an amazing change in Shanis.

"But I swear this to you. If I must, I will take up the Silver Serpent and bend each of you to my will if that is what it takes to make you stop killing your children and scourging your land. Lothan will once again be one nation, and will stand as one to weather the storms to come."

Oskar bit his lip. So much for the diplomatic, inspirational Shanis. Leave it to her to issue a challenge to several thousand people at once. He glanced at Aspin, whose blank stare revealed nothing. Fortunately, they did not seem angered by her words—only thoughtful.

"I am the one!" Karst shouted into the silence. "I bore the Silver Serpent to Calmut. I have already united the east, and I come with an army at my back. What does she come with? Nothing!"

"Then take up the sword." Shanis' voice was a calm counterpoint to Karst's rage. "Draw the Silver Serpent from its sheath, raise it up for all to see, and call upon its power. I will not try to stop you. Show us you are the one."

Karst was dumbstruck. His lips moved, but he spoke not a word. His knuckles shone white and his clenched fists trembled. His eyes flitted to and fro like the mouse cornered by the snake.

"Endgame," Aspin whispered in a voice almost too low to be heard. He smiled and nudged Oskar. "Look! Krion is holding the sword."

A Malgog clan chief stood, holding the Silver Serpent by its sheath. "Come, Pedric Karst. You claim to be the bearer. Take up your sword."

The young man had no choice. Making his way across a footpath that spanned the quakewater, he stood almost nose-to-nose with Krion. He turned to cast a defiant glance at Shanis before grasping the hilt of sword.

The effect was instantaneous.

Karst gasped and tremors racked his body, but he did not release his grip on the sword. With spasmodic jerks, he inched the gleaming sword from the scabbard. Sweat poured in rivulets down through the dried dirt and blood on his face. Using his left hand to steady his right arm, he lifted the sword above his head.

And then he screamed.

The sword clattered to the ground, and Karst fell next to it, clutching his right hand against his body and convulsing. When the spasms abated, he rolled over onto his side and vomited into the quakewater. Afterward, he did not try to rise, but lay trembling in the dirt.

Krion ignored the young man, but instead looked expectantly at Shanis, who took her time crossing the quakewater to stand before the chief.

At this moment she was every bit the girl Oskar had grown up with, her face shining with a self-confidence bordering on fearlessness, and her eyes issuing a challenge to all who met her stare. Keeping her eyes on Krion, she knelt down, took the sword in her hand, and stood. She now turned about, looking each clan chief in the eye, as if daring any of them to speak.

She thrust the Silver Serpent into the air. Sparks danced around the blade for an instant, and then a bolt of pure white light erupted forth from the tip. It shot skyward, piercing the gray clouds, which rolled back like ripples on a pond, letting blue sky shine through.

The silence broke all at once as every man and woman cried out as one. All around him, people jumped up and down, raised their hands in the air, and cried out in triumph. This outpouring of sheer joy was so unlike anything he had previously experienced with these people, who had always seemed so morose and downtrodden.

When the tumult died down, the clan chiefs rose. Krion spoke first. "Shanis Malan is the true bearer of the Silver Serpent."

Every clan chief repeated the affirmation, until only Horgris remained. The big Monaghan did not merely speak the words, but raised his fists and shouted for all to hear.

"Shanis Malan do be the bearer of the Silver Serpent!" As the crowd roared again, he dropped to one knee and bowed his head. Soon, others followed suit, until Oskar and Aspin were among the few who remained standing.

Some of the Lothans, however, apparently had no intention of kneeling to Shanis. The young men who had arrived with Karst remained standing, as did a few others scattered throughout the crowd. None of them looked directly at her, but stole glances out of the corners of their eyes and whispered amongst themselves.

Shanis did not notice. The Lothans were showing no signs of rising, and the silence now bordered on interminable. She looked at Oskar, frowned, and mouthed, "What should I do?"

Oskar could not help but grin. He shrugged and looked to Aspin, who motioned that the Lothans should stand.

"Y-you may rise!" Though her voice was uncertain, she had once again drawn the mask of supreme confidence over her visage.

A roar went up again as the Lothans stood as one.

"What do we do with this one?" Culmatan had to shout to be heard above the din, and his voice carried to where Oskar stood. He indicated Karst, who was now sitting up, still clutching his hand against his chest.

Shanis scowled at Karst. "See if someone can treat his hand; then let him go."

"I need no help!" Karst clambered to his feet, his face beet red. "I am leaving here for now, but mark my words. I shall be back to take my revenge." He tried to stagger away, but Horgris grabbed him by the collar and held him fast.

"Kill him!" One of the nearby Lothans bellowed. Others quickly took up the cry.

Shanis held up her hand to stymie the shouts. She stepped directly in front of Karst, so they were almost nose-to-nose. It seemed to Oskar that the space between them might erupt in flames, so intense were their stares.

"You may go and none shall harm you." The crowd fell silent at her words. "But if you or yours should dare take up arms against any Lothans, I promise you shall die by my hand." She continued to stare unblinking at Karst, whose jaw worked, but he made no sound.

For a moment, Oskar feared Karst would try to attack Shanis. He took a step toward her, and immediately felt Aspin's hand on his shoulder, pulling him back.

"She is doing fine. Do not interfere."

Of course there was no need for Oskar to try and help. Horgris still held Karst by the collar, and he and the other chiefs could intervene should they deem it necessary. Oskar released the breath he was unaware he had been holding.

Karst stared for a moment longer before muttering a curse, turning, and trying to pull away from Horgris, who maintained his grip for a moment, then let go, causing the young man to fall face-first to the ground. A few jeers and guffaws rang out, but most continued to watch in silence. He wasted no time regaining his feet and stalking away. Some in the crowd moved aside to let him pass, but others took obvious pleasure in making him worm his way through.

Oskar noticed that those who had not knelt to Shanis were also leaving. "How can they follow him?" he muttered. "He has made a fool of himself."

"Some people will only believe that which they want to believe." Aspin kept his voice low as he spoke. "Some will not accept a woman as a leader."

"But they revere Badla, almost worship her. She is the reason they have been at war all these years." He still could not believe that the dispute over whether to commit the great warrior queen's remains to water or earth had led to so much death and devastation.

"For some, she is merely their excuse to go to war. There is a difference. Many will follow Karst because conflict is all they know and all they care about. I fear we have not heard the last of him or them."

Somewhere in the distance, a cry arose, followed by a chorus of shouts, some gleeful, others indignant. The sound drew closer, and Oskar could make out chants of "Badla! Badla!" amidst the cacophony. A dark shape wended its way through the throng, coming ever closer to the circle where Shanis waited with the clan chiefs.

A dozen Monaghan men were carrying what looked to Oskar to be an ornately carved tree trunk, worn smooth by weather and age. And then he remembered. The Lothans used tree trunks as coffins. They were bringing forth the mortal remains of Badla, the celebrated warrior queen. He remembered that, after her death, while the Lothans argued over where her mortal remains should be interred, sorcerers had magically preserved her body. Oskar shuddered at the thought that she lay inside that hollowed-out tree looking exactly as she had on the day of her death. There was something unnatural and almost sinister about the thought.

As they entered the circle of stones, the warrior in the lead called out for all to hear. "The warriors of the Green Mountain Clan do bring Badla to Calmut! All honor be to the Green Mountain!" The few shouts of approval from the other members of the clan were drowned out by derisive cries from the rest of the Lothans.

"The Green Mountain did steal Badla from the Mud Snakes!" one Malgog shouted. "They did take her while under the peace of Calmut!"

"Badla was no inside Calmut." The Green Mountain spokesman shook his fist at the accuser. "You did encamp far from the city!"

Suddenly, it seemed everyone was shouting. Oskar could not make out a single word in the din. Even the chieftains were arguing. He could read Shanis' lips as she shouted for everyone to stop, but no one heard her. Her face was beet red, and Oskar could tell that she was moments from doing some damage with that sword of hers, but he could think of nothing he could do to help.

A group of Mud Snakes charged the Green Mountain men who held Badla high overhead. Above the throng, Oskar watched the casket move to and fro with the ebb and flow of the crowd. It wobbled, teetered...

...and crashed to the ground.

Those who saw what had happened uttered a collective gasp and stood in mute surprise. Those who could not see continued their arguing, but word quickly passed through the crowd, and peace reigned again.

The craftsmanship of the log casket was such that it had looked to Oskar to be one single piece, but as it struck the ground, a previously indiscernible lid came free and the body inside tumbled to the ground.

Oskar gaped at the remains of the warrior queen. She lay contorted like a grotesque marionette, gazing up at the sky through sightless eyes. He could not stop himself. He approached the body, drawn forward as if pulled by an unseen force, his gaze never leaving the face that was so like....

Shanis pushed her way through the crowd, but stopped short when she saw Badla. "What madness is this?" Her voice quavered and the blood drained from her face as she stared transfixed at the body that lay before her.

"Shanis," Oskar whispered, looking first at Shanis, then down at the body, and then back up at Shanis. "She's you!"

Chapter 37

The soft knock startled Jowan from his quiet reflection. It was well known that no one was to interrupt him during this time, save for matters of only the greatest importance. His heart pounding and his neck prickly hot from annoyance, he took a moment to gather himself before responding. As High Priest, he went to great pains to always appear to be in complete control, regardless of how he truly felt.

"You may enter."

Gemel entered, looking abashed. He dropped to one knee and lowered his head.

"You may rise. Now, what is it, Gemel?"

"Holiness, there is word of the prince." Gemel's words came out in a rush. "He entered the city a short while ago and is being escorted to the palace as we speak."

"And which prince would this be?"

Gemel's face reddened. "It is Prince Larris, Holiness. The second prince."

Jowan suppressed a smile. If only Gemel knew the truth. It was too bad Larris was not attempting to slip through the city on his own, which would be very much in character for the impulsive young prince. Were that the case, Jowan could simply send out the temple guard to bring Larris to him. With the prince guarded, however, that was not an option. Too many potential witnesses. If he could not take Larris, he would have to settle for the document.

"Word must be sent to those inside the palace. The prince is in possession of a certain document that I must have before it reaches the king."

Gemel screwed up his face as he always did when he was trying to decide how to phrase an objection in a way that would not offend Jowan.

"The prince will doubtless need to bathe and make himself presentable before being received by the king," Jowan continued before Gemel could interrupt. "Considering the unique position of one of our agents inside the palace, it should be a simple matter to take the document then, should it not?"

Gemel smiled. "That it will, Holiness. I shall send word immediately." He paused. "May I ask why this document is of such great importance?"

Now Jowan did smile. He folded his hands, leaned toward Gemel in conspiratorial fashion, and lowered his voice to a whisper. "The prince has been corrupted by the wildlings of Lothan. He has abandoned the Seven, and now he seeks to spread his heresy to Galdora. If I could stop him from reaching the palace, I would, but I cannot do so without rousing the king's ire. It is essential that we have that document before great damage is done. Can I rely on you?"

"Absolutely, Holiness." Gemel's eyes gleamed. "I promise; it shall be done."

"Highness, you are dirtier than I have ever seen you." Melina scrubbed Larris' back with a coarse wool cloth. The trail dirt came away in broad streaks, revealing swathes of skin turned pink from the scrubbing. "And I have seen you quite filthy in your lifetime." She poured warm, scented water over his back, sluicing away the grime.

"You don't have to remind me." Larris grinned up at her. Melina had tended both princes from birth, and they treated her, if not like a mother, then like a member of the family.

Orphaned as a young child, she had been taken in by the Temple of the Seven and raised there, first helping with the cleaning, and later the cooking. She had been spared the life of a ritual prostitute, the fate of most of the desperate young women who found their way into the temple, when Timmon, a kindly old priest who worked as a healer, had taken a liking to her. Contrary to the rumors whispered around the temple, there was nothing unsavory about their relationship. Amused by her sharp tongue and strong will, Timmon had taken her under his wing, and taught her to read, write, and do sums. Eventually, he permitted her to assist him with his daily work.

When Melina was fifteen, Timmon was called to the palace to attend to baby Lerryn. The child had a high fever which no one had been able to bring down. While Timmon puzzled over the illness, Melina held and comforted the baby. She had leaned down to nuzzle his head when she spotted something everyone else had missed—two tiny red dots behind his ear. The child had been bitten by a rare spider, and Melina's discovery saved his life. The king and queen had been so impressed by Melina they had made her Lerryn's nurse that very night. She had not wanted to take the position, but Timmon had insisted. It was not long before she learned why.

"I do think I am perhaps too old for you to still be giving me my bath." Larris' voice brought her thoughts back to the present.

"Royals do not bathe themselves, Highness. I am, however, satisfied that no sores or injuries requiring my attention lurk beneath this layer of dirt." She glanced at the serving girl who had just entered carrying a fresh set of clothes for the prince. "Sarill, will you finish for me?"

Sarill took the cloth from Melina and began scrubbing. The weary prince sighed and let his chin fall to his chest, and his eyes close. Melina scooped up his soiled clothing and his leather bag and made to leave.

"You may leave my bag here," Larris called. Apparently his eyes were not completely shut.

"I can leave it in your chamber for you, if you like." Melina tried to keep her tone nonchalant. Obviously, the document was in this bag.

"There is no need."

Melina laid the bag down, her mind working at a rapid clip. She moved back to Larris' side, her eyes narrowed and her mouth twisted into a grimace, as if she had spotted something distasteful. He looked up at her and arched an eyebrow. She pretended to give his hair a close inspection. After a minute's probing, she sighed.

"Vermin," she muttered. "Have you perhaps been sleeping in barns?"

"Since leaving home, I have slept in every sort of place you can imagine." He shook his head, a look of resignation on his face. "Let me guess. Lye soap?"

"Precisely." Melina looked at Sarill and adopted a commanding tone. "Two washings should do it. Use a towel to keep the lye out of his eyes, nose, and ears."

Sarill winced as she handed Larris a towel and took up the bar of the strong lye soap they kept on hand to kill lice, mites, and skin pests. Larris covered his face and ears with the towel, and Sarill began to scrub.

"It stings!" Larris grumbled. "Isn't there anything else that can do the job without burning my skin off?"

"Why do you think it works so well, Highness?" Melina smirked. The soap would do him no harm, though his skin would be red and tender for a day. Making certain Sarill was concentrating on her task, she opened Larris' bag and quickly found what she was looking for. She slid the rolled parchment into her baggy sleeve, retrieved the bundle of dirty clothes, and left the bath chamber.

She left the soiled clothing with the laundress and went directly to her suite of rooms, all the while expecting Larris to come chasing after her, demanding to know what had become of his stolen paper. When she reached her quarters, she locked the door behind her and sat on her bed, catching her breath.

The temple had frequently asked her for information, and she had always been happy to provide it. Her devotion to Timmon, and gratitude to the temple for saving her from the streets, had made it easy for her to comply. But they had never asked her to take anything. What was so important that they would instruct her to steal from the prince?

She took the document out and held it in her lap, staring at it. I should return it to Larris' bag and tell the temple there was no document. She immediately dismissed that thought. She doubted she could come up with another ruse that would distract both Larris and Sarill long enough for her to return it.

The document was not sealed. She unrolled it with care and read it hastily, her eyes constantly flitting to the door. She gasped as the meaning of the words sank in.

Lerryn had abdicated? It could not be!

Before she could contemplate the weight of that news, she heard approaching footsteps in the corridor. Whispering a curse, she hurried to the window. The mortar around one of the stones below the sill no longer clung to the stone, though it still fitted perfectly in place. She removed the stone, and slipped the rolled parchment into a hollow space behind it. Replacing the stone with care, she waited, her pulse pounding in her ears as she listened. The footsteps passed her door and kept going, and she allowed herself to breathe again.

What was she going to do? What would Larris do when he found the document was gone? How had the temple known, and why did Jowan want it so badly?

She sagged onto her bed and propped her head in her hands. She needed to think.

Chapter 38

Shanis looked down in numb disbelief at the face of Badla, the famed warrior queen of Lothan. She did look like Shanis, but it was like looking at her reflection in a rippling pond. It was an imperfect image of her. The differences were subtle, but they were there. Aside from being older than Shanis when she died, Badla was leaner, her shoulders not quite so broad, and her hair a lighter shade of red. Overall, Shanis thought Badla looked just a shade more feminine than her. Otherwise, however, the resemblance was frightening.

The clan chiefs stood transfixed as Shanis knelt beside Badla. Culmatan leaned over to Horgris. "Could Badla have been her vardoger?"

"Nah. A vardoger do be a ghostly thing, a premonition come to life, and no very long before the person it do represent. Badla did live." His voice was filled with wonder. "It can mean only one thing."

Before he could elaborate, Aspin strode into the circle. "Badla is your great-grandmother, Shanis."

Shanis gasped and sprang to her feet. How could it be true? Her father would have told her. It was impossible.

"Badla did have no children!" Culmatan's voice lacked certainty even as he disputed Aspin's words. "She did no marry, and she did die childless."

"I am afraid you are wrong on both counts." Silence reigned as everyone strained to hear Aspin's words. The saikur raised his voice. Shanis could tell by the tingle that washed over her that he was magically enhancing his words so all could hear. "As you know, Badla was the child of the son of a Malgog clan chieftain and the daughter of a Monaghan chieftain. She was the last ruler to be recognized by both peoples of Lothan." Aspin was a masterful speaker, and he paused just long enough to whet the appetites of those listening.

"Badla foresaw the conflict which has plagued your nation. She knew that neither the Malgog nor the Monaghan would accept any man as king save one of their own. It seemed to her that she was destined to die alone. Her fate would permit her no other choice."

Shanis felt a lump in her throat. It seemed she had more in common with this woman than physical appearance.

"But fate had other plans for her. She fell in love with a young man, whom she married in secret. Her enemies learned of her new husband, and murdered him, but not before the two of them conceived a child."

Shanis found herself just as engrossed by this tale as everyone else. She held her breath, waiting for him to go on. The faint tittering of a threshel was the only sound she could hear.

"Badla hid her pregnancy, and after her daughter was born, she placed the child in the care of a select few—a Lothan secret society. She gained her revenge on those who had slain her husband, but at great cost. She was killed in the fighting that ensued, and the kingdom was torn asunder by her death.

"Badla's descendants were kept safe. Her daughter, Bennell, married a Malgog, and they bore a son, Addan. Addan married a Malgog woman, and they had two children: a son who died young, and a daughter, Janel, who married Colin, a Malgog of the Black Mangrove clan." Voices from out in the crowd expressed surprise at this news. Apparently there were those here who know, or knew of, her father. "They had one child." Aspin turned to face Shanis. "Shanis Malan, the Bearer of the Silver Serpent, and Badla's true heir!"

In the space between heartbeats, Shanis contemplated Aspin's words. It was not possible. Then again, how many times had she thought that very same thing since leaving home? Already she had come to accept her role as Bearer, and as leader of Lothan, and she had suspected for a while now that Colin was of Malgog descent. Really, was being Badla's descendant truly that far-fetched in light of all the things that had happened?

Culmatan was the first to find his voice. "Begging your pardon, Seeker, but how can we accept this? It do seem like a Seeker's trick, meaning no offense, of course." Muttered whispers floated through the air, but no one else spoke up.

Aspin did not react to the words, but stared at Culmatan until the man lowered his gaze. "I do not lie. And there is at least one other here who can attest to the truth of my words."

An expectant hush settled on those assembled, until, finally, Krion stood. The clan chief of the Black Mangrove slowly turned, as if he could look every Lothan in the eye. The suspense stretched like a bow ready to loose.

"The saikur Aspin speaks the truth." The sudden flurry of surprised conversation cut off the moment he raised his hands. "Long has the Black Mangrove Clan protected the secret of Badla's line. We protected this secret even from our own. Colin's name was not always Colin Malan. He is my son."

Shanis felt her knees sag, and she only just caught herself before she crumpled to the ground. Her father was the son of the Black Mangrove chieftain? That meant that Krion was...

"I am Shanis Malan's grandfather. And I am proud to stand before you and declare that she is not only the Bearer of the Silver Serpent, the one prophesied to unite the clans, but she is also Badla's true heir."

His words hung in silence. It seemed that everyone was as surprised as she. Finally, Horgris raised his fist and cheered. Soon, everyone joined in.

"Let them hear us in Karkwall!" Horgris cried. "Let Orbrad know that Lothan do have a true queen!"

As the triumphant cheers cascaded over her, Shanis took a tentative step toward Krion. His steely eyes softened, and he dropped to his knees and bowed to her.

"No, Grandfather," she whispered, taking him by the hand. It felt more than a bit odd to name him such. "Please stand."

He rose, and looked into her eyes with an expression that seemed to take in her entire being. "You are a fine woman," he whispered. "I am humbled to know that I had some small part in bringing you into this world."

There was so much she wanted to say, so many questions she wanted to ask him, but the words would not come. She squeezed his hand and felt him return the gesture, his callused palms rough on her skin.

"You must do something about Badla." His lips barely moved, and his voice was low enough that only she could hear. "You are the only one who can."

She looked down at Badla's body, and the memories flooded her mind: children dead, cities destroyed, all over where a body should be put to rest. Earth or water? Was it truly so important that it was worth ripping apart a nation? Anger coursed in her veins, warming her body that had been numbed by shock at Aspin's and Krion's revelations.

Earth or water?

Her first instinct was to draw the Silver Serpent and burn the body right there. She had never used the sword to create fire, but she somehow knew she could do it. It was as if the sword was whispering to her, eager to share its knowledge. That would not do, though. Fire was of Arscla.

Earth or water?

And then her eyes fell on the quakewater. Yes!

She knelt and gathered Badla into her arms as gently as if she were picking up a newborn. She carried her great-grandmother to the edge of the pool of quakewater, the liquid earth at the center of the ring of stones. As gently as she had picked Badla up, she laid her in the water, and silently watched as she slowly… slowly… sank beneath the surface.

As if a spell had been broken, angry shouts arose and men pressed in on all sides. She sprang to her feet, drew the Serpent, and swept it in an arc. All around her, men fell back as if struck by an invisible blow. How had she done that?

"Enough!" Her voice boomed like thunder. She supposed Aspin was aiding her. "Badla's body has been returned to the earth and the water, that Dagdar and Boana might be pleased." She knew little of the god and goddess, but it felt right to invoke their names. "The clan war is ended. No more are we divided as Malgog and Monaghan. Lothan is a single, united land! We are one people!"

"All praise the wisdom of Shanis Malan, Bearer of the Silver Serpent and Badla's true heir!" The cry arose from somewhere in the crowd. Shanis realized immediately that it was Oskar who had called out, but the fact that it was not a fellow Lothan seemed to be lost on the crowd, who gradually began to chant Shanis' name.

"Shanis! Shanis!"

The chanting subsided as the clan chiefs circled her, and all dropped to their knees. She was thankful it was at an end, for she had felt more than a bit foolish standing there, receiving the kind of praise reserved for royalty. She needed to say something, but what? Larris had filled her head with advice, but nothing about how to tell a cheering throng to go away and leave her alone without offending them.

"You honor me." That was weak. "A great task stands before us, and I must consult with the clan chiefs." That was a little better, though not much. How to disperse them? "I ask that you return to your camps and pray that Dagdar and Boana will grant us wisdom." That was the best she had to offer, and thankfully, it appeared to be working. Some continued to cheer, but gradually, the crowd broke apart as the onlookers drifted away. Doubtless, there would be more merrymaking than praying, but it made no difference to her, as long as they were not killing one another.

She felt a firm hand on her shoulder, and she turned to see Krion smiling at her. "You did well."

"Thank you, Grandfather." The name still felt strange on her lips, but she supposed she would grow accustomed to it.

"There is a place nearby where we can meet."

Shanis signaled for Aspin and Oskar to join them. The remnants of the crowd gave way as the chieftains made their way to a stone roundhouse with a south-facing door and narrow, vertical slits set all around. The conical roof was made of poles, mud, and leafy branches, and appeared to be brand-new.

Horgris noticed her staring at it. "We did hope we would have reason to use this meeting house again. I do be glad we were right."

As the last person entered, guardians of Calmut took up positions outside, assuring they would remain undisturbed. When all had settled around a rough-hewn wooden table, another obviously recent addition, Culmatan cleared his throat.

"I can no believe you did do that to Badla." He paused. "I do think it was wise. Shocking, impulsive, but wise."

"Shanis is nothing, if not impulsive." Oskar's face reddened, perhaps feeling he was the last person who had a right to speak in this group. The chieftains seemed to feel the same way. Some frowned at him, while the rest ignored him entirely.

"Oskar is here because he is a trusted friend and I value his opinions," Shanis said. "He is also well-read, and he knows me better than the rest of you put together. For those reasons, he has leave to speak his mind whenever he sees fit." That had been one of Larris' suggestions; have someone close to you whom you could trust to always tell the truth, even if the truth hurt. "And he is right about me. If I know something is the right thing to do, I am not one to dawdle." A few of the men chuckled uneasy, forced laughs.

"I would like to know what you plan to do about Karst." Labar scowled, clearly bitter over the defection of most of his Mud Snake clan.

"Nothing right now." She knew this would be unpopular, so she hurried on. "Our first order of business is to rebuild our kingdom. Generations have been decimated by these wars. For Lothan to be a powerful nation again, it must be allowed to grow, and its people to regain their former strength."

"But how can we regain that strength with Orbrad sitting in Karkwall and Karst sitting in the east? We must not be weak in the face of our enemies." Jayan argued.

Shanis gritted her teeth. How could these people continue to look for reasons to fight? Had they not had enough yet? "I have made it clear that I will heal this land. The clan wars are over." She also suspected, based on what the Keeper of the Mists had shown her, that Pedric Karst was not their greatest threat, but she did not feel that this was the proper time to discuss it. The vision had been too nebulous. She needed to understand the vision for herself before she could persuade anyone else. "If Pedric Karst makes war against us, or so much as crosses the Igiranin, we shall fight him. Otherwise, we will deal with him in due time. Right now, our goals are to reunite and rebuild."

"If I may be heard?" Aspin's voice was serene, but it carried a tone of insistence. Shanis nodded to him.

"The situation in Gameryah has become precarious. Kyrin and Galdora are at war, and there is concern that a new frostmarch is at hand."

The men let this news sink in. Horgris and Culmatan, having traveled with Aspin, were already aware of the happenings outside of Lothan.

"And what of these threats?" Jayan asked.

"There is much I do not understand," Shanis admitted. "But these threats are further evidence that we must no longer fight amongst ourselves. We must be strong for what is to come. In the meantime, I need to learn more about our people, the history of this sword, about everything, really."

"Karkwall." Horgris folded his arms and looked around at the other chiefs. "That do be where we must go."

The fool man! After what Shanis had just said, he still wanted to go after Orbrad. She was about to upbraid him, but Aspin cut across her.

"Why do you say that, Horgris?"

"Two reasons. First," he held up a thick finger, "we can no be truly united without a properly crowned queen. We do accept you," he nodded to Shanis, "but many of the people will no accept you until you do be properly crowned, and rule from the throne." Shanis was ready to tell him just how foolish those people were, but she could see in his eyes that he already knew what she was going to say. "Second, Karkwall do have an extensive library. There be no better place to begin if you do want to learn about our people and...other things." His eyes flitted to the Silver Serpent and then back to her.

The other clan chiefs nodded in agreement. Of course, they probably saw this as nothing more than an excuse to make war on Orbrad.

"But Larris and Oskar searched that library thoroughly." She turned to Oskar. "You said there was virtually nothing there about the Serpent."

"That is true. Larris was surprised and disappointed at what we found. He felt the library did not live up to its reputation. Sorry," he hastily added. "I intended no offense."

"None was taken." Krion made a placating gesture. "Orbrad would not have permitted you to see anything of true worth. The location of the real library is a closely guarded secret. If you want to learn about the Silver Serpent, that is where you must begin your search."

"You want to lay siege to Karkwall? I've been there and seen its fortifications. That city could hold out for an eternity. Besides, I don't want the citizens to suffer. They are Lothans as much as any Malgog or Monaghan." The darkened faces around the table indicated that the others did not necessarily hold to this opinion.

"We might no have to do much fighting at all," Horgris said.

"What do you mean?" Shanis' blood raced. Though she fully intended to make peace her priority, she knew that, at some point in the future, she would have to deal with Orbrad, and probably Karst. Was it possible to remove Orbrad without a protracted siege, and more of the suffering she'd witnessed?

"Certain plans have been in place for quite some time." Krion exchanged glances with Horgris. "We have already sent the necessary messages. If you will accept our counsel, it would be wise to take a strong fighting force and move in that direction with all due haste. It will make you appear decisive, and put you in a position to take advantage of the situation, should our plan prove fruitful."

Shanis met each man's eyes in turn. Was this merely a ruse by which they hoped to continue fighting? She didn't think so. Though a few of the chieftains appeared surprised at Krion's words, most of them looked at her with expressions that were both grave and earnest. She recalled another bit of Larris' advice: You have to trust someone. Choose your advisers wisely and listen to them. She believed she could trust Horgris. He had given her no reason to doubt him. And somehow, she knew she could trust Krion.

"Very well. You may tell me about these plans, and then I have some plans of my own that we shall put into place as soon as this council has concluded."

The sun had hidden its face by the time the meeting ended, a ruddy smear across the horizon the only evidence of its passing. Shanis lounged by her campfire, thankful for Oskar's presence. Her friend lay stretched out on a bedroll, tossing crumpled leaves into the fire. Her campsite was now ringed by guards—something to which she would have to grow accustomed now that she was to be queen.

"I have to confess, I loved the looks on their faces when you told them that each clan would have to provide a young man and young woman from among their clan's leading families to be married to members of opposite tribes. Even Horgris looked like he was going to choke."

"It was Larris' idea. Not only will it form ties, tenuous though they might be, it produces healthier children to marry outside of your own circle. I intend this to be the first of many such marriages."

"They liked your rebuilding plan a little bit better, but not much." Each clan had been assigned the task of rebuilding a city or town within their own lands. Shanis' added wrinkle was to pair each Monaghan clan with a Malgod clan, and those clans would be responsible for rebuilding both towns. It was a small thing, but her father had taught her that working alongside a man was the best way to get to know him. Any inroads she could make in turning two tribes into one nation would be progress.

"It occurs to me," Oskar hesitated, his eyes still on the campfire, "that you will soon be a noblewoman, royalty even."

"That occurred to you only now? We've been talking about it all afternoon."

"No. It just occurred to me that you and Larris could wed if you wanted to."

It was as if an icy hand had squeezed the breath out of her. She couldn't marry Larris! It was impossible. "I don't think so." Her voice was scarcely a groan.

"Think about it. He's not going to be king. Lerryn is first prince. Consequently, Larris will simply need to find a suitable match. And what better way to solidify relations with Lothan than to marry the queen?"

"But..." She cleared her throat. "How would they feel about me marrying an outlander? They bowed to me today, but many of them have to be suspicious of me because of my upbringing. Marrying Larris might seem to them proof that I want to bring Lothan under Galdora's influence."

"Possibly." Oskar rolled over onto his back and stared up at the sky, tapping his chin as he thought over the problem. "But if you marry a Lothan, you will have to choose either a Malgog or a Monaghan. Either way you're going to offend half of your populace."

Shanis let her chin fall to her chest. The full impact of the day's events seemed to finally sink into her very being. She heaved a sigh that bore every ounce of weariness and hopelessness she had ever felt.

"Why did this happen?"

"What do you mean?" Oskar continued to stare at the sky. Despite his words, she suspected he knew exactly what he meant. She got up, walked over to where

Oskar lay, and nudged him with her toe.

"Move over."

Surprise filled Oskar's eyes, but then a smile split his face, and he scooted aside to make room on the blanket.

Shanis stretched out next to him, and together they lay gazing up at the heavens.

"Do you remember when we used to look up at the stars and you would tell me the stories of the pictures we saw there?" She could almost believe they were ten summers old, lying in a field in Galsbur with Hierm on her other side, all of them hoping their parents would not realize they had slipped out during the night.

"I remember."

"Promise me," she swallowed a lump in her throat. "Promise me that, no matter what else changes, our friendship will be like the pictures in the sky. I need one thing in life that I know will always remain the same."

She felt Oskar take her hand in his and give it a firm, reassuring squeeze. No words were necessary.

Chapter 39

"**Ambassador Amil to** see you, Highness." Bertram bowed to Orbrad, King of Lothan, who acknowledged him with a frown and an almost indiscernible wave, indicating that the ambassador should enter.

Amil did not wait for Bertram to usher him inside. He swept through the door and into Orbrad's private study. Bertram closed the door behind him. He seemed to be the only person the king trusted anymore.

"Your Highness, I appreciate your seeing me on short notice." There was no trace of irony in his words, and his bow was respectful, but the three of them knew Orbrad had no choice but to receive dignitaries from the surrounding kingdoms. Their acknowledgment of his kingship was as tenuous as his hold on the capital city and the surrounding land. He had never been a true king.

"I have come to inform you that Diyonus can no longer stand by as an army masses on its western border."

"Army?" Orbrad gripped the arms of his wooden chair and leaned toward Amil. "There is no army. It is the same rabble it has always been. Malgogs stirring up trouble."

"I beg to differ, Highness. The fighting among clans that you have been unable to quell has ended." Orbrad shifted in his seat but did not contradict him. "An organized force of Malgog, Monaghan, and even a few Galdorans has taken control of the lands surrounding the Igiranin River from the Galdoran border to the salt swamps near the coast. They are rebuilding the cities that were abandoned during the clan wars. This is permanent."

He paused to let his words sink in. Bertram already knew all of this and more. He had let Orbrad in on as much as Amil seemed to know. Doubtless, the ambassador was holding back information as well. Amil drew a rolled sheet of parchment from his cloak.

"In the interest of its own security, Diyonus shall take control of the Harriland before this new army does so. This document cedes that land to Diyonus. We shall, of course, pay you." He reached into his cloak again and withdrew a small leather pouch. "Your signature is required to make this official."

Orbrad, red in the face, reached out his trembling hand to take it, but Amil drew it back.

"I respectfully suggest that His Royal Highness should think long and hard before refusing to sign this document, much less tearing it to bits or tossing it into the fire."

Orbrad froze. Amil had obviously read his mind. He took two deep breaths and sat up straight. He was barely maintaining his composure.

"That is my land." His voice shook with rage. "Mine!"

"I tire of this." Amil turned to Bertram. "Leave us."

"You will not give orders in my chamber!" Orbrad looked as if he would explode from rage.

"By your leave, Highness." Bertram made a quick bow and slipped from the room, thus creating at least the minutest illusion that it was Orbrad who had dismissed him. Turning the corner, he slipped into an alcove behind a faded tapestry. He pressed his ear to a small hole in the wall.

"...both know that you have no kingdom. At best, you are the equivalent of an earl, maintaining control of nothing more than the lands within a day's ride of your castle. The Diyonan council has been exceedingly patient, waiting to see if you would give them any reason whatsoever to believe you could one day take control of your kingdom. You have not."

Bertram winced. Those who dealt with Orbrad on a regular basis went out of their way to maintain the fiction that he ruled Lothan in more than name. This would be painful for him to hear, and the ambassador's words had rendered him silent.

"You have two choices in this matter. You may cede the Harriland to us, in which case we will continue to recognize your kingship, and maintain diplomatic relations with your court. Your other option is, of course, to refuse to sign this document, in which case we shall make it our official position that you are a failure and a pretender to the throne, and we will make our peace with whomever emerges as clan leader from the gathering at Calmut."

"How do you know about that?"

"Never you mind how I know. I must have your answer. I suggest you choose the former."

"I will have to think about it." Bertram had never heard Orbrad sound more defeated than he did right now.

"Very well. I shall give you until you get up out of your chair to make your decision."

A ringing silence filled the air, as Amil's words sank in.

"Very well. I'll sign your freezing document, and to the snows with you and your council."

"I am pleased that we have been able to reach an agreement. I have two more copies here, if you will sign them as well. You may keep one for yourself, of course."

Bertram could no longer bear to listen. Orbrad was a fool, and was getting what he deserved, but he took no joy in listening to the man being humiliated. Amil was taking much too much pleasure in his work today.

He slipped out from his hiding place to find a young man in livery waiting for him. The boy looked embarrassed and would not meet Bertram's eye.

"What is it?"

"Master Carl sent me. He said if you were not with the king, I should wait by this tapestry. I was not meaning to spy."

"It is of no matter." Carl was an ostler, but he also kept Bertram's pigeons; those that carried messages outside the normal channels of communication in and out of the castle. Perhaps more important, Carl was a member of the Order of the Fox, a group dedicated to the reunification of Lothan. "I assume you have something for me?"

The lad bent down and drew a tiny roll of parchment from inside his boot, and handed it to Bertram.

"Give Carl my thanks. And you are not to speak of this to anyone."

The young man frowned. "The pigeons or the tapestry?"

"Both. And if you do not hold your tongue, I shall hear of it. Am I understood?"

"Yes." The young man bobbed his head. He took a hasty look up and down the corridor before pulling down the neck of his tunic, revealing a fox medallion on a leather cord.

Bertram smiled. This one could be trusted.

When the young man had gone, he unrolled the slip of paper, knowing he could easily hide it should anyone approach. The message was not surprising, but still his heart pounded as he read it.

The fox bites its tail

End of book two of The Absent Gods.

!

The Gates of Iron

Part 1-Through the Gates

Chapter 1

"This feels wrong." His fine clothing and freshly-scrubbed skin seemed alien to Larris after spending so much time riding, sleeping out of doors, and bathing in streams. He smoothed the front of his silk doublet and sighed. Why had he ever envied his brother Lerryn's place as the eldest and heir to the throne? Now that Lerryn had abdicated and Larris' path to the throne was clear, he would have given anything to be out on the road again. Instead, he found himself in his private chamber in the royal palace, waiting for an audience with the king. Beams of light shone through the narrow windows, reflecting on the marble floor and shining on the tapestries that adorned the wall, yet to him it all felt drab and empty.

He wanted to be with Shanis.

His heart sank at the thought of the fiery girl he'd left behind. He could see her green eyes and soft, red hair as clearly as if she were standing there in front of him. She had hated him at first but, in time, he'd won her over. He smiled at the thought of any man completely winning such a strong-willed woman. In any case, their divergent destinies had taken them along different paths.

Allyn poked his head into Larris' bedchamber. "Are you ready?" His longtime friend was one of the few people in the world who felt no compunction at entering the prince's chambers without first announcing himself. He paused, stared at Larris, and frowned. "What's wrong with you?"

"Not much. Just pining for fresh air and a little danger to keep me entertained."

"You're beginning to sound like Lerryn. Not that I disagree, mind you. I'm already feeling claustrophobic." Allyn made a face and ran a hand through his long blond hair. "Your father isn't going to be pleased when you give him the news."

Larris heaved a sigh. "I suppose we should get on with it. The longer I wait, the angrier Father will grow. Then again, his ire has been simmering for months. Perhaps he's reached his limit." He opened his wardrobe and took out the worn leather bag in which he'd placed Lerryn's letter of abdication. He looked inside and gasped. The letter was gone! Heart racing, he made a hasty search of the wardrobe bottom in case it had fallen out of the bag, but it was not there. What could have happened to it? Until Allyn arrived, no one else had entered his room.

"Is there a problem?"

Larris looked up, dizzy from surprise and confusion. "Lerryn's letter is gone." Upon publicly surrendering his place as the heir to the Galdoran throne, Lerryn had written out his abdication and sent it with Larris to give to their father, King Allar.

"How?" Allyn rushed to his side, snatched the bag away, and peered down into it, as if his sharp eyes might see something Larris hadn't. "Has the bag been out of your sight?"

"No. I've kept it by my side the entire time." That was mostly true, but it had, technically, been out of his sight for a few moments when he'd bathed. "Melina!" he shouted, striding out into his sitting room, where the woman who had cared for him since birth waited.

"Yes, Highness?" Though Melina had seen nearly forty summers, no gray touched her hair and her eyes shone with youthful vigor. Right now, she looked and sounded puzzled, even concerned, but gave no sign of feeling any guilt.

"There was a document inside my bag. What happened to it?"

She cocked her head to the side. "A document, Highness?"

"Yes. The only time I haven't had my eyes on it was when Sarill scrubbed my hair because you said I had lice." Larris couldn't believe he was accusing a woman he regarded as a second mother. But who else could it be? He expected his words to wound her, but instead, they seemed to inflame her temper.

"What exactly are you suggesting?" Melina put her hands on her hips and thrust out her chin. "You think I would steal this paper of yours, whatever it is? More than twenty summers I have served your family. I cared for you and your brother, and you accuse me of treachery? If His Highness's opinion of my character has fallen so low, perhaps he wishes me to leave his service."

"If I may." Allyn's voice, usually dry with sarcasm, was soft and hesitant.

"Of course you may," Larris snapped. "When have the three of us stood on ceremony when we're alone together?"

"Evidently, things have changed. When did Highness ever accuse me of thievery?" Melina snapped.

"Oh, stop with the Highness bit already." Larris slumped into a nearby chair and gazed at the two of them. "What is it, Allyn?"

"Can you say for certain that the paper was still in your bag when we entered the palace? The streets are packed with refugees and they were all trying to touch you. Someone might have slipped a hand into your bag, hoping to find food, and grabbed the first thing his fingers closed upon."

Larris gave a thoughtful nod. They hadn't made it far into the city before someone had recognized him. His escort had done its best to keep the wave of commoners at bay, but some had indeed managed to lay hands on him.

"People are desperate," Allyn continued. "Anyone could have done it."

"You're right." He turned to Melina. "I'm sorry. The situation is complicated. Right now, I can't give you the explanation you deserve, but I hope once you know the reason for my distress, you will forgive me." He held out his hand.

Melina tensed, and then her stony expression melted into a warm smile. "That won't do." She stepped forward and wrapped him in her gentle embrace. "Of course I forgive you, child." She gave him a tight squeeze and then stepped away. "But don't do it again." She wagged a finger at him. "I haven't forgotten how to administer the rod."

"Of course not." He rose from the chair and straightened his doublet. "I suppose it's time to give Father the good news."

"Your Royal Majesty, I present His Highness, Larris Van Altman, Second Prince of Galdora!" At the herald's words, a buzz of conversation rose, but quickly faded as Larris strode into the throne room.

Like wheat bending in the wind, the courtiers bowed as he passed through the beams of colored light that streamed through tall, stained glass windows. The more reticent of the attendees peered around the marble columns that lined the hall, but some were so bold as to leer at him, making no attempt to hide their curiosity or amusement. Everyone had apparently heard the story of the return of the prodigal prince.

He kept his head high and his eyes focused on his father, King Allar Van

Altman, who stared at him with a serene expression Larris knew to be a façade. Larris and Allyn had left the palace under a cloud of secrecy, telling no one where they had gone or why, and had been gone for months. If he knew Father, the king was at this very moment debating whether or not to send for the headsman.

Larris reached the foot of the dais, dropped to one knee, and lowered his head. He waited. King Allar was clearly dragging this out in order to shame his wayward son. Larris felt his cheeks heat. Embarrassing him in front of the entire court might be justifiable, but it would make things more difficult in the long run.

Finally, the king relented. "You may rise."

Larris stood, taking in his father's disapproving stare and his mother's beaming smile. Beloved by Galdorans, Queen Arissa was a plump, motherly woman with a kind heart and a ready smile.

"Father, I am pleased to see you looking well." That was a lie. He was not at all pleased to see his father, at least, not under these circumstances, and King Allar did not look well. He had lost a considerable amount of weight, and a sickly yellowish tinge marred his face. Larris grimaced. Allar was not a young man, but neither was he in his dotage. Had the king taken ill?

For his part, Allar offered no courtesies in return. "You disappeared. Ran away like a child and abandoned your duties here. I would never have expected it from a son of mine."

Duties? Larris had been given no responsibilities aside from than keeping his head low and never stepping out of his brother's long shadow. This, however, was no time to argue.

"One so irresponsible is not fit to wear a crown," Allar continued. "For this reason, you shall enter the priesthood. The temple has reserved a place for you."

Icy shock froze Larris to the core. He was scarcely aware of the low murmur of conversation all around him at this surprising turn of events. The priesthood? It could not be! He was now the heir to the throne. Even if he wasn't, he would never take the vows. He would leave again, and return to Shanis, and for good this time.

"Unless." Allar paused, "you can offer a valid reason for your prolonged absence."

Larris breathed a sigh of relief, opened his mouth to speak, and then hesitated. He would, of course, tell his father the entire story, but not here in front of the court.

"With respect, I request a private audience with Your Majesty."

Whispers rose again at his words. Most were too soft for him to hear, but a few of those in attendance, those either bold or foolish, didn't bother to keep their voices down.

"What is he hiding?"

"He's too ashamed to face the court."

"Foolish boy."

Larris' cheeks still burned, but he held the king's gaze.

"What could you possibly have to tell me that cannot be said in front of our loyal subjects?" Allar made a sweeping gesture that took in all the gathered courtiers, and Larris could not miss the slight tremor in the king's hand. Something was very wrong with his father. "Perhaps you ran away on some urgent matter of state of which I remain blissfully unaware?" Titters of laughter rang through the hall.

Larris cleared his throat. "That is precisely the situation." The laughter died. "I humbly apologize to you, my mother, and all the people of Galdora for the secrecy that surrounded my departure and for my prolonged absence. I do not expect to be forgiven, but I hope in time to regain your and their trust. I ask again, with respect, that I be granted a private audience before I offer my explanation."

Allar considered this for a long moment. Finally, he nodded. "Very well. Court is ended for today."

Grumbling, the courtiers made their way out, obviously displeased at missing out on seeing the prince brought low. A few cast baleful glances in his direction. Finally, the throne room stood empty, save the royals and the King's Guard. Queen Arissa rushed down to wrap him in a tight embrace.

Larris looked over his mother's head at his father, who remained ensconced upon his throne. To Larris' surprise, a solitary tear slid down his father's cheek and into his silver-flecked beard.

"We thought you were dead." Arissa's trembling whisper pierced Larris' heart. He had anticipated their anger, but not their hurt.

"I am truly sorry. I promise you, I had good reason."

He gently pulled away from Arissa and they all retired to a side chamber and sat down in overstuffed chairs. A serving woman brought mulled wine and bowed her way out, not quite managing to hide her look of curiosity.

When they were finally alone, Larris began his story. He told them of Lerryn's plan to find the Silver Serpent and use its power to defeat Karin; of his own distrust of Xaver, Lerryn's recently-deceased vizier; his worry about Lerryn's love of strong drink; and his decision to take Allyn and go in search of the Silver Serpent himself.

"The Silver Serpent?" Allar scoffed. "How could both of my sons be taken in by such a fable?"

"We found it."

Allar choked on his wine and required a moment to recover. "You...found it?" he rasped, his watering eyes wide with shock.

"Our companion did. She's a Galsburan named Shanis Malan."

"Galsbur? Wait a moment." Allar held up his hand. "You are telling me that the Silver Serpent is real and is now in the hands of a village girl? A commoner?"

A sudden urge to defend Shanis reared up inside of him. "She is hardly common. She is of royal Lothan stock, the sole living descendant of Badla, in fact, and is right now in the process of uniting the clans."

This time, Allar dropped his goblet, spilling blood red wine all over the lush, Diyonan rug. "Are you trying to kill me, boy? How many shocks can a man take?" He rose unsteadily, wobbled to the window, and looked up at the clear blue sky. "We are at war with Kyrin, Karst is fomenting rebellion in the south, an unknown force invades from the west, the Lothan clans are putting aside their war, and you permit the most fearsome weapon in memory to slip through your hands."

"I had no choice. Please hear me out." Larris recounted the rest of his tale, describing how the prophecy, despite his and Lerryn's best efforts, had been fulfilled in its own way. "No one can touch the sword but Shanis and therefore only she may control its power. She is the one destined to bear it," he finished.

Allar looked tireder than Larris had ever seen him. He returned slowly to his chair and sat down. "Do you have any other bad news?" He managed a weary smile.

His heart was in his throat. How would his parents receive this next bit of information? "Lerryn has abdicated."

Allar stiffened. His lips moved, but he made no sound.

"No!" Arissa gasped.

"He says Shanis used the power of the Silver Serpent to cure him of his need to drink. Now that his faculties are no longer muddled, he believes he is worthy only to lead soldiers, not a kingdom." Larris shifted uncomfortably. He had entertained the same thoughts about his brother many times. "He sent me and a few companions here and took his men west to meet the invaders."

"Was it witnessed?" Allar snapped.

"It was witnessed by me and Allyn, my friend Hierm Van Derin and his wife, and the men of the White Fang."

Allar and Arissa exchanged unreadable glances. "I don't suppose he put it in writing," Allar sighed.

"He did." Larris' mouth was suddenly so dry he felt he could scarcely move his tongue. He took a gulp of wine and swallowed hard. "But it was stolen."

Allar's breath left him in a rush and he slumped forward and buried his face in his hands. When he finally composed himself, he could find no words. He sat, shaking his head.

"I fear your father has endured enough surprises for one day." Arissa picked up a bell and rang for the serving woman. "Send two guards to escort His Majesty to his chambers." The young woman returned with the guards in short order, and they helped the king to his feet and escorted him out of the throne room. When they were gone, Arissa ordered the serving woman to send the royal physician to see to the king.

"What is wrong with him?" Larris asked. "He is too young to be failing so fast."

Arissa looked twenty years older. She pursed her lips, the lines on her face clearer. "We don't know. The strain of ruling is some of it. The situation in the kingdom is dire and having both of his sons vanish without a trace did not help matters." She lowered her gaze for a moment and Larris' heart fell along with it.

"I am sorry. I won't disappear again. I promise."

"I know you won't." Arissa gave his hand a squeeze. "We must sort out this situation with Lerryn. First, we need to find out if he is even alive."

"No word about the battle, then?"

"No." Her eyes took on a faraway cast. "I fear the worst. Your father sent messengers, but none have returned."

"Can we truly spare no forces for the conflict in the west?" Larris remembered what Tabars, captain of Lerryn's elite force, had told them. All of Galdora's armies were committed to the war with Kyrin, their enemy to the north. "Will no one come to our aid?"

"We are stretched thin. Your uncle has offered to take soldiers west, but neither he nor your cousin can lead men the way Lerryn can."

That was true. Orman Van Altman was a solid if uninspiring man, and his son, Carsus, was hewn from the same tree. Orman had his share of sticking swords into affronted nobles but was sorely lacking in experience on the battlefield. If Lerryn was alive, he was sorely needed.

"I have to find Lerryn. I'll go tonight." He rose, but Arissa grabbed his wrist and held on tightly.

"No. You mustn't leave the city again. At least, not while the circumstances are so dire. We must appear strong."

He sighed. "I understand. In that case, I promise I will stay, but I will take steps to see to it that he is found." Gently, he removed his mother's hand from his wrist, kissed her on the forehead, and bade her see to Allar.

He did not return directly to his chambers, but first visited the Chapel of the Seven. He was not religious, but right now, in the face of such a hopeless situation, he needed something to give him courage and strength. He lit a candle for each god and knelt before the altar, watching as the tapers melted away.

When the last was a mere lump of wax, he rose on stiff legs and strode out to the stables, where he commandeered a horse. He could not honestly say he felt better, but at least he now had a plan.

Chapter 2

Hierm took a deep breath, grasped the iron knocker, and rapped twice on the heavy wooden door. Heart racing, he squeezed Rinala's hand and listened to the sound of approaching footsteps. The door opened a crack, and one blue eye peered out.

"Hierm!" Laman, Hierm's older brother, swung the door open and caught him up in a rough embrace. Hierm felt taken aback at his brother's display of affection. The two had never really gotten along. "Mother," Laman called back into the house, "it's Hierm!" A cry of surprise sounded from somewhere inside, followed by the sound of running feet, and then Laman was shunted aside as Faun Van Derin wrapped her arms around him and began sobbing, her face pressed against his chest.

"I cannot believe it," she said. After a full minute of joyful tears, she finally stepped away and mopped her eyes with her sleeve. She reached up and laid a hand on his cheek. "It truly is you, flesh and blood. The gods have finally smiled upon us."

"I am sorry for the way I left, and for being gone so long." Hierm, along with his friends Shanis, Oskar, and Khalyndryn, had left their home in Galsbur without so much as a word to their families. They'd all had their reasons, at least, they'd thought so at the time, but seeing his mother's relief drove home just how much worry he'd put her through.

"And who is this?" Laman knitted his eyebrows as he noticed Rinala for the first time. Despite the girl's rough Monaghan clothing, his eyes betrayed no hint of the judgment Hierm had expected.

"This is Rinala, my wife." Hierm put a hand around Rinala's waist and drew her close.

Faun made no attempt to hide her amazement as she gaped at the girl who was now her daughter by marriage. Hierm could not say what caught his mother's attention first— Rinala's rough spun, travel-stained dress or her swelling stomach.

"As you can see, you're going to be a grandmother," he added unnecessarily.

Rinala bent her knee and made a perfect curtsy. "It is an honor to make your acquaintance, Mother. Your beauty is far greater even than my husband described."

Hierm had to grin. Throughout their trek to Archstone, the capital city of Galdora, Rinala had worked diligently to adopt a more Galdoran manner of speech. He had to admit when the girl set her mind to something, she attacked it with the tenacity of a hungry wolf.

"Well, then." Faun struggled for words. "I imagine you wish to bathe and change into a proper dress."

"I fear I have no other dress." Rinala looked at Faun, shamefaced.

This broke the tension in exactly the way Hierm had hoped. Faun, who had always wanted a daughter, began barking orders.

"Laman, go immediately to Madam Ross and tell her I need her right away. Tell her I want several dresses made, and if she isn't here by the time Rinala is out of her bath, I shall send for someone else." Laman chuckled and set off while Faun took Rinala by the hand and pulled her into the house. "Hierm, stoke the fire and put a kettle on to boil. A woman with child should not take cold baths. We shall be upstairs." Rinala threw a bemused smile in Hierm's direction as the two women disappeared up the stairs.

Hierm laughed to himself. Home for only a few minutes and he was already being ordered about as if he'd never left. It was comforting in its familiarity.

It was near dark when Faun and Rinala finally emerged from Faun's chambers. Faun had scraped and scrubbed every last speck of dirt from Rinala's body, filed her nails, plucked her eyebrows, and combed the snarls out of her hair. Hierm would not have known this, save for the fact that his mother described, at great length, all she had done to make his new wife "presentable."

"Madam Ross promised to have one dress ready by morning and the rest shortly thereafter," Faun said. "We shall, of course, have them taken in after the baby arrives." Gazing proudly at Rinala who sat curled up in a chair by the fire, sipping a cup of tea, Faun looked like a sculptor admiring her own work.

The transformation in Hierm's wife was striking. She had always been a lovely girl, but now her beauty was on display to full effect. She seemed to know it, too because she smiled at Hierm and gave him a seductive wink.

"It's a shame you would not let me trim your hair, dear," Faun said.

Hierm saw Rinala's eyes widen and recognized her prodigious temper beginning to flare. Apparently, cutting one's hair violated some Monaghan taboo. Not wishing to ruin the good mood, he placed a hand on his mother's elbow and guided her into the kitchen where a serving woman was preparing their meal.

"I need to talk to you about Rinala." He kept his voice low, so his wife would not hear though she already knew what he would be speaking to his mother about. "I will need you to take care of her and the child."

Faun blanched. "Take care of them? Are you leaving again?"

"No, but I have been offered a place at the Prince's Academy. They won't be able to live with me until I have finished my training."

"The Academy? But how?"

"Prince Larris is a friend of mine."

Coming on the heels of meeting Hierm's new wife and learning that she was about to be a grandmother, Faun seemed to find this tidbit unremarkable.

"Is that so? But you a soldier? Hierm, no."

"It's what I'm best at," he said firmly. "I can't run Van Derin and Sons. I'm neither Father nor Laman." He held up a hand to quiet her objection. "It is all right," he assured her. "I bear no ill will toward either of them. We are just different."

"But we need you," Faun whispered. "There has been no word from your father, or anyone from Galsbur for that matter. I have visited the temple every day praying for them. If something has happened to him, I don't know what I shall do."

Hierm swallowed hard. He and his father were not on the best of terms, yet the thought of losing Hiram weighed heavy on his heart. "I am sure he will be all right, and Laman is more than capable of running the business. Father has been grooming him for years." He found it strange to realize that, before he had left Galsbur, such an admission would have galled him, but now he knew it to be the pure truth. "I have to go to the academy. I gave Prince Larris my word."

Faun frowned. "How exactly did you come to know the prince?"

"The story is a long one. I'll tell you over dinner."

Dinner was a hearty stew with chunks of lamb and savory vegetables and a loaf of fresh bread. Faun apologized for the limited fare, but Hierm and Rinala assured her that, after months on the trail, it seemed a veritable feast.

As they ate, Hierm explained the circumstances of his departure from Galsbur so long ago. He briefly recounted meeting Larris and joining him in the search for the Silver Serpent. He omitted a great deal of the story, particularly the fact that, by now, Shanis was likely the leader of the Lothan clans. Faun, who had never thought much of Oskar and disapproved of Shanis outright, did not ask after either of them, but tears welled in her eyes when she learned that their friend, Khalyndryn, had died not long ago.

"So," Hierm finally finished, "Prince Larris expects me to present myself at the palace tomorrow morning."

Laman and Faun lapsed into stunned silence. Finally, Laman set down his wine glass and cleared his throat.

"That is quite a tale, brother. Let me make certain I understand. You are telling us that you are a personal friend of Prince Larris?"

Rinala rose to Hierm's defense immediately. "Every word is true."

"If you say so." Only someone who knew Laman well would recognize the patronizing tone that set Hierm's teeth on edge. "You do know we are at war on three fronts?" Laman asked. "Enlisting right now is suicide."

"What good is a soldier in peace time? Besides, I don't think Larris will give me a choice. The kingdom needs all the capable fighters it can find." He felt Rinala put her hand on his thigh and give him a squeeze. Born and raised in the midst of clan war, the girl was accustomed to her loved ones placing themselves in harm's way. He gave her a tight smile and looked at his mother. "What are your plans? Will you stay here?"

Her eyes fell. "If, I mean when, your father sends word, we will return to Galsbur."

"And what if…" Hierm could not say the words, but Faun evidently took his meaning.

"Then Laman will run the business and will also take up Hiram's post as Firstman."

"What is this Firstman?" Rinala asked.

"He is the leader of the council, and the most powerful man in Galsbur," Faun explained.

"And this council, they will just give Laman the job?" Rinala frowned over her cup of tea. "In Monaghan, a man who wants to lead must earn it."

Laman stiffened but held his tongue. He took a long drink of wine and stared daggers at Rinala.

"I wouldn't expect a girl to understand leadership." For the first time since their arrival, Faun looked at Rinala with a hint of disapproval.

"My father be Clan Chief of the Hawk Hill," Rinala said, slipping back into her familiar speech patterns.

A sharp knock at the door cut off Faun's retort. She and Rinala exchanged dark looks while Laman answered the door.

A resonant voice boomed through the house. "His Royal Highness, Prince Larris Van Altman, requests an audience with Hierm Van Derin."

"A-all right," they heard Laman stammer. He gave way to the prince and a uniformed guard.

Hierm, Faun, and Rinala made to stand, but Larris motioned for them to remain seated.

"Please do not get up on my account. I apologize for the intrusion, my lady," he nodded in Faun's direction, "but I must speak with your son on a matter of great urgency. Is there somewhere private we could talk?"

"There is a garden out back." Hierm scarcely choked out the words. It was the first time he had seen Larris dressed in his royal finery. Gone was the cheery, curly-haired youth whose brown eyes always seemed to carry secret knowledge. In his place stood a well-groomed, confident young man who bore little resemblance to Hierm's traveling companion.

"Very well. Ladies, again my apologies." Larris made a small bow.

Faun was too shocked to reply. Rinala smiled, enjoying her new mother's surprise. She winked at Larris and then blew her husband a kiss. The simple act eased Hierm's nerves and he managed a real smile as he led Larris out into the walled garden.

"I need your help," Larris began immediately. He quickly recounted the day's events, ending with the precarious issue of the line of succession. "My father is ill. With the document lost, it something happens to him it will be chaos."

"What is it you want from me?" Hierm couldn't see how he could assist with any of this.

"We need to find Lerryn. We need his skills as a commander and we need to resolve the questions about the line of succession. If Lerryn is dead, we need proof." Larris leaned against the garden wall, plucked a flower from a nearby climbing vine, and absently shredded the petals.

"We have proof," Hierm said. "Witnesses: me, Rinala, Edrin, Hair, Lerryn's soldiers. If they survived."

"Forgive me, but the word of commoners will carry little weight. The assumption would be, if I were behind this ruse, a commoner would be more likely than a noble to be bribed or intimidated. It's absurd, of course. There's more than enough corruption among the nobles." Larris sighed and tossed the shredded blossom on the ground. "In more peaceable times, it might not be so difficult, but with war and rebellion, the throne must appear strong and my family united." He barked a rueful laugh. "I don't even want to be king, but I'll do what I must."

"So, you want me to go with you to look for Lerryn?" Hierm's heart sank. His wife was expecting, he was so close to fulfilling his dream of entering the academy, and he saw little chance his mother would retain her unusually good humor if he announced he was leaving again.

"I can't go. If something happens to my father and both of his sons are missing, it would be a disaster. And with the abdication document missing, I have to assume a conspiracy is at foot. Allyn suggested it might have been taken by mistake, but I don't think so." Larris set his jaw. "You're the right man for the job. You know the lands to the west."

"Not all that well."

"Well enough. What's more, I trust you."

Hierm felt his resistance crumbling. "What about Rinala and the baby?"

"I know, but you have a few moons left until the baby comes. You should be back long before then." He reached out and put his hand on Hierm's shoulder. "I know I ask a great deal, but I need you."

"Why not Allyn?"

"I have already set him a task." Larris dropped his hands to his side and his expression hardened. "I will make it a royal order if that will help you with your wife and mother."

"It might at that." Hierm managed a smile. "Am I to go alone?"

"Edrin and Mattyas will join you." He referred to two young men from western Galdora, who had joined Lerryn on his separate quest to find the Silver Serpent.

"I suppose they're disappointed not to begin their study at the academy?"

"Not as disappointed as Mattyas is that I didn't get to him before they cut his hair."

Hierm had to laugh. "I can't wait to see that. Can I still call him Hair? I don't think I can call him by his actual name."

"I agree. They will be here in the morning with horses and supplies."

Hierm groaned. "The sooner I leave, the sooner I can return, I suppose."

"That's the spirit." Larris headed toward the door but halted after a few steps. "Can you do me one more favor?"

"What's that?"

"Wait until I'm gone before you tell Rinala."

Chapter 3

"What are they doing over there?" Shanis reined in her horse and pointed toward a place where men and women were hacking away at the thick undergrowth.

"Clearing out shrubs and creepers," Heztus replied.

"I know that. But why?"

"Oh. You should have asked." Heztus gave her a wink.

Shanis heaved a sigh, managing a tiny smile in the process. Since her friends had departed, the dwarf had kept her company, and he seemed to have made it his mission to keep her spirits up. He was also a helpful advisor whose genial manner made it easy for him to move among all the clans gathered around Calmut.

"Once upon a time, there was a sizable city here. People have begun reclaiming it. There's even talk of settling here, or at least establishing a presence for each clan."

Shanis nodded. "I wish we could do something about the divisions between clans. We're united, but we have a long way to go."

"Patience. The changes you've made are a fine start if for no other reason than you've given all the clans a single person on whom to focus their anger."

One of Shanis' first actions upon being recognized as the ruler of the newly-united Lothan was to arrange cross-clan marriages, seeking to form bonds where none had existed before. Most of the clan leaders and a few of the betrothed saw the wisdom in her actions, but many more were angry. She couldn't blame them, but knew it was the right thing to do.

"They do say you should no be making them marry until you do the same," Granlor said. Granlor was a young Monaghan warrior who'd appointed himself Shanis' bodyguard back when she first proclaimed herself as the bearer of the Silver Serpent. Realizing he'd said too much, he coughed into his fist and looked away.

"When she marries, it won't be to a Lothan." Heztus drew a sharp dagger and absently trimmed his nails. "She can't choose a Malgog over a Monaghan, or vice-versa, lest she drive a new wedge between the clans. It will have to be an outlander."

Shanis hoped her face did not reflect the way her heart fluttered at Heztus' words. Prince Larris, as the second son, was not the first in line to inherit the Galdoran throne. But she didn't dare hope.

"I won't be marrying any time soon, in any case. I have too much to do."

"Like laying siege to Karkwall and claiming the throne?" Heztus asked a bit too blithely.

"Heztus, do you remember when I told you how much I value the fact that you never prevaricate or mince words? I think I've changed my mind." She spurred her horse forward, leaving the two men hurrying to catch up.

They cantered down what had recently been a footpath, but was now a small thoroughfare, worn down by thousands of feet and hooves. They soon came upon a clearing where Gillen, the fair-haired apprentice bone woman of the Hawk Hill clan, stood in the midst of a cluster of girls and young women. Shanis could not hear what she was saying, but it was clear the woman was teaching. Several other bone women stood nearby, listening and occasionally nodding in agreement.

Shanis reined in, dismounted, and handed her reins over to Granlor as soon as he caught up. As she approached, Effie, a bone woman of the Black Mangrove clan, turned to greet her.

"What's all this?" Shanis indicated the gathering with a nod of her head. "Do all of them want to be bone women?"

"Not exactly." Effie placed a light hand on Shanis' elbow and steered her away so they would not disturb the instruction. "Some do, but others want to learn from us. Bone women's skills are varied: some are strong in healing, others know herbs, some give wise counsel, while some even know magic."

"Do any know sorcery?" Shanis was surprised to hear the question pass her lips, but she was keenly interested. With Aspin, the seeker, gone, no one remained to instruct her in her newly-discovered talent.

Effie pursed her lips. "It is considered impolite to ask. Of course, you did not know that." She thought for a few moments before answering. "At least two of us do— do not ask me to tell you who; it is not my place to do so. There are probably more, but I cannot say for certain. It will be their choice to reveal it when they are ready."

Shanis sighed. Of course, it couldn't be that easy. "What is Gillen teaching them?"

"A simple spell to sooth a crying baby. She taught the other bone women last night. She knows a number of spells none of us had ever heard of. This sharing has already broadened everyone's knowledge."

Shanis had assumed that all bone women had similar skills. Learning that this was not the case had given her an idea.

"Who trains new bone women?"

"The bone woman of a clan gives such instruction as she is able and keeps a few of her most skilled students as apprentices. If two clans are at peace, they will exchange apprentices so knowledge may be shared."

"We are all at peace with one another now," Shanis observed. "What if there was a place where all the clans could share their knowledge with one another?"

"You mean, like a school?" Effie looked doubtful.

"Exactly. Apprentices wouldn't be limited to what their own clan can teach them. Your knowledge would grow exponentially."

"Who would be in charge? The bone women must attend to their clans."

"How about the elders who are no longer able to fulfill their duties as they once did? Their bodies are weak, but the knowledge is still there."

"Interesting." Effie touched a finger to her chin and looked up at the ragged patch of blue sky visible through the dense cover of greenery. "Anyone with a particular skill could be a teacher. It would not have to be restricted to bone women."

"It could also be a place where the sick are tended to." Shanis grew more excited as she spoke. The ideas were pouring forth faster than she could voice them. "If all the clans' healing knowledge is pooled in one place…"

"I see. Very well." Effie cut her off in mid-sentence, turned, and hurried over to the bone women who were watching the lesson. After a few minutes of intense conversation and several annoyed glances from Gillen, who was still trying to teach her spell, the women gathered around Shanis and began peppering her with questions.

"This school you are starting, where would it be?"

"Who would be in charge? We will no take orders from clan chiefs."

"I hope you don't expect us to create war magic for you. That is not what bone women do."

Shanis held up her hands to stem the flow of words that threatened to engulf her. She wanted to tell them it was just an idea, and they should forget she'd suggested it, but she was a ruler now and need to act like one.

"The school would be here." It made sense. Calmut was in a central location, and it was a place all Lothans held in high regard. "The bone women would, of course, be in charge."

The women exchanged satisfied smiles.

"Answerable, of course, to the crown." That wiped their grins away. "My yoke is light, I assure you. I expect this to be a seat of learning, and a place where those in need can come for help. All the things that bone women do, I want you to learn to do them better, and share them with all the clans. No one may hold back knowledge from anyone, including me. And if anyone wants to teach or learn 'war magic', as you call it, you will permit them to do so. I don't like war any better than you do, but the better prepared we are to defend ourselves, the less likely others are to attack us. Do you accept my conditions?"

"The clan chiefs will never approve," Maisie, a young woman of the Hawk Hill clan said.

"It's not their decision; it's mine." Shanis knew she was testing the limits of her authority in this. She did not yet wear the crown, and the Lothans were not mere serfs ready to bend the knee to any so-called noble. Leading them was like riding a wild horse bareback: you held on tight and tried your best to nudge them in the proper direction without being thrown. In this case, however, she would not bend.

Why shouldn't the bone women have a certain degree of autonomy and a measure of power? And the gods help the first man who told her that women could not be trusted with power or responsibility. "What will it be?"

"Yes," Effie said, and the others added their assent.

"If I may make a suggestion?" Heztus had sidled up to her unnoticed. "There is an old temple not far from here which I believe will suit your needs. It will require a great deal of work to make it fit for habitation, but the roof is solid and there is a large block of penitent cells that could be converted to living quarters."

"Assemble a team of workmen and begin immediately," Shanis said.

Heztus looked like he'd just stepped in a pile of goat dung. "I don't believe I'm the best person for this job. The men do not like to take orders from a dwarf, you see."

"We will see to it you do have all the help you need." Jamma, a woman with silver-streaked red hair and skin like old leather, spoke up. "There are young men and boys aplenty in our clans who do spend too much time playing at swords and not enough time at honest work."

"The girls can help too," Maisie added. "And we will be there to make certain no one shirks their responsibilities."

"Wonderful." The expression on Heztus' face made it clear he thought it was nothing of the sort. He turned pleading eyes to Shanis. "I assume you wish me to serve in a supervisory capacity? I'm really not much of a laborer."

Shanis had to laugh. "Just see to it that the work gets done to their satisfaction." The bone women turned on Heztus and all began giving orders at the same time.

Shanis spared one sympathetic glance at her friend and then looked around for Granlor. He waited nearby with their horses, looking at the bone women with a sour expression on his face.

"You have something to say?" Shanis asked.

Granlor shook his head.

"A wise choice." Shanis swung up onto her horse and heaved a sigh. "Let's find the clan chiefs and tell them what I've done."

Chapter 4

"That's Vatania?" Oskar scarcely managed to choke out the words. He'd been to Karkwall and thought himself prepared for a big city, but this was something else entirely. Far below them, where the Blue River twisted its way south and east, the outskirts of the city blanketed the world in a jumble of wood, stone and smoke. Dirt roads clogged with traffic, mounted and afoot, meandered toward the city walls, just visible in the distance. And beyond them, lay the inner city and, Oskar knew, the sea.

"That is part of it," Aspin said, guiding his horse down the winding road.

Oskar hesitated for a moment, still mesmerized by the vast sea of human habitation that lay before him, and then hurried to catch up, his horse bouncing him roughly in the saddle.

"How long will it take us to get there?"

"That depends on what you mean by 'there.' We'll reach the outskirts of Vatania in less than hour. After that, another hour to the city walls, and the Gates."

Oskar shivered at the mention of the fabled headquarters of the saikurs, so named for the iron gates at its entrance. He forced his mind back to what Aspin had said. Another hour after entering the city proper?

"The city is that big? I thought once we were inside the city it wouldn't be so far." Oskar tried, but could not paint the picture in his mind's eye. It was too vast.

"The distance is not so great. What will slow us down are all the people we will have to navigate around. The closer you draw to the Gates, the slower the going." Aspin sounded as if he would rather be anywhere but here. His temper had grown noticeably shorter since they had crossed the border.

From central Lothan, they'd traveled northeast through Diyonus and then here to Vatania, a coastal city in southern Cardith. He'd been thrilled at the prospect of seeing the great cities of Diyonus, with their fabled rooftop gardens, but their travels had taken them through rural areas, and the few stops they made had been in villages not much larger than his home of Galsbur, where he'd grown up. Still, he'd enjoyed the trek through a country about which he'd read and heard tales.

Along the way, Aspin had intensified Oskar's training, instructing him in a variety of subjects as they rode, until Oskar felt as though his head would explode if he learned one more fact. The evenings were devoted to practicing with the quarterstaff, at which Oskar was competent, and sword forms, at which he was hopeless.

Each night, just before they drifted off to sleep, Aspin warned him of all the things he should not reveal to anyone within the Gates: Shanis, Larris and Lerryn, The Silver Serpent, the Keeper of the Mists, the re-unification of the clans, the lost city of Murantha, the Thandrylls, the warning signs of a new Frostmarch. Essentially, anything interesting that had happened to him during his travels was taboo. Now, as they drew ever closer to Vatania, Oskar wondered if he was in any way prepared for what he would face beyond the gates of iron.

Oskar sighted the iron gates that barred entry to the saikurs' headquarters long before he and Aspin reached them. Set between two high, crenelated walls of gray stone, they stood higher than the tallest building in Galsbur. Admittedly, that was less than forty spans, but still, the gates were impressive. Drawing closer, he saw the runes carved upon their surface. Common wisdom held that they were defensive spells that rendered the gates indestructible, and they cast curses upon any who attacked the walls, but Aspin had confided in him that the symbols merely made the iron impervious to rust. Of course, there had been a twinkle in his eye when he said it—one of the few traces of humor in the otherwise stolid man.

The gates stood open, a squad of guards barring the way. One guard stepped forward as Oskar and Aspin reined in. He stood ramrod straight, his eyes fixed on a point somewhere in the distance.

"Who seeks to pass beyond the Gates of Iron?"

"Aspin, a saikur."

Silence. Finally, Aspin cleared his throat and looked pointedly at Oskar.

Flustered, Oskar managed to stammer out the words Aspin had taught him. "Oskar, one who humbly seeks admission to the Gates."

Wordlessly, the guard stepped aside, and they rode in.

"You'll have to do better than that." Aspin's placid expression remained unchanged, but the disapproval in his voice was impossible to miss.

"I will." Privately, Oskar wondered if could really do this. Suddenly, the very idea of a farm boy from Galsbur studying to be a saikur, or seeker as they were commonly known, seemed the greatest of follies.

They rode through a forested area which made the Gates seem as if it were set apart from the surrounding city. The woods soon gave way to a broad, manicured green space, and beyond it, the foreboding towers of the Gates.

Aspin led the way to the stables, where they dismounted and turned their horses over to the stable hands. Oskar patted his mount, a chestnut stallion named Oaken, and whispered a word of thanks for bringing him safely to Vatania. It was something his father had taught him to do. The stable boy heard him and nodded his approval. Oskar slung his saddlebags over his shoulder, hefted his quarterstaff, and followed Aspin.

By the time they reached the front steps, Oskar felt like he'd swallowed a bullfrog. His stomach heaved and cold sweat dripped down the back of his neck. Every step he took seemed an insurmountable task, but he soldiered on until they stood at the front doors. Here, they were once again met by guards, one of whom asked their names. This time, the question was no mere formality. He passed word to a messenger who hurried away, returning minutes later with a brown-robed man with a wan face and receding hairline.

"Aspin." The man's nod was polite if perfunctory. "The prelate will receive you in his study immediately."

"Thank you, Nolan." Aspin turned to Oskar. "Good luck, young man. Work hard and learn all you can." With that, he turned on his heel and disappeared into the huge, gray granite castle.

Nolan crooked one finger, indicating Oskar should follow him. The high-ceilinged entry hall was built of the same granite as the exterior and lit by torches that glinted off the flecks of mica embedded in the rock. There was no time to take in any more detail than that because they soon left the main passage into a smaller hallway. Three turns later and Oskar was thoroughly lost.

They finally came to a halt in front of a closed door. A graying man with broad shoulders and a wide brow answered on the third knock.

"A new member of the novitiate to see you, Inceptor." Nolan bowed.

"Thank you. You are dismissed." The man turned to Oskar. "Come inside." He gestured to a wooden bench in front of a cluttered writing table. Oskar took a seat and the man settled into a chair.

"I am Inceptor Darhon. I will be responsible for you during your time in the novitiate." He moved aside a stack of papers, uncovering a leather-bound book. The binding was cracked and the pages brittle, and he opened it with care to a place he had marked. "Your name and your home, please."

"Oskar Clehn, from Galsbur in Galdora."

Darhon picked up a ragged quill, entered the information, and then blotted the entry with sand. When he finished, he set the book aside and fixed his gaze on Oskar.

"Why do you want to enter the Gates?"

"I want to learn." Aspin had told him to keep his answers simple, and that was the simple truth. He'd always loved learning.

"What do you wish to learn?" Darhon's voice betrayed no emotion.

"History, logic, magic, sorcery. Everything, I suppose."

"Why do you seek this knowledge?"

That wasn't so easy to answer. How did you explain the thing that, more than anything else, made you who you are?

"I've always sought knowledge for its own sake. I read every book I could get my hands on and listened to every story the elders told." He shrugged.

Dahron began shuffling papers, but the questions continued.

"What will you do with the knowledge you glean from this place?"

Oskar shook his head. "Something good. I don't know, I suppose I'll learn that too." He felt he was failing the interview. Dahron would probably send him on his way in short order. He was, after all, just a farm boy.

"Do you wish to be a saikur?" Dahron still looked down at his papers, but his tone was sharp.

"I suppose I do." Oskar kicked himself. Why hadn't he considered his answer? Aspin had warned him to take care of what he said.

Dahron looked up and smiled.

"If you aren't certain now, you shall soon find out." He laid his papers down, laced his fingers together, and locked eyes with Oskar. "You will begin as a novit, with no status. I may dismiss you at any time for any reason: violating rules, failure to attend classes or see to your duties, showing a lack of promise. Any reason at all." He fell silent and waited for Oskar to nod that he understood before continuing.

"Leave your personal effects here. They will be returned to you."

Oskar winced. He owned nothing of significant value, nor was he attached to many of his few possessions, but there was his book. In his youth, he'd copied sections from Lord Hiram's books, and when he left Galsbur, he recorded their travels, copied passages from books in the great library at Karkwall, mapped their journey, and even made rubbings of glyphs in the lost city of Murantha. It now comprised a thick bundle of papers wrapped in coarse leather and bound with twine. He hated the thought of giving it up, even briefly, but what choice did he have?"

"Do you have any questions?" Darhon asked.

"Could I get a list of the rules?"

"Learning the rules is part of your novit training. I suggest you do so with all due haste. Now, follow me."

An hour later, Oskar found himself bathed, de-loused, and garbed in an itchy tunic and hose. He was issued two spare sets of clothing, a coarse blanket, a surprisingly comfortable pair of boots, and a plain, brown cloak, the twin of the one the Thandrylls had given him so long ago. Aspin had kept it, thinking it a bad idea for Oskar to show up at the Gates already dressed like a saikur. Heart pounding, he stood outside the door to his dormitory. The page who had led him here smirked at his hesitation and pointed at the doorknob. Heart in his throat, Oskar opened the door and stepped inside.

The conversation in the room ceased. Three young men sat on bunk beds to his left and right. Directly opposite the door, a window looked out over the forest and onto the city. Oskar would have been eager to take a look were he not so nervous. He forced a grin.

"I'm Oskar."

"It's about time we got some fresh meat in here. I'm tired of being the new kid." A young man with light brown skin and glossy black hair stood and offered his hand. "I'm Naseeb, and these piles of horse dung are Whitt and Dacio." Whitt, a bulky blond, and Dacio, an angular youth with a crooked nose and dirt brown hair, added their greetings. "Toss your things on the empty bunk above mine. It's almost third bell."

"What does that mean?" Oskar hated feeling ignorant, but his only hope of learning his way was to ask as many questions as possible and hope no one steered him in the wrong direction.

"It means food." Whitt slid down off his top bunk and landed on his booted feet with a thud. "It's not tasty, but there's always plenty, and you look like you could use a little feeding up."

Oskar blinked. All his life, he'd been on the heavy side, but long months of travel, mostly through wilderness, living on trail rations, and practicing with his staff, had wrought a change in him to which he was not yet accustomed. He was tall and broad of shoulder, but he'd lost his girth, and his cheeks were no longer plump.

"Food will be welcome." He tossed his bundle onto the bunk— his bunk.

"Don't forget your cloak," Naseeb said. "Never leave quarters without it."

"Thanks. I asked the inceptor about the rules, but he said I had to learn them on my own."

His three roommates laughed.

"Darhon does that to everyone. Just pay close attention to what we say, and never forget a word, and you'll be fine." Naseeb's dark eyes twinkled. "Now, let's go before I shrivel up and blow away."

The smells of cooking reached Oskar long before they entered the dining hall: the aroma of freshly baked bread and something spicy. His stomach rumbled and his new companions laughed.

"Your stomach might not thank you for what you're about to feed it." Naseeb led the way into the dimly lit room. Tall, narrow windows cast slivers of orange sunlight across the rows of trestle tables where men of varying ages, all clad in brown robes, sat conversing around bites of bread and mouthfuls of a thick, brown stew.

As they joined the line of men waiting to be served, Whitt began to speak in a low tone. "All the men working the serving line are novits or low-level initiates. When they serve you, nod once and say, "Thank you." Don't say anything else, but don't forget to thank them."

"How about the fellow with all the ear hair?" A tall man with a pronounced widow's peak and thick sideburns paced like a caged animal behind the serving line.

"That's Master Moylan. Don't let him hear you talking about his ear hair. He's supposed to have tried every remedy to get rid of it, but every time it only grows back thicker." Whitt's expression turned grave. "If he speaks to you, address him as Master and don't look at him with a speck of defiance. He'll have you scrubbing pots with your hair if he thinks you're not showing the proper respect."

Oskar felt his spine stiffen as Whitt continued to explain proper conduct and forms of address for the masters, the proctors, the guardsman and his lieutenants, even the prelate. Oskar had always been one to put his boot in his mouth on occasion, so a misstep was inevitable. He just needed to keep them to a minimum and hope none were too egregious.

They found seats at the far table. Oskar dug into his bowl of stew. The meat was stringy and the vegetables undercooked, but after weeks on horseback, with only a few stops for proper meals, it tasted delicious. When he finally sopped the last morsel from his bowl with a crust of bread, he looked up to see the others staring at him.

"You might want to slow down next time. There are no second helpings."

Naseeb gestured with his spoon. "And you wouldn't want Master Moylan thinking you a glutton."

"Does he really pay attention to how fast a person eats?"

"He pays attention to everything. Here, you can have the rest of mine." Dacio slid his bowl, still half full, over to Oskar.

"Thanks." Oskar decided conversation might help him eat slower. "So, what lessons do we take?" His new friend explained that there were seven courses of study: History, Logic, Wisdom, Alchemy, Combat, Magic, and Sorcery. There were no courses on Seventhday, and while Sixthday mornings were devoted to either Combat or Sorcery, the remainder of the day was theirs.

"You'll need that day," Dacio said, "for study."

"What's the best course?"

"Combat," Whitt said, as Dacio and Naseeb answered "Logic" and "Magic" respectively.

"Can we at least agree History is the worst?" Whitt looked at his friends, who nodded.

"I love history." Oskar thought of the hours spent hidden away, reading Lord Hiram's books. "At least, I love books of history."

"It's not the subject; it's the teacher. Master Sibson once bored a student to death. I mean he literally died of boredom in the middle of a lecture."

Oskar looked for signs of jest in Whitt's eyes but saw none.

"He didn't die from boredom." Naseeb was doing tricks with his spoon- rolling it between his fingers and flipping it around his thumb and back again. "He died because his heart stopped beating."

"Because the lecture bored it to death."

"You're both wrong," Dacio said. "He tried mixing his own dream elixir, but he made it too strong and it stopped his heart."

"And why did he take the elixir? Because he couldn't stand Master Sibson's lectures." Whitt folded his arms across his chest and rocked back in his seat, waiting for Dacio's rejoinder.

Dacio rubbed his long nose thoughtfully. "Fine, but the boredom didn't literally kill him."

Oskar had to laugh. He already felt at home. Before he could ask about the rest of the teachers, someone called his name.

"Oskar Clehn?"

He turned to see a brown-robed man standing behind him.

"Yes?"

"Proctor Basilius wishes to see you. Follow me."

Puzzled, he collected his spoon and bowl and rose from his seat, but froze when he saw the frightened looks on his friends' faces.

"What does Basilius want with you?" Naseeb whispered. "He's…"

Whatever Basilius was, Oskar didn't find out because the man called his name again.

"We'll take your bowl," Dacio said. "You'd better go."

Oskar turned and followed his guide, wondering what, exactly, a proctor could want with him.

Chapter 5

Proctor Basilius stood with his back to the door when Oskar entered the office. Hands folded behind his back, he stared out the window. He was a broad-shouldered man with thick, yellow-white hair that hung to his shoulders. When he finally turned around, he arched an eyebrow at Oskar.

"Why did you not announce yourself?"

"I didn't want to interrupt." How had he already managed to run afoul of the man?

"What, pray tell, was I doing that you thought you should not interrupt?"

"Thinking? I think." He forced himself to meet the man's green-eyed stare.

Finally, Basilius' stony expression cracked and he twitched his cheek in something less than a smirk. "Don't mind me, boy. It's my duty as a master to take the measure of our novits. I merely wanted to see how you comported yourself."

Oskar felt he'd made a poor showing, but merely nodded. He and Basilius took seats in front of a cold fireplace, and Basilius stared at him far too long for comfort. Finally, the proctor broke the silence.

"Tell me how you came to the gates."

"Aspin brought me." This was one of the many areas in which Aspin had coached him not to reveal too much.

"I understand he sees great promise in you." Another twitch of the mouth. "Where did the two of you meet?"

"In Lothan." Wait! Was that the story he was supposed to tell, or should he have said they'd met in Galsbur? He'd been forced to learn so much in such a short time, that he couldn't possibly remember it all.

"A dangerous place. What is a young Galdoran doing down there?" Basilius kept his tone conversational, but his gaze hardened.

"I'm ashamed to admit it, but I left home seeking adventure." He hung his head, hoping the prelate wouldn't see the lie in his eyes. "I didn't know where I was going and, next thing I knew, I was in Lothan."

"I understand that the clans have united." Basilius stood, moved to a corner cabinet, and withdrew a bottle of wine and two glasses. "What is your assessment of the situation?"

"I don't know. Aspin found me and I traveled with him." He accepted a glass of red wine, but did not drink. As he gazed down into the depths, the deep crimson put him in mind of blood. "We saw lots of clans traveling, but that's all I know."

Basilius took a long drink, letting the silence hang in the air. Finally, he set his glass down. "Where were they traveling?"

"I'm not sure. Aspin talked with them. I tended the fire, practiced..." He realized he was providing more information than the prelate had requested, and fell silent.

"It's not unusual for a saikur to begin a novit's education before he is officially enrolled at the gates. What did you practice?"

This was not consistent with what Aspin had told him, but the proctor didn't seem bothered. "Some weapons training, quarterstaff mostly."

"Sorcery as well?" Basilius' smile calmed the wave of anxiety that rolled over Oskar. "I can sense it in you." He sat up straighter and smoothed his robes. "One of my areas of responsibility is to oversee Master Ashur, who teaches sorcery. I take an interest in novits who show a pronounced ability. I'd like to assess you."

Oskar's heart raced and his throat was tight, but he choked out a reply. "I haven't learned much."

"Relax. I am not testing you. I only want to measure your capacity for channeling power. All right?"

Oskar felt anything but all right, but he nodded and straightened in his seat.

"Look directly into my eyes." Basilius' voice was velvet. "Allow your focus to narrow until all you see are my pupils. Black circles in a haze of gray."

It was an odd feeling, looking into the man's eyes like this. Aspin had never used this technique with him. As the proctor guided him, he relaxed and opened himself to the energy all around him.

It started as a trickle, and then a flood. Power rolled through him, sharpening his awareness, intensifying his senses. As he gazed into Basilius' eyes, his pupils seemed to grow, until, suddenly, Oskar was engulfed in blackness. He tried to look away, or even close his eyes, but he was entranced.

And then the first memory came.

Drifting up like bubbles from the bottom of a pond, came a series of disjointed images: riding through the forest with Aspin, his first sorcery lesson, practicing the quarterstaff with Allyn. He tried to control his thoughts, but something seemed to reach inside his mind and draw them forth: Shanis holding the Silver Serpent aloft, Khalyndryn's lifeless eyes.

With a cry of pain, he broke free of whatever power gripped him. Basilius jerked back as if he'd been struck a sharp blow. They stared at one another, Oskar panting from the effort, the proctor looking bemused.

"Sorry," Oskar finally said. "I don't know what happened."

"It is all right. You are a novit after all. I shouldn't keep you any longer." Basilius rose, strode to the door, and opened it for Oskar. "Sleep well. You'll want to be ready for your first day of training."

Oskar mumbled a hasty word of thanks and bowed his way out of the office. He'd paid little attention on the way here, and had to ask directions twice before finding his way to his room. When he arrived, he found his roommates all still awake.

"What did Basilius want?" Naseeb asked.

"I'm not exactly sure." He gave a brief accounting of his meeting with the prelate. When he came to the assessment of his strength, he paused. "This is going to sound strange, but at the end, it felt like he was trying to draw memories out of me." He let the words hang there, waiting for them to laugh.

But only silence greeted his words. Naseeb and Whitt exchanged a hasty glance while Dacio coughed and looked away.

"What?"

They all held their silence for a few moments, and then Naseeb sighed. "There are rumors about Basilius. It's said he can read minds."

Oskar considered this. It had felt like an outside force was thumbing through his memories like the pages of a book. If that was the case, then Basilius had known Oskar was hiding information about his time in Lothan. He took a deep breath and let it out in a rush.

"You said rumors. What else do they say about him?"

Naseeb shook his head. "Not tonight. It's late and I don't like talking about him." His face brightened. "A page brought your things. I guess Darhon didn't find anything that concerned him." He tossed Oskar a brass key and indicated a wooden trunk in the corner. "That's yours. If you lose the key, you'll have to ask Darhon for a new one, and he'll make you regret it."

Oskar winced at the thought.

"Oh, and a saikur brought you this." Naseeb handed him a canvas bag. Oskar opened it and smiled. It was his cloak the Thandrylls had given him. Aspin must have brought it to him. He felt a pang of disappointment that he'd missed him. He would have loved to tell Aspin about his meeting with Basilius.

Leaving the cloak in the bag, he went to his trunk and unlocked it. There were his belongings, such as they were. His clothing had been laundered and mended. A lump formed in his throat as he looked at the reminders of the time he'd spent traveling with his friends. He wondered how Shanis was managing in her new role as leader of the Lothans. Was Hierm a father yet? Had Allyn recovered from his ordeal battling with the spirit that sought to possess him? And how was Larris faring back in the palace at Archstone? Then he thought of Khalyndryn, and tears welled in his eyes.

"Are you all right?" Whitt half-rose from the edge of his bed.

"Yes, I just…" The words froze on his tongue. He'd just realized something was missing.

His book.

Chapter 6

Where is she *going at this time of night?* The cold, rough stone pressed into Allyn's cheek as he hid in the shadows of the alleyway. The moon cast the street in silver light, but few were out this time of evening. It was an hour for thieves, and no time for a governess to be about.

Melina was apparently trying to move unseen and was making a poor job of it. She stopped and started, flitted from shadow to shadow, and kept looking all around.

Allyn would have laughed if the situation weren't so grave. Larris needed to find out what had happened to his brother's letter of abdication, and he was convinced Melina had something to do with it. He wondered if she had the letter on her person. Of course, accosting her would do no good. Even if she was the guilty party, he'd have to search her and, if she didn't have it on her person, he and Larris would lose any chance of finding it and discovering who was pulling her strings.

"You have to be working for someone," he whispered. "What use would you have for that letter?"

Melina turned onto a side street and Allyn had to hurry to catch up, moving along on silent feet. He peered around the corner and froze. She was gone! That couldn't be. She had only been out of his sight for a matter of seconds. Gritting his teeth, he stepped out into the street and looked around.

His eyes fell upon a single door at the back of a massive building. That had to be where she had gone. Getting his bearings, his heart lurched when he realized where he was—The Temple of the Seven!

He moved with haste back into the shadows and caught his breath. His thoughts churned as he considered the implications. If Melina were here to visit the sanctuary, which was highly unlikely in the middle of the night, she'd have entered through the front door. This proved it. Someone in the temple was meddling in the royal family's affairs, but to what end?

He considered returning to the palace immediately and reporting to Larris, but thought the better of it. Melina was very likely delivering the letter right now. If he could retrieve it, and find out for whom she was working, it would save a great deal of trouble. Steeling his nerves, he moved to the door and tried the handle. Locked. He'd have to enter by the front door.

He paused on the front steps, lowered his hood and made sure his cloak covered his belt knives before entering.

Shadows cloaked the sanctuary, with only the meager glow of a few candles to light his way. Statues of the seven gods sat in alcoves on either side, their odd number giving the room a strangely unbalanced feel.

A fat priest sat dozing behind the altar rail. Allyn fished a coin out of his belt pouch and dropped it into the bowl. The priest started at the sound of clinking metal but nodded and closed his eyes again as Allyn lit one of the candle stubs on the rail and knelt to pray. Soon, the man was snoring again.

Allyn scanned the altar area and spotted a poorly concealed door set in the back wall. He rose, slipped over the altar rail, and crept to the door. Taking one last look to make sure the priest was still asleep, he opened the door and stepped inside.

"Very good." Timmon smiled as he read Lerryn's abdication letter. "You have done well, daughter. Your faithful service to the seven will not be forgotten."

"I'm glad you are pleased." The priest was the closest thing to a father Melina had, which was the only reason she had served as his informant on the affairs of the local family for all these years. She took a shallow breath and forced the words out. "Forgive me, but I don't understand why the temple is interested in interfering with the line of succession. Larris is a reliable young man and will make a better king than Lerryn would have."

"It's not something that can be easily explained. And we do not intend to interfere. We simply need time to study the situation and make sure the outcome is what is best for the future of our nation." Timmon folded the paper and tucked it inside his robe. "You need not worry. We have only Galdora's best interests at heart."

Melina jumped as the door behind her opened. She snapped her head around to see the king's brother enter the room. "Lord Orman?"

He forced a smile, but not before a flash of anger mingled with surprise flitted across his face. "Melina. The hour is late for you to be at worship."

"I was just delivering something. I should go now." She took a step toward the door on wobbly knees, but Orman grabbed hold of her arm.

"No need to leave on my account. When I am in need of counsel, I prefer to visit when no one is about. The commoners do love to talk."

"I imagine they do." She'd never been so frightened in her life. Her head buzzed and she felt as if she were floating far above her body. Nothing made sense. Neither the temple's interest in the business of the royal family nor their previously-unsuspected connection to Orman, who had never, as far as she knew, shown any sign of being religious. She didn't believe Orman was here for counseling, and they both knew it. She looked longingly at the door. Even if she could break free of Orman's tight grip, she'd never get away.

Timmon stood and cleared his throat. "Melina was just leaving."

Orman's grip loosened as the priest took Melina by the elbow and guided her out.

As they navigated the silent halls, she permitted herself to relax if only a little. She'd escaped the situation, but what would happen when she and Orman were back at the palace? Would he suffer her to live now that she knew of his connection to the temple, or would he treat her as an accomplice, knowing she could not report his actions without admitting to treason? It was a knot she couldn't untangle. She would have to flee; there was nothing else for it. She had a horse, a gift from the royal family, and enough coin to get well away from Archstone.

"Here we are. I fear I cannot offer you an escort back to the palace. You understand, of course?"

Melina nodded and embraced Timmon.

She didn't see the dagger before he thrust it into her heart.

Allyn wound through the empty hallways of the Temple of the Seven. He moved silently through a corridor lined with empty studies, then through a dining hall and into the area which, by the snores he heard, housed the sleeping quarters. This was useless. He had no idea where he was going and, by now, Melina was likely long gone. His chance of discovering whom she was meeting and why was lost.

He retraced his steps, hoping he wouldn't be discovered, as he could offer no believable reason for being here, and he really didn't want to kill a priest.

Back in the sanctuary, he found the priest still snoring. Relief mingling with disappointment at his failure, he made his way back out onto the street. He took a deep breath of the damp night air and tried to sort out his thoughts. He felt as though he'd discovered something important, but he knew so little. At least he could point Larris in the proper direction.

As he passed through a row of pubs and inns, all dark, a shape lying on the ground caught his attention. His hand went to the hilt of his long hunting knife and he approached with caution. As he drew closer, he realized it was a body. Somehow, he knew who it was even before he knelt over her, pressing his hand to the wound in her chest.

Melina!

Chapter 7

"My children! Where are my children?" The woman tried to reach Pedric Karst, newly-crowned King of Kurnsbur, but his men held her back. She beat at their arms before crumpling to the ground in a heap. She looked at Karst through a curtain of lank, black hair. "I know you've taken them, you monster!"

Karst kicked his horse's flanks and trotted away. He didn't care what happened to the brats of Malgog filth. When they were well clear of her, he slowed to a trot. Down a steep embankment, the Igiranin River wended its way south toward the lands of the Black Mangrove clan, the only barrier to his establishing a port city. He dismissed the thought with a shake of his head.

"What did happen to her children?" he asked Jakom, who, along with Arlus rode alongside him.

"They were needed for the temple, Majesty." A hint of bitterness touched Jakom's voice.

Karst considered this. Instituted by his father, Rimmic Karst, the temple had operated outside of his writ since he'd seized control of northwestern Lothan and united it with his family's duchy of Kurnsbur in southeastern Galdora. He supposedly ruled here in Salgo, the new city that would be the capital of the new nation of Kurnsbur. Commoners bowed their heads when he passed, yet the priests looked down their noses at him. It was time for that to change.

"I think it's time I paid a visit to the temple."

"I don't think they would welcome that." Jakom kept his eyes fixed on a spot in front of them, but he couldn't stop his ears from turning red.

"What are they going to do? Bar my entry?"

"They have a force of guards who might do just that." Jakom raised his hand to forestall Karst's protest. "Remember, Majesty, your father established the temple as an independent entity. Those who answer to a god cannot answer to civil authority as well."

Arlus rode up beside him and pointed to a place where the river narrowed. "The perfect place for the bridge, no? Less distance to span."

"Don't change the subject. I want to know what is happening in the temple." He felt his temper rise and his hand went to the hilt of his sword without thought.

Jakom noticed and his eyes widened. "Forgive me, but is that necessary? You know I serve faithfully, but your father has made it clear that you are to lead the nation and the military but leave the temple to its own devices."

Karst took a deep breath and got his temper in check. He wondered if his father had set him up as a puppet leader. That seemed to be Rimmic's plan, but Pedric had other ideas.

"Let me make myself perfectly clear. My father is not in charge. I am. Is that understood?"

Jakom nodded. "I just don't think it would be wise to interfere with the temple. The work they are doing is important to your father's, I mean, your plans."

"All the more reason I should know what they are doing." He wheeled his horse about and put his heels to its flanks. A warm sense of satisfaction surged through him. Finally, he was taking control.

The temple was a circular, terraced structure of mud bricks, rising to a peak nearly two hundred hands high, easily the tallest structure in Salgo. Flowers, shrubs and fruit trees grew in the terraces, and a few temple servants tended them. The ever-present column of white smoke poured from the chimney at its apex. Karst grimaced. It was a far finer place than his own quarters—something else that would have to be remedied soon.

He dismounted, tied his horse off, and signaled for his men to follow. Striding forward, he drew his sword and held it low at his side. Padin, Danlar, and Arlus immediately followed suit. Behind them, a cluster of soldiers followed along, looking darkly eager for a fight.

"Your Highness, surely weapons are not needed?" Jakom drew his own sword and hurried to keep pace.

"Not if the guards don't try to stop us." Karst turned to Jakom. "You almost sound frightened. Do I need to replace you as my personal guard?"

"No. It's just that, it's not the guards that frighten me." He grimaced, glanced at Karst, and then hurried on ahead. "Make way for His Royal Highness, Pedric Karst, King of Kurnsbur!" he bellowed.

One of the guards lowered his spear and took a step forward before backing off. Two temple guards against twelve armed men would stand little chance.

Karst scowled at the guards. "Have you forgotten how to show proper respect?" Each man dropped to a knee and lowered his head. "Disarm them," Karst told Jakom and Padin, and they hurried to obey.

"You may rise." The guards stood and eyed him warily. "I wish to see the high priest. Lead me to him."

"Your Highness, he is leading worship at the moment and cannot be disturbed."

"I have not yet had the chance to worship in our temple. It is time I rectified that. Lead the way." He put steel in his words and emphasized them by pointing his sword between the man's eyes.

Both guards rose and stalked into the temple.

"Kill anyone who offers resistance." Karst sheathed his sword and tried to suppress his jangled nerves. It would not do to appear afraid. He was king here.

Candles set in alcoves offered faint light within the dark corridor. The passageway circled the base of the structure, winding inward. They passed a few closed doors and a narrow staircase but encountered no guards, nor anyone from the temple.

The deeper they penetrated, the more oppressive the darkness grew. Karst imagined he could feel its weight pressing down on him. The stale scent of wood smoke and something more acrid hung in the damp air, and he felt a throbbing, pulsing vibration all around. He wanted to ask if anyone else felt it but feared it would be seen a sign of weakness, so he kept his silence.

Finally, the corridor ended at a barred door. Here, a single guard waited. He looked at Karst with a bemused expression but lacked the temerity to challenge him. Finally, he dropped to a knee and averted his eyes.

"I would see Malaithus." Karst poured all the authority he possessed into the words.

"I fear that is impossible. The High Priest is in worship right now and cannot be disturbed." The guard did not look at Karst, but his voice was strong.

Karst turned to Padin. "Bring me his head."

"No!" The guard sprang to his feet. "I mean, His Holiness has given us strict orders. Anyone who disobeys is…" He blanched.

"Is what?" Karst asked.

"Your Highness, you will have to see for yourself." He turned, removed the bar from the door, and opened it just enough for one man to slip through at a time.

Perhaps fearing an ambush, Jakom entered first. Padin and Danlar followed. Karst took a moment to set two of his men to watch over the guard and make certain he did not raise an alarm, before entering the chamber with the remainder of his men bringing up the rear.

The sanctuary was thick with the same smoke that poured from the top of the temple. Karst wrinkled his nose. Here was the source of the acrid smell he now recognized as burnt flesh. Beams of light from windows high above sliced through the haze, revealing a ring of priests lying prostrate on the floor, encircling a fiery pit and a stone altar. The high priest stood with his back to the door. A child lay bound on the altar and two more lay weeping nearby, their wrists and ankles tied with thick rope. A single guard stood over them, his attention fixed on them as if he could not bring himself to look at what transpired on the altar.

As a drummer, hidden somewhere in the haze, pounded out a primordial beat, the High Priest, Malaithus, raised an obsidian knife and plunged it into the chest of the child on the altar. The priests all around him began a rhythmic chant which was soon picked up by a large chorus of voices.

In the haze, Karst had not noticed the peasants seated around the outer wall. They swayed to and fro and chanted in a monotonous rhythm. He considered the scene. He and his men could deal with a handful of priests and guards, but a hundred or more zealots maddened by religious fervor could be dangerous if something set them off.

The priest removed the child's heart and held it aloft, blood streaming down his arm. As the chanting rose to a crescendo, he hurled the heart into the fire. The congregants roared in ecstasy as the flames turned icy blue.

There was a sudden, oppressive weight in the air. Karst staggered and put his hands to his head. He felt like something was squeezing his mind, beating down his will. All around the worshipers were falling face-first onto the packed earth floor. He dropped to a knee and gritted his teeth, fighting to maintain control. What was happening to him?

The chanting sharpened into a single word that echoed mournfully through the sanctuary.

"Wake... wake... wake..."

"My Lord." Jakom's voice shook. "What is that...*thing*?"

Karst forced his eyes open and looked up at the roiling cloud of smoke. Terror silenced his scream.

Chapter 8

Oskar left breakfast early. He didn't want to be late for his first-ever class at the Gates, and he had a stop to make along the way. His heart raced as he hurried down the empty hall. He wasn't sure he should be doing this, but he had no better idea.

Inceptor Darhon was seated at his desk when Oskar arrived at his office. He looked up but didn't speak.

"Inceptor, may I ask you a question?" Oskar's heart pounded in his chest so furiously he was surprised Darhon couldn't hear it. Darhon continued to stare. Since he hadn't declined or sent Oskar away, Oskar decided to ask his question. He cleared his throat and shuffled his feet. "I received my belongings last night."

"That is not a question."

"No, but one of my items is missing. It's something that has sentimental value and I would like to have it back. I wondered if it might have been... misplaced."

A long moment of silence greeted his words, and he wondered if he'd given offense. Finally, the inceptor took a deep breath, exhaled, and reached for a quill. "If an item was withheld, it is because it is regarded as potentially harmful to you or other novits."

Oskar thought this an absurd stance to take, considering the novits were learning sorcery, magic, and combat, but he kept that thought to himself. "It was a book.

Rather, a collection of writings."

Darhon dipped his quill and began scribbling. "Books are given to Master Corwine, the keeper of the archives. He will return it in due course. Good morning."

The dismissal was plain. Oskar wanted to know when he could expect the book's return but thought the better of it. He made a hasty bow and hurried on to his first class.

He arrived just as everyone was taking their seats. His appearance drew several stares and a few whispers as he sat down on a bench beside his roommates. One young man, blond with pale blue eyes, turned and looked him up and down. He answered Oskar's polite nod with a sneer, then whispered something to the youths on either side of him, who chuckled and stole glances in Oskar's direction.

"That's Agen, Shaw, and Dronn. They're from wealthy families in northern Cardith and think they're better than everyone else. Steer clear of them." Naseeb scowled at the backs of the young men.

Oskar grimaced. He'd imagined those in training to be seekers would be above such pettiness. He was about to say so when the master entered the room.

Sorcery was taught by Master Ashur. A bald, spindly man with pinched features, he spoke in a low tone that forced the listener to strain to hear him. It also served to sharpen their focus. Oskar found himself leaning forward, eager to take in every word.

Today's lesson was about focusing energy into the tiniest space possible. All sorcery, he reminded them, was a matter of a person gathering in the life forces all around them, and focusing them upon an object.

"The uninitiated assume that all sorcery is, by nature, destructive. We, of course, know better." Ashur gave them a look that promised stern correction to anyone who did not know better. After explaining the theory, he led them out the side door onto a terrace brimming with greenery.

If he didn't know they were on an upper floor, Oskar would have thought they'd walked out into a garden. Fruit trees grew in giant clay pots, grape vines wound around the terrace rails, and potted ferns hung from hooks all around.

"Find a partner, pick a few grapes, preferably the overripe ones, spread out, and practice."

Oskar was about to ask which of his roommates would partner him when Master Ashur's voice rang out. "New boy. Come here!"

His throat tight, Oskar hurried over to where Ashur waited. "Yes, master?" He hoped he hadn't somehow broken one of the rules Darhon had warned him about but refused to share with him.

"Are you a beginner? That is, have you channeled power?"

"Yes. I mean, I have channeled power. Some."

Ashur nodded. "That is very well. You have much to learn in order to catch up with the rest of the class." He pursed his lips as one of the students missed his grape entirely and managed to singe the hem of his robe. "To some of them, at least. Now, show me what you can do. Reach out." He folded his arms across his chest and took a step back.

Most of the class was focused on the lesson, but Oskar caught sight of Whitt, Naseeb, and Dacio watching him. Agen and his friends had also taken an interest.

Oskar took a few breaths to calm his racing heart, opened himself and reached out. He immediately understood the reason for the terrace's abundant plant life. It provided an ample supply of life force from which to draw. He let the power flow in, felt it course through him, and realized Ashur had not told him what to do with the power. Hastily, he looked around and his eyes fell on Agen, who snickered and pointed at Oskar.

"Look at the country lout." He didn't bother to keep his voice down. "He has no business here."

Oskar didn't think. He reached out with the power, as Aspin had taught him, formed it into a wall, and gave Agen a shove that sat him down hard on his backside. Agen sat there in the middle of exploded grapes, looking shocked and angry.

"Very good." Ashur nodded once. "You are prepared for the coursework. On the other hand, using sorcery against a fellow member of the Gates is strictly prohibited. It is the first rule of the Gates. You shall remain behind after class to clean the terrace. This evening, report to the kitchens to work off your demerit. Now, find a partner and continue the lesson." The master turned his back and started circling the room, watching the students who had immediately returned to their work.

Oskar didn't know whether to feel proud or disappointed. He'd proven his worth but, in his very first class, had earned himself a punishment. And, by the look on Agen's face, he had made an enemy.

"That couldn't have gone much worse." Oskar stared down at his feet as they descended the stairs.

"Oh, I don't know about that." Naseeb gave him a friendly pat on the back. "You could have failed to channel."

"If I had failed to channel, I'd never have knocked Agen down and wouldn't have landed myself in the kitchens on my first day."

"Had you failed," Dacio interrupted, "Agen would have seen you as an easy target and made your life miserable. Now he has to take you seriously. As for kitchen work, don't worry about that. Everyone steps a toe out of bounds here and there."

"Except you," Naseeb retorted.

Dacio ignored him. "Honestly, don't fret over it. Master Ashur respects skill, and you clearly have it, especially for a novit. Not many of us have sufficient control to do what you did to Agen."

"All I did was push him." Oskar tried not to smile. His gran had always said, "Don't take your prize pig to town." As a child, he'd thought it was a warning to be careful with the things you treasured. It was years before he realized it meant not to be overly proud. Still, the compliment was welcome and reassured him that perhaps he wasn't entirely out of his depth here.

"Most of us have little control over the amount of force we use," Whitt said. "You used just the right amount. You'll have to teach me how you do it, that is if you aren't too tired from scrubbing pots tonight."

Now, Oskar permitted himself a smile. "Actually, I had thought of visiting the archives. Are we allowed to visit so late?"

"Novits are not permitted in the archives," Dacio said. "You must be an initiate."

Oskar's heart fell. Browsing the Gates' legendary collection of books and scrolls was the thing he'd been looking forward to the most. He'd just have to work hard to reach initiate status. But there was still the matter of his book.

"I don't actually need access to the archives; I just need to ask about my book." He went on to explain about his missing book and what Darhon had told him. "I suppose I could ask Master Corwine about it."

Naseeb blanched, quite a feat considering his dark complexion. "I wouldn't bother Master Corwine." He looked around before lowering his voice to a whisper and continuing. "He's the touchiest of all the masters. Anything can set him off, and he's unforgiving."

"I'm sure he'll return your book in time," Dacio added. "Just be patient."

They reached the ground floor and followed their classmates out into the walled grounds behind the main tower. Here, a cobblestone path wound through a formal garden, tended by several robed men.

"Are those saikurs tending the grounds?" Oskar asked, noting the men's apparent ages.

"Yes," Naseeb whispered. "Every man at the Gates is expected to contribute in some way. Tending the grounds is preferable to scrubbing floors. Some consider it meditative while others are assigned the duty as a penance for unsanctioned behavior."

"I'm surprised they'd make such a punishment public."

"They don't. You never know if a man is working off a punishment, taking his regular turn, or simply doing something he enjoys."

As they passed a bush laden with dark blue berries, a seeker bearing a full basket stepped out into the path. It was Aspin. Oskar opened his mouth but remembered Dacio had warned him that novits were not to speak to seekers unless spoken to. It was not, he claimed, a rule, but a custom and a sign of respect. He nodded instead, but Aspin seemed to look right through him. Oskar felt a flash of hurt, but it dissolved in the face of a sudden thought. Was Aspin serving a penance? He'd mentioned to Oskar that he'd been away from the Gates for some time. Perhaps he was embarrassed for Oskar to see him like this.

All thoughts of Aspin were quickly forgotten as they reached a grassy swath of land and the other novits began stripping off their robes and removing their boots. Puzzled, Oskar followed suit. Before he could ask what they were doing, the students took off at a quick jog. Groaning, he followed along.

He caught up with Whitt, who was bringing up the rear.

"What are we doing?" Though his travels had made Oskar leaner and stronger, he still wasn't one for running, and his lungs were already complaining.

"Warming up. We do this before every class. Just follow the group and try not to come in last."

Oskar thought he stood little chance of finishing anywhere other than the back of the pack. They reached a stone wall, turned left, and ran along its length. Above the heads of those running in front of him, he saw his fellow novits clambering up a steep hill.

"We're allowed to go around, right?" he panted.

Whitt grinned and gave him a friendly push up the hill. They scrambled up the slope, slid down the other side, and started running again. They were losing ground on the others.

"Looks like I'm going to be last." His side burned and he feared he would heave up the last of his breakfast.

"Maybe you should shut up and focus on running." Whitt put his head down and picked up the pace. Oskar tried to keep up but found he could not. He turned another corner and hurdled a series of logs, scarcely clearing the last one. He stumbled and fell, landing hard on his hands. Absently, he remembered he was supposed to roll on his shoulder or something like that, but he was too tired to care.

"It's just past that clearing. You'll make it."

Oskar hadn't noticed the young man seated against the bole of a tree. He had long, red hair and a crooked smile, and he grinned at Oskar from his place on the ground. Oskar thought his name was Garent.

"I was in the lead for the first time in weeks until Agen tripped me. I think my ankle is broken."

Oskar heaved himself up to his feet and staggered over to look at Garent's ankle. "It's swollen," he said.

"Really? I hadn't noticed." The note of amusement was evident in Garent's voice.

"Why did Agen trip you?"

"Because he's an ass who doesn't like to lose." Garent tried to rise, but he paled and slumped back against the tree. "When you get to the finish, tell Master Lang I'll be going to the infirmary as soon as I am able."

"I'll help you. Come on." Ignoring Garent's protests, Oskar hauled the young man to his feet, slipped an arm around his waist, and helped him limp to the finish.

As they reached the grassy area where they'd shed their cloaks, Agen and his friends chanted, "Last! Last! Last!" They cut off at a single glance from the master.

Master Lang was a barrel of a man. His arms and legs were like tree trunks and his neck looked nearly as thick. He wore his black hair shaved down almost to his scalp, save a long tail in the back. He stalked toward Oskar and Garent, his face red and his slate gray eyes narrowed to slits.

When he reached them, he knelt to examine Garent's ankle. He scrutinized it, stood, and turned to face the class.

"Novit Garent is one of the fastest runners in the class. Who here passed him by when he fell?"

One by one, every student raised his hand. All except Agen. Oskar wanted to protest but was too intimidated by the bearish Lang to interrupt.

"You were all so desperate to avoid finishing last that you left him behind." Lang's low rumble sounded like a roar in the silent field. "All of you except the new boy." He didn't spare Oskar a second glance. "Everyone except him, run it again."

It was a measure of Lang's authority that no one so much as frowned before starting off, save Agen, who shot Oskar a baleful look before following the group.

Lang called out to a seeker who was trimming a hedgerow and instructed him to take Garent to the infirmary. The seeker hurried to the task, as quick to obey the master as any novit.

Interesting.

"Do you have a name, or do you prefer New Boy?"

"Oskar Clehn."

"Tell me about your fighting skills, Oskar Clehn."

Oskar hesitated. He didn't have any skills to speak of, but he doubted that was what Lang wanted to hear. "I'm a fair wrestler, and more than fair with a quarterstaff."

"What else? Bow? Sling? Your accent tells me you're from the west. Don't all you frontier folk learn to hunt?"

"Not really. I'm a farmer." He couldn't think of anything else to say.

"Today we're working the sword. I suppose it's too much to hope you know how to use one."

Aspin had given him a few lessons but Oskar was so hopeless that he thought it better to leave that to himself, so he shook his head.

"You have a great deal of work ahead of you." Lang turned and walked away.

Oskar waited while the rest of the class finished its second lap. They returned, panting and dripping with sweat. A few cast baleful looks his way. How many new enemies had his good deed made him?

Lang didn't give them time to rest. He barked a few sharp orders and they each took a wooden practice sword and formed up in single-file lines. Oskar found a place in back, hoping to draw as little notice as possible. The master led them through a series of basic strikes, blocks, and forms. Aspin had worked on all of these with him, but he still was terrible with the sword.

When the warmup ended, Lang demonstrated a form called rippar, a defend and counter technique. He ran through it three times and then instructed the students to pair off and practice. Stomach clenched, Oskar looked around for a partner. He caught Dacio's eye, but before he could make his way over to his roommate, Lang's voice rang out.

"Clehn! To me!"

Oskar's shoulders sagged as he turned and navigated the throng of students to where the master stood. He had a feeling a round of remedial lessons were on the way. When he reached the master, he was even more unhappy to see Agen standing there.

"You have a great deal to learn and I don't have time to baby you."

"I wouldn't expect you to, Master," Oskar protested.

"Agen, here, has volunteered to teach you the basic forms. He's the best in this class with the sword, so you'd do well to learn all you can from him. You might never become a competent swordsman, but you'll remain a novit until I think you can wield a blade without cutting your own toes off. Get to work."

Agen motioned for Oskar to follow him. "We'll begin with blocks and footwork," he said over his shoulder. "Start by learning to keep yourself alive. You can learn to kill later." He seemed to be taking his role as instructor seriously, which gave Oskar a small measure of comfort. Perhaps the incident in Sorcery class had given Agen cause to, if not respect Oskar, at least not discount him entirely.

Agen selected a spot partially sheltered by trees, far from Lang, who was bellowing at one of the students. Oskar was grateful not to have his shortcomings fully exposed to his classmates, but that soon changed.

After reviewing all the basic blocks and defensive stances, Agen took a step back and raised his sword. His lips peeled back and his eyes sparkled.

"Defend yourself," he said and sprang to the attack.

Oskar deflected the first two sword strokes, both aimed at his face but he was too slow to stop the third. Agen's sword cracked him across the knee and he grunted in pain.

"Never assume a pattern. Be ready for a strike at any level." Agen readied himself again.

Reluctantly, Oskar raised his practice sword, vowing to do better this time.

Unfortunately, this, and all the subsequent times were no better. Time and again, Agen attacked him with the quickness and ferocity of a striking viper, letting Oskar block a few strokes before delivering a painful blow until Oskar could scarcely stand or raise his sword.

Agen followed every attack with brief instruction or correction. Oskar couldn't deny he was learning, but Agen was making it as painful as possible. The youth was undeniably gifted. Oskar had only seen a few people work the sword with such skill: Shanis, Hierm, Prince Lerryn, and Pedric Karst came immediately to mind. Agen was close to them in skill, and he took full advantage as he beat down his pupil's feeble defenses.

When Lang's shout finally rose above the clacking of swords, telling them it was time to leave, Oskar let his sword fall to his side and sighed. This had, without a doubt, been the most painful hour of his life.

His head exploded in a white hot flash of pain and a loud pop made his ears ring. The next thing he knew, he was down on his knees, holding the side of his head. What had happened?

"Last lesson of the day," Agen's voice whispered in his ear. "Never take your eyes off of your opponent." Agen picked up Oskar's sword and strode away.

Oskar watched through watery eyes as Agen returned the practice swords and approached Master Lang. Cold fury washed across the pain and he heaved himself to his feet. He wasn't going to let the master or any of his classmates see him down on his knees. Spotting Naseeb and Whitt, who were donning their boots and robes, he hobbled over to them.

"Are you all right?" Naseeb asked.

"Fine." He dropped to the ground and pulled on his boots. "Just stay close in case I can't get back up again." As he donned his robe, he spotted Agen and his friends laughing as they left the ground. He had no doubt what they found so funny. He only hoped Agen wouldn't be his instructor in every class.

Chapter 9

"Our emissary has returned from Diyonus." Krion's frown told Shanis that the news was not good. "Until you hold the throne, they consider you just another rebel leader."

Shanis looked at her grandfather, and then around the circle of clan chiefs, all of whom appeared on the verge of speaking. She already knew what each would say; they had discussed this many times.

Horgris cleared his throat and stood. "We understand you no want to keep fighting, and we do respect it, but this fight be inevitable. The rest of the world do see you the same way as the Diyonans."

"As will our own people, eventually, if you do not seize the throne," Krion added. "I know you do not want a return to clan war."

Shanis held her silence for a few moments. Her instinct was to start raging about the injustice of it all and the stupidity of the Diyonans, the Malgog, the Monaghan, all of them, but she'd learned a few lessons about leadership, and one was not to lose control of your emotions where others could see you.

"Has Orbrad responded to our messages?" Orbrad currently sat on the throne in Karkwall, the capital of Lothan but ruled little more than his city and the surrounding area. Nonetheless, he was king if in name only. Shanis had sent messengers to him, pointing out that the clans were now united against him, and urging him to abdicate.

"Not directly," Krion said. "Our spies have learned that the first messenger was locked up in the dungeon, where he soon died, and the second beheaded. Apparently, Orbrad wanted to send the head to you, but he has no idea where we are and he killed the only man who could tell him."

"Orbrad do be a fool," Culmatan of the Blue Stag clan rumbled. "How can he rule Lothan, and not know of Calmut?"

"There be a lot of things Orbrad don't know," Horgris chortled.

Shanis raised her voice to be heard above the laughter that rang out through the room. "Have you forgotten what I told you about the ice cats and the army my friends and I saw in the mountains? Remember what the seeker told us—there is reason to believe a new Frostmarch approaches."

"All the more reason for us to unite our nation before it happens," Krion said gently.

"Your grandfather be right, though," Culmatan said. "The people do be getting impatient and we fear the peace will not hold. It is not just the little things, like the marriages and that witch school, but you do refuse to take back the lands in the east that the usurper holds. You must act." The other chiefs nodded their agreement.

"Don't start with me about the school. I've made my decision about that and it's final. Besides, I'd like to see you try to dislodge the bone women now that they've settled in."

"And more come every day," Culmatan grumbled. "Calmut do be full of witches and even a few wizards. In any case, Karkwall matters most."

"Understand, we are not hungry for war, but there are times war is necessary." Regret hung heavy in Krion's voice. "You must take Karkwall and claim the throne. Then, when the other nations recognize you as queen, we can see to the east, hopefully with allies at our backs. It is possible that, under those circumstances, Pedric Karst would see reason."

"I doubt that." Shanis knew enough about Pedric Karst to know he could hardly be called reasonable, and that he would not give up easily. She stood and walked slowly around the room, her eyes on the ceiling. The truth was, she had made her decision about Karkwall the previous night though it pained her. She could not, however, appear to make this decision in haste.

When she thought she'd held them in suspense long enough, she turned and faced the clan chiefs. Some looked at her in nervous anticipation, while others met her eyes with dull stares, assuming she'd continue to insist on peace.

"What do we have to do in order to take Karkwall?"

The chiefs all spoke at once, each with his own plan of attack. The chatter quieted when Krion raised his hand.

"Let us first review what we face: the strongest city walls in Gameryah protecting a fortified keep. The city is well provisioned so a siege would be a protracted affair."

"It is the only way." Labar, chief of the Mud Snake clan, rose to his feet. "Seal the city off, and pound the walls with siege engines until they fall."

"And then face another siege at the keep," Jayan, chief of the Red Water, replied. "They can hold out a long time. Orbrad is stubborn."

"Do you have another suggestion?" Labar asked. "Besides, we have the Silver Serpent on our side." He turned to Shanis. "Can you bring down the walls with it?"

"Possibly." The truth was, Shanis had not tested the limits of the sword's power. She used it for healing and little else, but she had no doubt it could be turned to destruction.

"Another reason we need to take Karkwall," Krion said. "The library there might help us understand the extent of its power."

Shanis sighed. "Very well. It is time to make preparations." Shanis felt the burden of her decision settle upon her shoulders. She would be leading men and women to their deaths, the exact opposite of what she had hoped to accomplish, but she understood the reason. "I want each clan of the Monaghan, and only Monaghan, to leave behind a small force to protect Calmut and all of those who remain here. The city is being rebuilt and that is a fine thing. We cannot stop living every time we go to war." A few of the Malgog chieftains protested, and she silenced them with sharp words. "We cannot fight a war on two fronts and Monaghans are less likely than Malgogs to take it upon themselves to reclaim the lands in the east from Karst. We shall see to him soon enough."

They did not like it but saw the wisdom in her words. One by one, the chiefs left to prepare their forces to march.

"Grandfather, if you and Horgris would remain behind, I need to speak with you." Shanis waited for the other chiefs to leave the room, and then called for Heztus to join her. The dwarf had been waiting outside with Granlor, who guarded the door.

"I've been thinking about my escape from Karkwall," she began when they were all settled around a small table. Orbrad had imprisoned Shanis and her friends in the dungeons beneath the castle. They had escaped with help from members of the Order of the Fox, a group dedicated to the reunification of Lothan — a group of which Horgris was also a member. "Horgris, how much help can we count on from the inside?"

"I can no say." The big man shifted in his seat and scratched his ample beard. "No one knows for certain how many members the order do have, nor who they are. I do have a few contacts within the city."

"Grandfather, you said we have spies in Karkwall. Can we get more men inside?"

"We can try, but as soon as Orbrad finds out we are on the march, he will seal the city tight."

"Which will make it all the more difficult to coordinate an attack with our people on the inside," Heztus observed. "It will be difficult, if not impossible, to get word to them."

"Not if some members of Horgris' order are manning the walls." She and the chieftain exchanged knowing looks. "We need to alert the members of the order, and our friends on the inside, to be ready."

The others nodded. Shanis sent for bread, cheese, and wine, and began to outline her plan. It was going to be a long evening.

Chapter 10

Oskar was elbow deep in hot, soapy water when the kitchen master called his name.

"Novit Clehn! A saikur to see you."

Oskar turned away from the stewpot he was scrubbing and saw Aspin standing in the doorway. He was looking around the kitchen as if unsure where Oskar was, despite Moylan having just called to him. It took Oskar a moment to remember Aspin had wanted to downplay the fact that they knew one another.

"Master Moylan, would it be permissible for me to take this young man off your hands? I've been asked to give him remedial lessons and I fear my time is short."

At the words "remedial lessons," Moylan gave Oskar a nasty grin and some the other novits working the kitchens snickered.

"Of course. I was nearly finished with him anyway."

Oskar ignored the glances from the other novits as he dried his hands and straightened his sodden robe. Some whispered comments about "country louts needing extra lessons" and snickered. The pain from what felt like a thousand bruises hobbled him as he followed Aspin through the back door of the kitchen and into an empty hallway. He'd been so distracted by his various hurts that he'd made a poor showing in his first Logic class. His slow response time had frustrated Master Dac Kien, who had finally thrown up his hands in frustration and muttered something about starting a fire with wet logs. At least, that's what Oskar thought he heard. The brown-skinned master, whom everyone said hailed from beyond the Sun Sands, spoke with a pronounced accent.

A sharp pain in his leg yanked Oskar's thoughts back to the present, and he glanced at Aspin. "What did you need to see me about?"

"Not here," Aspin whispered. He led Oskar along a series of deserted corridors, finally coming to a halt in a turret with a window overlooking the city. "I'll make this brief. I believe the world faces a danger much greater than the wars between Galdora and Kyrin, or the instability caused by Duke Karst."

"The Frostmarch," Oskar whispered.

"Yes, and the Silver Serpent is the key to defeating Tichris."

Oskar winced at the mention of the Ice King's true name.

"We know so little about Serpent lore," Aspin continued. "The prophecies about it are few, and the way it seems to work for Shanis contradicts what I thought I knew about it. I had hoped to spend time here continuing my research in hopes of finding something that will help Shanis, but I've been watched since our arrival, and now the prelate is sending me away."

"Where?" Oskar felt panic welling up inside him. Although the two of them had not been in contact, the knowledge that Aspin was at the Gates, close by should Oskar need him, had been a source of comfort. Oskar was out of his depth, and now he was losing the closest thing to an ally he had.

"To Kyrin. They want me to try and negotiate peace between the Kyrinians and the Galdorans." He shook his head and turned toward the window. "It's futile, but I must try. This is the worst possible time for Kyrin to dredge up old grudges."

Oskar moved to the seeker's side. The sun had gone down and all around the city, lanterns and candles twinkled in windows. He still could not believe so many people could live in a single place. "Why are you telling me this? What can I do?"

"I need you to do the research for me. The Frostmarch could begin any day and if we don't know how to defeat the Ice King, all is lost."

"Do the research? I'm a novit. I can't access the archives. Even if I could, why me? There are plenty of people here older and wiser who probably know the place better than I."

"Things are complicated here. There are many factions, each with their own agendas, and they trade in secrets like a farmer trades in produce. I know I can trust you. I can't say that about anyone else, save the prelate."

"Could he grant me access to the archives?"

"No!" Aspin turned on Oskar, his eyes burning. "You must not let anyone know I've given you this charge, not even the prelate. Do nothing that might arouse suspicion."

"All right, but I still don't see how I'm going to get inside."

"You found the lost city of Murantha; you can find your way inside the archives."

The mention of Murantha reminded Oskar of his missing book, and he told Aspin the story. The seeker's brow furrowed as he listened.

"Odd. Of course, I've never known a novit to bring a book along with him, so perhaps it's not that unusual that Corwine would want to give it a closer look. Once Corwine realizes it is no more than your personal journal along with excerpts from books you've read, I'm sure he'll return it."

"But I wrote about our search for the Silver Serpent, about finding the Ramsgate, Thandryll, and Murantha. And there are the glyphs, of course."

"Glyphs?" Aspin's voice was sharp as a knife.

"The interior walls of the buildings in Murantha are covered in glyphs. I made several pages of rubbings." He shrugged. "I supposed I thought I might translate them some day."

"You never told me about the glyphs. Never mind. You had no reason to." Aspin began to pace. "If anyone asks you about the portions of the book relating to the Serpent, you must tell them it was merely a story you heard along the way. Something you recorded because you found it entertaining."

Oskar nodded. "I suppose I need a story about the rubbings as well."

"Possibly. Make it a simple lie and do not change your story." Aspin froze and held up a hand. Footsteps echoed somewhere in the distance. "We are almost out of time," Aspin whispered.

"What am I looking for, exactly?"

"Anything we don't already know about the Silver Serpent. Its history, prophecies, whatever you can find."

Oskar considered this. He was aware of two such prophecies: that the bearer of the Silver Serpent held the key to the survival of the Galdoran monarchy, and that the bearer of the Silver Serpent would reunite Lothan.

"I'm relying on you. Tell no one what you are doing." Aspin gave Oskar's shoulder a squeeze and sent him on his way.

Oskar's feet felt heavier with each step as he returned to his quarters. Making it through his novit classes was a daunting enough prospect. Now, with Aspin's task added to his burden, it all seemed impossible.

His sleep was filled with fitful dreams, most of which involved Shanis being attacked by minions of the Ice King, and he woke nearly as tired as when he'd lain down. As his roommates stirred, he rolled over, put his head in his hands, and groaned.

"You all right?" Whitt asked. "It's only your second day of classes. You're not going to make it if it's already taking that much of a toll on you."

"I'm sure landing himself on kitchen duty didn't help," Dacio added as he tugged on his robe. "That's hard work."

"Not nearly as hard as having Agen beat me with a stick for an hour." Oskar's work in the kitchens and the assignment from Aspin had temporarily distracted him from his aches and pains, but today he felt them all over. His arms, legs, and sides were a mass of bruises, plus a few dark patches where Agen had tried to skewer him with his practice sword.

"No need to worry about that today," Naseeb said with annoying cheerfulness. "Just lots of boring classes on the schedule. No combat training."

Oskar supposed he should be grateful for that, but the prospect of sitting in wooden chairs all day was hardly more appealing than sword practice. His father had taught him the best way to get rid of soreness was to work it out. Of course, that advice was more helpful after a long day of working on the farm. He doubted exercise did much to alleviate the pain of bruised ribs.

He dressed and followed his friends to the dining hall, limping until they reached the doorway. He was determined not to let Agen see him in pain. Fortunately, Agen and his friends were nowhere to be seen. They sat down with a group of fellow novits and while his roommates chattered, he ate his porridge and bacon in silence.

"What are you hiding?" Naseeb's voice was so low it scarcely carried to Oskar's ears.

"Nothing, I'm just tired and sore." Oskar took a sip of caf, the dark, bitter drink that, according to Dacio, came from somewhere across the Sun Sands.

"Bollocks. There's something on your mind, and you're doing a lousy job of hiding it. Come on. Tell me."

Oskar considered telling Naseeb the whole story. He would love to have an ally in this, and he felt he could trust Naseeb. But, Aspin had instructed him to tell no one about his charge. Then again, he could ask Naseeb's help getting into the archives without telling him why he needed to get inside. His gran would have said he was dancing with a badger, but right now he didn't care. He felt beaten down and completely alone, and he needed a friend.

"I need to get inside the archives." He took another sip of caf and looked at Naseeb, who appeared nonplussed.

"You can't. Your book isn't worth the trouble you'd get in if they catch you. They might turn you out."

"It's not about my book. I need to get inside for another reason. I can't tell you why, but I promise it's important. Will you help me?" He waited, heart pounding, wondering if he'd placed his trust in the wrong person. What if Naseeb told on him?

"I'm afraid I can't. I don't know how to get inside the archives. I suppose you could pick the lock if you know how, but Master Corwine's quarters are near the entrance, and you'd have a difficult time getting past him. I hear he rarely sleeps."

"I don't know how to pick the lock in any case. We've got to figure out something." Oskar felt as though a giant hand were squeezing his chest, constricting his breathing. He couldn't do this. It was impossible.

"But why do you need to get inside if not to recover your book?"

"I need to help a friend." He wondered how much more he could say without going against Aspin's orders.

"I don't understand. If your friend needs something researched, why doesn't he do it himself?" Naseeb filched a slice of bacon off of Whitt's plate and munched it while Oskar considered the question.

"She can't. I mean, he can't."

Naseeb laughed. "You don't even know if your friend is a man or a woman? You'd better pay close attention during lessons in case we cover that topic."

Oskar threw the last bit of his own bacon at Naseeb but missed badly. The bacon landed in the hood of an initiate who sat with his back to them. The two boys fell to laughing until Dacio hushed them.

"Master Moylan is looking this way," he hissed.

Oskar wiped his eyes with his sleeve and sipped his caf. He was already coming to enjoy the drink. Finally, he regained his composure.

"It's hard to explain. What I need to do will help more than one person. I wish I could say more, but I'm not allowed to."

"Not allowed? That means you're doing this on someone's orders. So, you're either working for someone inside the Gates who doesn't want to risk someone finding out what he's researching, or else you're working for someone on the outside, in which case you could be executed as a traitor."

"It's not someone outside," Oskar hurried, and then caught himself. "Look, I'm not going to say anything else since I can't seem to help saying too much. You're too clever by half, which is why I need you. Will you help me?"

Naseeb considered the question for a moment, and finally nodded. "All right. I'll see if I can come up with something, but I will not go in there with you, and if you mention my name, I'll deny everything. Understood?"

"Yes, and thank you." Oskar raised his cup but, before he could take a drink, someone banged into him from behind, causing him to spill the contents all over the table. The people around him scrambled off the benches with cries of surprise and annoyance. Oskar whirled around to see Agen grinning at him.

"So clumsy of me. Would you like me to get you another cup?" His smile said he was anything but sorry.

Fists clenched, Oskar made to rise, but Whitt shoved him back down.

"Master Moylan is coming this way."

Sure enough, the kitchen master was stalking toward them, his face red. As he strode through the hall, a wave of silence rolled ahead of him, and all the initiates and novits looked around for the source of his ire.

When he arrived at the table, he stared at the pool of caf, his jaw working and his expression unreadable.

Out of the corner of his eye, Oskar saw Agen and his friends moving away. Of course Agen wouldn't take any blame for what happened.

"What happened here?" Moylan asked after a lengthy silence.

"Someone bumped into me and I spilled my caf," Oskar said. "I'm sorry."

"And you just sat here. Who did you think was going to clean up your mess? Perhaps you think I am a servant?"

"No, not at all. I just hadn't gotten up yet."

"Perhaps another night's work in the kitchens will teach you to move more quickly. Report here tonight at the same time as last night." Moylan's gaze dared him to object, but Oskar was no fool.

"Yes, Master. Again, I'm sorry."

Apparently satisfied, Moylan gave a curt nod, turned on his heel, and headed back toward the kitchens. Gradually, quiet conversation rippled across the dining hall. Disheartened, Oskar gathered his plate and cup and went off in search of a cloth with which to clean up his spill. Today promised to be no better than yesterday.

Chapter 11

The sun hung high above the horizon when Hierm, Edrin, and Mattyas, who still preferred his nickname "Hair" despite his newly-shorn locks, rode into Galsbur. The village looked much as Hierm remembered, save the stockade wall surrounding the center of town. The wood was charred and broken in places, and a wide swath of land had been cleared all around, the land trampled. Clearly, there had been a battle here. Hierm's throat tightened as he wondered who had survived... and who had not.

A gate stood open and unguarded, and they rode into town unnoticed. Few people were about at this time of morning. Most would be tending their crops or about other tasks.

"It seems like forever since I was here last," Hair said, looking out across the circle of green grass in the center of town.

"The tournament." Even after all the time spent on the trail together, Edrin remained a man of few words.

Guided by prophecy, or so he thought, Prince Lerryn had held a tournament in Galsbur. Hierm had competed in the sword, Edrin in archery, and Mattyas in wrestling.

Hierm guided his horse along the path that circled the green and stopped in front of the warehouse that belonged to his family. His stomach lurched as he took in the scene. Both the warehouse and his family home alongside it bore signs of abandonment. Weeds grew thick in his mother's flower beds and the windows were dusty. And although it was the middle of the day, the warehouse was closed up tight.

He dismounted, tied up his horse, and told his companions to wait. An icy certainty pouring over him, he ran first to the warehouse, trying every door, and finding them locked.

"Father!" he called, banging on the office door. There was no answer.

He ran to the house and found it, too, to be sealed up tight. He brushed a thick netting of cobwebs away from the window and peered inside. He saw nothing. He banged on the door and called several times for his father, hoping, irrationally, that Hiram was perhaps ill and in bed. After several futile minutes, he gave up.

The looks that Hair and Edrin gave him held too much sympathy for his liking. He untied his horse and mounted up without acknowledging them. Turning his mount about, he put his heels to its flanks and set off at a trot for the inn. Perhaps someone in the common room would know where his father had gone.

"Maybe he headed to Archstone to find your mother," Hair offered, trotting alongside him.

"We would have passed him on the road."

"Perhaps." Hair lapsed into silence as they approached the inn.

Hierm hesitated before dismounting. He wanted his father to be alive, but something told him that the worst had happened, and he wasn't ready to hear it. He and his father had had their share of rows, the last few the worst. Hierm had left

Galsbur before the two of them could patch up their differences. Now, he wondered if he would ever get the chance.

He climbed the steps of the Dry Birch, the inn run by Khalyndryn Serrill's family. Khalyndryn. His heart sank. Would he have to be the one to deliver the news of her death, or had Lerryn already told them?

Two men sat inside: one a thick-set, fair-haired man, the other a mountain of a man with dark, shaggy hair. Master Serrill and Colin Malan. Colin's eyes widened and he lurched to his feet.

"Hierm!" He embraced Hierm roughly and greeted Hair and Edrin. "It's good to see you, boy. How have you been?"

"I'm all right. Have you seen my father?"

The dark look in Colin's eyes answered his question. Dizzy, Hierm dropped into a chair and buried his face in his hands.

"I am sorry." Colin pulled up a chair and sat down beside him. "You should know he died bravely— defending the village from an invading force. We sent a messenger to your mother in Archstone. Something must have happened to him."

Hierm fought to maintain his composure. He had a task to complete, and he couldn't fulfill it by sitting here weeping over the dead. He raised his head as Master Serrill set out mugs of ale for Hierm and his companions. And then he remembered another death.

"Master Serrill, I need to tell you about Khalyndryn."

"It's all right. I already know. Prince Lerryn told us the news." The innkeeper turned and hurried away.

"What about Shanis?" Colin asked. "Lerryn told me she was well and in Lothan, but that was all he said."

Hierm hesitated. Would Colin believe what he was about to tell him? "She was well last I saw her. There's something you should know." He took a gulp of ale to buy time, but he could think of no way to ease the man into the story.

"We went in search of the Silver Serpent. And we found it." The clatter of breaking glass rang out on the other side of the common room. Master Serrill had dropped a mug, and he now stood gaping at Hierm. "It seems Shanis is the one destined to bear it."

Surprisingly, Colin merely stroked his beard and nodded.

"When I left, she was headed to a place called Calmut."

"They want to make her queen, then?" Colin asked sharply.

"Some do. There is, apparently, an impostor who also claims to be the bearer of the Serpent." He took another drink, letting the lukewarm, frothy drink slake his thirst.

"I feared the day would come. How is she?" Colin asked.

"She's as ill-tempered as ever." They shared a laugh, and Hierm recounted the story of their flight from Galsbur, meeting Larris, their search for the Silver Serpent, and, finally, their return to the lands of the Monaghan. Hair and Edrin, who had never heard the story, listened with interest. "They recognized her as one of their own and accepted her as leader," he finished.

"Her mother was Monaghan and a descendant of Badla, their great warrior queen. I am a Malgog."

This should have been a surprise, but now, having met a few Malgog, Hierm saw the resemblance.

"My father is Krion, chief of the Black Mangrove clan," Colin continued. "I took Shanis away after her mother died. Since she is Badla's heir, I always knew there was a chance she would be the one destined to bring the clans together, but I hoped it would not be the case." He sighed. "I should go to her. I've been away from her too long."

"But Colin, we need you here." Master Serrill sat down opposite Hierm. "You are the closest thing we have to a leader, and no one else knows how to fight like you do."

Colin's shoulder's twitched once in a silent, rueful laugh. "We have plenty of men who've been blooded. Besides, the invading army is broken. We're safe for the time being."

"What do you mean?" Hair spoke for the first time. "You think they'll re-form and come back?"

"There were shifters and ice cats among them." At this, Hair sat up straight and Edrin dropped his mug. "I don't know what their purpose was in coming here, but I have no doubt a new Frostmarch is coming. And when it comes, none of us are safe."

"We encountered ice cats on the road," Hierm said. "I didn't want to believe it could be another Frostmarch." He drained his mug, wiped his mouth, and looked at Colin. "You mentioned Prince Lerryn. Was he killed in the battle?"

Colin looked down at the table and spun his mug in his big hands. "We don't know for certain, but we think he survived. He fought and killed a shifter. After the battle, I found tracks that I believe are his heading off into the forest."

"You could pick out one man's tracks in the midst of a battlefield?" Hair sounded impressed.

Colin shrugged. "Only one of his soldiers survived—a man named Tabars. He went off in search of Lerryn, but I doubt he'll find him. Tabars is a good fighter, but he's no woodsman."

"Unlike you." Hierm took a deep breath and let it out in a rush. "Colin, we need your help. We've been sent here to find Prince Lerryn and bring him back to Archstone. I don't know if you've heard, but we are at war with Kyrin, there's a rebellion in Kurnsbur, and there are…" he hesitated, "other problems. We need Lerryn, and I'm no more a tracker than Tabars. Will you help us?"

Colin sat back and looked a Hierm. "Those are someone else's problems. Shanis needs me."

"If another Frostmarch is coming, Galdora can't be at war on two other fronts. Shanis is working to unify Lothan. We need to find Lerryn so we can keep our own country united," Hierm argued.

"He's right." Master Serrill stood and wiped his hands on his apron. "Be thankful that your daughter is alive and well. What's a few more weeks before you go to her if it means we're better prepared for what lies ahead?"

Colin's face darkened. "Just once," he mumbled, "I'd like to do what I want to do." He looked around the table at Hierm and his friends. "Very well. You three rest here while I gather provisions. We'll leave at dawn."

Chapter 12

"**I feel like** someone hung me upside down for an hour." Whitt stole a glance over his shoulder to make sure Master Sibson was not within earshot. "My head is stuffed full of useless facts. I hate history."

"It wasn't that bad." Oskar had to laugh. The truth was, he enjoyed history and the lecture on the Godwars had fascinated him. He couldn't see how anyone could resist the stories.

"It's all the same: this god's followers did this to that god's followers, so they joined forces with another god's followers and on and on and on." Whitt sighed. "I'll never keep all that useless information in my head."

"It's hardly useless. Think of all the things saikurs are called on to do that require understanding people's values and traditions. How could you negotiate a peace treaty, for example, if you don't know the history between the nations involved?" Oskar felt odd engaging in such a debate on only his second day of classes, but this was something he felt strongly about.

"Well said," Dacio agreed. "I'm sure I've said similar things to our friend here." He arched an eyebrow at Whitt. "But he doesn't listen."

"Fine. You two history lovers can help me study for the next exam. Or sit next to me so I can copy." Whitt winked to show he was kidding. At least, that's what Oskar hoped it meant.

They made their way along the dark corridor toward the classroom where Master Lepidus taught Alchemy. Oskar had seen the master from a distance, and he was quite a sight, with frizzy white hair that stuck out in all directions, and he walked like a dizzy hen. He wondered if the man's teaching style was as eccentric as his appearance, but when he asked his friends, they just smiled.

The room was empty, save a group of three in the far corner: Agen, Dronn, and Shaw. Deep in conversation with his friends, Agen had his back to Oskar and the others, so he was unaware of them as they entered. That was fine with Oskar. He wasn't afraid of Agen, as long as they weren't dueling with swords, but he hated the way Agen grinned at him, clearly relishing the memory of yesterday's combat class.

"After dinner in the hall that leads out to the combat grounds," Agen whispered. "By the side door that leads into the back of the archives. You know—behind the tapestry of the two knights."

Shaw cleared his throat and Agen snapped his head around. He shot Oskar an angry look and the three fell silent.

Wonderful, Oskar thought. The one time he was actually interested in something Agen had to say, and he interrupted it. Unlike the other classrooms he'd been in, this room did not have individual desks, but rows of long tables, and he and his friends chose seats on the second row.

"Did you hear that?" he whispered to Naseeb. "There's a side door into the archives."

"Agen's not the most reliable source. Besides, the very day you announce you want to find a way into the archives, he lets something like that slip? That's too great a coincidence for me."

"I didn't announce it. You're the only person I told."

"I'll wager one of them overheard you and now they're trying to wind you up."

With a wave of his hand, Naseeb silenced the retort Oskar was preparing. Master Lepidus had entered the room.

The wild-haired man didn't look like Oskar's mental image of a master, but the lesson was interesting and Lepidus clearly had a sharp mind. Oskar had been surprised to discover that, at the Gates, Alchemy consisted of much more than failed attempts to turn lead into gold. It also included herbs, potions, and what Lepidus called "chemistry."

Today's lesson was on the properties of Redroot. For once, Oskar's rural upbringing was a positive. He correctly answered two questions, earning an approving nod from the master. The good feeling lasted until he volunteered that, when mixed with their grain, Redroot alleviated colic in cattle. Master Lepidus actually took a moment to write that down, but the laughter and derisive comments from the rest of the class made Oskar's cheeks burn.

Magic, taught by master Zuhayr, kept his mind occupied for the entire hour as they learned a spell that caused a small ball of light to float in the air just above the palm of one's hand. Casting a spell was much more than repeating the proper words; it had to be recited in exactly the right pitch and cadence and with a certain amount of focus. By the end of class, only Oskar, Dacio, and Agen had mastered it, though Whitt managed to set his roll of parchment on fire, earning him an evening with Oskar working in the kitchens.

When class was over, rather than return to their quarters, Oskar and Naseeb took a detour along the corridor that led to the combat grounds.

"I think you're making a mistake," Naseeb insisted.

"Yes, you told me. I'm just curious if there's even a door here." He inspected the tapestries and found that several displayed two or more knights. "Keep a lookout for me." Oskar ignored the dark-skinned boy's sarcastic reply and started pulling tapestries away from the wall and checking behind them. His progress was interrupted several times by people heading out to or in from the combat ground. Each time, he and Naseeb fell into false conversation until they were alone again. It wasn't until they reached the far end of the hall that he found something behind the last tapestry.

"There *is* a door here." He stole a glance up and down the hall, and then tried the knob. It turned and the door gave way with a scraping sound, revealing a set of stairs that climbed up into the darkness. "It must lead up to the higher levels of the stacks," he whispered, pulling the door shut and letting the tapestry fall back against the wall.

"Master Lang's coming," Naseeb whispered. They froze as the combat instructor entered the hall and fixed them with his steely gaze. "You come for extra sword instruction, Novit Clehn?"

"Ah, yes, that is, I came to ask if there might be a time I could come for instruction." It was as good a lie as any to explain his presence here, and he did need the help.

"I can give you an hour after mealtime this evening."

"I'm afraid I have to work in the kitchens." Oskar looked down at his feet.

"Again? Not off to a good start, are you? Very well, then. Tomorrow after mealtime. That is, if you don't land yourself in the kitchens again." Lang didn't wait for Oskar to reply but swept off down the corridor.

Oskar and Naseeb followed slowly, letting the distance between themselves and the master grow. When he turned a corner out of sight, they paused.

"Perfect! I'll get extra instruction tomorrow evening, which will give me an excuse to be in this hallway. I'll try the door then."

Naseeb gave him a long look and sighed. "I don't suppose there's any way I can talk you out of this?"

"I have to do it. I wish I could explain more, but you'll have to trust me."

"All right, Oskar. Just remember, if you're caught, they're likely to do worse to you than give you kitchen duty." Naseeb grimaced.

Oskar wondered what they would do to him. Put him out of the Gates, perhaps? It didn't matter. If he could do something to help Shanis fight the next Frostmarch, he had no choice.

"Well, then, I guess I'll just have to avoid being caught."

Chapter 13

The next day was Thirdday, which mean he had the same course schedule as Firstday: Sorcery, Combat, and Logic. Oskar made another good showing in Sorcery and was feeling like today was his day when he completed the warmup for Combat class not too terribly far behind his classmates, survived the second run, and reached the green to discover today's lesson would be the quarterstaff.

Suppressing a grin, he selected a staff of the perfect length, weight, and thickness. Allyn had worked with him on quarterstaff during their travels and said Oskar was an adept, even gifted, pupil. Master Lang led them through the basic movements, and the familiarity of the exercises brought a smile to Oskar's face as he remembered the time spent on the road with his friends. He wondered where they all were and what they were doing right now. He supposed Hierm had entered the prince's academy and was learning the skills of a soldier.

When the warmups were finished, they donned leather gloves and padded jerkins and paired off.

"I don't suppose the farm boy would care to try his skill?" Shaw stood grinning at Oskar. "Agen grew bored with you and said I could have a go if you have the courage."

Oskar was happy to oblige, confident this was a fight he could, if not win, at least acquit himself well in. The quarterstaff wasn't a gentleman's weapon, and he'd been told Shaw hailed from a wealthy family here in Cardith. He hid his enthusiasm behind a reluctant shrug, even pretending to look around for his friends as he and Shaw took their places.

When Lang called for them to begin, Shaw sprang forward and lashed out with a sweeping stroke that Oskar deftly parried and circled away. Not wanting to give away too much, he remained on the defensive as Shaw, his confidence growing with each stroke that went unanswered, attacked with reckless abandon.

Oskar waited as Shaw tired himself out. Finally, Shaw's hands fell too low and Oskar struck, cracking Shaw across the back of one hand, followed by a thrust to the gut that forced the wind out of him. Shaw stumbled backward and Oskar swept his feet out from under him. Shaw hit the ground hard and, unable to catch his breath in order to yield, raised his hands in surrender.

"Well fought, Novit Clehn." Master Lang didn't smile, but there was a twinkle in his gray eyes.

"Thank you, Master." Oskar bowed his head, in part to hide his smile. It felt good to receive a compliment.

"You clearly have some skill with the staff. I think your time would be better served working at the sword." He turned and called for Agen, who hurried over. "Another round of sword with Novit Clehn, if you please?"

Agen agreed, waiting until Lang turned away before giving Oskar his most wicked grin. "I see you abused my friend." He shot a glance at Shaw, who sat rubbing his hand where Oskar had struck him. "That just won't do. Let's find the practice swords, shall we?"

Oskar's shoulders fell. How quickly a good day could turn bad.

"Very good." Lang actually managed a smile as he lowered his practice sword. "I already see improvements in your defense."

"Thank you." Oskar needed to improve quickly. He now had fresh bruises on top of the old ones inflicted by Agen during their lessons. If he could reach the point where he could work with the class instead of receiving individual instruction from his sadistic classmate, he'd likely endure much less pain. "I'm working as hard as I can."

"I hear you're a passable student at Sorcery and History as well." Agen chuckled at Oskar's surprised expression. "You don't think the masters talk to one another?" He glanced up at the sky. "It's growing late. We should stop for the evening." He took Oskar's practice sword, turned and walked toward a nearby outbuilding, and indicated with a tilt of his head that Oskar should follow him. "You have an unusual background," he said, fishing a key from his belt pouch and unlocking the door.

The combat yard was a surprisingly peaceful place this late in the evening. No one was out practicing, and the adjoining gardens were nearly empty. Oskar noticed one saikur, his hood pulled up over his head, wandering through a small orchard. The quiet and the crisp evening air reminded him of nights at home on the farm, or around the campfire with Shanis, Hierm, and the others.

"I suppose you don't get many farmers here."

Lang chuckled again. "It isn't that; it's the traveling you've done."

Oskar missed a step. "I'm sorry?"

"Word is, you've been to Lothan and also to the mountains in the West. That's unusual for anyone. Lothan is a dangerous place and the mountains are simply not somewhere anyone travels." Lang stepped inside, replaced the practice swords on their rack, and stepped back out into the fading light. "Why would a farm boy from Galdora travel there?"

"Who told you I've been to the mountains?" Oskar tried to keep the note of suspicion out of his voice. He thought he'd kept that part of his journeys a secret.

"It's common knowledge among the masters. Zuhayr was the one who told me. I think he had it from Proctor Basilius."

"Oh." How had Basilius known about that part of his trip? Had he seen it when he invaded Oskar's mind? And if he knew that, what else did he know? "I did go to Lothan, but not into the mountains."

"Again, why would a young man who, by all accounts, has a good head on his shoulders, travel into the midst of clan war?"

"We didn't hear a great deal about the outer world in Galsbur. I had heard tales of the castle at Karkwall and it was the foreign city closest to where I grew up. I quickly learned otherwise." He shrugged.

"Did you know I'm a Lothan?"

Oskar shook his head. "I didn't know for certain. I take it you're a Malgog? You have the black hair though your eyes are lighter than any I've seen."

"You've seen many Malgog?" Lang raised his eyebrows. "How much of the country did you see?"

Oskar cursed inwardly. Freeze his careless tongue! "I met them in Karkwall."

Lang frowned but didn't question his story. They walked through the garden area, its trees and shrubs casting inky shadows on the dusk-shaded ground. "I left long ago. The clan war was fruitless. I've heard rumors that someone has united the clans, but I doubt it. It's an impossible task."

"Perhaps some day." Oskar could think of nothing else to say without taking the risk of giving away more than he ought to.

Lang fixed him with a level look and nodded once. They entered the castle in silence and bade one another a good night when they parted ways. Oskar waited for the sound of Lang's footsteps to fade away, and then doubled back.

He kept a sharp eye out as he made his way toward the hidden door, but he was alone. When he reached the tapestry, he looked around one last time before pushing it aside, opening the door and stepping inside.

He whispered the spell he had learned in his last Magic class, and a ball of blue light, no bigger than a robin's egg, appeared above his palm. A dust-coated staircase rose up before him. The stone walls on either side were constructed of precisely-hewn blocks fitted so neatly together that it appeared no mortar had been needed in construction. He wondered if it was craftsmanship or magic that held the place together.

As he approached the staircase, he noticed that the dust on the floor was disturbed and, on the first step, he spotted a boot print. He looked around more carefully now and spotted dangling cobwebs torn by someone passing this way recently. The realization both comforted and worried him. The knowledge that others used this passageway made it seem less forbidding, but it also raised the possibility that he might bump into someone. He supposed if he heard footsteps, he'd snuff out his light and run, and hope he didn't break his neck on the way down the stairs. Heart racing, he took a deep breath and mounted the stairs.

The climb through the dark seemed endless, with the steep staircase making the occasional turn, which told him the passageway likely ran along the outer walls of the archives. Based on how long he'd walked, he figured the stairway led to the top floor. That was fine with him, as it would place him far away from Keeper Corwine's quarters.

He paused at a landing, leaned against the wall, and struggled to catch his breath. He was exhausted from today's double measure of combat training, and his bruised body screamed in protest. If he had to climb much further, he might just sleep here tonight. The thought reminded him of all the times Mistress Faun had chided him for laziness, and the memory brought a smile to his face. Grinning, he moved on.

Beyond the landing, the stairs rose in a wide spiral. This must be the tower that topped the archives building. At long last, the staircase ended. Panting, his damp hair hanging in his eyes, he staggered over to the door that lay in front of him, turned the knob, and pushed. When it didn't budge, he threw his shoulder into it, and it banged open.

A light breeze chilled his sweat-soaked body. Pinpricks of light danced before his eyes, and a dizzying sensation of extreme height washed over him.

All these things registered in the split second before his feet went out from under him and he fell toward the gaping darkness below.

Chapter 14

"I don't know what to do." Pedric Karst took a sip of wine and winced at its bitterness. He glanced across the table to where Jakom sat, his eyes cloudy and thoughts seemingly far away, and then looked around the common room of the newly-constructed inn. A musician sat in the corner, plucking at his lute with an air of disinterest. He looked familiar, with his puffy, black hair and weathered cheeks, but Karst couldn't place him. There weren't many new arrivals in Salgo, at least, not yet, but once things settled down, his city would draw travelers from Diyonus, Galdora, Lothan, and Cardith. The problem was, he doubted things would settle down until he dealt with the temple. Perhaps the king shouldn't be seen in a common room, but more and more he was coming to realize it was an empty title. The temple wielded the real power. "Whenever I come near the temple, I feel…" He couldn't finish the thought.

"Overwhelmed?" Jakom scratched his chin and looked down at his own, untouched cup of wine. "I've never experienced anything like it. It was as if some force was trying to… not exactly take over my mind, but dominate it."

Karst nodded. On his first visit to the temple, he'd scarcely been able to make his retreat once he felt the force of will emanating from the thing floating above the altar. Now, the power had grown stronger, so much so that he couldn't come within shouting distance of the place without experiencing the strong urge to fall to his knees and abase himself. The experience had been so powerful and upsetting that he had not been able to bring himself to talk about it until now.

"What do you think it is?" he whispered.

The look in Jakom's eyes made it clear they both knew to what Karst was referring.

"I can't say for certain. It was as if the thing were forcing my eyes away when I tried to look at it. But it seemed to be human in shape though larger than a man." Now, Jakom attended to his wine, raising it to his lips with a trembling hand and draining it in three hearty gulps.

"Parts of it were transparent, and others more solid, as if it were not yet fully-formed." Karst shuddered at the thought. It galled him to admit his fear and confusion, but he'd never experienced anything like this. The closest had been when he tried to hold the Silver Serpent. The experience, though only for an instant, had felt much like his visit to the temple— overwhelmed by a power that made him feel tiny by comparison.

"And why the sacrifices? Do you think they're, I don't know, feeding people's souls to that thing?" Jakom winced, then signaled the serving girl for a cup of wine.

As Karst sat in silent contemplation, he began to take notice of the musician's song.

"…a thousand lives I will feed you, a thousand souls shall bleed for you, the god of…"

"You!" he snapped. "Come here!"

Nonplussed, the musician set his lute back in its case and approached Karst. He wore a red and yellow cloak and his chin whiskers were twisted into a hands-length braid. His weathered face was somehow familiar.

"What is your name?"

"Skedane. Sandrin Skedane." His tone was respectful, but there was a twinkle in his eye that Karst didn't care for.

"You will address me as 'Your Majesty.' Now, where do I know you from?"

"Galdora, my lord." Skedane hesitated. "You could say I rescued your neck from the headsman's axe."

Now Karst remembered. The man had wrestled him away from Shanis Malan before Karst could run her through. "What happened to your fancy cloak, Master Skedane?"

"It's in my bag, Majesty. Not proper for a simple common room."

"Yet you wore it with pride in Galsbur, a farm town."

"The prince was there, and I hoped to gain his notice. I've played in many a noble house, but never a palace." Skedane made a wry smile. "As you can see, I was unsuccessful."

"And you came to Salgo to witness the birth of a new city, a new nation, and tell our story? Perhaps you hoped to gain my notice?" Karst poured all the sarcasm he could muster into his words.

"I won't claim that was my plan when I passed this way. I was headed to Diyonus, but when I learned what you have planned here, the idea captivated me. Carving out a chunk of land and forming your own nation is ambitious."

"And you'll compose a song about me? Perhaps write my story?"

Across the table, Jakom snickered.

"If you'll forgive me, your Highness, whether you end up the most powerful ruler in Gameryah or a martyr with your head on a spike, it will make for a gripping tale."

Karst tensed. His palm itched and he almost reached for his sword, but he calmed himself. A good leader didn't lose control at a few words. He needed to maintain a more controlled and dignified air.

"I'm glad to hear you would find my death entertaining."

"Forgive me, that isn't what I meant. Every nation has its history: its heroes and martyrs, its institutions, its gods…"

Karst cut off Skedane's words with a wave of his hand. He had just remembered why the man had gained his notice. "Tell me about the song you were just singing."

"It is from the Ragar Saga. He was a Halvalan king of old who raised a god to do his bidding. I overheard snatches of your conversation, and that particular song sprang to mind."

A chill ran through Karst and he could not find his voice. To cover his hesitation, he motioned for Skedane to sit down.

"What do you mean, he raised a god?" Jakom asked before Karst could recover his wits.

"Ragar was a weak king, so he attempted to raise a god in order to gain power over the warring factions in his kingdom."

"What was it about our conversation that reminded you of this story?" Karst took another sip of wine and steeled himself for the answer.

"Several things: the way the god gradually gained strength, the way its presence overwhelmed those who came near, and, of course, the sacrifices."

"How does one raise a god? Is such a thing even possible?" Karst's voice was a whip crack, making Skedane flinch.

"I am no expert, but I have learned a few things over the years. A god draws its power from its worshipers. The number of worshipers, the frequency and intensity of said worship, the depth of belief, and the sacrifices made in its name." He cleared his throat and cast a look of longing at Karst's wine, but Karst wasn't feeling magnanimous at the moment.

"I suppose a human sacrifice would be more powerful than other sorts?" He knew some commoners would sacrifice animals or a portion of their crops, but nobles merely gave coin to the priest, who would then make a symbolic sacrifice of a chunk of meat.

"Indeed, Majesty. That, according to the songs, is the most powerful magic there is."

Karst looked to Jakom and could see they were thinking the same thing.

"I need to see Malaithus right now."

He still felt the dark presence as he approached the temple, but his anger shielded him from the worst of its effects. He demanded, and received, an escort to the High Priest's chambers. Reaching them, he hammered on the door before he could be announced.

"Malaithus! I want to talk to you!"

The door opened a crack.

"Your Majesty, it is late to be calling." Malaithus peered out of the door with a bemused expression on his face. His eyes, dull with weariness, sharpened when Karst stepped into the light. "What is amiss?"

"You tell me." Karst brushed past the sorcerer and closed the door behind him, leaving a nervous-looking Jakom outside.

"I don't understand. Have I given offense in some way?" Malaithus cast a wary glance to Karst's belt, where Karst's hand rested on his dagger. Malaithus was a sorcerer, but he was as susceptible as any man to a knife in the heart, and he knew Karst's temper well. He moved toward the table in the middle of the room, but Karst blocked his path, keeping the two at close quarters.

"You aren't just worshiping a god; you're trying to raise him, aren't you?" Karst slid the dagger a few inches out of its sheath, ready to strike should Malaithus give even the slightest hint of summoning power.

Malaithus exhaled, and the tension visibly drained from his body. "I wanted to tell you, but your father made me swear to keep it to myself until he decided to tell you himself."

"I found out on my own, so your conscience is clear. Now, tell me everything. Understand, my patience is wearing thin."

Malaithus took a second look at the dagger and seemed to make up his mind. "It is true. Our new nation is small and surrounded by enemies. We've made a good start, but when their war with Kyrin ends, Galdora will seek to bring Kurnsbur back into the fold, and who knows what the Malan girl will do? Your father believes raising a god to be our sovereign will give us the power we need to preserve our independence, and even expand our power."

Karst fell silent. It was hard to believe, but he'd seen and felt the evidence for himself.

"Even if he succeeds, the other nations have gods. What difference will it make if we have one too?"

"Gods come and go. Have you heard of Lellor? Antua?" Malaithus seemed to be regaining some of his confidence and, when Karst shook his head, went on. "They are gods from history who are now gone. Their worshipers lost their zeal and eventually died away. That seems to be what is happening with the Seven. They once touched the world directly, and their conflicts nearly tore us apart."

"The Godwars," Karst whispered.

"Exactly. But where are they now? They have been absent for so long that, even those who keep the faith begin to view them as mythological." Malaithus, apparently no longer fearing for his life, sat down at the table and Karst joined him a moment later.

"Do you truly think they are gone?"

"Perhaps not gone entirely, but diminished. Magic draws its power from the gods and, if the histories are at all accurate, magicians today cannot begin to approach the wonders that were done in the time of the Godwars and before."

Karst finally freed his dagger and spun it absently on the tabletop as he considered Malaithus' words. He'd heard this all before. "Didn't you tell me that your magic was becoming stronger?"

"It seems to be," Malaithus agreed, "but only by a fraction. My best guess is that the power is derived from the emergence of our new god."

"I was told that gods in turn draw their power from their worshipers. With our small numbers, how can we hope to match even the meager presence of the seven?"

"There is more to it than sheer numbers. The worship of one true believer is worth more than the rote prayers of a hundred casual followers." A pensive silence hung between them as Malaithus shifted in his seat and rubbed his face. "And then, there are the sacrifices." Karst scowled and Malaithus hurried on. "Understand, we are careful who we choose."

"Like children?" Truthfully, Karst didn't care about the children of some filthy Malgog, but he wanted to keep Malaithus off-balance. Already, he was feeling the rising god's presence, and he focused on his anger to try and shut it out.

"Only those who are dying anyway, from fevers or injuries and such. The same with the adults, as well as some who speak too loudly against you."

"I suppose you expect me to believe you are supporting me." Karst tried to force a laugh, but only managed a huff of breath.

"I don't expect you to believe me, but it is the truth, all the same."

"When you and the temple have held yourself above me all this time?" Karst was on his feet, his dagger trembling in his vise grip.

"Your Majesty, we are shaping a tool for your use, nothing more, and nothing less. We have been about our work." Rising, Malaithus placed his hands palms-down on the table and leaned closer. "I have not included you because I did not wish to create friction between you and your father, but know that the temple is yours."

Karst wanted to believe but clung to his ever-eroding skepticism. "How can I believe you?"

"Now that you know the truth, come to the temple and take part in worship. We are raising the god of the nation you lead. Think of the power you will wield when you harness his might. You could drive out the remnants of the Black Mangrove clan and give our new nation the access to the sea that we so crave."

Karst nodded. It made sense. Or was it the god's overwhelming presence breaking down his resolve as his anger ebbed?

"The temple is yours," Malaithus repeated. "All that remains is for you to accept our god as your own."

He reached out a hand. Perhaps by his own choice, perhaps compelled, Karst took it.

Chapter 15

Oskar shouted out in surprise as he slid down the steep roof. The world seemed to slow around him and the dark emptiness beyond the roof's edge appeared to grow larger, like a beast opening its gaping maw. He flipped over onto his stomach and scrabbled for a handhold, but could not find his grip. The roof tiles were slick and, for an instant, he wondered if it had rained in the brief time he had spent climbing the steps.

His mind immediately returned to the present. He was slowing a little though he couldn't completely arrest his fall. He pressed down hard with his feet and, for a moment, his toes gained purchase, but then the roof tile broke away and he began to descend again.

"Help!" No one was around to hear his cry, but it seemed the thing to do. A sharp pain lanced through his arm and something yanked him to a halt, the tips of his toes hanging over the edge. He looked up and saw that the sleeve of his cloak had caught on a nail head. The fabric was stretched to the tearing point and he realized with sickening certainty that it was all that lay between him and certain death.

Heart pounding, he reached across with his other hand and worked a fingernail behind the head of the nail. He let out a long breath and looked around. It was full dark now, with only a faint glow from the cloud-draped moon by which to see. To his right, there was nothing. A few feet to his left, however, just below the edge of the roof, a stone gargoyle leered down at the city. But could he make his way over to it? Carefully, he shifted his leg, and for a stomach-churning instant, he slid downward a few inches.

"I've got to get over there," he panted. "I can't cling to this nail for the rest of my life."

"So give me your hand and I'll help you."

The voice startled him so much that he jerked and lost his tenuous grip on the nail head. With a ragged ripping sound, his robe tore free. He cried out in alarm, but almost as soon as he began to slide again, someone grabbed him by the wrist. His rescuer's hand was small and didn't quite encircle his wrist, but the grip was strong.

"I can't do this by myself." The strain was evident in every word. "You've got to climb over to the gargoyle."

Dizzy from near panic, Oskar put everything he had into the effort, all the while wondering when he'd feel the falling sensation that would precede his death. Finally, his foot lodged against something solid: the gargoyle. With this foothold supporting his weight, he was able to crawl up onto the roof where he sat panting like a winded dog.

"So, how did you manage to fall? The roof isn't that steep."

Now, free from the fear of death, he realized his rescuer was a girl. She had raven hair, and milky skin that seemed to shine in the moonlight. The tight, dark clothing she wore failed to hide her curves, and he had to force himself not to stare.

"You're a girl."

"Don't tell me you've got a problem with a girl saving your life. Did it somehow offend your manhood?" She crossed her arms over her chest and looked down with a touch of disapproval in her blue eyes.

His eyes flitted to the dagger on her belt, then back to her eyes, and he laughed.

"I don't see what's funny." Her hand slipped to the hilt of her dagger.

"Nothing, it's just that you remind me of a friend of mine. She's perhaps the best I've ever known with a sword."

"Truly? Does she live here in the city?" The girl dropped to one knee in front of Oskar.

"No, she's in Lothan." A pang of regret struck him and he realized, not for the first time, that he missed his friends terribly.

"One of the wild women, then. How did you come to be friends with a Lothan?"

"We traveled there. She stayed and I came here for training. And the women there aren't wild. I mean, they're tougher than women here." He hesitated when the girl cocked her head to the side and eyed him dangerously. "I mean, they learn to fight, but they don't usually do it unless they're forced to. They take care of their families, bully their husbands, and do pretty much the same things women here do.

The girl stared for a moment and then giggled. "That's funny. For a moment, I almost believed you."

"It's true!" Oskar didn't know why he cared if this girl thought he was telling the truth or not, but suddenly it seemed of great importance that she did. He quickly told the story of how he, Shanis, Hierm, and Khalyndryn had left their village and traveled to Lothan, and how his meeting with Aspin had brought him here. He left out a few details, such as the fact that he was now friends with Prince Larris. If she already doubted his story, adding that in was sure to convince her of his prevarication. "I don't care if you believe it or not." That was a lie, but it seemed the thing to say.

She gave him another long look. "Look me in the eye and tell me you've been to Lothan." Oskar did just that. She leaned in so close their noses almost touched. He felt her breath on his lips and shivered. Finally, she sat back.

"All right, I believe you. We're going to have to spend some time together. I have a feeling you've got lots of stories to tell, and I like stories." She stood and stretched, and Oskar was once again all too aware of her many curves. "I'm Lizzie, by the way."

"Oskar."

"You never did tell me what you were doing up here." She looked around as if the reason lay hidden somewhere in the darkness nearby.

"I was trying to find a way inside the archives."

"You mean you can't just walk in?" She took him by the hand and hauled him to his feet. "That makes no sense."

"No, I'm still a novit." He took one step and his feet shot out from under him. He fell hard on his back, his breath escaping in a rush.

"Gods! Don't you fall again." Lizzie grabbed a handful of robe and kept him from sliding down the roof. "Haven't you walked on a roof before?"

"No, but that's not the reason. My foot just slipped out from under me." He held out his hand, conjured the blue light, and examined the sole of his boot. A thin sheen covered the bottom.

"What is that?" Lizzie touched a finger to the shiny patch. "It's greasy." She turned toward the door through which Oskar had come. "Can you shine your light over there?"

Oskar hadn't yet learned how to direct the beam, but he raised his hand, spilling the light all around.

"There's a patch of whatever this is just below the door, and you can see a streak of it running down the roof where you slid." She turned and frowned at him. "Did anyone know you were coming up here?"

"Maybe." Despite his noncommittal answer, he knew exactly who the culprit was. Agen had baited him into coming up here, and despite his friends' warnings, he'd charged up here like a bull in mating season. Idiot!

"Take off your boots and I'll help you back to the door."

His stocking feet weren't ideal for climbing a steep roof, but with Lizzie's aid, he made it back to the door without further embarrassing himself.

"Well, I guess this is goodbye."

"Hardly. You owe me a life debt, and until I decide it's repaid, you haven't seen the last of me." She winked, sending a shiver through him.

"How can I repay you?"

"Meet me here at moonrise two nights from now. And try not to fall."

Chuckling ruefully, he agreed. He turned toward the door and froze. There was no handle.

"Um. Do you know another way in?" He had wanted to at least make his exit with a shred of dignity intact, but it was apparently not to be.

"I wondered how soon you'd notice. Move it, big man." She drew her dagger, slid it into the crack between the door and the wall, and worked it back and forth. Moments later, it swung open. "And that's one more thing you owe me. For that, I think you should bring me a surprise when next we meet." She reached up, kissed him on the cheek, and slipped away into darkness.

Oskar gazed at the spot where she'd vanished, his hand pressed to his cheek and wondered what had just happened.

Chapter 16

"Hand it over, boy. And don't make no sudden moves if you don't want to end up skewered." The mounted man prodded Kelvin's chest with the tip of his spear and grinned, displaying rotting teeth turned brown from chewing laccor root. The group of men surrounding him laughed as if this were the funniest they'd ever heard.

Kelvin couldn't believe he'd let himself be caught unaware. When marauders killed his family and burned their farm, he'd managed to escape. But when he finally stopped to rest, they caught up with him.

He wore his bow and quiver across his back, but even if the bow was strung, he likely couldn't nock and loose a single arrow, much less four of them, before the man ran him through.

"Come on, now. It's all needed for the war effort."

"You expect me to support the Kyrinian side?" The words were bitter on his lips. Word was, Kyrin's armies had invaded deep into northern Galdora, and the two sides now stood at a stalemate. The villages of the northwest lay seemingly forgotten by the king, who focused his efforts on protecting the cities of the northeast. Here, roving bands of soldiers, most likely deserters, terrorized the countryside.

"I'd watch my tongue if I were you. These parts will soon be part of Kyrin, so you ought not to make any enemies for yourself." He prodded Kelvin again, harder this time. "Belt pouch and backpack, now!"

The soft thrum of hoof beats drew the man's attention. He turned to look for the approaching rider, and Kelvin, seeing his chance, ran for it. He dove directly beneath the man's horse, causing the beast to shy and almost step on Kelvin's head. He rolled, sprang to his feet, and ran for the forest.

He made it ten paces before a sharp pain brought him to his knees. He fell face-down on the ground, ears ringing and hot pain burning his scalp. He rolled over and tried to regain his feet, but a boot to the face sent him back down to the ground. He looked up to see a burly man with a shaved scalp climbing down from his horse.

"You were warned. Now we've got to make it hurt, so as to teach you a lesson." The man reversed his spear and raised it high overhead, ready to club Kelvin again, when a rider burst from the tree line.

He was a tall man, broad of shoulder, with curly brown hair and sun-bronzed skin. He rode leaning forward in the saddle with his sword bared.

Kelvin's assailant had only an instant to look up in surprise before the rider was upon him. A blur of steel flashed in the morning light, and the Kyrinian slumped to his knees, hands pressed to the gaping wound in his throat. The warhorse leaped over Kelvin, wheeled, and charged the three remaining Kyrinians. One hurled a spear at the rider, who moved his head an inch to his left, letting the projectile slide past him. His calm demeanor and economy of movement seemed to unsettle the Kyrinians, all of whom began to bark confused orders at once.

The newcomer bore down on the spear-thrower, changed directions at the last moment, and shot past him, slicing him across the shoulder.

The Kyrinian roared in pain, the short sword he had drawn falling from limp fingers. Cursing, he put his heels to his horse's flanks and galloped away.

The two remaining marauders seemed to have recovered some of their wits. They drew their swords and spread out. Whichever of them the man attacked first, the other would try to take him from behind. If the newcomer realized this, he didn't seem to care. He charged.

This time, he didn't veer away but plowed into the Kyrinian. Kreege, his highly-trained warhorse, sent the man's smaller mount to the ground. He then wheeled his horse around in time to parry the other Kyrinian's blow.

Kelvin stood and took in the scene in an instant. His rescuer was driving the mounted Kyrinian backward, but the man he had unhorsed was climbing slowly to his feet. Without thinking, Kelvin grabbed his bow, strung it, and nocked an arrow.

The last mounted Kyrinian went down, clutching his eyes where the newcomer's sword had slashed him. Meanwhile, the unhorsed marauder drew a throwing knife and took aim.

Kelvin's arrow took the Kyrinian through the cheek, slicing through flesh and knocking out a few teeth on its way out. It wasn't the finest shot he'd ever made, but it did the trick. The Kyrinian roared, dropped his knife, and stumbled away. In a moment, it was over. The rider rode him down, dismounted, and finished off both Kyrinians with cold efficiency, plunging his dagger into each man's heart in turn.

When he was finished, he cleaned and sheathed his blades, then turned to look at Kelvin, his brown eyes keen with interest.

"Thank you for the help. That was a well-placed shot."

"You're welcome." Kelvin was keenly aware of his youth and his ragged clothes. How must he look to this confident stranger? "I know you could have dealt with them all without me, but I wanted to get my licks in. They killed my family and burned our home." At that admission, his throat clenched and his knees wobbled. He'd forced those thoughts from his mind when he fled, focusing only on survival, but now they returned in full force.

"I'm sorry to hear that. Sit down and I'll have a look at your wound."

Kelvin put his hand to his stinging head and it came away covered in blood. It took all the resolve he could muster to remain on his feet. Something made him want to impress this stranger. He barely flinched as the man bathed and bandaged his head.

"My name is Kelvin," he offered.

"I didn't ask." The man stood. "It's a minor wound. Avoid any more blows to the head, and it should be fine in a few days." He replaced the items in his saddlebag and wandered around the clearing, inspecting the bodies. "Kyrinians. Deserters from their main force, I imagine."

"It's a problem throughout these parts. There's no one to stop them." Kelvin unstrung his bow and began rifling through the dead Kyrinian's pockets and belt pouches. He felt no compunction in doing so; they had already taken everything from him.

"Why don't the people who live here stand up to them?" The man turned his back to Kelvin, inspecting the gelding his warhorse had knocked down.

"We're farmers. We can't stand up to trained fighting men." Kelvin rolled the Kyrinian he was searching over onto his stomach and relieved him of his cloak. It wasn't fancy, but it was of good wool and dyed a dark green that would blend in well in the forest.

"You stood up to them." The man was looking at him now. "Find a dozen more like you who can handle a bow and won't flee in terror at the first sign of danger and you can deal with a few bandits."

A surge of pride at the man's praise dueled with an urge to defend his brethren. "Maybe it there were only a few bandits. But still, it's not that simple when you're in farm country. It isn't like a city where people live at close quarters and you can easily band together. We see one another at market, and that's about it."

The man shrugged. "So you have to do a spot of riding in order to spread the word. Speaking of riding, take this horse. It's in good condition and seems to have an even temperament."

He handed the reins to Kelvin, who stroked the creature's flanks. He'd never had a horse of his own.

"You still don't understand. Suppose I decided to go from farm to farm, trying to pull everyone together to fight the bandits. First off, no one's going to follow someone as young as me. Even if that were not a concern, every man wants to protect his own farm. He's not going to leave everything he has unprotected to go off on a fool's errand that'll likely get him killed. Everybody wants to protect his own."

"Like cherries for the picking." The man shook his head.

"What's a cherry?"

"Never mind." Close by, another of the Kyrinian's horses cropped a patch of wild oats, and the man began to search its saddlebags. "Where were you headed before they caught up with you?"

"Nowhere. I was just running. How about you? What is a city man, and probably a soldier considering the way you fight, doing in farm country?"

The man froze. After a long pause, his shoulders sagged. "Atoning for my sins."

"I don't understand."

"You have no reason to." The man walked the horse over to where his own mount waited, shifted his saddlebags to the new horse, and mounted up. "I suppose I'm purging the land of vermin."

"I want to help." Kelvin surprised himself with the sudden exclamation.

"No."

"Please. I have nothing left: no family, no home. If I die, no one will miss me. I might as well do something useful until then." He fought to keep the pleading tone out of his voice.

"Make no mistake, if you were to follow me, it would be to your death. I've had enough of that for a lifetime."

"You'll have to kill me then because I'm going to follow you. At a distance if I must, but I'm coming along." He was amazed at how calm he kept his voice. The renegades who had destroyed his life were dead, but it wasn't enough for him. He wanted revenge on the Kyrinians. All of them. "Besides, you said we could make a difference if enough of us banded together. With you as a leader, we can do just that."

"No." The man's eyes flashed hot but cooled just as quickly and he let out a sigh of resignation. "Follow along if you must, and try to keep up." Without another word, he wheeled his mount and trotted away.

Chapter 17

"**The walls of** Halholm stood for seven centuries, never breached by an enemy force. Strengthened by magic, they required no repair. Not ever. It was said that the stones were imbued with bits of moonlight that made them sparkle, but inspection of the ruins revealed that it was actually quartz and mica." The corner of Master Sibson's mouth twitched. "Despite its location near the disputed border between Halvala and Riza, the city maintained its independence. That is until its walls were demolished in a single day." He paused. "The first day of the Second Godwar."

Silence reigned in the classroom. Oskar held his breath, eager for the story to continue.

"In the spring of the year 3413, Henar, King of Riza, decreed that Halholm and the surrounding lands were part of his kingdom and sent emissaries to the city with a copy of the declaration and a demand for taxes," Sibson smirked and several students, mostly those from cities, chuckled. "Halholm sent its reply in the form of the heads of the members of the Rizan party, each with a fist-sized stone stuffed in his mouth.

"Rizans, of course, worship Kordlak, the god of stone, and found this reply to be more than a political rebuff, but heresy of the highest order, and declared war on Halholm. Kordlak apparently agreed because he led the Rizan forces into battle."

Oskar's hand shot up, almost before he realized what he was doing. "You're saying the god himself actually fought against humans?"

Agen turned around and made a confused face. "Considering he fought in the First Godwar, I don't know why that should come as a surprise." A few of the novits laughed, but most shook their heads at Oskar or simply ignored him.

"Ah, yes. You were not here when we discussed that particular war. The gods did, in fact, take a direct hand in human conflicts on occasion. When they did, it was a terrible sight to behold." He cleared his throat and resumed his lecture. "Being the god of stone, Kordlak had an unmatched affinity with stone. He marched up to the city, arrows bouncing off his granite-hard skin, and literally tore the walls apart."

"How?" Naseeb asked.

"If the stories are to be believed, he pressed his hands into the walls and yanked out great chunks of stone. When a section of wall collapsed, he moved on to another."

"There was nothing they could do about it?" Phill, a stout Halvalan youth with rust-colored hair and a florid face, asked. "I mean, can a human fight a god?"

"Anyone can fight a god. Whether or not he can do that god any damage is another question entirely." Sibson waited for laughter that did not come. "Let me answer this way. Could an ant fight you?"

Phill grinned. "Up until the moment I stepped on it."

"How about one hundred ants?" Sibson's tone made it clear he was working up to something.

"I'd take a few bites before I managed to crush them all, but I'd recover."

"How about ten thousand?"

"I'd run."

Everyone laughed at that, and Sibson nodded.

"Fighting a god is much like that. Given enough tiny hurts, even the mightiest god will fall. The difference is, even ten thousand would not be enough." Sibson gave that a moment to sink in. "Being the source of all magic, gods have at their disposal power beyond imagining. They are stronger and more resilient than humans. They are fearsome enemies, to be sure. But the greatest challenge in combating a god or goddess is overcoming his or her will. Men who approach a god's physical manifestation find themselves unable to think clearly and must run lest they be overwhelmed." He paused. "Unless, of course, some external force gives them the strength to fight. Such as, another god fighting for the opposing side."

Sibson waited for more questions, but none came. Returning to his lecture, he told of the destruction wrought by Kordlak, and how, one by one, the other gods joined in the battle—some intent on stopping Kordlak, others entering on his side. When the Second Godwar finally ended, all of Gameryah was devastated.

Oskar was so caught up in the lecture that he was startled when Sibson announced that class was over for the day. He sat, contemplating what he had learned while the others filed out.

"Is there something you need, Novit Clehn?" Sibson stood over him, looking down not unkindly.

"Sorry, Master, this is all new to me. It's a great deal to take in."

"I suppose it is," Sibson agreed. "I fear the subject matter has become a bit stale to me, given that I've lectured on it at least once a year for more years than I can count."

"How many Godwars were there?"

"Only three conflicts are named Godwars, but history is filled with minor conflicts between a handful of gods." Sibson chuckled. "Minor, that is, in terms of the numbers of gods involved. From the human standpoint, there was nothing minor about them."

"When was the last one?"

Sibson scratched his head and looked up at the ceiling. "3468, I believe. That was the last time the gods did battle."

Oskar froze. An idea had just come to him but did he dare try it?

"Master Sibson, as you pointed out, being new to the Gates, I've missed a great deal. Might I have your permission to visit the archives so that I may study up on the First Godwar and anything else I might have missed?" His heart raced as he awaited the master's answer.

Sibson gazed at him through hooded eyes. "Novits may not visit the archives. Besides, the curriculum is circular. Anything you missed will come back around in time."

Oskar's heart sank.

"However, it would benefit you to at least have a passing acquaintance with the first Godwar as we move forward. I will write a note asking that you be permitted to borrow Saclan's *Godwar*. It is not heavy reading, but it will give you a passing acquaintance with the subject matter."

Oskar forced a smile and thanked the master. While Sibson dug out a quill, ink, and sand, and wrote and then blotted the note, Oskar reflected on all he had learned today. Something was bothering him.

"What happened to the gods? The seven, I mean." Oskar knew that history was sprinkled with the names of other gods who seemed to have died out along with their worshipers. "They were involved in human affairs for thousands of years and then, suddenly, they're... absent."

"That does seem to be the case." Sibson handed him the piece of parchment. "Not only have they not taken a hand in our affairs for some time now, but their touch on the world is lighter. Magic today is much weaker than it was during and prior to the Third Godwar."

Oskar nodded. This was something he already knew. Something still bothered him.

"Where do you think they went?"

Sibson managed a faint smile. "No one knows."

"What kept you?" Naseeb asked when Oskar arrived at their alchemy class.

Oskar showed him the note.

"Not what you were hoping for," Naseeb said. "For what it's worth, you're the first novit I've known who's gotten to borrow a book from the archives."

"Yes, but it doesn't get me any closer to gaining access to the archives. I just hope I can learn something useful in time."

"In time for what? Wait, is that another of those things you can't tell me?" Naseeb asked.

"I'm afraid it...what is it?"

Naseeb's eyes had grown unfocused and his expression calculating. "You might not be as far away as you might think. Give me a minute." He turned and whispered something to Whitt, who frowned and shook his head. Naseeb whispered something else Oskar couldn't quite make out and made an emphatic gesture. Whitt flinched and then his shoulders sagged as he relented.

"What did you say to him?" Oskar whispered.

"As you're always telling me, it's better if you don't know. Just remember to act surprised."

"Better you hadn't told me anything. Then I really would be surprised."

Naseeb rolled his eyes and turned to look at Master Lepidus, who was beginning his lecture.

Lepidus discussed the properties of dragonroot, a sample of which lay on each table. Dried and ground, it could be used in a poultice to cure infection, or mixed with certain leaves to alleviate the pain of a toothache. It was the juice, however, that gave the root its name. In its purest form, it was more flammable than naphtha, but if it were brought slowly to a boil, it became a strong liquor— one which only the wealthy could afford, and could only be drunk in small amounts.

"I like to add a pinch of mint leaves just as it begins to boil," Lepidus said, "but the Master Dac Kien tells me that on the other side of the Sun Sands, they prefer ground orange or lemon peels." He narrowed his eyes and mimicked a stage whisper, "I hear Proctor Basilius puts bull stock in his."

A brief, stunned silence gave way to uproarious laughter among those students who knew exactly what bull stock was, followed by another ripple of laughter as they explained the joke to their fellow novits.

"You will use a press to squeeze the juice from your root. Add water. Then you will slowly heat it," Lepidus said once the class had returned to some semblance of order. "Bring it to a boil, and keep in mind, it is flammable. You won't have enough juice to do any serious damage, but you could suffer a painful burn if you aren't careful. And..." he paused for dramatic effect, "the five students with the lowest marks will be drinking your concoctions, so don't poison them. He winked to show he was joking, and the novits, once again laughing, set to work.

The surprise came a few minutes into the lesson, when Whitt lost his balance and fell backward, upsetting Agen's flask. Agen cried out in alarm as a brilliant flash of white light filled the room. Oskar shielded his eyes and, when he opened them, Naseeb was gone.

It took Lepidus a minute to sort things out. The fire had only singed the cuff of Agen's cloak, but it had incinerated his lecture notes. Lepidus instructed Whitt to provide Agen with a new set of notes, and then warned him that any more accidents would earn him an evening in the kitchens.

Oskar felt something bump against his shins and looked down to see Naseeb crawling beneath the table. The dark-skinned youth rose just before Lepidus went to get a new root for Agen and his friends.

"Where did you go?" Oskar asked as everyone returned to work.

"I'll tell you later." Naseeb then turned to Whitt. "What were you thinking? That wasn't the plan."

"My way is more fun," Whitt said. "I wondered, why make a fire at our table when I could set one at Agen's instead?"

"I'll copy those notes for you," Oskar said, "as I suspect this has something to do with Naseeb's plan to help me, whatever that plan might be. I'm just glad you weren't sent to the kitchens. I couldn't have covered that one for you."

"Lepidus rarely punishes us. You have to step far out of bounds or blunder several times to get in his bad books," Whitt said. "Besides, it would have been worth it."

The remainder of the class passed without incident though Lepidus surprised them by taking a sip from each group's flask. He briefly calmed Agen's anger at Whitt by proclaiming him and his table mates "future brew masters," but then ruined the moment by clutching his throat and gagging. By the time class was dismissed, Oskar had decided Lepidus was his favorite instructor.

Back in the room, Naseeb dug two small roots from a pocket within his robes and held them up. They looked like tiny, pink carrots. "Here's what we need. Better than magic. Now, give me Sibson's note."

Puzzled, Oskar handed him the note. Naseeb opened it and read aloud.

"Please allow Novit Clehn to borrow Saclan's Godwars. -M Sibson"

Oskar watched as Naseeb ground up the roots, added water and spread the resulting paste over the words *'borrow Saclan's Godwars.'* Almost immediately the gooey substance began to change color: first gray, then charcoal, and finally, inky black. Grinning, Naseeb took out a small knife and scraped it away.

The words were gone!

"That's nice, but what now?" Oskar asked.

"I happen to have a gift for copying handwriting." Naseeb took out his quill and ink and added the words *'use the archives.'* "There," he said handing the paper to Oskar. "Now you have permission from a master."

Oskar examined the note carefully. Naseeb's script was a perfect match for Lepidus' own handwriting. It would probably fool the master himself.

"What if Keeper Corwine still won't let me in?"

"I can only cut your food. I can't chew and swallow it for you." Naseeb flashed a wicked grin. "Corwine doesn't mind the desk. It's usually an initiate, sometimes a saikur. Choose a time when an initiate's at the desk and dare him to countermand a master."

"All right," Oskar said. "I'll do it today."

Chapter 18

A thin sheen of cold sweat coated Oskar's brow by the time he reached the archives. The closer the moment came, the more certain he grew that this would not work. He was a novit. He was not allowed inside.

When the archives' arched entryway came into sight, he stopped and leaned against the wall to catch his breath.

"Why am I doing this?" he whispered. "Aspin can search the archives when he returns. He doesn't need my help." This, of course, was not entirely true. Aspin had told him that he did, in fact, need Oskar's help.

He thought of all the times he'd hidden in Lord Hiram's warehouse, poring over one of the few books in Galsbur. Back then, he would have given anything to be here in this great center of learning, soaking up all the knowledge the masters had to offer without fear of getting chucked out for sneaking into the archives. It wasn't fair. Did he truly owe Aspin so much?

And then a face came unbidden to his mind. Shanis. He remembered their childhood and the affection he'd always had for her. He thought of her sincere desire to bring peace to Lothan, a sentiment he'd never thought the hot-tempered girl could possess. She was his lifelong friend and one of the people who mattered to him most. If a new Frostmarch approached, and the evidence suggested that it did, she would need help.

"You aren't just doing this for Aspin," he whispered. "You're doing it for her." Emboldened by this conviction, he strode into the archives.

The young man at the desk didn't bother to look up from the book he was reading.

"Name?" he drawled.

"Oskar Clehn."

Now, the young man did look up. His forehead crinkled as he looked Oskar up and down, and then consulted a scroll.

"You are not on the list. Are you an initiate?"

"No. I mean, I have a note." He thrust the doctored sheet of parchment into the young man's hands.

"I have never heard of a novit being granted access to the archives." He ran his finger across the words as if he could detect a forgery.

"I'm brand new and woefully behind. Master Sibson believes that, with enough extra effort, I can catch up, but I have some holes in my knowledge that are making it difficult for me to keep pace with the rest of the class." He'd rehearsed this line and hoped he didn't sound as wooden as he feared.

"I really should consult with the keeper about this."

"Feel free, if it will hurry things along," Oskar bluffed. "All I know is Master Sibson expects me to be caught up on several historical periods by next class, which is only two days away. He's in quite a temper about it."

"So this is only temporary?"

"Yes. Just until I can catch up." Oskar's heart skipped a beat. Might he actually pull it off?

"Which the master expects you to accomplish in two days." The young man rolled up Oskar's note and tapped it on the table, considering. "Very well. Being a novit, you won't know your way around. What periods of history are you studying?"

"The Godwars, and…" his mouth had gone dry. "The Silver Serpent."

"I beg your pardon? If you're studying the Godwars, you won't need to know anything about the Silver Serpent for some time yet. That doesn't come up until much later. Besides, there's not a section devoted to it. You'd have to scour texts from various periods in order to find a mere mention of it."

"Sorry. I thought it was a weapon used in the Godwars," Oskar improvised. "At least, that's the way the story was told in my village."

"You're thinking of the Frostmarch. Stick with your lessons and you'll get to that soon enough." The young man told him where he could find information on the Godwars, reminded him that the archives closed at the evening bell and returned to his book.

"May I have my note back?" Oskar reached out to take back the piece of parchment, but the young man slid it away.

"Sorry, all notes are turned over to Keeper Corwine for his records. I'll be working the desk for the next several days and I'll remember you so you won't need the note."

Panic welled up inside Oskar. When Corwine saw the note he would immediately know that something was amiss, and it would take only a word with Sibson to learn the truth. What an idiot he'd been! Sneaking into the archives was bad enough, but he'd forged a note from one of the masters. This could get him and his two friends chucked out. He had to get that note back!

"All right, then. Thank you." As he walked slowly away, he watched from the corner of his eye as the young man placed the note in a basket behind the table. Perhaps Oskar could manage to get hold of it on his way out.

Unable to do anything about it at the moment, he figured he might as well take advantage of the fact he was actually inside the archives! All his life, he'd heard tales of the wondrous library at Karkwall in Lothan. Having seen it during his travels, he now knew that it paled in comparison to this place. There looked to be as many books and scrolls on this floor alone than in Karkwall's entire collection. His eyes roamed over the shelves and he felt something like hunger stir inside him.

He took a moment to look around. In the center of the room, robed men sat at a long table, poring over thick tomes. Every one of them used a floating ball of light to illuminate the area around him. Good thing he'd already mastered that trick. He realized there were no lights in the archives, save the glow from the saikurs' and initiates' spell light. He supposed an open flame inside a tower filled with old paper would be a bad idea.

The Godwars books were shelved in the collection on the third floor, and he used his glowing light to make his way there. This floor was arranged the same as the first floor, with rows of shelves in concentric circles and a long table in the center. A lone saikur sat there, reading, and did not look up when Oskar entered, which was fine with him. Hoping he didn't encounter anyone who would know he didn't belong, he began his search.

Time seemed to lose all meaning in this dark, silent place. He had no idea how the shelves were organized, and few books had printing on the spine, so he ended up wandering through the stacks, opening books at random and flipping through. The snatches of text he read covered a variety of topics, all of which he would have loved to explore, but he knew time was short.

He found nothing about the Silver Serpent, but finally located the books covering the First Godwar. Figuring he should at least complete the task Master Sibson had set him to, he found the book, *Godwars*, and stood in a corner out of sight and read until evening bell.

He assumed he would have to sign the book out, and hoped that when he did, he might find a way to distract the young man at the table long enough to retrieve his note, but when he reached the first floor, his stopped short. Keeper Corwine now stood behind the table, helping his assistant, who was furiously signing out books for a long line of saikurs. That tore it. Oskar was not about to let the keeper see his face. Dousing his light, he retreated to the stairs and stuffed *Godwars* inside his robe. What was one more violation in light of what he'd already done today? He waited until a group of initiates passed close by him. They paid him no mind when he fell in beside them. Trying not to look guilty, he walked out the door.

It was not until he reached his room and stowed the book in his trunk that he was able to breath normally again, but that relief was short-lived. There was still the matter of his note. What was he going to do?

Chapter 19

"I am afraid he is dying." Jowan the Archpriest of the Temple of the Seven, shook his head as he turned away from King Allar. His face betrayed no emotion, but his eyes were troubled. "I am truly sorry, Your Majesty."

Larris put his arm around Queen Arissa's shoulders, but his comfort was not needed, at least, not at the moment. Queen Arissa maintained a calm exterior and her face was a mask of determination.

"What ails him, exactly?" Her voice held a hint of challenge.

The priest shrugged. "Age. His body grows tired and is no longer operating as it should."

"Age," Arissa repeated. "His Majesty is barely fifty summers. He is hardly an old man."

"Some men decline faster than others. Ruling takes its toll on a man, as does, believe it or not, spending too much of one's time sitting on a throne or at table."

"My father was a great soldier in his day." Larris clenched his fists, struggling to match his mother's calm. "He fought the Kyrinians more times than I can count."

Jowan raised a liver-spotted hand. "Please understand, it is not my desire to diminish your father's achievements, Highness. I only point out that it has been a long time since he spent his days in the saddle, and a few more since he found himself on the front lines. I sincerely regret that I can do no more than prescribe a restorative draught."

"But it won't return him to health?" Arissa asked.

"No. It will strengthen him and perhaps prolong his life." The priest opened his bag and withdrew a stoppered vial of viscous amber liquid.

"I'll see to it that he gets it." Larris snatched the vial away from the priest with unnecessary force, but right now, he didn't care what the priest thought of him. "How much of it and how often?"

"One spoonful in the morning and another in the evening." The priest looked back at the king, who lay sleeping, and winced. "I should give him the first dose just to see how he reacts."

"It's a general restorative. There should be no reaction." Larris took the man by the arm and steered him toward the door. "I'll send for you if there is a problem. Thank you for your time and attention."

Allyn waited outside, along with two guards. Larris set his friend the task of escorting the priest back to the temple and closed the door.

"That was discourteous of you," Arissa said though her tone was one of curiosity rather than disapproval.

"I don't trust him, or anyone else from the temple, for that matter." He hurried on, forestalling her argument. "Mother, I promise I have my reasons, but I can't share them right now. I only ask that you trust me."

"When will you tell me?"

"As soon as I can. I give you my word." He moved to the window seat, settled onto the thick cushions, and looked out across the city.

Arissa took a seat beside the king's bed, took Allar's hand in both of hers, and kissed his knuckles. "I assume you've had no word about your brother?"

"Not yet, but I have people searching for him."

"What shall we do if your father passes before Lerryn returns? We have no proof that he abdicated, so you cannot take the throne." She sighed. "We can't keep the severity of your father's illness a secret for much longer, and this is not the time to be without strong leadership. The war with Kyrin, the rebellion in Kurnsbur, the goings-on in Lothan..."

"And the coming Frostmarch," Larris added. His mother did not reply. She still refused to believe such a thing was possible, but her self-delusions would not change the reality of the situation. "There is one possibility we have not considered." He took a deep breath. Arissa would not like this suggestion. "If Lerryn died in battle, the succession issue would be solved."

"You said his body was never found."

"That is true." He'd received a message from Hierm confirming there had been a battle in Galsbur, won at great cost by the Galdorans. All but one of the White Fang, Lerryn's elite cavalry unity, had died in the battle, and all of the bodies had been recovered. Lerryn's body, however, was missing, and the locals believed he had survived. "But no one else knows that. If I send men to Galsbur and they return with a coffin, who's to say it's not Lerryn inside? We could say the body is in no condition for him to lie in state. We announce his passing, spread the story of his heroic death, hold a state funeral, and no one will be the wiser."

"Until he does return, and then what?" Arissa asked, her voice now trembling with anger.

"He won't return. At least, not in a public way. He made it clear that he does not consider himself fit to rule."

"I won't hear of it." Arissa rose from her chair. "If I dare spread such lies, I will publicly denounce you."

"Mother, you said it yourself. We must have strong leadership."

"And how secure would your seat on the throne be once the truth comes out? We can make any announcement we like, but there are people in Galdora who know the truth. Sooner or later, the story will make its way back here, assuming it hasn't already. The closed casket would only fuel the rumors."

Larris wanted to argue, but he saw the wisdom in her words. He nodded his grudging acceptance.

"Your uncle can serve as regent until the problem is settled."

Larris was on his feet in a flash. "No. Orman is needed in the field. He says this latest batch of troops is almost ready though the gods only know what has taken him so long to train them. I can rule as Prince Regent for the time being. I'm going to be king anyway."

"You have not yet earned the respect of the court. The memory of your disappearance is still fresh in too many minds, and that is the only thing most people at court know about you. And the Regis does not yet trust you." The Regis was the small council that advised the king.

Arissa closed the distance between them, put her hands on his shoulders, and drew him close. "Remain strong. We will find our way."

"I will." He gently broke off the embrace. "I think I should be the one to hold court today. As you point out, I need to change the way the nobility think of me. Not being a soldier, I can't earn their respect on the field of battle so I will have to do it another way."

Arissa gave him a long, speculative look, and finally nodded. "I think that is an excellent idea. Will you want me there to keep you from making a mess of things?" She managed a half-smile.

"Yes. Let me take the lead, and if you feel I'm headed in the wrong direction, take out your kerchief and dab at your brow. How does that sound?"

Now his mother did smile. "You are already thinking like a leader."

"I'll be there in an hour. There are some things I need to take care of first." He kissed his mother on the forehead, gave his father's hand a squeeze, and headed for his private quarters.

"Nothing to report, I'm afraid." Allyn whirled the blood red wine around in his glass but did not drink. "The priest had no interest in conversing with someone as lowly as me and certainly didn't invite me into the temple for a chat."

"If you'd let me grant you a title, you'd receive better treatment. I could marry you into a noble house and everything." Larris took a sip of wine and enjoyed the outraged expression on his friend's face.

"You know I don't want that. At least, not in the near future." A sly smile creased his face. "Speaking of marriage, I know someone who needs to find a nice young woman and produce an heir. Surely your mother has mentioned it."

"She has." Larris had now lost interest in his wine. There was only one woman he had any interest in marrying, and she was not a royal. At least, not yet. "I'm putting her off for now."

"Marrying a Diyonan might motivate them to help us crush the rebellion in Kurnsbur."

"Or I could marry a Halvalan or Cardithian in hopes they would intervene in the Kyrinian war." He lowered his gaze to his abandoned glass of wine. The red liquid reminded him of all the blood that would be spilled before the conflicts came to an end, especially if there were another Frostmarch.

"I know what you're thinking and you know it cannot be." Allyn's voice was surprisingly gentle. "You will sit the Galdoran throne, and Shanis will rule Lothan. It is not a match. If Lerryn had not abdicated, it would be a different story."

"I don't care to discuss it right now. We have too much to attend to at the moment, and I have to be in court shortly." Rising from his chair, he fished the bottle of restorative from a pocket inside his cloak. "Do you know of a reliable herb woman here in the city?"

"No, but I can doubtless find you a few in short order."

"Splendid. Find two of the best and have each of them examine my father separately. I don't need to tell you, it must be done in secret."

"Of course. I'll dress them as chambermaids. What is in the flask?"

"This is the restorative the priest wants to be given to my father. Have it tested for poison." He handed the bottle to Allyn.

Allyn eyed the flask as if it were a coiled serpent. "Do you honestly think they would be so foolish as to put the evidence of their deceit directly in your hands?"

"They killed Melina. I don't know if they conspired with her, or simply wanted to guarantee her silence about something she'd discovered, but right now, there's nothing I wouldn't put past them."

Chapter 20

"How did it go?" Naseeb grinned as Oskar sat down at the table in the dining hall.

Oskar shook his head.

"They didn't believe the note was real?" Naseeb let the chicken leg he'd been gnawing on fall back onto his plate. "Are we in trouble?"

"Oh, the note fooled them. At least, it fooled the fellow minding the store. The problem is, they keep all such notes and pass them along to Corwine."

"We've got to get it back." Naseeb slapped his palm on the table. "If Master Sibson finds out I forged his signature, I'll be turned out at once."

"I'll tell them I forged it. No need to bring you or Whitt into it. You were only trying to help me, after all." Oskar hoped it wouldn't come to that, but he couldn't see how he could avoid it.

"I don't want you to get chucked out either. We've got to do something."

Oskar shrugged. "Any suggestions?"

"Not really." Naseeb chewed on his lower lip and gazed into the distance. "I suppose we could sneak down there tonight and try to get inside."

"Maybe. I can't believe they would make it easy to get inside. The door might even be magically warded." Oskar rubbed his temples, trying to stave off the dull pain rising in his head. "If I can't come up with a better idea, I'll try the door. I don't want you to go, in case I'm caught."

"We're in this together. Besides, I don't have anything else to do tonight."

Oskar remembered that he, in fact, did have something to do. "I've got to go. I'll let you know about tonight." Rising, he took an apple from his plate and pocketed it inside his robe. It might not have been what Lizzie had in mind when she said to bring her a surprise, but right now he was too distracted by his own problems to think of something better.

"You're late."

Oskar jumped as the words rang out in the darkness of the stairwell.

"Lizzie?" His voice came out in a rasp. "What are you doing in here?"

"Keep your voice down," she whispered. "You weren't exactly nimble up on the roof, so I thought it would be safer to meet you down here. You're more likely to survive a tumble down some stairs than a fall from a rooftop."

He strained his eyes to see in the dark, but the blackness was absolute. Remembering himself, he extended his hand and called up the circle of light. A few paces away, Lizzie shielded her eyes.

"Next time warn me before you do that."

"Sorry." He let the light fade to a dull glow. Like the last time he'd seen her, she was clad in tight, dark clothing that would have caused a scandal in Galsbur. He looked away, grateful that the darkness hid his discomfort.

"Where's my surprise?" she asked.

Oskar handed her the apple.

"Oh! I never get fresh fruit unless I steal it from the grounds here. Most of the time, it's not worth the bother. It seems you people love your midnight strolls in the orchard." She bit down on the apple with a loud crunch.

"You steal things from the grounds? But you're…" Oskar stopped himself in mid-sentence.

"I'm what?" Lizzie smiled. "A girl?"

"You're too pretty to be a thief."

"Right." Lizzie rolled her eyes. "I've heard that more times than I care to think about, usually from fat old men who reek of sour wine; men who have to be taught to keep their hands to themselves."

"No, I really mean it." Oskar's mouth was dry. "I like your eyes and your smile."

"Nice try. 'You have pretty eyes' is the line young men use in hopes you won't notice what they're really looking at. Maybe that worked with your farm girls back home, but you'll have to try harder to sway me." She sat down on the stairs, took another bite of the apple, and smiled as he struggled for words.

"Not me," he finally said. "I'm just the fat boy who likes to read."

Lizzie's eyes narrowed. "Does fat mean something different on the farm than it does in the city?" Smiling at the puzzled look on Oskar's face, she reached up and poked him in the belly. "You, my bear of a friend, might be clumsy, but you're hardly fat."

Oskar put a hand to his stomach and was surprised to realize what remained of his soft middle had melted away. He knew his travels had firmed him up, but he hadn't realized how much of a change it had wrought in his physique. He had to stop himself from flexing his arms just to see how much his muscles had developed.

"I swear, I don't know what to make of you." Lizzie finished her apple, pocketed the core, and indicated with a tilt of her head that he should sit down beside her.

Oskar settled uncomfortably on the stone steps and she leaned her head against his shoulder. He veritably tingled at her touch. He hadn't had many opportunities to enjoy such closeness with a girl and wasn't quite sure what to do now. Should he put his arm around her? Heart racing, stomach turning somersaults, he shifted so he could snake his arm around her waist, and succeeded only in jostling her.

Lizzie sat up straight. "Sorry. I didn't mean to make you uncomfortable."

"It's not that, I was just moving around." His mind seemed to be moving at half speed. "The steps are uncomfortable." He reached out and clumsily took her hand. For a moment, he wondered if she'd pull away, or even reach for her belt knife, but she took his hand in both of hers and rested it on her knee. They sat there in the dim light until the companionable silence turned uncomfortable. He racked his brain for something to talk about.

"The other night I asked you if you know a way into the archives. Do you?"

"I might. I know my way into quite a few places I shouldn't. What's in there that's so important to you?"

"Mostly, I need information, but that's a long story. Right now, what I need the most is a document." He told her about the forged pass.

Lizzie's eyes grew serious and she fixed him with an appraising look. "You acted so shocked at the thought of me stealing fruit, but now you want me to break into your archives and steal something for you. You're not the most honest fellow in the world, are you?"

"I suppose not," he admitted. "I'm desperate. Can you help me?"

Lizzie made a show of considering his request. "I can," she finally said, "but not for free."

"I have a little money, but it's back in my quarters."

"Not money. I want a story."

"A story?" He knew plenty of stories— some from the books he'd read, others heard on the porch of Master Serrill's inn or at his grandfather's knee. But what sort of story did she want to hear?

Lizzie seemed to read his thoughts. "Not that kind of story. I want to hear about the world outside of the city. I've never left, and I suppose I never will." Her face fell. "Tell me a story from your life, and make it good. I want to believe I'm really there."

Oskar had listened to stories all his life, but he'd never tried to tell one of his own creation, and he had no gift for description, so he figured he should start with something familiar. He began with his home of Galsbur. He described the various shops that ringed the emerald oval of the town green, and the great tree with the odd carvings on its surface. Warming to his task, he soon found it easy to paint pictures with his words. He recalled with great clarity the Vulltu River, the sound it made is it rushed over the rocks, the way its icy water numbed his toes when he dangled his feet in the water, and its pure, clean taste. Soon, the words seemed to pour forth of their own volition. He lost his train of thought once when Lizzie shifted onto her side and laid her head in his lap, but he recovered quickly. He talked about his friendship with Hierm and Shanis, and soon had her in stitches with tales of Shanis' prodigious temper. When he told the story of how Shanis, in a fit of rage, had climbed up onto the roof of her house and used her sword to hack a hole in the thatched roof, Lizzie's eyes popped open.

"You're lying." She poked him in the chest for emphasis.

"May the gods strike me down if it's not the truth."

She sat up. "You're a good storyteller, but it's getting late. I need to hurry if I'm going to get your paper back."

"I should go with you."

"No. I'll need you to keep watch. Besides, I can move quickly and quietly in the dark. I doubt you can say the same." She didn't wait for him to argue with her but stood and mounted the stairs. Oskar followed along behind. "Can you at least try to be quiet? You walk like a runaway draft horse," she whispered.

Shanis and Allyn had tried to teach Oskar how to move silently in the forest, but that mostly involved him not being foolish or clumsy enough to step on dry leaves and branches or brush against shrubbery. He'd never advanced to the point where he learned how to properly place his feet. He tried tiptoeing but found that difficult on the steps, so he settled for walking on the balls of his feet, which at least kept the heels of his boots from clacking on the stone steps.

"Better," she whispered. "Next you can work on your breathing. You sound like an ox with a cold."

Oskar stifled a laugh. In some ways, Lizzie reminded him of Shanis.

They'd climbed for no more than a minute when Lizzie came to a stop. "It's right here," she whispered.

"What is?" Oskar focused on the light that hovered in front of him and it shone brightly. He saw nothing to distinguish this spot from any other.

"The way in." She knelt and ran a hand along the riser in front of her. "Found it." She drew her knife and pushed it into the stone until it stopped and then rotated it a quarter turn to the left.

Oskar sucked in his breath as the stair slid back, revealing a dark opening.

Lizzie slid gracefully into the hole. A moment later, she stuck her head back out. "Tell me exactly where to find your paper." She listened intently as he gave directions. "All right. I'll be back soon. Whatever you do, don't pull the knife out. If you do, I'll be trapped."

Smiling, Oskar let his light die. He settled down on the steps to wait. He strained to hear any sound that might warn of someone approaching, but he heard nothing. Finally, a soft, shuffling sound came from the hole, and Lizzie climbed out a moment later.

"Did you get it?" Oskar asked.

"I did."

Oskar heard the sound of the step moving back into place, and then he felt her take his hand.

"Come on. Let's get out of here." She didn't sound afraid, but there was a tension in her voice that hadn't been there before.

"What's wrong?" he whispered as they pounded down the steps.

"I don't know how, but someone knew I was there. I heard footsteps coming in my direction. I barely got away."

"Probably a spell of some sort." He wondered if such a thing were possible. He could ask Master Zuhayr, but if word got around that someone had broken into the archives, the question might raise suspicion.

"I had to eat your letter, you know," Lizzie said.

"What?"

"I couldn't risk getting you into trouble if I got caught, so I destroyed the evidence."

"How did it taste?"

"Like chicken." Lizzie giggled. They paused at the bottom of the stairwell. She opened the door, looked up and down the corridor, and finally stepped out. "I'm going to sneak out through the grounds. You should stay away from the archives tonight. Find a different way back to your quarters, just to be safe."

"When can I see you again?" Oskar blurted before he had time to stop himself.

"Two nights from now. Meet me at the top of the steps at moonrise."

"I don't know how to thank you," he said. "I'd have been in serious trouble if you hadn't gotten that letter."

"You are getting deeper in debt to me. Next time, I want a better present than an apple." Suddenly, she took his face in her hands, rose up on her tiptoes, and kissed him hard on the lips. "Goodnight," she whispered. And then she was gone.

Oskar stared at the spot where she'd stood a moment before, glad no one could see the foolish grin spreading across his face. For an instant, he considered following her, but knew he'd never find her. She moved like a shadow.

A noise behind him caught his attention, and he whirled about to see a figure disappear around a corner. Who had it been? He hastily stripped off his boots and took off at a run down the hallway. He was surprised to discover he actually could move quietly and quickly when he put his mind to it. Reaching the corner, he paused and peered around. The figure was moving at a fast walk, not looking back. This stretch of hallway was long and straight, and Oskar risked being seen if he followed too closely, but he had to know who it was. Heart in his throat, he took off again, this time at a trot. His gentle footfalls sounded like thunder to his ears, but the figure up ahead continued on, seemingly unaware that Oskar followed.

He was twenty paces away when he froze. Up ahead, a sliver of moonlight shone through a tall, narrow window, and as the figure passed through it, Oskar recognized the fair skin and pale blond hair.

Agen had been spying on him.

Chapter 21

"I've never seen so many people in such a small town." Hierm reined in his horse and sat staring at the masses that filled the forest and open fields around the town of Wilham. Some had built makeshift huts while others slept underneath wagons or stretches of canvas. On the whole, they were a pitiful lot, dirty and despondent. Here and there, a few men cast envious glances at Hierm's pack horse, whose burden was light, but likely held more food than any of these people had seen in some time. One man, a big fellow with wild, red hair, took two steps out into the road but stopped when a tiny woman took him by the arm and whispered something in his ear.

"Refugees," Colin said. "Most of them from the north, I'll wager, since the war's still going on up there. Some might have fled from the army we faced in Galsbur. That one," his eyes darted to the red-haired man, "looks like one of the mountain folk."

"I have a feeling we won't find Lerryn here," Hierm said. They'd been on the road for a week and had learned precious little— a few reports of a man fitting the prince's description passing through the countryside, headed north and east, plus a recent tale of a group of farmers, led by a stranger on a warhorse, driving off bandits that had been waylaying travelers on the road to Wilham.

"So do I, but someone here might have seen him or heard rumors." Colin's dark eyes scanned the crowd as if the prince might be found there. "Supplies will likely be expensive and hard to come by, but I suppose I should at least try. Foraging will be difficult as we get closer to the battle lines. The land will likely have been picked clean."

"We can take care of that if you like," Hair offered.

Colin shook his head. "I have a bit more experience at this than you do. Plus, I'm less likely to be robbed than the three of you." It was a measure of the force of Colin's personality as much as the young men's regard for his prowess that none of them disagreed.

"We'll ask after Lerryn," Hierm said.

"There's an inn up ahead. I'll meet you in the common room." Colin took the pack horse and rode off down the lane.

Hierm led the way to the inn, where they dismounted and tied their horses to the hitch by the front steps. A blocky man armed with a cudgel stood at the bottom of the steps. He looked them up and down for a moment, and then stepped aside.

"I'll keep an eye on your horses," he said.

"Thank you. Can I pay you for your trouble?" Hierm reached for his belt pouch.

"I'm a peacekeeper, not a servant." The man spat on the ground. "Just don't stir up any trouble and we'll be square."

"Wouldn't dream of it," Hair said smoothly and swept up the steps, the others following along behind.

The common room was almost empty. Two weedy men in travel-stained cloaks hunched over mugs of ale, speaking in low tones. Nearby, a burly man sat turning a cup in his hands and gazing out the dirty window. Something about the man looked familiar to Hierm, but before he could consider the matter further, a chubby serving girl interrupted his thoughts.

"Can I get something for M'Lord? Anything at all?" She flashed a gap-toothed smile and scooted in close so that her ample breasts brushed against his shoulder.

"Ale," he said, feeling his cheeks burn. "For all of us."

"Any food for you?" she asked. "We've got some vegetable stew and day-old bread."

"That will be fine."

"There won't be nothing else?" She gave him a wink. When he shook his head, she thrust out her lip. "Too bad. If you change your mind later tonight, I sleep upstairs— the little room at the end of the hall."

Hierm didn't know what to say to that, so he sat quietly and endured his friends' good-natured ribbing.

"Since she seems to have taken a liking to you, you can be the one to ask her if she's seen the prince." Hair ran a hand absently over his head and frowned. His formerly long hair for which he had earned his nickname was still far from short; it nearly touched his shoulders but was a far cry from its former length. "I can't wait until I graduate the academy and can grow my hair again."

"I don't know how you stood wearing it so long," Edrin said. "I couldn't bear my neck getting so hot."

"They wear it even longer on the other side of the Sun Sands," Hair said.

"And you crossed the Sun Sands when, exactly?" Hierm asked.

Hair made a rude hand gesture.

"Now then, you shouldn't treat M'Lord so." The serving girl had returned, bearing four mugs of ale.

"Who is the fourth mug for?" Hierm asked.

"An extra for you, M'Lord. Unless you want to invite me to sit down." She pursed her lips and fixed him with what he supposed was intended to be a smoldering look, but came off as more of a confused frown.

Hierm cursed his fair complexion as he felt himself blush again. He cleared his throat and sat up straighter. "That's a grand idea," he said, remembering he needed to extract information from her. "Sit down and take your ease."

"Oh." Now it was her turn to blush. "I'm sorry, M'Lord. I was only teasing. The master would have my head if I consorted with patrons while I was on the job." She emphasized the last three words.

"That is regrettable," Hierm agreed.

"I'm willing to make it up to you later." She rested her elbows on the table, pushing up her cleavage until Hierm feared it would break free from the fabric that struggled to hold it back.

"You can begin making it up to me right now," he said. "What is your name?"

"Sandra, M'Lord."

"Well, Sandra, first of all, you can stop calling me 'Lord.' That's my father, not me." He faltered for an instant, the still-fresh grief from the news of his Lord

Hiram's death washed over him.

Sandra nodded uncertainly.

"We are traveling north and east, and we are concerned about our safety. What have you heard about the towns and villages in that direction?"

"Well, there's bandits, of course. Mostly soldiers who abandoned their posts for easier pickings in the countryside. Some manner of fighting going on, too, or so I hear."

"So we stand a good chance of running into the Kyrinian or Galdoran armies should we travel much farther?" Hair took a sip of his ale and eyed her over his mug.

"Just the deserters causing trouble."

"So who's doing the fighting?" Hierm asked.

"According to the rumors, somebody's trained up a whole mess of common folk and they've been going about fighting the bandits and deserters. Got their own little army, they do."

"Are you sure?" Edrin asked.

Sandra shrugged. "Some of the locals have gone off to join up— those too young or too old to fight in the regular army. One of them came back to buy supplies. He was in here this morning, him and a few others. They told me all about it."

"Who leads them?" Hierm's heart raced. This had to be Lerryn.

"A soldier. At least, he used to be. No one knows his name, but they say he's handsome as a god and fierce as a demon. His band has gotten so big he finally had to set up a headquarters. He's got them organized and trained, and he sends men all over trying to keep the countryside safe."

"Where is this headquarters?" Hierm demanded, sharper than he intended.

Before Sandra could reply, a voice cried out.

"They's trying to take your horses!"

The innkeeper, a carving knife in one hand, pointed out the window. "Quick! Markus is trying to hold them off."

Hierm sprang and ran for the door. Hair and Edrin followed.

Outside, Markus, the guard, stood beside the horses, swinging his cudgel in a wide arc, to keep the crowd at bay.

"These lords got plenty." The big red-haired man they'd seen earlier thrust an accusing finger at Markus' chest. "If they won't do for those of us that's in need, we'll take it for ourselves."

"We don't steal from one another in these parts. The constable's on his way," Markus said. "You'd best disperse before he and his men get here."

"Let him come!" another man shouted. "Him and two deputies ain't enough to stop all of us."

"They won't be alone!" Hierm said. He descended the steps and moved to stand next to Markus with Edrin and Hair flanking them.

The red-haired man's eyes took them all in. "You think there's enough of you to stop us?"

Hierm assessed the situation. They were badly outnumbered. No one would blame him if he drew his sword. Or would they?"

A stone flew through the air and grazed his temple, cutting his contemplation short. He reached for his sword, but the red-haired man was on him in a flash, knocking him backward. Hierm brought his knees to his chest and kicked out, knocking the man to the side. He rolled to his feet, ducked a wild punch, and drove his fist into his assailant's gut. The man was solidly built, and the punch had little effect.

Hierm tried to dodge a second punch, but the tightly packed crowd made movement difficult. The man's fist caught him a glancing blow above the ear, and he stumbled backward, struggling to keep his balance.

Everything seemed to move in slow motion. Markus flailed about with his cudgel. Hair sidestepped a man's charge and, with a deft move, threw his hip into the man and flipped him over his back, sending him flying through the air. Edrin had fought through a forest of grasping hands and retrieved his bow, which he'd left tied to his saddle. Unable to string it, he now held it like a staff, laying about with it as the crowd closed in on him.

Hierm grabbed his attacker by the hair, yanked the man's head down, and drove his knee into the man's nose. The attacker cried out in pain but kept fighting. He wrapped his arms around Hierm's waist and drove him to the ground. Hierm's breath left him in a rush, and he struggled to raise his arms to defend himself against the blows that now rained down on him. The situation was hopeless. They were going to die here at the hands of this desperate mob.

And then, someone flew through the air and knocked Hierm's assailant to the ground. Hierm froze for an instant, and then recognized the man they'd seen in the common room— the one who'd looked familiar. The man didn't offer to help Hierm to his feet but looked around for someone to fight. He lashed out with tight, compact punches and elbow strikes that broke teeth, crushed noses, and set knees to wobbling. He was like a boulder rolling downhill. No one could stand in his way.

Hierm regained his feet, sucking in deep breaths, and looked around. Though a few men still struggled, most of the mob was drawing back. Over the ringing in his ears he heard a deep voice shouting out.

"Stand down or we'll thump your skulls for you!" A hollow thud and a cry of pain underscored this proclamation.

The few remaining fighters broke free of one another and stepped back. Three men clad all in purple waded through the crowd. Each carried a cudgel and wore a length of rope and a long knife at his waist. The man in the lead, a short, blocky man with shoulders like a blacksmith, wore a gold starburst pinned to his tunic. The constable had arrived.

The attackers who remained on their feet all broke and ran, but neither the constable nor his deputies tried to stop them. The constable stopped in front of Markus, tucked his thumbs in his belt, and looked the man up and down.

"What have we here?" The constable's voice betrayed no emotion.

"The crowd tried to steal these horses," Markus said. "At least, they wanted the men's supplies. We tried to keep them back; didn't use no blades or nothing."

The constable surveyed the scene. Three men lay unconscious. Two others were awake but too injured to rise. Hierm and his friends were battered and, in Edrin's case, bleeding, but appeared reasonably hale.

"No blades," the constable repeated. "That's good. Otherwise, I'd be forced to…"

"Constable!" one of the deputies barked. "We've got a dead man here. Somebody crushed his skull."

Hierm looked at the man who lay at the deputy's feet— a man whom he had assumed was unconscious. Sure enough, the side of his skull had been caved in. Trickles of blood flowed from his ear and nose.

"Perhaps one of your men did that with his cudgel?" The man from the common room, the one who had intervened on their side, offered.

"A cudgel didn't do this," the deputy said. "It was a stone. A big, round one. See how his head's dented in a circle?"

"None of us used a rock," Markus said. "But some of the mob was throwing them."

"It's us, now, is it?" The constable rocked back on his heels. "You know these men?"

"They're paying customers. They caused no trouble until the mob stirred things up." The innkeeper said from his position at the top of the steps. His pristine apron indicated he'd watched the fight from the safety of his inn.

"Be that as it may, can either of you say for certain who did or did not pick up a rock and club somebody?" The constable looked from the innkeeper to Markus. Both paused for a moment before shaking their heads.

"All right, then. I'm going to ask you all to come with me. I would take it as a kindness if you didn't try to flee, otherwise, my deputy on the roof," he inclined his head toward the inn, "will have to waste a crossbow bolt on one of you and the three of us will be obliged to fight the rest."

"What about them?" Hierm made a sweeping gesture that took in all the men on the ground, plus the ones who had run away.

"We'll take them in as well," the constable said. "Drag them, rather. When they wake up, we'll question everyone and try to get to the bottom of things. Markus can stay. He couldn't very well have picked up a rock when he's got two hands on the cudgel. But I would appreciate some help getting the injured men to the jail."

Markus nodded.

"Now," the constable said to Hierm, "are you coming peaceful like, or are we going to fight?"

Hierm looked at Edrin and Hair, who shrugged. There was no point in fighting. Whether they went for their weapons or their horses, the deputies would be on them in an instant, and then there was the crossbowman on the roof to consider. "We'll come with you."

The constable smiled and gave a curt nod before turning a wary eye on the other man. "And you?"

The man looked up at the deputy on the roof, who appeared to have correctly identified him as the most dangerous of the four who were being arrested, and held his crossbow steady, trained on the man's chest.

"All right," he finally said, "I'll come. But I warn you— I'm a member of the prince's guard, and I won't abide injustice. Not for me nor any of these men."

Now Hierm recognized him. It was Tabars, Lerryn's second in command. Was he searching for Lerryn too?

"You have my word," the constable said. "Now, if you'll all drop to your knees and place your hands behind your backs?"

They did as they were told. One deputy hastily bound their wrists while the other used a single length of rope to string them together, securing it around each man's ankles, leaving only enough room for them to waddle along.

"We'll tend to your horses and keep your possessions safe until this matter is disposed of," the constable said.

"How long will that be?" Tabars' quiet words dripped with malice.

"That all depends. If we get a confession, everyone else is free to go immediately. If we go to trial, we'll have to wait until the local lord makes his visit here. Shouldn't be more than three moons."

Hierm said nothing but his heart pounded in his chest. Three moons? What if, by the time they were released, Lerryn had moved on? Even worse, what if they weren't released at all? Unwilling to consider the possibility, he kept his chin up and focused on the back of Tabars' head as the deputies led them through the town and into the jail. It was not until the bars closed and locked behind him that he surrendered to the black thoughts.

Chapter 22

"I always knew you'd be the first of us raised to initiate." Naseeb clapped Dacio on the shoulder. "You know what this means, don't you?"

Dacio, still looking as shocked as he had when he'd been called away from dinner to face the masters, shrugged. "It doesn't mean much. I'll still take the same courses, sleep in the same bed, put up with the same annoying friends."

"No, you thickwit. When a man is raised to initiate, he buys the drinks," Naseeb said.

It took Dacio a moment to understand his meaning. "But novits aren't permitted to leave the Gates."

"We're supposed to sneak out with you," Whitt interjected. "It's such a long-standing tradition that it's practically expected."

Oskar shifted uncomfortably on the corner of his bed. Since the close call at the archives, he'd tried to stay out of trouble though he still met Lizzie a few nights a week. But, in that case, she was the one out of bounds, not him.

"I was just raised," Dacio said. "I don't want to lose my status the same night."

"You won't," Whitt assured him. "If anyone sees us, we'll tell them we went out on our own and that you tried to convince us to return. Besides, it's high time Oskar experienced Vatania." He turned a broad grin in Oskar's direction.

"What? You mean you have?" Oskar asked.

"Of course. Every novit sneaks out sooner or later, and I think your time has come."

An hour later, Oskar slipped over the wall that separated the forested outskirts of the Gates from the city. Beyond this wall stood a row of brick buildings, and beyond them, the smoky glow of the lamps and torches that lit the city streets.

He followed the others over the wall, along another alleyway, this one lined with broken cobblestones and smelling of sour wine and stale urine, and out onto the main street.

"I expected it to be..." Oskar began.

"Nicer? Cleaner? More majestic?" Naseeb asked.

"I suppose." After spending so much time at the Gates, Oskar had forgotten just how ragged and even dirty commoners looked. He immediately kicked himself for the thought. He was no noble; he was one of them. Was this how Larris and Allyn had thought of Oskar and his friends when they first met?

"This is Southgate," Whitt explained. "It's not the worst part of town, but you won't find a member of the Gates here."

"We're here," Oskar noted.

"Yes, but we're clever and devious." Naseeb swung an arm around Oskar's shoulders. "Now, let's go spend up Dacio's purse."

Oskar tried to maintain a stoic expression as they wandered the streets though he was eagerly taking it all in. This was, after all, only the second time in his life he'd been in a city. It wasn't that he cared what strangers thought of him, but he figured a young man who looked fresh off the farm would make a ripe target for pickpockets or worse.

The first tavern they visited stank of sweat and vomit. At the far end, a tired-looking man in a threadbare orange cloak plucked out a somber tune on his lute. Most of the patrons ignored him, conversing in loud, drunken voices. Oskar and his friends stayed long enough for Oskar to enjoy his first taste of vakka, a clear, white liquid that burned like the sun on its way down but left behind a pleasant, minty taste. Once he recovered from the first, scorching swallow, he was eager to try more.

"Oh no, my friend," Naseeb said. "The night is young and you have much yet to experience. Too many of these and you won't see anything else the rest of the night."

"Hold on. This is supposed to be my celebration." The expression of feigned offense on Dacio's face cracked into a grin almost immediately.

"And what better way to celebrate than to see our friend Oskar properly debauched?" Whitt pushed away from the table, tossed a copper at the foot of the lutenist, and headed for the door.

They wandered the streets, fending off oily men selling all manner of amusements, most of them alleged mind-altering liquids that Oskar suspected were little more than cheap, strong liquor mixed with a few herbs. The working girls were out in full force as well, and though Oskar had previously been exposed to their sisters in commerce on his visit to Karkwall, he still found himself blushing at their propositions.

As they rounded a corner, he noticed a couple, a young woman and a much older man, standing in the shadows. He knew he should look away from what was most likely an intimate business transaction, but his senses told him something wasn't right. The young woman stood with her back against the wall, her posture rigid. The man had his hands pressed against the wall on either side of her, keeping her in place. As his eyes adjusted to the darkness, Oskar saw the man's hungry look, and the expression of discomfort on the woman's face. And then his heart lurched and he veered toward them, closing the distance in a few steps.

"Lizzie!"

Lizzie looked up and the man turned slowly toward the sound of Oskar's voice.

"Find yourself another whore. This one is…" Oskar's fist stopped him in mid-sentence. His knees buckled and he hit the ground hard.

Lizzie gaped, and her eyes moved from the man on the ground up to Oskar's face.

And she slapped him hard across the ear, making his head ring.

"You stupid ox!" She emphasized each word with a punch to his chest. "I'm trying to work here."

"Work?" Had Oskar heard her correctly? His ears still rang from her slap. "I didn't know you sold yourself," he stammered.

This time, Lizzie slapped him on the other ear.

"You know better than that. He was my mark. I let him kiss me a little. Meanwhile, I make his purse a little lighter, and then make an excuse and slip away."

"Do you know how dangerous that is?"

"No, Oskar, I had no idea." Her tone was as flat as her stare. "I don't need help from you or any other man. I've been taking care of myself for a very long time." She knelt and scooped some coins out of the man's purse. The man began to stir, so she kicked him in the temple with the precision of a craftsman working at a delicate project. The man went limp again. "If I were you, I'd drag him into the alley and get out of here. I'm sure he didn't get a good look at you, but who can say for certain?"

Oskar looked down at the unconscious man and realized what he'd done. In his moment of anger and jealousy, he'd attacked someone. He could end up in jail for this, and then they'd turn him out of the Gates for certain.

"I'll do it. You should probably make yourself scarce. He knows exactly what *you* look like." He looked up and was surprised to see that Lizzie was already gone.

"We'll help you," Whitt said. Now that the fight, if that's what it had been, with Lizzie was over, his friends had come to join him. "Someone get his legs." Whitt grabbed the limp man under his arms while Naseeb held his ankles and they carried him away. When they returned a few moments later, they were laughing.

"It isn't funny," Dacio said. "And Oskar's girl was right. We should get away from here and fast."

"Not funny?" Whitt said as they started walking. "Oskar the book-loving farmer can't spend one evening in the city without getting into a brawl and getting slapped by a beautiful woman. That's funny."

"Also, I tied his ankles together," Naseeb said. "He can untie it in a thrice, but he'll fall on his face at least once before he knows it's there." He turned to Oskar. "Are you going to tell us who that girl was?"

Oskar shook his head. "I guess she's no one to me anymore. Evidently she hates me."

"Hardly," Dacio said. "If she didn't care for you, she wouldn't have gotten so angry with you."

Oskar frowned. "That makes no sense."

"Only because you know nothing about women," Dacio said in a matter-of-fact tone. "But what do I know? I live in a castle filled with men, and my roommates are the ugliest bunch of blighters this side of the Ice Reaches."

They continued to tease Oskar as they wended their way through the dark streets. He didn't mind. Being ribbed over problems with a girl was a new experience for him, even if he didn't know what he was to Lizzie, if anything at all, now that he'd incurred her wrath.

Up ahead, the sky glowed with the collected light of what must have been a hundred or more lamps. Drawing closer, he saw that the lamps ringed a pit around which a crowd had gathered in a roped-off area. Whatever was happening in the pit had their full interest, and they cheered, groaned, and roared as they watched.

"They're fighting tonight." Whitt quickened his pace. "Excellent."

A dark man, as broad as he was tall, collected a coin from each of them and drew the rope aside so they might enter.

"Any of you going to be fighting?" the man asked.

"Perhaps," Whitt said.

"If you do, you get your copper back," he said.

Privately, Oskar thought he'd pay more than a copper to *avoid* a fight. He endured enough bruises in training. What was this all about, anyway?

They worked their way into the crowd until they could see down into the pit. The sloped sides were roped off halfway down, allowing the onlookers to move in closer without blocking others' views.

Inside the pit, two men, sweaty and bleeding, circled one another. One man, a pale fellow with a scarred, shaved head, held his meaty fists low and gasped for breath. The second, a man with light brown skin and glossy black hair, was lean and frail-looking compared to his opponent, but clearly had more energy. He feinted with his left hand and when his opponent raised his own hands to block, lashed out with a vicious kick to the liver. The crowd "oohed" and, for a moment, shaved-head stood frozen. Then, agony spread across his face and he crumpled to the ground. The brown man moved in and landed a series of punches to his fallen opponent's head before a man in a red tunic hauled him off and waved him away.

The winner raised his hands in triumph as cheers and coins rained down on him. After enjoying the accolades for a few moments, he stooped and gathered up the coins. Nearby, the loser had regained his feet and Oskar was surprised to see a number of coins lying at his feet as well.

"Why are they throwing money to him? He lost."

"The money isn't necessarily given to the winner; it's sort of a way of praising a man for fighting well," Whitt explained. "It's rare, but sometimes the loser gets more money than the winner if the crowd prefers his style of fighting or his effort."

"People think this is fun?" Oskar grimaced. He didn't see the appeal.

"Only the uncivilized among us." Dacio frowned at Whitt. "This is supposed to be my celebration or have you forgotten?"

"We won't stay long. Only until I've had the chance to earn a few coins." Whitt moved to the rope and waved his arm until he had the attention of the man in red, who nodded and beckoned for him to come on.

"What is he doing? Is he bereft of his senses?" Oskar turned pleading eyes on his friends. "We've got to stop him."

"Go ahead. Go down there and drag him out." Naseeb laughed. "Of course, the crowd will probably tear you apart for interfering with the fights, but it's your choice."

Oskar hesitated. Really, there was nothing he could do. He was Whitt's friend, not his father. The best he could offer was to cheer his friend on and hope for the best. He held his breath as the contest began.

Whitt came in low, hands raised. The dark-skinned man circled, lashing out with quick punches that Whitt blocked with ease. Whitt threw a haymaker, and his opponent dodged it and stung Whitt with a sharp kick to the calf, grinning all the while.

Oskar groaned. Whitt was obviously too slow and sloppy to win. This promised to be an ugly contest, and painful to watch.

As the match continued, nothing changed his mind. The brown man circled while Whitt lumbered after him, occasionally swinging a meaty fist that never quite found its target. His opponent peppered him with jabs that Whitt managed to block with his thick arms, and kicks to the leg that didn't appear to faze Whitt, but must have been painful.

As the slow dance continued, the crowd grew impatient, and soon the onlookers began hurling insults down on the competitors.

"Fight, you snow-blighted cowards!" one particularly drunk man bellowed. A few others took up the cry.

The words had no visible effect on Whitt, who endured much worse abuse from Master Lang during combat training, but his opponent took notice.

The man struck with blinding fury, his lightning fast strikes stinging Whitt like a swarm of hornets. A few found their marks, but most did no damage. In a matter of seconds, the man's energy ebbed, and he circled away. His chest heaved and sweat poured off of him, the droplets forming tiny craters in the dust at his feet.

Whitt struck. With a speed he had not previously displayed, he caught his tired opponent up by one leg and bore him to the ground. In a flash, Whitt straddled the man and pounded his elbow again and again into the man's unprotected temple.

It was over in a matter of seconds. The man lay unconscious in the dust and Whitt stood with his arms upraised, fists clenched, soaking in the adoration of the onlookers who had only moments before called him a coward or worse. Coins flew through the air and he scooped them up and filled his purse. He pushed his way through the crowd, most of whom were calling for him to fight again, and made his way back to his friends.

"You look surprised," he said to Oskar. "You didn't think I could take him?"

"Things appeared to be pretty grim there for a while."

Whitt threw back his head and laughed. "How many combat classes have we taken together? Surely you knew I wasn't really that slow."

The truth was, between trying to catch up to the other students and watching over his shoulder for Agen and his cronies, Oskar had little attention to spare for others in class. He had no idea what Whitt was capable of in combat.

"Never mind." Whitt held up his purse, now heavy with coin. "Let's spend some of these good people's money."

Whitt chose a nearby alehouse where two young men, one tall with broad shoulders and red hair, the other dark-haired and wiry, performed. One juggled while the other played the flute. They weren't bad, but Oskar had a feeling neither would ever make court bard.

By his second tankard of ale, the world became an absolutely delightful place. His worries were soon forgotten as Oskar basked in the joys of music, conversation, and friendship. The yearning for adventure and knowledge that had ached within him all his life were gone. It was remarkable that he, a poor farm boy, would find himself here in the greatest city in Gameryah.

"Excuse me, sir. Would you care to dance?"

Though ale clouded his thoughts, he knew that voice immediately. He looked up to see Lizzie standing over him, but she looked very different. Gone was her tight, utilitarian clothing. She now wore a blood red dress that showed far too much of her breasts and calves. She'd scrubbed her face clean and applied some of the face paint that rich women and whores used to make their cheeks pink and their lips crimson. She wore her glossy black hair down over her shoulders. All around him, he saw men staring at her. He couldn't blame them. She was beautiful.

"Well? Are we going to dance, or should I find someone else?" Already, a few men had stood and were moving in her direction.

Oskar stood, wobbled a bit from too much drink, and put a hand on the table to steady himself. He was surprised two tankards had done this to him, but then he remembered the vakka he'd drunk earlier. It was potent stuff. The drink dizzied but also emboldened him. "I would love to dance with you." He put an arm around her waist and pulled her close so he could whisper in her ear. "But you will have to teach me how."

She laughed and led him to the front of the room where a handful of couples and a single, extremely drunk, old man, danced a jig. Lizzie guided him through the steps, and he found that, despite his condition, he wasn't entirely hopeless on the dance floor. Combat training had improved his coordination and made him if not exactly nimble of foot, moderately coordinated.

After a few dances, they retired to a table in the corner. Smiling inwardly at the envious glances cast in his direction by almost every man in the place, Oskar ordered wine, but barely sipped his. His head was clearing and he hated the befuddled feeling that came with too much drink.

"Where did you get the dress?" he finally asked, mostly because he couldn't think of anything else to say.

"I killed a woman and stripped it off her dead body. It took me a while to find someone wearing one just the color of blood. That way, the stains don't show. Cutting someone's throat is a messy business." She took a small sip of wine and gazed at Oskar over her cup.

His lips moved, but he couldn't speak. How could such evil lurk behind those beautiful blue eyes?

Lizzie broke into laughter. "You're so gullible. It's simply too easy with you."

"What? You mean you didn't kill anyone?"

"Of course not. I stole it a long time ago. I didn't think I'd ever have a reason to wear it, but I took it anyway." She paused. "Do you like me this way?"

"No. I mean, yes, you're beautiful, but…" He couldn't find the words.

"But what? Isn't this the way you want me to be? A helpless little girl who needs a big, strong man to protect her so she doesn't get her dress dirty?"

Now it was Oskar's turn to laugh. "You are more like my friend Shanis than I realized. I understand. I shouldn't have tried to rescue you."

"You're right. You shouldn't have. I walked all the way here dressed like this and didn't feel unsafe for a moment. I can handle myself better in a city than you'll ever be able to."

"Please know, I didn't do it because you're a woman." His cheeks burned and he took a long drink of wine solely for an excuse to break eye contact with her. When he finally set his cup down, she was still staring at him.

"I'm waiting."

It was as if the ice had frozen his tongue. He could not form a single word.

Under the table, Lizzie tapped her foot. Finally, she sighed and stood and looked down at him in amusement. "I'm leaving now. Alone. If you try to follow me out of some misplaced desire to keep me safe, you will never see me again. I don't need you. Not in that way." She moved around the table and leaned down to whisper in his ear. "But I do love you." She kissed him softly, eliciting a few hoots and whistles from men at nearby tables.

Oskar watched in stunned disbelief as she wove her way gracefully through the common room and out the door. As if in a trance, he wandered back to the table where his friends sat.

"I told you," Dacio said.

"I can't believe you let her go after that kiss," Whitt said.

"I had to. She said if I followed her, I'd never see her again."

"In that case, I'd better follow her." Naseeb rose to his feet.

"I really don't think she needs us," Oskar said. "She knows how to take care of herself."

"It's not her safety I'm worried about," Naseeb said. "I just spotted Agen and his lackeys. They're following her."

Oskar sprang to his feet, all worries about Lizzie's ire forgotten, but when he reached the street, she was gone and Agen and his friends were strolling along, chatting amiably. As they walked by, Agen looked in Oskar's direction and smiled. Oskar didn't know what that meant, but he was sure it wasn't good.

Chapter 23

Hierm's eyes flew open as a loud clang jolted him from his half-daze. He looked up to see the jailer, a veritable beast of a man with broad shoulders and no neck, standing silhouetted against the lamplight from the front room.

"Time to eat," the jailer rumbled. He pushed a small, greasy sack and a water skin between the bars.

"Why, it's just like dining in the common room of the finest inn in Galdora," Hair said, "though the serving girls are not nearly as attractive here."

Hierm managed a smile. "Let's see what's on the menu." He opened the bag and saw four crusts of bread and four strips of dried meat. He took his share and passed it to Tabars, who also took his bread and meat and offered it to Edrin, who shook his head.

"Eat," Tabars said. "I want you at full strength for when we get out of here."

Edrin reluctantly accepted the food and passed the bag along to Hair.

Hierm tore off a chunk of bread and chewed it slowly. The single cell in which the four of them sat was scarcely large enough to hold them all. Outside, the jailer sat down in a wooden chair, propped his feet on a stout table, folded his arms across his chest, and stared resolutely at the front door.

"Speaking of getting out of here," Edrin said around a mouthful of bread, "do you have any ideas about how we're going to manage that?"

Tabars shook his head. "Not yet."

"How about the window?" Edrin glanced up at the small, barred window set in the back wall.

"No good. Even if we had a chisel, it would take all summer to chip away enough stone and mortar to remove the bars, and even then none of us are small enough to slip through." He took a swallow of water. "The only way I can see is to get the jailer to open the door, or at least get the keys away from him and then overcome him, but looking at him, I'm not sure even the four of us together are up to the task."

"There's one thing I like about him." Hair pointed at the jailer. "He's proved to me that the stories are true. Trolls do exist."

Hierm and Edrin snickered, but Tabars remained deep in thought.

"The constable's not such a big fellow," he finally said. "I believe I could take him if he's alone and unarmed, but he didn't impress me as being foolish enough to give me the chance." He heaved a sigh and leaned back against the stone wall. "Let's get some rest. Perhaps I'll manage to dream up an escape plan."

They lapsed into a dark silence, but no one slept.

Hierm wasn't certain how much time had passed, but after what felt like hours, Hair rose and moved to inspect the bars that kept them in.

"There's got to be a way," Hair whispered.

"I think there is," someone said in a low voice.

Hierm looked up and saw a familiar face peering through the window. Colin!

Tabars stood. "I remember you from the battle."

"And I you. Here, take these." Colin slid a hammer and chisel between the bars.

Tabars chuckled. "I can't break out with these."

"I don't need you to break out," Colin said. "I need you to create a distraction. You'll know when it's time."

"Very well." Tabars took the hammer and chisel and turned to face the others. "When this starts, you three stay away from that jailer. I don't want you tangling with him. Leave him for me."

Hierm privately thought that, if it came to a fight, he'd do his best to help though he didn't know how much difference he'd make. He picked up the food bag and twisted it nervously in his hands.

From the front room, a sharp knock sounded at the door, and the jailer sprang to his feet, upending his chair.

"Who's there?"

"Constable needs you." Colin's muffled voice scarcely carried to their jail cell. "There's a ruckus in the refugee camps. We can't settle them without you."

The jailer took two steps toward the front door and then hesitated.

"Constable says I ain't never to leave when we've got prisoners. Not never."

Hierm's heart sank. So the jailer wasn't quite as stupid as he looked.

"I know," Colin said from the other side of the door, "but this time he says he really needs you. I'm to watch them while you go knock some heads."

A wicked grin slowly spread across the jailer's face. He turned and looked at his prisoners. "I don't suppose they're going anywhere." He turned and reached to unlock the door, but froze. "Wait a second. Who are you? You don't sound like you're from around here."

"That's it. He's not going to open the door." Tabars turned to the window and began hammering.

"What's that racket?" the jailer yelled. "What are you doing in there?" He turned and stalked toward them, looking every bit the troll Hair had called him earlier. He stopped short of the cell, saw what Tabars was doing, and chuckled. "Give me those. Don't make me come in there and take them away from you." He frowned as realization slowly dawned on him. "Hold on. Where did you get those?"

Just then, something slammed into the front door. The jailer slowly wheeled about. Another crash and the door flew open and Colin burst into the jail. The distraction had bought him enough time to get inside.

With surprising speed for a man his size, Colin closed the distance between himself and the jailer. He threw his shoulder into the jailer's chest, knocking him back against the bars, and followed up with a solid punch to the brute's jaw.

Hierm saw his chance. While Colin pummeled the jailer with a flurry of kicks and punches, Hierm reached through the bars and yanked the food sack down over the man's head. The jailer roared in anger and thrashed about, trying to pull the bag free, but Hierm held on tight.

With the jailer's hands occupied, Colin now had an easy target. He lashed out with a vicious kick to the larger man's groin and followed with another to the kidney. The jailer cried out in pain and wobbled, struggling to maintain his feet. Colin now aimed a precise kick to the side of the man's knee, buckling it. The jailer sat down heavily, grabbing at his injured joint, but Colin put an end to his struggled with a kick to the temple, rendering him unconscious. He relieved the brute of his keys and opened the cell.

"We must hurry. It's the middle of the night, but there's a chance someone heard me knock the door in."

"He's got our weapons." The words nearly stuck in Hierm's throat and came out in a croak. He found himself uncomfortable around Colin. All his life, Shanis' father had been the soft-spoken man who patiently endured Shanis' monumental fits of temper. He'd never suspected the man possessed such deadly skill.

Colin nodded and hurried to the front room where he opened a strongbox and retrieved their belongings, while Tabars, Edrin, and Hair dragged the jailer into the cell and bound and gagged him with strips torn from the food bag. Colin locked the man inside and hung the keys on a hook by the desk.

"He won't be out for long. Follow me, and don't make a sound." Leaving the candle on the desk burning, he led them out into the damp night and closed the broken door behind them as best he could.

Hierm felt as if a target had been painted on his back. He felt that at any moment someone would raise a cry or loose an arrow at them. His heart pounded with such force that he imagined it would wake everyone in town. It was not until they passed through a thick patch of forest and emerged into a clearing where their horses waited that he allowed himself to relax.

"How did you manage to recover our horses?" he asked.

Colin smiled. "I have a way with horses and I can move at night without being seen or heard." He raised his hand, forestalling further questions. "There is no time. I mean to be well clear of this place by sunrise."

They walked their horses in silence until Colin gave the signal, and then they mounted up.

"Where to now?" Hair asked as he swung up onto his horse.

"I collected a few rumors in town," Colin said, "and I think we're close to catching up with Lerryn."

Chapter 24

A thick blanket of clouds shrouded the moon. Oskar sat on the roof of the archives building, gazing down at the city. The twinkle of lights from houses far below looked like tiny stars, and he imagined for a moment that he was a god looking down on his creation. He managed a rueful grin. Such a thought must have stemmed from his choice of reading material.

He'd been sitting here three nights running, reading *Godwars* and hoping Lizzie would show up. So far, she had not. Perhaps tonight would be the night.

He summoned the tiny ball of blue light, making it just bright enough for him to read, but not so bright that he would be spotted from any distance, and opened his book. He quickly found himself drawn in by the details of the legendary war. With all the things that had changed in his life, his love of books had remained a constant. The words on the page came to life in his mind and he could imagine himself there in the midst of it all.

He'd only read for a short while when he found himself yanked back to reality by what he read.

"This isn't right," he said.

"Talking to yourself again?"

He jumped and dropped his book, but managed to catch it before it slid away.

"Stop doing that to me. One of these days, I'm going to fall off and it will be your fault."

"One of these days you'll learn to keep your eyes and ears open. You never know who or what might be sneaking up behind you." Lizzie sat down beside him, pulled her knees to her chest, and laid her head on his shoulder.

Oskar tensed. He knew it was wrong for him to let things continue with Lizzie. Their feelings for one another were growing stronger. She had told him she loved him, and he thought he felt the same way, but he was going to be a saikur, and that left no room for a woman in his life; not even one as beautiful as Lizzie.

She caught him staring at her. "I can tell you've got something on your mind. What is it?"

He hesitated. What should he say to her? His first impulse was to tell her how he felt about her, but how he felt and what he knew he ought to feel for her were at odds. Would he be doing her any kindness by sharing his feelings, knowing he could never act upon them?

"Lizzie, how much do you know about saikurs?"

"I know they're stuffy old men who wear ugly brown cloaks." She flicked the sleeve of Oskar's cloak. "And they spend entirely too much time with their noses buried in books. At least, one of them does." She looked meaningfully at Oskar's book.

Oskar managed a smile. "I'm not a saikur yet, but I hope to be."

"That's nice." She cast a thoughtful look at him. "So, what do you people do, exactly? Besides walk around and look self-important, I mean."

"Lots of things. It depends on your field of study. Some of us become healers, others scholars."

Lizzie pretended to yawn and then dropped her head onto his shoulder and pretended to fall asleep. "Boring."

"We don't all have boring jobs. Some are warriors, others travel the world, gathering knowledge or working as ambassadors."

Now Lizzie perked up. "That's a little better. I think you should be one of those. When do we leave?"

Oskar's insides fluttered at the word "we." Thief or no, for such a beautiful girl to think the two of them could have a future together... Well, it wasn't something he'd ever thought would happen to him. But he knew it couldn't be.

"Lizzie, a saikur can't ever get married."

She threw back her head and laughed. "Who said anything about getting married?"

"That's how it's done in the town where I grew up. You find someone you," he swallowed hard, "love and you get married."

Lizzie raised an eyebrow. "Look around you. Are you in your village anymore?"

He looked out at the night-blanketed city and then at Lizzie, and shook his head. "I suppose not."

Lizzie sighed. "I declare, it's going to take everything I've got to whip you into shape. I'll try to explain this to you, so listen carefully. When you are finally a seeker, or whatever you call yourselves, you're going to take me with you. We're going to see the world together. I'll watch your back and I'll be your companion."

She put an emphasis on the last word that sent a tingle through parts of his body he preferred not to think about at the moment. He shifted uncomfortably and continued to gaze into her eyes.

"That is," she began, wrapping her arms around his neck, "unless you don't want me."

His resolve crumbled. "I love you," he blurted.

"Why wouldn't you?" she teased. "I'm lovable." She pushed him onto his back and smothered him with kisses.

Some time later, it might have been minutes or hours for all his muddled mind could gather, they lay side by side looking up at the night sky. Lizzie's head rested on his arm, which had gone numb, but he didn't want her to move. Not ever. He lay there, feeling her warmth pressed against him and listening to the soft sounds of her breathing, and wondering how long it would take him to become a full-fledged saikur. Would she wait for him?

Lizzie finally broke the silence. "Does the moon look different in other parts of the world?"

"It's the same no matter where you go. It goes through the same cycles and everything."

"Cycles?" she asked.

"You know: full moon, half-moon, sickle moon."

Lizzie rolled onto her side, facing him. "And they're the same wherever you go? That's disappointing. You educated people take all the wonder out of the world."

"Not all the wonder," he said. "I once faced down a golorak and accidentally called down lightning on it." Seeing her confused frown, he told her about the creature that could best be described as a giant frog with a tough hide and razor sharp teeth. Before he could tell the story of how he'd dispatched one of them, she punched his chest.

"That's not a true story. Stop winding me up." She pressed a finger to his lips and shushed him before he could protest. "I'm not listening, so don't bother. If it were a true story, you would have told me before now."

"It never came up before," he protested. "It's not as if I killed it on purpose, so it wasn't heroic. Back then I didn't even know I was capable of sorcery."

Lizzie's expression grew serious. "It doesn't really matter to me, you know."

"What doesn't?"

"What you choose to do. I know how you feel about your books, and I'll still love you even if you decide to be a boring old librarian instead of an adventurer. Of course, we won't get to spend as much time alone together if you're a librarian as we will if we go on the road."

Oskar felt his face turn scarlet and hoped she couldn't see.

"Speaking of books, what are you reading?" She picked up his book and held it up in the moonlight.

He scowled and considered pressing the issue of the golorak, but decided against it. One day she would meet his friends and they would confirm the story. "It's called *Godwars*," he finally said.

"What's it about?"

Oskar frowned. "Um, it's about the Godwars."

Lizzie punched him again. "I know that, you ox. I mean, what's happening in the part you're reading now? Something in there got your attention just as I arrived. Whatever it was, you said it made no sense."

It took him a moment to remember what he'd been thinking about before she and her soft lips had interrupted him. "It's the final Godwar. It just... ended."

"That was a good thing, right? I mean, the songs all tell of the death and destruction the wars wrought."

"But wars don't just end. They wind down. There are negotiations, battles won and lost, concessions made, treaties signed. But that didn't happen here. Best I can tell, the rulers of all the nations disappeared, never to return again, and soon afterward, everyone lost the will to fight and just went home. But that's not the strangest part."

"What is?"

"The gods disappeared too. One day they're leading armies, shifting alliances, and battling one another; the next, they're gone. And I mean gone."

Lizzie looked up at the sky and tugged at her ponytail as she considered this. "You're saying there are no more gods?"

"I don't know. They haven't been seen since. What's more, magic comes from the gods. Before the Godwars, and during them, people could do amazing things with magic, but since the gods disappeared, we can do very little."

"But you can still do magic, so the gods are still around," Lizzie said.

"Right. At least, that makes the most sense, but it seems like they're far away or something."

"Why are you reading about the Godwars, anyway?"

"I've been trying to learn more about the Silver Serpent. I thought it was created before or during the Godwars, but there's no mention of it."

"You said your friend Shanis already has the Silver Serpent, so what does it matter?" Lizzie asked.

"I don't know," he admitted. "Aspin told me to research it. He thinks the Silver Serpent holds the key to stopping the next Frostmarch."

Lizzie shivered and snuggled up against him and he pulled her close. "I thought the Frostmarch was a fairy tale. I guess not, huh?"

Oskar shook his head.

"In that case, I suppose you should keep looking. I still think this Aspin fellow owes you a better explanation. You aren't his slave."

"I'm a novit and he's a saikur. Besides, I've always had someone telling me what to do: my parents, the Van Derins, and here at the Gates it seems like everyone gets to tell me what to do. It feels natural to me."

"If you're good at following instructions, that bodes well for me," Lizzie said.

"I don't suppose you're answerable to anyone, are you?"

"I wouldn't say that. It's true I have more freedom than you, but we thieves hold one another accountable through the guild. We can't step on one another's toes. I work the stretch between Beggar's Cove and the Red Way. I can't work anywhere else unless I'm reassigned. I'm mostly a rooftop girl. I slip inside houses and take what I want, but I also pick pockets from time to time. I'm not allowed to do anything that would call undue attention to my neighborhood. I can't steal too much from the same person, and I can't slit throats unless it's in defense of my life. If I think someone needs killing, I have to take my case to the guild. They get to decide, and if they agree with me, they'll send an assassin to do it. I'm not allowed."

Oskar found it almost inconceivable that such talk could come from a beautiful girl like Lizzy, but he supposed people could grow accustomed to anything. He remembered the Lothans, who thought of war the way he thought of a rainy day—a simple, often unfortunate, fact of life.

"Are you free to leave Vatania?" he asked. "Or will the guild try to stop you?"

Lizzie considered this. "I am allowed to leave, but if I do I can never come back. We keep an eye on one another's comings and goings. If one of our number starts meeting with the wrong sorts, we know about it. If one of us leaves, however, we have no way of knowing what he or she has been up to or for whom that person might be working. So if you leave, you don't come back. It is known."

"Do they know you've been meeting with me?"

"Doubtful. I'm good, you see, and I've never once given cause for suspicion. But if they knew, they'd definitely keep a closer eye on me. Of course, the Gates doesn't care about things like local crime. It's the constables, soldiers, and petty functionaries I need to avoid. Unless I'm cutting their purses." She flashed a wicked grin.

"Speaking of people to avoid, there's something I need to tell you." He told her about Agen trying to follow her.

Lizzie sat upright. "One of your weird magical friends was after me and you didn't do anything?"

"He's not my friend." Oskar felt that declaring Agen his sworn enemy would be a touch too melodramatic, so he left it at that. "And I did follow him, but when I got outside, he had already lost sight of you."

"I told you not to follow me," she said. "And you ignored my wishes?"

Now Oskar was completely flustered. "But you just said…"

Lizzie laughed. "You're too easy, you know that? I'll keep an eye out for him, but I'm not easy to catch." She looked out at the horizon, where the thin, gray line of the sea announced the sun's approach. "I'd better go. I have work to do and you need sleep." She brushed her lips against his cheek and then she was gone.

Chapter 25

Shanis looked down upon the open plain that surrounded Karkwall, the capital city of Lothan. Nothing stirred outside the city, but armed men stood guard upon its massive walls. This would be no easy battle. Even once they breached the city walls they would have to fight their way uphill and then break through a second ring of fortifications that protected the castle. The conquest would come at a steep price, but she supposed it must be paid.

"Those walls have never been breached," Krion said, staring out at the city.

"We will be the first," Horgris spoke as if it were a foregone conclusion.

"If we can find a way to do this without loss of life, we will," Shanis said. Their plan was to surround the city, keeping their troops out of range of the siege engines but in plain sight. Hopefully, once Orbrad realized he had no hope of victory, he would surrender. "Surely Orbrad will see reason."

"From what I've heard, Orbrad and reason do not go well together," Heztus chuckled.

"Neither did Malgog and Monaghan until now." Shanis scowled at the dwarf who quickly adopted a look of contrition.

Her forces began to take up their positions all around the city and soon hammering filled the air as they began construction of the siege towers and catapults that would be used in the assault.

It was not long before the city gates opened and a group of riders approached bearing a flag of truce.

"Horgris and I will see what they have to say," Krion said.

"I'm going too."

"Are you insane?" Heztus blurted. "Even if we meet them well out of range of their archers they have catapults, ballistae. It would take only one lucky shot to kill you and I don't doubt for a second they would sacrifice their own men if it meant killing you."

"Gillen can protect me. She knows shielding spells." The young bone woman had agreed to join her and provide added protection. Despite her youth, she had proved to be highly intelligent and exceptionally powerful. "Besides, I have the sword."

Heztus frowned. "Tell me," he said softly. "Can you use that sword for something other than healing? I've never seen you do anything else with it."

"I could use it to cut off your head. It would spare me much annoyance."

Heztus laughed wickedly.

Shanis urged her horse forward before anyone else could try and talk her out of what she was about to do. It was not in her nature to sit back while others took action, and even something as simple as riding out to meet the king's envoys made her feel as if she were doing something.

The five men who came out to meet her were all soldiers. None appeared to be armed with anything other than a sword. As long as she kept her distance, they should pose no threat, especially when she had Gillen, Heztus, and three skilled warriors along with her.

"I don't see Orbrad," she said. "Tell me, where is your brave leader?"

"His Majesty would never condescend to grant an audience to a rebel, and an outlander at that," one of the soldiers snapped.

Horgris cursed and Krion silenced him with a hard look.

"I assume you have a message from him?" Shanis said.

"The King orders you to throw down your weapons and surrender." The soldier's cheeks reddened as Heztus and Horgris began to laugh. "He reminds you that no army has ever conquered this city. Only his mercy will save you. Do not throw away your lives for a hopeless cause.

The man's words were too close to her own thoughts for Shanis' liking, but she was now committed to this course of action and it was too late to change her mind.

"I have a message as well, not just for Orbrad, but for the entire city."

The soldier smirked. "We shall deliver your message to his Majesty, of course, but I doubt he will be willing to pass it along."

"No need. I can deliver it myself." She glanced at Gillen, who nodded and began to whisper softly. Shanis drew the Silver Serpent and lifted it high. "I am Shanis Malan." Her voice boomed like thunder, amplified by Gillen's spell. "I am descended from both Malgog and Monaghan, and I am the granddaughter of Badla. By right of blood, I declare myself Queen of Lothan."

The envoys from the city appeared surprised, even shaken, but whether it was due to her proclamation or the use of magic, she could not say. She sheathed her sword and they visibly relaxed.

"Anyone could make that claim," one of them muttered.

"Look at her," said another. "You can't deny the resemblance."

The voice was a familiar one. Shanis took a closer look at the soldier who had, until this moment, remained silent and kept his face hidden beneath his hood. She was surprised to recognize Martrin, a soldier who had helped her and her friends escape from Karkwall many months before. And he was a member of the Order of the Fox.

"That's hardly proof," the soldier who had been doing most of the talking said. "Besides, all Monaghan women look alike." His smile melted away as Horgris reached for his sword.

"You can no deny her courage," Horgris growled. "Unlike your play king, she stands in sight of your walls and makes her claim."

The soldier looked at Shanis. "We are wasting time. What are your demands?"

"Unconditional surrender. All soldiers will have a place in the new, united army of Lothan. I will rule with the help of a group of advisers, one from each clan, and one from the city. Karkwall may choose its own representative." She ignored the stares from her escorts whom she had not yet advised about that particular plan. "I further pledge safe conduct for Orbrad and his family to the country of his choosing."

"Impossible."

"Then I shall take my case to the people." Once again, she spoke in the magically enhanced voice. "Soldiers and citizens of Karkwall, your forces are woefully outnumbered. The clan wars are over and now the full might of Lothan stands before you. I do not wish for anyone to die. Open your gates to us and let us heal our broken nation."

"Foolishness," the soldier said. "I remind you again that no army has ever breached these walls."

Shanis smiled coldly. "None of them bore the Silver Serpent. Orbrad has until sunrise to open the gates. When the first ray of sun touches the walls, I will bring them down."

"We will give your message to His Highness," Martrin said, "though I imagine he has already heard what you have to say."

"You do that." Shanis wheeled her horse and rode away, all the while praying to the gods that the foolish King would see sense for the first time in his life.

Chapter 26

"It's almost morning." Gillen peeked her head through the tent flap. "We should make ready."

Shanis sat up and rubbed her head. Her sleep had once again been troubled by strange dreams in which the gods ran rampant across the earth.

"What's wrong?"

She shook her head. "Nothing, just tired." She glanced up at Gillen. "I don't know why it never occurred to me before, but you don't talk like a Monaghan."

Gillen smiled. "Thank you. I find people take me more seriously when I 'no do speak like this.'"

Shanis couldn't help but laugh. She dressed quickly and stepped out into the damp, chilly morning. Granlor, who had taken to sleeping outside her tent despite the presence of guards, was there waiting for her.

"I don't suppose Orbrad has opened the gates?" she asked.

"No, but it no be sunrise yet." They strode through the camp to where Horgris, Culmatan, and Krion sat by a campfire. They all looked up when she arrived.

"Granlor tells me the gates are still closed. Any word from members of the Order of the Fox? Might we hope to receive help from the inside?"

Krion shook his head. "Not likely."

"Are you certain? It's early. Perhaps something can yet be done." She held her hands close to the fire, enjoying its warmth.

The three men exchanged dark looks. "There is something you need to see," Krion said. The men stood and they returned to the rise where yesterday they had looked down upon the city.

"Look at the gate."

Shanis stared through the semi-darkness. It took her a moment to realize what she was seeing. Bodies hung from the walls on either side of the main gate.

"Who are they?"

"They do be two members of our clan," Culmatan said. "Members of the order who have been living in the city for two summers, waiting for this day."

"I think we can consider this to be Orbrad's reply." Krion turned to Shanis. "We have no choice. We must attack."

Shanis sighed. She had hoped it would not come to this, but she saw no way out. "Very well. Let it begin."

Shanis watched as the first rays of dawn struck the gates of Karkwall. The corpses remained there for all to see. Perhaps Orbrad thought it would intimidate the attackers, but from the reactions she had heard among her people, it served only to fuel their rage and strengthen their resolve.

While thin ranks of troops still encircled the city, well beyond the range of Karkwall's defenses, she held the bulk of her forces in the forest, ready to serve as a surprise for the city's defenders when the moment came.

She kept hoping the gates would open, but it didn't happen. Finally, with a sick feeling in her gut, she gave the order for the attack to begin.

Horgris raised a horn to his lips and gave three short blasts.

Catapults rolled into place and began pounding the castle walls. Most were aimed at the gates, seeking to bring them down, while others hurled burning oil onto the ramparts. The first shots fell short, but they soon adjusted and began to hit the castle.

From within the city, Karkwall's own weapons returned fire. The first efforts were far off the mark, but the subsequent shots came steadily closer as they found their range.

Shanis bit her lip as the missiles finally flew on target. Would her plan work? Just as the stones descended beneath the height of the tree line, something strange happened. The stones seemed to strike an invisible dome and bounce away. Shanis smiled as shouts of surprise arose all around her. She hadn't been certain her plan would work, so she'd kept it to herself until it was tried.

"Did you do that?" Krion asked.

She shook her head. "I placed a bone woman in each crew. They'll keep the protective shields up for as long as they can." She knew fatigue would set in sooner or later, but she hoped her forces could strike quickly and forced the defenders to lose heart.

Heztus glanced up at her. "I wish I could see the looks on the faces of the soldiers inside the city right now."

Shanis' forces continued to pound the city walls while the defender's efforts continued to fail.

"Now it's your turn," Krion said. "Strike while they are confused and disheartened."

Shanis' stomach began to churn. She had never used the power as a weapon and wasn't sure she could do it. Aspin had taught her a bit about both magic and sorcery, and she understood the principles. If she could manage it, she might be able to bring this battle to an end.

She drew her sword and dropped to one knee. If her experiences in healing were any indication, this would be an exhausting task and she didn't want to collapse in front of the men and women who counted on her to lead them. Behind her, Gillen moved to stand beside her in case Shanis needed defending.

She thought about the times she had used the sword for healing She'd opened herself to its power, allowed it to flow through her, and then focused it on what she wanted to do. She took a deep breath and opened herself to the sword. She felt the power begin to stir, and she reached out with her thoughts, focusing on the south wall of the city, which had, by design, been subjected to only minimal bombardment.

An otherworldly force rose up inside her. Her limbs began to twitch of their own accord, and strange thoughts filled her mind—she felt a hunger, a desire to consume the very stone from which the city walls were constructed, and she found herself momentarily struggling to maintain control. She focused the hunger and poured it into the strands of her thoughts and cast them like a net over a two hundred span stretch of the city wall. Immeasurable power poured forth from the sword, flowing across the open space and filling the web of thought.

What is happening?

Just like healing, she did not quite understand what she was doing or how, but she somehow knew it was right.

The power clung to the wall like strands of ivy and slowly began to penetrate the stone. The hunger inside her rose to avarice and the strands of thought and power, *the will*, Aspin had called it, divided and divided again.

All around her, the crashes and cries of siege warfare faded away and she felt as if she were actually there, inside the stone, her essence flowing through it. Slowly she took control of the power and she spread the threads of energy through every block of the wall.

Cracks formed in the stone. She felt them growing, felt the rock divide and divide again. She was aware of the defenders on the wall cry out in surprise as the wall beneath them shifted. The rocks continued to split. What had begun as huge blocks of stone split into chunks the size of boulders, which then shattered into smaller chunks. It continued on, breaking down again and again until she had reduced the entire stretch of wall to a shifting mass of pebbles held loosely in place by the power of the Silver Serpent.

The alien awareness battered at her mind again. She held it back, but its intent filtered through. She understood. The blend of thought and power was like a whip that stretched across the battlefield, ending in countless, living tails of energy that continued to consume the stone. She focused her will and sent out a sharp burst of energy, cracking the whip and sending the crumbled remains of the wall flying apart.

The defenders had fled when they first felt the wall quaking, but now the bits of stone that shot out in every direction cut them down. Shanis felt each man fall. It was as if every bit of stone was a part of her. She felt it shred flesh, break bone, and rip apart the ballistae that sat atop the south wall. She heard the cries of the dying and the excited roar that rose from her own ranks as they saw the walls come down. She felt the hoof beats and footfalls as her previously-hidden troops poured forth from cover and charged toward the gaping hole in the wall. Ordinarily those troops would have been forced to endure a rain of projectiles as they crossed open ground. By concentrating their attack on the front gate, they'd enticed the enemy to move the bulk of their troops there, and the force of the Silver Serpent's attack had cleared what remained of the south wall of its defenses.

Atop the remaining walls, a ripple of awareness flowed through the defenders as they realize their south wall, what remained of it, anyway, stood undefended. The fire from the defenders' war engines abated as they sought to redirect them toward the attackers. A few officers managed to rally their troops and lead them toward the gaping hole in the outer wall.

"Can you bring down more of the wall?"

Shanis scarcely recognized Krion's voice. The hunger to consume remained, but her will was diminishing, and the power that flowed through her had been reduced to a trickle. She tried to gather her will, but she had nothing left. Like a guttering candle, she felt her connection to the sword flicker and die.

"I can do no more," she whispered. "That took everything I had." She closed her eyes and concentrated on remaining upright.

Krion placed a hand on her shoulder. "You did enough, granddaughter."

She opened her eyes and watched as her troops poured through the hole she'd opened in the wall, crushing the meager defenses the city had managed to muster. All along and inside the walls, defenders fled toward the inner keep. Shanis could see little of what was happening, but she knew that the combined forces of Malgog and Monaghan would slaughter any who stood in their path.

"Will they make it to the inner city?" she asked.

"Some will, but they won't be able to keep the gates open long enough to let most of them in," Krion said. "Not with our troops charging in."

When the defenders were in full retreat, her remaining forces charged. No one remained to fire upon them, and soon the main gate stood open and her forces controlled the outer wall and keep. Within minutes, they had turned Karkwall's own siege engines on the inner city and commenced bombardment. Soon afterward, the inner city's defenders began to return fire.

"Call our troops back," Shanis said.

"No," Krion snapped. "Not when we have the advantage."

"The advantage will be short-lived if they charge straight into the inner city's defenses. Now that Orbrad has seen what I can do, he will have to surrender. Let us not waste lives in the interim. If we want a united Lothan, it won't do for us to slaughter our future allies."

Krion scowled, but he obeyed. He raised his war horn and blew three sharp blasts. All around the battlefield, others heard the order and blew their own horns.

Soon, the attacking forces broke off and rallied outside the walls which now provided shelter against the bombardment from the inner city. In the midst of the attackers marched a long line of prisoners captured in the fighting. She breathed a sigh of relief that at least some lives had been spared.

"Gillen," she said, "I think it's time to send Orbrad another message." Once again, her voice boomed. "You have seen that your walls cannot withstand our attacks. Do not throw away your lives. You have until morning to surrender."

Somehow, she knew the stubborn king still would not listen.

Chapter 27

The sharp knock at the door startled Oskar. He looked up from the book he was reading and frowned. "Who could that be?" It was late, almost time for lights out.

"Why don't you open the door and find out?" Whitt asked.

Oskar flashed a dark look at his friend, rose and went to the door. When he opened it he was surprised to see inceptor Dahron standing there.

"Novit Clehn, you are summoned to the office of the prelate." He didn't wait for a reply, but turned and strode down the hall.

Oskar shot a confused glance at his roommates, all of whom gaped at him, before following along. What had he done to draw the prelate's attention? Did Denrill somehow know about Oskar's secret excursions into the archives or his late night meetings with Lizzie? Was Oskar about to be turned out from the Gates? His stomach turned somersaults and his mind raced as he followed along behind the inceptor. By the time they reached the prelate's office he feared he would vomit.

Darhon turned to face him. "Remove your cloak and hand it to me."

With trembling hands Oskar complied. This was the end. It had to be. Why else would he be stripped of his cloak? What would he do now? What use did anyone have for a half-trained novit?

"Step inside."

Head hanging, Oskar shuffled into the candlelit chamber and stopped just inside the door. He heard it close behind him like the sound of a prison cell.

"Novit Clehn," Prelate Denrill's voice rumbled through the dimly-lit room, "you may approach."

Sighing, he walked forward. As he moved through the semi-darkness he quickly realized that he and the prelate were not alone. A long, narrow table ran in front of the prelate's desk and behind it sat the seven proctors. To their left, all of the masters stood ramrod straight. What was happening?

He stopped a few feet shy of the table and waited.

"You are here because the masters believe you are ready to be raised to initiate," Denrill said.

Oskar's knees nearly gave way from surprise and relief but he managed to remain upright, and he gave a single nod.

"Today you will be tested to evaluate your fitness for your new rank. I must now ask you if you are ready to proceed." The prelate's gaze bored into him. "Before you answer know that you may refuse once and return to your studies as a Novit. If you refuse twice, you will be turned out from the Gates. Now I ask you, are you ready?" He said the last three words in a booming voice that nearly made Oskar flinch.

"I am ready." He wished he had managed to put more confidence into his voice, but it was all he could do to answer at all. Now a new kind of fear coursed through him. He had had no time to prepare. What if he failed? He decided against asking that question, fearing it would somehow count against him. *Do your best*, he told himself. *That is all you can do.*

"Master Ashur, you are first."

The soft-spoken master of sorcery stepped forward and Oskar moved back a few paces to give him room.

"Explain the difference between sorcery and magic."

Oskar knew this one. Aspin had taught it to him as one of his first lessons. Behind Ashur, he saw Proctor Basilius make a face, clearly disapproving of such a simple question.

"The sorcerer channels life force, converts it into energy and redirects it to a place and purpose of his choosing. The magician makes a plea to the gods." It was an overly simplified answer, but it seemed to satisfy the master.

Ashur reached into his pocket and pulled out a live mouse. Holding it by the tail he handed it to Oskar. "Drawing life force from this creature, boil the water in that pot."

Oskar looked in the direction Ashur pointed. A cauldron stood on stone blocks near the window. It would take a great deal of power to bring it to a boil, but he could do it. The trick, he knew, was to draw upon the mouse's life force without killing it. The life force of a living creature, when handled properly, could provide substantial energy. Only the tiniest fraction would be required to perform the task at hand. It was considered reckless, if not evil, to kill a living thing by drawing too much of its life force, save in the direst of circumstances.

Carefully, he focused his will and reached out to the mouse dangling from his fingers. He connected with it, felt its energy, felt its beating heart. And then as if unraveling a single thread from a garment, he drew a trickle of energy and directed it toward the cauldron. The mouse didn't make a squeak, so delicate was Oskar's touch.

The next bit required a measure of care as well. Direct all the energy onto the cauldron at once and he would bore a hole through it. Exercising control, he slowly heated the pot until wisps of steam rose from the surface. He increased the flow of power only a bit and soon came the welcome sound of boiling water.

"Excellent. That will be all." Ashur made a small bow which Oskar returned.

Next came Master Zuhayr, who quizzed Oskar about the nature of magic before asking him to perform a few tasks of increasing difficulty, all of which Oskar managed with ease. Master Sibson peppered him with questions about history, his favorite subject, and Oskar thought he acquitted himself well. And so it continued until the only master who remained was Master Lang.

The burly combat master turned, grabbed something that was leaning against the wall, and tossed it to Oskar. A quarterstaff! His weapon of choice! Oskar had only a moment to get a proper grip on it before Lang drew a knife and leaped forward.

Surprised, Oskar scarcely deflected the blade and danced away. He immediately knew he had done the wrong thing. In an actual fight, the proper move would have been to follow up the deflection with a blow from the staff to keep his opponent off balance. His instinct had told him not to hurt Master Lang, but he immediately realized how foolish that thought was. Lang could beat him with ease. This was about Oskar displaying his skill.

Lang thrust with the dagger and Oskar cracked him across the back of the wrist and followed with a stroke aimed for Lang's ankles. The master avoided the attack and struck again, feinting low and thrusting high. Oskar had seen the move countless times but still scarcely managed to dodge it. He sprang to the side and struck out, aiming for Lang's elbow. The master moved like a cat and the staff whistled through thin air. Oskar, however, had anticipated the dodge and thrust with the butt of his staff, managing to catch Lang on the kneecap. He was gratified to see that Lang actually gave the slightest wince when the blow struck home.

His success was short-lived. Lang double-feinted and then kicked Oskar's staff, loosening his grip on the weapon. Before Oskar could recover, Lang lashed out with his other foot and sent the staff clattering across the floor.

An inexperienced fighter would have moved away, but Lang had taught his students better than that. The moment he lost his grip on his weapon, Oskar struck with a short jab that caught Lang in the throat, followed by a kick to the stomach that sent his instructor stumbling backward.

Lang raised his dagger, poised to bring it down on Oskar's head. It was not a move an experienced fighter would try, and Oskar knew in a flash that this was part of the test. He crossed his arms, caught Lang by the wrist, and drove his knee into the master's groin. A lesser man would have collapsed, but Lang merely grunted, roughly shoved Oskar away, and stepped back.

"Well done," Lang said.

Oskar nodded in thanks. He had feared the blow to the groin might get him in serious trouble. The standard move was to control the opponent's wrist and twist the arm until your opponent released his weapon, but Lang was much too powerful for that to work. Apparently, Oskar had made the right choice.

"Novit Clehn, you may approach." The prelate beckoned to him and Oskar, weary but relieved stepped forward, trying not to wobble as he walked.

"Do the proctors have any questions for this candidate?" the prelate asked. One by one the proctors shook their heads. Oskar's shoulders sagged with relief. It was over. But then Basilius cleared his throat.

"I have questions for this candidate." The looks of surprise on the others' faces told him that this was an unusual request. "Novit Clehn, tell me what you know about the Silver Serpent."

Proctor Greguska interrupted. "Forgive me, Prelate, but history is my purview."

"Forgive *me*," Basilius replied, "but magic and sorcery are *my* areas."

Prelate Denrill gave Basilius a long, hard look. "Novit Clehn will answer the question," he finally said.

"The Silver Serpent is a weapon of unknown origin. It is prophesied that the bearer of the Silver Serpent will unite the clans of Lothan. Tradition holds that the bearer will also fight in the next Frostmarch, but no known prophecies explicitly state such." Basilius continued to stare, as did the other proctors, so Oskar went on. "It was formed in the shape of a longsword and contains power."

"Sorcerous or magical?" Basilius asked sharply.

Oskar's reply was automatic and came before he had a moment to think. "Both."

"Impossible. Magical power is derived from the gods and thus cannot be stored inside any object. A limited amount of sorcerous power, however, can be stored within the proper vessel." Basilius crossed his arms and sat back in his chair. "I think perhaps this candidate would find further study useful."

"Shanis Malan, the bearer of the Silver Serpent, has used its power to heal people. I have seen it." He immediately knew he had overstepped, and the small smile on Basilius' face told Oskar that the proctor believed he had just won whatever game he was playing.

"Objection," Basilius pronounced each syllable, "withdrawn."

"Very well." Denrill sounded relieved. "What say you, proctors?"

Proctor Subal rose from his chair and said, "I say Novit Clehn shall be raised to initiate." The next five prelates stood and repeated the words. Finally, they reached Basilius, who remained seated.

"I abstain."

Denrill frowned. "I would have it be unanimous."

Basilius would not meet the prelate's eye. "Still, I abstain."

The expressions on the other proctors' faces ranged from discomfort to outright anger. Clearly this was more than an unusual occurrence. It was apparently a serious breach of protocol. Perhaps even a personal affront to the prelate.

Denrill regained his composure at once. He stood and proclaimed in a loud voice, "I declare Oskar Clehn be raised to the rank of initiate. Kneel, Initiate Clehn."

Oskar dropped to one knee. The prelate came forward carrying a pitcher which he upended over Oskar's head. Oskar shivered as the cool water sluiced down the back of his neck and soaked his tunic but inside he felt warm. He had been raised to initiate! What was more, now he could freely use the archives.

Chapter 28

Larris swallowed the lump in his throat and looked down the table at the arrayed members of the Regis, the small council that aided the king in running the kingdom. His father was dead, having passed away only five days earlier. His funeral that morning had been a small one, much less than King Allar had deserved, but the war made a grand state funeral impractical. Allar was gone, but Larris was not king. No one was king, nor would anyone be, until Lerryn's status was resolved. Was Lerryn still alive and, if so, where was he?

Mazier, vizier to the late King Allar, cleared his throat. "Your Highness, if you are ready to begin?"

"Of course. I thank you all for being here at this difficult time." It was perhaps a silly thing to say. They were required to be here, but he saw no harm in a bit of courtesy. He looked around the table at those assembled. To his right sat his uncle Orman; Hugo, a military envoy representing the Galdoran army; and Rayburn, the aging commander of the city watch. On his left were Mazier; Edwin, the Silvermaster, who managed the finances for the crown; and Jowan, Archpriest of the Temple of the Seven. Larris' gut twisted at the sight of the man. He'd had the restorative Jowan had given King Allar tested, and it was found to be safe, yet he could not escape the feeling that the temple was somehow behind Allar's rapid decline and death.

He noted a significant absence. "Why isn't James here?" James was a saikur who had, for many years, served as a liaison between the Gates and Archstone.

"He is not needed at this time," Orman said. "The decisions we will make today regarding the future of the kingdom can be made without his input. We all know the situation."

All around the table, the others nodded in agreement.

"I, for one, feel the Gates exerts too much influence on sovereign nations." Jowan folded his arms and leaned back in his seat. No one disagreed with him though Hugo shifted uncomfortably.

"Do you have something to say?" Larris asked Hugo. "Please do not stand on ceremony. You have a right to speak."

"I would simply like to point out that the saikurs are currently negotiating to bring an end to this war. Would it not be prudent to include them in our discussions, as what we do here could impact the negotiations?"

"I agree," Rayburn rasped. "If we appear to be distancing ourselves from the Gates, it could make us appear vulnerable. Kyrin must see that we are united with all of our allies."

"Are we? What have our allies offered us, save platitudes? None have supported us. None!" Hugo pounded his fist on the table for emphasis.

Larris could not disagree. The nations of the north were hesitant to involve themselves in Galdora's dispute with Kyrin and, and to the south, Diyonus was devoting all of its troops to protecting its own border from the growing army in Kurnsbur.

"What *is* the status of the war with Kyrin?" Larris asked.

"If I may, Your Highness. There is a small matter that requires our attention. A formality, really," Mazier said apologetically. "Until we address the issue of the succession, no one is truly in charge of this body. It would be inappropriate to continue in this manner until the situation has been resolved."

"It cannot be dealt with at this time," Larris said. "I have sent men in search of Lerryn, and they have reason to believe he is still alive. Until he is found, I think it most expedient for me to serve in his place."

Rayburn nodded, but the others exchanged uncomfortable looks. Larris' heart sank. He knew how this conversation was about to go. He had already had the same discussion with his mother. Determined not to make it easy for them he waited.

"If you will forgive me, Highness, we have discussed this at length," Mazier said.

"We have?" Larris interrupted, emphasizing the word 'we.' "Please refresh my memory as I do not recall having had this discussion with anyone in this room."

"Nor do I." Rayburn scowled at Mazier.

Mazier could not suppress the frown that flashed across his face, but he was quickly all smiles again. "I should have made myself clear. Some of us," he glanced from Orman to Jowan, "have had occasion to discuss our current situation. It was not our intention to leave you out of the discussion. We merely found ourselves in the same place at the same time and naturally this is a subject which concerns us greatly. So…" He turned his palms up and shrugged.

"And what fruit was born from this accidental conversation?" Larris hoped he did not sound as sardonic as he felt. Right now, he needed the support of the Regis or at least a majority of it.

"We agree that your brother is still alive," Jowan began, "and is, therefore, the rightful king. We further agree that someone should serve as regent until he returns." He paused and glanced at Mazier, who nodded. "It is our opinion that appointing you in that capacity could fracture the kingdom."

"What do you mean?"

"We do not know how long it will take to find Lerryn." Jowan's brow furrowed. "His prolonged absence has not gone unnoticed. Some believe he is dead while others consider him unfit to rule. If you step in as regent, many will begin to think of you as the true king while others would see you as a usurper. This could cause division, and perhaps rebellion."

"Further rebellion, you mean," Hugo interjected

"True. We cannot ignore our current situation." The high priest gave Larris an apologetic smile. "I do hope you understand. This is an uncomfortable conversation and I do not wish you to think we do not value your input. We rejoice that you have returned to us."

Doubtful, Larris thought.

"Who do you suggest should serve until Prince Lerryn is found?" Edwin asked. His furrowed brow suggested that he too had been excluded from the machinations and was not happy about it.

"We believe that Lord Orman is best suited to serve. His Grace is not in the direct line of succession but is part of the royal family. The court knows and trusts him." Mazier looked around the table as if challenging anyone to contradict him.

Orman sat looking down at his hands. Finally, he looked up. "I will reluctantly accept this position, but only if I have the support of the Regis."

Larris fought the sudden urge to roll his eyes. Orman knew he could not serve without this group's blessing. His humble words were merely for show.

"Is there any further discussion on the subject?" Mazier asked.

"I support Prince Larris," Rayburn said, "but I will accede to the wishes of the Regis. We should be united now more than ever."

Larris' heart fell. His only hope had been for Hugo, Edwin, and Rayburn to come down on his side, thus splitting the vote.

"My sentiments exactly," Edwin said. "But I hope that, in the future, we will keep our conversations about such important matters inside the council chamber." He cast a meaningful look at Mazier, who gave a single nod.

After that, the result was a foregone conclusion. The Regis voted by acclamation to make Orman the new regent. Larris surrendered the seat at the head of the table to his uncle and sat down alongside Rayburn, who gave him an apologetic smile before turning his attention to Orman.

"Now," Orman began, "as my nephew correctly pointed out, we should discuss the status of the war efforts." He turned to Hugo.

"We are struggling" Hugo said. "I won't deny it. Kyrin continues to push us back along the border. We are giving ground slowly, but giving ground all the same."

Orman frowned. "My sources tell me otherwise. It is my understanding that the front has stabilized."

"As I said, we are giving ground slowly, but I would hardly say the front has stabilized." Hugo paused, waiting for a reply. When none came, he continued. "The situation in the south is difficult to assess. We have not managed to get a single spy into the lands controlled by Karst. Rather, not a single spy we sent in has returned. For that reason, there is very little we can say for certain about the situation. We know that he now controls the entirety of the former Duchy of Kurnsbur."

"It is not a *former* duchy," Orman said. "It is and will always be a part of Galdora. The rebellion does not change that fact."

"You are correct, of course." Hugo made a small nod in Orman's direction, which Larris' uncle returned with a smile. "Karst also controls a large portion of Eastern Lothan. The Malgog seem to have given up without a fight. They appear to have abandoned that part of their kingdom."

"Their civil war has moved east," Mazier said. "The bulk of their forces now lay siege to Karkwall."

"They'll destroy themselves soon enough." Rayburn shook his head.

"Don't be so certain," Larris said softly

"The ambassador from Diyonus is here at the castle," Mazier said. "He is, needless to say, concerned about our situation, but he was reluctant to discuss the situation on his nation's border. What, if anything, can you tell us about that?"

"Nothing definite. As far as we know, Karst has not attempted to cross the border into Diyonus, but every sortie by the Diyonan army has been crushed."

"How can that be?" Jowan asked. "A collection of rebels and stray Lothans against a trained army? I think that demonstrates the value of gossip."

"We hear the same story from every source." A note of defensiveness crept into Hugo's voice. "I cannot speak to the size or strength of Karst's forces, but it is clear that they are much stronger than we anticipated."

"That settles it." Orman rubbed his hands together. "Our first priority is to make our kingdom whole once again." His eyes locked on Hugo. "A significant number of soldiers have just completed their training, have they not?"

Hugo nodded. "A full legion and two cavalry units."

"Excellent. That should be more than enough to smash this rebellion in Kurnsbur. Once that has been accomplished, we may turn our full attention to the Kyrinian front."

"But my Lord, these are green troops. They have never seen battle." Hugo looked shocked

"And what better way to bloody them then against a collection of rabble? Better they cut their teeth in Kurnsbur than against Kyrinian regulars."

"We should mix them in with veteran troops," Hugo stammered. "One does not send such an inexperienced force into battle as a single unit. It simply isn't done."

"Good. Karst will not expect it." He turned to Rayburn. "I will need you to cull the ranks of the city guard of all veterans who are of fighting age. Send them to the Academy for induction."

"My Lord?" Rayburn gaped at Orman. "What few men I have who fit that description have all completed their terms of service and chosen to leave the army. They have wives and children."

"A life of leisure is not a luxury Galdora can afford during a time of war. They will serve or they will hang. Am I understood?"

"Yes, my Lord, but you will leave my guard woefully depleted."

"If we do not win this war, there will be no city for you to guard."

Hugo cleared his throat. "We have no experienced commanders in the city at this time. I shall have to send word to the front before you can take the troops to Kurnsbur."

"Nonsense," Orman said. "I shall command them myself."

Silence reigned around the table. Larris found himself at a loss for words. This was an unexpected turn of events to say the least. Just as his uncle had seized power, he was going to leave the city? What was his game? He glanced at Jowan, who, alone among the members of the Regis, appeared unsurprised. Was it Orman's plan to strip Archstone of its defenses and leave it in so vulnerable a position that the temple could step in and seize power? But why? It made no sense.

"Uncle," he began, "you are needed here. We have just named you regent. How will it stabilize the kingdom for you to leave immediately, taking all our troops with you?"

Orman dismissed Larris' question with the wave of his hand. "I will still be regent. The Regis can rule in my stead. Mazier will chair the meetings and Carsus will sit in my place."

Larris grimaced at the thought of his cousin taking up any sort of a position of authority, but there was nothing he could do about it. "I don't like it. The idea of you leaving…"

"Please tell me you, of all people, are not about to chastise me for leaving the kingdom in its hour of need."

Larris felt his cheeks go red. As much as he hated to admit it, his uncle was correct. Both he and Lerryn had done that very thing and not too long ago. What could he say about it?

Taking his silence for acquiescence, Orman rose. "I believe that ends our business for today. Commander Rayburn, I will expect those men in the morning. I plan to leave within the week." He immediately turned on his heel and strode out of the room.

Larris, Rayburn, and Edwin exchanged glances. Larris sensed he at least had two allies, but what could they do? He needed to understand his uncle's plan, whatever that was.

He hurried back to his quarters and sent for Allyn, who arrived in short order.

"There is something you need to know," Allyn said as soon as the guard closed the door.

"What is that?"

I intercepted a message to Orman from the temple."

"How did you manage that?" Larris asked

Allyn shrugged. "I followed the messenger and knocked him out before he reached the palace. I lifted his purse so he'll think he was robbed." He handed Larris a small sheet of parchment.

The message was brief.

Do not fret. Karst says the time is at hand.

Chapter 29

Shanis closed her eyes and breathed in the silence. No more pounding of siege engines. No more battle cries. For a few hours, all was still.

Inside the command tent, the clan chiefs awaited her. Most still disagreed with her decision to break off the attack for the night, seeing it as a sign of weakness on her part. She still contended that the people of Karkwall were not the enemy, and she wanted to keep as many of them alive as possible until Orbrad was removed from power. And if her plan worked, that would happen tonight.

Ordering Gillen and Granlor to wait outside, she stepped inside the tent. Heztus followed behind her.

The tent was poorly lit and the air thick with smoke and sweat. A small part of her wanted to order them all to bathe, and she smiled at the thought.

"What were our losses?" she asked, settling down at her place in the circle.

"Minimal," said Krion. "Most of the defenders broke and ran when the wall went down, so there was little resistance."

"Good. Now that we have our way in, we can put a stop to this in short order."

Krion frowned. "What do you mean we have our way in?"

"We control the outer wall. That means," she looked at Horgris, "we also control the tunnel through which my friends and I escaped the city."

Everyone turned to Horgris.

"What is she talking about?" Krion asked sharply.

Horgris sighed and explained how he and other members of the Order of the Fox had helped Shanis and her companions escape from Orbrad's dungeon. "I do know where the gate is, but I do not know the way through the tunnels."

"Martrin does," Shanis said. "Is he still on our side?"

"I believe so, but we can no reach him," Horgris replied. "He do be close to Orbrad. It be risky to try and communicate with him."

"We have to assume that the tunnels will be guarded," Culmatan said, scratching his beard. "But the idea do be worth exploring. We should send in some men to scout it out."

"I've already done that," Shanis said. "Many are still exploring, but those who have reported back say the tunnels are lightly guarded. We should be able to get men into the inner keep and open the gates without me blasting them apart. Orbrad would have to surrender."

"It could work, but it could also be a death trap," Labar, chieftain of the Mud Snake clan, said.

The chieftains debated the plan for some time, finally agreeing to wait until all the scouts returned before sending in a small group of armed guards.

"All right," Shanis said, rising to her feet. "I'm going to get some rest. Send Heztus to get me when you're ready to send men into the city."

The chieftains stood and bowed respectfully as she departed. Outside, she quickened her pace, forcing Granlor and Gillen to hurry along in order to keep pace. As soon as she was out of sight of the meeting tent, she changed directions and headed out of the camp.

"Wait!" Granlor had the good sense to keep his voice down. He and Gillen ran to catch up with her.

"What are you doing?" Gillen asked.

"I'm not waiting for any scouts," Shanis said. "I'm putting an end to this tonight."

Chapter 30

"This pass would make for an excellent ambush site." Lerryn gazed down at the narrow pass, mentally placing his troops and planning his strategy. They would hit hard and run fast. As long as they didn't get caught up in hand-to-hand fighting, they should be able to bloody the Kyrinians and get away safely.

It galled him to have to resort to such a strategy. He wanted to stand and fight, but he knew that if he did, his ragtag forces would be crushed.

His forces. The very thought made him grin ruefully. How had he come to this? After the battle of Galsbur he'd set off on his own without a plan, save to somehow atone for the poor choices he'd made. Soon he'd found himself waging a one-man war against the bandits, mostly deserters from the Galdoran and Kyrinian armies, who marauded across the countryside.

And then he'd met Kelvin. Against his better judgment, he'd permitted the young man to join him. From that point on it seemed he could not go anywhere without gaining followers. The single pebble had started an avalanche.

Now he led a respectable force. Most of them were farmers who had lost their homes and families and whose desire for vengeance outstripped their fighting skills, but the lot was far from hopeless. Many of the men were skilled hunters and he'd put their archery skills to use. He'd also collected a number of veterans who had stepped in as officers, training up his makeshift army.

Soon they'd scoured the western lands of bandits and were now working their way east. As they journeyed, they'd continued to gather volunteers, but also some regulars— men who had become separated from their units, or sometimes the remnants of units that had been decimated. Now he finally had a force that could, if not stand toe-to-toe with a Kyrinian unit of similar size, at least acquit themselves well in a fight, particularly if Lerryn chose the ground and fought on his terms.

"Do we have enough to defeat them?" Kelvin asked. "We've doubled in size over the last two weeks."

"Of course not. We can only hope to slow them down until the Galdoran reinforcements arrive."

"Reinforcements of which there is still no sign." Kelvin didn't know Lerryn was or had been, First Prince of Galdora, and Lerryn wondered if the knowledge would change how the young man spoke to him. Probably not.

"They will come. They have to." Lerryn tried to picture the geography of the region. This pass and the river beyond were the only natural barriers before the invaders would hit rolling, open farmland and have a clear path to Archstone. It was critical that they do what they could to slow these invaders and whittle down their numbers.

"But the soldiers who have joined us…"

"Are soldiers, and thus not privy to the decisions of kings and generals. Archstone will send out forces to meet this threat." Privately, he wondered if that were true. He hadn't a shred of evidence that his father was even aware of this invading force, much less that he was sending troops.

Kelvin grimaced but acquiesced. "Max is coming."

Max was one of the veterans who had joined them. A skilled cavalryman, he led the unit that had dubbed itself the White Fang, named after Lerryn's elite squad, all of whom had died in defense of Galsbur. He had considered asking them to choose another name but decided it wasn't worth the bother.

Max halted a few paces away and made a perfunctory bow. "There is someone here to see you, my Lord."

"You know what to do. Assign him to a squad, give him bread and a spear, and hope to the gods he knows how to use the latter."

"Begging your pardon, but he says he is here to see Lerryn, First Prince of Galdora."

Lerryn tensed, his heart drumming in his chest. "Then he is in the wrong place."

Max shrugged. "He described you perfect-like. Says you'll know his name. It's Tabars."

Despite his annoyance at his identity finally being revealed, Lerryn's heart leaped. Tabars was alive!

"Send him to me."

Max peered at him through narrowed eyes. "So it's true, then?"

Lerryn nodded. "I was First Prince. Not anymore." From the corner of his eye, he saw Kelvin gaping at him.

"In that case, I hope you'll forgive us for treating you like one of us. We didn't know."

"I didn't want you to know, and it was a welcome change to be treated like what I am— just a simple soldier."

"You're far more than that." Max bowed again, this time deeply, and hurried away, returning in short order not only with Tabars, but also with Colin Malan, Edrin, Hair, and Hierm Van Derin.

Tabars pressed his fist to his heart in salute. "Highness."

"I no longer hold that title. You know that."

Tabars looked down at his feet. "I don't know what else to call you."

"Call me Lerryn. After all these years, you've earned that much and more." He greeted each in turn and then stood back, arms folded. "I assume you didn't stumble upon my by accident. What do you want?"

Hierm cleared his throat. "Your brother sent us. Sent me, Hair, and Edrin, that is. We sort of picked up Colin and Tabars along the way."

Hierm then launched into a lengthy explanation, by the end of which, Lerryn wondered if perhaps he should start drinking again. Of course, the very thought of strong drink made him want to wretch. Whatever Shanis Malan had done to him, it had worked thoroughly.

He considered all that Hierm had told him: Lerryn's father was dying, there was no proof of his abdication, the temple appeared to be plotting against the royal family, and Galdora's forces were stretched to the breaking point.

"You are needed in Archstone, Highness," Hierm said.

"Don't call me that." Lerryn knew how peevish he must sound, but he didn't care. "I abdicated, remember?"

"As a matter of fact, I don't recall anything of the sort." Tabars grinned wickedly.

"Nor do I." Hierm scratched his head in mock-thoughtfulness. "Does anyone remember hearing anything about an abdication?" Grinning, the others shook their heads. "Unless you have it in writing…" Hierm shrugged.

"Mind your tongue when speaking to your prince." The words were out before Lerryn even realized what he was saying. No one replied. There was no need. "I can't do it," he said after a long silence. He turned a pleading look to Tabars. "You know what I was like."

"Yes, I do. On your worst day, you were the finest commander and best fighter I ever knew. No one can lead men like you can."

Lerryn grimaced. "I drank too much, I trusted the wrong people. I was weak."

"But that's not who you are now," Colin said. "I saw what you did in Galsbur. You were the very picture of what a leader should be. And look at what you've done here. You raised an entire army without even intending to if the men I've spoken to are to be believed."

"They follow me because I'm a fighter. That's all I'm fit for."

"Begging your pardon," Max said, "but I'm one of those men and it's a sight more than that. You command, but you also listen and take counsel. You're fair in your decisions and in the way you treat us. Besides that, there's just something about you. You make the people around you braver, you make us believe. I should have seen you for what you were."

"You are meant to lead," Tabars said. "You can stay out here leading a small group of men and fighting small skirmishes and tell yourself it's payment enough, but if you truly want to make amends to Galdora for your past sins, real or imagined, do it by serving her in the greatest capacity possible. Take up the mantle of First Prince and give all you are and all you have to your nation."

Lerryn felt his resistance crumbling, yet he stubbornly held on to his doubts.

"I shall consider what you say, but we have more pressing concerns at the moment. Van Derin, I want you, Edrin, and Hair to get to Archstone with all due haste. I'm sure at least one of my men knows the quickest route to get there. Make certain Larris knows there's a large Kyrinian army coming at them from the northwest. If our forces are concentrated in the northeast, it's possible they are completely unaware of this particular threat, despite my hopes to the contrary. Tell him I'll do all I can to slow them down but I can't hope to defeat them. Unless he can get help, either from our own forces or from our allies, it will be up to him to defend the city. The entire war might depend on him."

Chapter 31

"You can no go by yourself," Granlor protested. "This place be far too dangerous."

They stood inside the dark corridor that ran through Karkwall's outer walls. It was through this very passageway that Shanis and her friends had escaped their imprisonment in the dungeons beneath the castle.

"You presume to tell me, your queen, what to do?" Shanis felt like a fool saying this, but it gained the desired result.

"No, but I must keep you safe. I did make a vow."

She could tell by his resolute stare that he would not be moved. She had half expected that.

"I'm going too." Gillen's face was pale, but her tone was firm.

"Fine, you can both go with me, but don't do anything to draw attention to yourselves."

"You mean like carrying a giant sword across your back?" Granlor nodded at the hilt of the Silver Serpent that jutted up over her shoulder.

"Right. Well, it can't be helped. I have to have it with me if I have any hope of succeeding. Besides, if all goes as planned, no one will see us until we're inside the throne room."

"We are going inside the castle?"

"How else am I going to kill Orbrad? Devin here will show us the way." She pointed to the grizzled warrior who had just stepped out of the darkness. He was a member of the Order of the Fox who had made contact with Horgris after the battle. "Now, stop your yammering and come with me." Before he could argue she started off down the corridor.

"I don't remember much about my escape from Karkwall," she said to Devin. "We escaped from the dungeons through a tunnel that led into a stable. From there, Martrin took us into a different passageway and led us through the outer wall where we met Horgris."

"I know just the way," he assured her.

As they walked, the silence enveloped her, leaving her alone with her thoughts. Was this the proper course of action? What if she died or was taken prisoner? What then would hold Malgog and Monaghan together? Had she, once again, let her impulsive nature take over? Perhaps, but she could not abide the thought of more lives lost unnecessarily. She had to reach Orbrad and either make him see sense or, if she had to, end his life and, with it, his rule.

Of course, that came with its own set of problems. If it came to killing him, could she even do it? Execute someone? She had to. It would be wrong to make someone else do it for her though the thought turned her stomach.

"What will you do about the princess?" Granlor whispered.

She winced. She still had not made up her mind about Orbrad's fifteen-year-old daughter.

"If she lives, she will be a threat to your crown."

"No, she won't," Shanis snapped. "My line is from Badla. Orbrad is a pretender. Once he is dethroned, it won't matter what his child does."

"She is old enough to marry," Gillen said. "You could arrange it. But you would have to choose someone you trust. Perhaps a prince from somewhere far away."

Her stomach fluttered at the words "marry" and "prince." Thoughts of Larris flooded her mind and she was thankful for the darkness that hid her blushing. If she succeeded, she would be the queen of Lothan— royalty, just the same as Larris. The greatest obstacle standing in their path would be removed.

"The way out is just up ahead." Devin's voice jolted her thoughts back to the present. "Let me take a look."

A sliver of gray light sketched the shape of a door only to be blotted out by his dark frame. "The way is clear at the moment," he said. "Here is my suggestion. Many in Karkwall believe tonight will be their last night on this world. There has been a fair bit of carousing and wenching. I don't expect many to be on high alert, no matter what orders the king has given." He paused. "Stay close to me and Granlor. If we encounter anyone between here and the street, he and I will pretend to be deep in our cups and the two of you will be our..."

"Whores?" Gillen asked.

Devin coughed into his closed fist. "You'd only be pretending, my lady."

Gillen chuckled. "It's fine by me. Let's go."

Smiling, Devin pushed the door open, slipped an arm around the witch woman, and stepped outside. Granlor reached for Shanis.

"Don't touch me with any body part you don't want cut off," she warned. "I'll stay close to you," she added, regretting her shortness with the young man who had done nothing since she met him save try to keep her safe.

"Do you want me to carry your sword?" he asked. "It would look less suspicious if I wore it."

"No. I want it close at hand should I need it." The sword was useless to anyone but her. No one else could so much as hold it without experiencing excruciating pain. Granlor was correct, though. If she wore it across her back, no one would believe their ruse. She pulled the scabbard off of her shoulder and leaned on the oversized sword like a walking staff. In the darkness, with Granlor close to her side, it just might work.

It felt odd strolling casually down the street, knowing someone could put a bolt or arrow in her back at any moment. Once again, she questioned the wisdom of her decision.

Gillen seemed to read her thoughts. "Do you wish me to cast the web of protection?"

Shanis considered the question. "Not unless it seems as if we are in immediate danger. Save your strength."

They strode along through the cold night. Here and there they spotted people moving in the darkness, but no one took notice of them. It felt as if a pall were cast over the city as if all of Karkwall held its collective breath.

"The stable is close by," Devin said. He quickened his pace and the others hurried to keep up. The stable was in sight when a voice rang out in the darkness, stopping them short.

"Devin, what are you about?" A rangy man in palace livery leaned against the alley wall. He held a mug in both hands but seemed sober.

"Hello, Nigel. We're just having a bit of fun on the last night of my life." Devin cast a meaningful glance at Shanis and Gillen.

"It won't be my last night. If it goes badly, I'll surrender first thing. They say that girl is a wild one, but she doesn't sound so bad to me."

Shanis gripped her sword but held her tongue.

"Don't let anyone hear you say that," Devin warned. "They'll have you in chains for sure."

"True enough." Nigel cocked his head and frowned at Granlor. "I don't believe I know you."

Granlor nodded thoughtfully. "I've seen you about. I suppose I'm not very memorable." He covered his Monaghan accent and dialect well.

Nigel nodded slowly. "I'm sure we've passed another on the street at some point. Well, I'll not keep you from your fun. But I don't think there's a room available anywhere in the city. The ones that aren't being used to tend the wounded are filled up with men like yourselves."

"Oh, I think the stable will do fine for us." Devin reached out and pinched Gillen on the rump.

As soon as Nigel had wandered out of sight, Gillen drove an elbow into Devin's ribs. "What do you think you're doing?"

"I had to make it look believable," he said, rubbing his side.

"Just be glad you didn't try that with me," Shanis said. "Now, let's get inside before any more of your friends arrive."

They slipped inside the stable and closed the door behind them. Shanis breathed a sigh of relief. They weren't out of the woods yet, but it felt good to no longer be out in the open.

"Where's the trapdoor?" Gillen asked.

'It's inside the stall over there." Devin pointed to the far corner of the stable. "But that's not where we're going."

"What?" Shanis said. She realized Devin had betrayed her. She'd kill him for this! But before she could draw her sword, torches blazed to life all around her.

A dozen grim-faced men armed with crossbows surrounded them. She quickly considered the situation. There was nothing she could do. She could never summon the Silver Serpent's power before the bolts flew. She'd foolishly walked into a death trap. Perhaps Gillen could call up the shielding spell, but one glance told her that the young bone woman had reached the same conclusion Shanis had— there was no time.

"What is this?" Shanis poured all her rage into the words.

"This, Your Majesty," a voice said from behind her, "is how this battle ends."

Chapter 32

Shanis turned and recognized the speaker immediately. Martrin! The man who had helped them escape from Karkwall. But he was a member of the Order of the Fox. Then again, so was Devin. Rage burned inside her. For a moment, she didn't care if she was killed. She wanted to hurt someone.

"Traitor!" she hissed.

"No! Wait!" Martrin held up his hands. "You misunderstand. We are here to help you."

She frowned. "What do you mean?"

"My apologies, Majesty. I should have handled this better, but I'm so accustomed to keeping secrets that Devin didn't even know the full plan."

"Why don't you tell me now?" Devin looked affronted. "You said you knew a better way in, but you didn't mention surrounding us with armed men."

"These men are all members of the Order of the Fox, and some of our most loyal. They will take you to Orbrad."

"Just like that?" Shanis asked. She wanted to believe him.

"Orbrad has locked himself in his throne room and is protected by his most devoted guards. No one can get close to him."

"So, even if I had come up through the dungeons as I intended, I'd still have to fight my way through the guards to reach him."

"Exactly, but we have another way. Orbrad is not seeing anyone, but I think he would open his doors if we brought him the leader of the rebellion. He's dying to put your head on a spike and hang the rest of you from the front gate."

Granlor took a step forward. "You mean to bring her in chains?"

"I think rope will suffice," Martrin said. "I'll slice it almost all the way through so you can snap it at a moment's notice." He hesitated. "We will have to take your sword." He eyed the Silver Serpent nervously.

Shanis considered this. She had no reason to distrust Martrin, but what did she actually know about him? Yes, he had aided her before, but if he had turned his coat, he might be taking her to her death. Then again, if he intended her harm, his men would have opened fire the moment she stepped inside the stable.

"All right," she said. "But Granlor carries my sword."

"Very well. He should wear this." Martrin removed his green cloak and handed it to Granlor, who donned it and then slung the Silver Serpent over his back, being careful not to touch the hilt. "Orbrad doesn't know my men by sight, so he won't realize anything is amiss." He turned to Devin and Gillen. "You two will be prisoners also. I'll saw through your bindings as well."

"All right, but what do we do when we get there?" Devin asked.

Martrin smiled. "Just follow my lead."

Shanis kept her eyes straight ahead as they marched through the streets, into the palace, and up to the throne room. Inside, she was a mass of nerves. Up ahead, the guards whispered amongst themselves. Apparently, word of her supposed capture had spread, and she feared one of them might try something foolish before she could defend herself. But they only cast dark stares in her direction. One man called out something obscene, and Martrin's men played along, laughing and making jokes about the wild girl who would be queen.

She ignored their taunts. She had more pressing things on her mind. The moment of truth neared. Her plan to kill Orbrad had seemed a simple one when she had conceived it, but the reality was something different. Killing was not entirely foreign to her. Back in Galsbur she'd stabbed to death a man who had tried to assault her, but that had happened in a moment of desperation, she'd fought to defend herself at times, and she knew lives had been lost when she'd destroyed a portion of the city wall earlier in the day, but this was something entirely different. Could she kill a man in cold blood? Could she look him in the eye and run her sword through his heart? Revulsion welled up inside her. She had only consented to unite the clans in order to end the clan wars and save lives. Taking Orbrad's life ran contrary to what she stood for or tried to stand for.

The guards, apparently mistaking the expression on her face for fear, jeered.

"Not so brave now, are you sweetheart?"

"Didn't think you'd have to pay for what you did?"

"Come over here and I'll give you a good spanking!"

"Look at the witch. She's an ugly one."

Anger welled up inside her, strengthening her resolve. She raised her chin and swept a baleful gaze across their ranks. They fell silent. Not so brave, after all.

A single guard stepped forward and greeted Martrin with the ritual clenched fist across his heart. Martrin returned the greeting.

"I bring the rebel leader, Shanis Malan, to the king for the dispensation of justice," Martrin said.

The guard looked Shanis up and down. "So this is her? Why do you need so many guards for one girl?"

"Three prisoners total." Martrin indicated Devin and Gillen. "Both women are witches, so I thought it prudent to take added precautions."

"That one looks familiar." The guard frowned at Devin, trying to place him.

"A traitor. We caught him leading these two into the city."

"Plenty of traitors about these days. Is it safe to bring them before the king?"

Martrin laughed. "They are witches, not sorcerers. They can't cast spells if their hands are bound."

That was patently false, but the guard, obviously not recognizing the absurdity of the statement, nodded sagely. He turned and rapped three times on the door. Moments later, the doors swung open and Martrin took Shanis by the elbow and shoved her roughly inside.

"Now," he whispered.

Shanis yanked her wrists apart, snapping the few threads that bound them together. Behind her, crossbow bolts sang through the air and voices cried out in pain and alarm as they found their marks in the bodies of Orbrad's guards.

"What is this?" a shrill voice cried. Orbrad sat stiffly on his throne, pressing his ample girth backward as if he could vanish inside it. Queen Agnes and Princess Sophie stood to his right, holding one another tight and staring wide-eyed at the intruders. To his left stood a thin man with a pointed nose and silver hair—Bertram.

Bertram was the king's steward, but Shanis had observed on her previous visit that the odd man seemed to also have the king's ear as a royal advisor. He was not a member of the Order of the Fox, but he had previously conspired with Martrin to free Shanis and her party when they'd been imprisoned.

Two guards survived, and they stood flanking the king, swords upraised, looking uncertainly at Martrin.

"This is the end of your rule, Orbrad," Martrin said. Behind him, Granlor, Shanis, and Devin drew their swords.

One of the guards took a step forward.

"I wouldn't try it," Martrin said to the guards. "This is over. Don't die for a lost cause."

"Don't listen to him. Protect your king!" Orbrad shouted.

Shanis heard Gillen whisper, and then the guards began to sway. In a matter of seconds, both went limp and fell to the ground, their swords clanging uselessly onto the stone floor.

"Hurry. They won't be asleep for long," Gillen said.

"Witchcraft!" Orbrad's eyes were like saucers.

Granlor and Devin relieved the guards of their weapons and bound their wrists with rope. By the time they opened their eyes, they lay helpless on the floor.

"How can you do this to me?" Orbrad blathered. "You are a traitor, Martrin."

"My loyalty is and has always been to a united Lothan. To that end, I support the one person who can heal our wounds— the rightful queen."

Shanis stepped out from behind Granlor and Devin. Orbrad rose halfway out of his seat but froze. His lips worked furiously, but he managed only choked sounds.

"You are out of options," she said. "Your forces cannot stand against us, and now you cannot stand against me. Abdicate, and let this all be at an end."

"I refuse." Orbrad's tone was like that of a petulant child. He sat back down on his throne and gripped the seat cushions as if to keep himself from being dislodged.

"You really don't have a choice. Abdicate, and I will send you and your family into exile with enough gold that you may live out your lives in comfort somewhere far from here."

Martrin raised an eyebrow at the promise.

"I would sooner die, and so would my wife and daughter. We are the royal family and we will not live out or lives as refugees."

"Father, please listen to them," Sophie pleaded. She was a plain-faced girl but didn't share her parents' girth. "We don't have to die."

"I'll grant you a new title," Shanis invented wildly, "and you can make a suitable match for your daughter."

Orbrad shook his head, making his jowls wobble. "You will have to kill us all."

Agnes and Sophie began to cry. Orbrad turned and scowled.

"Stop that. We are the royal family of Lothan and we will die bravely. The history books will speak of our courage and devotion to the throne."

Beside him, Bertram reached inside his robe and drew out a knife. The light glinted along its surface as he pressed the blade to the king's throat.

"Wait!" Shanis cried, but it was too late.

With a deft movement, the steward opened Orbrad's throat and stepped back, watching with grim satisfaction as the surprised monarch clutched his throat, trying in desperation to stanch the flow of blood. Beside him, Agnes and Sophie screamed.

It was over in a matter of seconds, but to Shanis it seemed an eternity, but she forced herself to watch as the king expired. Finally, he slumped down, the front of his doublet soaked in crimson.

Ignoring the wails of the queen and princess, Bertram wiped the blade of his knife on Obrad's cape, slipped it back inside his robe, and then turned and bowed to her.

"Welcome to Karkwall, Your Majesty."

Chapter 33

"You are working hard. I only hope that's work for one of our classes." Naseeb gave Oskar a disapproving look. "You don't have time to work on your extra project."

"Do you think I don't know that?" Oskar closed his book, stretched, and yawned. Since his elevation to initiate, it seemed like his nose was always in a book. Though they still took the same courses as novits, initiates were given extra assignments to study independently until they were deemed ready for disciple status, at which time they'd be paired with a saikur whom they would shadow and assist, thus gaining real-world experience. For Oskar, that was years away.

"Have you made any progress?" Naseeb asked.

"I don't think so. I'm gathering all the information I can, but I don't feel like it's anything new or helpful—just confirmation of what I already know."

The collection of papers Oskar called his "book" lay unbound on the desk. Naseeb began absently shuffling through them until he came to the rubbings Oskar had made from the walls in the lost city of Murantha shortly before he and his friends had found the Silver Serpent

"What are these?"

Oskar frowned. He hadn't given much thought to the papers. He had wanted to keep them mostly for sentimental reasons, but with all of the resources available at the Gates, they seemed superfluous at best.

"Just some rubbings I made during my travels."

Naseeb scratched his head. "These glyphs look familiar. I swear I've seen their like before, but I can't say where."

Dacio joined them and took one of the pages from Naseeb. He held it up to the candlelight and leaned so close that his nose almost touched it. "I've been making a study of ancient writing. Would you mind if I borrow these? Perhaps there's something in the archives that would help me translate them."

"All right," Oskar said. He was so distracted by his task that he didn't really care what Naseeb did with the rubbings. "Just don't lose them."

"Where exactly did they come from?" Naseeb asked. "Somewhere pretty old I would imagine."

"Murantha."

"What?" Naseeb and Dacio cried in unison. Even Whitt sprang up from his bed and gaped at Oskar.

"You are telling us," Naseeb said slowly, "that you have been to the lost city of Murantha?"

Oskar realized how surprising, even absurd the statement must sound to his friends. He hadn't intended to let that bit of information slip. It was one of the many topics Aspin had ordered him not to discuss, but he was tired of keeping so many secrets. He decided that his friends could be trusted. "That's right. I thought I'd mentioned it."

A flood of questions ensued and Oskar spent the better part of an hour recounting the tale of how they had met up with Prince Larris and eventually found the lost city.

"Why didn't you tell us this before?" Whitt marveled.

"I'm not really supposed to talk about it. I'm relying on you all to keep the secret. Besides, would you have believed me? And even if you thought I was telling the truth, you would probably think I was boasting."

"I can't believe this," Naseeb said. "All this time I thought you were just another country oaf and now I discover you're, in fact, a hero." He playfully punched Oskar on the shoulder.

"So the civil war in Lothan is sort of your fault," Whitt said.

"It's not his fault. He just helped a little bit." Naseeb said with a wink.

Oskar managed a shy smile. He hadn't done anything important in his life until he and his friends had left Galsbur. Receiving praise was still an unusual and uncomfortable experience.

"Oskar, these could be important." Dacio shook the paper in his hand. "Your research is about the Silver Serpent, which was hidden at Murantha. Until you found it, that is," he added. "If we can translate these glyphs, there might be valuable information here."

"Feel free," Oskar said. "I'm willing to try anything." He paused. "Just remember—let's keep this between the four of us, all right?"

"Agreed," they all said.

Dacio looked up from the sheaf of papers and frowned.

"What is it?" Oskar asked.

Dacio pointed to the bottom of the door to their room. A shadow was just visible as if someone were standing there. Oskar stood, moved quietly to the door, and threw it open.

Oskar recognized the brown-robed man who stood in the doorway, hand raised as if about to knock. He had escorted Oskar to meet Basilius on Oskar's first day at the gates. How long had he been standing there and what might he have heard?

"Initiate Clehn? Proctor Basilius would like to see you." His face red with embarrassment, the saikur hurried away.

Oskar exchanged glances with his friends. He was certain no good would come of this meeting.

Proctor Basilius waited in his sitting room. He didn't rise when Oskar entered and bowed respectfully.

"Initiate Clehn," he said. "Please sit down." His firm tone and flinty gaze told Oskar that this was going to be an uncomfortable meeting.

Oskar took the closest chair and waited for Basilius to continue.

"I have heard some things that are of great concern to me," Basilius began. "I understand you have been keeping company with the wrong sort of people. Or should I say, the wrong sort of *person*?"

Oskar was not certain where the proctor was going with this though he assumed this was another of the proctor's attempts to fish for information about Aspin, so he thought it best to remain silent. He did his best to appear politely confused.

They sat in silence until Basilius grew impatient.

"You are aware that we do not allow women at the Gates. And we do not enter into relationships with women?"

Oskar's stomach fell. Basilius knew about Lizzie. "I'm sorry?" he managed.

Basilius scowled. "Don't play coy with me, Initiate. I know you have been keeping company with a woman of ill repute."

Oskar made a small gesture with his open palms but did not reply.

Basilius stared at him from beneath hooded lids until he finally let out his breath in a sharp exhale. "Initiate Clehn do you or do you not know a woman named Elizabeth?"

"It doesn't sound familiar." That wasn't technically a lie. Lizzie had never told him that her name was Elizabeth. "What is her surname?"

"She claims not to have one. But I am sure the constable will extract it from her in short order." Basilius stared at Oskar, trying to measure the effect of his words.

Oskar somehow managed to remain calm and outwardly relaxed. "I'm sorry Proctor, but I fear I can't help you. Incidentally, who told you that I know this person?"

"Where a proctor gets his information is not the business of an initiate."

"I only meant…"

Basilius slapped the arm of his chair. "I don't care what you meant. You are far too arrogant for a boy of your station and skills. I realize Aspin is Denrill's favorite, and you are Aspin's creature, but a prelate's term of service is not necessarily for life. Sooner or later every man is called to account for his misdeeds. Think upon that." His face turned beet red. "This meeting is at an end. See yourself out."

Oskar stood, bowed, and headed for the door, trying to remain calm. Inside, his nerves were jangled. Confused thoughts whirled through his mind.

"It's a shame you don't know the young lady," Basilius said as Oskar opened the door. "Perhaps you could have given evidence to her good character at the trial."

It took everything Oskar had, all of his self-control, to not turn around and confront the proctor, but he knew it would not do any good. It would only confirm that he had a relationship with Lizzie. He closed the door gently behind him and did not quicken his pace until he was well out of earshot.

When he returned to his quarters, he threw open the door. His friends looked at him in alarm.

"What's wrong?" Naseeb asked.

"I need your help."

Chapter 34

Larris strode along the northern stretch of Archstone's city walls, looking out into the distance as if he could see the armies that threatened his kingdom. Somewhere in the distance, Galdora's forces struggled to hold back the armies of Kyrin, and he was powerless to do anything about it. Orman had left three days earlier, taking with him the bulk of the city's troops. All that remained was a skeleton force guarding the city, plus a handful of the rawest recruits at the academy. The war was far away, yet he keenly felt his city's vulnerability. A stiff breeze lent a chill to the cold feeling running down his spine. Something bad was about to happen. He was sure of it.

"I still don't know what my uncle is playing at," he said to Allyn, who walked beside him. "Assuming the regency and then immediately leaving the city?"

Allyn ran a hand through his hair. "We know he's in league with the temple. I can only assume there's some sort of power grab in the works, but for the life of me I can't see how taking all the troops south fits in."

Up ahead, two guards, one tall and dark, the other short and fair, lounged against the parapet. As Larris drew closer, they stood at something close to attention.

"What is this?" Allyn barked. "You do not salute your prince?"

With a slowness bordering on insolence, the two men pressed their fists to their hearts and made awkward bows.

"I'll have your names," Allyn said.

"May I ask who you are?" The taller guard's eyes bored into Allyn. "You aren't the prince."

"He's the man who is going to defenestrate you both if you don't give him your names," Larris said, managing to suppress his grin at the sight of the man's bulging eyes.

The shorter guard spoke up immediately. "It's Edgar and Marcus. Please forgive me, Highness, but please don't defenes...whatever that word was. I prefer women, you see."

Allyn rolled his eyes. "By all the gods. We're relying on the likes you to protect our city?" He turned to Larris. "We're doomed."

Larris ignored the comment though he thought his friend had a point. He turned to the guards. "When guard changes, report to Commander Rayburn for remedial training."

"Yes, Highness," they said in unison. Each bowed again and then snapped to attention.

Larris and Allyn continued their walk. When they were out of earshot, Allyn cocked his head. "Don't you have to have a window in order to defenestrate someone?"

"I think you're right, but they didn't know that." He stopped, turned, and leaned against the parapet. Dark clouds hung low in the distance. "A storm is coming."

"In more ways than one," Allyn agreed.

Larris nodded.

"I quit."

Allyn turned to him and frowned. "What do you mean?"

"I'm finished with this life. I'm going to take Mother, and you if you want to come, and find Shanis. I'll be her consort, or whatever it is she wants me to be. I deserve to be happy, don't you think?"

Allyn's jaw dropped. "You can't be serious."

"I'm not. I just wanted to say it aloud to try it on for size. A part of me wants it, but I could never do that."

Allyn let out a slow breath. "I can't decide if I'm relieved or not. I would give much to be out on the road again. I can't breathe in the city." He tugged absently at his collar. "But I would no sooner leave right now than you would. I've been sworn to you and your house for as long as I can remember." He stiffened, his eye wide.

"What is it?"

"Let's keep walking." Not waiting for Larris, he turned and strode away. "I just realized something. I think I've seen the dark-haired guard before."

"Where?"

Allyn fixed him with a long, measured look before answering. "At the temple."

Larris resisted the urge to look back at the two guards. No need to let the men know they'd drawn undue attention to themselves. "If the temple is insinuating itself into the city guard, we need to do something about it. Let's talk to Rayburn."

They met with the grizzled commander of the guard in Larris' private chambers. He knew the fact they were meeting here would draw attention, but at least the trusted guards outside his door would make certain that no prying ears would hear their discussion.

"With so many men of fighting age joining the army, the pickings have been slim for the guard. Mazier took it upon himself to bring in a sizable number of new recruits. I can't say whether or not they have a connection to the temple." Rayburn frowned down at his scarred hands. "Forgive me, Highness, but I don't trust Mazier or Jowan."

"Neither do I." Larris turned to gaze out the window at the gray day. The pieces were coming together. Orman was in league with the temple, and Mazier had clearly favored Orman for the regency. The Vizier had now taken the unusual step of recruiting men for the city guard. If he were taking it upon himself to filter men loyal to the temple into the guard, could a coup be in the offing?

Allyn seemed to have come to the same conclusion. "We need to keep you safe, Larris. If we find out that Lerryn is dead, they need only to dispose of you and Orman becomes Jowan's puppet king. And then how long before the monarchy is set aside in favor of a temple-dominated council?"

"I won't go into hiding," Larris said. "I'll have to rely on you to watch my back." He turned to Rayburn. "I assume you have a record of which men were brought in by Mazier?"

"Of course."

"Split them up. Pair as many of them as you can with men whom you know to be loyal and incorruptible, and tell those men to keep an eye on these new recruits. Assign the rest to tasks that won't afford them opportunities to cause trouble. Keep your ear to the ground for connections any of your men might have to the temple. And turn away any recruits Mazier sends you. Allyn will begin the search for new guards."

Allyn glanced at him in surprise but did not argue.

"I understand, Highness. I'll get to it immediately. By your leave?" Rayburn had scarcely risen from his chair when a sharp knock came at the door.

"Enter," Larris said.

Theron, a sturdily-built veteran guardsman, opened the door. "Your Highness, Master Hierm Van Derin to see you. He isn't exactly fit to be received, but he insists you will want to see him immediately."

Larris' heart pounded double-time. "He is correct. Send him in."

Van Derin did look a mess. He was covered in trail dust from head to foot, and the dark pouches under his eyes said he sorely lacked sleep. "Your Highness." He bowed deeply and his knees buckled. He would have fallen on his face had Allyn not caught him around the middle. "Sorry," he said as Allyn half-carried him to a chair. "I fear I haven't taken the best care of myself the past few days. Hair and Edrin are with me and they're not in much better shape."

"Send for food and water," Larris said to Allyn. "And an herb woman," he added. "I don't trust the healers. Make sure the other two are cared for as well." He turned back to Hierm. "Tell me everything. Is Lerryn alive?"

Hierm held up a trembling hand. "Time is of the essence. Unless a miracle has happened in the time since we set out for Archstone, you can expect a Kyrinian army to arrive here in a matter of days."

"How..." Larris began, but Hierm spoke over him.

"They came from the northwest through farm country. Lerryn has theories about how they managed to slip through largely undetected, but that doesn't matter now. What is important is that you prepare the city's defenses."

"The prince is alive, then?" Rayburn asked.

Hierm nodded. "He started out fighting bandits, deserters mostly. He managed to gather a decent-sized force of fighting men. He will do what he can to slow the Kyrinian advance, but slow it is all he will be able to do. It's a large army. You'll need every available soldier to man the walls."

Larris sank into his chair. "We have no soldiers. My uncle took them from the city three days ago." He pressed his fingertips to his temples, feeling the beginnings of a headache coming on. "What," he asked, "are we going to do?"

Chapter 35

"That's the jail." Whitt pointed to a low stone building. Dim light flickered through the barred window on the front door. He turned to Oskar. "Are you sure about this?"

Oskar shook his head though hidden as they were in the darkness he doubted they could see him. "Not at all, but I have to get Lizzie out of there."

"What's your plan?" Naseeb asked.

"I'm going to blast the door open, find her, and escape. I need you two to cover my back while I do it." He bit his lip, wondering what dangers he might face one he got inside. Were many jailers on duty? If so, what would he do? He didn't want to hurt anyone, but they might force his hand.

Whitt's jaw dropped. "That is the stupidest plan I've ever heard."

"Do you have a better idea?"

"Every idea is better than that idea. I thought you knew what you were doing."

"Seriously," Naseeb said. "We'd never have left our room if we'd known what you had in mind. Even if you succeed, you'll be turned out for certain."

"He's right," Dacio said. "We need to think about this."

"Quiet." Naseeb raised his hand. "I see Agen. He's coming this way."

Sure enough, Agen was approaching from the opposite direction. The tall youth was trying to keep to the shadows and failing miserably. Oskar and his friends exchanged looks. There was no need to ask why Agen was there. Apparently, he had heard about Lizzie and hoped to catch Oskar outside the city without permission.

As Oskar watched his nemesis approach, he was struck by an idea. He hastily whispered instructions to his friends, who nodded and smiled.

They all trained their eyes on Agen and Naseeb began to whisper the incantation for somnus, a spell that made its target drowsy. So far, he alone among their class had developed an aptitude for it. Soon, Agen began to blink and rub his eyes. The spell was taking effect. He stumbled forward until he was no more than twenty paces from their hiding place.

Oskar joined in with a spell called caligo, which created a cloud of mist around Agen. As soon as Agen was shrouded in fog, Whitt sprang from their hiding place. He covered the intervening space quickly and silently, slipped up behind Agen, and clubbed him across the back of the head. Agen wobbled and his knees buckled, but Whitt caught him and dragged him into the alley where the others waited.

Oskar turned to Naseeb. "We need ale. Quickly, before he wakes."

Naseeb held out his hand. "Coin?" Seeing the expression on Oskar's face, he winked and hurried away, returning in short order with a mug of ale. "I had to pay for the mug too. You owe me."

"Fine." Oskar took the mug and sloshed the ale all over the front of Agen's robes, and then poured the rest down the young man's throat. Agen gasped and began to choke. Whitt rolled him onto his side and pounded him on the back until Agen's coughing fit subsided.

"You three hide," Whitt said. "I know what to do." The powerful young man hauled Agen to his feet, slipped an arm around his waist, and began singing loudly. Moments later the door to the jail opened and a skinny man with a sour face peered out.

"What's with all the noise?" he snarled.

"Sorry," Whitt said. "I tried to quiet him down, but he's not himself."

"It's late," the jailer said flatly.

"I know. I'm just trying to get him back to the Gates. I mean, the city gates."

"The Gates, you say?" The jailer's brow furrowed. "Come here."

"Please, your Honor," Whitt said. "He got some bad news today and went out on his own. My friends and I have been looking for him all evening."

Agen began to stir a little. "Where am I?" he mumbled.

The jailer stepped out into the street and hurried toward Whitt and Agen.

As soon as the man reached the middle of the road, Naseeb dashed to the door and slipped inside.

"You two are too young to be seekers, and I know the rules as well as you do," the jailer said. "I'm required to report this to your masters." He stopped in front of the two young men and sniffed the air. "He reeks of ale, but you seem to be all right."

"He's never done anything like this before. I'm just trying to get him back so he can sleep it off. Isn't there anything you can do?" Whitt asked.

The constable hesitated. "There's nothing I can do for your friend. I'll let you go this time, but I'll need your name."

"It's Shaw," Whitt said, providing the name of one of Agen's closest friends.

"All right. Help me get him inside and then you can go." The jailer and Whitt dragged Agen toward the front door.

Oskar watched, heart racing. Naseeb, the quickest of their group and easily the best at hiding, had gone inside to assess the situation, and with luck, find Lizzie. But even if he managed to find her and get her free, they'd never slip past the jailer now. Oskar might have to resort to main force after all. He was about to step out from his hiding place when Naseeb appeared in the doorway.

"Who are you?" the jailer barked.

"His friend." Naseeb pointed at Agen. "We've been looking for him, but I see you've found him."

"I found him and I'm keeping him. I'll send word to the Gates and let the masters send someone for him. Now the two of you get out of here before I decide to detain you as well." The jailer hauled Agen through the door and closed it behind him.

Naseeb, grinning, hurried over to Oskar.

"Did you see her?" Oskar demanded.

Naseeb nodded. "Just wait."

A few minutes later, the door opened again and Lizzie walked out, followed by a tall, oily-looking man with a shaved head.

Oskar couldn't contain his surprise. "Lizzie!" he called.

She turned around, spotted him, and broke into a grin. "Give me a minute," she said to the tall man, who glanced at Oskar and smirked. She hurried over and took his hands in hers. "What are you doing here?"

"I was going to try and break you out." He felt his cheeks warm as he said it.

She smiled. "That's sweet, but there was no need. We have an understanding with the constabulary. I'll have to repay the guild for the bribe, but I'll be fine."

Oskar didn't know what to make of this bit of information, but Lizzie only laughed at his confusion.

"I'll explain later. I have to make my apologies to the guild. I'll meet you tomorrow night." She gave him a quick kiss on the cheek and hurried away.

Whitt gazed admiringly at her receding form. "That," he said, "is some girl you've got."

Chapter 36

"It's a slaughter down there!" Kelvin loosed another arrow into the confused ranks of Kyrinians who struggled to fight their way up the steep sides of the pass. The bright sun shone down on the black-and-gold clad Kyrinians, and their cries filled the air on what would have otherwise been a beautiful day.

"Why don't they run?"

"They have no choice but to press forward," Lerryn said. "The bulk of their army is behind them. They can't go back now."

The attack had gone off just as he had planned. His forces had remained hidden while the Kyrinians sent advance scouts to probe the pass and had not attacked until the enemy was fully committed. The first riders had spurred their mounts forward and tried to make it through the pass, but the rain of projectiles fired and hurled down on them had brought every man down before he reached the other end. Of course, Lerryn's men had a few surprises waiting for them on the other side, as well.

As the bodies began to pile up, the Kyrinians had no choice but to engage with the attackers. Their archers attempted to return fire, but few of their arrows found their marks. Meanwhile, the infantry tried to advance, but they fell before engaging with Lerryn's troops.

"How long can we keep this up?" Kelvin asked.

"Until we run out of arrows. Or until they get enough men up the slopes to push us back. We'll have to retreat before that happens, though."

"Oh." Kelvin sounded disappointed. "I sort of hoped they'd just keep riding through the pass and we'd keep shooting them down."

Lerryn laughed. "If only it were that easy." The Kyrinian's numbers would soon prove too much for his force, but he was making them bleed, as he had planned. He watched as his forces repulsed another charge, but another line formed almost immediately and charged again. Each attack made it a little farther up the hill. Lerryn's forces were already running low on arrows, and now his men were choosing their targets carefully, reluctant to waste a shot. Gradually, they gave ground.

"That didn't last long." Kelvin was proving to be an astute pupil. "I suppose I should get ready?" At Lerryn's nod, he took out the battered war horn he'd taken off a dead Kyrinian weeks before, pressed it to his lips, and waited.

Lerryn watched, knowing he had to time this exactly right. He needed the Kyrinian attacks on both sides of the pass to ebb at the same time, giving his own troops the chance to disengage and get clear of what came next.

"Now!" he shouted.

Kelvin blew two long, loud blasts. All along the pass, their forces unleashed a final torrent of arrows, spears, and rocks and then turned and retreated to the top of the pass. Seeing their enemy in full retreat, a cheer went up among the Kyrinians. They rallied and began to climb the steep hills en masse. Behind them, troops continued to pour into the pass.

"Wait until they've almost reached the top," Lerryn whispered to himself. "Now!"

A single sharp blast from the horn, and then an odd moment of almost quiet fell across the battlefield as the Kyrinians looked for an attack that did not come.

And then a deep, hollow rumbling filled the air. Up and down the battle lines,

Lerryn's men tipped boulders over the edge and sent them tumbling down onto the surprised Kyrinians. Confused shouts rang out as men turned and tried to flee downhill, only to run into line after line of their own men who were intent on driving forward.

The boulders did their grisly work, crushing every man who stood in the way.

"Again!" Lerryn shouted.

Kelvin blew his horn, and rows of archers armed with flaming arrows stood and fired down into piles of dry shrubs, grass, leaves, and sticks Lerryn's men had planted all over the hillsides. In a matter of minutes, the entire pass was filled with thick white smoke as the gentle breeze that flowed through drew the smoke like a chimney. The Kyrinians would find it hard to see and even harder to breathe.

At Lerryn's command, Kelvin sounded the retreat. As they rode away, Lerryn managed a smile. The attack had gone as well as he could have hoped. They'd dealt a blow to the enemy's morale and reduced their numbers in the bargain.

"Are you sure they won't come after us?" Kelvin shouted.

"No." He supposed it was possible the Kyrinians might pursue them, but that would be a victory in itself. They'd have to divide their forces and spread out across the countryside in order to chase down Lerryn's forces. "I wish they would, but I fear they'll keep straight on until they reach Archstone."

The sun was an orange ball on the horizon when they met up with Tabars and the squad of cavalry he now commanded. Lerryn could tell by the look on his old comrade's face that something was wrong.

"What is it?" he asked as soon as he reined in at Tabars' side.

"We routed them. The enemy is in full retreat."

"But that's good, isn't it?" Kelvin asked.

Lerryn shook his head. "It's not good; it's impossible."

"They tricked us. Somehow they knew we were here, and they sent in just enough men to convince us the army was coming through the pass. Their main force now has at least a day's march on us, perhaps more."

Lerryn took a deep, calming breath. The Kyrinians had sacrificed at least a thousand men just to gain a march on him. His only hope had been to slow the enemy down in order to buy time for Larris to prepare Archstone's defenses.

He had failed.

Chapter 37

Oskar sighed and turned another page. He flipped hastily through the book, scanning the words but not digesting them. He knew what he was looking for, but had not found it yet.

Since being raised to initiate, he had spent as much of his limited free time as possible in the archives. He would have liked to have spent more, but it wouldn't do to fall behind in his studies immediately after being raised. Especially since Basilius had not supported him. He would do everything in his power to prove the man wrong. Then again, the proctor's objections to his candidacy had more to do with his connection to Aspin than to any reservations about Oskar as an initiate. Of that he was sure.

He closed the book, set it aside, and picked up another. He had given up searching through volumes of history and now focused on prophecy. It seemed, though, that the weapon was not the subject of a great deal of prophetic lore. He had read and reread what he could find, but it all was familiar to him. For the first time, he considered that he might fail at the task Aspin had set him.

This new book was useless. It was written by a tribesman who lived in the mountains of Riza. Written in verse, it spoke of thieves, princes, and murder. It might have made for an interesting read, but it was not what he needed right now. He set it aside and picked up the last of the books he'd taken from the shelves: a tiny volume the size of his hand. It's cracked leather cover and yellowed, brittle pages spoke of age. It looked promising, but the spidery script was difficult to read. It would take some time to work his way through it.

"There you are. How did I know I'd find you in the darkest corner of this place?" Dacio pulled up a chair and sat down beside him. "We should go somewhere else and talk."

Oskar turned and frowned at his friend, whose face was pale. Dacio's eyes darted to and fro and he tapped his foot with nervous energy.

"What's wrong?"

"I have something to tell you and I don't want Agen to hear."

"Is he around? I'm surprised they let him out of the kitchens." Oskar grinned. Since his arrest, Agen had been scrubbing pots as a punishment.

"I saw him when I came in. He greeted me in the usual way." Dacio made an obscene gesture and Oskar laughed. "This is important and I don't want to be overheard."

Oskar stood and looked around. No one was in sight. "Just tell me now and say it quietly. We only have a few minutes until mealtime."

Dacio hesitated. "All right. I've been working on translating your glyphs. The rubbings you made captured only bits and pieces of writing. The first one I translated is incomplete, but it paints a compelling picture. I came looking for you as soon as I finished this bit." He drew a rolled parchment from within his robe and handed it to Oskar.

Oskar looked around again to make sure no one was watching and then opened it. He began to read, slowly at first and then faster.

> *like a curse upon the nations*
> *feared the world would be torn apart.*
> *gathered in the holy place*
> *I freely give my life*
> *surrendered her life upon the blade*
> *the temple shook as Vesala was drawn into*
> *by the power of ultimate sacrifice*

Oskar's blood turned to ice. Hands trembling, he rolled the parchment up and looked at Dacio. Now he understood why his friend appeared shaken.

"I have not yet translated the other pages, but at a glance it looks like the same story was written over and over on the walls of the city you visited. They aren't all exactly the same so if I translate them all I might be able to piece most of it together." From the look on his face that was the last thing Dacio wanted to do.

"Please do." Oskar's throat was tight and he could barely speak. "But I think we both know what you will find."

Muffled cries broke the silence. They both sprang to their feet before realizing that the disturbance came from down below. They heard footsteps and saw that the few men who had been studying on this floor were now hurrying toward the stairs.

"I wonder what's going on," Dacio said.

"I don't know. Let's find out." Oskar tucked the book of prophecy into his robe and stood.

"You go. I think I'll finish up the translation while I've got this place to myself. Forgive me, but I'd like to have this out of my hands as quickly as possible." Dacio took out the remainder of Oskar's rubbings, laid them on the table, and set to work.

Oskar hurried down the stairs and found the main floor of the archives empty. Whatever was happening, it wasn't here. Out in the hallway, he met Whitt and Naseeb coming in his direction. Both looked as frightened as Dacio had been.

"What is it?"

Whitt grabbed Oskar by the arm and hauled him back inside the archives. "Something is happening," he said in a low voice.

"But why do we…"

"Not now!" Naseeb made a slashing gesture with his hand. "Whitt, stand by the door and warn us if anyone comes this way and try not to look suspicious."

"Yes, Sir. Anything else, Sir?"

Naseeb rolled his eyes. "Please."

"That's better." Whitt sauntered over to the archives entrance, leaned against the wall, and gazed out at the milling throng.

"Something is happening. Something bad. The word is, Basilius is trying to take the prelate's chair."

The news hit Oskar like a slap. "How could he? Surely he doesn't have the support of enough proctors, nor that of the masters."

"If the rumors are true, he's not going about it the usual way. No one can say for certain because that entire wing of the Gates has been barricaded." Naseeb swallowed hard. "By magic."

"Are you saying he is staging a coup?" Oskar couldn't believe his ears.

"I'm not saying it, but everyone else is. Oskar," Naseeb whispered, "everyone is saying Basilius is a coldheart and he's got a legion of followers inside the Gates. They're saying the second Frostmarch is beginning."

Oskar's head swam. "Once the Silver Serpent was found it was only a matter of time, I suppose. But I still can't believe Basilius is a follower of the Ice King. He's a nasty piece of work but he…" Oskar didn't know how to finish the sentence.

"Whether it's true or not, you have to get out of here. If Basilius succeeds, he'll be the most powerful man in the gates and you'll have no one to protect you from him. If he fails, he and his followers will be desperate. Who knows what they might do?"

"Where would I go?" But as soon as he had asked the question, Oskar knew the answer. "I have to get to Shanis."

Just then, Whitt hurried to their side. "I overheard two saikurs talking. They say Denrill has been deposed and some of the proctors and masters are dead. Basilius had men planted throughout the Gates waiting for him to give the word. Some are trying to make a fight of it but it isn't going well. Everyone's confused and afraid and no one knows who to trust. It's every bit as bad as we feared."

"I say we get out of here. We'll find somewhere safe until things settle down here if they ever do." Naseeb turned to Oskar. "Have you seen Dacio?"

"He's upstairs." Oskar wanted to tell his friends what Dacio had learned, but now was not the time. "Do you think you can make it back to our quarters?" Naseeb nodded. "Good. Get Dacio, go back to the room and gather as many of our things as you can, and meet me in the city just over the wall at the far side of the combat ground."

"What are you going to do?" Naseeb asked.

"I'm going to find Lizzie."

Oskar made his way through the crowded hallway, trying not to draw any more notice than necessary, but no one paid him any mind. Everyone seemed to be either exchanging gossip or debating their next move. A few had already gathered their possessions and were headed for the front gate. He wondered if they would be permitted to leave, or if Basilius had taken measures to stop anyone from fleeing. If so, he hoped that he and his friends would be able to get away. Surely the proctor did not have enough men to seal the entire perimeter.

When he made it out the back door, he quickened his pace, breaking into a sprint when he reached the combat ground. He'd scale the wall, head into the city, and search for Lizzie until he found her. He supposed he'd start where he'd seen her before, in the area around the alehouse he and his friends had visited when Dacio had been raised to initiate.

So distracted was he by his plans that he almost failed to notice the flash of movement out of the corner of his eye. He ducked as something flew past his head and clattered against the wall. A knife. Muttering a shielding spell he looked around for his attacker.

"Basilius told me not to kill you, but I'm sure he will understand if it happens by accident." Agen stepped out from behind a tree, a wicked grin spreading across his face. "I hated you from the start, and then you landed me in jail. It's time for you to pay." He made a cupping gesture and flung his empty hand toward Oskar, who stepped out of the way. The ball of energy burst against the wall behind him, spraying shards of stone everywhere.

"You don't want to kill me," Oskar said. "If you did you wouldn't have wasted time with that ridiculous speech. 'Time to pay?' You've seen one too many mummers' shows."

Agen hurled another ball of energy which Oskar easily sidestepped.

"And you should only use that spell when someone's back is turned. It's too easy to see what's coming." As he spoke, Oskar moved toward the wall, hoping for an opportunity to get away. "Why don't you get out of here before you get hurt? Basilius will never know you saw me."

"He'll know, farm boy. He'll know because I'll show him your body." Agen began walking forward, eyes alive with malice. "You never belonged here. You're a country lout who relied on your friends and on the masters who doted on you. But there's no one here now but you and me. Aaaah!" Agen began batting at the hem of his robes which had suddenly burst into flame.

Oskar turned and dashed for the wall. While Agen made his speech, Oskar had been whispering a fire spell and the fool hadn't even noticed.

He reached the wall in five strides and began to climb its rough surface. He was almost at the top when something yanked him back. He hit the ground hard, the breath leaving him in a rush. He opened his eyes in time to see Agen raise his booted foot.

He rolled to the side as Agen stamped down where Oskar's head had been a moment before. Oskar climbed to his hands and knees, trying to focus his will, but Agen's foot sailed through the air and caught him on the side of the head. Had it been a direct blow Oskar would have been rendered unconscious. Still, it made his ears ring.

He managed to suck in a ragged breath as Agen drew back his foot to kick him again. Oskar hurled himself forward, caught Agen by the leg, and bore him to the ground.

Despite his bookish nature, back in Galsbur Oskar had been a fair wrestler and the training he had received under Master Lang's tutelage had strengthened his body and honed his skills to a fine edge.

Using his weight to keep Agen down, he rained down punches onto the young man's face. Agen blocked a few, but most found their target. Agen bucked, twisted, and jerked, trying to dislodge him, but Oskar maintained his balance. In a matter of seconds, Agen's face was masked in bright red blood.

"You'll have to kill me," Agen said through split lips.

"Only if you're stupid enough to make me." Oskar rose up and Agen, feeling the absence of weight on his chest, turned over in a flash and tried to crawl away. It was what Oskar was waiting for. He came down on Agen's back, slipped one arm around his neck, and squeezed. Agen squirmed and clawed at Oskar's arm, but his grip held fast.

It was over in less than a minute. Agen's body went limp as he lost consciousness. Exhausted, Oskar wobbled to his feet and looked down at his fallen opponent.

"Are you going to cut his throat or should I?" Oskar whirled about to see Lizzie perched on the wall, grinning like the cat who got the cream. "Oh, don't look at me like that. If you'd gotten into any serious trouble, I would've intervened." She slid gracefully down off the wall, slinked over to him, and wrapped her arms around his neck. "But you did well. I'm impressed."

Although his world, or at least this little corner of it, seemed to be falling down around him, Oskar couldn't help but smile. He slipped an arm around Lizzie's waist and leaned down to kiss her.

"Hold on." She pushed him away, turned toward Agen, who was beginning to stir, and kicked him in the temple. Agen flopped back to the ground. "Now, where were we?" She kissed him deeply, but not long enough for his liking.

"What are you doing here? I was coming to find you."

Lizzie laughed. "Now that would have been something to see. You trying to find me in the city. Nice joke, country boy." She saw the expression on his face and made a tiny frown. "Don't look at me like that. You know I'm right. Anyway, the city is abuzz with word of the little... problem you're having here. I wanted to find you and make sure you're all right."

"I am for the moment, but the man who has taken over hates me and he wants to know what I know about Shanis and the Silver Serpent. I'm getting out of here before he catches up with me and I want you to come too."

Lizzie didn't hesitate. "Yes." She kissed him again, this time in a much more satisfactory fashion. They might have stayed like that for hours, but they were soon interrupted by the arrival of Oskar's friends.

"I might have known. Men are dying, the Gates is falling apart, Basilius is probably after you, and you stand here kissing a girl." Naseeb looked down at Agen. "What happened to him?"

"He decided to kill me."

"That didn't work out for him, did it?" Whitt asked. Agen began to move again and Whitt kicked him in the groin. "Always wanted to do that." He and Naseeb tied Agen up with his own shoelaces, stuffed a sock in his mouth and hid him beneath some nearby bushes. "That should keep him for a while."

They divided their possessions and stuffed them into packs they found in the nearby armory.

"I didn't have time to steal any food," Naseeb said, "but we have money, so we'll make do."

They armed themselves, Whitt and Dacio with swords, Naseeb with a bow and quiver, and Oskar with a staff and belt knife. When they were ready, they all turned Oskar.

"Where to first?" Dacio asked.

Oskar found it odd to be thrust into a position of leadership. He considered the question. He needed to get to Shanis, but he wasn't certain where she was, or that the five of them alone could make it to her without help.

"Archstone," he said. "To find Larris."

Chapter 38

"They will be here within the hour." Allyn's blank face matched his emotionless tone. "Our scouts say it's a sizeable force."

"We need only to hold them off until help arrives." Larris hoped he sounded more confident than he felt. He knew the chance was small. Their allies had thus far proved unwilling to offer aid, and even if they did, it would take weeks for help to arrive.

"I'd like to know where that saikur disappeared to," Allyn said.

Larris had sent for James, the saikur who served as liaison between Archstone and the Gates, hoping he could use the saikurs' unique form of communication to send for help more quickly, but the man's quarters were empty and no one knew where he'd gone. Larris feared the worst.

"I can't imagine he'd flee the city. He's a saikur," Larris said.

Allyn barked a bitter laugh. "Why not? Everyone else has."

"That's unfair. Where would we be without those who remained?" Desperate for bodies to man the city walls, Larris had sent agents out amongst the masses of refugees, signing on any man with fighting experience or who looked like he could handle a weapon. They were a weak lot, to be sure, but better than nothing. "If nothing else, the city will appear well-defended. And I can't blame the rest for fleeing. I only wish we could have taken them all inside the walls."

"If the Kyrinians breach our defenses, those who fled to the countryside will be better off than those of us inside." Allyn bared his teeth in a wolfish grin. "But I plan on taking out my share long before that happens."

"Let us hope it doesn't come to that." Larris and his friend exchanged a long look and clasped hands.

"Don't get sentimental on me." Allyn looked out at the horizon and frowned. "Riders approaching."

Indeed, a small contingent of men riding under a banner of truce, no more than a dozen, were galloping hard for the city. They reined in just beyond the range of the archers on the wall. At this distance, Larris could easily make out their black and gold uniforms.

"Kyrinians," he said. "I wonder what they want."

"They want us to surrender." Allyn scowled in the Kyrinians' direction. "They wouldn't come all this way just to ask for a cessation of hostilities."

A sudden, reckless urge came over Larris. "Let's go. I'll ride out to meet with them."

"You're an ice-blighted fool if you think you're going to expose yourself to enemy fire no matter how small a force."

"I'm not letting the council negotiate on the city's behalf. For all we know, the temple is in league with Kyrin. I need to get out there before Jowan and Mazier open the gates to them."

"That won't happen," Allyn said. "I took the liberty of sequestering the non-military members of the Regis inside the council chamber for the duration of the battle. I knew you wouldn't approve, at least not officially, so I didn't tell you."

Larris smiled for the first time all day. "Nicely done. Now, we need to decide who we can trust to meet with the Kyrinians."

"I don't think that will be necessary. They're coming closer."

Sure enough, the Kyrinians were slowly riding toward the city gate.

"Brave or foolish," Larris said.

"Expendable, more like." When the men were within hailing distance, Allyn called down to them. "That's close enough. What do you want?"

"We want to speak to King Allar Van Altman." The speaker was a wiry man with thinning, blond hair and a hawkish nose.

The mention of his father's name was like a punch to Larris' gut. Of course, this army that had been traveling in near-secret across the countryside would not be privy to recent events.

"I am afraid you are too late," Larris said. "He went to be with the gods several days ago. I am Larris Van Altman and I speak for Archstone and for all of Galdora."

"My sympathies, Highness." The man made a quick bow of his head, and his companions followed suit. "I will make this brief. We have a force sufficient to overwhelm your city, but would prefer to spare both sides unnecessary casualties. Kyrin's terms are simple. Galdora returns to us our ancestral lands north of the Whiterush River. Lands which we, incidentally, hold right now."

Since Galdora had been carved out of Kyrin and Lothan to serve as a buffer between the two nations, and as a refuge for the hard-put members of Kyrinian society, Kyrin had coveted the strip of fertile farmland in northern Galdora and had tried on more than one occasion to reclaim it by force.

"No." Larris was not about to surrender land for which so many Galdorans had sacrificed their lives to defend.

"Forgive me, Highness, but your position is untenable. Your forces are spread out all over your kingdom and no allies are coming to your aid." He said the last in a loud voice intended to travel as far up and down the wall as possible. Larris heard muttering among the guards as they considered the man's words. "We will give you until morning to consider our offer. Discuss it with your Regis. I am sure they will see that none of the brave men of this city need die for the sake of a parcel of land hundreds of leagues away. Land you no longer control."

Larris was about to reply that his answer would be unchanged on the morrow, but Allyn nudged him.

"We need every second we can get to prepare our defenses," he whispered.

Larris grimaced. Allyn was right. "Very well. But do not expect my answer to change. We are more than prepared to repel any attack you send against us. A Galdoran man fears no yellow-haired northerner."

At these words, a ragged cheer rose up among the defenders who stood within earshot.

The Kyrinian smirked. "As you wish. If you see reason by sunrise, lower your flags and open your gates. If not, we attack." He bowed, wheeled his horse, and rode away.

"Well then," Allyn said. "That bought us a little time."

"I only hope we can do something useful with it." Deep down, Larris knew it was a faint hope. They needed a miracle.

Chapter 39

I don't think we can hold them much longer." Sweat soaked Allyn's blonde hair, but he appeared unharmed. That alone seemed a miracle in the midst of the pitched battle. As promised, the Kyrinians had attacked at dawn and had not relented since.

Larris looked across the battlefield at the enemy forces which were already rallying for another charge. Just beyond their ranks, siege towers were being wheeled into place. A bad situation was about to get worse.

The Galdorans had fought bravely, bleeding the Kyrinians in every clash. The veterans they had culled from the ranks of refugees provided solid leadership, strengthening the resolve of their less-experienced comrades. They used their defenses to good effect, but their own losses were taking their toll. A few of the enemy, carrying scaling ladders, had actually surmounted the walls on the last attack. If they came again in force, he doubted the defenders could hold them back this time.

"I want the catapults firing for all they're worth as soon as the siege engines are in range. We have got to bring them down," he ordered.

"They will go for the gates at the same time—both the main and the postern." Rayburn cleared his throat and spat over the wall. "They'll spread us thin and look for any opportunity to break through. Once they get a toehold in the city..." He didn't need to finish his sentence. Without the walls for protection they would quickly succumb to Kyrinian's superior numbers.

Larris looked up and down the ramparts, appreciating for the first time how severely their ranks had been depleted. New faces had appeared to take up the defense of the city: old men, young boys, and women. None of them should have been needed to fight, but everyone seemed to understand this was their last chance. He had been pleasantly surprised to find virtually no dissension in the ranks. Given their present circumstances, he had expected more people to advocate surrender. The

Galdorans' deep-seated hatred and distrust of the Kyrinians appeared to have won out.

No sooner had that thought passed through his mind than a loud voice rang out from somewhere close by.

"We must surrender! Surrender or we will surely die!"

Larris looked around and saw a man in Temple robes walking along the battlements. The defenders watched him go by and Larris could tell by the expressions on their faces that some of them were close to following his instructions.

"Someone needs to close his mouth," Larris said. His patience with the Temple was at an end.

Allyn drew his bow and took aim at the priest.

"Not like that." Larris pushed the bow down. "Not everything I say is a direct order."

"I'll remember that." Allyn lowered his bow.

Larris managed a smile and shook his head

The priest's gaze fell upon Larris and his eyes widened. He pointed a bony finger in the prince's direction.

"You! What have you done with the archpriest? Where is he?"

"The archpriest is performing his duties as a member of the Regis," Allen shouted. "You should be about your duties as well. There are wounded who need your care." The temple priests had been helping to care for the wounded.

"There would be no wounded if you would see reason. We cannot fight so many. Your hubris will kill us all."

"You want to surrender?" Larris asked. "Very well." He turned to Rayburn. "Put him in a catapult and send him to the Kyrinians so that he may negotiate surrender terms." The priest blanched, turned, and ran. Larris laughed, but he had no time to savor his small victory.

"Everyone down!" Rayburn shouted.

The Kyrinian's war machines had opened fire again. Huge boulders hurtled through the air, crashing against the city walls. One struck close to where Larris stood. He felt the ground quake beneath his feet and shards of broken stone flew through the air, peppering him with tiny, sharp fragments. Under cover of the attack, the siege engines rolled forward, supported by the mass of Kyrinian troops.

"Archers hold your fire!" Rayburn shouted as a few nervous defenders released arrows that fell well short of their intended targets. "Wait until they are in range. I will give the order."

The Galdorans catapults opened up. One managed to find its target, smashing a siege engine. A cry of alarm went up from the Kyrinian ranks as the siege engine toppled into their tightly-packed ranks. The other catapults missed their targets but the boulders they hurled tore holes in the Kyrinian line, holes that were immediately filled by more soldiers. As the siege engines drew within bow range, the defenders sent flaming arrows at their targets. Some found purchase in the wooden towers and began to smolder.

In response, the Kyrinian archers raked the wall with their own hail of arrows. Cries of pain up and down the line told Larris that some had found their marks. With a roar, the front ranks of the Kyrinian troops charged forward. Though the enemy archers continued to fire, the defenders stood bravely, giving back as good as they got. All along the line, Kyrinian soldiers fell. Larris grimaced at the bloody work.

"Ladders!" Someone shouted

The first rank of Kyrinians had reached the wall and were throwing up siege ladders. The defenders immediately responded. Women and children tossed stones and any other heavy objects they could find down onto the attackers while men used long poles to push the ladders away from the walls. Larris saw a young woman raise a burning oil lamp above her head, ready to fling it down onto the enemy when an arrow took her in the throat. She collapsed without making a sound, a look of surprise filling her dying eyes. The lamp shattered, spilling burning oil all-around. Larris turned away, wincing. It was not the first tragic death he had seen during the battle, nor would it be the last

Though none of the soldiers bearing ladders had breached the walls, they had served their purpose, occupying the defenders so that the siege towers could be rolled into place. Three towers had made it across the battlefield intact and now their doors fell open, forming drawbridges that led onto the city walls. The sounds of hand-to-hand fighting rose up all around as defenders were forced to abandon their posts in order to meet this new threat. Down below, a thunderous crash told Larris that the enemy was also battering at the front gates. They wouldn't last much longer

"Your Highness!" A young man in the uniform of a city guard ran up to him, made a hasty bow, and dropped to one knee.

"There's no time for that! What is it?"

"The enemy broke through the postern gate. We drove them back and got it closed again."

"Then why are you telling me? We have a battle to fight."

"The enemy didn't actually break through. Some of our own opened the gate for them. They were men from the temple." He paused and drew in a long, ragged breath. "They were shouting something about it being time for the Seven to give way to the One."

Larris didn't have time to suss out exactly what that meant. Save for the fact that he now had proof that the Temple was on the Kyrinian side.

"Our officers are dead and the one they call "Hair" is in charge. He wants to know your orders."

"Tell him to hold a few of the temple men for questioning, and kill anyone else who even looks like he is attempting to aid the enemy. Take no further prisoners."

The youth gave a single nod, hopped up, and dashed away.

"Not that it will matter," Larris muttered. He could no longer deny it. The battle was almost over, and they had lost.

Somewhere in the distance a horn sounded its tinny note. Probably Kyrinian reinforcements. He looked around at the defenders who now fought with desperation against the men who had breached the walls. He saw Hierm run a man through, kick the body off of his sword, and turn to face two more Kyrinians. Beside him, Rinala, clad in her Monaghan garb, fought with two long knives.

He had led them all to their deaths. Had the priest been right? Was it his hubris that had brought him them to this end? Should he have agreed to the enemy's terms? He supposed it didn't matter now. Tightening his grip on his sword, he strode into the thick of the fight. If he was to die, he would take as many Kyrinians with him as he could

The horn sounded again, this time closer. Someone grabbed his shoulder and spun him around. It was Allyn. His friend was shouting something, but Larris could not make it out, so great was his rage and battle lust. He shook his head and tried to focus.

"What do you say?"

This time, Allyn's words swam through the fog in Larris' mind.

"It's Lerryn!"

Larris looked in the direction Allyn pointed and let out a triumphant shout. A new army had appeared on the horizon, and though he could not see the face of its leader, he could make out the banner of the White Fang, Lerryn's elite unit.

"Van Derin told us that Lerryn had gathered only a modest force, a ragtag one at that," Allyn said. "But those are regular troops, and plenty of them. How is it possible?

"I don't care. What matters now is that we hold the city. We can't give up now." As loudly as he could, he cried out, "Prince Lerryn has arrived! We are saved! Fight! Fight for your prince and rightful king!" Sword held aloft, he ran along the walls shouting words of encouragement. Behind him, he could hear Allyn doing the same. Soon the defenders echoed his cries and the message ran along the walls ahead of him until he no longer needed to spread the word himself.

Heartened by this stroke of good fortune, the defenders struck back with vigor. The attack began to falter. Down below, the Kyrinians heard the war horns and were now aware of a new army at their backs. Larris watched as their officers attempt to rally the troops to meet this new threat.

The newly-arrived Galdoran army closed in. Arrows flew and black and gold-clad men fell. The two forces closed in on one another, and as the Galdoran foot soldiers charged into the ranks of Kyrinian's, a contingent of cavalry broke away, circled the Kyrinian flank and swept along the wall, driving the attackers away from the front gate. Another unit veered off in the opposite direction, most likely heading for the postern gate.

Their main force now caught between the city walls and a superior force of Galdorans, the Kyrinians, who had seemed on the verge of taking the city, began to drop their weapons and call for surrender. A tumult arose along the city walls as the defenders rejoiced. Larris caught Allyn up in a rough embrace, and then turned to clasp hands with Rayburn, who scrubbed his teary eyes with a bloody sleeve. He saw Hierm and Rinala embrace, and relief flooded him that his friends have survived. He hoped Hair and Edrin had survived the fight at the rear gate.

Down below, he spotted Lerryn looking up at the walls and when their eyes met his brother grinned and raised his sword in salute. The defenders began to shout Lerryn's name, singing the praises of the prince who had rescued them in their direst hour. Larris smiled. His brother would be a beloved king.

The tenor of the chant began to change. Larris felt hands grabbing him, and then he was hoisted up into the air. He realized that the people who are no longer calling Lerryn's name, but his own.

"Come on, Larris," Allyn chided. "At least give them one smile."

Relief flooding through him, Larris raised his fists above his head and cried out in exultation. They had done it!

Chapter 40

Larris met his brother at the gate. Despite the dirt, sweat, and blood that marred Lerryn's face, the first prince looked vigorous. Whatever changes his time away had wrought, they had been for the better.

Smiling, Lerryn slid down off his horse and embraced his brother.

"I am so happy to see you," Larris said. "I had heard you were still alive, but I dared not believe it."

"I've never felt more alive." Lerryn didn't elaborate, but Larris took his brother's meaning. "There is someone you should meet." He gave a mysterious grin and motioned to a man who had just dismounted. "This is Colin Malan."

It took a moment for the name to register with Larris. "You're Shanis' father."

"That I am." Colin Malan was a veritable bear of a man: large, dark, and powerfully built. But his smile was genuine, and his dark eyes friendly. "I understand you and my daughter are friends."

"Yes sir, we are."

Colin laughed. "A prince calling me 'sir.' Now that is not something that happens every day. It is a pleasure to meet you, Highness."

"Please, call me Larris." He offered his hand and tried not to wince at Colin's powerful grip. "After all, you are the father of a queen."

Colin's eyes widened. "I had not heard."

"I don't know all the details, but sources tell me Shanis has taken the throne of Lothan."

"That is good. I hope I will be able to see her soon." He glanced at Lerryn, whose expression had turned grave.

"We have much to discuss," Lerryn said.

"Indeed we do," Larris agreed. "Let us speak alone for a moment." He and his brother drew away and Larris broke the news of their father's death. Lerryn's expression did not change, but Larris could see the hurt in his brother's eyes.

"I wish he had lived long enough to see that I've changed. There is much about my past I'm ashamed of."

"He never stopped loving you," Larris said. "There is more I need to tell you, much more, but we can talk as we walk."

Escorted by a contingent of city guard, Larris, Lerryn, Colin, Hierm, Rinala, a young man named Kelvin, who seemed to be Lerryn's ward of sorts, and Tabars, whom Larris learned was the only remaining member of the original White Fang, made their way to the palace. Along the way, Larris filled his brother in on the situation with the temple, the letter of abdication, and the status of the regency. Once inside the palace, they spoke briefly in private. By the time they left the room, they had formulated a plan.

Jowan sprang to his feet as soon as Larris opened the door of the chamber where the Regis was being held.

"You have held us prisoner here long enough! I will…" His words died in his throat when his eyes fell on Lerryn.

"Your Highness, it is a great relief to see you alive." Mazier rose from his seat and bowed deeply.

Jowan recovered himself quickly. "Indeed it is. Forgive me, but your brother's behavior has been most unseemly. He has imprisoned us here with no news of what transpires outside these walls."

"Imprisoned?" Lerryn glanced at Larris before turning back to the men at the table. "That is a serious accusation you have leveled against my brother."

"We are here, aren't we? You can see with your own eyes."

"What I see is that my brother has taken steps to keep the members of the Regis safe while he lays his life on the line to defend this city. And since you are all still alive, it would appear that his efforts have been successful."

Jowan gaped at Lerryn. "Highness, I assure you, our incarceration here was not voluntary."

"I am certain what the archpriest means to say is that we were reluctant to remain here where we felt we were of no use," Edwin said smoothly. "But we see the wisdom in his decision."

Larris suppressed a smile. The silvermaster was one of the few whom he knew he could trust.

"I know we are all wondering," Edwin continued, "how goes the battle?"

Lerryn and Larris exchanged glances. "You tell them," Lerryn said.

"We won," Larris said. "My brother and his army arrived just in time."

"We were only in time because Prince Larris skillfully defended the city, keeping the enemy at bay until we arrived."

Larris managed to maintain his dignity, but only just. Lerryn had never paid him a compliment about his leadership skills. "I've been meaning to ask you, how did you come by an army? The last we heard you had only a modest force at your disposal."

"We should sit." Lerryn motioned to the table. Not waiting for the others, he took the seat at the head and the others joined him. When they were all seated, he began. "Unfortunately, Rayburn and Hugo will not be joining us as they have duties to which to attend. The situation has changed dramatically. Kyrin has withdrawn its forces from our territory. I found myself at the head of an army only because we crossed paths as they made their way back to the city."

"Why has Kyrin withdrawn and why have we not heard about it?" Mazier asked.

"You would have heard about it upon the army's return. It is a new development." Lerryn paused, his face grave. "As to why the enemy has given up the fight it is because they are now facing an invasion on their western frontier much like the one we faced a short while ago. In fact, Riza and Halvala are also fighting invaders, and I would not be surprised if forces are once again threatening the western borders of our nation and that of Lothan."

"In that case it is essential that you assume the crown as quickly as possible," Edwin said. "Ordinarily we would treat the occasion with greater fanfare and grant you the honors you richly deserve, but circumstances demand otherwise."

Lerryn made a dismissive gesture. "It is not important. We have the defense of our nation to think of."

Jowan cleared his throat and looked around nervously. "Highness, there is a small matter which must be resolved. A rumor is going about that you abdicated your position as heir to the throne."

Lerryn looks surprised. "Who would spread such a rumor? Have they any proof?"

"We heard a rumor that there is a document, signed by you and witnessed by others."

"Forging a document is a serious offense," Lerryn said. "Forging a royal seal is punishable by death. If such a document exists, I should love to see it. I would take a personal interest in tracking down the forger."

Jowan and Mazier exchanged glances. Larris wanted to laugh as he watched realization dawn on their faces. If they produced the document now, they would not only have to explain how they came by it, but defend themselves against an accusation of forgery.

Jowan was not yet ready to surrender. "Your brother witnessed your abdication, as did his manservant, the entirety of White Fang, and at least one other. You surrendered your position before you went west to fight the invaders."

Lerryn slowly turned his head, eyebrows raised and gazed at the archpriest, who quickly withered under the Prince's stare.

"At least, that is the rumor," he added weakly.

"A rumor that can easily be put to rest." Lerryn slapped his palms on the table. "Brother, did you witness me abdicate my position as First Prince?"

"I did not." It was a lie, and it pained Larris to tell it, but he knew it was the right thing to do. Lerryn was the man to lead Galdora. His brother had changed for the better.

"I regret to say that only one member of the White Fang survived the battle in the west. He has taken it upon himself to guard my person and is standing outside right now."

Larris went to the door and summoned Tabars. The grizzled veteran looked out of place here, but he faced the Regis with the same confidence he displayed in battle.

"Ask him," Lerryn said to Mazier.

The vizier cleared his throat. "Did you witness His Highness abdicate his position as First Prince of Galdoran?"

Tabars shook his head.

"On your honor!" Jowan said shrilly.

For a moment, Larris feared they were sunk. Tabars was nothing if not honorable, but he was also more devoted to Lerryn than any other man alive. Furthermore, he had agreed with the rest of them: Lerryn should be King. The kingdom could not be divided, and that is exactly what would happen if the succession were thrown into dispute.

"I will thank the priest not to question my honor," Tabars said. "You serve the gods, but I serve this nation. I have bled for it. And I say His Highness did not abdicate and I will cross swords with any man who says otherwise."

"I believe that settles it." Edwin grinned. "Unless one of you is in the mood for a duel."

No one spoke. After a long silence, Tabars bowed himself out.

"Very well. I trust that the Regis will make the necessary arrangements for my coronation at the earliest possible convenience." Lerryn stood. "Because, gentlemen, in case you fail to reach the conclusion for yourselves, a new Frostmarch is upon us."

Part 2- Frostmarch

Chapter 41

He still remembered his name. Whatever else Pedric Karst might have forgotten, his name remained. Pedric Karst, king of the new nation of Kurnsbur. Oddly, it seemed he could remember little else. Where had he lived and what had he done before he came to this place? He concentrated, bringing all his faculties to bear on the subject. Flashes returned to him: childhood memories, his mother's face, learning to fight with the sword, and an image of a beautiful yet terrible red-haired girl. He couldn't remember who she was or how he knew her, but the very thought of her set his teeth on edge and his heart racing. Who was she?

Several times he had considered asking someone, but that would mean admitting to the gaping holes in his memory. In fact, so much was missing that he couldn't properly call them holes. It seemed that little of himself remained anymore. The only thing he could focus on was the mission. Kurnsbur would conquer all of Gameryah for their new God.

A knock came at the door and he rose quickly, smoothing his robes and running his fingers through his hair. He didn't feel like a king. In fact, he couldn't remember a time that he ever felt like royalty though he must have at some point, else he wouldn't be in the position he was today. But until he recaptured those memories, he needed to look the part.

"Enter!"

Padin, the prodigal son of a Mud Snake clan chief, and one of his self-appointed bodyguards, stuck his head inside.

"My Lord, an army is coming. Your father says you are needed at once."

His father. Rimmic Karst was the true leader here, unless you counted the priests of the temple, whom he suspected were pulling his father's strings.

"Very well." Karst strapped on his sword and followed Padin out into the bright morning sun. As they strode through the dirt streets, people stopped and bowed to him. Karst scarcely noticed. When he did meet someone's eye, he often imagined that he could see within them the same mottled thoughts which plagued him. Of course, that was impossible. Confusion was hardly a disease that could be passed from person to person. All around them were signs that Salgo prepared for war. Groups of men, some little more than boys, drilled with spears or practice swords. Others practiced archery. Most of the women he saw worked at practical tasks often reserved for men, hammering out spearheads in the smithy or working as fletchers. Very little of what would be considered normal activity in a city took place here. Everyone worked with a unified sense of purpose. So unified, in fact, that it felt mildly disconcerting. Karst contemplated this for a moment, but the thought seem to slip away as quickly as it had come.

"Here he is. Welcome, Majesty." Rimmic Karst's bow was respectful and his tone sincere. For whatever reason, he continued to maintain the fiction that Pedric was in charge.

"I understand an army approaches. Why have we not put men on the walls?" Their capital city of Salgo was protected only by a wooden stockade, but in the face of the enemy it was far better than nothing.

"I fear His Majesty has been misinformed," Rimmic said. "An army approaches, but they are not the enemy."

"Who are they, then?"

"Allies from Galdora. Just arrived from Archstone." The speaker was an officer whose name Pedric could not quite recall.

"I didn't realize we had allies in Galdora, and certainly not in Archstone." He grimaced. He hoped this was not another thing he had forgotten

"We do indeed," Rimmic said. "We should open the gates and welcome them."

Karst knew this was not a suggestion, but he pretended that it was. He paused as if considering his father's words and gave the order. Without hesitation, the soldiers unbarred the gates and swung them open. As they parted, he saw in the distance a mass of troops moving their way. Some small part of him protested. The Galdorans viewed him and his followers as rebels. Where was the wisdom in allowing them to walk inside without resistance? But this thought, like so many others, faded as soon as it appeared.

A small cluster of riders broke away from the main force. Four guards and a bannerman escorted a tall blond man of middle years. They rode inside, stopped at a respectable distance, and dismounted. The blond man came forward and bowed deeply.

"My lords, I am Orman Van Altman."

"You are welcome in Salgo, Lord Van Altman," Karst said. Van Altman. Why did he know that name? "I must confess I am surprised to see you here. My advisors have not apprised me of our alliance." A flicker of annoyance flashed through his mind and for a moment, his resolve strengthened. "Perhaps you could explain to me how a Galdoran army has come to support me?"

Everyone within earshot looked around nervously, but Orman merely smiled.

"Loyalty to one's king and country is a fine thing," he said. "But loyalty to one's god is paramount, would you not agree?"

"Indeed I would. Nevertheless, what assurances have I that your army shares your loyalties? Surely you cannot have converted all of your troops to the worship of our new god in so short a time." No sooner had he spoken the words than he felt as if a great weight were pressing down on him, seeking to crush his spirits and muddy his thoughts. He fought against it with the greatest of efforts.

"You are a wise man, Majesty," Orman said. "My men do not worship our god, that is true. In fact, they believe we are here to fight you and that I have come into the city to negotiate the terms of your surrender." Orman and Rimmic seemed to think this was a great joke, but Pedric was not amused.

"They will not find us easy meat," he snapped. "Your numbers are respectable, but ours are greater by far."

It was the truth. Ever since the construction of the temple, men had flocked to Salgo to follow him. First a trickle, then a flood. They came from all over, though the core of his army was still comprised of his father's loyal subjects from Kurnsbur, and the disenchanted Lothans who supported Pedric. What was it they were disenchanted with? He still could not remember though it seemed important.

"You are correct. And together our armies will be formidable indeed." Orman smiled as if that were a sufficient answer.

"You need not worry." Rimmic put an arm around Pedric in a fatherly manner. "We have a plan." He turned to Orman. "Lord Orman, would you care to visit the temple and pay your respects to our god?"

"I would indeed."

They turned and headed toward the center of the city. No one asked Pedric to join them, but he assumed it would be expected. Inwardly fuming, he quickened his pace and fell in alongside his father.

"What is this plan?" He said in a voice so soft that no one but Rimmic would hear.

"Simple," he said in an equally quiet voice. "We pretend to surrender the city. As soon as his troops are inside, our god will bend their wills to his. In a few days' time, he will be ready to move. Our god's plans are already in motion all over Gameryah, but ours is the battle that matters the most to him. When all is done, we will be exalted above all others."

There were so many questions Pedric wanted to ask, but he found himself unable to voice them. In fact, with every step, his mind grew cloudier. By the time, they reach the temple, he once again knew little more than his own name.

They ignored the guards as they entered the temple. As always, he felt the overwhelming presence of their nascent god. Approaching the altar felt like walking through deep, shifting sand. With each step, he felt as if he were sinking deeper and deeper.

Blood drenched the altar, the remnants of the sacrifices the priests now performed around-the-clock. Their god had grown stronger, and his form seemed to have solidified though it was difficult to tell for certain beneath the hooded robe he wore. Two things Karst could not fail to notice: their god was powerful, broader of shoulder and taller by a head than the largest man he had ever seen, and his skin shone with icy blue light.

They all dropped to their knees and began their whispered prayers. Time passed. He could not say how much, for such things couldn't be measured in the presence of a deity. One by one, each man stood and left the temple, stumbling as if in a trance, until only Pedric remained.

And then, for the first time, his God spoke to him.

Do you serve me?

"Yes. Yes I do," he stammered. Despite his occasional misgivings and the many questions that troubled him, right now he wanted nothing more than to serve his God. The divine presence filled him with a joy bordering on ecstasy.

You are king, and thus the first among my followers.

"I am. I shall lead your army to victory."

The god's laugh was sharp, like the sound of breaking ice.

I have many who can command an army. You I have chosen for a special task.

Karst's heart raced. He wanted nothing more than to complete this task for his god, though he did not know what it was. He didn't care. He only wished to serve.

Do you remember this girl?

The image of a tall girl with red hair filled his mind. It was the girl from his memories, and he suddenly remembered who she was.

"Yes, I do. I remember," he panted like a dog. "I hate her!" He couldn't remember why he hated the girl, but he didn't care.

You have been told I am the god of the hunt. Perhaps I am in a way because I am sending you out as my faithful hound. Find her, kill her, and bring me her sword.

And now he could sense her presence. She was far away, but he somehow knew exactly where she was. The urge to go after her was so strong that he wanted to turn and run, but something held him in place. The tiniest bit of doubt flickered in his mind. *Was* this the god of the hunt?

The god laughed again.

You are not wrong. I am not the god of the hunt. Open your eyes, faithful hound, and be the first to look upon my face. Then you shall know who I truly am.

He looked up at the glowing figure. With shining, blue-white hands, the god pushed back his hood.

Pedric Karst screamed.

Chapter 42

"Your Majesty, may I have a word?" Bertram did not wait for permission before entering the room. She didn't mind. The man knew more about ruling a kingdom than she ever would and she was grateful he had consented to stay on as her advisor. Of course, there was that pesky matter of him having murdered the previous ruler, but he had done it for her, and it wasn't the first time he had saved her. Still she was grateful that Heztus, Granlor, and Gillen were close at hand just in case.

"Of course you may." She sat up straighter in her chair and smoothed her dress. She hated the thing, but she was expected to dress a certain way in public. Of course, this place was not exactly public. She spent most of her time in this small room adjacent to the throne room. It was decorated with simple yet comfortable furnishings and the single window offered a view of a walled garden just outside. As was often the case, Heztus kept her entertained. The dwarf was a delight, full of funny stories and inappropriate jokes, but he was also intelligent and she trusted his judgment.

Bertram dropped to one knee before her.

"Stop that this instant," she snapped. "It's bad enough that people bow to me out there." She gestured toward the throne room. "I won't have it in private, at least not when there are none but friends present."

"Am I a friend, Majesty?" Bertram asked.

"I don't know what you are, but you've behaved as a friend to me so the term suits you as well as any. What is it you'd like to talk about, and don't say a word about choosing a husband and producing an heir."

"It is not that, I assure you. I fear I have grave news."

"Is there any other kind these days?" Heztus asked.

Indeed, since she had ascended the throne, the news had gotten progressively worse. One of the bone women in her service was familiar with the seekers' odd method of communication and had, after much effort, made a connection with a seeker in Archstone. Since then, news of the world had poured in.

The war between Kyrin and Galdora had ended, but only because the second Frostmarch had begun. All along the western border war had broken out. The worst of the fighting seemed to be happening in the north, where vast hordes of wild men invaded from the mountains. Lothan, however, had not been spared. Word had come to her from the clans who had returned to their lands of raids by ice cats and shifters, the fiercest of the Ice King's minions.

Meanwhile, the eastern nations were busy quelling revolts of coldhearts within their own ranks. Somehow, she knew this was only the beginning.

"As a matter of fact, I do have some good news too. Which would you like first?"

"Let's have the good news first for a change."

"Prince Lerryn has returned to Archstone. He and his brother Larris managed to defeat the invading Kyrinian force."

Shanis' heart skipped a beat at the mention of Larris' name.

"Prince Lerryn has assumed the throne and is marshaling his remaining forces for war. Or should I say, for the next war?" Bertram managed a small smile.

"Is the fighting in western Galdora not so severe?" Shanis asked.

Their situation is similar to ours. Some minor skirmishes along the border." Bertram shrugged. "Are you ready for the bad news?"

"No, but you're going to tell me anyway."

This time, Bertram did not smile. "This has not yet been confirmed, but I have it from reliable sources that the order of the saikurs is broken."

She clutched the arms of her chair and leaned forward slightly. "What does that mean, exactly?"

"There has been a revolt. Prelate Denrill has been overthrown and the survivors who were loyal to him have fled or have been imprisoned. The rumor is, the man who now leads there is a coldheart."

"Coldhearts among the seekers?" Heztus sprang to his feet. It was not an impressive sight given the dwarf's lack of stature. "How can that be?"

"I would assume that any man, or woman," Bertram added, his eyes flitting toward Shanis, "can fall under the Ice King's sway. It is our ill fortune that the most powerful group of magicians and sorcerers in Gameryah seems to be under his control. Of course, we do not know how many remain. With luck, it is only a small contingent who have given themselves over to that particular vileness. In any case, that is another problem for the government of Cardith to deal with." He grimaced. "And now for the worst of it."

"There's something worse?" Shanis asked.

"I'm afraid so. Spies have returned from Salgo. Karst has amassed a sizable army and has joined forces with a contingent of Galdoran troops. They intend to march on us any day."

"That makes no sense," Heztus said. "Karst is a Galdoran rebel. How could such an alliance have formed?"

"The Galdoran force is led by Orman Van Altman. King Lerryn's uncle. He is a coldheart." Bertram fixed Shanis with a level stare. "The temple in Salgo, using dark magic and the power of human sacrifice, has raised a god. They spread rumors that they were raising a minor, almost forgotten god, but the truth is much more terrible."

Shanis sank back in her chair. She thought she was going to be sick. "Tichris."

Everyone reacted immediately. Heztus cursed, Gillen gasped, and Granlor drew his sword and looked around as if the Ice King were somewhere in the room.

"The Ice King is close to his full power and he can bend men to his will. He now has a massive army under his sway and they will fight with a mindless unity of purpose. We must assume they will neither succumb to fear nor fatigue. We will have to kill them to the last man in order to defeat them."

Shanis placed a hand on the hilt of the Silver Serpent, which rested against her chair. She looked down at it, a grim sense of determination filling her.

"Or I will have to kill him," she whispered.

"You can no do that, can you?" Granlor asked. "I mean, it do be a god."

"Do you have a better idea?" She asked. "He was beaten once before. He can be beaten again." She stood and began pacing back and forth.

"If I may," Heztus began, "we should go out to meet him. If we hide behind these walls, his armies will ravage our lands and then lay siege to our city. If we meet them in the swamps in the east, we have the advantage. The Malgog know that place better than anyone, save those of their own who have turned their coats. We will make them bleed." He uttered the last declaration with cold ferocity.

"I agree." Bertram nodded. "Recall the clansmen who have returned to their homes and meet them with our full might on the ground of our choosing."

Shanis nodded. "Send word to King Lerryn and tell him the battle for which he has been preparing will be fought in Lothan. Ask him to come to our aid. I don't suppose we can expect much help from the other nations?"

Bertram shook his head. "Not while they are all on the defensive and not knowing where the next coldheart rebellion will spring up."

"I'll bet that was the Ice King's plan all along." Heztus pounded a fist into his palm. "Keep the nations of the north occupied while he wreaks havoc in the south."

"But why the south? What makes us so special?" Shanis asked.

Bertram fixed her with an incredulous look. "You are special. You are the bearer of the Silver Serpent. He will see you as the greatest threat in the world, perhaps the only threat."

"Well then, if he's coming after me, I guess I'd better be ready. Summon the Council. Tell them we are going to war."

Chapter 43

"I can see the city from here," Naseeb called down from his perch high in a chanbor tree. "We're almost there."

"Thank the gods. My backside hasn't hurt this much since the time the city guardsman caught me cutting his purse," Lizzie grumbled.

"He didn't have your arrested?" Whitt asked.

"I was only a little girl. I cried and pouted and managed to convince him I was a desperate, hungry orphan. He decided to teach me a lesson before letting me go. Of course, I think he enjoyed it. That spanking went on and on."

Oskar cleared his throat, interrupting this latest of Lizzie's uncomfortably honest tales.

"I think we should wear our cloaks. We might find it easier to get to Larris if we look like saikurs."

"I hate to break it to you," Dacio said, "but none of us fit the bill. At best we look like what we are—young men trying to pass as seekers."

"We are more than that. We have trained and, if need be, we could show them a thing or two to prove ourselves." Naseeb swung down from the tree and landed nimbly on his feet. "In any case, I think Oskar's idea is a sound one. It can't hurt."

As they approach the city they could see the signs of a recent battle: trampled earth, craters caused by war machines, broken arrows and spear shafts, and the occasional body that had been overlooked. It was a grim sight, but Oskar knew things would only be worse during the Frostmarch.

The travelers they had encountered along the way had all told differing stories, but with a few common threads. Everyone agreed that the Kyrinians had nearly overrun the city but Prince Lerryn, now King Lerryn, had arrived in time to save the day. The Kyrinian force had withdrawn and the refugees who had swamped the city during the war were gradually returning to their homes.

A line of people waited at the city gates, but Oskar steered his horse around them and rode to the front of the line.

"What are you doing? The line ends back there." Dacio pointed back behind them.

"Real saikurs would not wait in line and neither will we."

"Oskar, I think I am finally rubbing off on you," Lizzie said approvingly.

Oskar grinned but quickly set his jaw and adopted the expression of serenity that he had seen on so many faces inside the Gates. He reined in before a stuffy-looking soldier whose silver armband indicated he was an officer. The man's sharp eyes fell on Oskar. He prepared himself for the inevitable argument, but to his surprise, the officer nodded and waved them through.

"You're all gathering at the palace," he said. "The guards there will tell you where, exactly." He returned to his business, leaving the surprised group to ride on through.

"That was easy," Whitt said when they were out of earshot of the guards. "I wonder what he meant by 'you're all gathering at the palace'?"

"I'm not sure," Oskar said.

"Just when I pay you a compliment you go and say something like that." Lizzie shook her head.

"What you talking about?"

"Think about it. The only thing he knows about us is that the three of you are wearing brown robes. Obviously, all the men wearing brown robes are gathering in the palace." She paused, staring at Oskar. "Please don't make me explain it any further. I might have to reconsider my feelings for you if you do."

"No, I understand. It should have been obvious."

"The saikurs who fled are gathering here," Naseeb said. "That could be interesting."

Whitt cocked his head and frowned. "What do you mean?"

"I mean, are we still part of the gates? Are we under their authority? Will they treat us like the novits and initiates that we are?"

"I don't care how they treat me as long as they don't try to stop me from seeing Larris," Oskar said.

Lizzie grinned. "You know, I wasn't sure I believed your stories about being friends with a prince. I guess I'm about to find out whether or not you're full of wind."

"You thought I was lying? Why didn't you say something?"

"It didn't really matter to me. Everyone in my line of work lies all the time. I enjoyed your stories and that's what mattered. If it turns out you are telling the truth, I'm going to have to find a way to make amends for my lack of trust." The smile she directed his way made him warm under the collar and he decided to let the subject drop.

It was a long ride through crowded streets to the palace gates. Here the guards were better dressed and more attentive to their duties.

"I'll need your names, ranks, and where each of you is from. The seekers will send someone to verify your identities," a guard outside the palace gates explained.

"I need to get a message to Prince Larris," Oskar said. "He will want to see me as soon as possible."

The guard looked as if he were about to laugh, but his smile faded quickly. "Your leaders have been meeting regularly with King Lerryn and the Regis. If you have a message for someone in the royal family, send it through them."

Oskar gritted his teeth. It seemed that getting to Larris was going to be harder than he had hoped. He was considering just riding on through when a voice rang out from the crowd behind him.

"Oskar! Is it really you?" He turned and saw a tall, fair-haired young man pushing his way through the crowd toward him.

"Hierm!" He slid down off his horse and hurried to meet his old friend. Oskar introduced Hierm to his friends. He saved Lizzie for last and Hierm flashed a knowing grin at him.

"What are you doing here?" Hierm asked.

"There was an insurrection at the Gates. We managed to get away."

"I heard. Seekers have been arriving in the city for a few days now. I guess you've come to meet up with them?"

"Actually I need to see Larris as soon as possible." He lowered his voice. "It has to do with Shanis."

Hierm's face darkened. "I can get word to Larris. I'm known to most of the people in the palace. It's a long story," he added. "Why don't you wait for him at our house? We have plenty of room and I could introduce you to my son."

Oskar could not suppress the feeling of trepidation that came over him as he stepped into the Van Derins' home. When he had last seen Mistress Faun, he was nothing but a simple farm boy who worked for her husband mostly in order to sneak books out of his personal library. Faun had always looked down her nose at him and had treated him like a simpleton, a fiction he maintained so she would not suspect his actual motive for working there.

It was to his great surprise that, upon seeing him, she hurried over to him and caught him up in a tearful embrace. Awkwardly, he patted her on the back.

"I was sorry to hear about Lord Hiram," he managed.

"Thank you," Faun said pulling away and dabbing her eyes with the hem of her apron. She looked up at him and smiled. "Just look at you. You are no longer the boy who left Galsbur. Your parents would be proud to see what a fine young man you've grown into, and a seeker at that!"

For a moment, Oskar considered explaining to her that he was not yet a full-fledged saikur, but that didn't seem important right now. He introduced Lizzie, whom Faun also embraced. Whitt, Naseeb, and Dacio had decided to join the rest of the seekers in the palace.

"You are most welcome," Faun said. "Now come, there is someone you'll want to see." She took him by the hand and led him and Lizzie through the house to a back garden. Stunned by Faun's transformation, Oskar followed along a bemused grin on his face.

Outside, he found Rinala holding her baby and chatting with two men. One was

Hierm's brother Laman. The other was a dark haired brute of a man.

"Colin!" he exclaimed.

Shanis' father threw back his head and laughed when he saw Oskar.

"Who is this man in the brown robe? He looks like Oskar Clehn, but Oskar was a shy fat boy. This one looks like he can handle himself." He closed the distance between them in two strides and caught him and Lizzie up in a crushing embrace. "I hoped you were still alive. After what happened at the Gates we couldn't be sure."

"It was a close thing, but I managed to get away in time. Hierm tells me that Shanis has done well for herself."

"Indeed. She has finally claimed her rightful crown."

"Did you know all along? About the prophecy, I mean?" Oskar asked.

Colin nodded. "I knew she was descended from Badla on her mother's side, and that it was possible she could be the one. I hoped that by giving her a normal life in Galsbur she might avoid that fate, but I suppose it was meant to be."

"Is that why you let her learn the sword when it was something no other girl ever did?"

"She had to be ready, just in case."

"I imagine there is going to be a great deal of reminiscing tonight," Laman interrupted. "I'll pour us some drinks."

By the time evening fell, Oskar had washed off the trail dust, changed into clean clothes, and spent the day playing with the baby, whom they had named Hiram after Hierm's deceased father, and catching up with his old friends. Faun had actually coaxed Lizzie into a dress, which was cut so low in the front that Oskar couldn't look at her without blushing. They had spent the day eating, drinking, laughing, and forgetting about the world for a few hours. For her part, Lizzie went out of her way to draw forth as many embarrassing stories of Oskar's youth as she could, and the other Galsburans were happy to comply.

More than once he reflected on how much things had changed. They were equals now, no more lords and commoners. And the change that had come over Faun was nothing short of remarkable. He supposed it was a combination of the death of her husband and the birth of her grandson that had done the trick. Whatever the reason, he was glad of it. He almost felt like he was home again.

It was near dark when Larris and Allyn arrived, bringing Aspin along with them. Like the others, they teased Oskar about the changes that travel and his time at the Gates had wrought in him, and they enjoyed drinks and laughter until it was time to get down to serious business.

"Things are coming to a head," Aspin said without preamble. "The Ice King has risen once more. He has raised an army and intends to begin his conquest in the south. We don't know if he is on the move yet, but if not, he will be soon."

"Do you think he is going after Shanis?" Oskar asked

Aspin nodded. "We believe he sees her as his only real threat."

"Does she know?"

"Yes. As you are aware, we have means of communication far superior to messengers on horseback, and far quicker too. We are in contact with her. She is gathering her forces and intends to ride out and meet him."

"She will not be alone," Larris said. "Lerryn has decreed that Galdora stands with her. Our troops march in the morning."

"And what of the other nations? Will they support her?" Oskar asked.

"We are doing our best to convince them that this is the battle that truly matters," Aspin said. "But it is difficult when they are under attack as well. I have at least managed to convince all the saikurs who have gathered in Archstone to join us. Also, Shanis founded a school of magic in Calmut, mostly witches, but those who have the skill will fight for us as well." He took a deep breath. "Can I dare hope that you were successful in the task to which I set you?"

"I have had some success, but I don't know how much it helps us." Oskar described what he had learned about the nature of the Silver Serpent. Next, he produced Dacio's translation of the rubbings he'd made of the walls in Murantha. His friend had pieced it all together during their travels. Oskar read aloud.

"And the gods whom we worshiped had become like a curse upon the nations. They warred over petty causes until we feared the world would be torn apart. And the kings and queens of Gameryah gathered in the holy place. Before the sword, they stood and spoke the words, I freely give my life. Sarala spoke the words and surrendered her life upon the blade of the sword, and in the moment of her noble sacrifice she reached out to Vesala. And the temple shook as Vesala was drawn into the sword, for only by the power of ultimate sacrifice could a human impose his will upon a god..."

"It goes on like that, listing the monarchs who gave up their lives in order to draw the gods into the sword." He paused. "In the chamber where we found the Silver Serpent, we also found the tombs of all the Kings of Gameryah who are mentioned here. So, the Silver Serpent was not a weapon used in the Godwars. Its creation is what ended the Godwars."

"And I'll bet the absence of the gods is what opened the door for the Ice King," Larris said. "The first Frostmarch happened right on the heels of the end of the Godwars. But does this knowledge bring us any closer to defeating the Ice King?"

They all exchanged dark looks and a brooding silence fell upon the group. Finally, Aspin stood.

"I have always believed in the prophecy and that things happen in the way they are intended for reasons that we do not understand. Therefore, I believe that this knowledge came to you because it was intended to, and for that reason, I think it will help us."

"We should all get some rest," Larris said. "We have a long road ahead of us."

Chapter 44

Everywhere he went men stood in his path. Karst wanted to pull his hair out in frustration. As soon as The Ice King had issued his command, Karst had left to fulfill his mission. Perhaps he should have taken the time to plan, but the compulsion to kill Shanis Malan overwhelmed him. He could think of little else. Even the simplest things, like eating or stopping to rest, were far from his thoughts and required a supreme effort of will to perform.

Though he had hoped to complete the mission immediately, his best efforts had been stymied. The roads leading to the west were regularly patrolled by the enemy so he had been forced to take to the woods. The forest had soon given way to swamps. Not knowing the way through, he resorted to making a beeline toward that distant place where he somehow knew Shanis was. This had led him through some of the worst foulness he had ever encountered.

He had lost his horse in a pool of quakewater and barely escaped with his life. He been stung, bitten, and his skin was afire with nasty rashes from the myriad of plants he brushed up against. He'd never known such misery, but the will of his god drove him forward.

It had not been long before his own army had overtaken and passed him. The soldiers did not know that of course. He kept to the shadows whenever he crossed their path. He had enough left of his own mind to know that in his current appearance they would never believe that he was their king. Perhaps that ought to have bothered him. He vaguely remembered a time in his life when he desired nothing more than to be a leader of men, a ruler. Those things no longer seem to matter. The sheer ecstasy of being the chosen of the Ice King was all he cared about.

He caught a whiff of smoke and the aroma of cooking meat. He didn't know how far away the fire was. His senses seem to have heightened in the time since he had received his charge. He considered that, day by day, he was becoming less like a man and more like an animal, and his joy at being the chosen one could not completely dampen the feeling of unease this gave him.

He slowed his pace, not wanting to stumble into a precarious situation. Whether the men up ahead where his or the enemy's, he knew they would not welcome him.

Summoning all the will he still possessed, he forced down the urge to rush forward toward his goal. Instead, he crept along, careful not to make a sound. Soon he heard voices and loud cries. He closed the distance slowly until the swamp opened up into a large clearing. He ducked underneath the cover of the thick foliage and crawled on his belly until he could observe the scene unnoticed.

Close by, a group of men sat around a small fire. Beyond them lay many more campfires and a few tents. In the distance, he could make out tiny flickers that told him this was where the army, what was once his army, had chosen to make camp for the night.

The men closest to him were roasting frogs over the fire. He had always hated frog, but right now his hunger was so great that it seemed like a sumptuous feast. He recognized one of the men immediately—Paden, one of his most devout supporters. Perhaps Paden would share his food?

The invisible hand that drove his actions crushed that thought in an instant. No one could know of his mission. It was his alone. One of them might try to usurp his place and he couldn't have that.

But he was so hungry and, oddly enough, he realized that he longed for human interaction. He was not suited for solitary life, and he was not a hunting dog, no matter what the Ice King said. No sooner had that thought entered his mind than his head began to scream in agony. He felt as if powerful hands were crushing his skull. Fighting the urge to sick up, he squeezed his eyes closed and focused on his mission. Soon, the pain abated.

He laid there, eyes closed, until the sound of approaching footsteps on the soft ground drew his attention. He opened his eyes to see two temple priests, escorted by a dozen guards, approached the campfire where Paden sat.

"Your god requires your service," one of the priests said to Paden.

Paden's face went pale. "Requires me for what?"

"Come with us," the second priest said.

Paden's eyes widened in abject terror. He put his hand on the hilt of his sword. It was a measure of his fear that he could summon such resistance when the entire army seemed to have been bent to the will of the Ice King.

"Not me. Find someone else."

"You have been chosen," the first priest said flatly.

"But I do not worship your god. I am only here because I hate…" He couldn't finish the sentence. He pressed his hands to his temples and cried out in pain.

One of the priests nodded and a pair of guards rushed forward. They quickly disarmed Paden, bound his hands behind his back, and hauled him away.

The others nearby looked on with disinterest. Not a one of them raised an objection. As Paden's protests faded in the distance, they returned to their cook fire.

Something deep inside Karst wanted to object. For the briefest of instants, he thought about grabbing a sword and rescuing his friend. It was the right thing to do wasn't it? What sort of God killed his own followers?

Once again, the crushing pain filled his head. He fought it, but not for long. Moments later, he was once again a dog on the hunt.

Chapter 45

"**We must retreat**, Majesty." Blood streaked Krion's face and spattered his leather armor, but none of it appeared to be his own.

"Again?" Shanis snapped. "They've been pushing us back at every turn. I thought we'd have the advantage in the swamps." She pulled her cloak tightly around her. Winter had come early, and she had no doubt about the reason.

"We do. We have killed twice our number, perhaps more, but they have many more soldiers than we, and the Malgog among them know the swamps."

"I would no call them soldiers," Horgris said. The big clan chief had just entered the command tent. "They fight like they have a mind for nothing but war. They do ignore wounds that would fell an ordinary man. Or woman," he added quickly. "They fight on until they can no fight anymore."

"I should enter the battle, then. I'll make sure plenty of them won't be able to fight." Shanis grasped the hilt of the Silver Serpent, eager to draw on its power and wreak havoc among the Ice King's forces.

"You know we cannot risk that," Heztus said gently. "You are the only one who can fight the Ice King. If you are struck by a stray arrow…"

"Yes, yes, I know. You've told me this many times."

"And it appears we have to continue telling you, granddaughter." Krion folded his arms and gave her a reproving look. "Even without fighting, your contributions are invaluable. No one else can do what you can."

Shanis wanted to argue, but she knew it was a waste of time. Since the fighting had begun, she had been using her powers to heal the wounded. While her army had many who could tend to the injured, only she could perform miracles if that's what you called them. While the others tended to ordinary wounds, she saw to those with grievous injuries. She helped the most hopeless cases, bringing them back from the edge of death until she was spent. She knew her efforts made a difference. Many soldiers lived to fight on, thanks to her.

She thought about the first person she had ever healed and remembered that it was her urge to heal not only a few people, but an entire nation, that had led her to unite the clans. Now she was leading them into the worst sort of carnage. She knew that wasn't entirely accurate. The Ice King had given them no choice. They had no alternative but to fight. Still, she wished it were otherwise.

"Has there been any sign of him?" She didn't need to say whom she meant.

Krion shook his head. "It could be that he remains in Salgo. We do not know the extent of his power, but it is no great stretch to think his will would extend this far. He seems to dominate the minds of his soldiers. Even our people feel some hesitation when we face them."

"And as things stand now, I have no hope of getting to him. We would have to drive his army back before I could do that." A thought struck her.

"I see that look on your face. Don't even think about it." Heztus said.

"I don't know what you're talking about," she replied.

"You're wondering if you can sneak past their lines and make it all the way to Salgo without being found out."

"Are you a mind reader now?"

"No, but I can read you."

"It do be out of the question. It would be a much greater risk than you going into battle," Horgris said.

"I know," Shanis grumbled. "But I don't have to like it." She sighed and looked at her grandfather. "All right, give the order to fall back."

Chapter 46

"It's getting late and you need your rest." Lizzie slipped beneath Oskar's blanket and snuggled up against him. She laid her head on his chest and let out a small sigh. "Do you remember when I told you that I wanted to see the world?"

Oskar nodded.

"I was wrong. This is the most boring thing I've ever done."

Oskar chuckled. "Perhaps you should have been more specific about the sort of travel you were interested in."

Lizzie giggled. "I thought it went without saying that I didn't want to wander through the wilderness for days and weeks on end."

"You know me. You have to spell things out for me or I'll never understand." He slid an arm around Lizzie's shoulders and pulled her close. He still didn't see how so beautiful a girl could have any interest in him, but he had stopped trying to figure it out and simply enjoyed it. He hated the idea of taking her into a war zone, but he knew she would not be left behind. Besides, if they failed, nowhere in the world would be safe. This was a battle everyone would fight sooner or later.

"What are you reading?"

"The only book I thought to bring with me." He held up the small volume he had taken from the archives at the Gates just before he fled.

"Is it interesting?" she asked drowsily.

"No, but it's better than doing nothing." He angled the book to catch the firelight and turned to the next page.

"Doing nothing? If you think there's nothing to do at night under the blankets, you are in sore need of education." Lizzie ran her hand across his chest, rose up, and kissed him on the neck.

"Not with everyone around," he whispered.

"We're practically alone." She kissed him again.

They were hardly alone. Aspin, Colin, Larris, and Allyn slept nearby, as did Hair, Edrin, and Hierm, who had, after much shouting, convinced Rinala to stay behind with baby Hiram. A squad of soldiers ringed their camp, guarding the prince. Whitt, Naseeb, and Dacio were traveling along with the other saikurs, who were moving with the main force of the army. Despite their lack of privacy, Oskar was seriously considering giving in when he turned to the last page of the book and gasped.

"Did I nibble too hard on your ear?" Lizzie teased.

"It's not that. I have to talk to Aspin." He slid out from under the blanket leaving a surprised Lizzie staring daggers at him.

"Fine. *He* can kiss you on the neck tonight for all I care." She curled up on her side and pulled the blanket up over her head.

Oskar didn't give her a second thought. He could only focus on what he had discovered.

Aspin was still awake and he sat talking with Colin. They broke off their conversation when Oskar approached.

"What is it?" Aspin asked.

"I found something in this book of prophecy. I had so little success that I gave up on finding anything useful, but then I stumbled across this." His hand trembling, he passed the book to Aspin, whose eyes widened when he saw what was written there.

"What is it?" Larris asked. Apparently no one in the camp was asleep. Even Lizzie crawled out from under the blanket and joined them.

"It's a prophecy about a meeting of the bearer of the Silver Serpent and the Ice King."

"Is that a big deal? I mean, aren't there plenty of prophecies about that?" Lizzie asked.

"Every prophecy I have ever read says that the bearer will meet the Ice King at the final Frostmarch. What does this one say?" Larris sat rigid, his voice tight. Oskar knew why. Larris was in love with Shanis. He would not like what this prophecy had to say.

Aspin read aloud.

"*The Lord of ice shall rise up and all shall fall before him. The bearer shall meet him in the mists in the place of earth and water and there shall the choice be made. The ultimate sacrifice or eternal winter.*"

He closed the book. "The mists in the place of earth and water."

"Calmut?" Oskar asked.

Aspin nodded. "I think so. It fits, and at the rate Shanis' army is falling back, they will be in Calmut by the time we meet up with them."

"We'll be there in two days. Does that mean it's almost over?" Hierm asked.

"Possibly." Aspin rose and tugged on his robe. "I need to speak to King Lerryn. He should know what to expect."

"I'll go with you," Colin said weakly. He quickly turned his back on the others.

"What does the other part mean?" Lizzie asked. "What is the ultimate sacrifice? Does it have something to do with the glyphs Dacio translated for you?"

All eyes turned to Larris whose face was a mask of agony. The prince closed his eyes and pressed a fist to his forehead.

"We can't say for sure." Oskar scarcely managed to speak the words. All of this time he had envisioned Shanis emerging triumphant from a battle with the Ice King, but if this prophecy were to be believed, it would not be the sort of triumph he had imagined.

"That's true," Allyn said. "Prophecies are rarely what they seem."

"I don't care what any prophecy says. We're going to fight," Hierm said without conviction.

"And were going to win," Allyn added. "We always do."

Lizzie looked up at Oskar and her gaze softened when she saw the pain in his eyes. She wrapped her arms around his neck and pulled his head down to rest on her shoulder. "It will be all right."

Oskar drew her close and held on tightly. He wished he could believe her.

Chapter 47

Shanis was surprised at the changes in Calmut since she'd left there months before. It no longer looked like a lost city that had been devoured by the jungle. The streets and alleyways had been cleared of undergrowth and rubble, and the crumbling buildings that had not yet been repaired were at least free of foliage and detritus. All the rubble had been repurposed for the rebuilding of the city wall, which stood about twice her height. It was nothing compared to the defenses of a city like Karkwall, but it would have to serve.

The biggest change was the expansion of the school of magic. It no longer occupied a single building but had expanded to incorporate an entire street. Hundreds of women of all ages, and a surprising number of men had flocked to Calmut to join the school. Shanis didn't know how the word of the school had spread so far. She supposed it had something to do with the ability of magicians to communicate, something along the lines of how seekers communicated with one another. Gillen had recently mastered the skill and been exchanging messages with Aspin on Shanis' behalf for some time now.

"Most of the students are novices," Gillen explained, "and of those who are not, most have devoted their study to the healing arts."

"How many will be useful in a fight?" Shanis asked.

"About four dozen. Some of the elders could also fight in a pinch, but they primarily serve as instructors and leaders."

"Tell them, ask them, I mean, to begin teaching every combat skill they possess to as many students as possible. At minimum, perhaps some can learn the shielding spells that you use to protect me. Healing is important, but it might be that we will need every man and woman to fight."

Gillen nodded. She had been at Shanis' side since the siege of Karkwall and she knew what they faced. "I'll send word immediately." She flagged down a young woman who was on her way into the house of healing, spoke to her quietly, and sent the girl on her way at a fast walk. "Should we go inside?" Gillen glanced toward the house of healing.

Shanis suppressed a grimace. It galled her to cower inside while all around her, others were giving their lives to defend her. "Not just yet. I should at least see to the defenses."

"Horgris and your grandfather have that task well in hand," Heztus said. "If you like, I will make the rounds on your behalf and report back to you, but your safety is paramount. Right now, you are perhaps the most important person in the world."

"I can at least wait until the battle begins," she said. "There's no point in hiding until it's absolutely necessary. Just then, warning shouts arose from the city walls and her heart sank.

Heztus gave a wry smile. "It sounds like the time has come."

Shanis removed her hand from the soldier's forehead. She stood and wobbled a little on her tired legs. Healing was exhausting work, even with the power being drawn from the Silver Serpent.

"No matter how many times I see you do that, I never cease to be amazed." Hyda shook her head. The old woman whom Shanis had met so long ago had joined the school and risen to a position of prominence, and taken charge of the center of healing. "It be so much more than any of us can do. You healed a wound that would have claimed his life by daybreak."

"It isn't my doing. It's the sword." She staggered again, but it was not due to fatigue. Lately, the sword had been increasingly difficult to manage. It sometimes resisted her attempts to channel power from it and at night she was plagued by vivid dreams of the sword plunging into the hearts of robed and crowned men and women. She reflected that she was now queen and wondered if the sword hungered to plunge itself into her heart as well.

"Shanis! I mean, Your Majesty. You are needed."

She turned to see Heztus wending his way through the maze of injured warriors who lay in rows on the floor.

"What is it?"

"We are losing," he said flatly. "If help does not arrive soon, the city will fall. We can't retreat, as there is no defensible position for leagues to the west. If there is anything you can do to hold them back, now is the time."

"I'm coming." She hurried after the dwarf, leaving her ever-present pair of bodyguards to catch up. "Any word from Aspin?" she said over her shoulder to Gillen, who had snatched up her skirts and was rushing to keep up, with Granlor following close behind.

"Not since last night. He said they expected to be here sometime today. King Lerryn intended to march through the night."

"Good on him since the enemy has been fighting through the night."

Heztus led her up to the top floor of an ancient building just inside the city's eastern wall. From here, in the gray light of dawn, she could see most of the battle line without exposing herself to enemy fire. Up and down the line, the Ice King's forces were pressing the defenders hard. In some places, they even managed to surmount the wall, though they were quickly forced back or killed. Oddly, the enemy had neither encircled them nor attacked the western wall, but she didn't have time to speculate on the reason.

While Gillen summoned the protective shield, Shanis closed her eyes and reached out to the sword. Once again, it fought her. It felt as if it had its own will and it seemed to struggle to escape her control. Perhaps it could sense the presence of the Ice King. She concentrated hard and visualized what she wanted it to do. The same images that haunted her dreams flickered through her mind so fast she could scarcely recognize them. Figures whom she was now certain were ancient kings and queens died again and again, impaled upon the blade. She pushed them aside and concentrated.

"Any time now," Heztus said.

With supreme effort, she drew the power of the sword into her and hurled it out into the battle. A barrage of lightning bolts rained down from the sky, exploding through the ranks of the enemy forces. As if from a great distance, she heard Granlor retch at the site of scorched, broken bodies flying through the air.

She opened her eyes as a wave of fatigue swept over her. She dropped to one knee and rested against the windowsill. Down below, the defenders of Calmut had taken advantage of the enemy's surprise and indecision and were quickly sweeping the walls clean. Though some of the Ice King's forces continue to fight, the sudden carnage seemed to have overcome their will to fight. They began to draw back, some breaking into full flight.

"Are you all right?" Heztus hurried to her side and laid a hand on her shoulder.

She nodded. "I was already tired from healing, and that," she gestured toward the battlefield, "was almost more than I could manage."

"Let me help," Gillen said. "Draw some force from me. I will be all right."

"I can't." Shanis didn't elaborate. She thought it a bad idea to tell them that her grip on the Silver Serpent was so tenuous at the moment that she feared she would lose control of it entirely if she did not focus on keeping it in check. If she began to take even a trickle of life force from the young bone woman and the sword took over, Gillen might be consumed.

"Rest then," Gillen said. "The enemy is in retreat."

"Actually, they are not," Heztus said.

He was correct. Already the fleeing troops had rallied and were once again marching slowly toward the wall. Though they lacked the zeal of their earlier attacks, they nevertheless moved inexorably forward.

She watched as a hail of arrows cut through the first ranks. She wondered how soon before the archers ran out of shafts. There had been no respite from the fighting since the attack began, and she knew that soon they would have to resort to firing the enemy's spent arrows back at them. Even now, she could see that the volume and rate of fire had decreased noticeably since the beginning of the battle. Some of her warriors were now using crude slings to hurl rocks at the attackers. Interspersed amongst the soldiers, the magicians and sorcerers from the school, those who still had the energy to fight, hurled fireballs into the ranks of the Ice King's forces. Even these attacks were paltry compared to what they had been earlier.

"We should pull the magicians off the wall before they burn themselves out," she said.

"I suspect they realize that burning themselves out is nothing compared to what the minions of the Ice King will do to them if we lose the city," Heztus said.

Shanis watched as, despite the defenders' best efforts, the enemy continued to move forward. Once again, they seem to have lost any semblance of will and moved forward in a fearless, mindless wave.

"What be driving them?" Granlor had recovered his wits and stood alongside her, watching the battle unfold.

"That." Horgris pointed into the throng.

Shanis' heart fell. From somewhere within the heart of the enemy ranks, a figure had risen up. He stood head and shoulders above the rest and he glowed with a faint blue light.

The Ice King had come.

Chapter 48

Shanis sprang to her feet, all of her fatigue forgotten. Adrenaline coursing through her, she dashed down the stairs, out onto the street, and toward the city wall. The others kept pace with her, shouting warnings and urging caution, but she scarcely heard them. This was the moment she had been destined for and she would face it head on and without fear.

She clambered up onto the wall and looked out. The Ice King strode forward, radiating blue light and exuding power. No one could stand close to him. It was as if an invisible force pushed everyone away, or perhaps even his own people found his presence repelling. He raised his hand and pointed toward the city. As one, his minions surged forward once again and renewed their attack, weapons and voices raised.

Meanwhile, Shanis' own forces quailed. Weapons slid from numb fingers. Men fell to their knees. She had to do something. She glanced at Gillen, who seemed to know what she was thinking immediately.

"Stand and fight!" her magically amplified voice boomed. "I am with you, and we will not fail!"

Her words seemed to hearten her forces and once again, missiles flew into the enemy ranks, but the Ice King kept coming. She knew no one else could stop him. It had to be her.

"Can you cushion my fall?" she asked Gillen.

The young bone woman blanched and gave a single nod.

"Tell me when." Shanis' heart was in her throat as she heard Gillen whisper a spell.

"Now," Gillen said.

Shanis leaped off the wall. She felt the brief sensation of falling and then she slowed as if she'd plunged into deep water. Her feet touched the ground and she charged forward. She was aware of Granlor, Heztus, and Gillen leaping down off the wall behind her, and she cursed them for their foolishness.

The attackers parted before her until nothing stood between her and the Ice King. She looked upon him and revulsion welled within her.

He looked almost human. His hooded cloak had fallen back, revealing a hairless head and burning red eyes. Cracks ran through his pale blue skin and he gleamed like moonlight shining on snow. Waves of cold seem to roll off of him and she began to shiver uncontrollably. The Silver Serpent came alive in her hand. It jerked, trying to get to the Ice King. Suddenly aware of the danger she and everyone else was in, Shanis concentrated, trying to gain control of the sword's power.

Before she could make a move, Granlor cried out in defiance and charged forward to meet the Ice King's attack.

"Granlor, no!" She cried

It was too late. The Ice King didn't even raise his sword. With a dismissive swipe of his hand, he sent Granlor flying backward. The young Monaghan warrior smashed into the city wall with a sickening thud and fell to the ground.

Rage coursed through Shanis and with it came the power of the sword. The serpent mark on her chest burned. She sprang down off the wall and hurled all her power at the glowing figure.

The Ice King raised his own sword and sent a burst of power back at her. The sorcerous blasts, if that is what they were, met with an unearthly force. White-hot light met cold blue flame in the air between them. A crackle like lightning filled the air and the forces shattered like glass. The explosion tore through those closest to the Ice King and knocked others off their feet for a distance of twenty paces or more, but neither Shanis nor her enemy even felt it.

In two strides, she closed the gap between them and lashed out with all her might, pouring her will and her power into her sword stroke. The Ice King parried her stroke and the sound of their blades meeting shattered the air like the sound of a thousand panes of glass breaking.

The Silver Serpent was alive in her hands as she slashed, thrust, and parried. But no matter her efforts, the blade never came close to her enemy. As she fought, a powerful sense of hopelessness rose within her, and a voice whispered inside her mind.

You cannot defeat me. Many have tried and all have failed

"You were beaten before. By this weapon." She struck again with all her might. The Ice King laughed, a cold, hard sound, as he once again parried her stroke.

Is that what you have been told? Your ancestors poured all the powers of the gods into your sword, yet here I am.

He swung his sword again and Shanis scarcely managed to duck beneath the blade. She felt the cool breeze as it whistled inches above her.

"You were defeated!" She grunted, thrusting at him and dancing away.

I was delayed, but you cannot deny that I now stand before you, stronger than ever. Blood sacrifice has given me power beyond measure.

He swung his sword again, this time with such force that Shanis felt the blow all the way down to her ankles when she parried it.

She fell back, uncertain. Could she hope to defeat him? He was not wrong — whatever the legends claimed, he had not been defeated, at least not entirely. Furthermore, she still knew so little about the sword. She wielded it, yes, but she knew neither its limitations nor the full extent of its power. What a fool she had been to think she could stop the Frostmarch. Who was she, after all, but a spoiled, temperamental farm girl?

The Ice King read her thoughts.

You are beginning to understand. Surrender and you may live. You may all serve me. There is no use in fighting. Too many have already died for your folly.

Shanis winced and felt her will to resist waver. Something deep inside her wanted to obey. After all, many *would* die if she continued to fight, but if she surrendered…

Perhaps you are not as foolish as I had believed. Drop your sword and kneel before the Ice King.

Her resolve crumbling, she lowered her sword.

Chapter 49

"**The battle is** well underway, Majesty, and it is not going well." The look on Tabars' face was one of grave concern mixed with the same determination he'd always had even in the direst of circumstances.

Lerryn looked down from the small rise from which they could see the battlefield through the edge of the tangled forest. The Ice King's forces were concentrated along the north and west sides of the city. He could not see all the way to the south wall, but he could tell for certain that they were not attacking from the west.

"Why don't they have the city surrounded?" Larris asked.

"The Ice King is leaving them a path to retreat. The lands west of here provide few defensible positions until you reach Karkwall. If they abandon the city, they will be slaughtered." His mind racing, Lerryn assessed the situation in a glance. "Archers forward! Spears in support!

His commands were quickly passed through the lines and his troops formed up in solid rows. At Lerryn's command, Kelvin blew his war horn and a hail of arrows rained down on the surprised forces of the Ice King. Cries of pain and sharp commands rose up above the din of battle as their right flank turned to meet the new threat.

Lerryn looked at Aspin. "I need you and the seekers inside the city to help bolster the defenses. If you go in from the west, you should be able to enter unmolested. They've left that wall open."

Aspin nodded and began shouting instructions to the mounted throng of brown-robed men who waited nearby.

"Have our reserves form a wall and protect them," he said to Tabars. "Once the seekers are inside, the reserves should join them and aid in the city's defenses." The reserve force was comprised of the youngest and greenest troops. He expected little from them, but they would be better suited to fighting from behind a wall than out in the open. "You and the White Fang," he continued, "form a rear guard. When everyone is inside the city, sweep around to the south and take them in the flank. Slash and run but don't fully engage unless the situation dictates it. I want to give them lots to think about."

Tabars wheeled his horse about and gave the orders. Moments later, the reserves marched forward at double time. They were so young, Lerryn thought, some barely old enough to shave, and he was sending them to their deaths. Of course, he reminded himself if they did not prevail, their lives would be forfeit anyway.

"They will be all right," Aspin said. "We can provide some protection until they are in the city. After that..." He shrugged.

Lerryn nodded. He watched as the young men continued to file past. One fell to his knees and vomited loudly. Others looked so pale that he thought they might collapse there and then, but despite their fear, not one of them turned and ran. Soon they had formed a double wall of spears, with two rows of archers behind. The seekers swept around behind them, spurring their horses as fast as they could go, followed by Tabars and the White Fang.

Their presence went unnoticed by the main force of the attacking army, but a small contingent broke off and charged toward them. A few nervous archers released far too soon in the arrows fell uselessly to the ground.

"Hold!" Their commanding officer called. "Loose on my command!"

Lerryn tensed as the Ice King's forces released their own volley. Arrows whistled through the air toward his young troops.

"Shields!" The officer shouted.

But before his men could even assume a defensive posture, Aspin stuck out his hand and shouted a single word. The arrows bounced back as if striking an invisible wall and fell to the ground. The attackers saw this and hesitated, but then they charged again.

Another seeker had joined Aspin and the two of them hurled balls of fire into their ranks. Lerryn's men added another volley of arrows, and he was pleased to see that most found their marks. But despite the carnage, the remaining men continued to charge forward while the injured crawled as if driven by an unseen force. Lerryn returned his attention to the battle, confident that the seekers and his own troops would easily dispatch the remaining attackers.

Down below the battle raged. The arrival of his forces had caught the Ice King's troops unawares, but their sheer numbers and apparent mindless determination had helped them rally almost immediately. A large detachment had broken off and charged his position on the high ground. His archers were no longer firing in waves but released as quickly as they could nock, draw, and fire. The ranks of attackers fell like wheat before the scythe, but still they came, every fallen man replaced by two more. Lerryn drew his sword. It was time for him to enter the fray.

"Don't do it, Lerryn," Larris said. "I can lead the charge. You are the king. You are needed to command."

Lerryn looked at the faces of those around him: Larris, Allyn, Colin Malan, Hierm van Derin, Hair, Edrin, Kelvin, Oskar Clehn, his fierce-looking female companion, and the three young Seekers who had joined him. All nodded their agreement. He was about to acquiesce when he looked out and spotted a familiar face in the midst of the battle.

"I'm a fighter," he said. He reached out and squeezed Larris' shoulder. "The gods be with you, brother."

Larris nodded. "And also with you."

"If you will all excuse me," Lerryn said, "courtesy demands that I pay my respects to our uncle." He raised his sword, put his heels to the flanks of Kreege, his faithful warhorse, and shouted, "Cavalry, charge!"

"What do we do?" Allyn asked. "Should we get inside the city and try to find Shanis?"

It appeared to take a moment before his words registered with Larris, who was staring at the back of the charging cavalry as it plowed into the Ice King's forces. He shook his head as if coming awake. "I suppose we should."

Oskar shifted in his saddle, ready to ride when something caught his attention. In the midst of the battle, a circle had opened in the ranks of soldiers and a pale blue glow emanated from a massive figure that stood locked in battle with a tall, red-haired girl.

"There she is!" He pointed at the combatants.

Larris spotted them immediately. "We have to get to her!" He gave no orders, but kicked his horse and charged down the hill and into the fray with Colin close behind.

Cursing, Allyn galloped forward, trying to catch up with Larris.

Oskar turned to Lizzie. "You should be able to get into the city if you swing around west like the seekers did. I'll find you when this is over."

"No," she said flatly. "I stay with you."

Oskar knew a lost cause when he saw one. "Stay between us, then. We can shield you."

Lizzie laughed and shook her head. Here, in the midst of battle, with the Ice King in their sights and men and women dying all around, she showed no fear. "It will be as you say." She winked at him.

"Let's go." As one, they charge down the hill, following in Larris' wake. Up ahead, they saw him hacking his way through the confused tangle of battling warriors. Beside him, Colin was laying about with the ferocity of a wild beast. Allyn had dismounted and was firing off arrows with almost inhuman speed and accuracy. With no regard for his own safety, he took down every warrior who threatened Larris from behind. Hierm forged ahead, reaching Allyn just in time to ride down an enemy poised to thrust a spear through the young man's unprotected back.

As they rode, Oskar, Whitt, Naseeb, and Dacio began to hurl spells into the fray. It was a difficult task to accomplish from horseback, but they managed to blast a path for Larris to follow as the prince continued to fight his way toward Shanis.

Oskar stood in his stirrups, but he could no longer see her in the midst of the battle. Otherworldly noises, cracks like shattering ice, rang out across the battlefield and he knew she was still fighting.

"Look out!" Dacio shouted. He waved his hand and the force of his will sent an arrow flying off course.

"Nice one," Whitt said. "I wish I could..." The words died in his throat as a feathered shaft took him in the heart. His eyes widened as life fled from him and he slid off the saddle to the ground.

"Whitt!" Oskar cried. He wheeled his horse and tried to return to his friend's side. Another arrow flew, whizzing past his ear. He spotted the archer immediately— a man in a crimson Galdoran uniform perched high in a tree. Rage burned inside him and he remembered a place far away and a moment that seemed a lifetime ago when he had called down the lightning upon the golorak. He stretched out his hand and felt the power surge through him.

With a blinding flash, a great bolt of lightning struck the tree. It exploded with a deafening roar, sending earth, stone, and bodies flying in all directions. Oskar closed his eyes and when he opened them again, a smoking crater the size of a small house stood where the tree had been. Bodies, rather, body parts, lay all about and he smiled with grim satisfaction at the knowledge that his friend's killer was dead.

"No!" Something flew through the air at the corner of his vision and he wheeled to see Lizzie spring down off her horse onto the back of the silvery, catlike creature. The beast's claws whistled through the air, inches from Oskar, just as Lizzie opened its throat with one of her wicked looking knives. She hit the ground, rolled away from the thrashing beast. No sooner had the ice cat regained its feet then an arrow blossomed in its eye socket. Oskar knew it had to have been Allyn who made that shot.

He was about to look for his friend when Lizzie hurled another of her knives right at Oskar.

He had no time to react before the knife flew past him and struck a mounted warrior in the eye. Oskar gaped as the man fell to the ground.

"You can't expect me to have your back all the time. You've got to pay attention!" Lizzie yanked her knife from the dead man's skull and clambered back up onto her horse. "Now, keep your eyes open. Go!"

Lerryn was eager to fight but had no occasion to bloody his sword as he charged toward Orman. His cavalry encircled him, carving a path through the enemy ranks. He kept his eyes trained on Orman's blond head. His uncle sat astride his horse, shouting orders and flailing about with his sword.

As they drew closer, their progress slowed. The mass of soldiers, though none of them a match individually for his men, nonetheless proved a formidable obstacle due to their sheer numbers. Their charge slowed and up ahead, he saw the flow of the battle carry Orman off in the opposite direction.

Lerryn's heart raced. He had to get to Orman before someone else did. He wanted to be the one to finish the coldheart traitor. He urged his horse forward and began slicing his own path through the melee. His sword bit deeply into mail and flesh as he cut down every man in his way. He was aware that many of those he faced wore the uniform of Galdora. These were the rebel troops Orman had spirited away. He wondered if they were, in fact, rebels, or merely pawns under the Ice King's powerful sway. It did not matter. They were trying to kill him, and neither empathy nor sympathy would protect him.

He continued to battle, but no matter how hard he fought, Orman seemed to drift farther away from him. Would he ever get there?

No sooner had the thought passed through his mind than a bolt of lightning sliced through the air and erupted in a flash of light up ahead of him. He ducked his head and shielded his eyes from the flying debris. When he opened them again, he saw before him a large patch of burnt ground, and beyond it, his uncle.

Their eyes locked and Larris charged. Orman hesitated for only a second and then he too drove his mount forward.

They met in the center of the charred circle of earth. Their swords clashed and then they were past one another. Lerryn wheeled his mount and came forward again. He struck at Orman, who turned the blow and then the world narrowed to a single flurry of blades. Sparks flew and the sharp clang of steel on steel rang in his ears.

Orman's face was a mask of determination or was he under the same spell as his soldiers? His strokes were almost mechanical in their precision. He was an accomplished swordsman and had won many a duel.

"Hello nephew," Orman rasped as he struck out with his sword. "I understand you have usurped my position."

"No, I have merely claimed my throne," Lerryn said through gritted teeth as their swords clanged together again. "You shouldn't have left your son behind, you know. My dear cousin now rots in the dungeon along with your cohorts."

"It makes no difference. The Ice King has promised me the throne when the Frostmarch is over. My son and my loyal companions will be freed and we will rule while you and everyone you love lie beneath the ground."

Their swords came together again. Lerryn deflected the blow and thrust, opening a cut on Orman's shoulder, but his uncle didn't flinch. Orman struck again and once again Lerryn's counter-stroke found its target. But the wounds he inflicted were shallow and Orman continued to fight.

"Did I forget to mention?" Lerryn asked. "They are in the dungeon now, but they go before the headsman at sunrise tomorrow. You'll be hard-pressed to win this battle and reach Archstone in time. Sorry about that."

It was a lie, but it had the desired effect. The news of his son's impending demise cut through the force that dominated Orman's mind. Teeth bared, he roared and attacked with reckless abandon. Calmly, like a blacksmith at work, Lerryn turned each blow and gave back with vicious thrusts that left his uncle bleeding until, chest heaving and shoulders sagging, Orman managed one final swing that Lerryn easily ducked.

Smiling coldly, he drove his sword into Orman's throat just above his gorget. His uncle had only a second to open his mouth in surprise before blood poured forth, his eyes rolled back, and he fell lifeless to the ground.

The world around him seemed to return to Lerryn in a flash and he was aware of silver shapes coming at him from all sides. Ice cats! He had scarcely raised his blade when powerful claws tore into his flesh.

Chapter 50

As if in a daze, Shanis watched as the Ice King approached, his sword raised. The force of his will was so powerful, so utterly dominant, that only the tiniest part of her reacted. He had promised to spare her. Why was he going to kill her now?

Somewhere within her a tiny voice cried out. There was no life in surrender. What good was it to surrender if it meant subjugation? Death on the altar?

Surrender or I will kill you like I killed your friend.

A spark blazed deep inside her, and she felt that familiar, welcome anger burn inside her again. He had killed Granlor. She could not let him kill anyone else. Her strength returning, she gripped her sword and rose unsteadily to her feet. The Ice King roared, the sound like a winter wind inside her mind, and he came forward.

Out of the corner of her eye, she saw something flash through the air. Heztus had charged into the battle, and hurled a knife at the Ice King's head. On her other side, Gillen ran forward, flinging balls of fire.

The Ice King brushed both attacks away as if swatting flies. A mere flick of his finger sent the two tumbling to the ground.

And then the world exploded.

Somewhere nearby, a bolt of lightning burst from the clear sky, striking a tree and sending charred wood, scorched-earth, and the soldiers unfortunate enough to be standing in its vicinity, flying through the air.

It was all the distraction she needed. Shanis sprang forward, the power of the Silver Serpent once again coursing through her. For the first time, the Ice King fell back before the force of her onslaught.

Shanis fell into the familiar forms of swordplay she had studied all her life. She struck again and again, and now the Ice King was on the defensive. A strange sense of calm came over her. The sword had been a part of her for as long as she could remember and as she fought, she forgot the world around her. No longer did the Ice King's will batter at her resolve. No longer did she hear his voice inside her head.

She struck at him again and again, her blade coming closer and closer as he struggled to parry her strokes.

"You will never..."

Their swords met and blue and white sparks flew

"hurt my friends..."

Her vicious downstroke knocked his sword to the ground.

"Again!"

She thrust the Silver Serpent through his chest.

White fire burned where the sword pierced the Ice King's body. Ice shot along her arms and she wrenched her blade free and staggered backward. Cracks formed in the god's blue flesh, radiating out outward from the burning wound.

Before her eyes, the Ice King threw back his head and cried out in pain and rage as his body shattered into shards of blue ice.

Shanis fell to her knees, barely able to keep her head up. A mournful cry rose above the battlefield and she saw the enemy forces fall back and then break into full retreat. Bolts of lightning and balls of fire chased them back into the forest.

Shanis glanced back and saw to her surprise a line of men in brown robes standing atop the battlements. Seekers? All around them, men clad in crimson Galdoran uniforms had joined the defenders. Help had finally arrived.

She scanned the battlefield. A few of the Ice King's soldiers continued to fight, but many had dropped their weapons and stood with their hands above their heads, their eyes wide with confusion as if they had awakened from a terrible dream.

Or, perhaps it was she who was dreaming. In the midst of the retreating forces, she saw Prince Lerryn, make that King Lerryn, lop the head off of an ice cat. And to her left, was that Larris riding toward her?

She wanted to call out to him, but then something whispered her name. Something dark and sinister. She slowly turned her head toward the sound.

Vapor rose from the melting pile of ice that had been the Ice King. Instead of dissipating, it formed the shape of her vanquished foe and stood over her.

It laughed.

You think you have won? You did not defeat me. You fought a mere shadow of me. Look.

Shanis' blood seemed to turn to ice. Where the shattered remains of the Ice King had lain there now lay the body of a man. She recognized him at once. It was Arlus, one of the clanless who had refused to accept her leadership, and had gone to follow Pedric Karst.

My servant, the voice hissed. *Possessed by a mere shadow of my true self.*

Shanis wanted to cry out in frustration, but she lacked the strength. It could not be. She had thought she faced the Ice King but this... this specter had nearly beaten her. Hopelessness welled inside her, threatening to overcome her.

I am coming, and all shall despair

The final word echoed in her mind.

Despair

She tried to stand, but a wave of dizziness brought her back to her knees. As darkness slowly closed in on her, she saw a dark shape moving toward her. A bear of a man, his shaggy black hair drenched with sweat, rivulets of blood running down the blade of his sword. It should have been a fearsome sight but not to Shanis.

"Papa?"

Her consciousness fled as Colin Malan swept his daughter up in his arms.

Chapter 51

"My name is Pedric Karst." For the first time in weeks, Pedric Karst remembered everything. His memories had returned in a painful rush the moment Shanis Malan had driven her sword into the Ice King's heart. At least, he had thought it was the Ice King. Even now, he sensed the god's presence, distant yet still powerful. And though his hold on Karst had weakened, the icy hand still clutched his heart. He sensed Shanis Malan somewhere behind the city walls and the desire to drive his blade through her still burned inside him.

But he remembered.

He remembered with striking clarity his mother who had died so many years ago. He remembered her face and he thought that perhaps he had been a different person while she lived. He remembered the first time his father had put a sword in his hands and warned him of a world filled with people who wanted his blood. He remembered how he strove to please the man who grew more distant every day. And then other memories intruded. He remembered Calmut, Shanis Malan, and humiliation. He should kill her. Not for the Ice King, but for himself. For revenge.

He donned the cloak he had stolen from a dead Galdoran officer, pulled up the hood to shield his face, and stepped out of the shadows. The army, his army as he still thought of it, had retreated from battle, but already they were making preparations to resume the attack. The blank stares on the faces of the men he passed bore mute testimony to the return of the Ice King's sway. He had not been killed, nor even defeated, only stymied. Karst knew that wouldn't last.

No one paid him any mind as he strolled through the encampment. The men huddled around fires, tended the wounded, or sat staring off into space. As he moved among them, the presence in his mind grew stronger and along with it the urge to complete his task.

Angry words drew his attention and he ducked behind the cover of a nearby tree.

"You cannot do this to me!"

Karst knew that voice.

"I am the leader! You serve me!" Rimmic Karst, hands bound behind his back, stumbled past the spot where Pedric hid. He was escorted by a dozen warriors and behind them trailed a priest.

"We all serve our god," the priest said. "He has decided that this is how you will best serve him."

Pedric's hand went to the knife at his belt. They were taking his father to be sacrificed. He should do something. The thought brought another wave of excruciating pain shooting through his head. He clamped his jaw shut and suppressed the wail of anguish that threatened to give away his position. It was not his place to interfere. He had his own task to complete.

But it's my father.

Despite the agony, despite the compulsion to leave this place and go after Shanis Malan, he staggered to his feet and crept along behind the small group.

They laid Rimmic Karst on the stone altar and a group of priests circled around and began to whisper their prayers.

"But you promised me," Rimmic groaned, his resolve breaking. "You promised me I would see my wife again. I have done everything you asked."

"You will see your wife again. In the next life," the priest said.

"But I did all that you asked."

"You have been a faithful servant." The priest laid his hand on Rimmic's head and spoke in a soothing tone. "You must understand there is no greater power than that of sacrifice. The life of an ordinary person is worth very little. Aside from your son, yours is the greatest sacrifice that can be given to our god. Your spirit will be added to his and multiplied many times over."

"Not my son," Rimmic whimpered. "This is not his fault."

"You made him our king, and therefore as our god's highest adherent, his would be the greatest sacrifice of all." The priest produced a knife and held it high above his head. The moonlight glinted on its blade. "But take heart. If your gift to our god is sufficient, we will not need him at all. In a way, you are saving his life."

The blade flashed down. Rimmic Karst screamed. And then silence.

Pedric drew his knife and rose to his feet, but he got no further. The moment his father's life fled from his body the power of the Ice King returned. He felt it envelope him, surge through him, and with it a renewed, unwavering sense of purpose.

He must kill Shanis Malan.

Chapter 52

It should have been a joyful reunion. In fact, it had been, for a while. Shanis had awakened in a small room inside the house of healing to the sight of her father seated on one side of her bed and Larris on the other. She had cried more tears than she cared to admit, but she blamed it on fatigue and the death of Granlor. To her relief, Heztus and Gillen had been rescued by Oskar's friends, Dacio and Naseeb, and had suffered only minor injuries.

Over the next hour, while Hyda forced a series of bitter restorative potions down her throat, she enjoyed the company of her old friends. Hierm was now a father, and Oskar was barely recognizable with his seeker robe and a lovely girl seemingly attached at his hip. Allyn was still Allyn—dry and sarcastic.

And then there was Larris. The young prince refused to leave her side and he kept gazing at her so intently that she finally had to threaten him in order to get him to stop.

It had been delightful for as long as it lasted.

Now she sat clinging to Larris' hand as Aspin and Oskar explained to her that she must die.

That wasn't exactly the words they used, but it was a simple conclusion to draw.

"The Silver Serpent was not made as a weapon to fight the Ice King," Aspin explained. "It was in fact made to defend us against the gods."

"I don't understand," Shanis said.

"The wars between the gods nearly destroyed Gameryah. The gods didn't care how many mere mortals they trampled underfoot as they did battle. Finally, the nations came upon a solution." Aspen paused, cleared his throat, and glanced at Larris before continuing. "There is no greater power than sacrifice. The gods feed upon it."

"Doesn't sacrifice add to a god's power? That is how Karst and his followers brought the Ice King back, is it not?" Shanis asked.

"Yes and no. The taking of a life in the name of a god gives that god power. How much depends upon the person who was sacrificed. The greater, the nobler, the more faithful the sacrifice, the more powerful, but a sacrifice made willingly is the most powerful of all."

Shanis' throat clenched. The meaning was clear. She squeezed Larris' hand tighter.

"There is an ancient magic," Oskar said, taking up the explanation. "The greatest sacrifice of all is that of a king or queen. That person is a god's paramount subject. None stands higher. Therefore, no power can match the willing sacrifice of royalty." He shifted uncomfortably and looked down at his hands. "The rulers of every nation of Gameryah gathered together and, one by one, willingly gave their lives, and in the moment of their deaths they turned that power, the greatest power there is, against their gods." Tears welled in his eyes and he turned away.

"The Silver Serpent is not a weapon. It is a prison." Aspin looked into her eyes and she saw deep sorrow there. "It has power because the gods are trapped inside it."

"So that is why I can use it to heal. It's not merely a vessel of life force, but a source of magic, since magic comes from the gods." The pieces were beginning to fall into place. "And that is why I can do things without knowing what I'm doing or how to do it. The gods are reaching through the sword and touching my mind, taking hold of it."

Aspin nodded.

"Then she should be able to defeat the Ice King with it," Larris said. "The power of all the gods combined is greater than that of the Ice King. It has to be."

"It isn't strong enough," Shanis said. "It wasn't enough to destroy him during the first Frostmarch, and today I fought a mere shadow and nearly died."

Aspin sighed. The seeker looked wearier than she had ever seen him. "It seems the gods can only touch the world in a limited way. Look at the way their absence affected things. Magic and sorcery are mere shadows of what they were when the gods walked the earth."

"Then we must destroy the sword." Larris let go of her hand and rose. "It's the only way to bring the full power of the gods to bear against the Ice King."

"No." Shanis' mouth was so dry, her throat so tight with fear, that she was surprised she was able to speak. "A battle between the gods and the Ice King would destroy the world. Besides, you know what the prophecy says. 'The ultimate sacrifice or eternal winter.' What greater sacrifice could there be than the bearer of the Silver Serpent?" She was proud that she managed not to choke on the words though every part of her body resisted.

"The snows take your prophecy!" Larris clenched his fists, looking as if he were about to fall upon Aspin. "A few lines in a single book that Oskar found tucked away on a shelf. How do we know that the writer even knew what he was talking about?"

"It all fits," Aspin said softly. "I am sorry."

Shanis took Larris' hand. "Remember when this all started? Lerryn thought he could bend the prophecy to his will, but you knew otherwise. No matter what any of us did, the prophecy took control and things happened the way they were intended to. How long did that book sit on a shelf waiting to be discovered yet it was overlooked until the time of the Frostmarch? Oskar found it exactly when he was supposed to."

"I won't let you do it," Larris said through a curtain of unshed tears.

Shanis pushed back the threadbare blanket that lay over her legs and climbed to her feet. Oskar and Aspin politely looked away as she wrapped her arms around Larris and laid her head on his shoulder.

"There is no other way," she whispered.

Larris stood ramrod straight, and then his resolve broke. He wrapped his arms around her and pulled her close. "But what if you're wrong?" he choked, the tears flowing freely.

"The prophecy won't let it happen any way other than how it is intended. There's still hope." After a long moment, she drew away from him. "Who else knows about this?"

"Allyn, Hierm, Lizzie, Lerryn, Hair, Edrin, and your father," Oskar said.

"Papa knows?"

"He thinks we should destroy the sword. They all do," Oskar said.

"Then what that's what we shall tell them we intend to do. No one else needs to know the real plan. They might try to stop me."

"I think…" Oskar broke off, tears streaming down his face. He looked at her and nodded.

"That is the wise course," Aspin finished.

The Silver Serpent stood in the corner. Shanis picked it up and slung it over her shoulder. "We should do it right away."

"Now?" Larris asked. "Shouldn't you at least wait until morning?"

"They will attack again before morning. The sooner we bring this to an end the more lives we will save. Now, everyone wipe their eyes and put on a brave face."

Oskar mopped his eyes, took a moment to straighten his robes and stood. "We will give you two a moment alone," he said.

When the door had closed behind Oskar and Aspin, Larris seized her by the wrists. "Marry me first," he said.

"What?"

"Marry me right now, before we go. We'll find someone to do the ceremony." He hurried on. "I'm a prince and now you're a queen. That's what was stopping us before."

She reached out and brushed her fingers across his cheek. If she had ever known pain before it was nothing like what she felt now. The one thing she wanted, above all else, was within her grasp and she could not seize it.

"I will not leave you a widower. I know what it did to my father and I won't do it to you." She knew it would spare him no pain. If the shoe were on the other foot, her grief would be no less than if they were married, but it was all she could give him.

"I love you," he whispered.

"I love you." They stood there gazing into one another's eyes until she knew that if she didn't do it now, she never would. "You should probably stay here. I don't want you to see me…"

He gently pressed his finger to her lips. "I will stay with you until the very end."

Chapter 53

They moved quietly through the streets of Calmut. Everywhere they looked, soldiers stood guard but no one questioned them or tried to bar their way. After all, who would stand in the way of the Queen of Lothan, the Prince of Galdora, and four seekers, not to mention their armed escort?

The sacred grove where she had once submitted herself to the Keeper of the Mists lay just beyond the walls west of the city. Though the Ice King's forces had stayed clear of this area, they remained on their guard. When they reached the clearing where the standing stones framed the path beneath the sacred tree, they stopped and Aspin addressed the group.

"When we begin the ceremony, we must assume that the Ice King will sense it and will do everything in his power to stop us from destroying the sword." The others nodded, all apparently believing that was what Shanis intended to do. "King Lerryn's elite guard is on patrol a short distance from here and all of his forces are on high alert. Oskar and Larris will come with us. I will need their help in completing the ritual. I am relying on the rest of you to guard our backs. You are our last line of defense. If anyone, or anything, slips past the king's forces, it will be up to you to stop them. The fate of the world may rest upon it."

Shanis looked around at the others, all standing in a semicircle facing her. She took in each face, even the ones she barely knew. Her father, so ferocious yet so kind; Hierm, her best friend; Krion, the grandfather she had scarcely gotten to know; Allyn, so steadfast; Naseeb and Dacio, who were as loyal to Oskar as Allyn was to Larris; Lizzie, who clearly loved Oskar much more than the big oaf realized; Hair and Edrin, who had been there when all of this started; and Gillen and Heztus, whose loyalty to her never wavered.

"Thank you all," she whispered. "I can never repay you."

Colin and Krion came forward and the three shared a long embrace.

"You will be fine, my girl," Colin whispered. "Don't you worry about a thing. We'll see you when it's over."

Shanis managed a tight smile and turned away before her face betrayed her secret. Drawing her sword, she led the way into the mists.

The mist wrapped around Pedric Karst like a shroud, hiding him in plain sight. He had crept into the city, his Galdoran cloak sufficient disguise to avoid rousing the suspicions of the defenders. The ferocity of the day's battle seemed to have left everyone exhausted, with little energy left to question a solitary man walking down the street. Or perhaps it was something else.

He seemed to have become a creature of the shadows. He could slide into the darkness and no one even knew he was there. Was he still completely human? He didn't know.

He had followed the call, that strange presence inside his mind, which told him where Shanis Malan was. He had been unable to get to her—her room was too closely guarded. But he had hidden in the shadows outside her window and he had listened.

Upon learning her plan, he ran ahead and now lurked here in a place he knew all too well. The place where he had been disgraced. He would lie in wait for her and he would do his god's bidding.

He heard soft footsteps and he saw the faint outline of four figures moving through the mist. He drew his knife and tensed, ready to spring. When she came within his reach, he would plunge the knife into her heart and then his god's will would be done. He, the chosen one of the Ice King, would be exalted above all others. He would have the favor of his god.

His god...

The god for whom his friend had been sacrificed.

The god for whom his father's life had been taken.

The god for whom countless innocents had died on the altar.

Once again, the blinding pain threatened to crush his skull. His head swam and his knees buckled. He caught himself against the slimy wall and leaned there breathing heavily. When he could stand again, the girl was gone.

It didn't matter. He always knew where she was. Keeping his knife at the ready, he crept along behind them

Oskar didn't know whether it was the chill mist or his own nerves that made him shiver. Under a different set of circumstances, he would have been fascinated by his surroundings, overwhelmed by this fabled place of the mists. But not tonight. Tonight he was leading his friend to her death. Grief welled up inside him and he shunted it aside. If he dwelled upon it, he would give in, and all might be lost.

The ground beneath their feet was soft and steady as if they walked on a cloud. He lost all sense of time and distance as they moved forward through the swirl of white. Finally, without warning, the mists vanished and they stood in a clearing beneath a gray sky. Before them, a pool of quakewater encircled a small island upon which stood the largest tree he had ever seen. Ten men, arms spread wide, standing fingertip to fingertip could not have ringed it. Its height was beyond measure, its broad branches disappearing into the gray clouds high above. Strange, but familiar symbols were carved into its surface.

"It's a god's tree," Aspin said. "There are only a few like it in the world. This has to be the place."

"I've seen symbols like that before," Oskar said. He frowned, trying to remember, and then it came to him. "There is one on our village green. In fact, Colin told me that the Ice King's forces tried to destroy it when they attacked Galsbur."

"Perhaps the power of the god's tree is needed to perform the ritual. If that is the case, then it would serve him to destroy as many of these trees as possible."

"This is all very interesting, but can we please get on with it?" Shanis said.

Oskar almost managed a smile. Almost.

Stone steps led across the quakewater and onto the island. Shanis led the way, and Oskar brought up the rear. He noticed that the mist followed them across and, by the time he reached the other side, it had closed around the island like a curtain.

"I suppose we should begin," Aspin said. "Shanis, give Oskar your sword."

"That isn't going to work," she said. "No one can hold it but me, remember?"

Aspin nodded and scratched his chin. He looked around and his eyes widened. "Here." He pointed to the trunk of the tree where an oddly-shaped hole was... not *carved* into the surface, precisely. It was as if the tree had grown around an invisible sword hilt.

"It's like it was meant to be," Shanis whispered. She drew the Silver Serpent, reversed it, and slid the hilt into the hole. The sword locked into place. The blade now jutted out at a slight upward angle, its tip level with her stomach.

Tears streamed down Larris' face. He grabbed Shanis, kissed her hard, and then stepped away, his hands tucked into his armpits as if trying to prevent himself from interfering.

"Oskar, when I begin the ritual, direct your life force into the tree. Focus on the symbols."

Oskar nodded, unable to speak

"Shanis, when we reach your part of the ceremony, you'll repeat after me. And when we reach the end…"

"Yes, yes, I know what to do." If she were afraid, it did not show. Her face was a mask of determination.

Aspin took a deep breath and began the ritual.

Chapter 54

Knife in hand, Pedric Karst crept toward the sound of the seeker's voice. The mist grew thicker until he could scarcely see the ground beneath his feet. Cautiously, he moved forward until he found himself at the edge of a pool of quakewater. He hesitated. Had he gone in the wrong direction? The voice sounded so close. He must be in the right place.

As he strained to see through the dense curtain of fog, a light began to glow. Brighter and brighter it shone as the seeker's voice rose along with it. He could see faint shapes beyond the mist. One of them was Shanis Malan. He could feel her presence so close.

The light revealed a stepping stone in the quakewater. This was the path she had taken. Moving on silent feet, he continued on. Finally, as if looking through frost-covered glass, he saw them.

The Galdoran prince stood directly in front of him, facing in the opposite direction. To his left stood the seeker. The man was now deep into his ritual and his words had taken on the melodic tone of a chant. To his right, the younger seeker knelt staring at the sword, the hilt of which had been thrust into the tree. It was the sword that now shown with intense light.

And in front of it stood Shanis Malan.

In an instant, he understood. The conversation he had heard while eavesdropping on the house of healing made sense. She was the sacrifice! She was going to hurl herself onto the point of the sword. He could not let that happen. Killing her was his task. Gripping his knife tightly, he tensed, ready to attack.

Wait.

The Ice King's voice echoed in his mind. It was muffled and seemed to come from a great distance away as if this place somehow served as a buffer between him and the power that drove him forward.

You want me to kill her, he thought.

No. Let her do our work for us.

And the Ice King began to laugh.

Karst stood frozen in place at the edge of the mist. He had come all this way and now his god did not want him to finish the task? It could not be.

But the sacrifice...

Her sacrifice means nothing to me. She is not the ruler of my nation. You are. She does not know that she is about to die for nothing. All of their work has been for naught. They are about to give me what I want.

The Ice King laughed again, and the sound froze Karst's marrow. In his mind's eye, he caught a tiny glimpse of the Ice King's thoughts.

The seeker was wrong. The gods had been trapped inside the Silver Serpent because the greatest among *their own worshipers* had lain down their lives in sacrifice. When the girl threw herself onto the sword, she would accomplish one thing— she would remove the only remaining obstacle that stood in the Ice King's way.

Images flashed before his eyes: the Ice King's power extending across Gameryah and beyond. Lines of people marched to the temple like lambs to slaughter, all for the sake of extending his power. They would die like Karst's father had. He would move across the Sun Sands to the lands of the Far West, and then across the oceans. He would crush every nation beneath his feet. All would despair at his name.

I did this, Karst thought. *This is all my fault.*

The Ice King's laughter stopped

Come away from there.

It was a command, but the Ice King's words no longer held the powerful sway that it once had. The power of this place and the horror of his realization had restored Karst's mind.

Come away now!

Karst teetered and almost fell off of the stepping stone. The power of the Ice King battled with his own overwhelming desire to stop this abomination he had created. He felt as if he were being torn in two.

Come away or I shall come for you myself. I shall... The Ice King continued to speak, but his words grew fainter until Karst could not hear them in all.

The future he had witnessed was beyond imagining, and he was the author of the destruction.

My name is Pedric Karst, he thought. *My father was Rimmic Karst.*

He remembered his father, saw again his death upon the altar of the Ice King. His father hadn't believed in their horrible god. He had merely wanted to bring back his wife, Karst's mother.

His mother. And then another memory came to him the one memory of his mother that was stronger than all others.

He was young, exactly how young he could not say, but he recalled with vivid clarity, sitting on his mother's lap. Her arms around him holding him tight. She looked down at him, smiled, and kissed him on the forehead.

"You are a good boy."

I am good.

And then a powerful force like a physical blow drove him to his knees.

The Ice King was no longer far away.

He had come.

***

"Why are they attacking the city?" Tabars asked. He gazed off in the direction of Calmut as if he could see through the gathering fog and the thick walls to the battle that had resumed on the far side of the city. They could hear the sounds of battle and see the flashes of light from the balls of fire hurled by the defenders. "I thought they would come for us."

"So did I." Lerryn watched the sky with an unsettled feeling rising in his gut. Part of him felt he should be there, commanding his forces in the defense of the city, but he could not bring himself to cower behind the walls when here would be the battle that truly mattered. This was where he belonged. "Perhaps..." He broke off as shapes appeared in the mist. As they drew closer, he could make out their forms—ice cats.

"The attack is intended to be a distraction. They believed if they could draw all our defenders to the walls, the way to the sacred grove would be open."

"I guess we showed them." Tabars said.

Lerryn glanced at Kelvin, whose face was white as milk. He had ordered the young man to join the defense of the city, but Kelvin had ignored his command. It looked as though he was regretting his rash decision. It was too late now. The ice cats stood between them and the city.

Lerryn drew his sword and raised it high.

"This is the moment!" he called out. "Do not let them pass!"

A ragged cheer arose from the White Fang.

"Sound the horn, Kelvin."

A short blast and the men of the White Fang rode forward to meet the enemy. They were young and inexperienced, Lerryn mused, hardly the measure of the veterans of the original White Fang that had followed him into so many battles, but they were good men who had served him well. He hoped at least a few survived this day.

Bestial roars arose from the throng of ice cats. Frightened horses shied and whinnied while their riders shouted their battle cries as the two lines came together.

Lerryn's sword flashed and bit deeply into the nearest creature. All around him he saw ice cats fall, but he also saw soldiers pulled from their saddles and torn apart. There was nothing he could do for them except continue to fight. The battle raged on. Fur and blood flew. Shrieks and curses rent the night air. All around him ice cats and soldiers lay dying, but many fought on.

"Some of them have broken through!" Tabars shouted

"There's nothing we can do. We have enough to deal with here." Lerryn hacked the paw off an attacking ice cat, drew back, and thrust his sword through the beast's throat. The remaining ice cats scattered and his men gave chase, hoping to run them down before they reached the grove.

Larris wheeled his horse but stopped when a pale blue light shone in the distance.

"What is that?" Tabars gasped.

Time seemed to freeze. In an instant, Lerryn took in the terrible sight. If the shadow of the Ice King with which they had done battle earlier had been fearsome, it was nothing compared to the reality of the towering figure that strode toward them. Where his shade had glowed, the Ice King burned with angry blue fire and wherever he stepped frost spread across the ground. His very presence was so powerful that Lerryn could scarcely look at him, but he forced himself to meet the god's fearsome gaze.

"That," he said, "is how I will die." He kicked his heels into Kreege's flanks and rode out to meet the Ice King.

Hierm heard a roar in the distance as if thousands of voices were lifted as one. Sweat dripped down the back of his neck and he clutched the hilt of his sword for comfort. "I guess they're coming."

To his right, Dacio laughed ruefully. "I'm wishing I had paid more attention in sorcery and less in history."

"You'll be all right," Naseeb said. "You are the best in all of our studies." He made a thoughtful frown and then shook his head. "All right, not all of them but I still think you'll be all right. We are, after all, students of the Gates."

"I'll wager you a flagon of ale," Allyn said, "that I kill more them than both of you combined." He nocked an arrow and stared out into the fog with a sly grin on his face.

"Will the three of you shut your mouths? I'm trying to listen," Krion barked.

"Peace father," Colin said. "They are nervous. We all are."

Hierm glanced at Lizzie. The young thief clutched a knife in each hand and was trembling from head to toe. "You don't have to do this," he whispered. Take shelter in the trees until it's over."

She turned her pallid face toward him. "Oskar is in there." As if that ended the discussion she turned to stare off in the direction from which the cries had come.

"Here they come," Colin said. "Ice cats."

Closing on them fast, a line of the vicious creatures charged forward. Hierm had forgotten how fast they were. He couldn't help but marvel at the speed with which they chewed up the ground between them.

Allyn stepped forward and began firing. Again and again his arrows found their marks but a single shaft would not bring the beasts down unless it was perfectly placed. Just like the Ice King's warriors that fought through until the bitter end, the will of their master drove the beasts forward.

Gillen, Naseeb, and Dacio began flinging fireballs at the cats. They erupted in gouts of orange flame and the creatures squealed with feral rage, but still they came. Finally, one of the creatures fell, and then another. And then the cats were upon them.

All was chaos. Hierm thrust his sword at the nearest cat, driving his blade deep into its flank. It roared and lashed out, slashing him across the chest. He fell back and then Lizzie and Heztus leaped upon the beast, gashing it with their knives until it lay in a bloody, twitching heap.

Hierm whirled about, sword upraised. He saw Colin drive his sword into the heart of one of the beasts. Nearby, Krion was locked in battle with another.

Dacio went down beneath one of the massive creatures. Hierm ran to the young man's aid. He raised his sword and brought it down with all his might on the unprotected base of the ice cat's neck. He felt his blade cut through flesh and bone, and spurts of icy cold blood splashed his face. He stabbed again and again until it no longer moved. He threw his shoulder into its bloody side and rolled it off of Dacio and his heart fell at the sight. There was no hope for the young seeker. There was also no time to mourn.

Another cat flung itself at him, but it was taken down in midair by the twin spells hurled by Gillen and Naseeb.

Lizzie screamed and Hierm whirled about to see her desperately fending off another cat. She drove a dagger into its throat and his claws raked her face. Heztus ran forward, rolled beneath the beast, thrust two daggers up into its unprotected belly, and rolled free of its slashing claws. Hierm ran forward and finished the cat with a deft stroke of his sword.

The cats continued to try to break through their line, desperate to get inside the grove and into the passageway between the standing stones. Colin and Krion fought like wild men. Naseeb and Gillen hurled spells in every direction. Hierm chopped and hacked at every flash of gray he saw.

A cat sprang seemingly out of nowhere and caught Allyn from behind. The young archer went down and did not rise.

"We can't hold on much longer!" Heztus snarled.

A cold feeling of doom rose up inside Hierm. Perhaps this was the end.

Chapter 55

Shanis stood stock still. Cold sweat dripped down her face, and she repeated the words of the ritual as if in a trance. Beneath her feet the island on which she stood had begun to swirl and pulsate with the same bluish light that had filled the cavern beneath Murantha when she'd first found the Silver Serpent.

Before her eyes, the sword burned like a tiny sun, blotting Oskar and Aspin from sight. It was a good thing. If she had looked at either of their faces, her resolve might have crumbled.

She was desperately afraid, not of the pain, but of what lay beyond. What if death was a cold, empty place? What if there was nothing at all?

It made no difference. She had but one choice if she were to save everyone she cared about.

As if from far away Aspin spoke the final words.

"I freely give my life."

"I…"

"I freely give my life!" A voice behind her shrieked. She whirled about to see a tall, thin figure burst through the curtain of mist. She saw Larris reach out to grab the intruder. Steel flashed and Larris fell back, a knife hilt protruding from his stomach.

She had only the time to shriek "No!" and then the newcomer was upon her.

But he was not coming after her. He shouldered her aside and hurled himself onto the blade of the Silver Serpent.

Everything seemed to freeze as she tried to comprehend what had just happened.

And then the ground shook so violently that she was knocked off her feet. Oskar fell back, staring at the stranger who had, unbidden, given up his life in her place. Who was he?

But Shanis had no time to wonder. She hurried to Larris' side. The prince lay clutching the wound in his stomach. Blood soaked his tunic. The bloody dagger that had done the work lay discarded nearby

"Larris. Oh no." Tears streaming down her face she pressed her hands to his wound and tried to hold in his lifeblood, but she knew he was dying. Her life had been saved, and his taken from him.

Lerryn knew he stood no chance against the Ice King. The god could crush him with a wave of his hand, yet still he rode. For months now, he had sought to atone for his past transgressions. Finally, he had his chance. He knew he would die, but before he perished he would cast his defiance in the face of the Ice King. And he would die with his sword in his hand.

The Ice King held out his hand and Lerryn's horse skidded to a halt. The frightened beast began to buck and Lerryn jumped free. He hit the ground hard but regained his feet immediately. He raised his sword and began to walk slowly toward the terrible glowing figure before him.

The Ice King raised his sword…and froze.

The burning blue light that shone from his body flickered, and began to die. The frosty ground beneath his feet thawed and the Ice King let out a mournful wail that boomed like thunder in the night.

Lerryn didn't know what was happening, but he could recognize when the enemy was vulnerable. Fear coursing through every vein, he sprinted forward. He felt as though he were moving in a dream, scarcely able to lift his feet. In six strides, he reached the Ice King, raised his sword, and drove it into his heart.

A cold so intense that it burned shot up his arm and coursed through his body. Every muscle jerked spasmodically, but he could not let go of his sword.

Before him, the Ice King fell to his knees. Lerryn's blade shattered and he stumbled backward, his eyes still locked on the trembling god, whose unearthly glow was dying like a guttering candle. With an ear-splitting roar the Ice King fell face-first onto the ground.

And then he was gone.

Lerryn dropped to the ground, powerful shudders racking his body, but somewhere deep inside he felt warm.

"It's Pedric Karst!" Oskar shouted.

Shanis turned and gaped. Through a curtain of tears, she saw Oskar lean down and haul the young man's body free of the blade. As his lifeless form dropped to the ground, his hood fell back and Shanis recognized the familiar lean face and dark hair of the young man she had hated for so long. The young man who had died in her place.

"Where did he come from?" Oskar asked.

"Oskar, get away from there!" Aspin grabbed Oskar by the arm and pulled him away. "Look at the sword."

The Silver Serpent now pulsed with alternating blue and white light. It began to vibrate and then jerk back and forth as if trying to work free from the tree, and Shanis somehow knew that it was the movement of this sword that shook the world.

"What's happening?" Oskar said

"Karst is the King of Kurnsbur," Aspin said. "His sacrifice drew the Ice King into the sword, just like the rulers did when they formed it."

The blade emitted a high-pitched whine that rose above the rumbling of the earth.

"They're battling inside the sword." Shanis didn't know where the thought had come from, but she knew it was true. "The gods are fighting the Ice King."

As they gazed at the blade, which now writhed like its namesake serpent, cracks began to form across its surface.

"We should get out of here," Aspin said. "We don't know what might happen."

"No, wait!" Oskar shouted. "Shanis, you can heal him with the sword. Quick, before it's too late!" He grabbed Larris under the arms and dragged him closer to the sword.

Shanis could scarcely think, so great was her grief, but she was willing to try. Still nearly blinded by tears, she took Larris' hand and reached out for the sword with her other hand. Her hand closed on the point and she felt it pierce the flesh of her palm.

"Please," she whispered. "My life or his. My life or his. I freely give my life."

For the final time, she felt the power of the Silver Serpent flow into her, filling her, and then she poured it into Larris.

The power waned as the light from the sword dimmed. The force drained from her and her eyes grew heavy.

She was vaguely aware of blinding flash and a loud crack as the Silver Serpent flew apart.

And then all went black.

Epilogue

"Are you really going to wear a dress tomorrow, or will you wear your usual getup?" Hierm lounged against the low wall that enclosed the private garden just off the throne room at the palace in Karkwall. "You know we're all dying to see you dressed like a girl."

"I think a hunting shirt and breeches would look grand," Oskar said. "She wouldn't look out of place at all."

Shanis rolled her eyes. "I am a queen, and apparently a queen is expected to wear a dress at her wedding. Not that I'm happy about it." From her seat on the soft grass, she shot a dark look at Larris who raised his hands in mock protest.

"It's not my fault. It was the custom long before either of us came along." He dropped down to the ground beside her, laid his head in her lap and gazed up at the night sky." Besides, Lothan is your country. If you want to change tradition, that's up to you."

"This time tomorrow it will be your country too. I suppose I can wear a dress for one day," she sighed. "Besides, Mistress Faun spent years trying to get me into a dress. Considering she traveled all the way here to attend our wedding, it's the least that I can do." She absently stroked Larris' hair and gazed up at the stars.

It was late at night. All the evening's obligations had been met. She'd greeted more self-important nobles than she could count, eaten far too much food, and smiled until her jaws hurt. It was, as Bertram had reminded her, all part of being queen. She was still amazed that royals from all over Gameryah had come to Lothan for her wedding. She supposed she shouldn't be too surprised, though. Since the Battle of Calmut, as it was being called, her story had apparently spread far and wide. Now everyone wanted to meet the farm girl who saved the world. She didn't believe she deserved such accolades, but there was nothing to be done about it. For now, she put those thoughts aside and simply enjoyed being with her friends.

"I still can't believe Mother made the journey," Hierm said. "But it will be her last chance to see me, Rinala, and the baby for a while."

"So you're really going through with it?" Oskar asked. "You're going to live among the clans?"

Hierm nodded. "Rinala is the daughter of a clan chief and she feels it's her responsibility to help them rebuild their home. Besides, Lothan should be as safe a place to live now as any. No more clan war."

"Never again if I have anything to say about it," Shanis said. She turned to Oskar. "How about you? Once our wedding is over will it be time to start planning another?"

Oskar choked on his wine. "What's that?" he blustered. "No, Lizzie isn't exactly the marrying type. At least that's what she tells me. She says I promised to travel the world with her and she won't marry me until I've proven myself to be a man of my word."

"You're not going back to the Gates then?" Hierm asked.

Oskar shook his head. "I'm going to stay in Lothan for a while. I'll spend some time in Calmut at the magic school, and then Lizzie and I will decide where to go from there. Besides, Aspin says, even though the Gates has been reclaimed from the coldhearts it will be a long time before its reputation is restored."

"Does Naseeb ever plan on going back?" Larris asked.

Oskar grinned. "Naseeb will go wherever Gillen goes. The two have been inseparable since the battle."

Larris looked up at Shanis. "Perhaps there's a match to be made there if you're so eager to attend another wedding. Of course, I expect Lerryn to marry soon. He needs to get busy producing heirs to the throne. His only problem now is choosing between the suitors who all want to marry the man who killed the Ice King."

"Pedric Karst killed the Ice King," Shanis whispered.

Larris took her hand and gave it a gentle squeeze. "I know. We'll make sure his story is told. He did some terrible things, but in the end he was a hero."

"We lost a lot of heroes." Oskar gazed down into his cup.

Sadness welled up inside Shanis. The pain of losing so many who were dear to her still cut deeply.

Larris sat up, filled an empty cup, and stood. "Let us drink to fallen friends."

The others rose and formed a circle.

Oskar raised his cup. "Whitt and Dacio."

"Granlor," Shanis said.

"Khalyndryn," Hierm added.

Larris smiled sadly. "Allyn."

Shanis knew that the loss of his friend would haunt Larris for years to come

"They will not be forgotten," she said.

"They will not be forgotten," the others repeated.

They drained their cups and then stood in silence, listening to the whisper of the wind.

Finally, Larris sighed. "Now that I've dampened everyone's spirits I should be away to bed. It's almost midnight and it's bad luck for me to see the bride on our wedding day." He leaned down and kissed Shanis on the forehead. "I'll see you tomorrow."

"And every day after that," she said.

After Larris had left, she, Hierm, and Oskar sat there for a long time. None of them seemed to know what to say, but neither did they want to leave. It felt right that they should be here together again.

Finally, Oskar chuckled. "Do you remember the fight we had when Shanis and I decided to leave Galsbur?"

Hierm nodded. "You were going to travel to some place over the sea where women could be soldiers."

"Hallind. You know what I found out while I was studying at the Gates? It isn't even a real place. Your father's book had it wrong."

They all laughed. It felt to Shanis like her first real laugh since the war had ended, and for a moment she was transported back to Galsbur. They were simple townspeople again, youngsters with daydreams and small problems that seemed huge.

"Well, it sort of worked out," Hierm said. "Shanis got to be a soldier and you got to see some of the world."

"Do you ever wish we had just stayed home?" Oskar asked, his eyes fixed on some point in the distance.

"I don't think we had a choice," Shanis said. "The gods, or the universe, or the prophecy had bigger plans for us all." She reached out and took their hands. "But I'm glad that, at least for tonight, we're together again."

-End of The Absent Gods-

About the Author

David Debord is the pen name of action-adventure author David Wood. In addition to the Absent Gods, he is also the author of the Dane Maddock Adventures and several other titles. When not writing, he co-hosts the Authorcast podcast. He and his family live in Santa Fe, New Mexico. Visit him online at www.daviddebord.com.

Lightning Source UK Ltd.
Milton Keynes UK
UKOW04f1033290515

252539UK00002B/76/P